Sgt. Bellnapp's Secret

by Karl Reiner

AmErica House
Baltimore

Copyright 2001 by Karl Reiner.

First printing

ISBN: 1-58851-781-0
PUBLISHED BY AMERICA HOUSE BOOK PUBLISHERS
www.publishamerica.com
Baltimore
Printed in the United States of America

Dedicated to those who understand the corrosive influence of big money and the need for campaign finance reform.

April 2000

"Politics can be relatively fair in the breathing spaces of history; at its critical turning points there is no other rule possible than the old one, that the end justifies the means."

-Arthur Koestler, 1940

Leon Placke made big money lobbying in Washington, DC. He was the best of the Washington insiders, a master deal-doer. He was a fixer of the political problems that plagued important people and special interest groups. Placke had mastered the workings of the American political system, knew all of its weaknesses. Leon was shrewd, knew when to move, knew when to wait. The power brokers in the capital city of the United States, Republicans and Democrats alike, admired and respected Leon's uncanny sense of political timing.

The nation's Presidents came and went every four or eight years like clockwork. Being a separate branch of government, Congress followed its own yearly cycle regardless of who occupied the White House. Congress went into session with a great deal of fanfare, then debated endlessly, passed a mass of laws and adjourned. At every opportunity, its members scampered back to their home districts to tell the voters how much better they had made the world for them. None of the mechanics of government mattered much to Leon because he focused exclusively on getting things done for his clients. Always overlooking the underlying greed, the self-interest and the never ending struggle of competing interests to gain political advantage, Placke did well in Washington. Being the end product of 50 years of American political mutation, Leon Placke personified what the capital was all about as the new century began.

Placke had been at the top of the lobbying game, a respected power behind the Washington political scene. Then suddenly Leon became haunted by a phantom from America's past. It discombobulated his thinking processes until he could not tell the useless past from the highly profitable present. His former friends watched in disbelief as Leon lost control of his senses. For reasons no one understood, Leon Placke, the man who had become Washington's greatest lobbyist, turned his back on the profession that had made him wealthy and set out to change the very system he had spent years helping to build. To the dismay of the Washington establishment, Leon launched a crazy crusade to reform how Washington worked and to close down the city's lobbying profession. As Leon mentally disintegrated, he came to believe George Washington wanted him to lead the movement to change how the White House and Congress conducted the nation's affairs. What was more disconcerting than Leon's mental breakdown was the fact that his crazy ideas were catching on with the nation's citizenry. Placke was becoming a threat to trendy lifestyles enjoyed by Washington's prominent and powerful community of lobbyists. Something was going to have to be done about Leon and the sooner the better.

On one fortunate day Leon Placke was found dead. The police believed he committed suicide by imbibing a lethal cocktail composed of alcohol and barbiturates. Although Placke's death abruptly ended the downward spiraling career of the man who had once been Washington's most powerful lawyer and influence peddler, it was greeted with a large sigh of relief by those in the capital's influence industry.

Placke's body was discovered by a group of Civil War devotees who had begun a long day of visits to northern Virginia's Civil War sites at the railroad bridge (destroyed and rebuilt seven times during the war) which crossed the famous little stream named Bull Run. Later in the day, after viewing the few nondescript remnants of the mighty Confederate fortification line that once threatened Washington, DC, the group stopped at an antiquated house located at 5643 Mt. Gilead Road in Centreville, Virginia. The old house was of interest to students of the Civil War because it had been the residence of Confederate General Joseph E. Johnston during the first winter of the war in 1861-62. From this house, General Johnston conducted a series of venomous, on-going arguments with Confederate President Jefferson Davis in Richmond. Many students of the Civil War believed the Davis-Johnston feud, which grew white-hot while General Johnston was at Centreville, ultimately played a major role in the destruction of the Confederacy. Although the house had a degree of historical significance as the quarters of a Confederate army commander, it was also unique because it was one of the few structures in the tiny village surviving the firestorm of the Civil War. After a tour of the house, which struck the group as being too small and austere to have once been the residence of a famous general, the tourists walked toward a long, low mound of grass-covered earth located at the rear of the property. The pleasant looking ridge-like mound was the remains of an artillery position that had once been home to four cannon.

The group's lively discussion of how Civil War artillery inflicted a massive number of casualties abruptly halted when they came across Placke's body slumped against the base of a large tree, not far from the gun position. Also found lying next to the body were an assortment of eating utensils and an antique whiskey jug with the barely legible words "Strawderman's Finest" visible on its front. Although none of the investigating police officers could initially determine why Placke had the small jug with him, a later examination by experts determined the whiskey jug had contained the lethal concoction that Placke had consumed. The old jug was also worth approximately $150 because it was an authentic artifact from the 1860s.

What was immediately obvious to the police investigators was that they were dealing with the demise of a seriously mentally ill person. While searching the body, they found a number of notes in the pocket of Mr. Placke's expensive jacket. The short notations written in long hand enumerated a series of political reforms Placke was attempting to bring to the attention of the voters and the nation's lawmakers. The notes made it clear that Placke had obtained his ideas directly from George Washington. Apparently, Washington had often talked with Placke and urged him to speak to the American public. The score of reminder notes Placke had written to himself were on an expensive Placke and Associates, Inc. notepad. Police handwriting experts confirmed that Leon Placke was the author.

Initially, the sudden death of such a once powerful person raised a great deal of concern in official circles in Washington. Leon had been privy to many of the political secrets which those who wielded power in the nation's capital preferred to keep from public scrutiny. With the scandals of President Clinton's administration making politicians a bit nervous, there was almost a sense of joy in Washington when the police investigation concluded Placke's death was nothing more than the last desperate act of a man suffering from a severe mental disorder.

To confirm the police finding, investigators from the FBI and CIA quietly rechecked the facts of the case at the request of persons situated high in the nation's lawmaking establishment. In separate investigations, agents from both agencies found no possible connection between George Washington, the first President of the United States who died in 1799, and the suicide of Leon Placke. The possibilities of the notes being in code, Placke's involvement with a secret organization or other domestic or foreign political relationships were carefully checked. The results were negative. Placke had no major financial problems, there were no grounds for blackmail or indications of a love interest gone sour. Leon Placke was financially well-off, had been one of Washington's more successful lobbyists and moved in the city's highest social circles.

His former business acquaintances thought they understood why Placke took his own life. His odd belief that he was working on behalf of George

Washington to promote national political reform was proof enough of madness to satisfy everyone. The power elite of the nation's capital had been extremely unhappy with Leon's conduct during the last months of his life. Placke, once the ultimate Washington insider, had become increasingly critical of how the nation's lawmaking apparatus operated and he had no compunction about publicizing his nonsensical views. His relentless carping made all of Washington's lawyers and lobbyists uneasy. Many in Congress, the White House and the lobbying community had come to consider Leon as nothing more than a traitor to his class. His presence in the capital would not be missed.

Leon Placke's funeral was an event at which Washington insiders came to see and be seen. No longer an embarrassing problem to anyone, Leon was accorded treatment worthy of his former high status in Washington power circles. At the memorial service, Leon's many former corporate clients paid their final respects while they mixed with those of influence from Congress and the White House. Placke's former clients were deluged by offers of representation from lobbyists hoping to acquire Leon's accounts. Before the final oration had concluded, many deals had been struck among the whispering throng solemnly gathered to honor his memory.

Outside the funeral home, a group of 1,300 uninvited average people waited for a chance to pay their final respects to the man whose harsh reform message had been the most unwelcome of news to the sitting Congress. Near the main entrance were piled the wreathes, flower arrangements and condolence cards from people all over the United States. While he was increasingly despised by the political elite, Leon Placke had attracted a following in America's vast hinterland. Outside of Washington, the rumor began to circulate that Leon Placke had not committed suicide. It was said that he had been murdered by a cabal of tricky, powerful Washington special interests bent on derailing his plan to reform America's wasteful Congress and curtail the power of lobbyists.

It was with a great collective sigh of relief that Washington insiders greeted the news that no one else was implicated in the demise of the powerful lobbyist turned crackpot reformer. Perhaps the rumor that Placke had been murdered by the corrupt defenders of the political status quo would now quietly fade away. Since Placke had become a major annoyance to Washington's elite, not one of his former colleagues showed the slightest interest in learning what it was that had finally driven the distraught lobbyist over the edge. His former friends were genuinely delighted that Leon had departed life without creating any more problems for them. With Leon silenced, their attention focused on the legislative needs of clients and scheduling attendance at the multitude of fundraising events hosted by worthy members of Congress and politicians planning to run for high national office. It was all part of what public servants fondly like to call "conducting the nation's business."

Leon Placke was quickly forgotten as Washington focused on the coming presidential election, the political lessons being learned from the Republican failure to gain control of Congress in the 1998 elections, the tantalizing ramifications of the impeachment proceedings against President Clinton, American air raids on Iraqi installations and the $130 million appropriated by Congress to aid struggling hog farmers.

July 1799

When George Washington took over the management of Mt. Vernon's 2,126 acres upon the death of his half-brother in the 1750s, crop production was spiraling downward because the incessant growing of tobacco had depleted the soil. Already well-known as a gifted surveyor, the inquisitive Washington suddenly discovered a love of farming. As a result of his efforts, the size of Mt. Vernon and its surrounding farms eventually increased to 8,000 acres, of which approximately 3,200 were under cultivation.

George Washington, a veteran of the French and Indian War, the commander of the Continental Army during the Revolutionary War and the first president of the United States, was also a scientist at heart. His agricultural experiments included testing over 60 crops. Around 1765, he began growing less tobacco, switching to the production of wheat and corn. He was also a devoted horse breeder and trainer, keeping 130 of the animals on his farms. His fields adequately supported 600 sheep, but he had little success with his attempts to raise cattle. Washington's interest in the production of fruits and flowers led him to greatly enlarge the gardens and orchard in order to increase yields.

After 200 additional years of agricultural development, it is commonly known that the soil of the Mt. Vernon, Virginia region is best suited to corn, soybeans, mixed hay and small grains. Washington had to learn these lessons by trial and error, from observation and experimentation, because the standard agricultural practices so successful in England often failed in the harsher climate of Virginia. Wool producers in the temperate English climate easily obtained 11 pounds of wool from each sheep; Mt. Vernon's flock was lucky to produce three pounds per animal. As he struggled to combat the soil exhaustion which had become a problem in Virginia, Washington constantly sought advice from the leading agricultural scientists of the age. Over time, he made Mt. Vernon a diversified and successful farm venture as he experimented with fertilizer, animal manure and natural lime. He developed a sophisticated crop rotation cycle, planting grasses, clover and buckwheat to improve the plantation's worn-out soil. In an unusual procedure for the age, Washington purposely left the areas along the creeks in pasture to prevent soil erosion.

As he increased his knowledge of agricultural practices, Washington thought America could become the "storehouse and granary for the world." In a 1794 letter he wrote: "I know of no pursuit in which more real and important services can be rendered to any country than by improving its agriculture, the breed of useful animals and other branches of a husbandman's cares."

This deep-thinking man also had an uncanny appreciation for the application of technology to industrial production. In 1770, wishing to take advantage of the growing market for flour and other grain products fueled by the dawning of the Industrial Revolution, Washington decided to build a new gristmill at the head of Dogue Creek. It was a large commercial facility, accessible to ships which could move the barrels of flour to markets outside the region. Along with mills that he owned in Alexandria, Virginia and Pennsylvania, the Dogue Creek gristmill would make Washington one of the largest flour producers in the colonies.

In the 1780s, Oliver Evans, a native of Delaware, developed equipment to automate flour mills. His revolutionary new water-driven conveyor system moved grain and flour from place to place in the mill, sharply reducing the costs of milling. Among the first to be granted patents by the new United States government, many consider Evans to be the father of American industrial automation. Ever attuned to new technical developments and their application to his endeavors, Washington had the Evans-designed system installed in his mill in 1791.

Over time, Washington developed a sizable industrial complex on the mill property. By 1798, along with the mill, there was a cooperage manufacturing shipping barrels, a five still distillery producing whiskey, a hog fattening lot and stalls for 30 cattle. Washington saw to it that nothing arriving at the gristmill was wasted. What could not be turned into flour or whiskey went to feed the animals. By the standards of the day, the site was a beehive of productivity. The distillery ran at full capacity producing rye whiskey, bourbon and brandy. Coopers manufactured barrels for use by Washington's own businesses and for sale to other merchants. Grain wagons constantly made deliveries, the mill shook with the vibration created by operation of the two grinding stones, clouds of flour and grain dust hung in the air and sailors loaded barrels of flour and whiskey onto ships. Visitors to the mill must have stared at automated milling machinery in much the same way as we now gape at the latest innovations in computer technology.

George Washington's industrial complex provided employment for a number of the local inhabitants. One of these was Ben Strawderman. As Washington visited the site almost daily, Ben had many interesting conversations with the retired President of the United States on the ins and outs of making quality whiskey. The gristmill also catered to local farmers who paid a fee for having their wheat and corn ground. While waiting for their flour to be processed, these hard-working men often sampled the products of the distillery. On more than one occasion, a farmer had to sleep off the effects of the whiskey tasting in his wagon before he and his faithful team of horses could begin the journey home. Ben was a gregarious fellow and enjoyed the fellowship and conversation of the farmers. It broke the monotony of the sunup to sundown workday at the distillery. During his term of employment, he learned a great deal from Mr. Anderson, the distillery manager, and found that he had a talent for making whiskey.

The story of George Washington's business enterprises did not have a particularly happy ending. His last visit to the mill complex came on a bleak December day in 1799. The next day, Washington worked at Mt. Vernon in new-fallen snow and 30 degree weather, marking trees for a removal project. He was 67 years old when he died on December 14, 1799 from either an extreme form of tonsillitis, a streptococcus infection or diphtheria. Having had no children of his own, his holdings at the mill site passed through his will to his nephew. Over time, Dogue Creek silted-up, making the complex inaccessible to ships. Business declined and the facilities fell into ruin. By the late 1850s, most of the buildings had virtually disappeared. Overshadowed by Washington's monumental political and military contributions to the nation, his efforts in the fields of agriculture and business faded from national memory.

Unfortunately, few in Virginia shared Washington's thirst for developing agricultural knowledge and preserving land productivity. Between the American Revolution and 1850, approximately one million Virginians moved west as a result of the cycle of land ruination that Washington had hoped to change. For far too many farmers the standard practice was to clear the land, raise crops until the soil gave out, move to a new place farther west and start the vicious cycle over again. In the process, these migrants took their belongings, beliefs and at times, their slaves. The exodus from Virginia did much to promote the expansion of the country west of the Appalachian mountains and set in motion issues which would at a later date shatter the nation in a great civil war.

The Strawderman clan was no different from other Virginia families of the time. Many of Ben's kin and his descendants moved west with the flow of migration. Some went to Kentucky and Tennessee. Others headed for the lands of the Northwest Territory which would become the states of Ohio, Indiana, Michigan and Wisconsin.

At the end of the Revolutionary War, the new United States was viewed as the place to begin a life offering economic opportunity and freedom from political oppression. Immigrants from Europe and those without land in the original colonies east of the mountains saw that northwest of the Ohio River lay a land where good crops could be easily be grown in rich soil. However, because the current inhabitants, Native American tribes such as the Shawnees and Miamis were not willing to give it up, the settlers' journey to the promised land of Ohio could prove to be a costly one.

In the years preceding 1789, over 1,500 people had been killed while traveling on the Ohio River. The Shawnees in particular had become masters at enticing boats close to shore and killing passengers and crew alike. Because of this situation, President Washington moved to bring an end to the Indian menace on the western frontier. At his urging, Congress authorized the Virginia, Pennsylvania and Kentucky militias to crush the tribes. As part of the plan, in the summer 1789 construction began on a fort located on the north bank of the Ohio across from the mouth of the Licking River. Built next to the small village of Losantiville (which soon changed its name to Cincinnati) Ft. Washington was 180 feet square, two stories high and had strong blockhouses located at its four corners. Garrisoned by 300 troops, it was the largest and most impregnable military installation in the Northwest Territory.

Arthur St. Clair had been a moderately good general and a superb administrator during the Revolutionary War. Being a close friend of George Washington also helped him gain an appointment as governor of the Northwest Territory. He arrived at Ft. Washington in January 1790 with instructions from the President to organize an army, march north and build a series of forts. The energetic St. Clair had great difficulty in organizing his forces because the soldiers and supplies promised by the war department never arrived. It was not until October 1791 that he led a poorly supplied force of 1,400 from Ft. Washington. Marching in the ranks was John Strawderman, Ben's adventuresome young brother. He thought that serving a stint with the militia might lead to an opportunity for land acquisition in the new territory. He expected to be able to stake out a claim for himself at the campaign's conclusion. Following behind the troop column, in violation of St. Clair's orders, were a group of nearly 500 wives and camp followers.

About 23 miles north of Cincinnati, the little army paused to construct Ft. Hamilton. On October 24, St. Clair ordered a halt 44 miles north of Ft. Hamilton and constructed a second fort which was named Ft. Jefferson. While construction was in progress, 300 of the extremely unhappy militia soldiers deserted, taking with them about 200 of the camp followers. Worried that this group of hungry people would loot the supply train which was supposed to be following, St. Clair detached the First Regiment and sent it in pursuit of the fugitives. In a little more than one day, his effective force had been reduced to 920 troops as he sent away his best fighting unit. Lacking experience fighting Indians, St. Clair did not think to send out scouting parties. Not wishing to remain tactically blinded, the nervous militia troops began scouting on their own. They found growing evidence that a large enemy force was gathering in the vicinity.

On November 3, about 37 miles north of Ft. Jefferson, the army halted. The shivering and famished army would camp and wait for the overdue supply train to catch up. The construction of fortifications was put off until morning because the tired troops were going to be given a needed night's sleep. As a precaution against surprise attack, an advance guard post was established in front of the main camp. Had they known that a little over a mile away, 3,000 warriors led by Chiefs Little Turtle and Blue Jacket were spoiling for a fight, the troops would have foregone the rest and would have begun erecting fortifications immediately.

An hour before dawn, having become worried by reports the enemy was moving into position to attack, St. Clair had the army roused and organized for battle. Before any work could be done on defenses, the Indians struck. The impact of the attack quickly drove the forward guard back to the main body where a blistering fire from the army's main battle line temporarily halted the Indian assault. Unfortunately for St. Clair's little force, the cannon powder was so grossly defective the artillery could not maintain a steady rate of fire. As a result, most of the soldiers manning the unserviceable guns were soon killed or wounded. As the fighting grew hotter, General St. Clair, who was suffering terribly from gout, had the horses he mounted shot out from under him in quick succession. Although the general was in a great deal of pain, he led three bayonet charges on foot in order to blunt attacks. When the fighting began, the camp followers fled south in an attempt to escape the battle. Having no weapons, they were easy prey for the Indians who were moving in the army's rear. In less than a half hour, over two hundred were killed.

The new fallen snow in the fighting area was ground into a red slush as the battle raged for almost three hours. Powerful Indian attacks on both flanks and the rear finally forced General St. Clair to call a retreat. In a well executed move, his desperate troops managed to turn themselves around and fight their way through the Indians in the rear. The dejected troops left a trail of wounded all the way back to Ft. Jefferson, arriving there about dusk. Days later, the stunned residents of Cincinnati watched the remnants of the worst military disaster in the young history of the United States slog past. The statistics were grim: of the 920 men who had fought, only 24 remained uninjured; 264 had been wounded and 632 killed. Among those who would lie forever at the Wabash headwaters was John Strawderman. He fell in what may well have been the worst single defeat ever suffered by the United States Army at the hands of Native American forces.

The battle took on the proportions of a national disaster. General St. Clair was publicly derided and condemned. A congressional committee was appointed to investigate, interviewing over a hundred witnesses. At the end of the proceedings, Arthur St. Clair was exonerated. Despite the findings, his military reputation was ruined although he continued in his position as the territory's governor until replaced by President Jefferson in 1802. St. Clair spent the remainder of his life defending his conduct during the ill-fated expedition, dying in poverty in 1818.

Although upset by John's death, the promise of good land enticed others of the Strawderman clan and they had better luck. By 1860, their descendants were scattered across the old Northwest and many became prosperous in the fields of banking, manufacturing and railroading. Long forgotten were their Virginia roots. Politically, they tended to support the new Republican party, were staunchly pro-union and several were active in anti-slavery causes.

July 1861

"Cry havoc! and let loose the dogs of war,"
William Shakespeare, 1564-1616

By 1861, the only Strawderman remaining in Fairfax County, Virginia was William Strawderman who was living on a farm located on the north side of the Warrenton Turnpike not far from a small stream called Little Rocky Run. The farm was a little over a mile east of the decrepit little village of two dozen or so residences and buildings known as Centreville. The village and surrounding region had been in a slow economic decline for a number of years. When the land played out, people simply pulled up stakes and moved west. Never put into practice were the lessons of land fertility preservation so painstakingly learned by George Washington over 70 years before.

All things considered, Old Will, as William was called by those who knew him well, wasn't doing badly. He had a fairly sizable land holding, owed only a small amount of debt and was living rather comfortably for a farmer nearing 60 years of age. He had added acres to his farm in anticipation of a rise in land prices, but instead found himself trapped by stagnant land values. Between 1817 and 1830, the value of Virginia's land had fallen from $207 million to $90 million. As over a million people left Virginia for points west, the state fell from first place in national population ranking to seventh by the time the census of 1860 was taken. With so much free land available in the west and local crop yields low, Old Will realized he would almost have to give the farm away if he wanted to move on to greener pastures. So being relatively well off, he decided to stay where he was.

Centreville had its beginning as a coach stop on the road in colonial times. Originally known by the name of Newgate, there had always been a tavern or two serving the teamsters and travelers for as long as anyone could remember. It was a hard-drinking time and people liked a good whiskey to help settle the greasy food after a hard day of driving a team on the road or working in the fields. That social custom was Old Will's financial ally. At least one of George Washington's whiskey recipes had been handed down through the generations to him. He took great pride in producing a product which he believed would have met the great Washington's implacable taste in alcoholic spirits. Although he was a moderately successful farmer, making whiskey was Old Will's real claim to fame, his labor of love.

From the earliest days of the American Republic, many farmers had converted their grain, which was too bulky to transport over the poor roads, into whiskey which was easier to bring to market. Barely able to survive as it was, they flatly refused to pay the federal excise task imposed on whiskey. Their opposition to the tax flared into open rebellion in 1794, forcing President Washington to send troops to Pennsylvania to restore order. In keeping with this defiant tradition, William Strawderman gloried in his role as one who distilled and sold liquor illegally. His neighbors were of a like mind on the subject and saw nothing at all wrong with what he was doing.

In a glen, secluded by a dense growth of brush and second-growth timber on the hillside sloping down to Little Rocky Run, Old Will found a spring producing exactly the quality of water he thought Washington's distillery must have used. The whiskey still Old Will constructed near the spring was a thing of beauty. The copper cooking unit stood on a foundation made of stones and was located inside a rough three-walled shed that provided a fair amount of protection from the elements. Will named his beverage "Strawderman's Finest" and spent countless hours telling anyone willing to listen how he made the same fine quality whisky as was once produced by the first President of the United States in the county of Fairfax, Virginia.

Despite Old Will's pompous claims of links to presidential whiskey, it was generally agreed by area residents that he did make a decent drink. The village taverns were his steady customers. Old Will had been producing whiskey for so long that many travelers had gotten into the habit of asking for his product by name. As they sipped "Strawdermans Finest" to take the edge off of a hard day, countless tavern patrons let their imaginations wander with General Washington to places like Valley Forge, Trenton and Yorktown. Many of the travelers continued on to Washington city and in the hotel bars and the city's saloons retold the story of the Centreville man who claimed to be making a brand of George Washington's whiskey. As a result, Old Will made sales to a few of the hotels which served the visiting business and political elite of the nation's capital even though the bad roads made it difficult to deliver the jugs and barrels for much of the year. Business was good. If sales continued to increase, Will would have to hire someone to make the deliveries to his customers in Washington.

Old Will's whisky still had brought him a degree of local notoriety over the years. One of his better customers had been John Keene, owner of Keene's Mill on Pope's Head Creek. John was a pillar of the community, a hard-working and a hard-drinking man who had a knack for grinding fine

18

flour. One night in 1856, he got into a fight with a business partner named Billy Sanders over money owed. The affair started as an innocent social gathering when Billy came to the mill with two other men who were also acquaintances of John. As was their habit, the foursome had imbibed quite a bit of Strawderman's Finest before John and Billy got to arguing over who owed what to whom. As the discussion grew heated, the two carried the argument outside and blows were struck. John's famous temper got the best of him and he slashed Billy with a knife. The cut in Billy's stomach didn't look all that serious as the two other visitors hurriedly bundled the inebriated Billy into a wagon and drove over to Dr. Wallmark's house to get him stitched up. It turned out to be much worse than it looked. The knife gash had allowed a portion of Billy's intestines to protrude and although Dr. Wallmark did a fine job of pushing them back in as he closed the wound, an infection must have set in. Billy died two days later from the complications of the stab wound.

There was some disagreement among the two witnesses as to which party actually started the altercation and if John acted in self defense. Despite the conflicting statements, John was charged with first degree murder by the sheriff, who also happened to be Billy's brother-in-law, and a date was set for trial at the Fairfax Courthouse. John's defense attorney lined up five men to testify as to the sterling quality of John's character. Their testimony would support the defense's argument that Billy was trouble maker and that John had acted in self defense while being assaulted on his own property. The five character witnesses arrived at the courthouse early on the day of trial, and having become bored with the slowness of the proceedings while waiting to testify, went out to one of the wagons parked in the courthouse yard and opened a large jug of Strawderman's Finest.

By the time they were called to testify late in the afternoon session, all five were drunk. The enraged judge refused to hear the testimony of the five intoxicated men and had them ejected from the court. Without the supporting testimony of friendly witnesses, John's defense fell apart. The jury, being composed of somewhat sympathetic individuals decided not to hang John. Instead they sentenced him to eight years in the state penitentiary at Richmond. The drunk witness scandal rocked the community and brought out the temperance movement supporters in force. The court judge and the temperance people railed at the evil caused by excessive drinking in speeches and newspaper stories. During church services, Will Strawderman and his whiskey were denounced from several pulpits for doing the devil's work. He was providing a liquid temptation too strong for most men to resist.

To make matters worse for Old Will, two months later Washington

Mitchell died of exposure on the bank of Pope's Head Creek after becoming too drunk to seek to shelter on a cold night. The empty jug found by the body the next day had contained Strawderman's Finest. When he heard the news of Mr. Mitchell's death, Old Will thought it best to stay out of the town of Fairfax Courthouse for a time so things could cool down, but to his surprise business did not drop off. The courthouse incident and the demise of Mr. Mitchell, a man known for his good taste in whiskey, brought a batch of new customers to Old Will's door. Several of the new customers mentioned hearing of his product during church services and after praying for guidance, decided to give it a try. One of them later described Strawderman's Finest in glowing terms, "a good swig of it has been known to stop a man's watch, snap his suspenders and abruptly and violently burn the dust of a hard day's work from his throat."

Unfortunately, Old Will's expanding sales to the city of Washington were disrupted by political events. With the election of Abraham Lincoln of Illinois as President of the United States in November 1860, the country split apart like a ripe melon dropped on a rock. At first, Old Will and his neighbors treated the crisis almost as a joke. When hot heads in South Carolina left the Union in December 1860, one wise observer who knew the citizens of South Carolina well, was widely quoted as saying: "South Carolina was too small for a country and too large for an insane asylum." Many in the North and South continued to hope that cooler heads would prevail and the situation could be brought back to normal. In the inaugural address given on March 4, 1861, the lanky Lincoln didn't sound crazy or like a radical abolitionist to Old Will. Lincoln did not seem eager to bring on war when he said "In your hands, my dissatisfied fellow-countrymen, and not in mine, is the momentous issue of civil war. The government will not assail you. You can have no conflict, without being yourselves the aggressors. You have no oath registered in Heaven to destroy the government, while I shall have the most solemn one to preserve, protect and defend it."

Old Will listened attentively as the new president ended his speech with "We are not enemies, but friends. We must not be enemies. Though passion may have strained, it must not break our bonds of affection. The mystic chords of memory, stretching from every battlefield, and patriot grave, to every living heart and hearth-stone, all over this broad land, will yet swell the chorus of the Union, when again touched, as surely they will be, by the better angels of our nature."

Although Old Will thought it was a decent speech, it fell flat in the South. More deep south states left the Union to join the new Confederate States of America which established its capital at Montgomery, Alabama. As the situation worsened, Virginia hung tough for the Union right up to the end. It was not until the Confederates shelled federal held Fort Sumter in Charleston harbor on April 12, 1861 and President Lincoln called for 75,000 volunteers to put down the rebellion that Virginia pulled out of the Union. Virginia's secession dated from April 17, 1861.

The Centreville region of northern Virginia voted solidly for secession. Of course, there had been a degree of intimidation to silence the pro-Union people, but the fiery states' rights speeches delivered by all the local political leaders helped carry the day. It was clear to most Virginians that the South had been forced to act because the spirit of the Missouri Compromise, Compromise of 1850, the Kansas Nebraska Act and the Fugitive Slave Laws was being undermined. The Northern-run Underground Railroad and the spiteful book titled "Uncle Tom's Cabin" had done much to inflame sectional differences. As they went to the polls, Old Will and his neighbors were swayed by the argument that the gentle South had finally been pushed too far by a rapacious North determined to infringe on the constitutional rights of Southerners. Not long after Virginia joined the Confederacy, the Confederate government moved to Richmond, making that city the capital of the fledging new nation.

In his message to Congress on July 4, 1861, President Abraham Lincoln clearly indicated his determination to restore the Union when he stated "Having thus chosen our course, without guile and with pure purpose, let us renew our faith in God, and go forward without fear and with manly hearts." There was no longer any doubt that troops would soon be marching to force the South back into the Union by military means. There was also no doubt that the equally determined Confederates were going to resist. War was sure to come and it would begin wherever the armies met.

Old Will began to worry about the impact of the political changes on his whisky business and farm. Richmond was far away. He had never been there. He did know a few people who had journeyed to Richmond to visit John Keene in the penitentiary, but that was the extent of his knowledge of the place. Washington, with which he was familiar and which was an emerging market for his divine product, had suddenly become the capital of a hostile power. He did not know if he could continue to make deliveries to his customers in Washington with Confederate and Union guards patrolling all the roads. The grumpy soldiers manning the outposts weren't above helping themselves to an old farmer's liquid cargo.

Old Will didn't have to worry about the loss of the Washington market for long because business picked up from an unexpected new source. A large number of officers in new gray uniforms began frequenting the taverns of

Centreville. They talked a great deal about the natural defense line created by the ridge on which the village was located. A detachment of soldiers soon started work on a fort overlooking the turnpike as it came up the hill from the direction of Washington.

There was also a lot of talk in the taverns regarding the need for the new Confederate army to march to Washington and knock some sense into Abe Lincoln. There were endless discussions of war strategy. The visiting officers pointed out that Centreville had a high degree of military significance because it sat on the road from Washington to the vital rail junction at Manassas. A Confederate army moving on Washington or a Union army marching against Manassas was likely to come through Centreville. One kindly major, who had seen service in the war with Mexico, suggested it would be a good idea for the women and children to move out of harm's way until the issue was settled. None of the local residents paid the slightest heed to his warning. Everyone knew for sure the war would end after one battle. The Yankee scum would be taught a smart lesson by the valiant boys from the South and that would bring the end of the war. Fleeing to kinfolk located elsewhere was a disgusting idea. When one was sitting on the spot where history was going to be made, no one wanted to leave and miss the action. The major simply ordered another drink, sighed and said "For their sake he hoped they were right."

People who had never been 20 miles from the place they were born looked at the military maps on the walls and offered loads of advice. "Look here," one of the self-made strategists said, "Virginia is bordered by the Ohio River. We could send an army across it and march on Columbus and Cincinnati and knock out the Yankee communication lines. That would teach that damn hot bed of abolitionists a real lesson." Another chimed in, "send another army north through the Shenandoah Valley, and go after either Pittsburgh or Philadelphia. Such a move would truly slice the guts of the Yankee's will to fight." A third said, "we need to attack Washington, capture it and send Lincoln packing back to Illinois. If that doesn't finish the job, march to Baltimore and Philadelphia."

The veteran officers thought it was strange talk coming from people who had recently voted to create a new a nation of approximately 750,000 square miles in size. In all that vast expanse of territory, there were very few facilities that could build railroad equipment, munitions, muskets, cannon or the many other products needed to maintain an army in the field. One of the officers pointed this out the civilian patrons in the tavern as he said, "The war has to be short because our Confederacy lacks virtually everything needed to fight a long one." The local tavern patrons looked at him as if he had suddenly gone insane. Everyone knew for a fact that the war would be over in a few months at the most. What kind of morons were they letting into the army anyhow? This buffoon wasn't worth the price of another drink. Long war indeed! It would never happen in this day and age in Virginia!

Ruth Anne, Old Will's wife, enjoyed the new-found prosperity. The Confederate troops massing on the other side of Bull Run purchased chickens, eggs, hogs, and anything else edible from local farmers to supplement their boring army rations. The farm had done well, making more money in the past months than it had made in the entire previous year. Old Will was also selling all the whiskey he could produce. Things were looking up financially, perhaps the war wasn't going to be so bad after all. However, with all the younger men rushing to join the army, getting help was going to be a problem. Both of the local boys who had worked as temporary hired hands had already joined.

Ruth Anne was feeding the chickens and wishing she had three times as many because sales were so good, when she saw a mounted army courier pounding down the turnpike from the direction of Washington. She could see by his collar insignia that the grim-faced horseman was a lieutenant as he flashed past trailing a cloud of dust. The rider headed west up the hill to town and then turned down the Manassas road. Whatever he was carrying must be important because he was running his horse nearly to death in the July heat. Maybe he was heading for General Beauregard's headquarters. The fast-riding horseman made Ruth Anne nervous. She hoped he would remember to water the poor animal when he halted. Ruth Anne went to find Old Will because she sensed something was about to happen with the army.

General Beauregard stared at the copy of the deciphered message which had been smuggled out of Washington. It was from Rose O'Neal Greenhow, one of the most effective Confederate spies in the capital, and it contained the Union army's marching plans, troop strength and objective. The general had the highest regard for information provided by Mrs. Greenhow, the widow of a U.S. State Department official and a prominent Washington hostess. Highly effective at obtaining military information from Yankee politicians, she was an invaluable source. Beauregard tuned to an aide saying, "Get a copy of this to Richmond right away. Irvin McDowell's got 37,000 men under his command and has been ordered by Lincoln to march. Their first objective is Manassas Junction. Ask Richmond to send all available reinforcements here at once." Turning to another staff officer, Beauregard remarked, "Bill, this is excellent information. Order all the forward units pulled in. We will meet them along Bull Run and give them a good thrashing. Get every available soldier into position along the west bank of the stream.

I don't know how our Rose does it, but this army will be forever in her debt." With that said, he grabbed his hat and headed for the door. General Beauregard had an army to ready for action.

Acting on the timely information provided by Mrs. Greenhow, the Confederate government ordered General Joseph E. Johnston to move his troops from the Shenandoah Valley to Manassas. Johnston's troops would provide the winning margin for the Confederacy. Soon after the battle ended, Mrs. Greenhow received a secret message from the Confederate authorities which read "Our President and our Generals thank you. The entire Confederacy is in your debt. We rely on you for further information."

A bitter Senator Charles Sumner of Massachusetts later stated "Mrs. Greenhow is worth any six of Jeff Davis's best regiments." Arrested and confined to her home in August of 1861, she continued to provide the Confederates with Union military secrets garnered from visitors to her home. In January 1862, she was charged with espionage and treason and confined to the old Capitol Prison. There she continued her spy activities and, in a desperate bid to finally be rid of her, Union authorities deported her to the Confederacy in June 1862.

In August 1863, Mrs. Greenhow was sent abroad as an unofficial diplomat for the Confederacy. In that role she continued her intelligence gathering activities and regularly sent dispatches to Richmond. For reasons unknown, she decided to return to the Confederacy. She drowned when the blockade runner on which she had taken passage was driven aground by a Union warship at the mouth of the Cape Fear River in North Carolina on October 1, 1864. Whatever crucial information she was carrying went with her to the grave. Mrs. Greenhow (1815-1864) was buried with full military honors by the Confederates.

Ruth Anne's hunch had been correct. She and Old Will watched the steady procession of withdrawing gray and butternut-clad troops from the outposts marching on the turnpike. They didn't appear be in any great hurry as they headed for the fords on Bull Run. A sergeant, who was with the detachment falling back from Fairfax Courthouse, told the couple the Union Army had left its camps around Washington and Alexandria. The Confederates were moving into position along Bull Run on a front eight miles long, covering all the fords from Union Mills to the stone bridge which carried the Warrenton Turnpike over the stream. The sergeant didn't understand why the Yankees had chosen to come via the turnpike. He had lost a $2 wager because he had bet the Union troops were going to follow the Orange and Alexandria railroad tracks out of Alexandra to Manassas Junction. In the end, he supposed it didn't matter which way they came.

Wherever the Union army tried to cross Bull Run, the Confederates would meet them. He was confident the defense line along the stream would hold. "People ought not drink the water for a couple of days" he said, "because there will be a lot of Yankee blood in it after the shooting starts." The sergeant hastily took his leave. Will and Ruth Anne watched him trot to catch up with the detachment which was a good 100 yards down the pike by the time they had finished talking.

The lackadaisical artillery unit which had been casually working on the fort at the top of the hill also departed. Old Will watched from a distance as the six-horse teams were hitched to the field guns and headed toward Blackburn's ford. The rest of the unit's equipment was tossed into three wagons which shortly thereafter followed the tracks left in the dust by the guns. The partially completed fort didn't look too imposing anymore. Now deserted, it certainly wasn't doing much by way of controlling the high ground around Centreville. To Old Will, the artillery project just seemed to be a lot of wasted digging. All the gun emplacement construction had done was to make a mess out of what had once been a good field for crops. It would take the owner a long time to level the half-built fort enough so the ground could be plowed again.

It got very quiet. There was no traffic on the dusty turnpike. The July heat hung in the humid northern Virginia air, forcing man and beast to seek out shade. The Confederates had gone but where were the Yankees? The Union army had departed its camps around Washington on July 16, taking until July 18 to reach Centreville. It required nearly three days to move the army a little more than 23 miles because the enthusiastic troops were not well trained, lacked equipment and displayed poor marching discipline. Perhaps these deficiencies would not matter; this army believed it was going to win a victory and end the war before the soldiers' term of enlistment expired. As they sprawled in their camps around Centreville, the troops carried with them the last vestiges of a national innocence which would in a short time be forever shattered on the battlefield. Nothing would ever be the same again for these soldiers or the nation.

Old Will was flabbergasted when the mass of blue locusts finally descended on his farm. There had to be over 35,000 Union troops around Centreville. General McDowell established his headquarters on the south side of the turnpike not far from Will's house. The various division commands and their subordinate brigades established camps all along the turnpike and soon filled all the space south of the pike down to Braddock Road. A great blanket of enemy soldiers smothered the fields. Blue-clad troopers belonging to Hunter's Division began trampling Will's crops, dismantling his fences for firewood and attempting to steal his chickens and hogs. Although Old Will and Ruth Anne found it a bit disconcerting to suddenly be surrounded by troops with hostile intent, they quickly learned to cope with the reality of living next to an army.

Business, which had fallen to almost nothing when the Confederates withdrew, improved significantly with the arrival of the Union army. The Strawdermans sold out of fresh eggs every day, got top prices for their chickens and all the garden produce they wished to sell. Old Will did a brisk business with the officers and non-commissioned officers interested in supplementing their rations with a little whiskey. If he could keep the chicken-stealers and wood-snatchers at bay, they might make decent money from the unwelcome stay of the Union army. To accomplish this end, Old Will enlisted the help of his customers of higher rank. A number of extra generous whiskey portions were dispensed while Old Will pleaded for the safety of his property. This display of generosity to the saviors of the Union greatly helped the situation. The word soon went down the chain of command for the soldiers to keep their hands off the Strawderman place. As a result, the farm suffered far less damage than some of the others on which the Blue troops camped.

In Centreville on July 18, General Daniel Tyler, commander of the First Division, received orders from General McDowell to probe the Confederate right flank. At Blackburn's Ford, where Route 28 now crosses Bull Run, the troops of Colonel Israel B. Richardson's Fourth Brigade collided with the Confederates. The topography of the area favored the Union attackers because the north bank of the stream was higher, providing an excellent position for artillery. However, it was not going to be as easy as it looked because the Rebel troops were commanded by an obscure, newly-appointed general named James Longstreet. He was holding the ford with a brigade composed of three Virginia regiments. Longstreet had nearly 1,200 men in battle formation when the Union artillery opened fire and the Blue infantry advanced down the slope toward the ford, firing as they moved.

A number of the Virginia troops who found they didn't like being shot at, broke from the ranks and ran for the rear. Displaying the traits that would later make him one of the Confederacy's best generals, Longstreet moved among his men with a cigar firmly clamped in his mouth and a saber in his hand, ignoring the zipping bullets and stabilizing the battle line. Under Longstreet's direction, the Virginians rallied and repulsed the attack. In response, Union gunners moved forward two cannon and fired canister which sliced away the tree branches above the Virginians' heads. Colonel Richardson then ordered the Union brigade forward to renew the attack.

When they came into range, Longstreet's battle line exploded with return fire. His presence was noted everywhere along the firing line, calmly giving orders and steadying the raw troops. On both the Union and Confederate sides, small groups of men drifted to the rear, drained of courage and cured of their romantic notions of war.

In response to Longstreet's request for assistance, Confederate infantry and artillery reinforcements began to arrive. As he was overseeing the deployment of a newly-arrived regiment and riding in front of the ranks, its officers gave the order to fire. Longstreet dived from his horse to the ground, shots flying overhead. Only when he stood up, did the troops realize he had not been hit. The comments made by the irritated Longstreet were not recorded. The reinforcements blunted the attack, and Richardson's infantry force slowly withdrew. The opposing artillery units continued to duel, the firing could be heard in Centreville until dark.

"Military glory—the attractive rainbow that rises in a shower of blood."

-Abraham Lincoln, 1848

The brutal little fight at the ford was a harbinger of things to come. The Confederates suffered 68 casualties, the Union troops lost 83 killed or wounded. The Union wounded were taken back to Centreville, and the little village got its first taste of real war as the surgeons appropriated buildings for use as aid stations. The small losses, despite the high volume of fire and length of the engagement, were due to the poor marksmanship of the combatants. New troops had a tendency to aim high. Time and combat experience would correct the habit. In later battles, the casualty rate would approach 25 percent.

Richardson's poke at the Rebels convinced General McDowell that the Confederate lines south of Centreville were too strong to attack. After some deliberation, he revised his plans, and on Sunday, July 21, the bulk of his army moved north in a flanking movement around the Confederate defenses at the stone bridge. As the Confederates desperately turned out of their positions to meet them, the first battle of Manassas (Bull Run) got seriously underway. Although close at times, the battle slowly turned against General McDowell as Joe Johnston funneled his valley troops into the struggle. The final result was a Union rout and panic in Washington.

Between 4 and 5 p.m. on July 21, 1861, the Union army began to retreat. At first, it was an orderly withdrawal with the majority of the troops leaving as they had come, across Sudley ford and rejoining the Warrenton Turnpike in the vicinity of Cub Run. The retreating infantry, artillery and army wagons soon became mixed with the carriages of congressmen and sightseers anxious to leave the scene of the federal defeat. Sometime after 6 p.m., a Confederate shell smashed a wagon on the Cub Run bridge. With the explosion, panic set in and all remaining discipline among the Union troops disappeared. The retreating army disintegrated into a mob several miles long and a hundred yards wide in places as it fled madly back to Washington. Even by today's standards, it was probably the worst rolling traffic jam ever seen on the highway. The sketches made at the time show a mass of civilians, infantry, cavalry, wagons and artillery all intermingled in panicked flight.

The embarrassing affair became known as "the great skedaddle." Colonel Erasmus D. Keys of the 11th U.S. Infantry described the mess as, "Cavalry horses without riders, wrecked baggage wagons and pieces of artillery drawn by six horses without drivers, flying at their utmost speed and whacking against other vehicles, produced a noise like a hurricane at sea." The troops discarded packs, cartridge boxes and rifles as they retreated. Some soldiers cut horses from their traces and mounted them so they could flee faster. The road became littered with the abandoned equipment of war. Near the Cub Run crossing, the Confederates captured 14 cannon and a large number of horses and wagons abandoned by the routed Union army.

General McDowell thought he would be able to rally the army on the Centreville heights. However, the troops were too demoralized to make a stand and the unchecked retreat continued. Three brigades which had been in reserve at Centreville formed a rear guard and followed the dispirited throng back to Washington. They made good time. Although it had taken the army nearly three days to reach Centerville on the way out, the defeated troops got back to Washington in one night. To the green, poorly trained soldiers it was a horrid introduction to war. Few ever forgot the awful night journey.

The initial reports General McDowell sent to Washington indicated a Union victory was in the making. Upon hearing the good news, President Abraham Lincoln decided to go for a Sunday drive. When he returned, the frantic aides who had been searching for him informed the President the battle had been lost. Lincoln headed for the War Department where he read a grim dispatch from the field:

July 21, 1861

General McDowell's army is in full retreat through Centreville.
The day is lost. Save Washington and the remnants of this army.
All advance troops ought to be thrown forward in one body.
General McDowell is doing all he can to cover the retreat. Colonel

Miles is forming for that purpose. He was in reserve at Centreville. The routed troops will not reform.

B. S. Alexander,
Captain, Corps Engineers

The shock of the dreadful message burned the name of Centreville, Virginia indelibly into Abraham Lincoln's brain. He would remember the awful moment clearly for the remainder of his life. The somber President returned to the White House where he spent the first of the many sleepless nights that would be required by his quest to save the Union.

On July 18, Old Will and Ruth Anne heard the rumble of the guns from the direction of Blackburn's Ford. "Must be a big battle going on down near there," Ruth Anne said. Later in the evening, they heard from a passerby that the Yankees had failed to force a crossing of Bull Run. A whole pack of Yankees had been shot in the fight and Union surgeons had taken over the Methodist Church in the village to treat the wounded. Will thought it a shame that a house of God could be taken over by the Yankee army for use as a hospital. Then he remembered the income he derived from his dealings with the hated enemy, who were rather decent folk as individuals, and reconsidered. "I suppose a church could serve as hospital in a pinch. It just wouldn't be right to let them lie in the open," he muttered. His customers were not bad people. He hoped that none of his good ones had been shot. He did not care much about what happened to those who abstained completely from drink, they were no concern of his.

In the early hours of July 21, the Union army quietly marched out of the camps around Centreville. Most of them appeared to be heading in the direction of the stone bridge, but Will couldn't be sure. It wasn't too long after daybreak when the ominous rumble of guns began to drift in. Although it was at a greater distance than the previous fight at Blackburn's Ford, it sounded as though there were a lot more of the big guns. From the top of the ridge in the village, Will and Ruth Anne could see smoke plumes rising from the battlefield. A fair amount of traffic was moving on the turnpike. There was a steady stream of army wagons moving forward, couriers moving in the opposite direction and a number of fancy carriages from Washington on their way to view the battle. The sound of gunfire went on for most of the day, changing in clarity as the wind shifted direction.

In the afternoon, the first of the blue-uniformed soldiers trickled by the farm as they headed back to Alexandria or Washington. At first, there was only a few of them, but their appearance made Old Will uneasy. Many of the powder-smudged faces had a wild, crazed look in their eyes. What had these men seen to make them so fearful? Neither Will nor Ruth Anne could remember exactly when the massive tide of fleeing humanity engulfed them. As they later recalled, it was around 7 or 8 p.m. when the turnpike began to explode in noise and confusion. They could see an endless line of fast moving vehicles raising dust as they came down the hill from the village. It began with just a few baggage wagons, moving at top speed. The few soon turned into many with the horse and mule teams being pushed to their absolute limit by the profanity screaming teamsters who urged them on. Then infantry, cavalry and artillery units began to appear, competing with the wagons for space on the turnpike. The infantry soon spread out on both sides of the road, trampling crops, knocking down fences and anything else that got in their way. Wagons were abandoned as teamsters cut the teams loose and rode off. Some soldiers left the jammed road and headed across country through the fields of ripening crops. Old Will was not sure how long it took for the rolling riot of fleeing vehicles and men to pass his farm. He and Ruth Anne had never witnessed anything remotely like it in all the years they had resided next to the turnpike. It was late in the evening after the full moon had risen before they noticed a lull in the traffic. The once peaceful road that had uneventfully gone by the farm for as long as anyone could remember had turned into a turnpike of despair. Almost every conceivable type of military equipment lay scattered along the road, along with abandoned wagons, caissons and a cannon or two.

The night retreat of the Yankee army had been hard on Old Will's property, leaving a large part of his farm wrecked. Fences were down and livestock lost. Old Will figured he might as well try to salvage something by picking up a good wagon and maybe a spare horse or mule from the mass of military flotsam littering the road. If he didn't act promptly, he was certain the Confederates who would come with the sunrise would collect everything usable for themselves. They were welcome to the muskets and other military gear. Old Will was only looking for items he could use to repair the damage to his farm.

He headed toward Centreville, the moon casting a pale light on the littered road. As he crossed Little Rocky Run, Old Will saw two horses still hitched to a wagon, drinking from the stream a short distance from the turnpike. The other horses of the team was gone, probably taken by fleeing troops. As Old Will checked the animals he softly spoke to the tired animals, "Easy now. What a nice piece of luck. You seem to be in good shape. Nothing looks wrong with you other than being plumb tuckered out from all the running." While the horses grazed quietly on the stream bank grass, Will checked the contents of the wagon. Upon lifting the rear flap of the canvas wagon cover, he was greeted by the sickening smell of drying blood. He found himself looking directly into the open eyes of a pale-faced, dead soldier.

Old Will was stunned by the burning sensation the bullet made as it nicked his side. Next, he heard the booming pistol report. Will spun around and slid down against the rear wheel of the wagon, his side leaking blood. "Is the bushwhacking Rebel bastard dead?" roared the Union first lieutenant who was holding a smoking army-issued Colt revolver. Two privates cautiously came over to look at Will, their weapons at the ready. "No, he's still alive," one answered.

"Shooting is too good for the likes of him," growled the lieutenant, "Let's string him up from yonder tree and leave him dangling as warning to the other thieves and bushwhackers in these parts." Prodded by a musket barrel in his back, Will was roughly jostled into place under the large limb of a sycamore tree, his hands quickly tied behind his back. Despite Old Will's protestations that he was only a poor farmer searching for his missing livestock and had not killed anyone, a noose was fitted tightly around his neck. The five soldiers were about to hoist Old Will when a mounted officer who had ridden over to the execution site after checking the wagon gruffly asked, "Just what the hell do you think you are doing lieutenant?" The lieutenant turned, smartly saluted the colonel and said, "This bushwhacker killed the soldier in the wagon and was caught stealing army property. We are going to hang the murdering thief right here."

Colonel William T. Sherman was a bit bemused by the intensity of the answer. "The trooper in the wagon has been dead for a number of hours," he said. "He died from the loss of blood caused by an untreated gunshot wound. He probably was shot sometime during the battle and placed in the wagon by his messmates when the retreat began. Most likely died sometime while the wagon moved along the road. No one attended the wound. This farmer could not have done it. Where is his weapon? I think you have caught yourself the wrong man. This fellow here is no killer, let him go!" The soldiers untied Old Will, who stood unsteadily while nervously eyeing the group of soldiers. Colonel Sherman glared down at the shaking old farmer and sternly warned him, "The next time I buy something from you to drink, I expect you will give me your best price without any haggle. Now get back to your farm and stay out of the army's way! If you go wandering around in the dark again, you may not be so lucky the next time!"

As the soldiers headed back to the road, Old Will overheard Sherman talking to the young officer: "Lieutenant, I like your style. How would you like to be reassigned to my command when we get back to Washington? This disastrous day has proved nothing other than we are going to be in for a mighty long war. Good officers are going to have serve in the right outfits if we are going to have any chance at all to win it." The lieutenant was flattered by the gruff colonel's words. He agreed to request a transfer.

Old Will was shaken to the core. He had been shot and almost hanged in the space of 20 minutes. His wound, although bloody, did not appear to be life-threatening. The bullet had ripped a mean gash through the flesh covering his ribs. Still, it was painful. "Lucky for me, the crazy lieutenant hadn't taken more time to aim," he mumbled to himself. He would never forget the look of pure hate reflected in the young officer's eyes. The only other time he had seen anything nearly as bad was many years ago when Travis McCarton had come after him with a knife in one of the taverns one night. Some of the village wags, with nothing better to do than stir up trouble, had told Travis that Will was making eyes at his wife. Hot-tempered Travis had erupted in rage at the insult to his honor and came looking for Will. It had been a close call. If another patron had not brained Travis with a chair, Will would have been cut to pieces. After the falsehood had been exposed for what it was, Will and Travis had become good friends. Travis had been dead for years now, Will recalled. He had died when a skittish horse kicked him and smashed his guts. Horses could be dangerous. Maybe some day, someone would invent a safer way for people to travel.

From the south side of Centreville came the sound of gunfire as probing Confederate cavalry units slammed into Blenker's Brigade which was part of the rear guard covering the humiliating Union retreat. The brigade held its ground and traded lead with the cavalry as the halfhearted, disorganized Confederate pursuit ground to a halt. It grew dark as clouds slid across the moon and a slow, steady, warm summer rain began pelting the ground. The dust on the Warrenton Turnpike began to turn into the sticky mud which was the bane of travelers in northern Virginia.

Old Will's trembling finally stopped. He made a crude bandage out of a shirt he found in the wagon and wrapped it around the oozing gash in his side, securing it with a big knot. It had grown quiet on the turnpike. There was no use leaving the horses which had nearly cost him his life behind. So, miserable as he was from his ordeal and soaking wet to boot, he unhitched the animals. The dead soldier lying in the wagon continued to stare at Will with unseeing eyes as he led the horses around the rear of the wagon. "I don't even know you soldier," muttered Will, "But you damn near got me killed. May you rest in peace anyhow, whoever you are." With that pronouncement, Will began a slow journey back to the farm. There were a few military units moving on the turnpike, probably among the last to leave the battlefield. They paid no attention to Will or the jaded pair of horses he led. He was just one of many dispirited individuals heading for Washington on what had become a rainy night . He may have been one of the congressmen who had come out to watch the battle for all they knew. The soundly defeated soldiers had other things on their minds. Most of their enlistments had expired or would shortly expire. After they got back to Washington, they could go home. Their military experience had made them sadder but wiser men.

Old Will had reached his home by the time the Union rear guard slogged by his farm. As it retreated, the jurisdiction of the United States government shrank with it. By dawn, federal control hardly extended beyond the city limits of Washington, D.C. The Confederate tide would soon be lapping at the gates of the capital. In the White House, Abraham Lincoln was in deep despair.

As Ruth Anne did a proper job of re-bandaging his wound, Old Will told her how Colonel Sherman had saved him from the hangman's rope. Sherman was so nondescript and colorless that Old Will could not remember meeting him while the army camped at Centreville. Sherman lacked the flash and dash of the many other officers who had impressed Old Will with their military grandeur. While he would be eternally grateful to the nervous man with the reddish hair for saving his life, Will didn't think Sherman would turn out to be much of a soldier. He told to Ruth Anne, "We will probably never hear anything else about Bill Sherman again. I don't think he has what it takes to make a good military leader." "That may be true," Ruth Anne replied, "but since he saved your life, I wish him all the best. I hope he lives through the war and makes it back to his home when the fighting finally stops."

By late 1864, Will had to admit he had never been more wrong about anything in his life then in his assessment of the military prospects of William T. Sherman. As he recounted the details of their rainy night meeting near the Warrenton Turnpike to his rapt listeners, Will readily admitted that Sherman possessed hidden qualities of military genius not readily apparent to an observer back in the summer of 1861.

Old Will went to Centreville and saw for himself the carnage around the Methodist Church. There was a pile of vermin-covered human limbs lying outside one of the windows. The surgeons had taken down the door and used it as an operating table. It was still propped in position amid the pools of dried blood. On one side of the building were a row of dead soldiers waiting for the burial detail to come and take them away. On the other side of the stone structure, lying in shade, were a large number of wounded too ill to be moved to prison camps. They would most likely be sent to Washington under a flag of truce and accompanied by the doctors who had remained behind to treat them.

The victorious Confederates moved forward in pursuit of the routed Yankees. They had become almost as disorganized by victory as the Union army had been by its defeat. Units were all mixed up, rations were in short supply and many soldiers were out of ammunition. Though nearly everyone expected an attack to be made on Washington during the remainder of the summer, it never came. General Johnston told the government he needed more troops. He could not take Washington without them. Since Confederate President Davis was unable to supply the reinforcements, a stalemate developed. The Union army rapidly fortified the capital of the United States while its new commander, General George B. McClellan, labored to rebuild the shattered force into a viable fighting machine. Short of resources, Johnston's army had to be content with keeping the Yankees pinned in the capital. The military activity in Northern Virginia declined to the level of sharp skirmishes between opposing patrols.

Will spent the months following the battle repairing the damage to his farm. The Confederates, who held the positions around Washington, again became his customers. He did a good business in eggs, meat and produce. The Centreville taverns continued to purchase his whiskey, as did a number of officers and noncommissioned officers. Selling whiskey to the military was a touchy endeavor requiring a keen judgment of human nature. If Will did not carefully select his customers, he could easily fall into the clutches of the provost marshal who was valiantly attempting to curb the excessive drinking of the soldiery. Will knew that if the provost guards caught him, he would be put out of business for good.

What had been unthinkable only a few months ago, now became a prudent course of action for the area's residents. As a consequence of the damage inflicted by the armies sweeping across the land, the civilian farming population around Centreville began an exodus because their means of earning a living was gone. The damage caused by the armies shattered many dreams of a prosperous life in the new Confederacy, as Wilmer McLean, one of the prominent local citizens, learned. McLean was a local businessman and speculator residing at Yorkshire Plantation just across Bull Run in Prince William County. While seeking to ingratiate himself with the general and at the same time pursue business opportunities with the Confederate government, Wilmer invited General Beauregard to use his house as a headquarters.

On July 18, 1861, the McLean property abruptly came under Union cannon fire. Some time around noon, a shell exploded in the summer kitchen, ruining preparations for the general's dinner. After the conclusion of the battle and shocked by what he had seen, McLean moved his family down state to a little village called Appomattox. On April 9, 1865, the unlucky man's residence in the central Virginia village became the site of Lee's surrender to Grant. McLean had the distinction of having had the first and last major actions of the war in the east take place on his property. His place in the history books, however, came at a high personal price. The Yorkshire property suffered major damage in the fighting and from its occupation by troops. At Appomattox, Union officers purchased many of his furnishings as souvenirs after the surrender documents were signed.

The good times were gone for good and by late 1866, McLean, was virtually bankrupt. Although the family still owned many acres of farmland in Northern Virginia, it was almost worthless after the war. Land prices had declined from a pre-war price near $125 an acre to around $2.50. Like many other residents who had gone into the war with high expectations and the hope of a rapid Confederate victory, Wilmer McLean's fortunes never recovered. Given the continuing poor state of the local economy, he was forced to move to the city of Alexandria, Virginia around 1876. General Grant, then President of the United States, helped him obtain a job at the Treasury Department in Washington where he worked until 1880.

October 1861

After much hard work, Will Strawderman had his farm back in relatively good shape by October when President Jefferson Davis came up from Richmond to visit his generals. Old Will had heard of the meeting at Fairfax Courthouse between the President, Generals Joseph E. Johnston and P. G. T. Beauregard. "They are probably planning an attack on Washington before the good weather ends. It is high time they got around to finishing this silly war," Old Will told Ruth Anne. Rumor had it that the President's relationship with the two generals had grown cool during the past months due to personality and war policy differences. Now, the generals told the president they wanted 20,000 reinforcements before they would attack. After Davis informed them the supplementary troops could not be provided, all planning for the Confederate offensive in northern Virginia abruptly came to an end.

General Johnston knew he could not capture Washington with the number of troops available to him. Unwilling to attack, with bad weather coming and the Union army growing stronger every day, the army could not remain in its forward positions around the capital for the winter. A suitable defensive position had to be located for the army's winter quarters, one which would keep it within striking distance of Washington. The general's military engineers were instructed to find the strongest defensive position between Washington and Manassas.

Old Will was flabbergasted when on October 19, the army came back to Centreville. Work immediately commenced on a line of fortifications over six miles long, beginning in the valley of Cub Run and running west to east north of the village. On the high ground on the northeast side of town, the defensive line was linked at a large, imposing fort with another line of fortifications running south to where Little Rocky Run flows into Bull Run. From his farm, Will could see the cursing soldiers at work on the forts and the interconnecting trench lines.

The ugly line of fortifications stretched as far as Old Will could see. The miles of land defacing military earthworks had 13 large forts situated at key positions. Many of these forts were fronted with a 10 foot wide, six feet deep ditch. The sloping fort walls rose 10 to 14 feet above ground level, and were 20 feet or more in height if measured from the bottom of the ditch. Over 70 pieces of artillery could be mounted along the Confederate line. The descending slopes falling away from the line of fortifications offered perfect fields of fire for the cannon. The defensive line of earthworks was state of the art. It was constantly written about in Northern and Southern newspapers because the defenses around Centreville were among the strongest built in North America up to the year of 1861.

Old Will could see one big problem with the army's decision to hole up for the winter at Centreville. His farm was directly in the line of fire of the entrenched cannon glowering down on his property from their positions atop the ridge line. "Perhaps it would have been a good idea to leave," Old Will said to himself. "We might have been better off taking Wilmer McLean's advice." Wilmer had made no secret about his desire to get out of the way of the armies during the short good-bye visit he made to Will's farm prior to vacating the area. Wilmer had strongly urged Will to follow his example and leave. Wilmer foresaw nothing but trouble coming for the residents who remained between the warring armies. As he looked again at the artillery batteries ensconced behind their earthen forts, Old Will had a sinking feeling that Wilmer had been right. His farm was directly in the line of fire of the big, ugly guns.

"Honor has not to be won; it must only not be lost."
-Arthur Schopenhauer, 1851

Matthew F. Chambon quickly rose to the rank of captain in the Virginia state forces after Virginia left the Union. A 1859 graduate of the Virginia Military Institute, he had excelled in the study of artillery tactics taught by an eccentric professor named Thomas J. Jackson. After his heroic performance at the battle of Manassas, the professor everyone had thought to be more than a little odd became known as "Stonewall" Jackson. Because of his artillery background, Captain Chambon had been assigned the duty of sorting and readying for action the chaotic mass of guns which fell into the Confederacy's possession when Virginia seized the Federal installations within the state. He had been sorting, repairing and shipping the nearly 300 cannon acquired as a result of the takeover of the Norfolk Navy Yard. Shortly after the battle near Manassas, Captain Chambon had received orders to report to General Johnston's army in northern Virginia. He immediately became immersed in the task of positioning artillery and helping train the newly formed artillery units.

All in all, General Johnston was responsible for a 58 mile front which ran from Leesburg south through Centreville and on to the south bank of the Occoquan River where it joins the Potomac. Since such a long front was impossible to garrison, the vital points were fortified and patrols moved constantly throughout the area watching vigilantly for any enemy movement.

Although there were no major battles, clashes occurred near Dranesville, Pohick Church, Springfield, Burke Station, Annandale, Falls Church and Fairfax Court House. There was just enough action to keep everyone alert and on their toes.

"War is regarded as nothing but the continuation of politics by other means."
-Karl Von Clausewitz, 1780-1831

The autumn of 1861 was a time of high tension in northern Virginia. By the middle of October, the capital of the United States at Washington, DC was virtually blockaded. Captain Chambon helped place artillery along the Potomac River's Virginia bank, from a point south of Occoquan Bay to where the Quantico Marine base is now located. Once in place, the batteries began firing on Union navy and commercial vessels heading upriver to Washington. With the vital river transportation artery closed to commercial traffic, over 40 vessels were soon stranded below the batteries. Although the plucky Union navy constantly dueled with the Rebel guns and managed to maintain control of the river proper, the Potomac was effectively closed to all but the most daring ship captains. Feeling the pinch of the blockade, the prices of staples in Washington climbed and the daily number of rail cars moving to the city rose to more than 400 as federal authorities struggled to keep the city supplied. Although the federal government had proclaimed a blockade of Southern ports, Washington may have been the only partially blockaded city in the North or South at this stage of the war. Although the blockade caused the residents a high degree of discomfort and uncertainty, it had no chance of starving the capital into submission because of the vast array of logistical resources available to Federal authorities.

Still, Johnston's blockade was an embarrassment to the Lincoln administration. Naval vessels traveling to and from the Washington Navy Yard had to fight their way past the river batteries, a fact duly reported home by the foreign diplomatic community. It also greatly increased the cost of supplying Washington because the majority of commercial shipping would not risk running the Confederate fire. To counter any Confederate attempt to cross the river and stir up trouble in southern Maryland, General Joseph Hooker's division was sent to occupy the Maryland shore opposite Johnston's guns. As cooler weather arrived, the Potomac echoed with the sound of artillery fire as Hooker's long-range guns dueled with the Confederate batteries on the Virginia shore.

General Johnston concentrated the largest part of his 45,000 soldiers in the Centreville fortifications. As army logging parties moved across the countryside, the trees disappeared to satisfy the huge need for firewood, fortification construction and the winter huts for troops. Farmers who thought they had enough wood to last a hundred years suddenly found themselves with hardly enough fuel for cooking and heating for the coming winter. Old Will watched sadly as virtually all of his trees were taken to serve the Confederate cause. Beside meeting his domestic needs, it was becoming exceedingly difficult to find fuel for the still which was located a distance from his home. Old Will partially resolved the problem by dispensing an ample amount of liquid refreshment to the sullen wood cutting crews that came by the farm. He often found that a sizable stack of wood had been left behind after the wagons returned to the camps at night. In spite of the nagging wood shortage, business improved as the troops camped in the area. Everything edible on the farm was sold and the still ran at capacity to supply the taverns and army customers. Many of the officers were known for their ability to provide a measure of pleasant hospitality in the headquarters scattered around Centreville. Old Will, and the growing number of new competitors who suddenly emerged, did all they could to keep the military supplied with strong drink.

General Johnston was bedeviled by a shortage of cannon to place in his otherwise strong fortifications around Centreville. During the general's meeting with his senior officers and artillery specialists, Captain Chambon suggested cutting logs to cannon size, painting them black and placing them in the vacant gun ports in the forts. At first Joe Johnston didn't think much of the idea. What point would it serve? General Beauregard thought the captain's suggestion had a great deal of merit because the Yankee scouts would not be able to tell the real guns from the fake ones at a distance. The bogus cannon would help create an illusion of more fire power being available than the Confederates actually had. The Confederate commanders were well aware that General McClellan's growing army outside of Washington already outnumbered them. The fake guns might cause him to delay his attack during the remaining period of good weather. Captain Chambon was told to go ahead with his idea. The "Quaker Guns," as they were called by the troops, soon filled all the empty gun slots in the fortification line. Not aware of the ruse, Will Strawderman was amazed at the speed at which the vacant gun positions suddenly filled. Richmond must have sent artillery up here by the trainload!

Fearing a possible Confederate strike, the Union army began to fortify Washington. The city was soon protected by a rival defense line and over 60 forts. As General McClellan's army trained endlessly and grew stronger, he delayed attacking the Centreville fortifications. A reliance on faulty intelligence information led him to conclude Johnston had 90,000 troops behind his fortification line. Rumors of the impregnable Confederate defenses at Centreville began to filter through the Union camps around Washington. The name "Centreville" struck a degree of fear in the Union troops who would have to attack what was widely believed to be an appallingly strong position that offered its defenders every advantage.

As autumn waned, Johnston's army, too weak to move against Washington, awaited an expected attack behind its fortifications. General McClellan, fixated by the erroneous intelligence data, avoided doing anything but training the never ending stream of reinforcements flowing to his army. His troops, being in no hurry to march on the strong Rebel line at Centreville, complained very little. The rank and file of both armies breathed a collective sigh of relief when the rains finally made the roads impassable.

March 1862

Newly-promoted Major Chambon thought it had been a terrible winter. The army supply system had not functioned well at all. Excesses of some food items and baggage piled up, tying up valuable space in warehouses and rail cars while other necessary items remained in critically short supply. To lessen dependence on the roads which became impassable in wet weather, the army constructed a spur railroad line from Manassas Junction to the camps at Centreville. One Richmond newspaper reporter called it the first railroad line in the world built solely for military purposes. The major had never considered the railroad to be an instrument of war, but he was ready to admit it was playing a growing role in this conflict. The railroad certainly had helped alleviate the creaky supply situation because trains were able to run in all kinds of weather. The trains were fast too. Maintaining a speed of nearly 25 miles per hour was not difficult if the track was in good condition.

Although there had been little fighting during the long cold, damp winter, the army lost a large number of soldiers. The troops had been hit hard by diarrhea, dysentery, typhoid, measles and pneumonia. In one report he read, Chambon saw 3,400 troops listed as sick and unfit for duty. He knew a large number had also died, although he had not seen the report listing the actual numbers. "If this keeps up," the major told a friend over dinner one evening, "I am afraid that deaths caused by disease will be twice as high as battle casualties. The army succumbs to sickness at a higher rate than it does to fighting. Being in camp is actually deadlier than being on the battlefield." His dinner guest looked puzzled. He had never looked at the situation that way before. It was something to think about.

Major Chambon kept his log guns well-painted. As far as anyone could tell, the Yankees had yet to catch on to the charade. Major Chambon was aggravated by the fact that ammunition distribution for his real cannon was a problem. Too much of the ammunition was stored too far behind the gun positions. It would be difficult to keep the batteries supplied with powder, shot and shells once fighting started. A combination of faulty packaging and poorly constructed magazines had also led to the ruination of a large amount of gunpowder due to exposure to the elements. It would have to be replaced quickly.

The chill at army headquarters was not completely due to the late winter weather. Overly proud and too sensitive of his honor, Confederate President Davis had transferred General Beauregard out of Centreville in January after the president had been embarrassed by comments made in Beauregard's Manassas battle report. General Johnston was also feuding with Davis. At a secret planning meeting in Richmond, the president and general had discussed the army's withdrawal from the Centreville line. Joe Johnston had become enraged when the contents of the strategy discussion were leaked to the press by Davis or someone close to him. Now he and Davis were barely on speaking terms.

Johnston's senior staff officers had seen the reports from spies indicating General McClellan was promoting a plan to bypass Centreville completely and transport his army down the Chesapeake Bay on ships. The Union army would land at a suitable point and attack Richmond from the east. The strong Union navy would have no problem in keeping the troops supplied, an advantage not to be overlooked. Although opposed to the idea at first, Abe Lincoln was reported to be on the verge of giving his approval to the plan. Once the Union army moved, Johnston's army at Centreville would be flanked and in danger of being cut off from Richmond. McClellan's forces could travel faster by water than Johnston could march in the thawing late-winter mud. To avoid becoming isolated in useless Centreville positions, General Joe was going to pull his army back behind the Rappahannock River as quickly as possible. Northern Virginia was to be given up to the Yankees without a fight whether the idiot politicians in Richmond liked it or not.

When General Johnston abruptly gave the order to abandon the Centreville defenses, the army plunged into chaos. The soft, late winter roads created a horrendous problem for troops on the move. Most of the loaded wagons sank nearly to their hubs, making movement extremely slow even when they were hitched to double mule teams. Given little notice of the army's departure, the railroad had no time to gather enough cars to move the vast stockpile of supplies at Manassas and Centreville.

Because the Union navy controlled the Potomac, the Confederates were denied access to waterborne transportation. Major Chambon had to tell the general the big guns of the Potomac River batteries had to be abandoned because the guns were too heavy to move over the bad roads. The Confederacy could ill afford to relinquish the artillery, and although Johnston raged at the idea, he could offer no other solution. He would not consider, as Chambon suggested, delaying the withdrawal until the roads dried a little more. It was not an unreasonable suggestion. Unknown to the major, President Davis was also urging Johnston to delay withdrawing until the military stores in northern Virginia could be removed. General Johnston was not swayed by the arguments, so orders were issued to disable those guns that could not be moved. The Confederate blockade of Washington, which had choked off the river to Union shipping, was coming to an ignominious end.

General Johnston fumed when he learned of the massive amount of supplies his army would have to leave behind. Looking at the growing mountain of supplies piling up at the Centreville railhead, one officer sadly remarked, "I have a feeling we are going to miss all of this material later on. This may be the last time our army ever has too much of anything. It is such a damn shame that we have to destroy it because some fool can't arrange for enough rail cars to move it."

Despite General Johnston's protest that it was too close to the front lines for comfort, in 1861 the Confederate Subsistence Department established a large meat-curing facility on the grounds of John Chapman's mill located at Thoroughfare Gap. There were over two million pounds of curing meat at the site when word came that Johnston had decided to pull out of northern Virginia. Since the majority of the artillery units had already begun marching to the new positions far to the south, General Johnston yanked Major Chambon away from his artillery duties and sent to him to Chapman's mill to ensure the removal or destruction of the meat stores went as planned. When he arrived at the mill, the major found the place a madhouse. The furious subsistence officers did not want to destroy their valuable food supplies because of Johnston's ill-time evacuation decision. "Why the hell had he not informed anyone in Richmond of his planned evacuation?" they demanded. "The meat could have been easily shipped out of here before the army grabbed every available wagon and rail car, leaving no way for us to move this irreplaceable meat! Don't you stupid bastards at headquarters know soldiers have to eat in order to be able to fight?" an enraged red-faced butcher screamed at Chambon. The major quickly agreed with the man holding the cleaver that everything had certainly turned into one hell of a big mess.

Major Chambon did the best he could with the dicey situation. When D. H. Hill's brigade came down after withdrawing from the positions they had held at Leesburg, Chambon insisted they cram all the meat they could carry into their wagons. "How can the dolts passing themselves off as our leaders expect to win a war if they are so dumb they can't even make the simple arrangements necessary to move a pile of hams?" the disbelieving Hill inquired of Major Chambon as he surveyed the piles of meat. After the troops had taken their fill, local residents were invited to haul away whatever they could manage to carry. Even after meat was added to the load of every army wagon moving on the muddy turnpike, the major found he still had more than a million pounds which he had to keep from falling into Yankee hands.

Sadly and reluctantly, Major Chambon organized the biggest barbecue ever held in northern Virginia. As the remaining supplies were put to the torch, the smell of burning meat carried for miles. A devout army private slogging by the flaming piles prophesied to his mess mates, "God don't like it when you waste the good victuals he has provided. This army is going to starve from now on because of the terrible waste you see before you. You mark my words boys, mark them well! God always gets even when we do wrong!" With that bitter, offhand remark an army legend was born. From that time forward hungry Confederate soldiers would tell and retell the story of how God had cursed their army for the appalling waste of good food at Chapman's mill. The tale always ended with, "I tell you the truth boys, you could smell the sizzling meat for ten miles in all directions. Over a million pounds got burnt up for no good reason. I sure do wish we had just a little bit of it here with us now. It would be mighty nice to have just one of those wasted hams. Yes sir, it truly would be nice."

With the stench of blazing meat hanging in his nostrils, Major Chambon followed the Warrenton Turnpike back to headquarters at Centreville. Crossing the stone bridge on Bull Run, he had to stop and explain to the engineers busily planting the charges to demolish the bridge why the wind was carrying the smell of burning meat. Arriving at the Centreville railhead, he reported the destruction of the meat supply to General Johnston. "I hoped we could have saved more of it. It is too bad the government cannot provide us with more wagons and rail cars," the general said in reply to the report. He then instructed Major Chambon to remain with the rear guard and put the torch to the piles of supplies which could not be removed. "The last units will be marching out by tomorrow tonight," General Johnston remarked. "I want nothing usable left behind for the Yankees. See to it that nothing remains here but a pile of ashes by the time you leave. The rear guard will hold its positions until your work is complete. Then all of you clear out."

Major Chambon looked at the small mountains of equipment, excess personal clothing, tents, ruined wagons, caissons, horse harnesses and other military debris the army was abandoning and thought it would at least be easy to burn. His teams were soon setting fire to the piles scattered around the railroad terminus. Word had come from Manassas Junction that the warehouses located there were also going up in flames. Major Chambon was watching the heaps of discarded supplies begin to blaze nicely when one of them suddenly exploded, hurling a mixture of wagon parts, lumber and iron casings in all directions. In the sloppy haste of the evacuation, someone had inadvertently placed a number of barrels of gunpowder and an unknown number of dud artillery shells in the pile. The resulting explosion killed the three soldiers standing near the blast site outright. Major Chambon, who was some distance away, never knew what hit him. A piece of flying iron slammed into the side of his head knocking him senseless. A hurtling wagon wheel broke his left leg in two places and another chunk of iron sliced a gash down his right side as he went down. Of the five men injured in the blast, the four others luckily suffered injuries that were not life-threatening. All were treated at the site by a regimental surgeon who had been supervising the loading of the last of the army's medical supplies in a rail car. Although the doctor patched Matt Chambon as best he could, he did not think the major would survive the night because of his severe head injury. The major, the other four injured and three dead soldiers were hastily loaded on one of the last trains leaving the Centreville railhead and sent to Richmond for recuperation or burial.

General Johnston's army evacuated Centreville on a dreary March 9, 1862, leaving behind a countryside stripped of forage and provisions. Remaining behind in graves scattered over the hillsides behind the fortifications were the many soldiers who had died from accident or disease during the long winter the army had sat at the gates of Washington. In the rush to evacuate, no one had taken the time to remove the burial records. The rosters listing the number and the location of the dead were inadvertently burned with the rest of the material the army was forced to leave behind. Johnston's downcast rear guard slogged unmolested across the stone bridge spanning Bull Run. Shortly after the last man had crossed, the engineers blew up the span and joined the retreating troop column heading south on the muddy road. As they passed the ruins of the meat packing facility, the soldiers could not fail to notice the strong stench of overcooked meat hanging in the chilly night air.

Union troops probed forward cautiously on March 10 and found the Confederates gone. With the threat to Washington removed, the occupying soldiers amused themselves by inspecting the fortifications, wandering through the abandoned winter camps and admiring the Quaker Guns which had so worried them through the autumn and winter. Newspaper reporters mingled with the curious troops, and the Northern press promptly destroyed the myths surrounding Centreville. One reporter wrote: "The fancied impregnability of the position turns out to be a sham." After inspecting the Rebel fortifications, a reporter for the New York Tribune wrote on March 13, 1862: "Utterly dispirited, ashamed and humiliated, I return from this visit to the rebel stronghold, feeling their retreat is our defeat." President Abraham Lincoln was chagrined to learn the defenses at Centreville had been held by an army only half the size estimated by General McClellan.

In Richmond, Confederate President Davis was subjected to a great deal of criticism because Johnston's retreat resulted in a huge loss of supplies and gave up a substantial amount of territory without a fight. The bad news of the retreat in Virginia came on top of news of terrible setbacks in the west. In February, an unknown Union general named Grant had taken Ft. Henry on the Tennessee River and Ft. Donelson on the Cumberland. With the rivers thrown open to Yankee gunboats, much of the vital industrial capacity of Tennessee was lost to the Confederate cause. Nashville, with its war industries still running full tilt, was occupied by Union forces on February 23. Coupled with these disasters, Johnston's seemingly panicked retreat depressed morale in the South and raised grave questions regarding the competence of the civilian and military leadership of the Confederacy.

Will Strawderman had not made up his mind whether the Confederate evacuation was a curse or a blessing. He was standing by the side of the turnpike pondering the sudden change of events on March 11 when the Union commander, Major General George B McClellean, rode by with his staff to inspect the abandoned Confederate positions. Old Will thought the general was a fine looking man, one who looked like a general ought to look. Old Will swelled with importance when the general halted and asked if he knew where the Confederates had gone. Having heard some snippets of information from the departing Confederate troops, Old Will told the general that the Confederates had left in a great hurry to establish a new defense line along the Rapidan River. "They didn't have enough rail cars to move everything when they retreated, so they blew up a big batch of ammunition down by the railhead. I heard the explosion all the way over here," he added. To tell the truth, Old Will would have liked to see a sizable number of Union troops permanently occupy the Rebel works because his whiskey business could use an infusion of paying customers with the Confederates gone.

The winter-long stay of the Confederate army had soured relations with the farmers because the army's presence taxed local resources, resulting in an increase in the price of grain, cattle and hogs. In response to rising prices, the Confederate government seized goods, paying the reluctant owners fixed prices in Confederate currency. The farmers felt cheated because the amount paid by the unfeeling Confederate States' purchasing agents was below market value. In a high-handed manner resented by the locals, the army took what it wanted, leaving virtually nothing for local consumption. General Johnston had also made life miserable for the distillers in the region. He ordered their grain supplies confiscated because he believed the whiskey producers controlled the grain market.

Discipline had been a problem in the winter camps as the bored and lonely Confederate soldiers took to drink. After a couple of drunken soldiers in General Longstreet's division tried to kill an officer, they were tried by an army court. After the determination of guilt was reached, Longstreet ordered them shot by a firing squad. The executions took place in front of the entire division and many of the troops never forgot the sight of soldiers killing their own. After the incident, the army launched a serious effort to curb the amount of whiskey available to the rank and file. Wisely, Old Will began limiting his sales to officers and noncommissioned officers he could trust. To keep his still in operation, Old Will had to smuggle wagon loads of grain past the military check points and bribe officials to look the other way. It was a stressful undertaking. If General Joe Johnston ever found out what he was doing, Old Will knew he would be shot or sent to prison. Although his whiskey production declined somewhat and he had to increase prices, Old Will's customers seemed to understand that the problem was due to the war's disruption of economic activity and the general officers' efforts keep the soldiers sober.

As the first year of the war drew to a close, it had already lasted much longer than Old Will or anyone else in Centreville had expected. He found himself trapped in a land of desolation in which many of the necessities of life had disappeared or if available at all, had been priced out of reach. Old Will had a considerable amount of cash from the sales of his farm products and whiskey to the armies, but no livestock and little firewood. Not even in his wildest dreams had Old Will expected to see the day when no firewood was available. Now, because the armies had exhausted the local supply, he faced an acute shortage. He was not sure if his financial gain had been worth the trouble, having almost been killed once by the Yankees and having to constantly face the risk of imprisonment or worse if caught by the Confederate authorities.

Old Will never thought the war would cause him so much grief. While it gave him new business opportunities, at the same time the war made it harder to acquire the basic staples of life. Caught as he was between two armies, it was becoming harder to survive every day. His peaceful, uneventful life alongside the Warrenton Turnpike was gone. He began to believe the war was bringing personal and national ruination. Old Will saw the war as a monster let loose on the land by politicians who cared nothing for the fate of the simple farmers living in the path of the armies. Union or Confederate, it did not matter. They both burned your fences for fuel, stole your livestock and trampled your crops. Conveniently forgetting his own enthusiasm for war before the fighting began, Will took a large swig of his latest batch of whiskey and loudly damned Abe Lincoln and Jeff Davis for the problems they had inflicted upon him with their stupid war. Having gotten the rage out of his system, he shuttered when he thought about what the year might bring.

The engine pulling a string of box cars and a hospital car chugged slowly down the six mile military railroad spur from Centreville to Manassas Junction. After a wait of nearly an hour, it was switched onto the main line of the Orange and Alexandria Railroad. The weary railroad men were glad to see it cross the switches because it was the next to last train in a series of trains that had been frantically shuttling what could be salvaged of General Johnston's war supplies to a new supply base. The train moved uneventfully south through Culpeper Court House and on to Gordonsville, where the hospital car was detached and coupled to a train bound for Richmond on the Virginia Central line. At the rear end of the car, covered by blankets, lay the bodies of three dead soldiers. The five injured soldiers were arranged as comfortably as possible in the front end of the car. Major Chambon's broken leg had been set in splints, his gashed side stitched and his swollen head bandaged. Throughout the slow trip, he remained unconscious. With each passing hour, the doctor traveling with the group became more certain that the injured major would not survive.

A chilly dawn had broken by the time the train entered Richmond's north side, crossed Clay and Marshall Streets and pulled into the Virginia Central Railroad Depot on the south side of Broad near 17th Street. The dead were loaded into a wagon and transported to Oakwood Cemetery where they were buried with military honors. The injured were moved by army ambulances down Broad Street to the new Chimborazo Hospital located on the east side of town at the city line. After the battle at Manassas, a woefully unprepared Richmond had been flooded with casualties which had to be treated in hotels, houses and barns because hospital space was lacking. In response to the crisis in medical services, the Confederate government ordered the construction of five new general hospitals in Richmond. One of these was opened on Chimborazo hill in October 1861. As the war progressed, the hospital on the hill became known as Chimborazo Hospital. It would grow to cover over 40 acres. With a capacity of over 3,000 patients, the hospital would treat more than 76,000 sick and wounded through the course of the war. Chimborazo would come to be considered one of the best managed hospitals in the Confederacy. Its mortality rate of 20 percent was quite good by the medical standards of the nineteenth century. Large as it was, Chimborazo was not the largest military hospital in Richmond. Camp Winder on the west side of town would grow even larger as the tempo of the fighting increased.

The Confederacy would muster approximately 850,000 men into military service during the Civil War. Over 260,000 of these would be killed in battle or die as a result of wounds or disease. The soldiers injured in the explosion at the Centreville railhead were fortunate because plenty of empty beds were available at Chimborazo when they arrived. It was a quiet time at the hospital, there having been no large battles in Virginia since the armies had clashed at Manassas during the previous July. Almost all the wounded from Manassas had died or recovered and returned to duty or been granted medical discharges and sent home. Although several wards were filled with sick soldiers, the hospital was far from its capacity.

The four less seriously injured soldiers had their injuries treated and were assigned to beds in a ward, which was a really nothing more than a building made of white-washed pine boards. Within a few days, they were well enough to move about and help with hospital chores. Within two weeks, all had recovered enough to be sent home on medical furlough before returning to the army. The seriously injured Major Chambon was placed in an empty officers' ward where the surgeons changed his bandages and reworked the splints on his broken leg. They knew from experience that there was little they could do for serious head injuries because probing around the skull usually did more harm than good. Only time would tell if this patient would die or recover.

When he opened his eyes four days after arriving at Chimborazo, it was the first visible sign that Major Matthew F. Chambon of the Confederate States Army was not going to die, at least not right away. The first person the major saw upon regaining consciousness was Cyrus Bellnapp, a hospital orderly, who quietly told the major, "Well now, it's about time you came back to this world. Don't you go no place till I come back with the doctor." Cyrus left the ward and quickly returned with a surgeon who, after carefully checking Matt's vital signs, found the major able to see, hear and speak. Although there was some loss of hearing from either the blast or the blow to the head, the major was expected to make a full recovery. The broken leg appeared to be mending but it would be some time before he could move around on his own. It was so quiet on the Virginia battlefronts that, with the exception of the occasional addition of a few sick or wounded officers, Major Chambon had the ward to himself most of the time.

> **"Slavery is founded on the selfishness of man's nature—opposition to it on his love of justice. These principles are in eternal antagonism; and when brought into collision so fiercely as slavery's extension brings them, shocks and throes and convulsions must ceaselessly follow."**
>
> **-Abraham Lincoln, 1854**

Even when two or three of the ward's 40 beds were filled, the major received excellent care from Cyrus Bellnapp, the only orderly on duty in the ward most of the time. It was a somewhat peculiar situation because Cyrus was a 16 year old slave from Branefield plantation down on the James River east of Richmond, one of the first parts of North America to be settled by the English. By 1862, the region was blend of small farms, large plantations and untamed wilderness. For as long as anyone could remember, Branefield plantation had been owned by John Churchman, a crusty veteran of the Mexican War, who was dedicated to producing the finest quality agricultural products. Although the Bellnapps were slaves, they had been on the plantation for so long that the place was also considered their home. Churchman himself was somewhat unorthodox, having coolly dropped five charging Mexican lancers from their saddles with revolver fire during the campaign to take Mexico City. He was insistent on personally running a plantation which produced quality crops and put in long days in the fields to ensure that the work got done the way he wanted.

By 1860, vast economic changes driven by new technologies were sweeping through agriculture and industry. As one of the consequences, the 2,500 year old institution of slavery was dying throughout much of the world. The tension created by the rapidly growing economic power of the North and the South's rabid defense of slavery did much to widen the rift between the sections of the rapidly growing United States. Because the planter class of the South had dug in its heels, one of the cornerstones of Confederate policy was the insistence that slavery be maintained. That policy put the Confederacy at odds with the tide of history and greatly reduced the possibility of foreign intervention on the Confederacy's behalf. The Bellnapp clan thought little about these momentous events because they were too busy farming. Having a strong attachment to the land, their lives and labor were governed by the changing of the seasons, the problems of drought, early frost, animal diseases, and the fluctuations in commodity prices.

There were good years and bad. Each year brought a renewal of the continuing struggle with the fickleness of nature as they planted, harvested and tried to anticipate shifting market patterns driven by changing consumer tastes. Life was hard, but not impossible. There was always the nagging fear that it could get worse. The failure of a plantation meant bankruptcy for the owner and being sold at auction for the slave. Everyone in Virginia knew that life for a slave on the deep south plantations of Georgia, Mississippi and Alabama was a living hell. The fear of these harsh, far-off places served as a powerful incentive to do whatever was necessary to keep from ending up there. Laboring long and hard in Virginia was not all that bad when one considered the awful alternative.

Due to his expertise with the pistol and his quick temper, outsiders quickly learned to keep their distance from the eccentric Churchman, his slaves and his horses. It was a common belief among his neighbors that his service in the war with Mexico had left him slightly touched in the head. The Bellnapps made the best of the situation by taking to heart the dictum of Diogenes: "The art of being a slave is to rule one's master." They provided the skilled day-to-day labor needed to keep the enterprise profitable and over time probably developed one of the most workable master-slave relationships that existed anywhere in Virginia. Churchman knew that under the United States Constitution slaves were property and counted for three-fifths of a free person for taxation and representation purposes. He also knew they were human and treated them as fairly as Virginia's slave statues would allow. As a consequence of the arrangement, the plantation prospered as it supplied agricultural products to the growing industrial cities along the east coast.

With the manpower supply becoming tight, the Confederate government began pressuring plantation owners to rent slaves to the government for war work. A labor recruiting officer in Richmond was astounded when Cyrus Bellnapp presented himself along with a letter from Churchman in response to the government's summons. It had never occurred to Cyrus to attempt to escape as he made his way to Richmond because he saw the war as threat to his family's well being. Not having any idea of what a Northern victory might bring, the Bellnapps were was not willing to sacrifice the gains of their hard labor by supporting the enemy, even one with a vague promise to end slavery. They had seen too many scoundrels over the years to be taken in by slick talking strangers. Although they harbored no delusions regarding their status under slavery, they saw no other choice but to support the Confederacy. As with most people who have achieved a modicum of economic success, the Bellnapps had become adverse to radical changes of any sort. A war was underway and if the Churchman plantation was destroyed by it, they stood to lose their way of life.

Cyrus went to work on hospital construction, the income from his labor paid monthly into his owner's account. Although his neighbors thought him to be half crazy, John Churchman's insistence on teaching the latest techniques in agriculture and animal husbandry to his slaves was one of the reasons for the plantation's success. Away from the farm for an extended period for the first time in his life, Cyrus soon found that he knew a great deal more of how the physical world functioned than did the average free or slave city laborer. While helping construct hospital wards and kitchens, he also treated the minor injuries which struck the construction crew. So impressed were the Chimborazo surgeons with his understanding of basic wound treatment that he was assigned to the hospital on a permanent basis. He remained busy keeping the buildings in repair and by assisting the doctors when a rush of sick or wounded soldiers arrived. Because the Confederacy's new Richmond hospitals were rather empty places, the doctors and Cyrus had a great deal of time to lavish on the injured major who had been shipped down from Centreville.

Major Chambon's swollen head slowly returned to normal size although he would forever bear the scars. The loss of hearing was not considered unusual for an artillery officer. The surgeons knew that sooner or later most of the men who worked the guns came down with the problem. In a few weeks, the major had mended to the point where he was able to hobble about on crutches. Matt Chambon was fortunate that his smashed leg had not become infected. Once infection set in, the leg would have had to be removed because no one knew how to treat infection. Sometimes it made no difference if the doctor took off the leg, the patient died anyhow. Everyone knew that the risks were high even though the doctors tried their best. Although he would walk with a noticeable limp as a reminder of the explosion, Matt had a lot to be thankful for. He still had both of his legs. He and Cyrus also got along fabulously well as Cyrus helped him learn how to move around on the crude crutches.

After evacuating northern Virginia, General Johnston pulled his army back to Fredericksburg. The Union troops marched out of Washington, advanced as far as Manassas, then turned around and disappeared back into the defenses of the capital. In late March, transports carrying the lead elements of General McClellan's Union army began unloading troops at Fort Monroe at the tip of the peninsula between the York and James rivers. On April 4, they began to move toward Richmond, over 100,000 strong. On April 9, President Davis ordered Johnston to Richmond. The Confederates stalled McClellan's advance for a month at Yorktown. Then falling back, the retreating Rebels fought a rearguard action at Williamsburg on May 5. Backed almost to the Richmond suburbs by May 31, General Johnston launched a savage counterblow at Seven Pines which cost the combined armies 11,200 casualties.

Johnston also found himself numbered among the wounded. Hit in the right shoulder by a bullet and struck in the chest by a shell fragment, the general would be out of action for some length of time. Desperately groping for a successor, President Davis replaced him with an little known 55 year old staff officer named Robert E. Lee. People thought "Old Granny" Lee was a very odd choice because he had not done anything of note thus far in the war. There were few in the city of Richmond who thought this quiet, refined, old gentleman could save Richmond from the Yankees. Most simply assumed the inept Davis had bungled again by placing Lee in command.

The hospitals in Richmond, which critics had thought to be excessive in size and cost only a few months ago, were filled with the sick and wounded as McClellan's Union army pushed slowly up the Peninsula as it advanced on Richmond. Cyrus helped the doctors unload the incoming wagons of wounded, assisted the surgeons at the operating table and ministered to those lying in the wards. Hobbling around as best he could on his crutch, Major Chambon lent a hand by sorting the incoming wounded by the extent of injury and writing letters for the dying when there were no ambulances to unload. As the human wreckage from the battle of Seven Pines began flooding Richmond hospitals, the medical facilities were so overwhelmed that social convention had to be abandoned in order to keep the hospitals functioning. As a desperate, last resort in manpower-short Richmond, women were brought in to serve as ward attendants. Although many senior medical officers were appalled by the idea of a female presence in the hospitals, it was a wartime necessity. The social niceties would be have to be set aside if the masses of wounded were going to get any semblance of proper care.

"The cannon thunders...limbs fly in all directions...one can hear the groans of victims and the howling of those performing the sacrifice...it's humanity in search of happiness."
-Charles Baudelaire, 1821-1867

Wounded were coming from the Shenandoah Valley where the ex-professor now known as Stonewall Jackson was fighting hard and keeping two or three Yankee armies off balance. Given the scanty reports, no one knew for sure how many armies were in action in the Valley at any one time. In a miraculous feat of arms, General Jackson swept the Shenandoah clear of Union troops in a lightning-fast campaign that stunned friend and foe alike. The inhabitants of the Confederate capital were digesting this good news when suddenly, to the surprise of nearly everyone, General Lee revealed his true killer instincts. The army stopped retreating. There was fighting at Oak Grove on June 25. Then with a series of furious attacks, Lee went on the offensive and hit the Union army at Mechanicsville on June 26, Gaines's Mill on June 27, Savage's Station on June 29, White Oak Swamp on June 30 and Malvern Hill on July 1. As a result of Lee's furious attacks, McClellan was forced back from the gates of Richmond and driven to a new base on the

James River at Harrison's Landing. Lee's combat initiative had a high human cost, resulting in almost 16,000 Federal casualties and nearly 21,000 Confederate. Of the Confederate casualties, 16,261 were wounded. They were being brought to Richmond's hospitals as fast as the understaffed medical service could remove them from the battlefields in the wake of Lee's slashing drive.

A frantic Major Matt Chambon, not yet fully recovered himself, was moving around the hospital entrance on his crutch, helping unload the never-ending stream of ambulances, sorting the living from the dead, then those who could be helped by treatment from those with mortal wounds. Those of the wounded scheduled to see a doctor were further sorted by gut-shot, chest-shot and arm and leg wounds. Inside one of the operating rooms, Cyrus assisted a tired surgeon. As other assistants fainted or became ill and had to leave, Cyrus stood fast at his post readying arms and legs for amputation and stitching up the wounds as the surgeon finished his cutting and probing. They worked non-stop in a sea of blood and pain with the line of wounded, sometimes screaming men, growing longer outside the operating room door. The reports from Chambon and his ambulance unloading crew were all bad. The wounded were arriving faster then they could be processed. All the hospitals in Richmond were full. Every doctor was on duty and still the ambulances arrived with more grisly cargo. Bandages and other medical supplies were running out. In the distance artillery rumbled, signaling fresh loads of wounded yet to come.

Cyrus was shocked when the bleary-eyed surgeon asked, "Do you think you can handle a bone saw if I show you where to cut?" "I believe I can," Cyrus responded with a disbelieving sputter. "Good, let's give it a try," said the doctor. "Just don't forget to tie off the arteries and blood vessels. We have to operate faster if we are going to save the lives of these men. Too many have been untreated for too long and are dying on our doorstep."

Cyrus placed the saw on the shattered leg where the surgeon pointed and began to cut. He never forgot the feel of the saw or the sound it made as he performed his first amputation. The chloroformed soldier never knew his mangled leg had been removed and the stump stitched by a slave. The doctor set up a second operating table. After examining the patient, he instructed Cyrus what to do and then moved to the next patient waiting on the second table. After rendering treatment, he came back and checked the work Cyrus had performed, providing any necessary finishing touches. They worked thorough the days and nights, sleeping in snatches, no longer noticing the stench of gangrene and puss. Sometimes they were able to treat two patients at a time. At other times, only one if the wounds were multiple. In a hospital filled to overflowing with mangled soldiers, no one thought it strange that a slave had been promoted to become a full-fledged "bone-saw-man" without having had any formal medical training. In the military hospital's terrible world of mutilation and death, the focus had narrowed to a desperate struggle to maintain a minimal level of patient treatment. Anyone willing to help was welcome. The turnover was constant because few of those who volunteered could stand the strain for more than a few days.

"I have a deep sympathy with war, it so apes the gait and bearing of the soul."

-Henry David Thoreau, 1840

Richmond had become one vast hospital. On the east side of the city, Chimborazo was operating at capacity. On the city's west side, Camp Winder was also filled. The wounded were placed in private homes, hotels and warehouses. Plans were hastily made by Confederate authorities to expand the size of all the existing hospitals and establish new ones in any suitable buildings that could be found. The medical authorities faced a difficult task because space was in short supply. Richmond's pre-war population of 37,000 was swelling as workers flocked to the city's war industries. As the war progressed, the population would increase to more than 137,000, driving up the cost of living and taxing city services to the breaking point.

The sound of artillery fire faded in Richmond as General Lee turned his back on McClellan's army now sandwiched along the sweltering bank of the James River and marched the bulk of his forces north. As the flood of wounded and sick slowed to a trickle, the frazzled Dr. Wesley Hoffmann and his indispensable assistant Cyrus Bellnapp sat on the steps outside of the operating ward relaxing for the first time in weeks. The constant sound of hammers and saws indicated the construction crews were busy erecting new ward buildings. As fast as one was completed, it was filled with patients moved from temporary facilities in the city. Looking out over the growing complex of wards, kitchens, warehouses and a bakery, Cyrus said, "I believe this hospital will soon cover the entire hilltop at the rate it is growing."

"Most likely so," answered Dr. Hoffmann. "At the rate the casualties are coming in, they might as well keep right on building. It would be nice to have a few extra beds again for a change." Turning to Cyrus, he said, "I really appreciate the help you have given me. I don't know what I would have done without you during these past weeks. I think you have a real talent for medicine. After the war ends, you ought to give doctoring a try. You already have gained more experience working with me than most practitioners get in ten years."

"I had never thought about doing anything but working on Branefield plantation like my Pa and Grandpa. Do you think I could really become a doctor?" Cyrus responded.

Looking Cyrus straight in the eye, Dr. Hoffmann said, "If your master is agreeable, you can apprentice with me after the war ends. I would be proud to teach you because we have gone through a nightmare together here at Chimborazo, and so far we have managed to come through it. I should hope we would have something more normal to look forward to after the war ends. The war is changing things in medicine. Consider how well the women have worked out as ward attendants. I would not be at all surprised if they kept on working in nursing as a profession when peace comes. A few might even become doctors too."

"Have you noticed how many of the patients we treat in the morning seem to do better than the ones we work on in the afternoon? They seem to get less infection in their wounds. Why do you think that is?" the doctor asked.

Cyrus thought about Dr. Hoffmann's observation for a few moments before he replied, "Maybe it's because we treat them faster in the morning. Could the early daylight help the healing somehow?"

"I don't rightly know," answered Dr. Hoffmann. "Something is happening, but I don't know what is. Is it our procedures? Are we changing them slightly as the day goes on? Or is it some unknown factor related to the hour of the day? There has to be an explanation! If we observe our patients closely, we may be able to figure it out. It would help the advancement of medical science if we could get a handle on the reason why a higher percentage of our morning patients seem to do better."

A male nurse stuck his head out of the door, announcing more wounded were on the way. Wearily, the two men slowly got up, stretched and went back inside the whitewashed building. Stretcher bearers were already bringing a new batch of wounded to examined and treated.

Cyrus knew Dr. Hoffmann was on to something. But try as he might, he could not find a cause to explain why his morning patients had a higher success rate than those he treated later in the day. They often talked of the strange trend, but could find no reason for it. They observed and took notes when time permitted. Both were convinced there was a reason, but what? When he visited Camp Winder, Dr. Hoffmann asked if the surgeons there had noticed the same trend. They had on occasion, but there were times when the reverse was true. Sometimes on certain days, the patients treated in the afternoon did better. Many soldiers thought the hospitals only served as a place to die and avoided hospital stays at all costs. Because the surgeons did not want to create more morale problems by focusing on Dr. Hoffmann's time of treatment observations, it was agreed that nothing would be made public until a cause could be determined. There was no use worrying soldiers and government officials about something over which the doctors had no control and could not explain.

August 1862

Will Strawderman learned that General Lee had stopped the Yankee drive on Richmond. Stonewall Jackson was said to have completed a lightning attack that swept the Shenandoah Valley clear of Union forces. Jackson had crossed the mountains and joined in the fighting near Richmond. Now, the latest rumors had the combined forces of Lee and Jackson turning away from McClellan's army which was dug in on the James River under the cover of the Union navy's guns. Lee was moving north to intercept General John Pope's army which was pushing into central Virginia. Lee had turned out to be quite a fighter, so everyone knew another big battle was going to be fought when the armies met.

Pope's main supply base was the busy, sprawling quartermaster depot at Manassas Junction. Old Will sold whiskey to some of the U.S. Military Railroad crews running trains down to Pope's army and to the troops guarding the railroad bridge over Bull Run. The supply depot contained warehouses crammed full of all sorts of good things to eat, rail sidings were lined with ammunition box cars, and a corral was full of spare horses and mules. Old Will collected an assortment of canned oysters, meat, real coffee, dried vegetables and cash in payment for his deliveries of Strawderman's Finest brand of whiskey. He liked having the military railroad crews, quartermaster and guard troops as customers. They were not as touchy as the combat troops of either army had been. There also was no doubt about the fact that the Yankees had access to more than enough of everything needed by an army except whiskey. As long as he could avoid getting caught by the annoying provost guards, Old Will felt that the summer might turn out to be quite a profitable one. He thought it would be just fine if the Yankee supply depot stayed where it was for the rest of the war. The armies could keep on doing their fighting someplace else as far as he was concerned.

The first hint of trouble came with news of Rebel raiders wrecking two trains down the line. On August 26, General Jackson and his army corps composed of three divisions suddenly appeared out of nowhere and pounced cat-like on the Manassas Junction depot. His troops spent most of the next day eating their fill and cramming what supplies they could carry into their clothing and their limited number of wagons. Because communications with Washington had been cut, it took the Union authorities some time to figure out what had happened. When General Pope realized Jackson's corps was deep in his rear, he set his forces into motion in an effort to trap him.

Stonewall Jackson, however, had no intention of waiting around to be smashed by a superior force while his gaunt soldiers gorged themselves on captured supplies. He burned the railroad bridge and the supply depot before moving to a new position two miles from Bull Run and northwest of the first Manassas battlefield. As a diversion, Hill's division was sent to Centreville to fool the enemy into believing Jackson's entire force had withdrawn in that direction.

Old Will was in Centreville late in the day on August 27, 1862, delivering fresh jugs of Strawderman's Finest to the taverns. He was catching up on the latest gossip with a few of the patrons when General A. P. Hill's division came marching down the dusty road from Manassas Junction. Old Will, the tavern proprietor and the patrons rushed to the roadside to watch the troops pass. The dust-covered soldiers moved with the steady gait of veterans who wasted no motion and spoke few words. Even though they were in a region that would soon be swarming with Union forces, it was an unhurried, almost pleasant march. Unlike on previous visits, the troops paid little attention to the houses and gardens in the dilapidated little village because their haversacks and bed rolls were bulging with recently acquired supplies. The column leisurely made the turn in the road at the stone church and headed down the turnpike toward the stone bridge over Bull Run. There was no joy to the occasion because the soldiers and the people standing by the roadside sensed another battle was fast approaching.

A very unhappy General Pope arrived at the smoking ruins of his supply base around noon on August 28. Looking at the evidence, he concluded that Jackson had attempted to escape by retreating to Centreville, so he ordered his forces to concentrate there. The first Union troops arrived in the village about dark, but found no Confederates. By that time, Hill had completed his movement of diversion and rejoined Jackson. The reunited force had spent the day resting in the trees north of the turnpike, not far from the old battlefield.

The Centreville taverns filled up with blue-clad soldiers as the Union host gathered in the village. When asked the Confederate's whereabouts, Old Will honestly answered that the only troops he saw were headed for the Bull Run crossing. He had no idea where they had gone afterwards. Old Will sold his entire supply of whiskey and everything else edible to the officers and noncoms camped in and around the village. With the Federal supply base destroyed, the Yankees were very short of food.

General Jackson began to think that Hill's ruse may have worked better than planned because Pope's army was rapidly concentrating at Centreville. It could not be permitted to remain there while Jackson waited for General

Lee and the remainder of the Confederate army to arrive because it could not be attacked on those highly defensible heights. On the other hand, if Jackson provoked a battle too soon, the larger Union army would crush his smaller force before reinforcements arrived. Never one to avoid taking a calculated risk when a possible victory was at stake, Jackson decided to draw Pope's army away from the Centreville heights. All he had to do was find something to use as bait.

On the evening of August 28, unaware of Jackson's concealed position north of the road, elements of General Rufus King's First Division (Third Corps) was marching east on the turnpike toward Centreville to join General Pope. These unsuspecting Union troops presented the opportunity for which Jackson had been anxiously waiting. After scouting the Union column himself, Jackson decided to attack. Speaking softly, he instructed his officers: "Gentlemen, bring out your men." With those fateful words, Stonewall Jackson deliberately revealed the position of his troops and ignited the bloody second battle of Manassas. It all began at a rather undistinguished location called Brawner's farm, a place that soon earned a page in military history.

To their credit, the stunned Union troops did not break when the howling Confederates came storming forward from their concealed positions. The Union soldiers quickly faced left, established a battle line and returned fire. Separated by only 80 yards at some points, the Blue and Gray lines blasted each other for one-and-a-half hours. When darkness finally halted the firing, neither line had budged. Union losses amounted to 1,100 while the Confederates lost 1,200 including Generals Taliafarro and Ewell who were wounded. Almost one-third of the 7,000 men engaged became casualties in the furious battle on Mr. Brawner's property. It would be remembered as one of the toughest close-quarter fights of the entire war.

While making a delivery of whiskey to a group of officers camped on the ridge, Old Will heard the clamor of battle suddenly erupt as a large number of men and boys marching to Centreville on a hot summer's evening came to the end of their lives in an unexpected, furious twilight battle. Because General Jackson wanted to avoid fighting on the heights at Centreville, he had provoked a murderous beginning to a vicious battle that would rage for the better part of two more days. Old Will watched fascinated as the distant twilight was stabbed by the flashes of musket and cannon fire. "It looks as if someone has found Jackson for us," a captain remarked as he paid Will for the jug of whiskey. "It's more likely that Jackson has found some of our boys instead of the other way around," said a somber looking major. "There will be hell to pay one way or another in the morning. It's bound to be a big fight if Jackson is involved," he added while checking the contents of the cartridge box on his belt. He would be proven right. When the campaign of second Manassas closed on September 2, over 25,000 soldiers had been killed or wounded.

Old Will was in a state of shock. Only a little over year after the first battle, the armies were fighting again over virtually the same ground. The Yankees around Centreville left their camps long before first light. All day the guns roared as they hurled themselves at Jackson's battle line which stretched along the embankment of the unfinished railroad line. The turnpike filled with military traffic as a steady line of ambulances headed to the receiving hospital that had been setup by Pope's surgeons less than a mile east of Old Will's house at the point where the Willow Springs Branch crossed the turnpike. No one knew for sure how the battle was going, but Pope seemed to be determined to crush Jackson before Lee arrived.

After reinforcements arrived, a furious afternoon Confederate counterattack finally drove the stubborn Yankees from the field. The blue-uniformed soldiers streamed back in disarray to the heights around Centreville to regroup. Will watched as the sullen troops went into position along the ridge line. The road in front of his farm was jammed with ambulances moving wounded and stragglers drifting to the rear while reserve artillery units and reinforcements coming from Washington moved in the opposite direction. Will had a sickening feeling that if Lee attacked again the next day, the fighting would engulf his home.

Lee, however, was not going to launch a frontal assault against an army holding the commanding high ground. On August 31, he ordered Jackson's tired, dirty veterans to move around the Yankee flank. Departing about noon, rain storms slowed the march as they moved north, then turned east on the Little River Turnpike. On a clear and windy September 1, Jackson continued his movement around the flank of the Union army until he ran into a determined Union force led by Generals Kearny and Stevens near Chantilly. In a bitter battle fought in an early evening thunderstorm, Jackson's flank movement was brought to a halt by fighting in which both Stevens and Kearny were killed. By then, the badly rattled General Pope gave up any thought of further offensive or defensive action and ordered his army to withdraw to the defenses of Washington. Leaving their campfires burning brightly, the Union troops began to withdraw at 2:30 in the morning of September 2.

Everyone expected the fighting to continue because Pope outnumbered Lee by 63,000 to 49,000. To the north, Old Will could hear the occasional crack of gunfire as cavalry moving in advance of Jackson' main force skirmished with Union patrols. In the afternoon, he heard a massive volume of gunfire from the direction of Chantilly which lay northeast of his farm. The battle was not long underway when a massive thunderstorm blew through with a roar and soaked everything. From where Will stood, he could not distinguish the noise of the thunder from the sound of guns. As the fighting raged to the northeast, he was thankful that nothing was happening to the main body of troops holding the ridge west of his farm. That night, the road filled with retreating Union troops as they began to withdraw to Washington.

The next morning, the stench of death hung in the air. Wrecked railroad engines which cost $8,000 apiece and railroad cars ($500 each) were strewn along the Orange and Alexandria railroad tracks and on the sidings of the charred supply depot. On the battlefield, the dead were being hastily buried while many of the wounded crawled or walked into fence rows, ravines and creek bottoms to escape the heat, search for water and probably die alone and unattended. The Yankee hospital at Willow Springs had hurriedly packed up and moved to Fairfax Station, leaving behind the dead and those too seriously wounded to move. Will learned that a woman named Clara Barton had come to Fairfax Station from Alexandria on one of the ammunition trains to help tend the 3,000 wounded littering the grounds. When they withdrew, the Yankee railroad crews burned the facilities at Fairfax Station and loaded the wounded into empty box cars. Old Will thought about the irony of the situation. The army hauled ammunition by the trainload. Then some of the soldiers wounded by bullets and shells hauled by the railroad were themselves hauled away in the empty freight cars. The railroad was certainly proving itself to be a useful military tool, no doubt about that.

The Confederates bagged 7,000 prisoners in addition to the 30 pieces of artillery, a large number of small arms and the 38 wagons also captured. The quartermaster paid Old Will to help bury the dead Yankees at the hospital site and those found along the turnpike. His wife and the few other ladies remaining in the village tried to comfort the living unfortunates left behind. These were all cases with mortal wounds and all died within four days.

This latest round of fighting put Old Will out of business. Some of the 8,000 hungry soldiers straggling from Pope's army had taken everything edible from his farm. He was out of whiskey making supplies and had no way to obtain more because his horses and wagon had been stolen by the Yankees. His team and wagon were probably at Fairfax Station, or maybe even Washington city by now. He would have try to find them as soon as the armies got out of the way because there was nothing left in the war-ravaged region around Centreville for him to purchase. Everything he was going to use in the future was going to have to be hauled in from someplace else.

Finding the city of Washington too well fortified to attack, General Lee turned his columns north in a bold invasion of Maryland. With General McClellan back in charge, the Union army slid out of the Washington defenses in a effort to intercept him before he got too far into Northern territory.

With the armies gone, Old Will borrowed a horse and headed to Fairfax Station to search for his missing team and wagon. He had gone as far as Fairfax Courthouse when he ran into Clinton Stackhouse, an upstanding businessman and resident of Washington City. Clinton had been a clerk processing purchasing vouchers at the Treasury Department before the war. A strong Confederate sympathizer, Clinton had been recruited into Rose O'Neal Greenhow's ring of intelligence operatives when the war began. He found the work to his liking and continued in the trade after Mrs. Greenhow had been arrested and deported. During the past year, he had resigned from his administrative position and opened a brothel on 14th Street not far from the White House. The funding for his venture was provided by the Confederate Secret Service. Standing on a street full of other bawdy houses, his establishment was almost inconspicuous. His well-paid girls were trained to ask probing questions of their patrons and report the answers. Clinton spent the majority of his time at the establishment's bar, plying his customers with drinks and wheedling information out of them. It was a very low-key operation. Confrontations with the police were avoided at all costs. Clinton's prices were fair, the establishment well- run, and the food and liquor quality judged to be quite good by the prevailing brothel standards of Washington city.

Clinton Stackhouse found himself managing a gold mine. He was making much more money than expected from the business and he often obtained information useful to the Confederate government. When he met Will Strawderman, Clinton was in Fairfax Courthouse delivering a report on McClellan's troop strength to a courier who would rush it to Richmond.

His interest in the farmer grew when he learned, while being introduced by a mutual acquaintance, that Old Will was the producer of Strawderman's Finest whiskey. Whiskey helped loosen the tongues of the lonely War Department employees and military men who patronized Clinton's establishment.

Because he practically gave the stuff away when the right occasion arose, Clinton was always on the lookout for another source of cheap, reasonably good quality whiskey. Always a practical man, Clinton saw nothing in the regulations prohibiting him from reducing his business costs and increasing his profit margin while he nobly served the Confederate cause as a spy.

As long as neither his employees nor his customers caught on to the fact he was part of a spy ring, Clinton would survive and make a great deal of money in the process. To avoid arousing suspicion, he never asked obvious or leading questions of his customers. Clinton was always a sociable host who encouraged his patrons to talk as much and as long as they desired as he refilled their glasses. Of course, the Yankees were not all stupid and they were always on the hunt for spies. One small mistake was all it would take on his part and Clinton's charade would swiftly end with his head in the hangman's noose. To a small extent, Clinton sympathized with the overworked people who processed the endless flow of paper that lubricated the Union war effort, but all was fair in love and war and he had a job to do. Many of his patrons were so drunk by the time they finally got around to going upstairs with the ladies that they promptly passed out. These customers were left to sleep off the effects of the whiskey while the girl moved on to her next appointment and serviced another customer, earning twice the pay for half the work. The system worked well for all concerned. Clinton got access to useful military information, the customer enjoyed a sociable evening while gaining a massive hangover and the girls liked the idea of being paid twice.

The whiskey-making farmer didn't seem to be much smarter than a tree stump. The less the old man learned about his business, the better it would be for Clinton Stackhouse. Speaking with his best professional whorehouse owner's smile on his face, Clinton told Old Will that he had heard a lot of good things about his brand of whiskey and asked why none had been sold in Washington recently. Old Will mentioned his load of woes, the missing horses and wagon, the havoc wrought by the armies as they tramped his farm and the other hardships brought on by the war. After an hour's discussion, they agreed on the price for a sizable quantity of distilled sprits. If Old Will was unable to make deliveries, Clinton would send a wagon to the farm.

Clinton also mentioned he had an official pass to travel beyond the Washington defenses. He was able to go into the Virginia and Maryland countryside to procure fresh food and beverages for his establishment anytime he desired. The unrestricted travel pass made getting the whiskey to Washington a simple matter of arranging for a team and wagon to pick it up. As they shook hands on the deal, Clinton smiled to himself. He was thinking about George Washington's whiskey recipe playing a role in helping the South win the second American revolution. He was certain the father of the United States would not have minded. Clinton knew George Washington would have supported the South in its struggle to free itself from the clutches of the overbearing North.

Feeling much better now that he had a new customer to replace the lost supply depot and railroad business, Will rode down the road to Fairfax Station which was situated a little over three miles south of the Courthouse. Along the road, he passed an occasional abandoned army ambulance, broken wagons, dead horses and mules bloating in the summer heat, and the fresh graves of the Union soldiers who had died on the way to the railroad. To Old Will it was an indication that the warring governments were still paying a fair price to the contracted grave-digging crews.

When he arrived at what had once been Fairfax Station, Old Will found there was nothing left of the place. Evacuating U.S. Military Railroad crews had put the torch to the station building and the government warehouses. The only structure left standing was St. Mary's Church. And it was not in the best of shape, having been used as an operating room by Union surgeons. All around the church building Old Will saw the hastily dug graves of the dead who had been left behind. Amos Carter, whose farm was nearby, told Old Will the Yankees had burned all the wagons before they pulled out. Amos had managed to collect a number of horses he found running free, the railroad crews had been in too much of a hurry to shoot them. Perhaps Old Will's four missing animals were among them. He was welcome to take a look.

As they walked toward the woods where Amos had the horses penned, Amos talked sadly about the events of the past few days. Herman Haupt, the big boss at the U.S. Military Railroad headquarters in Alexandria, had gotten the army to send out a brigade of New Jersey troops on a train to check why the telegraph line had gone dead. They detrained at the Bull Run railroad bridge, advanced and had been shot to pieces by Jackson's troops. When the big battle began a day or two later, Haupt sent out a bridge repair crew and almost had the bridge rebuilt by the time the Yankees started to pull back. In the meantime, train upon train of ammunition and food had been unloaded at Fairfax Station in an effort to keep Pope's army supplied. The wounded were brought in and soon covered the hillside between the church and station. Amos thought there must have been at least 4,000 by the time they started loading them into the cars.

"It was a sight to behold," said Amos. "Yankees laid out everywhere you could see, moaning and groaning. I hope I never see anything like that again for the rest of my life." A lady named Clara Barton worked day and night tending the wounded. "She really got things organized and only had a few people to help her," Amos told Will. "As the Union army retreated, the railroad crews fired the buildings and returned to Alexandria. There was nothing left now except the dead and piles of cooling ashes."

Will was lucky. He found his missing horses among those Amos had collected as the Yankees fled. Amos was happy to let him have them back for the payment of a small boarding fee. Amos knew he would turn a nice profit selling the other horses to private parties or to the Confederate government, if he found no civilian takers. If there were no Confederate purchasing agents around, the Yankees would do in a pinch. At least you could spend their money in Washington.

Old Will's wagon was another matter. It was gone for good. The wagon had been burned with the other vehicles and equipment when Fairfax Station was abandoned. As he rode back to Centreville leading his string of recovered horses, Will's thoughts turned to the necessity of obtaining a wagon. He had to locate one quickly if he was going to haul supplies and make deliveries to Mr. Stackhouse in Washington city. Perhaps he could find a usable wagon closer to the battlefield. Deep in thought as he rode, he paid little attention to the wreckage of war littering the countryside. A man had to try to make a living, war or no war. Why was the damn thing going on for so long when the politicians had promised everyone it would be over in a matter of weeks? Will concluded that both Presidents Lincoln and Davis were nothing more than grand liars bent on bringing ruin to the country as they loudly proclaimed themselves to be doing otherwise.

Will Strawderman scrounged enough usable components from the abandoned army wagons scattered along the Warrenton Turnpike to build himself a wagon that was almost better than new. He also diligently gathered all the usable wheels and other parts he could fit into his barn. When he was finished collecting, he thought he had enough parts to assemble two additional wagons. It was a good feeling knowing he was going to be able to keep his wagon on the road for a long time. He was also glad he had acted quickly because the Confederate quartermasters were soon hauling away everything usable. Because they were in a hurry, they never noticed that Will had stripped a few wagons for his own use.

The Southern planter class looked at industrial endeavors with disdain and extolled the virtues of agriculture during the pre-war years. When the war did not end as quickly as expected, the Confederates found themselves with little of the manufacturing capacity needed to produce weapons, a total lack of standardization and a chaotic supply system. Although the Confederacy had taken over the seven federal arsenals located in the South, most of the 150,000 weapons acquired in the takeover were obsolete. To make matters worse, some of the most productive parts of the Confederacy's limited industrial capacity was lost early in the war when Union forces captured Nashville and Memphis in Tennessee and New Orleans, Louisiana.

Major Matthew Chambon was discharged from the hospital very lucky to be alive and partially disabled. While his other injuries had healed well, his damaged leg would require him to rely on the use of a cane. No longer totally fit for service in the field, the crippled major was reassigned to the Confederate Ordnance Bureau in Richmond. Its chief, Colonel Gorgas, had the almost impossible job of expanding the Confederate arms and gunpowder manufacturing industries. He promptly established large arsenals at Richmond, Virginia; Fayetteville, North Carolina; Augusta, Macon, Atlanta and Columbus, Georgia; Charleston, South Carolina and Selma, Alabama. Smaller facilities were opened at Danville and Lynchburg in Virginia and Montgomery, Alabama. The swift Confederate blockade runners sailing from Bermuda to Wilmington, North Carolina and from Nassau to Charleston, South Carolina and Savannah, Georgia were a tremendous asset to the armament program. They delivered close to 500,000 small arms before the Union navy blockade was able to effectively close off the Southern ports.

Major Chambon's first job was to expand and reorganize the iron deliveries from Cloverdale Furnace in Botetourt County, Virginia to Joseph Reid Anderson's Tredegar Iron Works located on the James River in Richmond. Tredegar had the only rolling mill in the entire Confederacy when the war began and also had the ability to build railroad locomotives. The artisans working at Tredegar would manufacture an astonishing 50 percent of the 2,300 cannon produced by Southern foundries during the war. As the demand for labor skyrocketed, Tredegar became an equal opportunity employer of sorts. African-Americans flocked to Tredegar, eventually making up half of the work force. Free blacks were paid salaries while slaves were leased from their masters.

Plagued by a lack of manpower, a shortage of raw materials, the lack of government credit and vexed by a poor transportation system, the Confederate Ordnance Bureau was a miracle of innovation and improvisation. Its sprawling Richmond Armory complex would produce 323,000 small arms during the course of the war while its Richmond Laboratory supplied small arms ammunition. So effective was the Bureau's work that when Lee surrendered his army in April 1865, his troops had an average of 75 rounds of ammunition per man. While many of the soldiers were in rags and had nothing to eat, ammunition was supplied right up to the end. Josiah Gorgas and his odd mixture of government manufacturing facilities, contractors and African-American workers had not let the Confederacy down.

October 1863

"As I would not be a slave, so I would not be a master. This expresses my idea of democracy."

-Abraham Lincoln, 1858

Despite the constant construction of new wards, Chimborazo Hospital always was filled as the sick and wounded were shuttled to Richmond from treatment stations behind the lines. Dr. Wesley Hoffmann and Cyrus Bellnapp labored in a world of death and pain as the casualties from Lee's Second Manassas campaign, the invasion of Maryland, Fredericksburg and Chancellorsville flowed into the hospital. Ether and chloroform were used when available as anesthesia. Whiskey and morphia substituted when other supplies were exhausted. Hoffmann and Bellnapp struggled with a grim set of mortality statistics. Approximately 60 percent of soldiers with gunshot wounds to the chest died. For those with stomach wounds, the chances of recovery were worse. Close to 90 percent of those so wounded died. For every soldier dying of wounds, two or three died of illness caused by dysentery, typhoid, pneumonia, smallpox, tuberculosis and measles. When the fighting slackened, the rate of disease increased as the soldiers idled in camp. The hospital was always filled to capacity.

General Thomas J. (Stonewall) Jackson had been accidentally shot by his own men during the battle of Chancellorsville. On a day in May, Dr. Hoffmann and Cyrus Bellnapp had walked down Broad Street and watched an engine pulling the single car containing the general's body slowly pass. Neither had time to see the general lie in state in the governor's mansion or at the capital building. The lines of somber mourners were too long and they could not afford to spend much time away from the hospital. The citizens of Richmond were deeply affected by the death of the general who had begun the war as a quaint eccentric and had gone on to become the hero of the Confederacy. He had been Lee's offensive sledge hammer and a God-fearing man to boot. Many in Virginia saw his untimely passing as a clear sign from God that the Confederacy was destined to lose the war.

Ever the long-odds gambler, Lee marched north in June 1863 after his stunning Chancellorsville victory, and in early July met defeat in a tremendous battle fought at the Pennsylvania town of Gettysburg. On the same day Lee began his dismal retreat in Pennsylvania, Vicksburg, the mighty fortress that denied the Union control of the Mississippi River, fell to General Grant after a long siege. Lee had been whipped badly and the Confederacy had been effectively sliced in two. As the decimated Army of Northern Virginia struggled to return to Virginia, it carried with it 12,700 wounded in a wagon train stretching nearly 17 miles. Another 6,035 soldiers too seriously injured to transport were left behind at the mercy of the Union victors. It took an agonizing number of days for the wounded to reach the hospitals of Richmond. When they finally arrived in the stifling July heat, many were beyond help.

The city of Washington was booming as the thousands of troops manning its defending forts or passing through the city on the way to the army in Virginia spent money in the town. In Centreville, the opposite was true and the economy continued to decline. There were shortages of everything Old Will needed to run his farm and operate the still. There were often times when he had to have Mr. Stackhouse purchase items for him in Washington city. Sometimes they would meet on the Virginia side of the Long Bridge, transferring the load of Strawderman's Finest from one wagon to another. Old Will would then load the grain and other goods provided by Stackhouse into his wagon and they would settle the bill. Stackhouse always paid generously in cash and included a little extra for Old Will's trouble. Mr. Stackhouse was a man who knew how to get things done in Washington, and Old Will was thankful for that. Stackhouse never had any difficulty passing the guards. He seemed to have a pass to everywhere and access to everything. Old Will believed Mr. Stackhouse had secret contacts someplace high in the army quartermaster department or in the Lincoln administration.

As Old Will headed the team back to the farm, he thought about the grim situation in Centreville. Much of the population had fled the devastation, so the taverns in the village did little business anymore. The once massive Manassas quartermaster depot was a weed-choked ruin because the Yankees had not rebuilt it after Jackson had destroyed it. This year things had gotten even worse. In January or thereabouts, General Lee had sent a lieutenant named John S. Mosby to Northern Virginia with orders to tie down as many Union troops as possible and disrupt the Yankee supply lines. Old Will had to admit Mosby was doing a good job of doing what General Lee sent him to do. Stretching from the gates of Washington to the Blue Ridge Mountains was an area now called Mosby's Confederacy. It was a region in which neither Union soldiers nor supplies were safe. As Mosby attacked wagon trains, railroads, army patrols and supply depots, the area became a no-man's land, a regular guerrilla battleground. The constant attacks by Mosby's Rangers hardened the attitude of the Union soldiers sent to stop him. They developed a deep hatred for the partisans and the civilian population that hid, clothed and fed them. At every chance, the Union troops took their revenge. Houses and barns were torched, crops and livestock destroyed. The Union authorities had also ordered anyone living near the railroad tracks to move or be held responsible for the damage caused by the raiders.

It was a downright ugly way to live. Will traveled with two loaded pistols, one in his belt hidden under his coat, the other stashed under the wagon seat. His dealings with Mr. Stackhouse in Washington city did not endear him to some of Mosby's hot-tempered band. Living in the Mosby-controlled countryside made him a suspected guerrilla supporter in the eyes of the patrolling Union cavalry. To be caught on the road after dark meant death by gunshot if either side caught you. At night, the wise householder also answered any noise on the porch or knock on the door with a shot, questions could be asked afterward. A climate of fear descended like a fog each evening as everyone scurried home to hide behind barred doors. Mosby might be providing an invaluable service to Lee's army, but in the process he was bringing economic ruin to a region already hit hard by the impact of the war. As the troopers and guerrillas clashed, more of the remaining residents gave up the nerve-wracking struggle and fled to safer places.

After the battle of Gettysburg, Lee's badly mauled army retreated to Virginia by way of the Shenandoah Valley, with General George B. Meade's Army of the Potomac moving slowly in pursuit. By September, the armies of Lee and Meade were sparring with each other along the Rapidan River south of Culpeper. In a desperate attempt to halt the Union drive which had punched deep into Tennessee, the authorities in Richmond detached two of General Longstreet's divisions from Lee's army and sent them to Georgia where they arrived in time to provide the winning margin in the battle of Chickamauga on September 19-20, 1863. The Confederates routed the Union army and drove it back to Chattanooga, where it was besieged.

It was now the turn of the U.S. government to undertake a desperate movement of troops. Two corps were detached from Meade's army and rushed to Tennessee by rail in what turned out to be one of the war's best coordinated railroading efforts. The troop shifts to the west had left Lee with approximately 50,000 troops while Meade had 80,000.

As soon as he learned of the reduction in Meade's forces, the crafty Lee went on the offensive, On October 9, his army was marching west and north around Meade's flank. By October 11, the Confederates had reached Culpeper. Although the army was advancing, conditions had sadly deteriorated since the previous year when General Pope had been forced back over the same ground. General Lee was so crippled by rheumatism that he was forced to ride in a wagon. His army was increasingly handicapped by shortages in men and materiel. Many of the best commanders were dead, transport was in short supply and the soldiers usually went hungry. Despite the difficulties, the tattered Rebel columns marched into Warrenton on October 13.

Ever the gambler, Lee hoped to intercept Meade at a point along the Orange and Alexandria railroad and force him to fight. However, Meade was not making any of Pope's mistakes as he pulled back to keep his forces between the onrushing Rebels and Washington. Lee's attempt to intercept the withdrawing Union troops at the Broad Run ford near Bristoe Station met with a decisive repulse. In a lopsided defeat, the Confederates lost 450 prisoners, five pieces of artillery and 1,400 killed or wounded. Despite the victory, Meade had no intention of giving battle on the ill-starred ground around Bull Run and withdrew rapidly past the old battlefields.

When the advancing Confederates reached the site of the destroyed Union supply depot at Manassas Junction, many remembered the feast it had provided them after Jackson had captured the place in August 1862. The Confederates found themselves back in a region stripped of supplies. Lee's rickety supply organization, short of wagons, mules and horses, was incapable of meeting the army's needs as it advanced. The railroad which had been mangled by retreating Union forces could not be repaired in time to be of use. To stay in northern Virginia would mean only slow starvation. If it was going to feed itself, the army had to move quickly into an area unspoiled by war.

Crusty General Meade halted when he found ground to his liking. His Army of the Potomac dug in along the great natural defense line formed by the ridges which ran north and south of Centreville. In a line of battle running from Union Mills to Frying Pan Church, 80,000 veteran troops readied themselves for Lee's attack. Aligned from south to north were the III Corps, I Corps, II Corps, and VI Corps. The V Corps moved into reserve between Chantilly and Jermantown. Meade's forces held these positions October 15 -18. Everything flammable overlooked by prior troop visitations was utilized to kindle the cooking fires. On the plains near Manassas, Lee's nearly 50,000 troops waited for orders and searched for food. The two armies created the largest concentration of troops gathered around Centreville during the war.

Meade might be criticized for being cautious, but he was not making a mistake by underestimating the aggressive genius of Lee. His army was on comfortable terrain and he had placed Lee in a position where he must attack. General Meade was hoping that Lee would push forward as he had done at Gettysburg, thereby providing the opportunity for another smashing repulse. Lee, knowing the strength of the Union positions, ruled out the possibility of a frontal assault. As he looked at the formidable Union line, he pondered his next move. The army could not stay in a fixed position long because of the horrendous supply situation. On October 16, a chill autumn rain drenched the region making movement impossible. As he sat in his tent suffering from an attack of lumbago, Lee sadly realized that his only course of action was to withdraw the same way he had come because he could not maneuver around Meade. The army was too weak to mount a sustained campaign in an area containing no supplies for man or beast. His resources and troops had been stretched to the limit. Slogging through the mud, his army began to withdraw on October 17.

All things considered, it had been quite a feat. Lee had maneuvered Meade into a 60 mile retreat from the Rapidan River to Centreville. By taking the offensive, Lee had forestalled any possibility of an attack by Meade during the remaining period of good weather. Now he was being forced to withdraw because of the critical lack of supplies and the fact that Meade had denied him the opportunity for a successful attack. Although no one knew it at the time, a military era ended at Centreville when Lee began to retire. It was the last time the Confederate Army of Northern Virginia would be on the offensive in the region.

The summer and autumn of 1863 had not treated Will Strawderman well. Along with the constant clashes between Mosby's Rangers and the Union cavalry that kept everyone on edge, it seemed as if a large part of the Yankee army had tromped through the area as it headed north to meet Bobby Lee in the big fight that took place in Pennsylvania. After the Union army had moved on, things had been relatively quiet for a few months. In October, the Union army had come up the roads from Union Mills and Manassas and dug in along the ridge line. Old Will thought for sure Lee would attack them this time, but nothing happened except for some minor skirmishing. Some of the officers visiting the taverns told Old Will that President Lincoln was unhappy because Meade let himself be put on the defensive. A series of testy messages passed back and forth between Meade's headquarters and the White House. Lincoln was probably looking around for a replacement for poor General George Meade.

The farm was a wreck. As they set up their camps, the troops squashed the few crops Old Will had managed to plant in the spring. Foraging army horses had eaten what the troops had not destroyed because the fences had again been taken for firewood. His cow and pigs disappeared into army cook pots. Old Will managed to save his team and wagon by giving a gift of whiskey to a major from a Connecticut unit. The appreciative major placed the barn and its contents off limits to the soldiery. After the armies moved on, a few more of the remaining residents pulled up stakes and departed. The dispirited people had no other choice because the armies had taken all their food and firewood. With nothing left to eat, they could stay and starve during the coming winter or move someplace else while the roads remained passable.

As the region became more desolate, Old Will had to spend top dollar and buy grain from as far away as Loudoun County, which had so far been spared most of the impact of the war. From the virtual cornucopia of a booming Washington city, Clinton Stackhouse graciously supplied the other necessaries Old Will needed to keep his still producing. In return, Will supplied all the Strawderman's Finest he could produce to Mr. Stackhouse's establishment on 14th Street. Strangely enough, although his farm had been rendered completely unproductive, Old Will had more cash than when he was a full-time farmer. His association with Mr. Stackhouse more than made up for ruined crops and the loss of business from the virtually empty Centreville taverns.

December 1864

"I don't know who my grandfather was; I am much more concerned to know what his grandson will be."

-Abraham Lincoln, 1809-1865

Sergeant Erasmus Henry Strawderman was an extremely unhappy man as he stumbled tired, cold and hungry over the frozen Tennessee roads leading south to Alabama. Moving with him was the floundering wreckage of the once proud Confederate Army of Tennessee, sent into full flight after the crushing disaster at Nashville. When General John Bell Hood, the army's commander, rode by with his staff, the disgusted Sergeant Strawderman and those marching with him began to loudly sing an irreverent song set to the tune of the Yellow Rose of Texas.

> *"So now I'm going southward,*
> *My heart is full of woe.*
> *I'm going down to Georgia*
> *To see my Uncle Joe.*
> *You can talk about your Beauregard,*
> *And sing of General Lee,*
> *But the gallant Hood of Texas*
> *Played hell in Tennessee."*

General Hood looked directly at Sergeant Strawderman as he passed the column, but never uttered a word. As he glared back at the general he had grown to hate, Erasmus muttered to himself, "Why don't you shoot me, you incompetent bastard and put me out of my misery! You wrecked our army and got many a good man killed, proving nothing other than you are a damn fool." Erasmus had served in General Patrick Cleburne's division, which was arguably the best unit in the west, since he had enlisted in the army in early 1864. General Johnston had been the army commander then, skillfully slowing Sherman's drive through northern Georgia throughout the summer. In what may have been the biggest mistake of the war, an uneasy President Davis relieved Johnston as army commander in July and replaced him with John B. Hood. Erasmus thought Johnston was a defensive genius who could have held Atlanta forever. Hood, on the other hand, was an overly aggressive fighter who continually underestimated the Yankees and was not at all suited

77

to command an army. Upon assuming command, he hurled his troops forward in bloody attacks that didn't work and lost Atlanta to Sherman in September.

As well as being a brilliant division commander, General Cleburne had the unenviable distinction of being the author of a radical paper recommending that slaves be recruited into the army and given their freedom if they would fight for the Confederacy. Although desperately short of manpower, the idea was flatly rejected by the authorities in Richmond. For having the audacity to suggest such an unorthodox idea, General Cleburne found himself ostracized by the political elite of the Confederacy. Although the general's chances for promotion were gone, his social disgrace had little impact on his troops. Sergeant Erasmus Henry Strawderman and the other soldiers already knew the political elite were never to be found on the firing line during battles. Since General Cleburne took good care of his men, they cared more about his ability to keep them alive in battle than his theoretical views on recruiting Negro troops. It mattered little to them how far from the mainstream of contemporary Southern political thought he seemed to be.

Hoping to force Sherman to withdraw from Georgia after the loss of Atlanta, Hood launched an invasion of Tennessee. At Franklin in late November, General Hood flung his troops forward in a head-on attack against entrenched Yankee positions. In a battle which did not have to be fought because the Yankees were going to withdraw if Hood would have had the good sense to let them go, General Cleburne was killed and his division and the others in the attacking force decimated. As a consequence of the fiasco at Franklin, when Hood's much reduced army reached Nashville in December, it was too weak to capture the city. Later in the month, the Union troops put an end to Hood's siege. They came out fighting, overran Hood's lines and sent the surviving remnants of his army fleeing south.

In the meantime, Sherman had a easy time in Georgia. He marched virtually unopposed across the state from Atlanta to Savannah, ripping the economic vitals out of the Confederacy and leaving a swath of destruction 60 miles wide in his wake. Erasmus thought about these events as he plodded south with a battered army that grew steadily smaller as it moved. Most of the men from Tennessee considered the war lost and were deserting in droves. The army, which had over 30,000 effective troops in its ranks when it invaded Tennessee, counted less than 16,000 as it fled the state. In the new year, they trudged into Mississippi headed for Tupelo where they huddled in cold camps without shoes or blankets during the coldest winter in many years.

February 1865

"No man is good enough to govern another man without that other's consent."

-Abraham Lincoln, 1854

In February, Sergeant Erasmus Henry Strawderman found himself with the troops being transferred to the Carolinas as a frantic Confederate Government tried to scrape together a force to oppose Sherman, who had begun an astonishing winter campaign. Sherman departed Savannah on February 1, and was spreading demoralization and destruction as he moved through the swamps and wetlands of South Carolina at the unbelievable rate of ten miles per day. He had to be stopped before he destroyed the Carolinas and marched into Virginia to link up with Grant. The fact that General Joe Johnston had been restored to command after Hood had resigned made Erasmus feel a little better about things. He had never been to the Carolinas. Maybe he could also visit Virginia and see where his forefathers lived. According to family tradition, the family's founder, Ben Strawderman, had his home on Dogue Creek not far from one of George Washington's farms. If he survived the war, Erasmus thought it would be interesting to see if he had any kin living in the vicinity.

Bank Street runs east to west across the south side of Richmond's capital square. Taking up a large part of the block bounded by Bank Street on the north, Main Street on the south, 10th Street to the west and 11th Street on the east was the former U.S. Customs House. The Confederate Treasury Department occupied the first floor of the building, its presses endlessly printing the nearly worthless paper currency that fueled the 15 percent a month inflation that ravaged the wartime Southern economy. On the third floor, President Davis had an office which he now rarely occupied, preferring, due to his infirmities, to conduct the majority of government business from a small office in the Confederate White House. The second floor of the building also saw little activity because it housed the State Department of the Confederate States of America. Secretary of State Judah P. Benjamin had a great deal of time to think because no foreign nation recognized the Confederacy as a sovereign state, thus leaving little work to do in the sphere of foreign diplomacy. When Union forces captured Fort Fisher on January 15, Wilmington, North Carolina, the last east coast port open to Confederate blockade runners was lost. The government in

Richmond was not only cut-off from the world diplomatically, but also physically because the Union blockade choked off the importation of vital war supplies and prevented Southern cotton from reaching foreign markets.

Judah P. Benjamin was a former U.S. senator from Louisiana and a loyal friend of Jefferson Davis, serving the increasingly embattled Confederate President in the posts of Attorney General, Secretary of War and Secretary of State. The ever-loyal Mr. Benjamin knew he was derisively called the "clerk of Mr. Davis" by the rapidly mounting number of Davis critics. As the Confederacy disintegrated, Davis became the most reviled man in the South, blindly blamed for the problems plaguing the dying Confederacy. Benjamin thought it odd that as Davis became more vilified, General Lee had become a beloved symbol. The glorification of the general was galling to the Secretary of State. Some congressmen even had the audacity to call for Davis to step down so Lee could replace him as a dictator. The intemperate suggestion came from the same Congress that had blocked the taxing of slaves and cotton, hindered war mobilization and done too little to increase the military manufacturing base. While it was true that General Lee was doing more with less than any other general in the war, it was also true that the Confederacy did not have the manufacturing capacity to provide the supplies necessary to sustain military operations in a prolonged conflict. Although he was being blamed in all quarters for the shortages, Davis could not wish rations, wagons, shoes, uniforms, medicine and tents into existence.

As he gazed into the dismal Richmond streets, the Secretary pondered over how the Confederacy was being done in by the illusions the politically powerful planter class of the South insisted were realities. The 2,500 year old institution of slavery was dying out throughout the world. Yet, one of the cornerstones of Confederate policy was the insistence that it be maintained. That policy put the Confederacy at odds with the tide of history and greatly reduced the possibility of foreign intervention on the Confederacy's behalf.

Southern cotton production reached four million bales per year in the late 1850s. In 1860, cotton exports accounted for a hefty $192 million share of the $334 million U.S. export total. When the war began, the Confederacy had bet heavily that the demand for cotton would force a lifting of the Union blockade of Southern ports. It did not happen. As cotton prices rose from ten cents to $1.10 a pound due to the blockade's increasingly effective disruption of the South's commodity exports, other market forces took over. Planters in other parts of the world rushed to put in cotton crops. U. S. wool production climbed from 40 million pounds to 140 million pounds per year as suppliers raced to fill Union army contracts. To fill the void in sugar production, Hawaiian cane plantings increased.

The Lincoln administration shrewdly followed a policy of permitting cotton to be traded and was able to draw a fair amount of the South's crop into Northern hands. Many of the same planters who had urged on the war also found it convenient to ignore the Confederate government's plea to burn cotton in order to keep it from the Yankees. They sold the valuable commodity to traders licensed by the U.S. Treasury Department. Secretary Benjamin had to admit there was a great deal of truth to the common Rebel soldier's lament that is was a "rich man's war and a poor man's fight."

Although a number of English mills dependent on Southern cotton were forced to close, the disruption was not serious enough to bring British government intervention. The products the Confederacy assumed to be indispensable to the markets of Europe and the North were being smuggled out of the South, produced elsewhere, or replaced by substitutes. Those who went to war believing "King Cotton" would bring foreign powers to the Confederacy's aid were sadly mistaken.

Davis, Benjamin and General Lee knew this. They also knew that too many of the goods brought into Southern ports by the blockade runners were destined for civilian consumption. There was more money to be made in luxuries, civilian clothes and alcoholic beverages than in hauling military supplies. As he pondered the pathetic state of the Confederacy, it was becoming evident to Benjamin that the government's days were numbered. Sherman was devastating the Carolinas, moving over roads Confederate generals believed to be impassable in wintertime. When Sherman joined Grant at Petersburg, Richmond would fall, and with it, the Confederate Government. Benjamin, being an astute lawyer, knew it would be wise to prepare for that awful eventuality.

When the Confederacy collapsed, Benjamin felt certain that its leaders would be hunted down, put on trial for treason and executed by hanging or a firing squad. Benjamin was not going to let the Yankee prosecutors have an easy time of it as they orchestrated their public spectacle of humiliation and revenge. On the floor next to his desk were two boxes approximately two foot square in size in which he had been placing items that would be invaluable during a trial defense. Both he and Davis might end up dangling at the end of a Yankee hangman's rope, but it would be only after a resolute defense that would give the Northern rabble something to remember.

The Confederacy had many sympathetic friends of influence in the North. Clement L. Vallandigham, a former Ohio congressman, Horatio Seymour of New York and Judge George C. Woodard of Pennsylvania were among the most prominent. They and many others in the Democratic Party could be counted on to apply all the political pressure they could bring to bear on

President Lincoln in order to force him to spare the lives of the defeated Southern leaders. Benjamin's plan to cheat the hangman included a legal defense arguing the constitutional right of states to leave the Union, and a behind-the-scenes program pressuring the Lincoln administration to be merciful. Any attorney worth his salt would have agreed with Judah Benjamin's decision to begin preparations while time remained.

Mr. Benjamin was uniquely qualified to judge the wartime political situation. Along with his duties as Confederate Secretary of State, he was also the head of the State Department's Secret Service, a shadowy organization with agents operating in the North and Canada. The management of the Confederate espionage system was the direct responsibility of Benjamin, although President Davis often intervened in the decision making process. One of their best agents had been Rose O'Neal Greenhow, who had provided invaluable intelligence before the Yankees had arrested and deported her. Another find was Clinton Stackhouse, who had been able to gain access to Union military plans by rather unconventional means. His timely information on General Grant's objectives during the spring and summer of 1864, had enabled Lee to check Grant's army at every turn and probably cost the Yankees 50,000 extra casualties as the battered Army of the Potomac slowly fought its way through tidewater Virginia to Petersburg.

Benjamin's secret service had spent $1,200,000 in gold attempting to influence the outcome of the 1864 election in the North. Few people actually knew how close the South had come to winning by clandestine political means what it could not achieve on the battlefield. The plan supported the Democratic peace platform by painting the war as a dismal failure to Northern voters. Benjamin's operatives paid subsidies to friendly newspaper editors, financed candidates running in opposition to Lincoln's policies and provided money to agitators to denounce the war and incite riots. By the late summer of 1864, no one gave the much despised Lincoln the slightest chance of winning the November election. The war-weary Northern electorate was ready turn him out and install a new administration pledged to end the war, even if it meant letting the South go its independent way. Judah Benjamin had watched in consternation as the Confederacy's hope of independence suddenly dissipated when Sherman captured Atlanta in September and General Early lost the Shenandoah Valley in October. In Northern eyes, the cities of Atlanta and Richmond had become the symbols of Confederate power. As long as they remained unconquered, the Confederacy stood strong. When Atlanta fell, Lincoln's discredited war policies were stunningly vindicated and the evil ogre from Illinois handily won reelection. The war would go on under Lincoln's administration until the Union was restored and the Confederacy vanquished. Judah Benjamin was often haunted by the thought that the removal of General Johnston had been the mistake that doomed the Confederate Government. If Davis had left Joe Johnston in command of the army, the defensive-minded general might have been able hold onto Atlanta until after Lincoln had been turned out of office.

Thinking about what might have been was no help in the current situation. Into a box went the list of Northerners who had worked for the defeat of Lincoln while in the pay of the Confederacy. They would be a useful source to tap for legal defense funds or in agitating for leniency during the trial. The list of Northerners who had illegally sold the Confederates arms, medicines and other war-related goods also went into one of the boxes for the same reason. The names of the disgusting abolitionists who bankrolled bloody John Brown in his murderous pre-war adventures in Kansas and Virginia had been collected by Confederate agents and submitted in a report to Richmond. It too went into a box, along with samples of pistols and medicines shipped south by Yankees willing to make a quick dollar by selling to the enemy.

As he packed, Judah wondered if Harriet Beecher Stowe had been paid by abolitionists to write the dreadful book which had so vilified the South. He smiled at the thought of dropping such a bombshell in court. It would be very uplifting to be able to tell the court that the despicable woman who brought on a war with her malicious writings had been paid by radical abolitionists to write those inflammatory falsehoods. She played a big part in the abolitionist plot to wreck the established social order of the South, no doubt about that. The Confederates knew her father collected money and shipped rifles to Brown in Kansas. Why did the North consider it admirable for a preacher of the gospel to kill innocent people by arming a fanatic lunatic to do the dirty deeds? The twisted workings of the Yankee mind made no sense at all to Benjamin.

Having space in one of the boxes, Benjamin looked around the office for something of bulk to fill the remaining space. His eyes fell on a report which had been sent to all cabinet officers by John S. Preston, Superintendent of the Conscription Bureau. Judah Benjamin remembered it as depressing reading when he digested its unsettling contents two days ago. According to Preston's report, the Confederacy, which had put 850,000 soldiers in the field since 1861, now had less than 160,000 on active duty. Preston went on to report over 150,000 soldiers were absent without leave from the armies of the Confederacy. The enormous list of Confederate deserters had been carefully organized by army, division and other sub-units. Many regiments and brigades had more men listed as deserters than they had on active duty.

Having no further use for the report, Benjamin used it as filler in his second box. It did the job quite nicely. Now tightly packed, nothing in the box rattled against the sides or lid.

The skyrocketing number of deserters indicated how dire the situation had become since the days after the victory at First Manassas when jubilant Confederate troops had fired a 100 gun salute on Capitol Square. General Lee's bedraggled army, now struggling to hold the 40 miles of trenches running from northeast of Richmond to southwest of Petersburg, was down to less than 60,000 men. It was losing the equivalent of a regiment a day to desertion. To further stress Lee's diminishing fighting ability, the Yankees were offering Rebel deserters $8 in hard cash for each weapon they brought with them. Lee could not be expected to fend off Grant's forces for very much longer. The campaigning season would begin with the drying of the roads and Lee's over-stretched lines were sure to be broken.

How to get his two boxes safely to a place near Washington where they could be hidden and easily retrieved when the need arose was a problem Judah Benjamin had not yet resolved. He did not feel comfortable using the regular couriers who traveled to Washington from Richmond, via Ashland and Taylorsville, then slipping across the Potomac River and journeying up through Southern Maryland. The Yankees had been increasing their patrols and some of his agents had been captured. Who could he consign the boxes to? If they were discovered in someone's home by the Yankees, the contents of the boxes would surely send the hapless homeowner directly to prison or to the gallows.

As he paced his office deep in thought, Benjamin picked up a folder from a shelf on the bookcase which stood against the wall. It contained old papers, mementos from the time he had served as Secretary of War. Seeking a momentary distraction from the dilemma of what to do with his boxes, he began to read the documents one by one.

Richmond, October 28, 1861

General Joseph E. Johnston, Centreville:
Just heard from Norfolk that the enemy's great fleet is going to sea,
thus indicating that the threat of attack on the Rappahannock was
intended to deceive us.

J. P. Benjamin,
Acting Secretary of War

Headquarters Department of Northern Virginia,
Centreville, January 16, 1862
Hon. J. P. Benjamin, Secretary of War:
Sir: I beg leave to urge the importance of filling, as soon as possible,
the grades of major and brigadier general now existing in this army. The
necessity of filling these offices is increasing by the absence of three
brigadier- generals, two of whom are members of Congress; the other is sick.

I have twice asked, by telegraph, for an officer of ability to succeed
General Whiting, but have received no reply. That command is an important
one, and should be exercised by one of our best officers; but those at my
disposal who are competent to it are indispensable in their present positions.
Most respectfully, your obedient servant,
E. Johnston, General

Judah Benjamin was wondering why he had kept the copies of old correspondence in his bookcase when he found one that brought deep a pang of regret. The flood of memories it evoked brought tears to his eyes as he slumped back into his chair to reread the letter:

Headquarters Valley District,
Winchester, Va., January 31, 1862
Hon. J. P. Benjamin, Secretary of War:
Sir: Your order requiring me to direct General Loring to return with
his command to Winchester immediately has been promptly complied with.

With such interference in my command I cannot expect to be of much
service in the field, and accordingly respectfully request to be ordered to
report for duty to the superintendent of the Virginia Military Institute at
Lexington, as has been done in the case of other professors. Should this
application not be granted, I respectfully request that the President will
accept my resignation from the Army.

I am sir, very respectfully, your obedient servant,
T. J. Jackson
Major-General, P.A.C.S.
(Endorsement)   Headquarters

Centreville, February 7, 1862
Respectfully forwarded, with great regret. I don't know how the loss of
this officer can be supplied. General officers are much wanted in this
department.
J. E. Johnston, General

Judah Benjamin, the Confederate Secretary of State, sat at his desk sobbing unabashedly as he recalled how shabbily he and President Davis had treated General Jackson in the days when they thought he had little in the way of military merit. Benjamin had very nearly driven the quaint Virginia Military Institute professor from the army only months before Jackson had stunned the North and South by ridding the Shenandoah Valley of Union troops. It had been one of the war's most amazing feats of arms. Later as a team, Jackson and Lee were unbeatable, defying all the odds and winning victories. Things might have been so different if Jackson had lived. If Jackson had not been killed, Lee might have been able to win the battle of Gettysburg. It pained Benjamin deeply as he squarely faced the awful reality laid out in the documents. He had mistreated Jackson because he had misjudged him. Jackson was not an idiot. He was a military genius and Benjamin had not been able to tell the difference. Benjamin sincerely wished there was some way he could make amends to the fallen hero. But there was nothing he could do because Jackson went to his grave over two years ago. The dream of an independent Confederacy that Jackson had so ably championed while he lived was also fading fast under the unceasing rain of blows delivered by Generals Grant and Sherman.

Judah thought back to the halcyon days of the winter of 1861-62 when Johnston's army had Washington almost blockaded. The Yankee papers were full of stories about the miles of impregnable Confederate fortifications around the village of Centreville. Northern and Southern newspaper reporters alike referred to them as among the strongest ever built in North America. The intervening years of war had brought massive changes with them. This winter, Lee's army was holding 40 miles of fortifications. The six miles of lines thought to be so substantial in 1862 would now be considered nothing more than a good skirmish line.

The army's glory days at Centreville were gone; they belonged to an age well-nigh blasted from memory. If Benjamin remembered correctly, General Johnston had resided at a place called the Jameson House in Centreville. Unfortunately for the Confederate war effort, President Davis and the general argued bitterly that winter, a time that deepened the animosity between the two men. Judah knew from experience that Davis was incapable of bending when his honor was involved. His rigidity had created problems with more than one general and had hampered his relations with Congress. One irritated detractor had described Davis as, "Cold as a lizard and ambitious as Lucifer."

In the realm of personality traits, Judah Benjamin knew General Johnston was no prize winner either. He was very cautious and extremely touchy about his dignity. Jefferson Davis, Benjamin admitted to himself, never forgot a slight or forgave the person who committed it. On the other hand, the moody Johnston never ignored the slightest perceived jab at his dignity. Johnston, as a subordinate general, could have made an attempt to be less provocative in his dealings with Davis. The simmering conflict between the president and general became a recipe for disaster. It wreaked havoc when Davis, under terrible strain in the summer of 1864, had grown tired of Johnston's prickly insinuations and relieved him of command. It was the decision that resulted in the loss of Atlanta. Benjamin wondered if someday in the future, a memorial would be erected in Centreville commemorating it as the site of the leadership dispute that eventually destroyed the Confederacy.

Then he had a flash of insight. Perhaps General Jackson had sent Judah Benjamin the idea from somewhere beyond the grave. It would be just like Jackson to do that thought Benjamin because Jackson would always do whatever he could to help the Confederacy. As he closed the memory-riddled correspondence file and placed it back on the shelf, Benjamin realized he had solved the problem of where to safely stash his two boxes of materials. The region around Centreville had been devastated by the war. Mosby's Rangers controlled the area at night, making it quite uncomfortable for any Union troops in the area. The village was less than an easy day's ride from Washington. Somewhere in those miles of vacant trenches, bomb proof magazines and forts had to be the perfect place to hide his two small boxes. All Benjamin needed to do was borrow a few soldiers who had once been stationed at Centreville and have them take the boxes to northern Virginia. The trip up and back should not take longer than a couple of weeks. When the soldiers returned to Richmond with a map showing the boxes' hiding place, Benjamin's plan to save President Davis, the other members of the cabinet and himself from the vengeful Yankee hangman would be complete.

Benjamin penned a note to Major General John C. Breckinridge, who had recently been appointed Secretary of War. Breckinridge was politically astute, having been Vice President of the United States before the war began. The general would certainly understand Benjamin's plan and supply the troops to carry out the mission. Just as Benjamin finished writing his note, the gas light sputtered out, leaving him sitting in the late afternoon gloom of a chilly winter's day. It was another sign of how hard life in Richmond had become. They couldn't even keep the lights working in the Confederate capital.

Like so much else in Richmond, the gas works were worn out. Although the workers struggled to keep the plant in operation, the deteriorated equipment could no longer do the job. The necessary replacement parts could not be obtained from foreign sources because of the blockade. This late in the war, no northern manufacturer would be willing to smuggle the parts to the Confederate government. Almost on a daily basis, the delivery of gas had to be reduced or shut off completely in parts of town. For many users, gas was only supplied during certain limited hours of the day. Not wishing to continue to work by candlelight, Benjamin gave the note to one of his assistants for delivery to Secretary Breckinridge and departed the dark office.

Secretary of State Benjamin liked to occasionally personally check the prices in the Richmond markets. It gave him a good feel for the economic condition of the city, a topic which came up often in meetings with President Davis these days. With pen and writing tablet in hand, he ordered his driver to detour the carriage to the market before proceeding to his elegant home located on the south side of Main Street between Fourshee and Adams.

In 1860, Richmond had been the proud cultural, manufacturing and commercial center of Virginia. With its prewar population of 38,000 now more than tripled with workers and refugees, it was the decaying capital city of a nation in the final convulsion of military defeat. The streets were falling apart and decent living space was unavailable at any price. Hotels and hospitals were always overcrowded. A criminal fraternity of speculators, counterfeiters and assorted riffraff constantly tormented the populace, making the imposition of martial law a necessity. In an era of high prices and a shortage of goods, the city purchased food for resale at fixed prices in order to alleviate a few of the problems faced by war industry workers. Benjamin had seen a notice stating Richmond's city council had passed an ordinance to combat fraud at the city wood yard and supply store. Violation would result in a fine of $50. Unscrupulous individuals were already at work debasing the city's feeding program. He hoped they could be stopped.

By early 1865, advancing Union armies had severed transportation connections in over 75 percent of the Confederacy's 750,00 square miles. As a result of the disruption, the army meat ration was down to a mere four ounces per day. While food was available in some areas, the lack of transport prevented delivery to Richmond. At the obscure country village of Appomattox Courthouse, a place Benjamin knew would never be famous for anything, food was selling at half the Richmond prices. Runaway inflation had become the scourge of the Southern economy. In 1861, one gold dollar equaled $1.03 in Confederate currency. By the late winter of 1864-65, it took $60 in Confederate money to purchase one gold dollar. Since wages did not keep up with the escalating prices, workers' living standards were continually compressed downward. Many of Richmond's people lived on the verge of starvation, lacked adequate shelter and as a result, were growing more bad-tempered with each passing day. The danger of riot was ever present, necessitating a strong police and military presence on the city streets at all times.

Benjamin took note of the prices as he strolled through the market accompanied by two armed guards in civilian clothing. There was little in the way of conversation. Some of the customers and vendors glared at him with unabashed malice as he passed storefronts and stalls. As a high government official, the common people held him partly responsible for the economic and military catastrophe that was growing worse by the day. Once safely back in his carriage, Benjamin checked the prices he garnered from verbal quotes or copied from signs. His findings gave a clear indication of how grim the level of daily life in Richmond had become. Benjamin knew the government was powerless to do anything about the economic situation. Feeling totally helpless, he looked over his appalling list of prices as the carriage headed for his home:

$45 Confederate for pound of coffee. There was none available that evening.
$100 for a pound of tea. Only one type was available.
$25 for a pound of butter of poor quality.
Flour cost $1,250 a barrel, quality uncertain.
Bacon was selling for $20 a pound.
A scrawny live hen, which would not have been sellable before the war, was priced at $50.
Quantities of poor quality beef were available at $15 a pound.

In these desperate times, the Confederate Congress increasingly attacked the administration of President Davis. Tired of the unending abuse, Secretary of War Seddon gave in to the relentless pressure and resigned. Everyone agreed that the new Secretary, Major General John C. Breckinridge, would do a better job. When Congress passed a law creating the position of General in Chief, President Davis appointed Robert E. Lee to the position on February 6, 1865. Congress yelled and screamed until something was also done about the inefficient commissary system. The bumbling Commissary General, Lucius Northrop, was pushed out. His replacement, Brigadier General Isacc M. St. John, was feverishly working to establish a reserve of three million bread rations and 2.5 million pounds of meat because if the army was going to continue to fight it also had to eat at least now and then.

No Confederate politician dared to contemptuously laugh at dead General Cleburne's suggestion to raise Negro troops any longer because General Lee himself was demanding it. Thousands of black soldiers were competently serving in the ranks of the Union forces while the South had exhausted its manpower reserve. A bill to enlist Negro soldiers passed 40-37 in the Confederate House, but went down to defeat in the Senate. In response to General Lee's plea, individual states began to recruit on their own accord. Two companies of Negro soldiers and their white officers were soon seen drilling smartly on Richmond's Capitol Square. Benjamin was not sure he agreed with the concept, but he knew the Confederacy had no other options. If it was going to have any chance of survival, it had to avoid losing the war during the next few months. Giving General Lee what he wanted seemed like a small price to pay for the chance.

March 1865

"With malice toward none, with charity for all, with firmness in the right, as God gives us to see the right, let us strive on to finish the work we are in, to bind up the nation's wounds, to care for him who shall have borne the battle, and for his widow and his orphan, to do all which may achieve and cherish a just and lasting peace among ourselves, and with all nations."
         -Abraham Lincoln, March 4, 1864

"I have been up to see the Congress and they do not seem to be able to anything except to eat peanuts and chew tobacco, while my army is starving."
         -General Robert E. Lee, March 1864,
expressing his dissatisfaction with the Confederate Congress.

Major General John C. Breckinridge sat at his desk in the Confederate States War Department, located in the former Virginia Mechanics Institute on Franklin and Ninth Streets, reading Benjamin's note for a second time. While he agreed with Benjamin's line of reasoning in making provisions to protect high-level Confederate officials in the very likely event of a post-war trial, he was not at all happy. Benjamin knew as well as he did that the army had no men to spare to carry out Benjamin's scheme. Most of the soldiers who were in the army when it held northern Virginia in 1861-62 had been killed in later battles. Those few still alive, if they could be found, could not be spared to carry two boxes to the abandoned fortifications at Centreville. Breckinridge gave serious thought to forcing Benjamin to assign the task to his own State Department dandies because Benjamin must have a few people to spare. With no foreign relations work to do, what did they do at State all day long?

Then General Breckinridge began to have second thoughts. The Confederate State Department had been wrong on every assumption it made in foreign affairs since the establishment of the Confederacy. Thanks in part to their series of misjudgments, the Confederacy had failed to gain diplomatic recognition from any foreign country. Therefore, it was very unlikely that the dolts at State could be trusted to get this box hiding job done correctly. Since his own life was also at stake, it was better to find someone in the army competent enough to carry out the important mission. If he left his future in the hands of the State Department, Breckinridge believed he might as well go ahead and hang himself now and save the Yankees the trouble of doing it later. Given its record of abysmal failure, State would just bungle the box-hiding mission like they had everything else.

Matthew F. Chambon had been promoted to Lieutenant Colonel. Since his discharge from the hospital in 1862, the crippled officer had made himself virtually indispensable to Colonel Josiah Gorgas, the Chief of the Ordnance Bureau, as he struggled to keep the Confederate armies supplied with cannon, rifles, shells, powder and bullets.

Lieutenant Colonel Chambon spent a great of his time at the sprawling, fire-spewing Tredegar Iron Works located on the James River and Kanawa Canal near the end of 4th Street. He became intimately familiar with every shop in the hot, dirty installation where men labored around the clock to produce cannon for the Confederacy. He checked and revised production specifications, certified iron deliveries and ran the firing tests on new cannon before they were accepted by the government. Chambon also knew the CSA Artillery Work Shops, which occupied nearly all the space between 7th and 8th Streets and Canal Street and Boyd Street, like the back of his hand. Here, in the former tobacco warehouses, the cannon were mounted on the wheeled gun carriages and equipped for war.

It appeared to Lieutenant Colonel Chambon that almost all the available space along Richmond's river front was dedicated to military manufacturing of some type. The Arsenal and Ordnance Shops between 7th and 8th streets manufactured the deadly rifled musket with machines the Confederates had recovered from the federal Arsenal at Harpers Ferry. Chambon knew its workings as well as those of the Nitre and Mining Bureau, situated at Franklin and 10th Streets. While working most of the time in Richmond, Matt had traveled to the Augusta, Georgia powder works and other facilities on several occasions to implement production change directives for Colonel Gorgas. Ordnance production turned out to be almost as dangerous as serving with a front-line unit. Due to the hectic production schedule, safety precautions slipped and there were deadly accidents and explosions. Chambon nearly met his end when the Richmond Laboratory's cartridge loading facility blew up in 1863, killing 30 workers. Had he arrived at the site a few minutes earlier, he would have been numbered among the dead.

The lieutenant colonel was on his way to give the new Secretary of War the latest report on ordnance production. While facilities were still producing at capacity, shortages of materials were rapidly developing due to the disrupted transportation network. If Union incursions were not halted, the entire arms production complex which Colonel Gorgas had built from scratch would grind to a halt by June. As he entered the Secretary's outer office, he bumped into Major General John C. Breckinridge himself. The general had seen Chambon hobbling around the War Department on his cane during previous visits. He was not an unusual sight because a large number of the staff officers had some type of injury which disqualified them from field service.

"Colonel Chambon," Breckinridge asked, "Weren't you with the army when it was at Centreville during the winter of '61-62?"

"Why yes," Chambon answered, "I was there the entire winter. I got this," he continued while pointing to his damaged leg, "from an explosion during the evacuation. Some damn fool buried live shells and powder in the piles of discarded equipment we were burning."

"Are you familiar with the gun positions, shot storage and bomb proofs in the old Centreville fortification lines? The houses in the village?" asked Breckinridge.

"Yes sir," Chambon answered. " I constructed a number of the artillery positions when we entrenched during the autumn. I don't think things have changed much up there since the army pulled out. I expect the magazines are almost like we left them, except for some water seepage. The water gets in easily if maintenance ceases. There was not much to the village, maybe two dozen houses at most. If I recall, there were a couple of good taverns, two churches and not much else. "

"You are just the man I have been looking for," replied the Secretary, slapping Chambon on the back to show how delighted he was. "I have an assignment for you that will take about two weeks. You are to report to Secretary Benjamin at the State Department. He will fill you in on the details. Oh, and also find at least one good enlisted man to take with you. When you return, report to me before returning to your duties with Colonel Gorgas. Turning to the aide seated at one of the desks, the Secretary of War instructed him to prepare the necessary travel passes for Colonel Chambon and one other individual to be named later.

Lieutenant Colonel Chambon found Secretary of State Benjamin to be a portly, jovial fellow. Their meeting was friendly enough, but Chambon came away from it with the feeling there was a lot more to Mr. Benjamin than foreign diplomacy. His instructions were quite specific. The Secretary emphasized again and again how important it was to maintain secrecy. Chambon was to have the two boxes of material waterproofed by the Navy Department. He and his assistant were to travel by canal boat to Lexington as inconspicuously as possible and there, purchase horses for the trip to Centreville. Under no circumstances was he to let the boxes out of his sight.

He was not to let anyone open the containers, nor divulge the details of his mission to anyone. Upon reaching the destination, he was to prepare a detailed map of the concealed location of the boxes. One copy was to be delivered to the Secretary of State upon return to Richmond, the other was for the Secretary of War. If for some reason he could not reach Centreville, he was to return to Richmond. If captured, he was to destroy both boxes before surrendering. Under no circumstances was he to allow the boxes to fall into Union hands. Chambon clearly understood whatever was in the two containers was more important to the Confederacy than he was. If necessary, he was to defend the boxes with his life. Still, it would be good to get out of Richmond for a couple of weeks. He had heard that food was still available in the countryside. He looked forward to eating a few good regular meals again.

Secretary Benjamin noticed Lieutenant Colonel Chambon used a cane as an aid when walking. As a parting gift, he presented him with one of the finest walking sticks Chambon had ever seen. After the Secretary showed him how to use it, the colonel realized the walking stick was really a weapon in disguise. The head of the stick was heavy enough to practically decapitate a man when thrust forward at close range. After being wound, the heavy spring hidden inside the shaft of the cane could propel a six inch long iron dart with enough force to kill a man 35 feet away. It was well designed and engineered. Four darts were neatly stored in the shaft of the walking stick. When Chambon looked skeptical during his explanation, the Secretary eagerly demonstrated the weapon by firing a dart into the side of the wooden bookcase behind his desk. By the way the dart penetrated the two inch thick oak board, Chambon could tell the thing was lethal, and not a toy as he first suspected. As he handed the walking stick to the officer, the Secretary laughingly remarked "I trust you will refrain from using this device in any saloon brawls you partake in during your off-duty hours."

He also handed over a signed authorization to draw $250 in gold from the Treasury Department. "Use it to pay for your travel expenses, horses and any necessary bribes. Bring an accounting of your expenses and any leftover money back when you return. Good luck and God be with you. The leaders of our government are depending on you." As he left the building, Matt Chambon wondered what other shadowy enterprises the jolly Secretary of State was involved in. The fancy walking stick he had been given was certainly not an instrument of diplomacy.

Chambon took the authorization to draw $250 in gold to the Treasury Department's vault section. After passing through the guards, he arrived before the desk of Andrew J. Clinton, the superintendent in charge of the gold bullion reserves of the Confederate States Treasury Department. Mr. Clinton was engrossed in writing his name in a variety of ways on a large piece of scratch paper. He wrote, "Andrew Jackson Clinton, Andrew J. Clinton, A. Jackson Clinton and A .J. Clinton" in flourishing signatures.

"Excuse me sir, I have a warrant to draw gold coins for certain anticipated expenses," said Chambon interrupting the honorable Mr. Clinton's signature practice session as he placed the paper on the desk. "Don't you know the Confederacy is almost out of gold reserves?" Clinton responded, while picking up the document. When he found it signed by the Secretary of State his manner changed. He knew it must be for an important espionage task of some kind. Andrew J. Clinton was one of the few people in Richmond who knew Mr. Benjamin also held another important government post, a very secret one. Then noticing that the injured army officer leaning on the fancy walking stick was staring at the signature samples on the paper, he defensively added, "I have only recently been appointed to this position of high trust by President Davis. I was trying to decide how my official signature should look." The implication in his comment was clear. Here sat a man who was politically connected to the highest level of the government. He was a person not be crossed. His critical duties at Treasury would also serve nicely to keep him out of the cold, filthy trenches around Richmond and Petersburg.

Mr. Clinton took the authorization, reading it carefully as he headed for the massive vault. After checking to ensure the signatures were authentic, he returned with a small bag of gold coins. Chambon counted the money, signed three copies of the treasury receipt and departed from the vault division. As he exited the building, he noted that Mr. Clinton's official signature had finally been decided as "Andrew J. Clinton." The colonel thought it was admirable that his visit had been a help in resolving a weighty issue for the poor fellow. As he headed up the street filled with gaunt, unsmiling faces, he also wondered how such an idiot managed to get himself appointed to a nice job like that.

Those buildings in Richmond not devoted to producing armaments seemed to have been converted to hospitals. Last year, Dr. Wesley Hoffmann told Cyrus Bellnapp he thought that there were at least 25 Confederate Government medical facilities in operation, maybe more. Regardless of the total number of hospitals, the sick and wounded kept coming to Chimborazo and its staff struggled valiantly to treat them. The 80 wards were always full, meaning over 3,200 patients were on the grounds. Shortages of basic foodstuffs such as salt, coffee, meat and flour often disrupted the feeding of convalescent patients. The lack of straw for stuffing mattresses and soap for cleaning hindered sanitation efforts. During the winter, the hospital bakery had been forced to close for the first time in the war because it could not obtain supplies. Oakwood Cemetery next to the hospital was filled. The army's dead were being transported to Hollywood Cemetery on the west side of town for burial.

In January, Cyrus had been devastated when Dr. Hoffmann was killed. The doctor had gone to the forward lines to help set up a first aid station when a misdirected artillery shell struck the ambulance in which he was traveling. It had not been intentional; the gunners may have miscalculated the range or the shell fuse may have been defective. It made no difference. Dr. Hoffmann was dead. Lost without his close friend and mentor, Cyrus began looking for a way out of the hospital where he had nobly served through the worst of the war. When Virginia began its program to recruit Negro troops, Cyrus obtained permission to sign up. He quickly rose to the rank of sergeant. With his previous medical experience, he was also the unofficial company surgeon.

Lieutenant Colonel Chambon was passing through Capitol Square near Ninth and Grace Streets, close to the Washington Monument and where President Davis had been inaugurated on February 22, 1862. On the other side of the Square, he could see a company of the new Virginia State Negro troops drilling. One of the sergeants looked vaguely familiar, so he hobbled over for a better look. "Well I'll be damned," he said. There in the front rank marched an old acquaintance from his days in the hospital. When the drill session ended, he asked Sergeant Bellnapp if he was interested in going with him on a mission to northern Virginia. Cyrus did not take much convincing since the company's training was nearly completed and he had grown to respect Chambon. Going to war with someone you respected was always better than taking the risk of going with a fool you didn't know. After checking the papers Colonel Chambon presented, the company lieutenant noted on the roster that Sergeant Cyrus Bellnapp of Virginia's Colored Troops was detailed to the C. S. Ordnance Department for a period not to exceed one month.

On Broad Street between Ninth and Tenth Streets, the Transportation Bureau maintained its offices and a large stable which sheltered over 100 horses, most of which were reserved for pulling ambulances. The authorization papers from the Secretary of War got the lieutenant colonel and sergeant the use of a shabby two-wheeled wagon pulled by a single horse for one day. As they headed east on Broad Street, they could see the majestic residence of Confederate President Jefferson Davis situated at the corner of Clay and 12th Streets on the hill above them. The pair turned the horse down hill on 20th Street and then east on Main, which carried them to the Confederate Navy Yard on the west side of Rocketts Landing. Before the Union blockade had closed down sea-borne commerce in 1862, ocean going ships filled the docks at Rocketts Landing. Now, the docks stood empty because Richmond's manufactured goods were denied access to the markets of the world. The Navy yard itself was quiet because the majority of the sailors and marines were serving the heavy guns in the fort at Drewry's Bluff, a key position that prevented Union ships from coming up river and bombarding Richmond. Although the Navy had no ships large enough to grapple with the Union vessels enforcing the blockade, the yard had plenty of tar and canvas with which to seal boxes. The sailor who did the work said he had waterproofed them good enough to last 150 years. "If they don't hold up, bring them back in 1995 and I'll do them again for you for free," he said. They all laughed at his little joke because the waterproofed boxes were probably the only things in Richmond that came with any kind of a guarantee anymore.

When it was completed in 1854, the James River and Kanawha Canal became a bustling commercial artery connecting Richmond to Buchanan, 197 miles upstream. The canal boat crews at the Richmond Turning Basin, where the canal boats were turned around, paid scant attention to the two soldiers who arrived with a sizable assortment of bundles and boxes, all of which had been thoughtfully provided by the Secretary of State. The speedy delivery of the odd cargo could not have been a consideration because the only mode of transportation slower than a mule-pulled canal boat moving at three miles per hour, was walking. The soldiers were going to Lexington by way of the James River and the north branch of the James, a distance of 155 miles. Although the bundles and boxes all looked the same from the outside, the soldiers kept two of the smaller ones near them as they spread their personal gear on the deck. The overworked boat crew had learned from experience not to ask questions of military passengers. These two were an especially peculiar pair, a crippled white lieutenant colonel and a Negro sergeant, probably one of the first to be mustered into Virginia's service. Each was armed with a hard-to obtain repeating cavalry carbine and a revolver. To protect against the winter chill each wore a captured blue Union army overcoat on which had been sewn Confederate badges of rank. The officer's uniform was the standard gray issue, although a bit on the very worn side. The sergeant wore a mixture of gray and butternut, no different from the many other uniforms they had seen.

The boat on which they had taken passage was the Marshall. It usually traveled the canal between Lexington and Lynchburg, not often coming all the way to Richmond. The Marshall was the most famous boat on the western stretch of the canal because in 1863 it carried the body of General Thomas J. (Stonewall) Jackson to Lexington for burial. A crowd estimated at 4,000 had met the Marshall as it pulled into the dock below the bluff occupied by the Virginia Military Institute. Now, the boat was merely a cog in the tenuous canal supply line that linked the besieged city of Richmond to the interior of Virginia. The crew picked up snatches of soldiers' conversation as the Marshall slowly moved upstream. Although attached to the Ordnance Department, they talked mostly of medical matters. From the way he discussed wound treatment, one would have thought the Negro to be an experienced surgeon of repute. They also argued the merits of horse breeds, obviously having plans to purchase some horseflesh in Lexington in order to continue their travel. To while away the hours as the Marshall moved through the locks and followed the winding course of the canal, the soldiers calculated and debated the number of horses killed in the conflict. They finally came to agreement on the astounding figure of approximately 1.5 million. With so many being killed, it was no wonder that horses were scarce and the price for the animals was steadily climbing.

As the boat passed through the war-weary towns heading for Lexington, the talk was all about the raid by General Sheridan's marauding cavalry. He left Winchester, Virginia, heading down the Valley Pike, passing through Harrisonburg and Staunton with at least 10,000 troopers. After he routed Jubal Early's sad little remnant of an army at Waynesboro, Sheridan hit Charlottesville and then moved down to the James River to smash locks and burn canal boats before linking with General Grant's army near Petersburg. The canal behind them would be closed until repairs could be made, so it looked as though the Marshall would not be returning to Richmond anytime soon. It was another sign of how badly things were going for the Confederacy. The Yankee cavalry, which earlier in the war had been totally ineffective in dealing with Confederate horsemen, now went anywhere it wanted with complete impunity. Once the pride of the South, the decimated Confederate cavalry was incapable of fielding the men and horses needed to halt Yankee raiders.

As the Marshall pulled into the dock, Matt Chambon could see the blackened ruins of his alma mater, the Virginia Military Institute, standing desolately on the bluff overlooking the canal. Torched along with other buildings in the town when General Hunter had swept into Lexington the previous June, the ruined building brought a deep feeling of sadness to the lieutenant colonel who had spent many happy days there as a student. Despite the devastation, the school had not closed completely. It was operating in Richmond's former Alms House. The building had been leased as temporary school quarters in December 1864. As Matt stared up at the charred ruins, he hoped the school buildings in Lexington would be rebuilt after the war ended.

It took awhile to find someone with a wagon who was willing to take them and their cargo into town because the people of Lexington viewed anyone arriving from Richmond with undisguised anger. Richmond officialdom was blamed for stripping the Shenandoah Valley of troops and allowing the fertile region to be destroyed by the marauding Yankees. What had once been the breadbasket of the Confederacy had been reduced to a wasteland, its once prosperous people rendered destitute and helpless.

As their rented wagon trundled slowly along Main Street crossing Washington Street, Matt and Cyrus caught a glimpse of the residence on Washington Street once owned by General Jackson when he had been a professor at the Institute. They continued on Main Street to the cemetery at the outskirts of town where the wagon halted briefly while they paid their respects at the General's grave. Returning to town, they found supper and lodgings for the night. The strange assortment of rags, bits of clothing, parts of horse harnesses, sail canvas and other odds and ends packed in the bundles were sold cheaply or given away. Lexington's residents scratched their heads in amazement as they tried to figure out why the two soldiers had gone to the trouble of hauling the contents of someone's attic all the way from Richmond. Chambon's offer to purchase horses brought no response from the sullen residents until he let it be known he was willing to pay in gold coin. Six horses were quickly offered for sale as word of the remarkable offer spread through the shabby town. Matt purchased the two best, paying top dollar for horses and saddles. One horse had brand markings indicating it had once been in the service of the Union, the other had no army markings of any kind. Its owner must have had it carefully hidden from the prowling government purchasing agents always on the lookout for horses.

Judah P. Benjamin was a man of honor, but no one's fool. He prepared a third box containing duplicates of the items he thought would be most useful in his legal defense program and stored it at his residence on Main Street. He could always hide it later if the situation required. It was an insurance policy in case the soldiers he sent to Centreville failed. Secretary of War Breckinridge agreed with his decision not to inform President Davis of the attempt to place the documents in a safe place near Washington. The haggard President had enough to worry about. As the war news grew increasingly dismal, President Davis seemed to become more defiant, insisting the Confederacy continue the fight against all odds. Both Breckinridge and

Benjamin would serve the President to the end, their honor would allow them to do no less. But they were realistic enough to know the Confederacy had precious little time left. General Lee was warning that Richmond could not be held if the horrendous problems caused by the lack of supplies were not ameliorated. In the Carolinas, General Johnston had been unable to halt Sherman's destructive advance.

Barring an unforeseen miracle, both Breckinridge and Benjamin agreed that Lee could not hold Richmond much beyond the first weeks of May. With the coming of good weather, General Grant's forces would move to dislodge Lee's shrinking army from its ever lengthening line of trenches. How long the war could be carried on after Lee evacuated Richmond was open to anybody's guess. As they sat in the elegantly appointed state dining room on the first floor of the Confederate White House awaiting President Davis, the thoughts of the two cabinet officers focused on how to guide the President to a course which would end the agony of the Southern people. Although he had done his level best for the Confederacy, Davis remained obstinate. He did not like to hear talk of defeatism and surrender. The President passionately believed in the righteousness of the Confederate cause and would not accept the fact that the war was irretrievably lost. He talked of breaking the army into small guerrilla units to continue the struggle after Richmond fell. In his agitated mental state, neither Breckinridge nor Benjamin could convince him to change his mind. The only good news they received was the notification of the adjournment of the contentious Confederate Congress on March 18. With its members out of the city, they would be free of the insults and verbal barbs flung by the administration's many congressional critics.

After purchasing a supply of edibles, Chambon and Bellnapp readied themselves for an early morning departure. They would travel over 160 miles through hazardous country in which Union and Confederate deserters lurked. The two mounted men would offer a tempting target. While Confederate guerrillas continued to control much of northern Virginia, it had become a backwater of the war. There was little action except clashes between Mosby's men and Union patrols. Contact with both would have to be avoided if the boxes were to get to where Secretary Benjamin wanted them to be. Carbines and pistols were checked and loaded. Each rider carried one of the precious boxes along with saddlebags of rations, extra ammunition, a canteen, a bed roll and a section of rubberized shelter cloth.

Lexington's residents paid no attention to the two soldiers when they departed heading north on a damp, chilly March morning, carbines at the ready. Their headgear was of Confederate origin, their warm overcoats had been Union issue. Sergeant Bellnapp carried with him a copy of one of those new photographs made by the set plate technique. Its advantage was a negative image that was reproducible in any number of copies. While in Richmond, he and Chambon had stopped by a photographer's studio located next to the Southern Literary Messenger Building on Franklin Street. Noticing the sergeant's interest in the portrait photographs on display, the lieutenant colonel suggested they have one made of themselves. The finished photograph showed a lieutenant colonel and a sergeant standing in the stiff, unsmiling pose required by the cameras of the period. Chambon purchased five copies and gave two of them to Sergeant Bellnapp. They were among his most treasured possessions. He carried a framed copy in his coat, the other safely packed in his saddlebag with a spare shirt and pair of pants.

They traveled the same roads taken in May 1864 by the 264 man Virginia Military Institute contingent as it rushed north to help General Breckinridge defeat an invading Union force at the battle of New Market. No one cheered their passage because the Shenandoah Valley had been knocked out of the war. General Sheridan had defeated General Early at Winchester the previous September and pushed as far south as Staunton. Halting his advance, he deployed his cavalry corps across the valley. The twenty-mile wide line of troopers began moving slowly north, driving livestock ahead of them and burning everything else. There was anger in the air, a rage born of bushwhacking and throat-slitting. As they moved, Sheridan's troopers took their revenge on the cowardly nightriders who shot soldiers in the back and than faded back into the civilian population. In such an environment, many a private home went up in smoke even when dwellings were supposed to be spared. The red in the valley that autumn was from burning barns and mills, not the fall foliage. For 92 miles between Staunton and Winchester, Sheridan's troops left nothing but smoking ruins.

Having smashed General Early's army for the final time at Cedar Creek in October, General Sheridan decided the time was ripe to cripple Mosby's home base. In late November, 3,000 Union cavalrymen poured into the area between the Shenandoah Valley and the Bull Run Mountains with orders to destroy all forage and subsistence. Barns, corncribs and harvested crops were burned. All horses, cattle and sheep were removed. It was a terrible retribution on a land that had for three years supported and lodged the guerrilla bands. In one day, one Union unit burned 150 barns, 100 haystacks and six flour mills. The region was left barren as Mosby's hornets were burned out once and for all.

The further north Chambon and Bellnapp traveled, the more desolate the landscape became. Only payment in gold would entice food and fodder from

101

the sullen farmers remaining on their ruined property. They slept in shifts, making sure the boxes and horses were never out of sight. Even so, trouble was never far away. On the night as they were camped in a abandoned farmhouse near Staunton, Sergeant Bellnapp shot and killed a Union deserter he caught trying to steal the horses.

Jacob and Sarah Bushong's farm was about a mile west of the Valley Turnpike, slightly northwest of the town of New Market. The newer of the two farmhouses on the property had been built in 1825 and enlarged by an addition built onto its rear in 1850. Also located on the farmstead was an older house built in 1818. On May 15, 1864, a battle engulfed the farm forcing the Bushong family to take refuge in the stone cellar of their home. A Confederate force under Major General John C. Breckinridge, which included the cadets from the Virginia Military Institute, attacked Union forces commanded by Major General Franz Siegel. The Confederates won the battle and the defeated Union troops retreated to Winchester.

Chambon and Bellnapp sheltered in the older dwelling on the Bushong farm as they passed through New Market. It was a clear, chilly, moonlit night. After cooking supper in the decrepit fireplace, they spread their rubberized ground cloths and blankets on the floor. Peering out of the windowless old house, they saw the moonlight reflecting from the white skulls and bones of some of the dead who had been buried on the farm after the battle. The incessant winter rains and snows had washed the soil from the graves. After ten months in the ground, the remains of the Union and Confederate dead looked exactly alike in the moonlight. A deep feeling of melancholy came over the pair of travelers as they prepared to bed down for the night.

The gloomy feeling remained with them as they rode north through a war ravaged countryside. As Chambon and Bellnapp halted to set up camp just before dusk a few miles north of Toms Brook, two unfriendly men claiming to be Confederate irregulars appeared without warning and attempted to rob them of their horses and supplies. The robbery attempt quickly turned into a close quarter gunfight that left both guerrillas dead. It began as Lieutenant Colonel Chambon argued violently with the two irregulars as he leaned heavily on his walking stick while twisting its head. When it became clear the visitors were bent on thievery and murder, the walking stick was suddenly raised, its tip pointed at one assailant as if to emphasize the point the officer was angrily making. There was a sharp twang as the taut spring released. The man screamed as he fell backwards, the end of an iron dart protruding from his chest, his revolver discharging wildly into the air. The startled second assailant fired at Chambon twice, missing both times as the lieutenant colonel dived to the ground. Before he could aim at the rolling figure and fire again, Sergeant Bellnapp's Colt revolver barked twice as he withdrew it from under his overcoat in a smooth motion. The first shot blew the top of the guerrilla's head off, the second tore through his chest. He was dead before he hit the ground.

Regaining his feet, Chambon dispatched the first guerrilla, who was writhing on the ground, with a single well-aimed pistol shot. "Damned if that wasn't close," he said as he put his finger through the bullet hole in his overcoat, "I felt that one go by." Bellnapp, who knew what was going to happen when he saw the walking stick begin to rise, nervously answered, "I never saw a crippled man move so fast in all my born days. You sure had him fooled good." They stripped the bodies of everything useful before dragging them to a nearby hollow and covering the corpses with soil and brush. They found the horses belonging to the deceased guerrillas tethered a short distance away and brought them into camp.

Later during the traumatic night, Chambon was standing guard when he heard a pitiful, appalling sound that sounded like a cross between a painful groan and mooing. His hair stood on end as he began to think one of the guerrillas they had buried must still be alive. But how could that be? Chambon had seen plenty of men killed by gunshot. Those two were dead for sure. By now, Bellnapp was also up and they could hear something crashing around in a thicket, the sad, groaning noise coming closer. They were ready to fire as soon as the creature, which must be fairly large judging from the sound it was making, became visible. With a deep sense of relief, they saw a milk cow with a severely distended utter amble toward them out of the darkness. The poor creature was bawling pitifully because it had not been milked for days. It must have wandered away from a nearby farm after its owner had been killed, perhaps by the two thugs now lying in their graves not far away.

"This is problem I can handle easily. I know all about cows, having worked on a plantation most of my life," Sergeant Bellnapp said as he squatted to milk the bovine which looked at him gratefully with its big brown eyes. Once relieved of the excess milk, the cow joined the horses contentedly cropping the emerging late winter grass. "We can't leave the poor cow behind. With no one to milk or feed it, it would surely die if we left it on its own. Anyway, it will be nice to have a supply of fresh milk traveling with us for awhile," Chambon said as they saddled the horses in the morning. Sergeant Bellnapp smiled to himself and made no response as he tied his saddle bags. He knew Chambon meant for them to try to find the cow a good home. The pair of soldiers mounted and headed for Thoroughfare Gap with two extra horses and a milk cow in tow.

Chapman's Mill was located at Thoroughfare Gap where the stream named Broad Run dropped 80 feet as its channel squeezed between the hills. The fast moving water provided ample power to operate the grinding machinery, ensuring the mill's commercial success. The site was picturesque, but the incessant combat and guerrilla activity in the area ruined John Chapman. The stress of operating a mill under wartime conditions drove Chapman insane, making him another of the many uncounted casualties of the war.

When they reached the mill in early evening, Lieutenant Colonel Chambon poignantly remembered his last visit in 1862 when the Subsistence Department's meat processing plant was located here. He saw the marks on the outside walls left by the impact of the bullets fired in August 1862 when Longstreet's corps had fought Union troopers at the mill while pushing through the gap on the way to join Jackson's force. As they prepared to cook supper in the sheltering ruin of the mill, Matt told Cyrus the story of how he had destroyed the meat supplies. Long used to scant rations, Cyrus had a hard time believing there was ever a time when the Confederacy had such a massive amount of meat in one place. His nose began to pick up the faint smell of the overcooked bacon he imagined still lingered in the walls.

As the Confederacy lurched to destruction, Richmond society began rereading the eerie, morbid works of Edgar Allan Poe. It was as if his writings expressed the sentiments prevailing in the doomed city. Orphaned in Richmond as a child, Poe grew up as a member of the Allan family. In later life, he returned to Richmond to edit the prestigious Southern Literary Messenger, eventually becoming the city's favorite literary son. Copies of Poe's stories and poems circulated among the medical staff of the military hospitals. They were also read at "starvation parties," the social gatherings at which no food was served because of its scarcity due to its non-availability.

The fire cast flickering shadows on the mill walls as the wind moaned through the ruined structure. Outside, the rushing water drowned out the sounds of the animals grazing. Now and then, only the tinkling of the cow's bell could be heard over the sound of the fast flowing water. Matt took a worn copy of the works of Edgar Allan Poe out of his saddlebags and began to read "The Raven" aloud.

"Once upon a midnight dreary, while I pondered, weak and weary,
Over many a quaint and curious volume of forgotten lore—
While I nodded, nearly napping, suddenly there came a tapping,

As of some one gently rapping, rapping at my chamber door.
"Tis some visitor," I muttered, "tapping at my chamber door—
Only this and nothing more."
    Ah, distinctly I remember it was in the bleak December;
And each separate dying ember wrought its ghost upon the floor.
Eagerly I wished the morrow;-- vainly I had sought to borrow
From my books surcease of sorrow—sorrow for the lost Lenore—
For the rare and radiant maiden whom the angles named Lenore—
Nameless here for evermore.
    And the silken, sad, uncertain rustling of each purple curtain
Thrilled me –filled me with fantastic terrors never felt before;
So that now, to still the beating of my heart, I stood repeating
"Tis some visitor entreating entrance at my chamber door--
Some late visitor entreating entrance at my chamber door;--
This is it and nothing more."

"The Raven" was popular among the soldiers manning Richmond's defense lines. Most could recite at least parts of it by heart. When Matt read the stanzas ending with the haunting "Nevermore," Cyrus, who was tapping his fingers on his carbine stock in time to the reading, boomed out, "Nevermore" in a deep, sad voice that echoed off of the interior of the mill's six- story high walls. As he read, Matt remembered how he had spent last New Year's Eve at the New Richmond Theatre at the corner of Seventh and Broad Streets in the company of a young lady. They attended the play "Black-Eyed Susan" and afterwards went to a late night reception at her home at which only water and a small amount of bread were served to the guests. The evening ended with a reading of several of Poe's stories, including, "The Raven."

The poem kindled somber memories of an incident that occurred at Chimborazo Hospital. As Cyrus remembered it, a young Mississippi soldier near death from wounds inflicted by artillery fire was brought into the ward. As there was nothing the doctors could do for him, Cyrus made the dying soldier comfortable as they waited for the end to come. The delirious soldier had been on the battlefield for at two days before the stretcher bearers found him. In his delirium he continually talked to a crow which had walked among the dead. "Mr. Crow," he said, "Don't you be pecking the eyes out of those dead men. Some of them were friends of mine. Don't be pulling on those guts, you leave them be, you hear! Go find yourself a nice field of corn and leave us alone. Go on, get away now!" Cyrus told Matt that crows were known to eat just about anything, bugs, frogs, seed, fruit, food scraps, dead animals and men. Crows and Ravens were related; they spent some discussing how a person could tell one from the other. "Maybe I'll write a poem about a crow on a battlefield someday," Cyrus mused. "You do that and you just might become as famous as Edgar Allan Poe," Matt replied as he got up to the check on the horses and the cow.

General Johnston's rag-tag army was doing its best to slow General Sherman's progress. Sergeant Erasmus Strawderman crouched behind a large tree watching the Yankee skirmish line advance relentlessly across the North Carolina field. Erasmus thought that on a good day, they might be strong enough to force old Sherman to cut his advance back by a mile or so. At the rate things were going, Sherman would shove them completely out of North Carolina and up into Virginia in another four weeks. Erasmus had seen a lot of North Carolina as the army backed up before Sherman's relentless northward drive. He wondered if Virginia would look much different.

The Confederacy had reached the end of its manpower resources. Lads as young as twelve and men in their seventies were being prodded into the firing lines. Being a jaded veteran, Sergeant Erasmus Strawderman didn't like being responsible for the welfare of the new recruits. Their wide range of ages and lack of experience made them easy targets for the boys in blue. As the Yankee line came into range, Erasmus pulled the hammer on his Springfield back to full cock in one smooth motion and squeezed the trigger as he had done countless times before. Through the cloud of black powder smoke, he saw the Union soldier in his sights fling his rifle into the air and topple backwards. In an almost instantaneous response, the other Yankee skirmishers returned fire. A bullet slammed into the tree to his front while another whined through the air on his left side. Looking to his right, he saw a nervous thirteen-year old soldier fire at a Yankee and miss. The boy jumped up and was running to the rear when two bullets simultaneously hit him in the back, pitching his lifeless body violently forward as it fell to the ground. The gray-clad men in line to the left of Erasmus also fired and began hotfooting to the rear amid a hail of return fire. Erasmus could not tell if they hit anyone as he darted between the trees, bullets clipping the branches as he ran. "Bet we slowed old Sherman up a whole five minutes worth this time," he yelled as he raced for safety. Someday he would like to meet the politician in Richmond who boasted, "One Rebel can whip ten Yankees any day." The idiot of a man obviously had never tangled with Sherman's troops. Erasmus looked forward to giving the fool a piece of his mind when he got to Virginia.

General William T. Sherman was riding with his headquarters staff, chatting amicably with Colonel Jefferson Beuhler of the engineers, when the sharp reports of rifled muskets echoed from near the front of the column. Since it didn't sound like much more than another feeble Rebel attempt to block his advance guard, the general continued his interrupted conversation. "That's interesting. You say your mother's maiden name was Sarah Strawderman and her side of your family hailed from Virginia before moving to Ohio and then on to Illinois?"

"Yes sir, that's correct. My mother says the first Strawderman lived not too far from George Washington's gristmill, on some creek whose name escapes me at the moment. Although she never liked to tell of it, he was known to produce a whiskey of fairly good quality," the colonel replied. Colonel Jefferson Beuhler had become one of Sherman's favorites during the history-making march across Georgia and up into the Carolinas. "Short Fuse" Beuhler and his engineers were responsible for setting the charges that demolished mills, factories, and warehouses. Working rapidly, Beuhler and his demolition men allowed the army to keep moving onward at a blistering pace. The nickname came from his habit of setting the shortest fuses imaginable on his powder charges and then running to safety. He had an uncanny knack for knowing the outer limits of the explosion's danger zone, reaching it mere seconds before the charges went off. He was often seen standing scant yards from where a rain of falling debris crashed to earth after being flung skyward by the blast. Beuhler and his engineers had become a familiar sight to the infantrymen as they ranged along the line of march, furiously blasting the Confederacy's economic infrastructure into oblivion. It was all part of Sherman's efficient system of waging total war. His staff scoured census reports for potential targets, the foraging bummers and advance guard ranging on the flanks and to the front, continually reported on facilities marked for destruction. The wooden structures were immediately torched, the more substantial edifices were turned over to "Short Fuse" and his tireless blasting crew. They were proud of the fact that no facility that fell into their hands ever produced anything for the Confederate war effort again. A substantial part of Sherman's supply train was dedicated to hauling Beuhler's blasting powder. Heavily guarded, it had priority over everything except ammunition and medical supplies.

Sherman smiled as he said, "I think I met some distant kin of yours right around the time of First Bull Run. An old fellow by the name of William Strawderman sold whiskey to our boys while we were camped at Centreville before the battle. I saved his worthless hide during the night retreat back to Washington. I will never forget that awful night, it rained on us most of the way back. Colonel Paxton was a new lieutenant back then. He was going to hang Strawderman for trying to steal a wagon and team our boys had left on the road. I talked him into leaving the old bootlegger alone. When we get to Virginia, you ought to stop by and see if Old Will made it through the war. His farm is on the Warrenton Turnpike, just before you go up the hill into Centreville. He had his still by Little Rocky Run, I think. Come to think of it, Old Will said his whiskey recipe had been handed down in the family from a Strawderman who worked at George Washington's distillery. It's quite likely he is the part of your family that stayed in Virginia."

Colonel Beuhler rubbed his chin as he replied, "You are probably right. We must be related along the line someplace. The war can't last much longer with us almost to Virginia. I'll plan to stop by and visit with William after this thing ends."

"If the Rebs had any sense, the war would be over by now," Sherman muttered. "Any government worth a tinker's damn would have known the war was lost after we took Atlanta. But these stubborn people keep on fighting, so we have to go on smashing things up. Sooner or later, they will realize they have been whipped. When they finally do, the war will end." With that Sherman gave his horse, Sam, a light prod with the single spur he wore on one shoe and began to move along the column of marching soldiers toward the sound of the gunfire. He sent an aide forward with a message for the advance guard to press the Confederates hard, bring on a battle if possible. The faster he could whip these people, the sooner his army could go home.

General Sherman wisely changed his strategy as the army crossed into North Carolina. Due to the high level of pro-Union sentiment in the state prior to the war, Sherman ordered his rampaging forces to limit their property destruction to war industries and other Confederate government property. Around noon on February 11, 1865, his motley, hard-marching army reached Fayetteville. As the army occupied the town, Sherman established his headquarters in the former federal arsenal which had been taken over by the Confederacy at the onset of the war. The arsenal property consisted of an extensive collection of light-colored brick buildings covering an entire city block. With its main entrance located on Adams Street, the well-landscaped arsenal grounds also served the town as a large municipal park.

In the late 1830s, the Ordnance Department of the U.S. Army selected Fayetteville as the site for the United States Arsenal in North Carolina because of the town's strategic location. It was halfway between the arsenals in Washington, DC and Augusta Georgia, between the coast and the mountains, and on a major north-south route. The 1850s saw the structural completion of the facility and the installation of rifle manufacturing machinery. In April 1861, North Carolina militiamen forced the surrender of the federal garrison and the state of North Carolina took control of the buildings. Renamed the Fayetteville Arsenal and Armory, the facility manufactured ammunition, repaired rifles and modernized muskets for the Confederacy. To house captured machinery, the Confederate government expanded the facility, adding a timber storage area, laboratory, rifle factory and several additions to the existing workshops.

The Fayetteville Arsenal and Armory produced two types of weapons for the Confederacy, the Fayetteville pistol-carbine and the Fayetteville rifle. Plagued by a lack of skilled workmen and constant shortages, the facility managed to produce only 10,000 new weapons between 1862 and 1865. The arsenal's greatest contribution to the war effort was the manufacture of munitions. The arsenal produced massive quantities of small arms ammunition, signal rockets and artillery shells.

General Sherman was sitting at a commandeered desk in the main building reading dispatches recently delivered by an army tug that had come up the Cape Fear River from Wilmington when Colonel Jefferson Beuhler knocked on the door, "You wanted to see me general?" "Why yes I do, colonel. As you can see this arsenal is in fine working order. I cannot afford to leave troops behind to garrison it, so it will have to be destroyed before we move on. I don't want this place to ever again produce so much as a single bullet for the Rebels. I want you to blow it up and knock down any remaining walls. Make it into a big pile of useless rubbish. How long do you think it will take to do the job?"

"We've got 18 separate buildings, the outer walls with workshops along them and the four big towers at each corner. From the size of it, I would say we could flatten everything in less than two days without any problem."

"Get started then. You have three days to finish because we need to rest the men a bit. While you are at it, blast the Fayetteville Times building in town too. That damn Rebel newspaper has published its last issue. It never says anything good about our army, so we will treat it like any other war industry. Put it out of business for the rest of the war. Our next stop will be Goldsboro where we will link up with the reinforcements moving in from the coast. We will also refit ourselves with the new clothes and equipment the quartermaster is bringing for us. We all could use a change of clothes, don't you think?"

"Yes sir, that is sure enough true. We look worse off than the Rebels. People also say you can smell this army coming long before you can see it," Colonel Beuhler said half-joking as he saluted the general and took his leave.

"Short Fuse" Beuhler and his demolition engineers went to work. They moved across the vast expanse of arsenal property burning everything that took to the torch. Then the magnificent brick buildings housing the workshops were blown up one at a time. The four massive tower structures and the outer walls were saved till last. When the blasting was completed, the few standing walls remaining were knocked down with battering rams. When Sherman's army departed Fayetteville, the arsenal complex was a large smoldering pile of ruins. Hardly a stone remained on top of another. The arsenal's proud days as a war production facility for the Confederate States of America were over.

Because of his views on the duration and the human cost of the war, there were many people who considered William T. Sherman to be slightly insane early in the war. Crazy or not, in one of the wisest military decisions ever made, General Ulysses S. Grant placed Sherman in command of the army assigned to capture Atlanta. The red-headed general from Ohio catapulted into national fame when his forces captured the city on September 2, 1864, saving Abraham Lincoln from political defeat in the autumn elections. With typical understatement, Sherman had wired President Lincoln: "Atlanta is ours and fairly won." The effect of the message in the North was electric. Gloom turned to euphoria overnight. One-hundred gun salutes were fired in Sherman's honor in a number of Northern cities.

It had been a hard-fought campaign; Sherman had lost 31,000 men fighting his way through north Georgia to Atlanta. Now, a war-numbed and grieving nation wanted the fighting brought to a close. What to do next was the question. The fighting in Virginia was at a stalemate. In Georgia, Sherman's army was deep in hostile territory with ever lengthening lines of supply. The Confederates, although severely battered, showed no signs of giving up. General Sherman had no intention of immobilizing his army by garrisoning Atlanta. He believed the war must be made even more terrible so it would demoralize the civilian population supporting the Rebel armies with food and military supplies. His name would soon come to symbolize the awful new doctrine of total warfare in which the destruction of the civilian economy is as an important objective as defeating the opposing military force.

The military doctrine of the era stipulated that an army could not survive in hostile country without lines of communication and supply. To attempt to do otherwise would bring disaster from starvation and attacks by enemy forces. When General John B. Hood's Confederate army began moving into Tennessee to draw the Union forces out of Georgia, Sherman acted. He sent part of his army to halt Hood, and ignored conventional wisdom by plunging deeper into Georgia.

It was an audacious plan, and the country waited anxiously for the results.

Something new had to be in the making or else Sherman's army was doomed.

Sherman's forces were not conventional; they had their own proud, distinctive style. Thousands in the ranks were under the age of 18, the majority of the lieutenants and captains in their early twenties, and most of the colonels under the age of thirty. The six commanders of armies, corps and divisions averaged 31 years of age. These troops were also used to winning. They had driven the Confederates out of Kentucky, conquered most of Tennessee, chopped the Confederacy in two by seizing the Mississippi River and fought their way into the vital rail and industrial city of Atlanta. They were cool and efficient in battle; discipline, however, was free and easy. Sherman had long ago canceled all drills and reviews, and reduced formality to a minimum. The troops fondly called him "Uncle Billy." He referred to them as "my little devils."

They traveled light. Most men carried a blanket wrapped in a rubber poncho, a haversack, 40 to 60 rounds of ammunition, and the trusty rifle. Sherman's entire headquarters fit into a single wagon. Although the army was battle-hardened, lean and stripped to the bone, it had its softer side. The marching columns were swarming with pets. A squirrel rode on its master's shoulder. Also there was an owl and numerous dogs riding on saddles, in wagons, and on caissons. "Old Abe," the pet eagle of a Wisconsin regiment, rode out of the flaming ruins of Atlanta proudly perched on a cannon.

With General Hood moving north, there were few Confederate troops to oppose Sherman in Georgia. With the rail, military manufacturing facilities and a good part of the civilian housing of Atlanta in ruins, Sherman cut his communications with the North and his army of 62,000 marched east on November 16, 1864. They moved in two wings on a 60 mile front to confuse the Confederates. The objective was Savannah on the Atlantic coast over 250 miles away. Along the route, everything of economic significance that supported the Confederate war effort was to be destroyed. Sherman's marching order to his troops began with: "The army will forage liberally on the country during the march." The troops tore up railroad tracks, heated them, and twisted them into useless spirals. Some artistic wrecking crews got so good they twisted the rails into the letters "US." Buildings went up in flames. The charred chimneys that marked the army's passing became known as "Sherman's sentinels."

It was total war administered to a defiant population in big doses and it brought results. Confederate civilian and military morale plunged to rock bottom. Army desertions began to skyrocket as troops departed to care for starving families. The loss of transportation and manufacturing capabilities turned an already bad supply situation into an intolerable one. Starvation and shortages began to ravage the Confederacy. On December 22, 1864 Sherman's army reached Savannah and linked up with Union naval units.

That Christmas the North was jubilant. The army had not been destroyed as so arrogantly predicted by Confederate authorities and many other observers. Instead, it had sliced the Confederacy in two for a second time and inflicted fatal damage to the South's war machine. To make matters worse for the Confederacy, General Hood's army was virtually destroyed in a battle at Nashville on December 15-16 by General George Thomas and the part of Sherman's forces sent to stop him. "Uncle Billy" had been vindicated on all counts.

That should have been the end of it with the onset of winter and the end of the campaigning season. But General Sherman and his hellions were on a roll. After refitting in Savannah, the army swept into South Carolina, much to the disbelief of Confederates who believed no force could travel over the soggy roads in winter. Sherman's soldiers took revenge on the first state to leave the Union by destroying everything as they marched. Columbia, the state capital, burned on February 17, 1865. Charleston, with its communications cut by Sherman's forces, surrendered to the Union navy which had been attempting to capture it for nearly four years.

During the campaign, Sherman's army scorched and plundered a vast region of enemy territory and left a wrecked plantation society in its wake as it tramped north to link up with General Grant's army hammering at the gates of Richmond. The unknown colonel who had saved the life of a Centreville moonshine maker on a rainy Sunday night, had gone on to become one of the most famous generals in America. He was striking the deathblow to the Confederacy and writing a new chapter on military doctrine in the process.

April 1865

Skirting the desolate villages of Hay Market and Gainesville, Lieutenant Colonel Chambon and Sergeant Bellnapp reached the Warrenton Turnpike. They passed through the Manassas battlefields, passing abandoned houses, shell-blasted trees, rotting wagons and the sunken graves of the dead. The temporary repairs made by the army to the bridge over Bull Run had collapsed into the waterway, forcing them to turn north and cross upstream at a farm ford where the stream banks were less steep. Retracing their route down the opposite bank, they soon were back on the turnpike. It was a turnpike in name only. The road had seen no maintenance in over two years and was virtually impassable to wagon traffic. The poor condition of the road made little difference to the local farmers because the road was the contested domain of Union cavalry patrols and Confederate guerrillas.

After crossing Cub Run, they left the Turnpike heading northward and soon reached the long-abandoned Confederate fortification line. The bleak trench lines and gun emplacements stood as haunting reminders of the time the mighty fortification line at Centreville riveted national attention as it defied the federal army for five months. The defense line was of no current interest to either army because its military usefulness ended when the fighting shifted to other fronts. As they crouched inside one of the forts whose 20 foot high walls were eroding in the winter rains and snows, the pair watched a column of 150 Union horsemen ride down the turnpike in the direction from which they had come. Their horses and equipment were in excellent shape, nothing like the poorly equipped Confederates they had seen in Richmond. Based at Fairfax Courthouse, the far-ranging Union cavalry's mission was to confront the guerrilla problem created by the rangers commanded by John S. Mosby. With the Shenandoah Valley and much of northern Virginia in ruins and Grant's army supplied by routes that bypassed this guerrilla infested region, the anti-guerrilla campaign had degenerated into a unpleasant military side-show that did nothing to affect the war's outcome as it continued to kill men.

Chambon, Bellnapp, the two spare horses and a cow followed the fortification line eastward as they searched for a suitable artillery magazine in which to conceal the two boxes Secretary Benjamin had entrusted to their care. The first seven they inspected were unsuitable because they had collapsed from neglect, become water filled or would be too difficult to camouflage. The odd little caravan moved along the high ground north of the virtually deserted village of Centreville and passed the massive forts which controlled the valleys of Big Rocky Run and Little Rocky Run. South of where the Braddock Road bisected the old defense line, Matt found what they had been searching for. Overlooking the valley of Little Rocky Run was a series of fortifications built to house 12 cannon. It was a gunner's dream location. The descending slope allowed a perfect field of fire in a 180 degree arc around the position. Due to the curvature of the slope, the artillery position was constructed 15 yards below the hill crest, placed there because it eliminated all the spaces attacking troops could shelter safely from the cannon fire.

It was one of the positions that Matt had constructed. On the reverse slope of the hill about ten yards down from the crest were three magazines which had been carved into the hillside. The deep layer of covering earth designed to protect the magazines from enemy artillery fire had performed its task well. They remained dry and virtually intact. Chambon and Bellnapp selected the smallest of the three as the best suited to their purpose and spent the remainder of the day carrying rocks to pack into the space around the two boxes. If the supporting timbers should collapse, the rock filled void would protect the boxes from being crushed and would prevent the accumulation of standing water. Chambon and Bellnapp were concealing the opening with sod when they were interrupted by three drunk Confederate guerrillas.

"What are you boys so intent on hiding there? " one queried. "Oh excuse me Colonel Sir," he continued in a mocking tone, "I didn't notice an officer was in charge of the digging detail you got going here. This sure is a surprise because we ain't seen no regular troops around here since Bobby Lee come through these parts for the last time back in October of '63."

Chambon noticed the jug of Strawderman's Finest dangling loosely from the glassy- eyed man's fingers as he responded, "I see Old Will has continued in the business of making whiskey. I remember sampling a bit of Strawderman's Finest when I was here in '61 and '62."

"Them was good days around here back then. Not sorry times like it is now. Old Will is still making his bootleg whiskey, sells most of it in Washington city these days. Mighty strange thing, if you ask me. He sells to the Yankees and we get told to leave him be. Beats all, if you ask me. He is about the only farmer hereabouts who can produce anything for sale. Most everyone else has been burned out or starved out and has moved on. Them that hasn't left is hanging on by planting a few crops, and raising a hog or two. Say Colonel, where did you come by the cow?"

Lieutenant Colonel Chambon knew he had a serious problem on his hands. His instructions from Secretary Benjamin were explicitly clear.

Except for the Secretary of State and the Secretary of War, no one was to be given the location of boxes. If the secret was to remain safe, these three drunken guerrillas would have to die. How could they be trusted to keep the location of the hiding place to themselves? " Picked it up when we came through the valley," he dryly replied to the guerrilla's question.

"Now don't that beat it! You all come out of the burned valley with a cow and two spare horses to bury something in an old powder storage bunker. Me and my partners got a right to know what you is doing in our neck of the woods! You see, we belong to the Rangers and we ain't in no mood to take crap from you regular army boys. You going to tell us what you buried there," the man said pointing to partially covered entrance.

As he fumbled with his walking stick, Chambon also managed to unsnap the cover of the revolver holstered on his hip. The move had been unnoticed. "Since you three are in the service of the Confederate States irregular forces, I will tell you if you promise to keep it a secret."

After the three men nodded an affirmative response, Chambon continued, "There are two boxes in there," he said pointing to the entrance with his walking stick, "containing Confederate Government state secrets. We have hidden them here as instructed by the Secretary of War. I don't know anything else about the contents, they were sealed when we took them in our possession. Now that we have the boxes buried, we have to return to Richmond and report this location to the Secretaries of State and War."

The guerrilla narrowed his eyes, expressing disbelief at Chambon's answer. "You telling me you come all the way up here from Richmond to hide two boxes in an old fort which ain't been used for years? Why would they send you to do that? Must be a thousand places around Richmond better suited for hiding stuff! You don't make any sense at all to me. Do you really think we're going believe a lame tale like that? I think you are hiding something of value you don't want to share with us." The man was growing visibly angrier by the minute.

Chambon calmly replied, "I told you all I know about the boxes. If you want to know why they were placed here, tell you commander to get the answer for you from the Secretary of War! I don't know the reason why he wants these boxes here! My job is to see it gets done!"

Another of the guerrillas who had been eyeing Sergeant Bellnapp broke into the conversation, changing the subject. "How come your slave is wearing an army uniform with sergeant's stripes on it?" he said pointing to Bellnapp's sleeves.

"It is because he is a sergeant in the Virginia State Colored Troops," Chambon coolly replied. "He enlisted in one of the first companies of colored troops raised by Virginia. There will be more to come. They were training in Richmond when we left."

"That is the damnedest thing I ever heard," spat back the guerrilla. "What half-witted politician came up with the idea? The idiot Jeff Davis or some buffoon in our useless Congress?"

"As I understand it," Chambon responded, "General Lee argued for the idea himself. The Negro troop bill he wanted implemented passed in the House, but failed in the Senate before Congress adjourned. Virginia has taken it upon herself to meet General Lee's needs by raising a body of Negro state troops."

Taken aback by the answer, the guerrilla mused aloud, "Well, if Bobby Lee wants it done than it must be a good idea. He's got more brains in his little finger than all the rest of them Richmond politicians put together. No sir, I don't like it worth a damn! I don't understand it! But if Bobby Lee says do it, it has got to be done! General Lee would never do anything to hurt his boys in the army. I ain't go no faith in Davis and his crowd of useless hangers-on, but I'd do anything for Bobby Lee, even soldier with slaves if need be."

The first guerrilla jumped back into the conversation. "What Marse Robert got to do to keep the Yankees out of Richmond ain't got nothing to do with the problem we got here! Colonel," he said looking at Chambon, "are you going to tell us the truth about what you stashed here? Don't tell us no more stories about secret missions because we ain't dumb enough to believe them. We ain't stupid enough to settle for a mess of chicken guts when we can have the whole hen. I think you are hiding something on your own, and it has nothing to do with government business! How do we know you are not a couple of deserters using a forged travel pass to hide stolen goods? Maybe we will wait till after you leave and then dig up the stuff ourselves. If there is nothing but papers in there, we will bury them again," he added with a laugh. "There is not a awful lot of much else for us to do right now anyhow, with the war moved down by Richmond and all," he added.

Lieutenant Colonel Chambon was saddened by the knowledge that nothing he said was going to dissuade the three drunken guerrillas of their notion of riches. These three part-time fighters could never be trusted to hold their tongues. Leaving them walking around Centreville alive was an invitation to failure. With no Confederate authorities available to turn the men over to, he was going to have to do the unthinkable in order to preserve the secrecy demanded by Secretary Benjamin. Even so, the odds of three to two were not good even with the element of surprise on his side. When Sergeant Bellnapp observed him twisting the handle of the walking stick, he loosened the cover of his holster. Chambon knew he was alert and ready.

"Colonel why don't you ride on out of here and leave us to finish covering the entrance for you? Never can tell when a Yankee patrol will come by. The longer you stay in these parts, the better the chances they will catch you. We could also use them two spare horses, if you would be so inclined to leave them with us," the bad-tempered guerrilla said as his hand edged slowly toward his holster. Chambon knew it was now or never. Once the guerrilla had his revolver out, the advantage would be all his. The tip of the walking stick rose quickly. The spring twanged as the dart drove deep into the man's chest, piercing his heart. His fingers clawed at the butt of his pistol as he toppled backwards. The revolver flopped from his lifeless fingers as he reached the ground.

The other two guerrillas, their reflexes somewhat slowed by the effects of alcohol and the surprise of seeing the walking stick in action, drew their weapons and began firing. Unfortunately for them, Bellnapp had the edge, being a split second faster. His first shot slammed into the second guerrilla, knocking him sideways and ruining his aim. His bullet missed Chambon by a good 12 inches. Bellnapp's second shot caught the third guerrilla in the groin, spinning him enough so that the shot he fired at the sergeant missed, slamming into the hillside behind him.

Chambon dropped the walking stick and drew his Colt. As the second befuddled guerrilla attempted to recover his balance and fire at Bellnapp, Matt dropped him with two shots to the upper body. As the third guerrilla, a bear of a man doubled over in pain, raised his revolver to fire a second a time at Bellnapp, the sergeant shot him in the chest. As he staggered under the impact, the guerrilla's revolver discharged, sending a bullet zinging between Bellnapp and Chambon. Bellnapp shot him again in the chest, while Chambon shot him through the side. The revolver finally dropped from his hand as the large man fell. "I didn't think we were going to have enough bullets for that one. He died hard," Chambon said as he moved through the cloud of powder smoke to check the deceased. All three of the guerrillas were goners.

Chambon didn't want to bury the bodies were they had fallen because fresh graves might attract attention. So they laid the bodies in a row while they finished concealing the magazine's entrance and Matt prepared two copies of a map. By using compass sightings based on easily recognized topographic features, anyone who could read the map location description and use a compass, could find the boxes with no difficulty. After the work was completed, Chambon and Bellnapp loaded the three bodies onto the horses and rode a couple of miles west. They buried the dead guerrillas in an area where many of the soldiers who died during the winter of 1861-62 had been laid to rest. No one would notice the addition of three new burial mounds in the neglected plot overgrown with weeds. As they dug the graves, Bellnapp began a conversation, "I sure hope what is in those boxes was worth killing three men for."

"We had no other choice. There was no way of knowing if they would keep their months shut. I told them the truth, but they refused to believe it," replied Chambon as he lifted another spade full of dirt from the hole he was digging. "They were men we could not trust. It was unfortunate that they came along when they did. Look at it this way Cyrus! Do you want to go back to Richmond and tell Secretary Benjamin we may have let his secrets fall into Yankee hands because we felt sorry for three drunk guerrillas? We were ordered to ensure secrecy at all hazards! The Secretary would be right to put us in front of the provost guard's firing squad for failing to follow his instructions, no question about that. It was a awful price those men paid, but this is wartime. Better them than us."

"I see your point," said Cyrus as a pulled one of the bodies into the grave he had completed digging. "Still it leaves me with a bad feeling. It seems like such a waste."

"The war has killed and ruined a lot of good men," answered Chambon as he slid another of the bodies into the shallow hole. "It started as a political struggle between the planters of the deep south and the industrialists up north. They let their differences get out of hand and the war came as a result. We play only a small part in it and with luck, we may live to see it end. These dead men might be the lucky ones because their troubles are over, ours are not."

"You got that right for sure," replied Cyrus. "The Union army stomped all over Branefield Plantation for almost a month when McClellan pushed up the peninsula trying to get his grubby hands on Richmond. I heard there is nothing left of my old home place. While the government pays poor old Mr. Churchman rent for me, he don't have much of anything else left. He is a refugee living with his kin on some little farm down by the Carolina line. Where will he get the money to rebuild Branefield when the fighting stops? All the work my family put into the place has gone for nothing. We don't have no place to go back to, unless we want to starve to death. Can't put in crops with no barns, mules or tools. My days on the big farm are gone for good. Doctor Hoffmann was going to help me get started in doctoring, but he got killed by a shell. I reckon about the only thing left for me to do is go around the countryside with you killing men who try to mess with some big government official's plans. I am about as bad off as an old mule too worn down to pull a plow."

"When this is over, I'll help you find a doctor to apprentice with. I probably would not be alive today if you hadn't cared for me at Chimborazo," responded Chambon. "I am sure we can find a surgeon or doctor to take you on. With all the wounded, there will be a need for surgeons for at least a year after the war ends." The mooing of the cow interrupted the discussion and let them know they had forgotten milking time. "Attend to the needs of our bovine friend while I put a mess of dry weeds on the graves. We don't want anyone passing by to notice they are fresh," Chambon said as he gathered an armful of dried plant stalks. When he was done camouflaging the graves, a person passing the overgrown field would not have noticed any of the graves were new.

"I noticed smoke coming from chimney at the Strawderman place when we were up on the ridge. Let's stop by and see if Old Will has any news. We could also leave our faithful cow with him. He probably could use it, judging from the sorry look of his farm," Matt said. "We might also snatch a night's sleep in his barn before starting back to Richmond."

The burst of pistol fire echoing across the abandoned fields from the ridge line during the afternoon alerted Old Will to the fact that someone was in the vicinity. The shooting could have been drunk soldiers settling a card dispute, guerrillas attacking someone, or chicken stealers caught in the act. Old Will could count on one hand the number of farms in the region occupied by their owners. Many of the houses in the village were also empty. Old Will attributed the economic decline directly to Major John S. Mosby and his rangers. The rangers might be adored in Richmond for the damage they inflicted on the Yankee army, but the retaliation provoked by Mosby's raids had brought economic ruin to the inhabitants of the region. When General Sheridan took charge of Union forces in the Shenandoah Valley, he didn't brother to hunt the rangers. He destroyed everything of military or economic value and left Mosby in control of a wasteland.

The war had not spared General Lee's property either. In 1864, with the cemeteries near Washington overflowing, Union authorities seized part of the Lee family property at Arlington, Virginia for use as a cemetery. Dead Yankees were planted in the general's garden. With close to 16,000 of them buried on Lee's property, Old Will seriously doubted the general would ever be able to move back into his house, surrounded as it was by dead Yankee soldiers. Old Will drove his team by the Lee place on his way to swap goods with Mr. Stackhouse. It was as an eerie sight. The big mansion known as Arlington House sat on a hill completely encircled by a sea of graves.

Business was way down in the Centreville taverns because few farmers were working the fields and sending products to market on the turnpike. Will

Strawderman's best customer was Clinton Stackhouse in Washington city. Mr. Stackhouse purchased nearly all the whiskey Old Will produced and provided him the necessaries that were no longer available locally. Old Will's wife, Ruth Anne, tended a garden, reestablished the chicken flock and kept a watchful eye on their five fine hogs. Old Will was thinking about trying to put in crops this season because it looked like the armies were finally gone for good. On the other hand, if the rangers and cavalry continued to clash, planting might prove to be a waste of time.

Near dusk, Old Will was visibly concerned as he watched two riders descend from the ridge and angle across the fallow fields toward his farm. Looking through the spyglass a Yankee captain had given him back in '63, Old Will could see the riders appeared to be dressed in the uniforms of the Confederate army. That was odd because there had been almost no regular troops in the area for nearly two years. Even more strange was the fact that one of the riders was a white man, the other a Negro. The duo seemed well-off, having two spare horses and a cow with them. They were obviously intending to pay a call at his house and Old Will thought it best to be ready in case the uninvited guests brought trouble with them.

Old Will had turned the farmhouse into a fortress with reinforced doors, solid window shutters and rifle slits in the walls. Inside, was a small arsenal of weapons provided over time by Union and Confederate patrons in payment for whiskey. Old Will had three Springfield rifled muskets, five revolvers and his favorite, a double- barreled, sawed-off shotgun. With Ruth Anne doing the loading, Old Will could hold the house against almost anything for a time. He called to Ruth Anne, telling her to get ready because company was coming their way.

Old Will was seated on the porch with the shotgun under a blanket as the pair rode up. Behind the door, opened a slight crack, stood Ruth Anne with two revolvers. "How do you do Mr. Strawderman," Matt said in greeting, " I'm Matt Chambon. Do you remember me? We met when I was here with the army back in '61and '62."

"There has been a lot of soldiers through here over the years, can't say that I remember you," Will responded as he looked hard into the lieutenant colonel's face. Ruth Anne, who had a better memory for people's faces stepped from behind the partially open door saying, "I remember him Will. He was the officer who got himself blown up about the time Johnston's army pulled out."

A hint of recognition flickered across Old Will's haggard face as he said, "That was a long time ago, back in March of '62. We heard you died on the train on the way to Richmond or wherever. Guess you didn't, since you are standing in front of my porch." Looking at the insignia of rank, he added, "Don't remember you being a lieutenant colonel. You must have got a promotion since then. By the way, what brings you back to this miserable part of the country this time of the year?"

Matt answered evasively, "Oh, we were passing through on business for the Ordnance Department when we found this cow wandering on the road with no owner anywhere in sight. We thought you might like to have her, she does give a good bucket of milk." The offer of a free cow made Old Will's day because the last of his animals had been taken by hungry soldiers a couple of months ago. Matt continued with, "Have you heard any news? We will be heading back to Richmond in the morning. Are the roads open?"

Old Will laughed, "No need for you to go there, General Lee evacuated the city. His army is on the run, heading west, I think. A telegram from General Grant came to Washington city with the news. A gentleman I do business with heard all about it almost as soon as the message arrived. One of his wagons came to my farm to pick up a load of whiskey yesterday. The teamster and guards told me about it while we was loading. They also said Richmond is in a bad way. Lee's army set fire to a big part of the city before he pulled out. The Yankees are trying to put out the fires."

Matt shot a worried glance at Cyrus. "Mr. Strawderman, did you hear where the government has moved to? What happened to President Davis and the cabinet, the government offices?"

"I heard Davis and the whole kit and caboodle of his worthless government left Richmond on trains bound for Danville. Its to become the temporary capital of the sorry, no account Confederacy." To emphasize his dislike of Davis and his government, Old Will spit a stream of tobacco juice into the mud.

"Well I guess we better make tracks for Danville instead of Richmond in the morning," Matt said while Cyrus nodded his head in agreement. " Do you mind if we stay in your barn overnight, Mr. Strawderman?"

"Be my guest," Will responded. "I'd invite you to stay in the house except the Yankees will burn the place if they find you here. If you stay in the barn, I can always say you got in there without my knowing about it. Ruth Anne will fix you supper and pack a few edibles for you to take with you. We have to get your horses into the barn and out of sight before a Yankee patrol comes by and sees you standing here." As he led the way to the barn, Old Will offered his profuse thanks for the gift of the cow. He looked forward with great anticipation to having a steady supply of milk and butter again.

A chill April rain beat steadily down on the barn roof as Matt and Cyrus prepared to bed down with their bellies full of good home cooked food. The horses and cow were contentedly munching grain in the stalls. At one end of the barn was a large stack of grain sacks that looked suspiciously like they came from an Union army supply depot. In the dim lantern light, they could see why the barn was so snug. The walls had been repaired with boards taken from ammunition boxes bearing the marks of nearly every arsenal in the North and South. Other boards from limbers, caissons, ambulances and supply wagons, with their CSA, USA and unit designations still readable, served to brace the roof and sections of the walls. "This place looks like it was built from the leftovers of at least two quartermaster depots," Matt noted as he prepared to turn out the lantern and take the first guard shift. Cyrus didn't hear him, he was already sound asleep, his blankets spread on a bed of clean hay.

Shortly before dawn, Cyrus caught a glimpse of two shadowy figures moving stealthily through the darkness toward the barn door. A rooster cackled defiantly as they passed the chicken coop. Cyrus nudged Chambon awake with a kick of his boot and both men, with carbines cocked, watched the intruders creep steadily forward. "They must be looking for horses," whispered Cyrus, "They passed right by chickens without stopping." Because Chambon and Bellnapp were staying inside, the barn door had not been locked. The intruders slowly and quietly pushed the door open wide enough to squeeze in. From their uniforms, Cyrus and Matt determined they were Yankees. One carried a pistol, the other a carbine, as they advanced slowly toward the horse stalls.

"Take the one on the left," Matt whispered, "Are you ready?" When Cyrus nodded, Matt squeezed the trigger. The intruders never had a chance as two carbines blazed almost in the same instant. The Yankee shot by Cyrus died in his tracks. The one hit by Matt rolled on the ground and made an ineffectual attempt to return fire. He died, unable to get off a shot, when Matt pumped a second bullet into him. The sound of the gunfire brought Old Will running from the farmhouse. "Damn," he said, "If the Yankees find these dead troopers, they will burn me out for sure. They will say Mosby's men bushwhacked them. These days, that's the price we pay for such goings on."

"Will, help us tie the bodies onto our spare horses and we'll get rid of them for you," Chambon responded. Then go find their horses, they must be tied close by and turn them loose. The Yankees will never know these men were ever near your farm." After following the men's tracks in mud, Old Will found the horses tied to a stump about a quarter of a mile away. After untying them, a swat of his hat sent the animals down the pike toward Fairfax Courthouse.

After saying goodbye, Chambon and Bellnapp rode across the fallow fields with two corpses tied across the saddles of the spare horses. They rode near the camouflaged site of the boxes whose secrets had forced them to take the lives of two more men. In the now familiar deserted burying field, they quickly added two new graves next to the three they had previously filled.

They would not travel through the Shenandoah Valley on the return trip. The route they selected would carry them south through Warrenton, Culpeper Courthouse and Gordonsville. Hopefully, they could intercept Lee's army at some point along its line of march as it moved west. Once behind the army's lines, they could continue on to Danville and deliver the maps to the Secretaries of War and State.

Clinton Stackhouse was a worried man. Although he was wallowing in the obscene profits his brothel on Washington's 14th Street generated, the fall of Richmond was a clear signal to him that the end of the Confederacy was fast approaching. From his strategic position as brothel owner, Clinton ably served the South as one of its better intelligence agents. Sooner or later however, the Union authorities would uncover evidence linking him to Secretary Benjamin's espionage ring. John Wilkes Booth, the noted Shakespearean actor, was also part of the Secretary's loose system of agents. The 27-year old Booth was too zealous and flamboyant for Stackhouse's liking. Booth also drank far too much, his head was seldom clear enough to be really useful. Unlike the rest of his family, Booth was an ardent Southern sympathizer obsessed with the rightness of the Confederate cause. However, like so many others who loved to talk a good fight, he did not love the South enough to give up his lucrative acting career. Despite all of his pro-Confederate diatribes, Booth never showed the slightest inclination of joining the Rebel army. Stackhouse was worried that the temperamental Booth, who loved hogging the limelight, might do something exceedingly stupid one of these days. He had already tried and failed to kidnap President Lincoln. Heaven only knew what the drunken actor lost in his unrealistic dreams of glory might do next.

Stackhouse had no intention of being in Washington to find out. He had no desire to remain in the city and run the risk of being hanged as a spy for a cause now hopelessly lost. He sold his brothel at market value, put his substantial amount of cash in U.S. Treasury bearer bonds and booked passage on a ship sailing from the port of Baltimore to San Francisco. He would make a new start in the west where his money would bring instant respectability and no one would know of his ties to the Confederate Secret Service. Close to 50,000 Yankee soldiers were lying in their graves due in part to the information Stackhouse had skillfully wheedled out of drunken soldiers, war department clerks and members of Congress and congressional staff. He had done his duty. Enough was enough. Clinton Stackhouse was looking forward to beginning a new life as a respectable businessman in California. He heard that there were good profits to be made in the Orient trade.

Lieutenant Colonel Chambon and Sergeant Bellnapp made camp for the night in an abandoned farmhouse outside of Warrenton. After supper, Cyrus was reading one of the old Washington newspapers that Ruth Anne had used to wrap the food she packed for them. "Who is Walt Whitman?" he asked. "Never heard of him," answered Matt. "What brought his name to mind?"

"He is a poet of some degree of fame in the North, I guess. One of his poems is printed in this newspaper. It's about a wound-dresser in an army hospital. It sure strikes home. It reminds me of the many days I spent working at Chimborazo Hospital " Cyrus responded. He began to read the Whitman poem aloud in a slow, measured voice:

"Bearing the bandages, water and sponge,
Straight and swift to my wounded I go,
Where they lie on the ground after the battle brought in,
Where their priceless blood reddens the grass the ground,
Or to the rows of the hospital tent, or under the roof'd hospital,
To the long rows of cots up and down each side I return,
To each and all one after another I draw near, not do I miss,
An attendant follows holding a tray, he carries a refuse pail,
Soon to be fill'd with clotted rags and blood emptied, and fill'd again."

"I dress the perforated shoulder, the foot with the bullet-wound,
Cleanse the one with a gnawing and putrid gangrene, o sickening, so offensive,
While the attendant stands aside me holding the tray and pail.
I am faithful, I do not give out,
The fractur'd thigh, the knee, the wound in the abdomen,
These and more I dress with impassive hand, yet deep in my breast a fire, a burning flame."

"He sure has the feel of being in an army hospital exactly right," said Matt, now giving Cyrus his full attention. "Being able to translate feelings like those into written words has to be a great talent. Walt Whitman will probably be a mighty famous poet someday if he keeps churning out words like those. I would like to hear all of it, read the whole thing again from the beginning."

Cyrus began reading Whitman's moving poem for the second time. "The Wound-Dresser by Walt Whitman," he solemnly intoned.

South of Culpeper, as they did a routine backtrack to check for pursuers, Chambon and Bellnapp spotted a group of six men intently following their tracks. Given the choice of running or fighting, they tilted the odds in their favor by setting up an ambush where the road dipped to cross a ravine. In a little over an hour the group rode into view following the horse tracks through the little valley that ran between two low, brush- covered hills. The lieutenant colonel and sergeant opened fire when the group began to ascend the slope on which they had hidden themselves. The first shots knocked the two lead riders from their saddles. Two more saddles emptied with the next volley. The two men at the rear of the column fired at the puffs of gunsmoke hanging in the air. Their well-aimed shots sent splinters and branches flying as they came uncomfortably close to where Chambon and Bellnapp were blazing away. The third volley from the ridge cut the remaining two riders down. Of the six pursuers, three were dead and one was bleeding profusely from the mouth, dying and unable to fire his weapon. Two were wounded, but able to return fire. It took several more minutes of trading lead before the last of the group was finally killed.

> **"Since an intelligence common to us all makes things known to us and formulates them in our minds, honorable actions are ascribed by us to virtue, and dishonorable actions to vice; and only a madman would conclude that these judgments are matters of opinion, and not fixed by nature."**
>
> **-Cicero, 106-43 B. C.**

Bushwhacking was a bloody art practiced without regard to fixed rules of conduct. It was a matter of the brutal basics of wartime survival, kill or be killed. Chambon cautiously circled behind the last living man on the road and, as the wounded man furiously worked to reload, unceremoniously shot him in the back of the head, his blood and brains splattering the ground as his body toppled. As the smoke slowly drifted away, the group of once fearsome highwaymen had the appearance of a batch of harmless rag dolls casually cast aside by a child after a hard afternoon of play. The transition from living to dead had been swift.

As he reloaded his carbine while staring at the lifeless bodies grotesquely sprawled along the muddy roadway, Cyrus muttered, "Whose side are these people on?" The odd mixture of blue and gray uniforms and civilian clothing made it difficult to tell if the dead men were Union or Confederate.

"They probably were a group of deserters who banded together to go into the robbing business," Matt answered as he tamped new charges into the empty cylinder of his revolver. "One thing is for sure. They aren't going to tell us anything about it now." They dragged the bodies, already attracting a swarm of flies, a few yards off the roadway and covered them with brush. Nothing found in the men's personal effects gave any indication of who they had been in life. Their horses, weapons and spare clothing were added to the growing hoard of booty which trailed behind the two riders.

A hint of spring was in the air as Matt and Cyrus traveled south, trading some of the items taken from the men they had killed to farmers for food and lodging. With the telegraph lines down, there was no reliable way to obtain war news. They knew that Richmond had been occupied by the Yankees and Lee was moving west, hotly pursued by General Grant's tenacious Union army. There were rumors of Lee moving through Amelia Court House and Jetersville. Part of Lee's army was cut off and forced to surrender at Saylors' Creek. Chambon and Bellnapp crossed the James River at New Canton and saw first-hand the damage General Sheridan's cavalry had inflicted on the James River and Kanawha Canal shortly after they made their leisurely trip to Lexington on it less than a month ago. Boats and warehouses were burned and lock gates demolished. It was going to take a great deal of costly repair work to get Central Virginia's vital commercial waterway back into operation.

Near the crossroads village of Maysville Courthouse, Chambon and Bellnapp ran headlong into outriders from Grant's army coming north on the same road. There were at least 40 Yankees in the party, moving slowly through countryside which as yet had been untouched by war. When they spotted the Yankees, Chambon and Bellnapp swung off the road and raced their horses into a small grove of trees surrounded on all sides by open fields. They had plenty of ammunition. Their plan was to hold the Yankees at bay until dark and then slip away after creating a diversion by stampeding the spare horses. As they crouched behind trees, the lieutenant colonel and sergeant saw the Union column come up the road at a leisurely pace and halt out of rifle range. Surprisingly, the seemingly unconcerned Yankees made no preparations to engage. The group waited as one of the riders dismounted and attached a white flag to a stick as he walked towards the waiting Confederates. When he got within hearing range he began waving the flag and shouting, "truce, truce!" "Now what do you suppose is going on," growled Matt as he watched the trooper come across the field. "Must be important, whatever it is, for him to risk his life like that," an equally perplexed Cyrus answered.

126

They held their fire as the Yankee moved closer. "Haven't you heard the news about Lee's army?" he shouted. "What are you talking about?" Matt shouted back, "We haven't heard anything about our army's whereabouts in days." By now, the truce flag waving Yankee was in normal speaking range. "General Lee surrendered his army to General Grant at Appomattox Courthouse on the ninth. Under the terms of surrender, all troops attached to the Confederate Army of Northern Virginia are to report to Appomattox for parole processing and mustering out. Boys, the war is over in these parts! When the other Rebel forces learn Lee has given up, I suppose they will be laying down their muskets too."

Thunderstruck, Chambon and Bellnapp stared at each other in disbelief as they lowered their weapons. "Are you sure?" a flabbergasted Matt managed to stammer. The trooper smiled as he responded, "If I was not, we would be shooting at you now. We going to spread the word as far as the James River. A goodly number of Lee's troops straggled during the retreat from Petersburg and they are now spread out all over the countryside for miles in all directions. It will take a few days for the word to get to all of them."

"What are we supposed to do now?" an incredulous Cyrus asked. "The rules are simple. Ride into Appomattox Courthouse, turn in your weapons and other C. S. army issued equipment. Once that's done, you'll be furnished parole papers. Then you can head home. No federal authority will bother you as long as you carry your parole and stay away from soldiering. That's the gist of the terms Generals Grant and Lee agreed to. We would appreciate it greatly if you would tell any other Reb soldiers you come across about the agreement. I would like to stay and jaw awhile longer with you boys, but we have a ways to ride yet today," said the soldier as he shook their hands.

"Don't that beat all," Matt muttered as he watched the soldier walk away. "The war is over for the Army of Northern Virginia."

"Have any trouble?" the Union trooper holding the cavalryman's horse asked as he returned to the column of troops waiting on the road. "Not a bit," he replied as he swung easily into the saddle. "They took it about the same as the others we have come across so far. Most are relieved to hear that it's all over with. Funny thing though, the sergeant back there was a Negro. Never saw a Negro Confederate soldier before."

"Come on, really? Why would any Negro in his right mind join the Confederate army?" asked the disbelieving trooper riding next to him. "That's one question I have no answer for," said the cavalryman. "There are many things about this war I am not sure I understand. Negroes serving in the Rebel ranks must be a very rare thing, given the Confederate government's insistence on maintaining slavery. There are probably about as many Negroes in Lee's army as there are rich New York City boys in our Army of the Potomac. Maybe the poor fellow couldn't buy his way out of the draft by hiring a substitute to serve for him." They both laughed at the absurdity of the thought. The day was pleasant and the duty was easy with the war winding down. They would soon be going home as victors. Having survived the fighting, they could laugh at almost anything now. Even the thought of Negro Confederate soldiers. It had been one hell of a tough war. At the very end of it, they find out Negroes are serving in the Confederate army. Damned if that did not beat all! It was something to write home about!

Chambon and Bellnapp watched the Union cavalry column move out of sight. It seemed like hours before either of them moved or spoke. Bellnapp was the first to break the silence. "Lieutenant Colonel Chambon sir! What are your orders? It appears the two of us have a real problem on our hands, being the army we belong to has gone out of business."

"You are right as rain, sergeant," said Matt feigning the same proper military demeanor Cyrus used. "It's a long way from here to Danville. If we don't get ourselves paroled with the rest of Lee's army, we could be shot by the Yankees as we try to catch up to Secretary Benjamin. We might as well take advantage of General Grant's generous terms before we try to do anything else."

"The Yankees always said they wanted to hang Jeff Davis from a sour apple tree. Does that mean they will hang the men in his cabinet when they catch them?" asked Cyrus.

"General Grant let Lee's army down real easy. I have no idea of how the Yankees will treat the political leaders. We do have an obligation to deliver the maps to Mr. Benjamin or General Breckinridge before we can call it quits for good," responded Matt. "There probably are some important papers they will need in those two boxes we hid at Centreville. Otherwise there would be no need for all the secrecy. It was the one thing Secretary Benjamin really insisted on."

About five miles down the road they met a man who had the latest news. Pat Fitzgerald was a crew member on one of the special trains that had transported the Confederate Government from Richmond to Danville on the night of April 2-3. Pat was returning to his family's home at Palmyra Courthouse to spend the next weeks awaiting developments. With the armies swarming all over the rail lines, the railroads were in chaos, the majority of trains were no longer running. On the return run from Danville, his train nearly reached the junction where the Richmond and Danville line crossed the Southside Railroad before they were forced to reverse direction to avoid capture. Having no desire to spend more time in Danville, Pat hopped off the train and walked the last few miles to Burkeville. There he found some friendly Yankee teamsters who were hauling ammunition to General Ord's fast-moving troops. They gave him a ride on one of their wagons as far as Appomattox Station. From there, he had been walking north toward the James River crossing when he met Matt and Cyrus. Accepting their offer of a free meal served on a stump by the roadside, the hungry trainman told them what he knew of recent events.

"President Davis along with the entire cabinet, except General Breckinridge who stayed behind in Richmond to oversee the evacuation, left Richmond on hastily organized special trains around 9 p.m. on April 2nd. The trains carrying the relocating Confederate government began arriving in Danville on the afternoon of April 3rd. President Davis opened a temporary office in the Southerlin mansion on Main street. The other cabinet officials are staying at different locations in Danville, I don't know where. Breckinridge was going to arrive later. He might be there by now, for all I know. Or, it is also possible the Yankees may have caught him. The Treasury Department moved the currency reserves to Danville on one of the special trains guarded by naval cadets. I heard it amounted to about $500,000 in double-eagle gold pieces, gold bullion and Mexican silver. That sure is mighty little cash for a government to have, don't you think? "

A grin spread across the face of Lieutenant Colonel Matthew Chambon at he thought about Andrew Jackson Clinton, the nitwit he had met while drawing money at the Treasury Department. He could see the pompous dolt frantically signing vouchers at his desk as the dying Confederacy's gold reserves were hurriedly removed from his vault. Andrew J. Clinton may have gone to Danville. Perhaps he was there now, signing the receipts needed to place the gold in a local bank vault for temporary safe keeping. His signature probably had improved after all the practice Clinton got signing papers during the past few days.

As he savored the first food he had eaten in nearly two days, Pat Fitzgerald continued his story. "Davis was expecting General Lee's army to march to Danville and make a stand before trying to link up with Johnston's army down in North Carolina. Now that Lee has surrendered, I don't rightly expect the government to stay on in Danville much longer. The Yankees will swoop down on the place and catch the lot of them with Lee's army now gone from the field."

"I learned Richmond got all tore up during the evacuation. The convicts got out of the state penitentiary when the guards abandoned the place. Mobs made up of the city's fine citizens roamed the streets looting government warehouses. The army set fire to the tobacco warehouses, munitions storage buildings and the arsenals as it pulled out. The wind and mob helped the fire spread. I heard the flour mills by the river burned because the fire got out of control! A big part of the city burned up in a fire started by our own soldiers, can you believe it? Everything between Eighth and Eighteenth Streets and from the river up across Canal and Cary to Main Street is gone. Real shame that is. Mind if I have some more of that?" Pat asked pointing to the chunk of salted ham and partial loaf of bread sitting between them.

"Help yourself. We have plenty," Matt replied. "Any idea what Davis and his cabinet are going to do next? Do you think Davis will surrender to the Yankees?"

"Not at all likely. He is not even thinking about giving up. The word around Danville was that he might try to make a run for it across the Mississippi and try to keep the war going from Texas. President Jeff has now got himself a government on wheels. As long as he can stay one step ahead of the Yankees, he can roll along issuing proclamations to the people. Read this one," he said between chews, pulling a crumpled paper out of his shirt pocket.

Matt took the paper, unfolded it and read aloud a proclamation written by President Jefferson Davis and addressed "To the People of the Confederate States of America."

"It would be unwise, even if it were possible, to conceal the great moral as well as material injury to our cause that must result from the occupation of Richmond by the enemy. It is equally unwise and unworthy of us, as patriots engaged in a most sacred cause, to allow our energies to falter, our spirits to grow faint, or our efforts to become relaxed under reverses, however calamitous."

"It is for us, my countrymen, to show by our bearing under reverses how wretched has been the self-deception of those who believed us less able to endure misfortune with fortitude than to encounter danger with courage. We have now entered upon a new phase of the struggle, the memory of which is to endure for all ages and to shed an increasing luster upon our country. Relieved from the necessity of guarding cities and particular points, important but not vital to our defense; with an army free to move from point to point and strike in detail the garrisons and detachments of the enemy; operating in the interior of our country, where supplies are more accessible and where the foe will be far removed from his own base and cut off from all succor in case of reverse, nothing is now needed to render our triumph certain but the exhibition of our own unquenchable resolve. Let us but will it, and we are free -- and who, in the light of the past, dare not doubt your purpose in the future?"

"Animated by that confidence in your spirit and fortitude which never yet has failed me, I announce to you, fellow countrymen, that it is my purpose to maintain your cause with my whole heart and soul, that I will never consent to abandon to the enemy one foot of the soil of any one of the States of the Confederacy. If by stress of numbers we should ever be compelled to a temporary withdrawal from Virginia's limits, or those of any other border State, again and again will we return, until the baffled and exhausted enemy shall abandon in despair his endless and impossible task of making slaves of a people resolved to be free. Let us not then despond, my countrymen, but relying on the never-failing mercies and protecting care of our God, let us meet the foe with fresh defiance, with unconquered and unconquerable hearts."

"Well what do you think about that?" asked Matt as he finished reading the document.

"Sure sounds to me like he is planning to keep up the fight. I wonder what he plans to use for an army with Lee's given up? The commissary agents already stripped the whole of the South to keep the armies fed up to now. I didn't see any of the accessible supplies Mr. Davis mentioned in the countryside we traveled through, did you?" responded Cyrus.

Patrick sputtered an anger-tinged response through a mouthful of food. "I tell you Mr. Jeff Davis has become demented. Last year, he sent General J. B. Hood back up to Tennessee. Lot of good that did us, Hood got his army annihilated good and proper at Nashville. General Sherman has been tearing up Georgia, South Carolina and North Carolina since he left Atlanta last November. Davis, despite all his extravagant talk of Sherman marching to ruination in Georgia, was unable to find troops to stop him. It was Georgia and the Carolinas that got ruined, not Sherman's boys. With Richmond done for, where are the bullets for the army Davis mentions in his proclamation going to come from? What are they going to do, shoot cow dung at the Yankees as they dash across the pasture fields this spring? Davis is too gone in the head to realize he has been whipped! The damn man ought to just give it up, hard as it may be for him to admit Abe Lincoln has bested him. I saw Jeff Davis in Danville as he was leaving the station. He looks like a sallow-faced, one-eyed, walking corpse. He is the perfect symbol for what is left of our once glorious Confederacy."

Pat Fitzgerald felt a great deal better as he resumed the journey toward his home. He had an interesting conversation, gotten his belly filled with food and had been completely outfitted by the two generous soldiers. He was mounted on the good horse they had given him, a loaded Remington revolver holstered on his belt. An Enfield rifle was strapped to the side of the saddle, three slightly used changes of clothes and blankets were neatly rolled behind it. A four day supply of food, a pocket watch and spare ammunition were tucked in the saddlebags. Having a horse to ride sure beat walking. It would speed up his trip home.

The two soldiers must have seen quite a bit of action from the looks of the clothes and equipment they had with them. There were bullet holes in a lot of it. The pair had been rather closed mouthed, not volunteering information on where they had been and what they were doing. Pat was wise enough to take the hint and not to raise the subject. Why they were riding through the countryside with many spare horses and all sorts of extra equipment was strictly their business. He was a bit surprised by their keen interest in learning where the Secretaries of State and War had relocated after the evacuation of Richmond. Why were they so interested in finding out the temporary location of the virtually defunct Confederate government? Why did they care? Those low-ranking troopers were never going to get to see cabinet officials. If they had any sense, they would avoid Danville altogether. Going there would only bring them trouble with the Yankees. There was no use in pushing your luck by trying to visit with the ineffectual politicians of a nearly expired government.

Thankful for the gifts his benefactors had provided, Pat let his mind turn to things of more immediate importance. He could make himself useful by helping with the spring work on the family farm near Palmyra Courthouse until the railroad got back into operation. Now that the fighting had stopped, the railroad company would start fixing the track, he was sure of that. It would not be too long before he had his old job back. USA or CSA, it made no difference, the railroads had to run. The name of the nation and the politicians running it might change, but the railroad track and rolling stock would always be the same. With everything falling to pieces around him, Pat didn't care one bit if the Yankees stretched the neck of Jeff Davis when they caught him. Thanks to the man's stupidity, the war had been lost. Davis should have been tossed out last year and General Lee brought in. The government should have given him the powers of a dictator. Now Pat and all the people he knew and loved were going to have to live with the mess Davis and his group of clowns had created. Pat could not believe he had once been so feeble-witted that he actually cheered for succession. He felt a great need to go find a priest and bare his soul by making a full confession of his political stupidity.

Chambon and Bellnapp were down to three spare horses and an

assortment of weapons when they reached Appomattox Courthouse on the afternoon of Wednesday, April 12, 1865. The remainder had been given to farmers along the way to the hamlet. Matt and Cyrus found Appomattox and its 150 inhabitants engulfed in a sea of Blue and Gray troops. The place where Lee finally lost his race with Grant and starvation, was about as nondescript as could be imagined. It consisted of a courthouse, county jail, tavern, a couple of stores and a scattering of homes.

Although Lee surrendered on April 9, administrative preparations delayed the formal surrender ceremony for a few days as Union authorities hurriedly set up printing presses in the Clover Hill Tavern. Army printers working round-the-clock got 30,000 blank parole forms printed and ready for distribution by the late evening of April 11.

General Grant issued orders to conduct a simple surrender ceremony that would not humiliate the officers and men of Lee's vanquished army. Early on the morning Chambon and Bellnapp arrived at Appomattox, Major General Joshua L. Chamberlain aligned his Union troops along the Richmond-Lynchburg Road. A short time later, marching at the route step, the Confederate columns led by Major General John B. Gordon came into view. At Chamberlain's order the Union line snapped to attention and presented the marching salute of carry arms. Gordon instantly realized the significance of the military courtesy and ordered his marching columns to return the salute as they marched by, honor answering honor. The Confederates marched down the length of the Union line, halted and turned to face the Union soldiers approximately 15 feet away. They fixed bayonets, stacked arms and placed their cartridge boxes on the ground next to the stacked rifles. They folded the battle flags, placed them on the equipment piles and departed.

It took the entire day to process the Confederate units as they marched up and repeated the procedure. Chambon and Bellnapp were near the tail end of the gray column, reaching the surrender field shortly before sundown. They were permitted to keep one revolver each along with their personal horses, but added their collection of other assorted arms to the large stacks of surrendered weapons. It would take the Union troops over two days to collect and load the war materiel Lee's troops left on the surrender field.

After turning in their arms, they proceeded to one of the many field desks to be registered and obtain a copy of the coveted parole paper. They pledged not to take up arms against the United States again in return for being allowed to return home and live unmolested by federal authorities. The Union soldiers processing paroles cast admiring eyes on Chambon's walking stick. Cyrus had a difficult time keeping a straight face as Matt politely explained the stick was gift from a dear friend and was the source of many fond memories for him. Cyrus smiled a little as he remembered that neither of them would be alive now if it had not been for the deadly surprise concealed inside the innocent looking walking stick.

As they camped with the Rebel troops on the last night the Confederate Army of Northern Virginia existed as viable military organization and ate rations furnished by the Union army, Chambon and Bellnapp learned President Davis had held a cabinet meeting in the temporary capital of Danville on April 10. However, the government was no longer there. Davis and his entourage had departed the city and were thought to be on the way to Greensboro, North Carolina, although no one knew for certain and few of the soldiers cared.

On Thursday, April 13, the Confederates began to leave Appomattox individually and in groups, on horseback and on foot, as they began the sad trek to back to their homes. As they ate a leisurely breakfast and watched the tattered Rebel troops begin to depart, Cyrus asked Matt what they should do next. "We'll never catch up to Benjamin or Breckinridge by chasing after them. By the time we get to Greensboro, if that is where they went, they will have moved on to another place. Let's go back to Richmond and see if they finally stay in one place long enough so we can deliver the maps and be done with this thing. There are people in Richmond who will learn of their whereabouts faster than we can," Matt said.

On April 16, they were on the road to Richmond when an Union cavalry patrol stopped them to check their parole papers. After looking at the documents, the sullen troopers showed them a copy of a telegram which read in part:

Washington, April 15, 1865

The President died this morning.
Wilkes Booth the assassin.
Secretary Seward dangerously wounded.

"Why would John Wilkes Booth, who is one of the most renowned actors in the land, assassinate President Lincoln?" a stunned Matt asked the cavalrymen. The answer was a terse: "We don't know yet. He might have committed the foul deed under orders from Jeff Davis or one of the members of his cabinet. There are many in Washington who believe the assassination of President Lincoln is part of a larger conspiracy. Good day, gentlemen," and the dour troopers rode off.

"If Davis, Benjamin or Breckinridge is involved in the assassination of

Lincoln, we have a new problem on our hands. Being on the losing side of a war is one thing. Murdering the president of the winning nation is quite another. The material we hid at Centreville won't do any of our leaders a bit of good now," Matt remarked to Cyrus as they urged their horses forward. As if to prove Matt correct, chilling indicators of reprisals to come soon emerged from Washington. The new President of the United States, Andrew Johnson, branded Davis and the other leaders of the failed Confederacy as criminals not eligible for parole. They were purposely exempted from the amnesty being extended to members of the Rebel military forces. The United States Government also offered a $100,000 reward to anyone assisting in the capture of Davis. The hunt for the leaders of the failed rebellion was on with a vengeance.

Chambon and Bellnapp were sitting beside the road having a bite to eat while the horses rested, cropped grass and drank from a nearby stream. Cyrus was toying with a brass belt buckle with the letters CSA on its front that he had taken from his saddlebags. He was trying to remember from which dead man the buckle had come when another Union patrol rode up and wanted to check their parole papers. The papers being in order, the patrol was making ready to move on, when one of the cavalrymen said: "Want to trade something for that belt buckle, Reb?"

Cyrus nonchalantly answered, "I might be interested, what have you got." The belt buckle had no meaning for him. He knew they had another four or five more, some Union, some Confederate, packed among the clothing. Cyrus figured the soldier must be new to the field for such a common military issue item to be of interest to him.

"I'll swap you an authentic copy of the letter surrendering Richmond for it," responded the trooper. "I got it near the junction of the Osborne Turnpike and the New Market Road. Guess it was about three miles south of the city line, the night Mayor Mayo came out to call it quits. Might be valuable someday as a remembrance of the night Richmond fell," he said as he handed the letter to Cyrus.

Cyrus took the document and read the simple, direct letter that ended Confederate control of the city of Richmond:

Richmond, Virginia
Monday, April 3, 1865
To the General Commanding the United States Army in front of
Richmond:
General,
The Army of the Confederate Government having abandoned the City

of Richmond, I respectfully request that you take possession of it with an organized force, to preserve order and protect women, children and property.

> *Respectfully,*
> *Joseph Mayo, Mayor*

Since he had more than enough belt buckles, Cyrus agreed to the swap. The letter would take up no space in his saddlebag. In addition, there was nothing to be gained by senselessly aggravating the Union cavalryman with a refusal. Cyrus could not imagine a day ever coming when the letter would have value. Who would ever want a reminder of the terrible night Richmond fell? It would be a long time before anyone he knew would want to see the letter again.

The mounted trooper continued speaking as Cyrus handed up the belt buckle: "Sure was one hell of a bad night, that was. When we got into the city, we had to quell rioting mobs and fight fires for the remainder of the night and all the next day. We saved the citizens of Richmond from fires started by Rebel troops, dispersed looting mobs and caught some of the convicts running loose. The capital of the Confederacy sure gave us a hot welcome. Yes sir, it was a welcome I'll never forget. Thanks for the buckle. Take care now, you hear."

Paroled Lieutenant Colonel Chambon and Sergeant Bellnapp entered Richmond's west side on Broad Street. Having some time on their hands as unemployed soldiers, they decided to ride by the houses of some of the late Confederacy's leaders. Mrs. Robert E. Lee and the general's children had been living at 707 Franklin Street, near Fourth, for nearly two years. The General had returned to the residence on April 15, after leaving Appomattox. To the astonishment of many citizens, the beloved former army commander had ridden nonchalantly across the temporary pontoon bridge from Manchester with a small group of aides. Matt and Cyrus were surprised to see groups of Union soldiers, ex-Confederates and civilians lounging on the sidewalk in the hope of catching a glimpse of the already famous general. "General Lee has the same parole as we do. As long as he abides by the terms, the new Union bosses of Richmond are duty bound to leave him be," Cyrus said as they rode slowly by the house.

At Eighth and Franklin Streets, they passed the residence of former Vice President Stephens, one of the many in the Confederacy who had bitterly opposed a number of the war policies advocated by Jefferson Davis. On the south side of Main Street between Fourshee and Adams Streets, they passed the shuttered house that had been the main residence of Judah P. Benjamin from 1861 until he fled the city during the Confederate evacuation. There were Union sentries on duty at the door. It was obvious from the litter on the sidewalk that the house had been thoroughly searched and ransacked. The house made Chambon uneasy. What was going to happen to them if Judah Benjamin was involved in the assassination of Lincoln? He and the sergeant could find themselves in a heap of trouble.

After asking discreet questions of a number of people, Matt and Cyrus confirmed Davis and his cabinet had departed Danville late on the night of April 10 and had gone to Greensboro, North Carolina. President Davis held an acrimonious meeting with General Johnston in Greensboro on April 12. On April 15, the fleeing Davis party, guarded by a small detachment of cavalry, was rumored to have left Greensboro possibly heading for Charlotte, although no one could be certain. Completely disgusted with Davis and his hopeless delusions of continuing the struggle, General Joseph E. Johnston was said to have opened capitulation discussions with General William T. Sherman somewhere near Durham, North Carolina.

"There is not much more we can do right now" Matt said as they continued their ride through the ruined city. "I might be able to find some temporary work at the Tredegar Iron Works. Since they've stopped making cannon, they might be go back into the business of manufacturing railroad rails. All the railroads in the South have a desperate need for new track and rolling stock. The canal company needs the iron components necessary to repair the locks if it is going to get the waterway back into operation. Tredegar will be busy if the works can be gotten running again."

"Chimborazo Hospital is still full of wounded and sick. I ought to be able to get my old job back until the hospital gets emptied out enough to close down. Should we meet every other night to exchange information on what we have learned about the whereabouts of Benjamin and Breckinridge?" questioned Cyrus.

"Sounds like a good idea to me," said Matt. "We still have gold enough to travel if they stop in one place long enough for us to catch up to them. I certainly would like to be rid of these damn maps and get this job over with."

"Amen to that," muttered Cyrus. "I'll meet you in front of St. John's church on Broad Street at 7 o'clock in the evening. Why are you looking at me like that?"

"In front of a church? That is fine with me, but I was sure you were going to suggest one of the taverns," Chambon responded.

When Cyrus Bellnapp returned to the hospital, the surgeons were more than glad to have him back. With the Confederate government gone out of existence, its currency was becoming totally unusable as a medium of exchange. The hospital staff had to resort to begging for donations of food, bandages and medicines from the Union occupation authorities and private sources. The state of Virginia and the City of Richmond were destitute. They could provide little or nothing to help the hospital.

The Yankees were more forthcoming. Their objective was to see the paroled patients healed and discharged as quickly as possible so the hospital, which was a functioning remnant of Confederate authority, could be closed. Although it was tough going at times, the staff managed to keep the hospital operating. Cyrus noticed that for the first time since 1862, no new patients were coming in to fill the spaces of those being discharged. With each passing week more beds and wards were emptied. He began to see it as the first sure sign that the war was really over.

Like so many other businesses in the South, the Tredegar Iron Works was technically bankrupt. It owed money to its suppliers of raw materials and to its employees. In return, the firm was owed money by the Confederate Government for the fulfillment of contracts. The problem was the debt was now uncollectible because the government had gone out of existence. The railroads and canal companies had need of Tredegar's products, but they had no funds with which to make purchases. With the transportation system destroyed, Tredegar could not move iron ore or fuel to the furnaces. If it was able to manufacture a product, it could not ship it much beyond Richmond's city limits. Matt Chambon found himself doing a great deal of work for which there would be no pay. He was working for shares in the defunct company based on a hope of a reward to come when Virginia's war-devastated economy began to recover.

All in all, Matt was no worse off than most other people in Richmond. Few individuals had any real money these days since the Confederate currency was becoming totally worthless. Those who had invested in Confederate bonds found themselves holding paper whose only value was for stuffing cracks in walls or covering broken windows. As the currency collapsed, everything had to be done by barter. No one could predict when a cash economy would emerge again. In the countryside, the farming situation was equally desperate. Unpaid returning soldiers had no money to purchase seed or tools. They would have to struggle to put in a crop with few mules or horses. Matt knew it was not going to be a good year for the businesses and farmers in the former Confederacy.

Richmond received the news of the surrender of General Johnston's army to General Sherman at Durham Station, North Carolina on April 26 with no show of emotion. The downhearted city had been expecting the bad news for almost two weeks. It was also learned that President Lincoln's assassin, John

Wilkes Booth, had been trapped and killed in a tobacco barn on the Virginia side of the Potomac on the same day.

As he moved forward slowly in the long line of General Johnston's soldiers processing for parole, Sergeant Erasmus Henry Strawderman seethed inwardly. He was thinking about the time wasted by the men of the army since the meetings between President Davis and General Johnston at Greensboro on April 12 and 13. Living in a world of false illusions, Davis rejected outright General Joe's suggestion to begin truce discussions. The blockhead of a President had babbled a stream of nonsense about raising additional troops by rounding up deserters and conscripting men who had avoided the draft. Davis and his toady Judah Benjamin, had no intention of allowing the war to end, although everyone else in the Confederacy knew it was a completely lost cause.

General Joseph E. Johnston's reputation among the troops in North Carolina soared when word leaked out of how he had bluntly advised Davis about hopelessness of his army's situation. Old Joe had been spiteful. He told the President the Southern people were tired of war. They knew they were whipped and would no longer fight for him or anyone else. The Confederate Government had no arms, money, credit or ammunition with which to continue the struggle Davis was advocating. His troops were deserting in large numbers every day. There was no choice but to surrender. When Lee called it quits up in Virginia the war, for all practical purposes, had come to an end. Davis had not said a word in response to the general's cutting commentary. He stared at a piece of paper which he constantly folded and unfolded.

Davis was unmoved by Johnston's harsh presentation. He was determined to try to reach the Trans-Mississippi region and carry out his grandiose plans for continuing the struggle. When the wretched remains of the Confederate Government fled Greensboro, Johnston was given $39,000 in gold to distribute to the ranks. Each soldier drew the princely sum of $1.15 to see him home. It seemed to Erasmus that the Richmond numskulls, whose incompetence and narrow focus on Virginia cost the South the war, had hurled a final obscene insult at the hard-fighting troops of the Confederacy's western army. "Damn Davis and his slick crew of smooth-talkers to hell, ten times over. They should have sent troops to help break Grant's siege of Vicksburg back in '63 and ought to have left Joe Johnson in command at Atlanta in '64," muttered Erasmus to man next to him as they shuffled along in the line going to the parole table.

A Union colonel of engineers was standing behind the junior officers and noncommissioned officers paroling Johnston's troops. As the lieutenant read off Strawderman, Erasmus, Henry, sergeant, the colonel suddenly took a great deal of interest in the ragged man standing before the table. After the formalities were completed he said: "Sergeant, please step over here for a minute."

Erasmus walked over to the colonel, saluted the officer and replied with a polite: "Yes sir, what can I do for you?"

"I heard your last name as Strawderman when it was recorded on the rolls. Was I correct?"

"Yes sir, my full name is Erasmus Henry Strawderman. I hail from back in Tennessee."

"My mother's maiden name was Strawderman. Her side of the family originally came out of northern Virginia way back when. She was descended from Ben Strawderman who lived near George Washington's property on Dogue Creek. Could it be that we are related in some way?"

"Lord almighty! It appears so. The old folks back home often told of how our family moved to Tennessee after the farm land in Virginia wore out and would not produce a decent crop. I have often heard stories about Ben. He was said to have made a good whiskey from a recipe given to him by George Washington himself. My father and my brother back home still produce a batch of it now and then, following the great man's tried and true formula which has been handed down from generation to generation."

"We must be related to each other. My mother, unfortunately, made little mention of Ben's whiskey. She does not like strong drink and may have purposely ignored that part of our common history in her telling of it. We are most likely distant cousins of some sort. Let's go sit on that log yonder and figure out our relationship."

Union Colonel Jefferson Beuhler and Confederate Sergeant Erasmus Strawderman spent the better part of a pleasant two hours sitting on the log discussing their family connections. Erasmus made mention of his desire to visit the home of his forefathers in Virginia before returning to Tennessee. They laughed about how both of them could have done it quite easily, if the war had continued for a few more weeks. Jefferson told Henry that there was at least one family member known to be living in northern Virginia. He knew that for a fact because General William T. Sherman had met him during the first major campaign of the war. William Strawderman farmed and made a fair amount of whiskey using George Washington's recipe. "Uncle Billy" Sherman himself had sampled the product on more than one occasion back in '61 and pronounced it to be "not too bad." It was agreed that the paroled Confederate sergeant could tag along with Sherman's troops on their march to Washington. "You can save your big $1.15 gift from Jeff Davis for later use," Beuhler told him.

In one way, Matt Chambon and Cyrus Bellnapp found themselves more fortunate than the other paroled veterans. The occupying authorities of Richmond issued regulations prohibiting the wearing of all Confederate insignia or designations of rank. This meant that all Confederate military buttons had to be removed from coats and jackets. Having collected a sizable amount of clothing during their trip to Centreville, Matt and Cyrus were able to outfit themselves in a mixture of civilian and Union army clothing. They were able to avoid the completely bedraggled look of the other veterans who, having no other clothes to wear, went about town in their old uniform coats and jackets minus the buttons.

May 1865

Matt and Cyrus met every other evening to exchange rumors regarding the movements of the fleeing cabinet officials. As time passed, it became increasingly obvious they might never be able to deliver the maps. They learned that General Breckinridge, the Confederacy's last Secretary of War, had separated from the Davis party on May 4, 1865. Fearing indictment for treason if he remained in the territory of the United States, he skirted capture as he moved through Georgia to Florida. Traveling at one time in a sloop he captured at gun point, Breckinridge got across the straits to Cuba, arriving on June 12. To finalize his often harrowing escape ordeal, he took passage on a steamer, reaching the safety of England on August 27.

Secretary of State Judah P. Benjamin bid his final farewell to President Davis on May 2. Disguised as a farmer and a Frenchman, the urbane "Brains of the Confederacy" trekked through Georgia and down the west coast of Florida where he hid for a time at the large Gamble sugar plantation near Tampa Bay. Narrowly managing to avoid capture on several occasions, Benjamin was reported to have arrived safely in Havana, Cuba around July 25. By late August, the portly former head of the Confederate espionage service was in London.

President Davis was not as lucky as his subordinates. Refusing to the leave the mainland because of his delusive dream of continuing the war from the west side of the Mississippi, he was captured on May 10 at Irwinville, Georgia by General Wilson's hard-riding cavalry troopers. By May 23, the disgraced former Confederate President was imprisoned at Fortress Monroe in Virginia, awaiting trial for treason.

On May 10, the same day Davis was captured, U. S. President Andrew Johnston issued a proclamation declaring "armed resistance to the authority of the Government of the United States at an end." It was the official end of the Civil War.

As soon as he learned Benjamin and Breckinridge were in England, Matt Chambon smuggled letters to them via sympathetic persons in the British Embassy in Washington. In his letters, he asked for instructions regarding the disposition of the maps. Should the copies be sent to them in London or turned over to someone else in Richmond for safe keeping?

Sherman's motley-looking army, proudly marching in its battered hats and tattered trousers, had knocked the economic underpinnings out of the Confederate war machine. They had destroyed one state capital, captured two others and taken a major seaport. With General Johnston's troops paroled and drifting homeward, the blue-clad host crossed into Virginia. Former Confederate Sergeant Erasmus Henry Strawderman traveled with the engineers supervising a string of mules, his parole paper safely tucked into the new shirt his recently discovered kinsman, Colonel Jefferson Beuhler, had provided. Although the majority of the mules originated from Missouri and Tennessee, the engineers named them for the cites of the northern states that provided the bulk of Sherman's troops. There was Cincinnati, Columbus and Cleveland, Indianapolis, Fort Wayne, Bloomington, Chicago, Peoria, Springfield, Des Moines, Davenport, Waterloo, Madison, Milwaukee, Duluth and Minneapolis. The cantankerous creatures had been with the army since it left Atlanta over six months ago and over a thousand blackened miles to the rear. Erasmus was taking a liking to Sherman's boys. They were not all that much different from his old messmates in the ill-fated Confederate Army of Tennessee. These Yankees could march as hard as any Rebel force he had served with and had proven themselves savage fighters when committed to combat. Erasmus also liked having enough to eat every day. That was the best change of all. He would stay with the army until they got to Washington. Then he and Jefferson would go see William Strawderman and visit their common ancestral home.

Sherman's forces arrived at Richmond on May 11 and halted for a few days rest. There was trouble almost immediately because the Union Army of the Potomac and Sherman's troops did not get along. The provost guard was doubled, then tripled in an effort to keep the brawling soldiers apart. Whenever contact was made, insults were hurled and fights began. Each army accused the other of not doing its fair share to win the war. The animosity exhibited by the two bodies of troops was so severe that the senior commanders planning the grand victory parade in Washington decided on arrangements to keep the armies apart. They would not be permitted to conduct an intramural brawl in the United States capital. May 23 was the day scheduled for the Army of the Potomac to parade down Pennsylvania Avenue. Sherman's hellions would strut their stuff the next day on May 24.

As the army went into camp, Colonel Beuhler rode to the city. He planned to visit some of sights in the captured Confederate capital and pay his respects to one of the staff at Chimborazo Hospital. One of his acquaintances, who was wounded and captured at Second Bull Run, had received excellent care from a surgeon's assistant named Bellnapp before being released in a prisoner exchange. The colonel wanted to thank the man personally for his kind treatment of his comrade in arms. Jefferson toured the former Confederate White House, now the headquarters of the Union occupation troops, visited the Capitol building and the burned district before riding east on Broad Street to Chimborazo Hospital.

It did not take Colonel Beuhler long to find Cyrus Bellnapp in the hospital's seedy wards. He was with a group of convalescent amputees wounded during the last days of fighting along the Richmond-Petersburg lines. Like many other Confederates, Bellnapp had not been paid since long before the fall of Richmond, so the colonel paid to have dinner brought in. As they ate in one of the silent ward buildings, the conversation turned to what Cyrus would do after the hospital closed. Cyrus told how his arrangement to pursue a medical apprenticeship ended when his mentor had been killed.

"Have you ever considered leaving Virginia and trying your luck in a new location? Would you consider studying medicine in another place, Ohio for instance?" Colonel Beuhler asked.

"I have never been out of Virginia. I don't know anyone in Ohio who would take me on. How would I find a doctor or a surgeon there interested in teaching me?" responded Cyrus.

Colonel Beuhler mulled over the question for a minute and then continued: "My cousin, Dr. Alexander Mason, teaches at the Medical College of Ohio in Worthington. He is getting up in years, but always keeps his eye out for good men interested in advancing the cause of medical science. I am sure he would like to have you as an apprentice or student. I would be honored to write a letter of introduction for you if you decided to make the journey."

"Oh Lord, yes. If he will take me on, I will gladly move to Ohio after affairs are finished here. The hospital is closing down, no new patients have been brought in since General Lee was chased out of Richmond," exclaimed Cyrus. He continued with his melancholy observations on how the famous hospital was being phased out of existence. "After the Union soldiers marched in, the staff was told to stay on and attend the patients. For a time, we were very short of food because the obstructions placed in the James to stop the federal gunboats also blocked supply ships from reaching the city. It took a number of days for the engineers to clear a passage so the steamboats could reach the wharves. Once the ships began to arrive, the federal quartermaster began to issue us rations, mostly cornmeal and codfish, at first. A lot of the sick men didn't like the cod because it had a mighty strong taste to it."

"The Union commander of Richmond wants to close all the Confederate military hospitals as quickly as he can. Our surgeons have been leaving, going back home or into private practice. As quick as patients get well, they are discharged. The bad cases will be transferred to other hospitals, I guess. Chimborazo Hospital will soon be an empty shell. Our 120 buildings, the wards, the ice houses, kitchens, mess halls, morgues, bathhouses, bakery and the brewery will disappear as people tear them apart for the lumber. This hospital treated more than 78,000 patients during the war. The physical part of it will soon be gone, but I will always carry the memory of this place in my heart."

"We all will have the memories of the war with us forever. It's the price we pay for doing what we did. We don't have it so bad when you think of all the men under the ground, they paid the highest price of all," Colonel Beuhler responded. He continued: "I will leave the letter of introduction with you. I will also send a letter from Washington to Dr. Mason, advising him you will be coming his way as soon as Chimborazo closes. Here is $40 in greenbacks to pay for your train ticket and help with your expenses. It is the least I can do to repay you for saving the life of my friend," said the colonel as he handed Cyrus eight five dollar bills. "Perhaps by the time you begin your journey, the railroad will be back in operation. You can take a train all the way from Richmond to Washington and connect there to Columbus." They continued talking about the war, hospitals and the future. It was late afternoon before they shook hands and parted. The colonel returned to Sherman's camps, Bellnapp to his evening duties. A warm spring breeze was blowing through the partially deserted hospital grounds on Chimborazo hill banging the unlatched doors and shutters on the empty buildings.

Sherman's soldiers continued their march north. On the way to their camps around Alexandria, Virginia, a number of the army's regiments made a detour to Mt. Vernon to visit President George Washington's home. They saluted the general's tomb as they marched by it, secure in the belief they prevented the nation he founded from splintering into fragments. The treasonous assault against the principles of government laid down by George Washington had been stopped dead in its tracks. The soldiers were proud of the work they had done in keeping Washington's concept of government alive and well.

During the late afternoon of May 23, Sherman's troops left their Virginia camps and marched to the streets around the Capitol in order to be fresh and ready for tomorrow's parade. The next morning, they were up for roll call at 5 a.m. At 9 a.m., the army stepped off down Pennsylvania Avenue with the regimental bands playing the Battle Hymn of the Republic and the tattered battle flags fluttering above the blue-clad host. The combat units passed the reviewing stand, each followed by its group of ambulances with blood stained canvas stretchers strapped to their sides. The Pioneer Corps, which had laid 400 miles of corduroy roads and uncounted miles of pontoon bridges, came with its portable pontoons. The men marched with their well-worn picks and axes on their shoulders. Colonel "Short Fuse" Beuhler rode at the head of his demolition engineers, some of whom were swinging lengths of burning fuse to delight the crowd. A roar from the onlookers went up when they saw one of the engineers' wagons containing small baskets full of rubble, each with a hand lettered sign denoting the name of a town along the route of the army's famous march. General Sherman smiled broadly as the ribbon and flower bedecked mules carrying casks of blasting powder passed in review.

There were very few people living around the village of Centreville. The majority of the pre-war residents seemed to have moved away for good. Very few had reappeared in the war-devastated area since Lee's army had laid down its arms. Will Strawderman was looking at the parcel of land he had planted with crops. Although it was nowhere near the farm's capacity, it was the largest planting he had made since the unfortunate spring of 1861. He was almost the only one in the entire neighborhood who had planted crops. His property was surrounded on all sides by the weed-filled, fallow fields of abandoned farms. With land prices at rock bottom, he could increase the size of his holdings by purchasing land for little more than the price of the unpaid back taxes. The only problem was that there was no one to help work additional acres.

"They have gone up," he muttered to himself as he thought about the quantity of worthless Confederate dollars he owned. As the Confederacy disintegrated in the spring of 1865, Old Will found himself extremely fortunate to have done little business with Confederates during the last two years of the war. If he had done more, his current financial losses would have been greater. His largest customer, Clinton Stackhouse, had paid for his whiskey purchases in United States coin and currency. The U.S. money, which was now the sole legal tender of the land, had maintained its value, giving Old Will purchasing power in an area filled with bankrupt Confederate bond holders, worthless Rebel dollars and uninhabited farms. Since the Confederacy had failed, its promise to redeem its currency in gold after a ratification of a treaty of peace between the Confederate States of America and the United States of America was worthless. With nearly everyone broke but him, the few critics of his business dealings in Washington had been effectively silenced.

Old Will saw the two riders coming down the turnpike from the direction of Alexandria. One was a Union officer, the other he didn't recognize. Trailing behind the riders were two fine looking mules with supplies of all sorts strapped to their strong backs. As it became clear the riders were heading for his farm, Old Will left the field and walked out to meet them. "Are you William Strawderman?" the colonel asked. When Old Will nodded his head in assent, the officer continued: "How do you do sir? Please allow me to introduce myself. I am Jefferson Beuhler, my mother's maiden name was Strawderman. This fellow here is Erasmus Henry Strawderman of Tennessee," he said pointing to Erasmus. "We believe we are related to you in some manner or fashion. Would you mind if we sit a spell and chat while we figure out the family connection?" The thought of kinfolk arriving out of nowhere to visit perked Old Will up. "You all set yourselves down here on the porch while I find something to wash down the road dust. Ruth Anne," he shouted, "come on out here and meet our company. Some of our kin folks have rode a mighty long way to see us."

The three men sat on the porch sipping Strawderman's Finest while they traced their kinship through the generations as the Strawderman clan moved from Virginia into Ohio, Indiana, Illinois and Tennessee. Old Will learned from Jefferson that there were a couple relatives living somewhere in California. By supper time, they had tracked the family lineage back to Colonial times and Ben's farm near George Washington's distillery on Dogue Creek. Old Will agreed to take them to the site of the Ben's farm in the morning. The team of gift mules would be a big help with the plowing even though they had been sold off as surplus from Sherman's demobilizing army. No one in the neighborhood need ever be told the mules had faithfully served the destroyer of the Confederacy before they arrived on the farm. The shovels, axes, hand tools and canvas the mules carried would also be useful as he expanded crop production and made repairs to the still.

After spending two days visiting the property which was once Ben's farm, the remains of Washington's mill and distillery on Dogue Creek and the Mt. Vernon mansion, the trio returned to Old Will's farm. Old Will spent a great deal of time during the trip attempting to convince Erasmus to stay on at Centreville and help him expand his farm holdings. Since Erasmus had more brothers back in Tennessee than were needed at the family farm, he decided to try his luck in Virginia. As soon as mail service was reestablished, he would send a letter home explaining his intentions. After he and Old Will got the fall harvest in, he would take some time off and visit his family in Tennessee. Hopefully by then, the trains would be running again. In the meantime, he and Old Will had some serious Strawderman family business to discuss. Old Will's recipe for Strawderman's Finest was not quite the same as the one used by the Tennessee branch of the family. They had to figure out how George Washington's whiskey-making recipe had gotten changed through the years. The question had to be resolved because it was a point of family honor!

With the dream of an independent Confederacy in ashes, the citizens of Richmond were reduced to the mundane task of making a living in an occupied city. It had been demeaning to have been dependent on the Union army for food rations during first weeks of occupation. The humiliation of having to accept Yankee handouts was compounded by the fact that the departing Confederate army had played a major role in causing the shortage when it torched the ration warehouses. Even though a large part of the city's industrial base was destroyed in the evacuation night fire, economic activity began to pick up as the Union troops maintained order. Four of the railroads serving Richmond were repaired and running again by May 1865. The bars of the Spotswood Hotel, the Exchange Hotel and the Ballard Hotel were soon filled with businessmen looking for investment opportunities in the humbled former Confederate capital. Within a year, the Tredegar Iron Works was back to almost full production, its equipment and supplies purchased with an infusion of Northern investment capital. Instead of inspecting cannon destined for the Confederate army, Matt Chambon was busily engaged in the production of railroad rails and other iron products for industrial use and civilian consumption. The employees worked the 11 hour workday standard throughout the U.S. at the time and considered themselves fortunate.

November 1865

In August 1865, Matt and Cyrus heard an interesting piece of news. The unemployed General Robert E. Lee had grown restless observing the terms of his parole confined to the house on Franklin Street. The general, who had rejected many more lucrative offers, had accepted a position as the president of the small, bankrupt Washington College in Lexington, Virginia. His salary at the struggling institution in the war-ravaged Shenandoah Valley was set at $1,500 per year. At the age of 58, the combative Lee was beginning a new life as an educator in a strange town. It was, oddly enough, the very same town in which his famous subordinate Stonewall Jackson was buried.

The pugnacious Lee had seen 121,000 of his soldiers killed or wounded during the war. That was 27,000 more than any other general on either side, including Union General Ulysses S. Grant, who had been branded a "butcher" by many Northern newspapers during his hard-hitting 1864-65 campaign. Lee's tactics had also taken a toll of his general officers. Lee lost two corps commanders, four division commanders, and 33 brigade commanders during the fighting. As he rode out of Richmond to begin a new career, the general didn't seem to care what others thought about his qualities as a military leader. He knew he had performed his duty to the best of his ability. What historians might write about him in the future did not seem to trouble him at all.

Matt Chambon received a response from General Breckinridge in September. The short note thanked him for successfully completing the mission to Centreville and asked him to hold the map until the former Secretary of War instructed him otherwise. Later in the month, Matt saw Cyrus off. He took a coastal vessel to Baltimore where he boarded a Baltimore and Ohio train bound for Parkersburg in the new state of West Virginia. He crossed the Ohio River by ferry and rode the cars of the Marietta and Cincinnati Railroad to Xenia, Ohio. There, he caught a train on the Cleveland, Columbus and Cincinnati Railroad that carried him through Columbus to Worthington. Dr. Mason warmly greeted him at the small depot when he arrived. As their carriage traveled to the medical college, he prodded Cyrus to tell him about his experiences while treating the wounded at Chimborazo Hospital.

The month of November saw a second hand-delivered response find its way to Matt Chambon from a writer in England. Former Confederate Secretary of State Benjamin thanked Matt for his services and asked him to hold his copy of the map for the time being. Benjamin would be in touch with him when he required the map.

Breckinridge spent three and one half years in exile in England, the Continent and Canada. Under the terms of President Johnson's Christmas Day 1868 general amnesty proclamation, General Breckinridge returned to the United States and resumed his law practice in Lexington, Kentucky in March 1869. In April, Matt received a letter from the former Confederate cabinet officer advising him to destroy the map because the amnesty had removed any need for the contents of the two boxes. Former U.S. Vice President, Confederate General and Secretary of War Breckinridge died at the age of 54 on May 17, 1875.

"The good lawyer is not the man who has an eye to every side and angle of contingency, and qualifies all his qualifications, but who throws himself on your part so heartily, that he can get you out of a scrape."

-Ralph Waldo Emerson, 1860

Judah Benjamin had a net worth of $20,000 when he reached England to begin the life of an exile at the age of 55. The man who had been considered one of the best lawyers in the South, took up the practice of law becoming a highly successful international lawyer. Loyal to Jefferson Davis to the end, he never discussed the activities of the Confederate secret service and declined to publish his views on the Confederate government during the book writing frenzy of the 1870s and 1880s. Benjamin died in Paris in 1884. Matt Chambon never received a response to the inquiry he sent to Mr. Benjamin after he destroyed Breckinridge's copy of the map. Matt waited another year, and then in keeping with the pledge of secrecy he had given the Confederate Secretary of State, destroyed Benjamin's map. Benjamin's two boxes of secrets would remain forever buried near the little village of Centreville, Virginia.

May 1900

When no links to John Wilkes Booth could be established and no proof of a Confederate government conspiracy to assassinate President Lincoln were found, Confederate President Jefferson Davis was released from confinement at Fortress Monroe in May 1867. Out of jail on $100,000 bail, Davis was never tried for treason. In later life, the unreconstructed ex-Confederate President wrote articles and published books, including his memoirs: "The Rise and Fall of the Confederate Government." He died on December 5, 1889 and was buried in a vault in Metaire Cemetery in New Orleans. In May 1893, Davis' body was removed from the vault and loaded on a funeral train making stops in the capitals of Alabama, Georgia and North Carolina. On May 31, a crowd of 75,000 watched the procession to Richmond's Hollywood Cemetery where a 21-gun salute was fired as the body was reinterred. In 1978, a joint Congressional resolution signed by President Jimmy Carter restored Davis's citizenship effective to December 25, 1868. The man who was almost universally despised in the South during the closing days of the war had his reputation restored by a later generation.

The martyred U.S. President, Abraham Lincoln, who pulled out all the stops as he waged a savage war to crush the Confederacy, lies buried at Oak Ridge Cemetery in Springfield, Illinois. His massive tomb was completed in October 1874 at a cost of $173,000. It was rebuilt in 1931 at an additional cost of $175,000. Lincoln, whose war policies nearly cost him the mid-war presidential election of 1864, has become the most respected of all U.S. Presidents.

Former Confederate sergeant and freed slave, Cyrus Bellnapp, completed his medical studies under the tutelage of Dr. Alexander Mason at the Medical College of Ohio in Worthington. When they discussed the germ theory the noted French Chemist Louis Pasteur had put forth, Cyrus excitedly related the observations which had so perplexed Dr. Hoffman at the operating tables of Chimborazo Hospital. Pasteur's theory neatly explained why there had been less infected wounds at certain times in the hospital. When the operating instruments and tables were clean, there were fewer germs. Pasteur's discovery radically changed medical thinking on the cause and spread of disease. Cyrus had barely digested the awesome implications of Pasteur's findings when Dr. Mason showed him a copy of the work English surgeon Joseph Lister had done in 1865. Lister had used carbolic acid as an antiseptic when treating compound fractures. Infection in wounds could be greatly reduced by the use of Lister's process. The conclusion was mind boggling. If germs were destroyed, infection could be controlled. Cyrus thought about all the war wounded who had lost their lives because the staff in the Chimborazo operating rooms had not known about the discoveries of Pasteur and Lister. As he dwelled on the almost endless rows of soldiers graves in Richmond's Hollywood Cemetery, he suddenly realized he had found his life's calling.

The age of sterilization and the use of disinfecting agents in hospital operating rooms had dawned. Dr. Cyrus Bellnapp became almost fanatical in his devotion to the notion of germs causing infection and the need to combat the little killers by improving sanitation practices. His lectures and writings on the subject developed a wide following because his recommendations were vividly illustrated by his first-hand accounts of germ-caused death in the hospitals and military camps of the American Civil War. The Medical College of Ohio was absorbed into the medical school of the Ohio State University in the 1880s. Dr. Bellnapp continued his research and teaching career at the University while his reputation as a renowned infection and disease fighter continued to grow.

True to the pledge of secrecy he had given Matt Chambon, Cyrus never discussed the mission to Centreville with anyone. Although they corresponded during the following years, the memory of the secret assignment they had carried out in the closing days of the war slowly faded as current events, the responsibilities of work and families occupied their time. Like most veterans of the Civil War, Cyrus stored his uniform, revolver and parole paper in a safe place in the attic of his home. Since he was employed in a Yankee hospital doing research work on bacteria, he never found a good reason to mention his relatively short Confederate army service to anyone. As the years went by, he began to consider it as something he had done when he was young and somewhat stupid. Still, he was proud of the fact that he and Chambon had accomplished what they had set out to do, even if their effort had served no useful purpose in the end. It had been an exciting and deadly time, they had been tested and it had made them life-long friends. He was proud to have played a role in it.

The national trauma of the Civil War slowly faded into the background as the United States outgrew its myopic sectional rivalries in the following years. The focus of the nation had shifted, occupied by current topics of interest. By the early 1900s, the United States of America was a Pacific Ocean power. America was in the throes of industrialization, the frontier was gone, people felt good about the country's prospects and a strong hint of imperialism was in the air.

In 1898, William McKinley, the 25th President and a Union army veteran of the fighting in the Shenandoah Valley during the Civil War, annexed the Hawaiian Islands. These peaceful tropical land specks, which had once been only of interest to the whaling industry, had become major sugar cane producers in response to the market disruptions caused by the Civil War. With an eye to marketing new products, entrepreneurs also opened the first pineapple cannery in 1892. After annexation, the military established bases to support America's vital national interests in the Pacific. Also in the fateful year of 1898, the U.S. quickly won the Spanish-American War. A number of the senior officers in the victorious U.S. Army had fought on opposing sides during the Civil War. Newspapers carried numerous articles on why the war with Spain should be considered the event that finally erased the North/South division in the U.S. military establishment.

As part of the peace settlement with Spain, the United States acquired control of the Philippine Islands. As an ugly harbinger of what the coming century would bring, 50,000 troops had to be committed to suppressing a guerrilla war in the newly acquired Philippines because many Filipinos were opposed to trading rule by Spain for rule by the United States. During the struggle which lasted until 1902, U.S. forces suffered approximately 6,000 casualties while the Filipinos lost a total of 250,000. One of the reminders of that long-forgotten conflict, a captured church bell, still travels with the U.S. Army's 11th Infantry.

On the other side of the Pacific, another emerging power was flexing its imperialistic muscles. Japan defeated China and took control of Korea and Formosa in 1895. In 1905, it emerged as a world power after dealing a military defeat to Czarist Russia in the Far East. President Theodore Roosevelt was awarded the 1906 Nobel Peace Prize for his role in mediating the peace settlement that ended the Russo-Japanese War. Although it was a great personal honor for the president, it was also a sign that henceforth the United States would be involved in Pacific affairs. And although no one could foresee it at the time, the ruthless military and economic expansionism of Japan would have dire consequences for the United States later in the century.

July 1911

"All quiet along the Potomac to-night,
No sound save the rush of the river,
While soft falls the dew on the face of the dead,
the picket is off duty forever."

                                                    -Ethel Beers, 1827-79

With the U.S. population standing at 94 million, the memory of the Civil War was becoming old history as the nation moved onto the international stage. Realizing that they belonged to a past age, Matt Chambon and Dr. Cyrus Bellnapp decided to attend the Manassas Jubilee of Peace, a celebration honoring the fiftieth anniversary of the Battle of First Manassas on July 21, 1911. Since they were getting on in years, they both understood the event would probably be their final chance to discuss the old days with friends. There would never be a better time or place for them because the region was the location where many of their war memories were made.

They arrived by separate trains only to find nothing looked as they remembered it. Over the course of the intervening years, much had changed. Not far from the site of the destroyed Union supply depot at Manassas Junction was the town of Manassas which had been established in 1868. Amid the commotion of hundreds of arriving old veterans, Matt and Cyrus found each other and rented a carriage to transport them to the battlefield. As they talked, Cyrus noticed Matt still carrying the lethal walking stick. "Does it still work?" he asked as the carriage moved down the dusty road. "Probably, but it has been unloaded since the war ended. I just couldn't force myself to get rid of it. Besides, it does help me get around and it does have a rather classy look about it," answered Matt. The well-worn walking stick was just like them, Cyrus thought. A relic from a past age when they both had been young and able, not old and feeble.

On the battlefield, Matt and Cyrus watched as over 1,000 veterans eschewed all thoughts of sectional hatred as they gathered to exchange remembrances of a distant, murderous time. In a moving ceremony which brought tears to the eyes of veterans and onlookers alike, the veterans of the battle met in merging lines and clasped hands on Henry Hill. These old soldiers were a dwindling living reminder of the vast armies of the North and South that prowled across the northern Virginia landscape a half century earlier.

Erasmus Henry Strawderman had remained at Old Will's farm after the war. Their purchases of vacant farm land had made them the largest landowners in the area by the time of Old Will's death in 1871. All the farm property was inherited by Henry with Ruth Anne's passing two years later. He had returned to Tennessee several times over the years to visit, but found farming and operating Old Will's still to his liking, and so had remained on the farm near the village of Centreville. Although the farms had slowly been brought back into cultivation, the village never recovered from the war. Most businesses shifted to Fairfax Courthouse or the new town of Manassas, leaving Centreville not much more than a dot on Civil War era maps. Erasmus married Elizabeth Sue Kincheloe and their noisy brood of five children had kept them busy. Now semi-retired himself, Erasmus turned over the farm operations to his two sons, although he continued to devote a considerable amount of time to the still. He had no interest in the ceremonies at the Manassas battlefield because he was a veteran of the Confederacy's ill-fated western army, attending the reunions on the battlefields of Tennessee and Georgia where he had once fought.

President Taft decided to travel to Manassas by motor car rather than by train. He departed Washington a little past noon on July 21 in a cavalcade of four vehicles filled with politicians, secret service men and his military aide, Major Archie Butt. The cars stopped briefly at Fairfax Courthouse where the party was welcomed by the mayor and downed a tasty lunch. As the little convoy headed to Centreville on the old Warrenton Turnpike now designated as Route 29, the president's party was severely jostled about as the cars bounced over the rutted road. It was agreed by the members of the president's group that this was the worst road they had ever seen. Barely 30 miles from Washington, they were driving through an economic backwater little changed since the Civil War. As they forded Willow Spring not far from the old Strawderman farm, one of the cars became stuck in the rising water caused by recent thunderstorms. The President and a few selected members of the party continued on in the steamer which was able to cross the flooded stream.

As he sat on his porch bending a replacement copper pipe for the still, Erasmus was amazed to see a car carrying the President of the United States speed pass the farm and come to a screeching halt a short distance down the turnpike at Little Rocky Run. This stream was also rising. Its water had become so deep the President's vehicle could not cross. Erasmus watched the gallant Major Butt wade into the chest deep water taking depth measurements. Now in danger of being late for the President's 4:15 p.m. scheduled arrival at Manassas, the party backtracked on the pike and asked

Erasmus for alternate directions. He was also asked to take his mule team and pull the car stranded in Willow Spring back onto dry land. Always happy to help the President, Erasmus jumped up, got a team of mules from the barn and pulled the vehicle from the stream. He watched the four automobiles disappeared over a hill as they headed back to the detour Erasmus had suggested. "My gracious, President Taft sure is a heavy fellow. He must eat at least six meals a day in order to develop the girth he's got on him. I don't expect the major is going to get dried out before they get to Manassas. He will have to stand around in his wet clothes while the President gives his speech," Erasmus said to the mules as he watched the cars speed out of sight. Forced by flooded streams to take the roundabout way suggested by Erasmus, President Taft was late. He did not reach Manassas till 5:45p.m.

The festivities climaxed on the evening of July 21, 1911 with the late - arriving President William H. Taft delivering a speech on the courthouse lawn in Manassas. A crowd of 10,000 citizens, politicians and veterans gathered to listen to him speak. Although the President was late in arriving, he was given a warm reception by the assemblage. His speech regarding the heroic deeds and sacrifices of the soldiers in Blue and Gray was a perfect fit with the spirit of the reunion. After concluding his speech, the President spent another half hour happily talking with the veterans. Around 8 p.m., he departed for Washington as a guest in a private railroad car. After having suffered through a very difficult arrival, President Taft decided not to tempt fate again by traveling by motor car.

As he was enjoying the reunion festivities, Cyrus thought he recognized a man wearing the uniform of an Union army colonel. "Excuse me sir," he said. "My name is Dr. Cyrus Bellnapp. You look very familiar. I believe we must have met before."

"We certainly have doctor. I am Jefferson Beuhler. I was with Sherman's army when we met in Richmond." Cyrus grabbed the man's hand and shook it vigorously. "I kind of thought it had to be you. But why are you at a reunion in Manassas? I thought you did all your fighting in the west."

"Uncle Billy Sherman fought here at First Bull Run. I came to honor his memory since having died, he can't come himself. It was something I felt I had to do because I was with him all the way across Georgia and up through the Carolinas. The general began his service in the war on this battlefield. I wanted to come and walk the field with the other veterans one last time. I think he would have liked me to do that for him. He was my friend and commander during some really rough times."

Cyrus introduced Jefferson to Matt. The trio spent the evening reminiscing about the war and the leadership abilities of Abraham Lincoln and Jefferson Davis. Who was the better general, Grant or Lee? Why did Davis sack General Johnston during the crucial Atlanta campaign? They also talked about the more recent fighting in the Philippines, the war with Spain and America's growing presence in the Pacific.

The next day, they paid a visit to the Strawderman farm where Erasmus warmly greeted them. Matt told how he met Old Will during the winter of 1861-62 when the Confederate army occupied the region, bringing the secessionist military forces to the very gates of Washington. With a great deal of pride, Erasmus told how he had continued making fine whiskey by following the time-honored recipe handed down in the family from George Washington's time.

Erasmus led the group to a tree-choked ravine that ran down the steep hillside and emptied into Little Rocky Run. There, neatly hidden among the dense second growth trees, was the whiskey still he had been continually improving over the years. It was a gleaming, all copper affair composed of a cooker which was over three feet in height and four feet in diameter. A copper cap which terminated in a long, downward slanting tube fit into the neck of the cooker. A copper coil connected to the cap tube and ran into a barrel of cold water. Near the bottom of the barrel, the tube came out through the barrel wall.

Erasmus happily explained how the still worked. First, he mixed a mash composed of ground, unsprouted, rye or corn kernels with water in the mash barrels located near the still. After the mash steeped for a few days, a small amount of malt, made from ground, sprouted corn kernels was added to the mixture. After working for several more days, the mixture changed into a low-alcohol, fermented beverage similar to beer. This concoction was poured into the copper cooker and heated to a boil. The alcohol bearing steam rose in the cooker and collected under pressure on the inside of the copper cap. The pressurized steam passed from the cap through the elongated cap arm and into the "worm" as the copper coil was called in the whiskey-making trade. As the steam traveled through the coil, the cold water condensed the steam into a liquid. As a last step, Erasmus filtered the condensed liquor through a funnel filled with pieces of cloth and hickory charcoal to help remove impurities. After filtering through the funnel, the new moonshine whiskey went into a jug and was ready to go to market.

Erasmus waxed eloquent as he told his visitors that moonshining was legally defined as distilling liquor without paying federal excise taxes. Since these hated taxes had been imposed on and off by the government since the 1790s and continuously since 1865, Erasmus was following a tradition of whiskey tax avoidance as old as the Republic itself. Erasmus was proud that

Virginia was doing quite well in the business of illegal whiskey production. According to his lawyer, who had obtained the information from government revenue agents, the state ranked third in the nation as a moonshine producer.

After returning to the farm, the group sat on the porch sipping and testing a new batch of Strawderman's Finest. Erasmus began to talk about the fighting in the western theater of war and how the U.S. and Confederate governments tended to ignore operations in the west because they were obsessed with Richmond and Washington. After about an hour, the pleasant banter finally drifted back to Virginia. Elizabeth Sue spoke up, mentioning a lingering family mystery. She had an older brother who rode with Mosby's Rangers on and off for nearly two years. The family believed he was killed sometime during the war's last days, but had no information regarding where or when. It was very strange, his body was never found and he was never heard from again. He and two other men had completely disappeared from the face of the earth. Although the Yankees denied killing him, what else could have happened to him? Matt and Cyrus became quiet as she spoke. They realized Elizabeth Sue's brother was very likely one of the men they shot and buried not far from the farm on an early April day nearly fifty years ago. The passage of so much time helped make it a little easier to eat the food prepared by the sister of a man they killed in order to protect the secret of Secretary Benjamin's boxes. General Sherman was certainly correct when he said war was hell. Matt wondered if the general had ever faced a situation like this.

After seeing Jefferson off on the train, Matt and Cyrus talked about the sad situation they found themselves in. It would be impossible for them to explain how Elizabeth Sue's brother died and disappeared without mentioning what they had been doing in Centreville during the closing days of the war. However much they would have liked to put her mind to rest, they could not do so. They would honor the oaths they had made long ago and remain silent. Although the principals were dead and the war was fast fading from national memory, a man's word was still his bond. They would take the secret entrusted to them by the Confederate Secretaries of War and State with them to the grave. Elizabeth Sue would have to remain one of the many thousands of people who never learned of the final resting place of a loved one killed in the war. It was not an uncommon state of affairs for those who had lived through the brutal conflict of 1861-65.

On rented horses, the two old men rode across the land they had last visited nearly a half century ago while in the service of the Confederacy. Farmers had knocked down many of the smaller earthworks and filled many of the trenches as they struggled to get the fields back into production. Many of the reference points noted when they prepared the location map in 1865 had disappeared by 1911, eroded by nature or removed by the hand of man. A tangled second growth of timber now covered many of the hillsides. As a result of the changes to the land, Matt and Cyrus were unable to find any trace of the magazine in which they had hidden two boxes. Benjamin's secret papers would remain secure for ever. Awash in their sad memories, they retraced their route in reverse as far as Chapman's Mill. There, the stream continued to plunge through the rocks as it had done in 1865. The mill had been restored to working condition around 1870 by Robert Beverly and was now known as Beverley's mill. The workers at the mill were amused by sight of the two old men wandering around the grounds talking about the war and trying to remember the words to a poem they had once known so well.

March 1952

When Matt Chambon died in 1915, his indispensable walking stick went into the coffin with him. No one thought to closely examine the stick he had used as an aid for as long as anyone could remember. He was buried with the full military honors due an officer of the Confederate States army. Dr. Cyrus Bellnapp, the Negro doctor famous for work on controlling infection and disease, died in 1923. As the doctor lay on his deathbed, his mind wandered back to drills he executed as an soldier on Richmond's Capitol Square. He talked of killing men in the Shenandoah Valley and traveling with a lieutenant colonel whose name could not be understood by those at his bedside. The final rendition Cyrus made of his Civil War experiences was dismissed by his family members as the hallucinations and ramblings of a dying old man. Everyone knew Dr. Bellnapp had worked at Chimborazo Hospital during the Civil War. No one had any knowledge of his service in the Confederate Army, so his last statements were not believed. They must have been about someone else he knew, possibly a long forgotten old friend. Dr. Bellnapp's picture was hung in one of the buildings of the Ohio State University's medical school. The students rushing down the corridor hardy gave it or the other pictures of medical pioneers a glance. They were too busy worrying about the present to have time to delve into the past.

On March 12, 1952, James A. Hard died at Rochester New York at the age of 111. He was the last combat soldier of the Civil War who had participated in the battles of First and Second Manassas, having served in a New York regiment. His death erased the last living connection to the fighting which had once swirled around Manassas and Centreville and the time when soldiers marched on the turnpike. He was also the last soldier who had seen the majestic Confederate fortification line around Centreville when it was in the national news.

March 1998

In January 1997, earth moving equipment excavating the site of a new McDonald's restaurant on Route 28 southwest of the old village of Centreville uncovered several sets of human remains. Construction work was halted as excited burial excavators painstakingly uncovered the rediscovered graves of an unknown number of Civil War dead. Onlookers flocked to the site to watch as bones, fragments of clothing, bullets and buttons were uncovered. Once collected, the remains were sent to the Smithsonian Institution in Washington for analysis. The Smithsonian experts confirmed the human remains were those of Civil War era soldiers, but no positive identification of the individuals or their military unit could be made. Although the local newspapers ran several stories covering the details of the historical find, it was not the first time graves had been uncovered in the area during construction. The location of many of the Confederate graves from the 1861-62 period had been forgotten by the end of the war. With information as to location no longer available, many of them were overlooked by the recovery crews that gathered the bodies for reburial in the years after the cessation of hostilities. The new restaurant was scheduled to serve the rapidly growing northern Virginia suburbs of the nation's capital. It was being constructed on the same field Lieutenant Colonel Chambon and Sergeant Bellnapp used to bury the five men they had shot and killed in 1865. The experts' estimate of the date of burial was nearly accurate, it was off by a mere three years.

In March 1998, Bob Vargo was excavating a trench for a new water line with his back hoe. The line was for a new house under construction on the ridge overlooking the valley of Little Rocky Run. During his years of working construction, Bob had learned to keep an eye out for artifacts as his machine pulled up the soil. There was a good market for old bottles, cooking utensils and military equipment. Two weeks ago, a friend of his had uncovered an odd-shaped bottle and almost tossed it away. Instead, he had the good sense to take it home. When he took it to an antique appraiser, it turned out to be from the Revolutionary War era and worth a $100. Every now and then Bob came across something of value. Civil War belt buckles brought him good money, as did insignia. He had found an untold number of bullets, two artillery shells and a cannon ball during the previous four days. Bob's collector instinct told him he was working an area that may have been an artillery position at some time during the Civil War. He was sure the items he uncovered would bring a nice price when he sold them to one of the dealers in military memorabilia he did business with on occasion.

Not long before quitting time, as he was ditching through the clay and shale on the reverse slope of the hill, Bob's hoe bucket suddenly stuck a mass of stones of all shape and sizes. When the hoe brought up fragments of old planks, Bob slowed down the machine because he knew he had dug into something man made. Working slowly and carefully, Bob's eyes widened as he saw a tarred box emerge along with the rocks in his hoe bucket two scoops later. Gently lowering the bucket, he shut off the machine and jumped down to examine his find. It was a box wrapped in material and sealed with pitch to waterproof it. Grabbing a shovel from the assortment of hand tools carried on the machine, he slid into the trench and, after a short dig, found a second box buried among the rocks. He dug it out, set it beside the first one and covered both with a tarp to conceal them from the prying eyes of passersby. The pitch covered boxes looked like they had once belonged on a ship because they had an unmistakable nautical look about them. What were they doing buried out here, miles from the ocean? Bob restarted the machine and dug through the remainder of the rock filled space, but found nothing but another rusty old artillery shell. After looking at the site again, Bob figured he had found an old a root cellar that had been dug into the hillside many years ago. Someone had carefully stored the two boxes in it and sealed the entrance. As he hurriedly parked the hoe for the night, Bob excitedly muttered to himself, "Whoever did it, hauled a lot of stones to make sure the boxes were well protected. There has got to be something valuable inside these old crates. Why else would someone have gone through all the trouble to hide and protect them?" He loaded his find into the bed of his pick up truck. He would open them in the privacy of his garage after supper. Bob drove home being careful to stay within the speed limit. He didn't want any cops nosing around his truck on this his day of days.

Bob had no intention of damaging the contents as he carefully cut through the musty box wrappings. Tucked inside one of the outer folds he found a note written on what looked to be a piece of old wallpaper. It read: "In obedience to orders, two boxes were stored in magazine number 11 on (smudged) April 1865. Matthew F. Chambon, Lt. Col., CSA, Cyrus Bellnapp, Sgt., CSA." Bob was elated. He had seen enough Civil War artifacts to know that CSA meant either Confederate States Army or the Confederate States of America. Since the note had been signed by two soldiers, he took it for granted to be the army designation. He carefully put the note aside because original letters and written materials had been selling well lately. He might be able to get $25 for the scrap of paper with its handwritten note of long ago.

There was nothing else of value in the three layers of box wrappings he removed. The coverings were made from a type of canvas or rubberized cloth which had stuck together, making it miserable stuff to work with. On the top of the fourth layer, Bob found something which might be valuable. It was the seal of the Confederate States of America strategically placed over the spot where the folds of cloth overlapped. The seal was still readable. Bob could see George Washington astride a horse in the seal's center, surrounded by a circle of grains or fruit. Around the edge of the seal were the words "The Confederate States of America February 1862." At the bottom of the seal were two Latin or Greek words: "Deo Vindice" which Bob didn't understand. He carefully cut away the section of cloth surrounding the seal on each box. A collector might pay a $100 or more for the pair.

One of the box lids had "C. S. Laboratory Richmond" stenciled on it. Bob thought that might make it valuable because it was a storage box for some type of military material. He removed a quantity of old documents and lists before he hit pay dirt near the bottom. His eyes nearly popped out of his head when he found a 44 caliber, six shot, army model Colt revolver in its original factory wrappings. Bob knew a great deal about the value of old firearms because he attended two or three antique gun shows a year. Just to be sure his find was the real McCoy, he checked his reference books. The marks on the revolver matched those listed. On the revolver's barrel was: "Sam'l Colt, Hartford, Ct." On the cylinder: "Colt Patent number 1605." On the pistol frame: "Colt's Patent." The revolver was probably worth close to $20,000 in its like new condition. The army model Colt had been the principal revolver of the Union army. Over 300,000 were manufactured by the Colt Company during the course of the Civil War and sold to the government at a cost of $17.69 each.

Anyone with a basic knowledge of firearms knew that Colonel Samuel Colt revolutionized the American handgun industry when he developed his revolver. Unfortunately for the Union war effort, Sam Colt died suddenly at the age of 48 in January 1862. However, his firm was able to continue its vital wartime weapons production as Colt's able assistant, Mr. Elisha K. Root took over the management of the company. In addition to revolver production, Colt contracted with the U.S. government to manufacture long arms. Colt sold 7,000 of its unique repeating rifle to federal units. The company also manufactured 75,000 Springfield single shot muskets under government contact. Another 40,000 Springfield muskets were manufactured under subcontracts from other firms. On February 5, 1864 a fire of unknown origin destroyed one of the main buildings at Colt's Hartford, Connecticut production complex. It was believed to have been set by Confederate spies seeking to sabotage Colt's arms production. Bob began to wonder why a new Colt revolver was in a box of documents that belonged to the Confederate government.

The second box yielded more documents and another Colt revolver. Still in its wrappings with the contact number and inspection stamps, Bob found a model 1861, 36 caliber, Colt navy revolver. Its barrel was marked: "Address Col. Sam'l Colt, New York, U.S. of America." Because of its mint condition, Bob figured it might be worth more than the army model because fewer of the 36 caliber pistols had been produced. His curiosity and greed being aroused, Bob began to read some of the unpacked documents covering the top of his workbench. He was stunned by what he discovered. During the Civil War, approximately 8,000 of the navy Colts and 35,000 of the army model had been purchased from the Colt company by fictitious firms headed by Northern industrialists sympathetic to the Confederacy. The phony firms were paid double the purchase price by the Confederate government when the smuggled weapons reached the South.

The arsenals of the Confederacy copied the successful Colt design as they established manufacturing facilities to produce revolvers. Plagued by a severe shortage of raw materials, the Confederate production effort was aided by ring of spies who covertly purchased barrels, cylinders, main springs, butt plates and other components stolen from the Colt works and smuggled to the South. The clandestine weapons purchasing program, theft ring and sabotage effort were controlled by Judah P. Benjamin's Confederate Secret Service. Bob read a chilling report from a Confederate agent confirming Confederate government involvement in the sabotage of the Colt factory. Richmond had not been pleased when only one building was destroyed by the fire. Bob saw another report indicating that the already ailing Samuel Colt may have been poisoned by adulterated medicine slipped into his home by a Confederate agent.

The next day, Bob took the revolvers to a friendly antique arms appraiser. The dealer had never seen two revolvers in such excellent condition and didn't believe Bob's story of finding them buried in the ground. He gave Bob a receipt for the pistols, telling him it would take another day to research the records and establish the market value of the weapons. As a matter of routine, he called the police to inquire if any antique revolvers had been recently reported stolen. The police had no theft report, but their interest in the matter was aroused when Bob Vargo's name was mentioned. Police records indicated Bob had been arrested twice during the past five years for digging up artifacts without the permission of land owners. The first incident, on private property near the Wilderness battlefield, resulted in Bob paying a $250 fine and receiving a suspended ten day jail sentence. The second incident on the National Park Service's Manassas battlefield, resulted in Bob doing 20 days jail time and paying a $1,000 fine. Bob had also been detained on suspicion of car theft, but no charges were filed. He had also been arrested twice for assaults stemming from fights in local bars.

For two years Bob worked in the building materials department of the Fairfax Home Depot. One day while not paying attention to what he was doing, he drove too fast around an outside corner of the building on a forklift loaded with 4' by 8' sheets of drywall. Bob slammed into a customer's truck, sending the heavy sheets of drywall flying in all directions. The forklift and the customer's vehicle sustained major damage and the drywall was ruined. Because the police could not prove beyond a shadow of a doubt that Bob started the fight they were called to break up, the assault charges against both parties were reduced to disturbing the peace. A local newspaper reporter, who happened to be passing by, got a good picture of the two men flailing away at each other amid the ruined drywall. The story and picture made page one of the next day's edition. The trial judge, not amused by the explanations offered by the pugilists, fined them $500 each and gave them a 30-day jail sentence which was suspended on the condition they keep out of trouble for the next six months. Despite Bob's self-serving protestations that it had been an accident, he was fired from his job. The probationary period resulting from the brawl in the Home Depot parking had not expired. If Bob was found to be involved in any wrong-doing in his revolver acquisitions, he would go to jail. The police, suspecting another theft from a federal park, informed the FBI which agreed to look into the matter.

"Greed is a bottomless pit which exhausts the person in an endless effort to satisfy the need without ever reaching satisfaction."

-Erich From, 1941

When Bob returned to the appraiser, he learned his two revolvers would probably bring over $50,000 at auction because they were specimens of a quality rarely seen in the market in recent times. The final selling price could easily go higher if the collecting community was informed of the uniqueness of the revolvers in advance of the auction date. Upon hearing the good news, Bob gladly paid the $100 appraisal fee and headed for the door, appraisal report and revolvers in hand.

As he prepared to enter his car, two FBI agents flashed their identification and politely asked if they could trouble him for a moment of his time. After reviewing the documents lying around Bob's garage, the agents turned him over to the local police with the suggestion he be held as a suspect in a possible case of grand theft and/or attempted sale of stolen property. Bob's probation was revoked and he found himself locked in the Fairfax County jail awaiting the results of the investigation.

Things might yet work out because he had been lawfully engaged in his work when he uncovered the boxes. This time there was no question of trespassing or digging without the owner's permission. As the finder, was Bob entitled to claim the documents and pistols? Although he might have to share the profits from the sale, he felt certain he would be entitled to a big part of the find because he had dug them up. Of course, that determination would have to wait until the cops were satisfied Bob had not stolen the goods from someone and planted them in the trench. Bob didn't mind being in jail for a few days while the case was resolved because the sheets were clean and the food was tolerable. His boss would be understanding because Bob was not the first member of the construction crew to land in jail. He might lose a few days pay, but his job would be waiting for him upon release. While Bob sat in his cell, the Colt revolvers and Confederate documents were sent by the FBI to the Smithsonian Institution for analysis and ownership tracing.

The Smithsonian analysts traced the Colt revolvers through the contract data packed with the revolvers and found the weapons had been sold by the Colt company to fulfill contracts with firms alleged to have contracts to arm and equip troops being raised by a number of Northern state governments. However, no record of delivery of the revolvers to any Northern federal, state, militia or law enforcement agency could be found. While cross checking records, enough of the serial numbers appeared on Union army inventory lists of captured or surrendered pistols to give the analysts a good indication the missing revolvers had ended up in the hands of the Confederate army. The analysts concluded the revolvers were bought from Colt under fraudulent contracts let by unscrupulous Northern businessmen who then smuggled the weapons to the Confederacy and pocketed a handsome profit for their troubles. The business and commercial enterprises of these unsuspected war profiteers prospered in the years after the Civil War. The descendants of the clandestine arms smugglers now included many of the big current donors to the Republican and Democratic parties in the northeast United States.

Suspicions that John Brown waged his campaign of terror with financing provided by Northern abolitionists also proved to be true. Benjamin's agents had uncovered evidence of the eight wealthy Northerners who had funded Brown's murderous attacks in Kansas. When Brown's raid on the federal arsenal at Harpers Ferry failed, his financial backers ran for cover. None of the contributors attended the hanging of John Brown at Charles Town, Virginia on December 2, 1859, although they did pay for his defense lawyers. In attendance at Brown's execution were other men who would soon leave their mark upon American history, among them were a Virginia Military Institute professor named Thomas J. Jackson and John Wilkes Booth, a noted actor.

"Man's mind is so formed that it is far more susceptible to falsehood than to truth."

-Desiderius Erasmus, 1509

Other documents revealed how the Confederacy hoped to achieve by political means what it had not been able to do by force of arms. Benjamin's operatives sought to influence the outcome of the Northern election in 1864 and send the hated Lincoln down to political defeat. They planted stories about the U.S. President's desire to destroy the constitutional basis of the national government, his being under the influence of a cabal of fanatical abolitionists and Lincoln's total lack of concern for the number of men his incompetent generals got killed on the battlefield. The rumor was also planted that Lincoln's preoccupation with the slavery issue was due to the large percentage of Negro blood cursing through the evil man's veins.

Anyone who spoke against Lincoln or printed articles denouncing the debased president who sent thousands of Northern boys to be slaughtered in a war they could not win, received Confederate funding. Agitators stirred up mobs of workers with tales of how Lincoln planned to enrich his industrialist friends by allowing free Negroes from the South to come North and drive down the wages paid northern workers. Funds were also provided to those who argued Lincoln had trampled on the Constitution when he denied the Confederate States the right to leave the Union.

There was a wealth of information in Benjamin's extensive files regarding the sums of money paid those who worked for Lincoln's defeat. One Indiana agitator listed on the Confederate payroll stumped southern Ohio, Indiana and Illinois denouncing Lincoln and his failed war policies in speech after speech. He always ended his fiery anti-Lincoln tirades with: "It's time to stop the senseless killing and let the South go. Bring our boys home." The analysts burst into gales of laughter when they discovered the man hell-bent on destroying the Lincoln presidency was related to several modern mid-western politicians who were well known for their use of Lincoln quotations in their speeches.

Based on the number of Southerners claiming to have had an ancestor who fought with General Robert E. Lee all the way to the final surrender at Appomattox, the analysts concluded Lee must have had 100,000 men with him at the time of his surrender. This figure was a good deal higher than the less than 30,000 names of soldiers paroled from the Army of Northern Virginia in April 1865. The mammoth list containing the names of over 150,000 Confederate deserters that Judah P. Benjamin had placed in one of the boxes, now gave the Smithsonian analysts another reason for merriment. It was evident from the records that a large number of modern Southerners who proudly boasted of their Confederate heritage had conveniently forgotten that their revered ancestor was in actuality a deserter. A number of U.S. senators and members of the House of Representatives were going to be humbled when the public learned that the Civil War family hero had deserted the dying Confederate cause. An additional large number claiming to be related to Confederate colonels, majors and captains were not going to be pleased to learn that the actual rank held by their distinguished ancestor was private or corporal. "This is proof positive that family memory has a wonderful ability to enhance the facts as time goes by," one of the analysts said to his coworkers as he began to cross check a computerized list.

The Confederate Secret Service smuggled bombs disguised as lumps of coal onto Union ships. When the bomb was shoveled into the ship's boiler, it exploded, setting the ship afire and maybe to the bottom of the sea. The pattern of espionage, political manipulation, bank robbery and sabotage outlined by Benjamin's documents led the analysts to believe that perhaps President Carter should not have restored U.S. citizenship to Jefferson Davis. Although there was no evidence of a direct order to John Wilkes Booth to assassinate President Lincoln, it was clear Booth worked at times for the secret service. Davis had fought savagely to destroy the Union, using every tool at his disposal. He failed only because his limited resources permitted him no wider field of action. Even so, Davis and Benjamin had come very close to success in the summer of 1864. If General Sherman had not taken Atlanta, Lincoln would have lost the election and been replaced by a president pledged to end the war by giving the South its independence. The Benjamin document collection dispelled any illusions the analysts harbored about the Civil War. It had not been a romantic adventure. It was a war waged by opponents who fought ruthlessly with all the means at their disposal, honorable and dishonorable.

May 1998

"In politics, what begins in fear usually ends in folly."
-Samuel Taylor Coleridge, 1830

Word of the work being done on the Civil War document hoard at the Smithsonian began to leak out. A bipartisan group of powerful Washington lawmakers interested in protecting themselves and their large campaign contributors from ridicule and embarrassment decided to bring the project to closure. Once it became clear to the bipartisan group that both well-placed Democrats and Republicans would suffer a degree of humiliation when the documents were made public, it was jointly agreed that this was not the proper time to embarrass members of the current administration, Congress and political donors with the truth about their forefathers' tawdry exploits. Why should anyone be interested in reading the names on a Confederate list of prominent Northern people opposed to Abraham Lincoln's Emancipation Proclamation?

The dredging up of derogatory facts regarding the shady dealings of the ancestors of many of modern America's political and financial elite was not the politically correct thing to be doing, even if it was historically accurate. Political contributors, whose family and business histories were disparaged in the research done in a government facility, could not be expected continue to make large political contributions. The lawmakers didn't want to be placed in the position of besmirching the reputation of a person's ancestors and then having to ask the insulted man or woman to contribute $5,000 at a fund raising dinner. Corporations were also extremely touchy about image issues. Contributions might dry up if the information in the Benjamin documents cast unflattering aspersions on the activities of the precursors of many of America's most politically active businesses. Of course, if the damaging historical information had only affected members of one political party, the situation would have been different. The research findings would have been announced with all possible fanfare by the party suffering no harm. That was the way Washington politics worked in the late 1990s.

Since members of both parties had a great deal at stake, the situation had to brought under control quietly and quickly and by someone who had the trust of the Washington establishment. The one person who could get the job done was the savvy, powerful, lobbyist Leon Placke. Armed with a letter of authorization from the Congressional Committee on Research, Placke swept

173

into the Smithsonian and took charge of the project. "It's too bad this information affects the members of both parties. It would have made great material to leak to the press," Leon said to no one in particular as he read the analysts' reports. Leon had no doubt that the analysts had done a thorough job. The documents were authenticated by tests run on the paper and ink. They were part of the records of the Confederacy. No similar documents existed in library archives because the majority of Rebel records were destroyed as the Confederate government abandoned Richmond. The analysts had sorted the documents, indexed and summarized the contents on computer disks. Leon smiled as he read the summaries. They contained a great deal of delectable information which, if made public, would deflate many egos of the first families of American politics and embarrass more than a few major U.S. corporations.

Leon knew the three analysts working on the project had been a little too talkative. Their discussions with their friends had alerted powerful politicians to the potential problem contained in the Benjamin papers. As a matter of law, Leon knew the analysts could not be charged with a violation of the security statutes because the documentary materials they were reviewing were over 100 years old. Another way had to be found to ensure the trio of analysts kept silent. So Leon stretched the truth a little. In a meeting with them, he stressed the need to keep the research findings under wraps because of the risk of upsetting delicate discussions currently underway with certain unnamed foreign governments. The junior analysts were so honored to be in the presence of the awesome Mr. Placke that they believed his every word. As a reward for their promise of silence in this grave matter of national honor, one analyst was sent to the United Kingdom and two to France for six weeks to the study the Confederacy's overseas shipbuilding program. At first, the director of the Smithsonian had balked at Leon's suggestion that the analysts be sent to Europe on what was obviously nothing more than an all expenses paid vacation. Within fifteen minutes after Leon had departed his office, the director received three icy calls from congresspersons involved with the institution's budget. They strongly hinted in no uncertain terms it would be wise for him to change his mind. The shaken director quickly reversed himself and approved the travel funds. Leon Placke had proved once again that he was not a man to be trifled with.

Leon turned next to the problem of Bob Vargo who was being held on suspicion of grand theft in the Fairfax County jail. While it was true the law was somewhat unclear as to the ownership of the two containers of valuable historical artifacts that Vargo had discovered, Leon's keen legal mind focused on broader matters. With the actual possession of an object being nine-tenths of the law, Leon felt he could beat back any legal challenge to the right of ownership because he had the boxes and their contents in his custody. The issue to be resolved revolved around Vargo because the man had seen too much. Like the analysts, the back hoe operator was going to have to be silenced. Leon thought about the matter for the better part of an hour, outlining his objectives and talking points on a yellow legal pad. Then he made three phone calls.

Everyone in a position of power in Washington knew the rules of protocol. Calls from the President, cabinet secretaries, members of Congress, supreme Court judges and Mr. Leon Placke were always answered immediately. They were never to be put on hold under any circumstances. The strange part of the protocol rule was that Leon Placke had no position of authority in the United States Government. He was the owner of a lobbying and public relations firm, half owner of a litigation support firm, and had a sizable stake in two political polling firms.

Bob Vargo was grateful to be out of jail. The nice man from an unnamed national security agency gave him a ride home, chatting all the time about his interest in Civil War arms and how the government wanted to reward Bob for his remarkable discovery. Bob was cautioned not to discuss the matter with anyone else. He would be driven to a meeting at the U.S. Department of Commerce at 1:30 p.m. the next afternoon. Bob was told to wear a coat and tie because he would be meeting very important people on a major issue of national significance.

The car picked Bob up at his home on schedule. About 20 minutes later, the vehicle entered Washington heading east on Constitution Avenue. The car made a left turn on 15th Street, made a right on Pennsylvania, another right on 14th Street, stopping in front of the main entrance of the Department of Commerce. Bob was told to go inside and proceed to room 2029B. Inside the building, Bob admired the ornate ceiling as he headed for the security desk. The building had been built before the Great Depression and had once been the largest federal office building in Washington. The security guard checked his driver's license and waved him through the metal detector. Another guard waiting on the inside of the detector said: "We have been expecting you Mr. Vargo. Please follow me."

They moved quickly across the shinny marble floor through a display touting government international trade programs and up the stairs to the second floor. Turning right after opening a heavy metal fire door, they moved down a long poorly lit hallway. Bob noticed a sign denoting the Office of Africa and another for the Office of South Asia as they passed the doorways of darkened offices. Near the end of the hallway, they came to room 2029B.

A large, expensive looking sign on the door indicated the room was the home of the Bureau of Historical Research. "You are expected, please go right in." said the guard as he opened the door.

As Bob stepped inside, a man came forward saying, "Mr. Vargo, I am delighted to make your acquaintance. My name is Leon Placke." He grabbed Bob's arm and shook hands. Mr. Placke introduced his colleagues as Mr. Fred Jones and Mr. Ron Smith, as they moved to take their seats at a conference table. Bob became a bit suspicious because Jones and Smith looked more like cops than historians. And Placke looked more like a high-priced lawyer than the head of a research bureau. The maps on the office walls indicated the place may have had more to do with the oil trade between the U.S. and the Middle East than historical research. Bob was smart enough not to ask prying questions when he sensed the law was around, so he made no comment other than introducing himself.

After they were seated, Leon Placke got right to the point. "Mr. Vargo how and where did you find two such fine examples of Civil War era revolvers?"

"The lawyer's truth is not truth, but consistency or a consistent expediency."

-Henry David Thoreau, 1849

Bob's suspicion that Placke was really a lawyer was confirmed when Placke pulled a yellow legal pad out of his briefcase. Bob also noticed the bulges under the coats of Smith and Jones, a good indication they were carrying arms. Bob did not want to create a big problem for himself with an unknown federal agency. So he answered truthfully, "I was digging a trench for a water line with my back hoe when I hit a pocket of stones and found the two boxes buried among the stones."

"Were the revolvers in the boxes?"

"Yes, there was one in each box."

"When did you open the containers?"

"Not until after I got home from work that night."

"Did anyone else see you take the boxes?"

"No. There was no one around when I loaded them in my truck."

"Did anyone else see you as you opened the boxes?"

"No. I was alone in my garage. No one was there but me."

"What else did you find?"

"A big batch of old Confederate government papers, reports, lists, things like that."

"Anything else?"

"There were two Confederate seals on the box lids. I cut them off."

"Did you read all the documents?"

"Only a few of them. There was some interesting stuff about spies and agents and a lot of political things that I didn't have time to read."

"As I see it Mr. Vargo, you could have a serious problem maintaining ownership of the pistols and documents. Under the laws of the Commonwealth of Virginia, which is where you found the property, the owner of the land may have a right to it. Also, your employer might be able to press a claim since you were digging the trench as part of your job. How long do you think it would take to settle a case of disputed ownership in the courts?"

"I don't have any idea. I have never been to court for a civil matter. When I go, it's because the cops drag me in. "

"It could take over a year and cost you $25,000 in legal costs. Justice may be blind in the United States, but it doesn't come free. Would you be interested in a cash settlement for your rights to the Civil War goods, if you got the money right away?"

Vargo thought a moment before replying, "I might be interested. How much are you offering?"

"Let me explain the deal first, so you understand the terms," Leon said. "You sign over to us all your rights to the boxes and their contents. We get the revolvers and documents and assume the risk of any court battle with other parties claiming an interest in the find. How does that sound?"

"Sounds fair to me if the price is right"

"If you agree to the terms we are offering today, I am authorized to give you a check for $50,000. But you must accept our offer immediately."

Bob nearly fell out of his chair. He was being offered 50 big ones for the right to items he no longer had in his possession. They were the same things for which he had been tossed into jail because the cops thought he stole them. He did not hesitate a second before responding to Mr. Placke, "You have got yourself a deal. Boxes, pistols, seals, wrappings and all for $50,000."

"Good, we have an agreement then. Ron, please loan Mr. Vargo your pen. He has a number of documents to sign," said Mr. Placke as he handed Bob a cashiers check and pulled a stack of forms from his expensive briefcase. Bob pretended not to notice the logo on the pen Ron had given him. It read: "Economic Analysis Section, Central Intelligence Agency." As Mr. Placke handed him the forms, Bob quickly wrote the number of the phone on the table on the palm of his hand.

Bob signed a document called a quit claim agreement in which he sold his interest in the artifacts. Next was a nondisclosure agreement. In it, he agreed not to divulge the price he received. The last document was an agreement to protect research property rights pledging Bob to silence. Under no circumstances could he discuss any facet of the transaction, the sale or how he found the items. The terms were stiff. If he violated the agreement, he forfeited the $50,000 and was liable for all financial damages. The trio spent over two hours making sure Bob clearly understood the implications of everything he was signing. Bob had no intention of violating any of the terms because he had a feeling one of these guys would kill him and not really brother with taking him to court.

After Bob departed, Leon thanked Fred and Ron for their assistance and took the sign on the door down. Leon returned to his office and placed labels on the government storage containers holding the two antique boxes of Confederate memorabilia. The containers were to remain sealed for 20 more years. Leon called the guards and sent the containers to the classified document section of the National Archives. As the containers left the building, Leon made phone calls to senior lawmakers from each party, stating the matter had been taken care of.

Having completed the task assigned him, Leon felt the need for a little relaxation, so he went to the Four Seasons Hotel to attend the party given for George Stephanapolous. George had served in President Clinton's inner circle and his unflattering book about the President had gone on sale in the bookstores this morning. George had landed a good job as an ABC political analyst and was going to make several million dollars from the sales of his book. Leon had no problem with the concept. Get into government, learn a few things that had a big payoff, get out of government and cash in. Leon was the most successful practitioner of that art the city of Washington had ever seen. Leon would not stay too long at the reception, just long enough to have a couple of drinks, a few bites to eat and see and be seen as he caught up on the political gossip. It would be interesting to see how many of George's former friends from the White House dared to show up.

After depositing the check, curiosity got the better of Bob Vargo. He called the number he had written on his hand during the meeting. A voice answered, "Office of the Near East."

Bob asked if the phone number was for the Bureau of Historical Research. "No such organization on this floor," said the voice at the other end of the line. "This is an international trade office at the Commerce Department. You probably dialed the number incorrectly. We don't have anything to do with historical research here. We deal strictly with economics and trade matters." Bob thanked the person for her trouble and hung up.

For the life of him, he could not figure out why a collection of old Civil War relics was so important that someone would go through the trouble of setting up a phony office just to fool him. Bob shrugged as he looked at the deposit slip. Whatever the reason, it made no difference. He had the money and his lips were sealed. There had been enough hints dropped at the meeting to let Bob know the consequences of breaking his agreement to keep silent would be more serious than a lawsuit. He knew that Fred Jones or Ron Smith would probably kill him if he so much as uttered a world about the pistols or documents he had discovered. Bob could tell by the sinister look in Mr. Placke's eyes that the man was not above ordering him murdered for the slightest infraction of the agreement.

Leon was annoyed by the overreaction in high places to the revelations contained in the Benjamin papers. He thought his friends in Congress had misjudged the matter completely. They should have ignored the matter and let the information go public. While it was true that a number of individuals, families and corporations that generously funded American politics might be embarrassed at the shady Civil War era doings, the problem would have blown over quickly. There would have been no lasting damage done to the family and corporate reputations of America's rich and powerful. The historical affair would been great conversation on the cocktail circuit for a few weeks, and nothing more. The ongoing scandals of President Clinton and the failed impeachment, in Leon's opinion, had clouded the judgment of Washington's political elite. In their state of mental disarray, they made a big mountain out of the very minor Benjamin papers molehill.

The potential problem the lawmakers feared had offered Leon an opportunity to please a bipartisan group of very nervous people. It was a chit he could collect at a later date when he needed their help on a matter important to him. He had buried the sordid details of human failing during the Civil War for 20 more years. They would owe him for the service for a long, long time. Leon made a note in his weekly planner to read up on Mr. Benjamin. Judah Benjamin was a man who looked ahead, he played a shrewd game in the battles of life. Leon believed Benjamin had shown great foresight in sending the documents to Centreville. In the event he and other Confederate leaders were brought to trial, Benjamin would have really made a fight of it. As Benjamin defended himself against the charge of treason, his voluminous document file would have enabled him to force a number of influential Northerners to come to his aid. Leon liked that, it showed a real touch of political class.

Leon Placke was party to the secret that no member of either political party ever mentioned to the voters during an election campaign. The voters never seemed to notice both Republicans and Democrats tended to spend equal sums of money once they got into power in Washington. Conservatives spent as freely as liberals when it came to being President or a lawmaker in Congress. At its founding, the government of the United States expected much from its citizens. Government service was seen as a temporary hardship to be endured for the common good of all. It was an interruption that dedicated individuals made in their lives, often at great personal cost. In the old days, a role in the management of national affairs often came at great personal sacrifice. Now it was seen as a reward to be milked for all it was worth during one's stay in the capital.

Leon was not sure when the concept of government service changed. Somewhere along the way, he knew the federal government had become the world's largest dispenser of goods and services, with national interest groups locked in a never ending struggle over how to divide up the federal tax dollar pie. Government service had ceased to be a financial sacrifice. The time spent in an administration post or in Congress was amply rewarded when one left office. The concept of public service being a hardship was the great charade that the Washington power elite fobbed off on the gullible national electorate.

Bob Vargo, the man who discovered Benjamin's documents, was a good example. He was a typical American, probably believing everything he saw on TV. It would never dawn on Bob to question why George Stephanapolous, who had put in a few years on President Clinton's White House staff, would make more money in one year from his book sales than Bob would earn in a lifetime. Tedious people like Bob labored long and hard for their daily bread and served only one useful purpose. Every April 15, the 134 million Bobs in the American labor force paid taxes to keep the magnificent system going. The money flowed to Washington in a never ending stream at the rate of $1.8 trillion a year. To Leon's way of thinking, politics was nothing more than an argument over how the sizable chuck of tax money got divided up. Power in Washington sprang from one's ability to get one's hands into the federal budget pie and dole it out to friends and constituents.

"To administer is to govern: to govern is to reign."
-Comte de Mirabeau, 1749-91

Leon knew the system well and had every intention of continuing to profit handsomely from it. When Leon had come to Washington straight out of law school 25 years ago, Clark Clifford was the reigning champion of those who profited from government service. Clifford had been a special advisor to

President Truman from 1946-50, helping to arrange the speedy recognition of the state of Israel in 1948. Clifford worked on the creation of the Department of Defense, served as an advisor to President Kennedy and filled numerous other high government posts through the years. Between his stints of government service, Clifford made tons of money selling advice through his law practice. He was among the first in Washington to see the opportunity in offering the services of a former government official to clients who needed help in dealing with the government. Of course, the more complex things could be made, the larger the amount of help that could be sold.

Clifford played the ultimate Washington game of cultivating an image that defied reality as he crafted a reputation as a man who could do no wrong. Eventually, after Clifford became the Chairman of First American Bankshares things began to fall apart for him. In 1992, he was indicted on charges stemming from the fact that First American was secretly owned by a foreign bank that was prohibited from owning banks in the United States. With his reputation in shreds, Clifford slowly faded from the top rung of the Washington scene. Until his death at the age of 92 in October 1997, Clifford never admitted any wrongdoing. Leon admired Clifford's moneymaking abilities, but felt he had gone overboard in maintaining his innocence. After all, a keen attorney like Clifford could have been expected to check out an issue as important as bank ownership when he agreed to get involved in the deal.

Leon decided he had a great deal more respect for Judah Benjamin than for Clark Clifford. Benjamin had not whined when things had fallen apart. He didn't spill out his guts in interviews. He kept his mouth shut, keeping his secrets to himself, taking them with him all the way to the grave. Clifford, on the other hand, had refused to speak with a young attorney named Leon Placke when the newly-minted lawyer arrived in Washington. The long-dead Benjamin had recently given Leon a good degree of leverage over the nervous members of the current Congress. Clifford had given him the brush off and nothing more.

Early in his career, Leon found he possessed the ability to clearly see the strategic long-term ramifications of political decisions. His shrewd political sense soon came to the attention of members of Congress, many of whom would remain in his debt until they retired or went down to defeat in elections. At the time, the Social Security Administration was in hot water with the voters because it took many months to process the first check going to individuals qualified to collect social security payments. Checks also often got lost or were made out for an incorrect amount. When the frustrated recipient contacted a Social Security office to get a problem corrected, in many cases nothing happened for an additional six to eight months. As a result, Congress was bombarded with complaints from irritated constituents demanding the mess be fixed so Social Security recipients could be paid correctly and on time.

At a meeting, conferees from the Senate and the House agreed it was time to fund the long-needed upgrade of the Social Security Administration's obsolete computer system. As the technical specialists outlined the hardware and software improvements that would reduce processing time and virtually eliminate errors, Leon had the brilliant flash of insight that made him famous in the halls of Congress. After the technical presentation was completed, Leon put forth the argument that it would not be politically wise to remove all the glitches. Many times, the only contact a voter had with a member of Congress was when he or she was desperate enough to lodge a complaint about a Social Security payment problem. When the member of Congress quickly got the problem resolved, the elated voter told friends and neighbors about the assistance rendered. In short, the Congressperson's intervention ensured a vote during the next election and gave the member a grassroots issue to discuss when visiting the voters back home. Leon drove home the point that it was a good thing to be seen defending the retired voters' interests against the entrenched, incompetent bureaucrats in the Social Security Administration. Did the lawmakers really want to remove the source of so much political goodwill?

Leon's presentation was met with a long, stunned silence. The facial expressions of those seated around the table told him that some in the room were clearly appalled by his audacious proposal. The senators and congresspersons present fidgeted uncomfortably as they mentally digested the contents of Leon's political bombshell. As he sat with his hands folded waiting for a response, Leon knew his career was on the line. If he had misjudged the situation, he had just become a Washington non-person. His phone would never ring again and the calls he placed would never be answered. Without political access, he could not function and he would be forced to leave town.

Finally, the senior senator present spoke. He thanked Leon for his astute reading of the situation. He had brought up a key point that they all had overlooked. Behind closed doors, the bipartisan group quickly agreed that it would be foolish to eliminate 100 percent of the errors when the Social Security computer system was upgraded. A ten percent error rate was going to be maintained because, as Leon had so wisely pointed out, it was good for constituent contact. As Leon departed at the conclusion of the meeting, the other staff members eyed him with new respect. Leon Placke was now seen as a man destined to do big things in Washington. He knew how the political system worked.

Leon met John D. Ehrlichman once or twice when Ehrlichman was President Nixon's domestic affairs advisor. Leon thought Ehrlichman would make a name for himself in Washington after he left the White House. Ehrlichman could have easily become the next Clark Clifford of Washington's powerful lobbying community. Instead, Leon was stunned when Ehrlichman was sentenced to federal prison for 18 months for his part in the Watergate scandal. Disbarred as a lawyer, Ehrlichman never worked in Washington again. All the time Ehrlichman invested in managing Richard Nixon's presidential campaign and working at the White House went for nothing. When Leon heard Ehrlichman had died in Atlanta, he thought about the man's lost income potential. The Ehrlichman affair showed clearly that not everyone with brains and potential made it to the big money circle of influence peddlers. It was a risky business, similar to farming in many ways. There was so much that could go wrong if one wasn't careful. Being able to maintain a facade of legal deniability for much of what one did during the course of the business day was very important.

Leon was able to borrow the room at the Commerce Department for his meeting with Bob Vargo because he was well-known to the Secretary and Assistant Secretaries of Commerce. The Department managed the business-friendly programs utilized by many of Placke's corporate clients. There were programs to promote exports, block imports, issue export licenses and promote minority business development. With U.S. exports running at $931 billion per year and imports at nearly $1.1 trillion, American companies were willing to pay well to see to it that their interests were well represented during government policy-making deliberations. A small change in a law or regulation could have serious consequences for the affected firms. It could mean the difference between profit or loss, a major unwelcome change could lead to CEO job loss. Leon liked to look out for the vested interests of the big oil firms fighting restrictions on oil imports and the use of alternate power sources even though the U.S. was importing more than 50 percent of the oil it consumed. The big firms paid for Leon's services well and promptly. As he accepted their money, Leon saw the correctness of their position more clearly.

Maneuvering behind the scenes, Placke masterminded the deal in Congress placing the responsibility for licensing industrial exports in the Commerce Department. Business groups knew Commerce would be more lenient in the interpretation and enforcement of regulations than the Customs Bureau which had a reputation of being a tough enforcer. Although the political deal fragmented effective enforcement of the nation's export controls, it pleased the business groups that contributed cash at fund raising dinners held for members of Congress. Things got a bit dicey when much of the equipment used by Iraq in its weapon production program was discovered by weapons inspectors to have slipped through the porous U.S. licensing system. For a time after the Gulf War, it looked like Commerce might lose control of the licensing program as the enraged public learned the details of Iraq's clever circumvention of Commerce's disorderly licensing system. After a few months, however, the furor died down. Members of Congress, Leon Placke and American industry breathed a sigh of relief as things returned to normal.

Leon also represented firms importing/exporting agricultural equipment, consumer goods and industrial products in their maneuvers to influence the position the U.S. government would take on trade issues coming before the Geneva-based World Trade Organization. It was good, steady business. Backed by a staff of 20 highly-paid economists and trade specialists situated in his spacious offices on Washington's prestigious K Street, Leon created the high quality economic analyses needed to support his client's position in the continual struggle to influence the direction of U.S. policy. He also assisted firms such as General Dynamics when they moved to acquire rival Newport News Shipbuilding. Placke's cleverly worded competitive assessment of the impact of the merger on the industry might just be the guarantee needed to ensure government approval. As companies devoured each other in the competitive American marketplace of the late 1990s, Leon Placke made lots of money.

Placke enjoyed watching companies battle to increase their share of the global market because he earned a great deal of money by assisting their effort. As he pondered his financial success, Leon idly leafed through a report someone had sent him. The summary stated seven million people had been killed in wars during the 18th century. The total killed jumped to 19.4 million during the 19th century. With less than a year to run, 111 million had been killed in wars so far during the 20th century. Leon thought the report was an interesting piece of research work. Perhaps one of his friends in Congress might want to hold a hearing or sponsor a symposium on the issue. It would be a sure way to get the coveted 30 seconds of exposure on the evening news. The event would show the voters that the weighty issues of the world were being properly handled for them in Washington. Appearing on the news regularly made it a lot easier for a politician to win the next election. Leon knew a man who could certainly use the beneficial media exposure. He would give him a call on the war deaths idea.

"Oh, duty is what one expects from others, it is not what one does for oneself."

-Oscar Wilde, 1854-1900

Sometimes knowing the right people led to embarrassing situations. When John Huang was appointed as the Principal Deputy Assistant Secretary for International Economic Policy at the Commerce Department in December 1993, Leon Placke went out of his way to make John's acquaintance. The Washington rumor mill had Huang pegged as a good friend of both President Clinton and Vice President Gore. That meant John Huang had access to the center of political power and Leon wanted to be numbered among his friends. Leon had a couple publicity photographs of Mr. Huang and himself taken by a photographer and hung them in a prominent location in his outer office. His visitors could not help being impressed by the fact that Leon had access to the President's inner circle. For a time things went well. Mr. Hung worked on the issue of most favored nation trade status for China, but also spent an inordinate amount of his time at the White House. With virtually no notice, he transferred to the Democratic National Committee and went to work as a fund raiser for the 1996 campaign, raising over $3 million. Leon kept in contact with John, they did lunch now and then, and Leon sent two $1,000 contribution checks.

By May 1997, Leon realized he had made a bad investment of his time and money because John Huang was on the front page of the Washington papers. Part of the $3 million he raised for the Clinton campaign had come from illegal foreign business sources and had to be returned. Mr. Huang's ties with the Indonesian financial conglomerate, the Lippo Group, were also under investigation. With Indonesia doing over $8 billion a year in trade with the United States, it was quite possible that Huang had passed some sensitive U.S. government trade policy information to Lippo. From its powerful position in banking and trade, Lippo stood to profit enormously from advance warning of any trade action the U.S. government planned to undertake.

Leon raced to his office on the day the story broke and took down the Huang photographs. He never again mentioned his close ties to the man who met with President Clinton 15 times between 1993 and 1996. The knowledge that Mr. Huang had also visited the White House 94 times on other business during the same period was no longer a marketable asset for Leon. When the Huang name came up in conversation, he had been transformed from a close personal friend into a person Leon Placke barely knew and saw very rarely. Leon also righteously pointed out the need to improve the government's trade information security program. It was a shame that data vital to the economic well being of the United States was so poorly protected. Perhaps new laws to correct the problem needed to be considered by Congress. Leon graciously volunteered his time to help the committee staff draft a new regulation designed to prevent future abuse.

Cynics said the Commerce Department was a dumping ground for the political hacks of both parties. While it was true the Department had an inordinately large number of political appointees on its payroll, Leon considered them to be part of the necessary overhead cost of making American democracy function. Everyone in Washington knew it took a great deal of money and time to win elected political office in the 1990s. Many of the people who gave their time to work on campaigns wanted to be rewarded for their efforts after the candidate won. Both parties played by the same set of rules and a two/four stint at the Commerce Department meant the political appointee was entitled to two years on the federal payroll in a position paying $60,000 to $120,000 per year and was entitled to take four overseas trips at government expense. During the two years the incumbent filled the position, he or she was expected to use the time wisely and cultivate the contacts necessary to line up a job to follow the arduous tour of duty in Washington. The large majority of the real work to be done was always to delegated to the 10 to 20 civil servants assigned to assist the appointee. Both political parties thought it was a good system because it provided a training program enabling those who had worked hard for the current party in power to move into the economic mainstream while being subsidized by the taxpayers.

Leon heartily agreed that those who labored in the political trenches deserved the rewards. America's taxpaying masses, many of whom who did nothing more for the democratic process than cast a ballot on election day, were merely paying their fair share of the actual and necessary costs of the national election process. For the most part, Leon believed the faceless American multitude was composed of nothing more than selfish people living in bucolic neighborhoods. They were politically unsophisticated, having no interest in life other than the accumulation of consumer goods. Leon thought it proper and just that a portion of their tax dollars went to those who fought the war for control of the national political agenda. Those who labored in politics ought to be rewarded for the expenditure of their time. Leon kept a quote from Newt Gingrich in his desk that read: "The idea that a congressman would be tainted by accepting money from private industry or private sources is essentially a socialist argument." It summed up Leon's feelings on the matter; he believed America had the best government money could buy and saw nothing at all wrong with the current state of affairs in Washington, DC.

Although the system of rewarding the politically active had come under increasing attack in recent years, Leon believed it was still working fairly well. Early in the first Clinton administration, the practice of politicization rose to new heights as the Commerce Department launched a series of foreign trade missions and allocated many of the top slots on the trips to business executives who had donated generously to the Democratic Party. In the wake of the embarrassing John Huang affair, the procedure had to be curtailed somewhat. At his Senate confirmation hearings in January 1997, the incoming Secretary of Commerce, William M. Daley, made a pledge to refurbish the Department's reputation. Soon after taking office, Secretary Daley, with much fanfare and an extremely heavy heart, fired 40 political appointees. It was the first increment of the 156 political positions he was pledged to eliminate over time. It had been a good compromise. The Republicans in Congress wanted action to show they were controlling waste, but not too much. If the Republicans won the next election, it would be their loyal campaign workers who would be lining up at the employment and travel feedbag housed at the Department of Commerce. The Republicans weren't stupid enough to abolish a good thing and the Democrats respected them for it.

In the competitive political environment of Washington, there were always new players pushing onto center stage. Leon watched as Peter S. Knight, a longtime aide and chief-fund raiser to Vice President Al Gore, took his place in the spotlight. Leon was impressed at the speed by which Peter Knight moved. When the Middle East peace initiative was signed on the White House lawn in September 1993, Peter had jumped on the opportunity. He became a founding member of Builders for Peace, an American private sector initiative to support the Middle East peace effort. The goal of the organization was to facilitate private sector business development and employment opportunities in the Palestinian territories. When the business community failed to appreciate Peter's vision of the bountiful business deals to come and failed to donate funds to the project, Peter was undaunted. Using his connections, he pressured the Agency for International Development into making a $500,000 grant to the Commerce Department. Commerce turned the money around and gave Builders for Peace the money in the form of another grant. A retiring staff member from the White House was given the job as the organization's executive director. A former democratic congressman from California and the president of an Arab-American group were paid to travel around the country making speeches. Businesspersons

187

were also invited to attend the organization's conferences and dinners in Washington. The program continued for three years before the absence of any results made providing additional funding too politically risky. The participants had a good time while it lasted. Those involved with the Builders for Peace program had made a number of good contacts and had been seen in important places in Washington.

Mr. Knight went on to become chairman of the Clinton-Gore 1996 reelection campaign. Sometime after the election victory gave President Clinton and Vice President Gore a second term, Mr. Knight was paid $1 million for unspecified legal and consulting work by a Tennessee land developer. There was a congressional investigation, but there was no proof that any of the campaign contributors had been helped by Mr. Knight in their quests for new federal business.

One of Knight's associates, Nathan Landow, had gotten the Cheyenne-Arapaho Indians of Oklahoma to contribute $107,000 to the Democratic National Committee. Landow was rumored to be developing a consulting contract paying him a ten percent commission for his efforts to help the tribe obtain the return of their tribal lands from the federal government. Leon was impressed with the ingenious nature of the arrangement because he knew the Clinton administration was accused in a class action civil law suit of mismanaging billions of dollars in trust funds held for Native Americans. There was no doubt about it, Mr. Knight was a brassy and bold rising star, a good person to know. Peter Knight was plowing new ground in the fertile financial consulting fields of Washington.

January 1999

It ever was decreed, Sir,
If a lawyer's hand is fee'd, Sir,
He steals your whole estate.

-John Gay, 1685-1732

Leon sat at his desk flipping through a thick batch of reports. The first one he looked at concerned the illegal drug trade. With drugs accounting for eight percent of the value of world trade, the illegal drug business had an annual turnover of $400 billion. Leon thought it was a lot of money, a good tidbit to remember for future cocktail conversations. Mentioning the mind-boggling statistic would show his genuine interest in the problems of society. The next report concerning the campaign spending reported to the Federal Election Commission was of more interest to him. The Republican National Committee received $70 million in contributions in 1998, leaving it debt free despite the poor showing the party made in the midterm congressional elections. While the Democratic National Committee had collected a respectable $54 million, it remained $6.5 million in debt. The large amount of money flowing into the coffers of the political parties was good news for the polling firms in which Leon held an interest.

Leon went through the latest poll results as he mulled over new ways to entice the parties to spend more of their dollars on political polling. His data revealed a hefty 53 percent of Americans had little or no confidence in the federal government. With barely 50 percent of eligible voters turning out for elections, the major parties were going to have to reinvigorate their party members to get out the vote. The ongoing Clinton administration scandals had taken their toll of voter confidence. In a recent poll, 63 percent of the respondents believed that elected officials put their own agendas before the national interest. Leon wasn't smiling as he read the bad news. Too many of the dummies outside of Washington were starting to catch on to how the game was played.

Placke was a depressed by the item announcing a federal judge had ordered the Department of Defense to pay General Dynamics Corporation over a billion dollars in settlement for a terminated fighter aircraft program. Leon had completely missed the action. Not even his litigation support firm had been involved in the case. Had they been on the ball, they should have gotten at least a $85,000 contract to computerize the litigation documents. Leon made a note to talk to his managers about missing the opportunity. Leon was beginning to think he ought to focus more of his energy on the defense and political sectors and devote less of his time to trade issues. Still, trade had paid him well. With foreign investors gobbling up treasury securities and corporate bonds at a record rate, the U.S. remained the world's biggest debtor. Foreigners owned $4.6 trillion in U.S. assets while Americans held $3.7 trillion in foreign corporations, real estate, stocks and bonds. Perhaps he should focus more of his time on helping the foreigners desiring to invest in the United States. It might turn out to be a profitable venture for him.

Turning away from the daily grind of business, Leon focused on the pleasant task of preparing the speech he would deliver at the annual dinner of the Washington Society of Solicitors, a social group composed of 685 of the most powerful lawyers and lobbyists in Washington. Although the society gathered informally many times a year to enable its membership to exchange information on the workings of government and key private sector firms, the dinner speech was the highlight of the organization's year. The unwritten goal of the Washington Society of Solicitors was to promote the exchange of information enhancing the income potential of its membership. The motto of the organization was jokingly said by the members to be: "There is no right or wrong side to any issue. Just make sure we get paid."

That Washington, DC had more attorneys per capita than any other city in the world was no accident. As the United States Congress churned out massive amounts of complex legislation, lawyers flocked to the fertile legal ground of the nation's capital. Attorneys labored in government enforcement agencies writing the regulations and rules necessary to enforce the new laws. Other attorneys lined up clients to test the laws in the courts, arguing their view of the true intent of Congress. The boundless legal opportunities in the fields of civil rights, safety regulation, environmental protection, deregulation of industries, consumer protection, health care, sexual harassment, international trade controls, tax law and monopolistic business practices created a fruitful paradise for lawyers in Washington.

As the various segments of American society waged an unending war to avoid paying taxes and shift the tax burden to others, Washington's lobbyists prospered. One of the proudest results of the Washington Society of Solicitors' behind the scenes work was the United States Tax Code, which over the years, had evolved into a hideously complex web of difficult to understand regulations. The impressive stack of tax code pages now stood over seven feet high and the society's goal was to add six inches to it every year. In addition to raising government revenue, the complex tax code served another unpublicized purpose. Thousands of lobbyists, attorneys and accountants were gainfully employed in helping the American masses deal with complex tax matters.

The simple act of raising revenue to support the functions of government had become extremely complicated in the United States. Leon saw the situation for what it truly was, a way for the legal class to garner a larger share of the wealth produced by the American economy. As he mulled over the remarks he would make at the dinner, Leon decided to title his speech "The Titanium Triangle of Success." It was an appropriate title because a number of promising young attorneys beginning their careers in Washington had been invited to the dinner. As the acknowledged informal dean of Washington's lobbyists, Leon was charged with the responsibility of giving the new people a dose of fatherly advice. They needed something to guide them as they took their places in the multitudinous ranks of Washington's lawyers and lobbyists.

Leon took the bull by the horns when he unflinchingly laid out his view of America in 1999. Forget the arcane views of America's founding fathers, he wrote. That is the stuff of high school history classes, totally irrelevant to life in today's Washington. The economic juggernaut that is the modern United States could no longer be run by a group of clod-kickers, who took a few years off from farming to serve the peoples' interests in Washington. Nor could the country be run by narrow-minded provincial merchants and small-scale industrialists who sacrificed a few years of their lives to serve in the capital. The bumpkins and laborers in the heartland might need their cherished old myths to hang on to for comfort, but Washington lobbyists had to deal with the stark modern reality of running the most powerful nation on earth.

The three branches of government, executive, legislative and judicial, enshrined in the Constitution by the nation's founding fathers had to be helped to function by the proud men and women of the Washington Society of Solicitors. They were the invisible, de facto fourth branch of government, Leon argued. Their unheralded work was vital to making the great American democracy function. Washington lobbyists were the grease that kept the cumbersome gears of the republic grinding. With the power to govern ineffectively split among the three branches of government, the lobbyists of Washington had to shoulder the awesome burden placed on them by the demands of the evolving American economic system. The cream of American society was here, in the capital, managing the affairs of the nation without the slightest acknowledgment or expression of appreciation from the nearly brain-dead masses comprising the bulk of the American public.

Leon went on to state he believed the members of the Washington Society of Solicitors deserved to be adequately compensated for the outstanding services they rendered to the nation. Leon ended this section of his speech with a stirring declaration stating the society had a sacred duty to ensure that government by its members and of its members was made safe for future generations of law school graduates. No one else in the country was going to look out for the interests of lobbyists; the members of the society had to do it for themselves. America provided no guarantees, it only offered opportunity to those willing to accept the challenge, Leon eloquently wrote in his remarks.

Leon shifted the focus of his remaining remarks to the bright, young, eager attorneys seeking to carve out lobbying careers in the seat of federal power. Leon warned of the fearsome pitfalls they faced, of seeing one's power base swept out of office by a fickle national electorate which changed administrations and the makeup of Congress with about as much thought as it put into buying breakfast cereal. It was nerve-wracking to have to watch as politicians were forced to market themselves to the uncaring masses in the same way as companies sold soap powder. In the expensive world of electioneering, a cleaver TV ad pushing the right voter hot button could swing an election in a matter of days. As part-owner of two prominent political polling firms, Leon knew that it was quite profitable to invest in the working infrastructure supporting the American political system. It bought him a larger return than the stock market.

Leon told how he forged a successful career for himself by strenuously following his theory of the unbreakable titanium triangle of success. To have a chance of reaching the top in Washington, one had to begin by constructing a triangle of legal knowledge and the right contacts. To build the first leg of a triangular career-supporting structure, an attorney had to go through the demeaning process of creating legislation for others. This meant laboring in the obscurity of a congressional committee, drafting legislation and pandering to various constituent groups as they pressured Congress to pass the laws bestowing favors on them. It was no secret in Washington that campaign contributors gave money in order to be able to influence the legislation in Congress. The pressure groups had their agendas and only fools believed anyone contributed to a political campaign out of the goodness of their hearts. With big business, labor, agriculture and a host of other groups contributing their many millions to congressional races, the stakes were high. While laboring in the halls of Congress, an attorney had to draft the proposed laws in silence and craftily wait until the right one came along. Watchful waiting was the rule because it was the key to later success.

When a law resulting in a large enforcement or administrative budget for the enforcing agency came along, it was time to begin work on the next arm of the career triangle. In most cases, the proposed legislation would also have the backing of a powerful, well-funded pressure group to help push it through Congress. When the law was enacted by Congress and went into effect, it was time to move to the Executive Branch of the government and become the administrator or the enforcer of the new regulations. Leon said it could take years of painstaking work to build up the needed support among politicians and interest groups to land the right job in the executive branch. Once there, the attorney had to devote more years to enhancing a reputation as a fair and impartial administrator who also knew how to look out for a pressure group's vital interests. With a little luck, one could easily move through two or three programs in the process of developing a following of loyal constituent groups. When one had assembled a solid base of power, it was time to set the last leg of the career supporting triangle into place.

The final and most dangerous part of the career building process was to leave government and become a lobbyist, perhaps also overseeing on occasion the litigation of cases in court. Times change and political power bases shift. The astute attorney had to instinctively know when to move with the changing political currents. As a lobbyist, Leon had often argued the exact opposite of the position he had taken a few years earlier when he had been enforcing the regulations. He had to endure the stinging barbs of numerous detractors who called him a hypocrite and a man of no fixed values as he moved forward relentlessly amassing a larger power base and increased wealth. Leon endured the insults and watched as one by one his less flexible detractors were engulfed and consumed by the changing political tides. Nursing their shattered dreams, they lived out their drab lives in America's vast heartland drafting wills, handling divorces and doing financial planning. Leon had immensely enjoyed having the last laugh as he watched those encumbered with scruples fade into oblivion.

The banquet of the Washington Society of Solicitors was held at the trend-setting Louis the Fourteenth restaurant, the best on Capitol Hill and a mere six blocks from the Capitol building. At a $135 per plate, the six course meal was guaranteed to be exquisite. The members sampled rare wines and chatted about the political events of the day during the two hours it took to consume the fine foods set before them. Finally, it was time for Leon to speak. As he rose from his seat at the head table and strode to the podium, Leon looked out at the 600 assembled guests. Here in one room were the people who got things done in America. Leon was proud of the role the group played in national affairs. He also noted with quiet confidence that virtually everyone in the room owed Leon Placke a favor. Having favors to collect any time he desired was another source of real power.

Leon's speech on the indispensable services Washington's lobbyists provided to the United States of America was a smashing success. Afterwards, as he moved through the assembled multitude shaking hands, the walls of the dining room reverberated as the adoring crowd chanted: "Placke, Placke, Leon Placke." While it was good to be loved and respected by your peers, in his heart Leon knew that in Washington it was often better to be feared. But the times were good. The economy was in its eighth year of economic expansion with the stock market pushing through the 10,000 level for the first time. The hours Leon could bill his clients for lobbying work were up. Bill Clinton might be the President of the United States, but Leon Placke was the undisputed king of the lobbyists, a position nearly as powerful.

Leon was putting the finishing touches on a $350,000 litigation support contract for the Department of Energy's Super Fund Program. He had spent the better part of two working days nailing down the details, much annoyed by the fact that his company manager had been so slow in capturing the contract. The woman has an MBA from one of the best schools in the country, Leon thought to himself. She needs to get off of her rear and hustle, these contracts don't fall from trees like ripe apples. Leon knew from experience it was extremely hard to get good help in Washington these days. Although he paid top dollar salaries, it seemed as though everyone wanted to talk about national policy issues, attend congressional hearings and write tattletale books about politicians. It seemed no one wanted to do any of the dirty detail work necessary to develop new business. Although he was going to read his manager the riot act, Leon was satisfied with the overall result because the contract would net him a nice profit.

The intercom buzzed, Leon picked up the phone and answered, "Good morning senator, how are you doing this fine morning?"

"Yes, I have been following the sale of the Washington Redskins football team. It's on the market for $800 million. The NFL owners just rejected the offer of one group because the deal presented was too leveraged for the other team owners' liking."

"I am sure another group is putting a package together. The trustees of the Jack Kent Cooke estate want the team sold to the highest bidder in accordance with the provisions of his will."

"I understand your position completely senator. You are absolutely correct. The NFL team owners are composed of the most obnoxious set of private-sector tycoons in the nation. You feel the need to knock them down a peg or two, do you? "

"Sure, I would like to have a stake in the team ownership. The Skins are the most financially successful team in the nation. Every home game is always sold out. You can count me in for $500,000."

"I'd be happy to front the deal for you and your friends. To recap your plan, we will put up $2 million in cash and then force the winning consortium of bidders to give us a $8 million share in the team's ownership. Quite a nice profit for pain and suffering the owners caused you by jerking the sports fans of Washington around, don't you think?"

" With you and your friends backing it, there is no way this deal can fail. We'll teach the arrogant rich boys they can't afford to ignore the advice of Congress. Just send over the cashier checks made out to Leon Placke Associates Limited Partnership."

"You may rest assured that no one will ever know you were personally involved. I will take care of all the details." After hanging up the phone Leon buzzed his administrative assistant and asked him to arrange a luncheon meeting with Bradley Atkins of the National Football League.

Bradley Atkins proved to be a hard man to pin down. Much to Leon's extreme displeasure, it took several days to get the luncheon meeting scheduled. Atkins obviously didn't have the slightest clue who he was dealing with or he would have been more responsive. He was one of those annoying people who simply did not understand that when Leon Placke called, you dropped what you were doing and took the call right away. Leon was going to enjoy teaching the dunce a lesson over a lunch that Atkins would never forget. Leon savored the thought as he headed to the parking garage in the basement of the building and got into his Porsche 911. Leon liked driving the $80,000 coupe. Its 3.4 liter, 296 horsepower flat-six engine delivered performance that defied description and impressed those who saw Leon driving by. The Porsche could hit 60 in 4.9 seconds, its top speed was 175 mph. Leon smoothly worked the 6-speed manual transmission as the car leaped out of the parking garage entrance into the traffic on K Street.

As he headed toward 14th Street, Leon saw Frank Duester, Ph.D. standing on the curb trying to hail a cab. The traffic respectfully gave way as Leon forcefully swung the Porsche curbside, rolled down the window and asked Frank if he needed a ride to the Hill. Frank, who was going to a hearing on interstate banking regulations at the Rayburn House Office Building, expressed his thanks for the lift as he hopped in. Frank was an economic guru who had been in Washington since the first administration of President

Ronald Reagan in 1981. A staunch fiscal conservative, Frank had been made an assistant secretary of the Treasury as a reward for his work in the campaign. He worked hard to make excellent contacts in the financial sector and after leaving government service, Frank's consulting specialty became federal banking and financial services laws.

Frank also proved to have what it takes to survive in the political arena. Leon had thought for sure that Frank was headed for political extinction when the savings and loan scandal exploded on the national scene. As the major architect of the of the legislation removing federal controls from the savings and loan industry while at the same time leaving the government liable to reimburse depositors for the industry's losses, Frank was struck a political setback when the savings and loans began to fold and the government was stuck with a mountain of debt. For awhile it had been nip and tuck as the politicians struggled to cleverly disavow their role in permitting the industry to run amuck. In the end, very few people went to jail and the Treasury Department forked out over $500 billion of the taxpayers' money to cover depositors' losses.

As the massive, embarrassing savings and loan fiasco came to its expensive end, everyone in Washington agreed a valuable lesson had been learned. In the future, there would be no more deregulation of industry while the government remained responsible for paying for the industry's mistakes. Frank survived the bureaucratic firestorm intact since big mistakes often go unpunished in Washington. He continued to do economic consulting work for the financial and banking industries. Leon thought Frank was a competent professional, netting close to $450,000 in profit from his activities during the previous year.

Every time he needed a complex economic analysis to obfuscate a touchy issue, Leon subcontracted the work to Frank. Frank could adjust economic data to support a desired conclusion better than any other person in Washington. He was clever, imaginative and never let facts get in the way of meeting a client's needs. If you needed economic data, charts and graphs to bolster a position, Frank Duester was the best person to provide it. His Ph.D. gave him credibility. When people in Washington saw "Prepared by Frank Duester, Ph.D." boldly listed below the title of an economic report, they immediately knew it was the very best economic analysis money could buy.

Leon dropped Frank off at the main entrance of Rayburn House Office building knowing that Frank would dazzle the sparsely attended hearing on banking deregulation with his economic expertise. Leon moved quickly through the Porsche's gears as the car sped toward the Louis the Fourteenth restaurant and his meeting with Bradley Atkins of the National Football

League. As he drove through the narrow streets of Washington's Capitol Hill district, Leon thought about doing more business with Frank Duester, Ph.D. in the future. The deregulation of the airline industry, which had been going on for years, had not lived up to its promises of delivering better service and lower fares to the consumer. In reality, fares were higher, seats had become smaller and flights were crowded and late in arriving. The flying public was generally unhappy with the results achieved thus far by the much touted move to get the government out of the aviation marketplace. As the pendulum of public opinion swung away from deregulation, Leon saw the opportunity for re-regulation emerging from the froth of the public's discontent. He and Frank stood to make big bucks if they jumped on the issue early. Deregulate and then re-regulate might just become the new legislative theme in Congress as America moved into the new century.

Leon ordered the seafood salad special and a glass of white wine for lunch while Bradley Atkins had the luncheon steak and a glass of beer. The atmosphere at the table was frosty because Leon was incensed over the fact that Bradley had taken his own sweet time in agreeing to the meeting. When he did the bidding of important people, Leon felt he had a right to be treated with deference and respect. The clown sitting across the table from him had no legitimate reason to avoid returning Leon's phone calls for three days.

As they ate, it began to slowly dawn on Bradley that he would have been better off if he had jumped through hoops when Placke first called. He didn't like the glint in Leon's eyes; Bradley felt like he was having lunch with a cobra getting ready to strike. There was something sinister going on here. Leon Placke, Bradley's friends had warned him, was known around Washington as the unofficial king of the lobbyists. As an uneasy feeling crept over him, Bradley began to wish he was someplace else.

After disposing of small talk about the weather, the coming football season and the high-quality food served at the Louis the Fourteenth, Leon got to the point: "Your team owners are jerking around the sports fans of Washington by not settling the Washington Redskins ownership issue in an expeditious manner. The drawn-out NFL selection process has made several members of Congress extremely unhappy."

"I fail to see how picking the new ownership of the Washington football team has anything to do with Congress," Bradley responded.

"Washington is a high- pressure city, the most powerful city in the world, in case you don't know. Decisions that affect the lives of millions of Americans are made here daily. Many of our national decision-makers unwind on Sunday afternoons by watching the Redskins games. It's part of the culture of Washington. Virtually all activity around the beltway stops when the game begins. Our already stressed citizens don't need the additional strain of not knowing who the new team owners will be. It's a very upsetting situation and many of the voters have asked members of Congress to do something about it."

"The NFL team owners have a right to take whatever time is necessary to pick a responsible new ownership group. There are many financial considerations to be considered. It shouldn't be such a big deal with the fans. Maybe they should pay less attention to the panic stories of the sports writers. The ownership issue will be settled in the very near future, believe me."

"Mr. Atkins, with offers of $800 million to purchase the team on the table, the ownership of the Redskins is a big deal, let's leave no doubt about that. I represent a small group of very influential investors who will pay the new team owners $2 million for an $8 million stake in the team. We believe that would be fair compensation for the pain and suffering the NFL owners have inflicted on members of Congress because of their sloppy handling of the ownership issue."

"Putting up $2 million for a $8 million share in one of the most successful football franchises in the United States sounds more like extortion than a honest business investment. I don't think the team owners will buy it."

"The act of disrupting the Sunday routine of the constituents of powerful politicians comes with a high price. Before you say anything else, let me give you the downside of my offer. Please ensure that your principals clearly understand the ramifications of what I am now going to tell you. Congress, in its infinite wisdom, has been very, very generous to the people who own football teams in sections of the internal revenue code. The NFL is also exempt from most antitrust laws. The real estate and business ventures owned by the team owners do quite well under the tax code when the deductions and the other provisions that reduce the tax burden are considered. If I don't have a positive answer to the offer I have laid on the table within 24 hours, you may assure your team owners that legislation will be introduced in Congress during the coming session to close tax loopholes and remove many of the specific business deductions now taken by team owners in their other classes of business enterprise. The changes in the tax law will generate an additional $9 billion in tax revenue for the United States Treasury. Of course, it will come out of the pockets of the people who own things like football teams, do you understand?"

When Bradley nodded in affirmation, Leon continued "Any chump can do the arithmetic. Your owners pay a measly $6 million to save their businesses $9 billion a year in tax deductions. It's a no brainer. Only a complete fool would be stupid enough to turn it down. My firm, Leon Placke Associates, will act as the agent for the members of Congress who do not wish to have their role in this matter made a matter of public record. I have a check for $2 million ready to present to the owners. Do you have any other questions?"

"No, none. I will pass your message on to the ownership committee within the hour."

"One final word of warning, Mr. Atkins. Don't even consider the possibility of going to the press with the matter we have discussed. If even so much as a single world leaks out, the deal is off and the tax law changes move forward. Play it straight and your team owners continue to save big bucks on taxes. Cross me, and you will find out just how dire the consequences of stepping on the wrong toes in Washington can be. Do we understand each other?"

"I understand the offer and the ramifications of rejection completely. While this is nothing at all like the negotiating I am used to conducting, I do believe you are capable of doing everything you said you would. I will get back to you as soon as possible with the owners' decision."

"It has been a pleasure having lunch with you on this fine day. Perhaps we can do it again sometime after this bit of business has been put to bed. I'd like to discuss the coming season's prospects with you. Which teams have the best chance of going to the super Bowl? Let's be sure to do lunch again sometime in the near future." Leon was smiling broadly as he ended the conversation.

As he and Bradley parted ways in the parking lot, Leon knew he had just cleared $500,000 for the few days of work he invested in helping his friends in Congress deflate the egos of the wealthy NFL football team owners. Leon felt good as he climbed into the Porsche for the trip back to the office. In his heart, he knew he was right in helping his friends make a little extra money because they deserved all the financial help they could get. Coming to Washington to be a servant of the people was an obsolete theory. It no longer applied to elected officials in the expensive political climate of the 1990s. Lining up the money necessary to finance election and reelection campaigns was what modern politics were all about.

"Old friendships are like meats served up repeatedly, cold, comfortless, and distasteful. The stomach turns against them."
-William Hazlitt, 1826

As Leon sat in traffic on 14ᵗʰ Street near the Washington Press Club waiting for the signal to change, he saw Sam Tomaso shuffling along in the crosswalk in front of the Porsche. Times had been hard for Sam since he had fallen from the ranks of the powerful. Leon knew Sam had been reduced to scratching out a living by doing freelance writing for a couple of obscure newspapers and working retail three nights a week. A person of such low status was not worth speaking to, so Leon made no effort to attract Sam's attention. As he watched the hunched figure moving along the sidewalk, Leon thought about the days when Sam was somebody in Washington worth knowing.

During the early 1980s, Iraq's emissaries to the U.S. capital began emphasizing their government's less strident foreign policy and renewed focus on internal economic development. Iraq wanted an end to war with Iran. In their desire to promote regional stability, the Iraqis expressed a willingness to support whatever agreement the Israelis and Palestinians worked out between themselves to resolve that festering issue. Since Iraq was viewed as a possible counterweight to Iran in the oil rich Persian Gulf region and appeared to be the less dangerous of the two, the administration decided to try a new Iraqi policy.

Had the long war with Iran brought about permanent alterations to Iraq's internal and foreign policies? The sudden emphasis placed on economic development and the desire for regional peace and closer cooperation with the United States were seen as signs that the war-weary nation was adjusting to reality. Sam Tomaso certainly thought so. He quit his job as a staff member on the House of Representatives' Foreign Affairs Committee and went to work as a lobbyist pushing Iraq's interests in Washington.

For a time, Leon had to admit, it looked like Sam had struck a gold mine. As if to emphasize the policy shift, Iraq was now willing to restore full diplomatic relations with the United States. In November 1984, ambassadors were exchanged for the first time in 17 years. In conversations with diplomats and business visitors to Baghdad, Iraq's Minister of Trade expressed a strong appreciation of American technology and encouraged greater commercial, technical and economic cooperation between the two countries.

Sam prospered as the American business community took note of the changes in Iraq. In 1985, he helped establish the United States-Iraq Business Forum to promote the development of commercial relations. The business potential was so great that the organization soon had over 50 members, including some of the largest U.S. corporations. Sam promoted the message that Iraq was on the road to developing regional political stability and internal economic liberalization. There were wonderful opportunities coming in the fields of energy, agriculture, finance, transportation, health and construction engineering. As he watched Sam preside over the forum's glittering Washington social events, Leon could see Sam had seemingly made the transition from the ranks of those who toiled for wages. He was the toast of the town, an honest-to-goodness foreign economic affairs prophet. As a man who had correctly predicted the future, Sam was deluged with invitations to speak.

A cease fire in August 1988 brought the eight-year Iraq-Iran war to a close. It had been the longest and bloodiest war in modern Middle East history, inflicting approximately one million casualties. The monetary costs to the combatants was in excess of $200 billion. With an end to the fighting, Iraq could concentrate its resources on replacing neglected infrastructure and expanding the nation's industrial base. Iraqi officials made it clear they believed the country's future prospects would be best served by moving towards a free market economy and increased commercial ties with the United States.

Sam Tomaso's consulting income skyrocketed as the Iraqi government began to give the country's private sector a greater role in the nation's economy and price controls were removed from some categories of goods. State-owned agricultural lands, poultry and dairy farms were being leased to private interests. The government announced plans to sell off light industries, construction companies and hotels to private investors. A ten-year tax holiday was granted to privately held industrial enterprises. Observers could all clearly see the slow drift away from the rigid socialist structure that had long been the hallmark of Iraq's economy.

It was all quite believable at the time because Iraq's oil production was heading towards three billion barrels per day and petroleum revenues were expected to earn $12-15 billion per year. Despite the harshness of the ruling regime, Iraq was a nation with acknowledged economic potential. The country possessed the land, water and population necessary to support solid economic expansion. With crude oil reserves second in size only to Saudi Arabia and ample supplies of natural gas, Iraq also appeared to have available the financial resources to fund continued agricultural and industrial development. These factors, along with the promise of continued economic liberalization, made the future look promising. Leon envied Sam's foresight as he watched him cash in on his Iraqi connections.

Unfortunately for Sam Tomaso, the full potential the Iraqi market offered American firms was never realized. As a consequence of the war, Iraq owed approximately $28 billion to non-Arab creditor nations and faced a severe short-term debt problem. Eighteen billion dollars in principal and interest payments were coming due over the next five years. Much to the dismay of the western banking community, Iraq proved uncooperative in its financial dealings. It actively played one creditor nation against another, kept much of its economic data secret, and refused offers to reschedule the debt over a longer, more manageable time period.

Iraq's obstinate behavior in the financial arena soon cast a pall on the attempts to expand commercial ties. Unknown to all outside the Iraqi ruling inner circle, Saddam Hussein had quietly decided to shelve the cooperative approach. The diplomatic discussions on regional issues dissolved into a stalemate that did nothing to resolve problems in the volatile Middle East. Chilling intelligence reports on Iraq's armament, missile development and chemical and biological weapons programs began to cast doubt on Iraq's peaceful intentions. The national leadership was not emphasizing the development of peaceful industries. It was focusing on rebuilding and improving the country's military might.

Was all the talk of economic development and goodwill orchestrated by Saddam Hussein merely a device to buy time before embarking on another military adventure? With the brutal invasion of Kuwait on August 2, 1990, Saddam Hussein stunned the world, smashed rapprochement with the United States, and callously crushed a neighboring state. A stunned Sam Tomaso watched helplessly as his world disintegrated. His US-Iraqi Business Forum closed its doors amid allegations that some of its member companies had circumvented American export control laws and supplied technology useful to Iraq's military build-up. The export-import bank of the United States suffered tens of millions of dollars in losses as its insurance program, which had guaranteed Iraqi payment for industrial goods purchases, covered the losses incurred by American corporations. The United States Department of Agriculture lost over $1 billion as it made good its guarantee to cover Iraqi payment defaults for the purchases of agricultural products. Washington decision makers watched in horror as the once rosy Iraqi government-to-government guarantees to make payment proved to be worthless.

As the coalition forces led by the United States of America went to war to drive the Iraqis out of Kuwait, no one in Washington wanted to be seen in public with Sam Tomaso, the Iraqi dupe. His phone calls were not returned; his invitations to lunch rejected outright. Overnight he went from being one of Washington's bright, bold international visionaries to an object of contempt. As the bombs began to drop and the big guns roared along the battlefront, Sam Tomaso became an individual to be avoided at all costs by Washington insiders. Federal investigators looked into his Iraqi connections for any irregularities and found none. In congressional hearings, Sam was derided and ridiculed for falling for the big Iraqi lie by many of the same members of Congress who had shown support for their constituent firms' efforts to penetrate the lucrative Iraqi market. They had often lauded Sam's effort to help companies sell products to Iraq over the dinners and drinks Sam graciously provided. Iraq had brutally double crossed America's foreign policy makers. With their voters marching off to war as a consequence, everyone in Congress wanted to put the blame on Sam Tomaso.

Sam was psychologically crushed by the vicious attacks mounted by his former friends as they disassociated themselves from him. His income quickly plunged and he was driven to financial ruin. Corporate executives who had once sought his sage advice on marketing to Iraq at $500 a session, spurned his offers to work for them as a janitor at $8 per hour. Sam was soon thrown out of his office for nonpayment of rent, his palatial home was repossessed by the bank and within a year he was in bankruptcy proceedings. Still, Sam stubbornly hung on to his dream of becoming somebody important in Washington again. He had been reduced to renting a cheap basement apartment across the Potomac River in one of the older, less expensive Virginia suburbs, struggling to make a living in retail and by taking any writing assignment which came along.

As he watched the haggard figure of Sam Tomaso move along the sidewalk, Leon hoped Sam would not attempt to speak to him. There was an unwritten rule in Washington for Leon to follow. One never made contact with a person who had fallen from a position of power and influence unless one was making an offer of temporary employment. Since there was nothing Sam could do for him, Leon saw no reason to waste his valuable time by engaging in conversation with one of Washington's biggest losers. Sam had his brief stay in the limelight when he was a big shot in international trade circles. When his world came crashing down, Sam should have had the good sense to leave town. No one wanted or needed a pathetic reminder of the Iraqi fiasco walking around the city. Sam's presence made the senior officials who had made a few of the mistakes in foreign policy a bit edgy. As he wheeled the Porsche past the dispirited figure on the sidewalk, Leon thought about the irony of the situation. Saddam Hussein had outlasted President Bush and probably would still be in power after Bill Clinton left office. Sam Tomaso, on the other hand, had become a complete non-person in the policy-making circles of Washington. Sam was walking proof that life could be tough when you reached the top in the capital. One mistake was all it took, and you were gone. Leon knew very few people ever got a second chance in this tough town.

Out of the corner of his eye, Sam saw Leon Placke' Porsche edge past him. He knew Leon was purposely ignoring him. "You goddamn, no good, selfish, bastard," Sam muttered as he trudged up 14th Street. Leon was always hanging around the edges of Sam's professional life when Sam was riding high. Leon attended his social functions because a number of Leon's clients also were interested in the Iraqi market. To help Leon, Sam provided him a good deal of economic information and excellent market intelligence at little or no cost. Leon had slapped his own price tag on the material and passed it on to his clients. Sam had acted in the hope of establishing a solid, professional relationship with the famous lobbyist. Hoping for a return favor some day when the need arose, Sam found his efforts had been in vain. When the war began, like everyone else in Washington, Leon severed his association with Sam. He never returned any of Sam's many desperate phone calls. As Sam struggled to keep his creditors at bay, Leon never acknowledged the receipt of Sam's resume and offer to work as a low-paid economic analyst. Leon had sat by impassively, never lifting a finger, as Sam was quietly flushed down the toilet by Washington's power elite.

Sam Tomaso had just left the office of the Kuwaiti-English language newspaper located in the National Press Club building after submitting a 1,000 word article on the American stock market, when Leon snubbed him. Sam thought about the insult on his way to his second job as a clerk in the retail store where he was scheduled to work until 10 p.m. In the morning, he would begin his new writing assignment for a Japanese-English language paper, an article on the American love affair with firearms. As he turned the corner from 14th street on to K street, Sam saw a familiar caterer's truck parked at curbside. The vehicle brought back a flood of memories from happier times because it was the same caterer Sam had employed to prepare the luncheons and dinners when he was entertaining. Sam stood by the rear of the truck admiring an empty tin of caviar, a half plate of leftover canapés and the partially filled bottles of fine wines that were sitting on the tailgate. It had been years since he tasted the delicious food of a catered Washington power meal, one where the heady issues of national importance were discussed and deals were done.

Sam's reverie was rudely interrupted by a snarling voice: "Get away from my truck, you damn bum! I'm not running a free soup kitchen for the likes of you! Don't even think about trying to grab any of my leftover food!"

Stunned by the harsh words, Sam turned quickly to see Andres, the catering firm's owner standing behind him with an armload of chafing dishes. " I am no bum, Andres. My name's Sam Tomaso. I used to be a customer of yours a few years ago, don't you remember?"

It took awhile for Andres to recognize the derelict standing before him as the man who had once been among his best customers. He finally apologetically replied: "Why yes, Mr. Tomaso, you used to run a business forum on Iraq, I think it was. It has been several years since I have last heard from you. I am sorry I didn't recognize you standing there. You look so much different. Is there anything I can help you with? I heard you left town shortly after the Gulf war. It is very nice to see you again, sir. Now if you will excuse me, I have to get this truck loaded. Running behind schedule you know."

Andres pushed past Sam as he slid the dishes onto the truck. "Are you all right," he continued. "You look terribly worn, not at all like you once did. Have you been ill?" As Sam stood in a silence of shame, Andres continued, somewhat flustered by the seedy appearance of his once prominent former customer, "We have a few nice leftovers from the luncheon, would you like me to fix you a plate to take with you Mr. Tomaso? No charge, a free reminder of the good times we once shared."

"No thank you," Sam replied as he turned away from the truck. "It has been good to see you again Andres."

"Likewise," responded Andres as he entered the truck.

The chance meeting with Andres drove home to Sam the finality and completeness of his failure. Even his former caterer had mistaken him for a down and out derelict. And it was true, Sam realized with horrible clarity. He was broke, working odd jobs and barely making ends meet as he frantically clung to the lowest rung of Washington's social structure. He was shunned by his former friends and clients alike. As he watched a limousine from one of the embassies move slowly down K Street, Sam sadly realized he was finished as a power broker in Washington. He had no money to contribute to political campaigns, no way to reenter the circle of the policy decision makers and lobbyists. He was merely a member of the dull class of people who labored for their daily bread at demeaning, boring jobs. His prodigious mental powers were unused and most likely would never be gainfully employed to their full capacity again. He was among the lowest of the low, nothing more than a common voter. That no good, double-crossing Saddam Hussein had done him in. How could he have been so stupid as to believe the Iraqi's sugar-coated string of unending lies? Sam realized he would be better off dead than continuing to live as a failure on the fringes of the capital's lower class. He had nothing worthwhile to do, nowhere important to go. Having tasted the elixir of Washington power, Sam knew he never again could be happy being nothing more than a plain American wage earner.

After finishing his shift and clocking out from his retail sales job, Sam walked slowly toward the Memorial bridge across the Potomac River, carrying some old brochures listing participants in trade missions to Iraq. He had organized those trade missions with the help of the U.S. Department of Commerce many long, painful years ago. Sam also carried a copy of the US-Iraqi Business Forum's 1988 directory that listed over 50 major American corporations as members. He reread the forward to the directory as he walked. In it, the Iraqi Ambassador to Washington had written: "Now that the Iran-Iraq war is hopefully behind us, Iraq is determined to mobilize and allocate all its resources and wealth to reconstruct and expand its economy and lay the foundations for prosperity and happiness of all our people."

How could Sam have been so foolish as to believe the propaganda line pumped out by the flunkies of Saddam Hussein? He had to admit his vision had been blinded somewhat by the dream of the profits he would earn from introducing American firms to the new Iraq. He had been completely fooled by the slick-talking Iraqis who had come to Washington spouting their cooperative line of lies. They had continued the charade for a long time. They talked of the mutual economic gain coming for both countries even as Iraq prepared for war. When the war began, the Iraqi ambassador in Washington got transferred to the sweet job of being Iraq's ambassador to the United Nations. He was living high on the hog in New York city, denouncing the UN embargo on trade with Iraq while Sam, who had wanted to make things better for the Iraqi people through economic growth, starved nearly to death in Washington, DC.

As he walked past the brightly lit Lincoln memorial, Sam sunk deeper into despair, believing himself to be a failure who had no options left. The Iraqis had cleverly used him as a pawn in their program of deluding the U.S. government. The Iraqis talked peace in Washington while they plotted to gain control of a larger share of Persian Gulf oil reserves. As a consequence of his misjudgment of Iraq's true intentions, Sam looked like a fool. Washington had no room for fools who failed, so Sam had been deserted by his friends and clients alike. From the middle of the bridge, Sam could see the moonlight reflecting from the white gravestones in Arlington cemetery at the other end of the bridge. On the top of the hill amid the graves of the Civil War dead sat Arlington House, Robert E. Lee's old home.

"The difference between Lee and me was that Lee was an nineteenth century military man while I was a twentieth century economic animal," Sam softly said to the bridge rail. "Lee sent thousands of men to die for a lost cause, but was treated with respect afterward even though he fought on the losing side in a war. Despite suffering military defeat, Lee was able to finish out his days as the respected president of a college. I made one small misjudgment regarding Iraq and, as a result, I will be shunned by the Washington establishment for the rest of my life. My one-time friend Leon Placke treats me like a piece of crap! He refuses to speak to me, conveniently forgetting the pile of money I helped him make. My former caterer feels so sorry for me that he offers me a free handout of leftovers."

For a long time Sam pondered the many injustices heaped on him by the uncaring elite of the capital as he stared down into the deep, dark waters of the Potomac. Around 2:30 a.m., when there were no cars or other pedestrians on the span, Sam climbed on top of the decorative railing and jumped, tightly clutching the mementos of his former days of glory to his chest. The Potomac is a tidal river. The tide moved Sam's drowned corpse back and forth along Washington's elegant waterfront several times before the drawbridge tender down river on the Wilson bridge saw the body floating in the water and reported it to the police.

February 1999

After driving silently by Sam without bothering to honk his horn or wave in recognition of his one-time friend, Leon returned to his office. One item of mail that caught his attention was an invitation to attend the grand reopening of George Washington's Grist Mill at 5514 Mount Vernon Memorial Highway in Alexandria, Virginia. Ordinarily, Leon would have declined the invitation because he wasn't much into the history of George Washington. What made this event worth attending was the fact that Al Gore, the Vice President of the United States and the administration's point man on technology issues, was going to cut the ribbon. The ceremony would offer Leon a chance for a photo opportunity with the vice president and a few minutes of private conversation. As a general rule, Leon never missed an opportunity to have his picture taken with high administration officials. The photos quickly became part of his office decor because they demonstrated to visitors that Leon was an important person. They were the visible proof to back his claim of having access to the leaders of the land. As a lobbyist, Leon was keenly aware that access to those who wielded power was the major ingredient of a lobbyist's success. To have an impact on the formulation of regulations and legislation, one had to be able to get inside the doors of those who made the big decisions. His ability to visit and talk to administration officials and members of Congress was why Leon's clients paid him the big bucks.

"Great is the hand that holds dominion over
Man by a scribbled name."
-Dylan Thomas 1914-53

To ensure he got to spend some private time with the Vice President at the gristmill affair, Leon sent a $1,000 check by courier to Mr. Gore's election committee. It was the first of many checks he would write for candidates during the coming election cycle, an expense of keeping the doors of power open to him. Leon knew the drill well. A few days before the event, he would call the Vice President's office and tell the administrative assistant he was a contributor and would like to have a few precious minutes of the man's valuable time at some point during the ceremony. The administrative person would check to see if Leon's claim was true and then block out a time period on the event schedule for a private meeting. Leon got his staff busy putting a briefing paper together, complete with the talking points he would raise on the issues his clients wanted brought to the attention of the administration. After the meeting with the Vice President, Leon's clients would receive a report outlining the Vice President's views of the points discussed. Leon liked to send the status reports along with the monthly statements for the services he rendered.

Leon always prepared well for important meetings. As he settled back into his chair, he called for his file on Al Gore, a man Leon found to be anything but boring. Before Leon could get started on the Gore file review, his phone rang. At the other end of the line was House Majority Whip, Tom DeLay asking Leon to contribute $2,000 for DeLay's project to help 10 vulnerable Republican House incumbents. DeLay wanted to have $200,000 to $500,000 in the bank for each of the members at risk by June 30, the first financial reporting deadline for congressional candidates. Leon knew when the Majority Whip asked for something, it was akin to a request that could not be refused. Leon told DeLay that he was delighted to help out the Republican party. A check for $2,000 was on the way. He would also be happy to raise another $4,000 from friends and send it along in two weeks. "That should keep Tom off my back for at least two months," Leon said to his desk lamp as he hung up the phone.

Leon had been around the Washington scene long enough to know money was the lubricant of American politics. Every elected politician in Washington needed massive amounts of financing to spend on campaigning. Long ago, Leon had learned that infusions of money kept the doors of power open; it was better than a master key to all the high-level offices in the White House and Congress. Leon generously provided whatever size contributions it took to get the job done. He passed the cost on to his clients as part of his overhead costs. Contributing to campaigns came with doing business in Washington, part of the expense for the work he performed, no different than copy paper or rent.

As he returned to his review of the Gore file after Congressman Delay's expensive little interruption, Leon had to admit that the Clinton-Gore administration was having an exceedingly good run despite the never ending string of scandals, including the first attempt to impeach a president in over 135 years. As long as the economy was good and no serious foreign policy blunders were made, the voters of modern America appeared to be in a mood to forgive almost anything. In a free market economy such as the United States, Leon could never quite figure out why the voters gave the president all the credit when the economy was good and heaped all the blame on him when times were bad. Anyone with a rudimentary smattering of economic understanding knew the president actually had only a limited amount of control over the nation's economic situation. One of the most useful advantages of modern American presidential politics was that the American people believed the president controlled the economy. It was proof Americans had become an apathetic lot, willing to believe almost anything any politician said.

It was a foregone conclusion in high-level Washington political circles that Al Gore would be the Democratic candidate for president in the year 2000. His major rival for the nomination, House Minority Leader Richard A. Gephardt, had already announced he would not battle Gore for the nomination in the primaries. Leon was planning to funnel $50,000 to the Gore campaign when the decision was finalized. When it became clear later in the year who the Republican candidate would be, Leon was prepared to spend another $50,000. It was an expense that came with every presidential election. It was a fact of life, a cost of doing business. No one ever said successful Washington lobbying could be done on the cheap. Exercising one's right to petition the government on behalf of one's clients had gotten to be very expensive in recent years.

Being vague was in vogue among all the presidential hopefuls casting about for supporters and funding sources and the Vice President was no exception. Leon was amazed by the continuous stream of clever stories flowing out of the Vice President's office in the hope they would be picked up by the newspapers. Al Gore was being presented as America's first high tech vice president. Al also claimed to be the inventor of the Internet because he had a hand in passing much of the legislation that made modern computer networks possible.

What was not mentioned in the press releases was the fact the Clinton administration had spent nearly $100 billion on computer systems to modernize government operations during the past three years. The government was spending $35 billion a year to hire technology contractors; some of the contractors would hopefully be willing to make political contributions. To further promote his technical image with voting public, Vice President Gore negotiated an accord with information industry executives making it easier for parents to control their children's access to online web sites.

Leon was impressed by the amount the government was spending on information technology. He saw he had been remiss in not paying more attention to the field. He had to begin wooing clients in the information technology sector; it was the fastest growing part of America's booming economy.

Leon knew everyone joked about Vice President Gore's wooden speaking style and stiff manner. In reality, Gore was a hardened political operative who played the game of politics to win. Al Gore was completely ruthless when it came to battling political opponents or working his staff hard. Vice President Gore, a man who often stated he was trying to make the world a better place for everyone, had an income of $197,729 in one recent year. His contributions to charity for that year amounted to only $353, not much for a person who had dedicated his life to improving human welfare, Leon thought.

The Albert Gore of Tennessee, who Leon studied, displayed driving ambition and a disciplined approach to reaching his political objectives. He was organized, tough as an old barn nail and extremely hard-working. No detail escaped his attention. After a lifetime in politics, Gore had mastered every aspect of the political game and had his sights set on becoming the next president. Gore seethed inside as the problems unleashed by the antics of the undisciplined President Clinton impacted on his chances for winning the next presidential election. When Clinton told a New York times reporter that he had private fears about the organization of Gore's campaign, Gore exploded. What the ramrod stiff Al Gore lacked in flashy brilliance and superficial public relations skills, he more than made up for in craftiness, attention to detail and organizational skill. Al Gore wanted to be the next president of the United States of America and was pulling out all the stops as he relentlessly moved toward his goal.

There was no doubt in Leon's mind that this cold, ruthless, calculating man had all the qualifications necessary for leading the nation. The gaining, maintaining and exercising power was what life in Washington was all about. Leon knew this political fact of life better than most, and deeply envied Gore for being able to make a go for the presidency. Leon often longed to be part of a president's power structure. Perhaps one day he would make the big personal contribution necessary to gain an appointment as an ambassador or assistant secretary of something or another in one of the federal agencies. It would be a fitting capstone to his career when he decided to get out of the lobbying business.

"Every country has the government it deserves."
-Joseph de Maistre, 1811

Leon believed the 2000 presidential campaign would set a new record for political spending. The brutal race to the White House was going to take money, lots of it. Vice President Gore was well aware of the money issue and had fielded a top-notch team composed of the most brilliant fund raisers in American politics. His team of hard-hitting money raisers was going to stretch the federal matching-fund raising rules to the outer limits of decency as they set in motion their plan to collect $55 million. Gore's ferocious fund raising machine had already gotten the jump on the other candidates. It was striving to raise $25 million during the current year, about $60,000 for each day of 1999. As a consequence of the need to raise campaign money, payment was being demanded for the past favors Vice President Gore had done for other candidates. By Leon's calculations, Gore had campaigned for 67 Democrats, participated in 123 fund-raising events and gave $1.3 million from his own political action committee to help other candidates during the off-year elections. Those who found themselves in political debt to the Vice President were now being recruited into the ranks of those who would labor long and hard raising funds for Gore during the coming presidential campaign.

At fund-raising dinners hosted by friends, Gore wooed Wall Street as he introduced his ideas on the economy and finance. Al Gore could not ignore Wall Street as a factor in his presidential calculations because it was the home of a huge number of million-dollar salaries and had the potential for turning out many big political donors if they liked the candidate's message. As he diligently worked the bastion of American capitalism, Al also feverishly courted organized labor. The AFL-CIO planned to spend $46 million on political activities through the 2000 election. Al Gore fully intended to get his fair share of those funds as he presented his lofty vision of the glory of honest labor and the rights of workers to an audience composed of the union hierarchy.

Leon noted that Gore's crack public relations staff was working overtime. Gore got good newspaper coverage when he announced the new federal guidelines for labeling over-the-counter drugs. The new rules would require manufacturers of 10,000 products to follow a strict format in describing a drug's uses, ingredients and dosage directions.

Gore made speeches stressing the need for community action to control gun violence. The community, he said, was a powerful force in American society. Leon thought it was a very profound statement with which no one of any political persuasion could disagree. When he promulgated the White House drug control strategy, Gore cited drug abuse as a problem with spiritual roots. As ways to reduce drug use, he called on Americans to improve the schools and provide economic opportunity for the less fortunate. As he raced to gather campaign funds, Gore reaffirmed his support for the real and meaningful campaign reforms that would correct the shortcomings of the present system he had mastered so well.

To enhance his foreign policy credentials, Gore hosted an international forum on the subject of bureaucracy. In his keynote speech, he called on world leaders to make their governments lean, nimble and creative lest they be left behind in the race for the greater productivity demanded by the new global economy. In his grand vision of the future, the conference would be the first phase of a new international coalition focusing on competitiveness.

The Vice President also met with foreign leaders such as Deputy President Thabo Mbeki of South Africa in an effort to display to the American voters his skills in foreign policy negotiations. Gore also assumed a visible role in policy formulation regarding NATO's operation in Kosovo. While this aggressive stance in support of human rights allowed the Vice President to display his knowledge of complex foreign issues, there were great political risks involved. The voters would remember Gore's role in crucial Kosovo policy- making if things began to go badly for America's interests there in the future. Leon could see Al Gore was no wimp. He was willing to take large political risks. That was one of the qualities required of a great leader of any type.

Gore's image had changed. He no longer seemed to be obsessed with protecting the environment at all costs. He was speaking out on such diverse topics as the economy, education, civil rights, healthcare and crime. In his hard-hitting speeches, Gore pledged himself to carry on the mission of building a better America for everyone, continuing the work so nobly begun by President Clinton. As he made speeches to the party faithful, Al Gore thundered from the podium: "We will create a 21st century America that is the brightest time our nation has ever seen. The issue we must squarely face is the kind of 21st century that we want to build for our children." In many ways Leon thought Gore sounded like a company CEO as he talked about reinventing the federal bureaucracy, setting new performance goals, cutting the workforce and saving money by working more efficiently.

"We need people to participate in our system to make it work. I'm grateful to have you here because you share my vision of the future," Vice President Gore said as he spoke to potential contributors coming through the receiving line of the $1,000 a plate halibut in lobster sauce dinners. Leon was immensely impressed by how fluent Gore had become in the obscure language of the political money raising game. Al had a real knack for making the donor feel special. Not one to shy away from the unpleasant tasks of fund raising, Al made countless solicitations for campaign contributions in person and by telephone. He also performed the tedious follow up chores of successful fund raising very well. Al Gore hosted thank you parties and sent large numbers of personal notes.

Leon's files held evidence that Gore also had made a few mistakes. His Buddhist temple fund-raising visit was considered by many political observers to be the low point of the 1996 campaign. There were the unseemly coffees hosted for political donors in the White House map room, the tasteless overnight stays in the White House Lincoln bedroom by high-rolling campaign contributors and the whopping $3.8 million in illegal contributions that had to be returned by the Democratic National Committee. Leon didn't consider these missteps to be anything serious in the overall scheme of the race for the White House. In the endless quest for campaign funds, one had to expect a few things to slip through the cracks. Even a man as dedicated and organized as Al Gore could not watch everything and everyone all the time. Like a good military commander who learns from failure, Al Gore had probably learned the hard lessons of his 1996 mistakes. Leon didn't think there would be a repeat performance of the embarrassing fiascoes in the coming 2000 race.

As he closed the file, Leon pondered the stakes in the ongoing race for the presidency. Al Gore was after was the most prestigious and powerful job in America. The president had custody of the domestic and international affairs of the world's third largest country. His decisions directly affected the lives of 270 million Americans. With a gross domestic product running in excess of $7.6 trillion dollars, the United States had the largest and most powerful economy in the world. There were 134 million souls in America's labor force, 182 million telephones in use and 11,000 airports with paved runways.

Leon's cursory review of national statistics confirmed his assumption that America was the mightiest of nations in the waning days of the 20th century. The U.S. president directly controlled the military establishment and oversaw $267 billion per year in defense spending. In military manpower availability, America had 69 million males between the ages of 15-49. With women clamoring for a greater role in the military, nearly another 70 million persons could be said to be available for the potential military manpower pool. Leon knew instinctively why Al Gore and the other presidential contenders wanted the job of president. It was the ultimate office in which to exercise power. It was at the very pinnacle of politics. After a four or eight year stint in the White House, there was no place higher to go. To be President of the United States was a power trip unequaled by anything else the world had to offer.

As a lobbyist and long-term observer of the Washington political scene, Leon had seen a long string of elected and appointed political people move through Washington. It never took long for them to become bored with whatever cause motivated them to come to Washington. Leon had watched how easily they slipped into the mode of pursuing the power necessary to enhance their position in the nation's capital. Year in and year out, it was always the same.

Sometime the change came quickly, sometimes it took a few years. But the metamorphosis from being a humble servant of the people to a Washington power monger always took place. In 1925, Richard Nixon had honestly told his mother: "Mother, I want to be an old-fashioned lawyer, a honest lawyer who can't be bought by crooks." Many years later at the time of the Watergate scandal, President Richard Nixon had long outgrown his naive youthful utterances. He had become willing to do almost anything to hold onto power and destroy his political enemies. The ceaseless political wars in Washington corroded the souls of Republicans and Democrats alike over time. The ancients had it absolutely correct, Leon knew. All power corrupts and absolute power corrupts absolutely. Washington, DC was a city filled with those proving the validity of that wise old observation over and over again.

As he thought about the many shortcomings of America's politicians and the enormous expense of running for elected office, the thought never occurred to Leon that as a lobbyist, a hired-gun for anyone willing to pay him to maneuver behind the scenes to affect the laws and regulations of the United States, that he was part of the problem that pundits said was corroding America's political soul. Having early in his Washington career developed the ability to never see himself as part of any problem, Leon considered himself to be a vital part of the American democratic process, a person who petitioned government on behalf of others. Like so many others in Washington, Leon knew the facts behind the sad state of American political life, but felt no need to say or do anything about the situation. Although he would never admit it to others, there was no money to be made by rocking the boat.

> **"Government is the great fiction, through which everybody endeavors to live at the expense of everybody else."**
> **-Frederic Bastiat, 1846**

Leon knew the federal government, with its annual budget exceeding $1.7 trillion had become a massive dispenser of funds and services to many politically well-connected special interests. Leon had no intention of telling the unsuspecting taxpaying masses just how dramatically the overhead costs of government had risen during the past years. While the Legislative Branch

(Congress) was able to operate at an annual cost of $196 million as late as 1962, the 1999 budget for the Legislative Branch came to a whopping $2.8 billion, making it by far the world's most expensive deliberative body.

Although its function was supposedly the creation of federal laws, Congress had evolved into one of Washington's major employers. There were approximately 31,000 employees on the congressional payroll providing assistance to the 100 elected members of the Senate and the 435 members of the House of Representatives. With its large staff, Congress had become an enormous year-round legislative mill. To justify the large number of personnel, Congress hardly ever went out of session anymore. To keep themselves busy, the staff members were forever on the lookout for new legislative initiatives to churn out. Leon had to admit that the unquenchable thirst for new legislation made his job as a legislative manipulator a lot easier. A power lunch at one of Washington's better dining spots more often than not resulted in the quiet introduction of legislation with terms quite favorable to the economic interests of Leon's clients.

Not to be outdone by the bloating of Congress, successive presidents had winked at the trend as they pushed up staff size and the cost of running the White House. The Executive Office of the President (White House) added councils, advisors and offices as the administrations came and went. The cost of keeping the president and his staff in business was now running at an annual rate of $300 million per year. In 1999, the Executive Office of the President employed approximately 1,000 paid staff. Another 160 persons were loaned to the White House by the other federal agencies that covered their salaries. Over a year's time, 1,000 unpaid volunteers were brought in to help with the strictly political task of making the party in power look as good as possible. Unfortunately, the volunteer and intern program garnered a massive amount of unwanted publicity during the Clinton administration because of President Clinton's hands-on policy regarding some of the female volunteers and interns.

One of the best kept secrets in Washington was that the President also got to fill over 3,000 high -level patronage positions scattered strategically throughout the various federal agencies. Some of these positions (at the cabinet level) paid $148,000 per year. An appointment to one of these coveted positions was what the campaign workers and large contributors hoped to get as a reward for their selfless service to financing and winning elections. Did the government really work better under the burden of over 3,000 political jobs paid for by the taxpayers? Probably not, but Leon knew no one in Washington was ever going to raise the question. How else was the winner of an election going to reward the most deserving of the campaign workers and contributors who had made it possible? There was strong bipartisan agreement in Washington that a change to the present system of political rewards would have a detrimental effect on the national political process. The large number of political appointees was viewed as part of the necessary overhead cost of maintaining America's wonderful political system.

As succeeding administrations centralized bureaucratic power in the White House, the staff had expanded in size. On any given day, the president's workers jammed to overflowing every nook and cranny of the buildings on the White House grounds, forcing many very important political people to work in tiny, obscure office spaces. It was a very demeaning situation for those who had helped to elect the president and then come to Washington to assist the president in governing the nation. Because the congestion had put an unbearable strain on the presidential facilities, the National Park Service had quietly prepared plans, with broad bipartisan support of course, for a $300 million overhaul of the 200-year-old White House property. Because the White House was the symbol of the power of the American presidency, no political personage was going to question the expense. When the work was completed, the 5,000 tourists who came through the White House every day would enjoy seeing how well their tax dollars had been spent.

Growing a little cynical, Leon smiled to himself as he thought about Vice President Gore, who was an integral part of the massive and expensive White House complex, challenging the leaders of 32 federal agencies to make significant reductions in the number of federal employees working in their agencies. In his heart, Leon knew the Vice President would never challenge himself to reduce the size of the self-important White House staff. Because it was vital to the exercise of modern political power, it would remain completely free from the management oversight Vice President Gore cleverly focused on the federal agencies. It had not always been that way. Washington old- timers had told Leon that less than 100 people worked at the White House at the height of World War II. The expansion of Congress and the Executive Office of the President was another sign of how much the American political process had changed. Changed, but not improved, Leon realized.

As an astute political observer, Leon also knew that Gore was not quite telling the taxpayers the entire truth in his speeches touting the Clinton administration's government manpower reductions. Leon was not particularly shocked by the shading of the facts Gore used in his speeches because the omission of relevant data was a common device used by both political parties when it was to their advantage. In 1962, when the U.S. had a population of 186 million, there were 2,515,000 federal civilian employees and an additional 2,840,00 serving in military uniform. The total number of federal employees came to 5,355,000. The number of employees working for state and local governments at the time was 6,549,000.

In 1997, as the second term of the Clinton-Gore administration got underway, the U.S. population had grown to 268 million. The federal government employed 2,787,000 civilians; the number serving in the military had been reduced to 1,474,000. All told, 4.2 million people worked for the federal government in one capacity or another. Although the total number of federal employees was clearly down as the Vice President often stated in his speeches, the number of individuals employed by state and local governments had increased to 16,911,000. Despite the emphasis on reducing the size of the government sector, the actual result of the Clinton administration's program had been the shifting of government employment from the federal to the local level. Leon was not sure whether the Republicans or the Democrats had benefited most from this subtle transfer of government functions. The blessings must have fallen equally on both parties Leon surmised, because if they had not, one party or the other would be raising the subject as a national campaign issue. Leon knew that in matters such as these, nothing was said by either party if both parties had equal access to the trough of government spending. Federal, state or local tax dollars, it made no difference to politicians as long as they were able to keep their hands in the till.

Two days later, Leon received the news of the demise of Sam Tomaso, who reportedly had jumped into the Potomac River and drowned. There would be no memorial service of any kind. Sam's distraught and long-suffering wife was taking the body back to southwest Missouri for burial. She would remain there, resuming her career as an elementary school teacher. Just as well, Leon thought. It would save him the $50 flowers would cost and allow him to avoid having to admit he was once an acquaintance of a man who had been duped by Iraq. Leon didn't need any reminder of how close he had once been to a failed foreign policy. Having your name associated with a policy failure of any type was not good advertising if you were in the lobbying business in Washington.

Leon found the affair at George Washington's gristmill to be boring in the extreme. He had sacrificed his valuable time to attend because he wanted to be seen in the company of Vice President Al Gore and spend a few private minutes with the Vice President pushing his client's special business interest agendas. Leon fidgeted in his seat under the expensive tent on the lawn as the speakers discussed George Washington's experiences as a surveyor, farmer, mill owner, whiskey distiller, soldier, army commander, framer of the Constitution and first president of the United States. While Leon readily admitted George Washington must have been one hell of a man, the fact that Washington was such an upright, principled, stick-in- the-mud didn't sit well with him. Washington had probably been too busy doing useful things to have been willing to spend much of his time listening to the lobbyists of the period.

To make matters more unbearable for Leon, the perimeter of the tent was lined with a copy of virtually every known painting of George Washington. The visual tribute to Washington had been tastefully done. The paintings on their easels had been highlighted by just the right amount of carefully placed accent lighting. Although it was an impressive display of art, one of the paintings especially annoyed Leon. The stern eyes of George Washington seemed to bore into him every time he glanced at the portrait. As the ceremony wore on, Leon's dislike of the Washington painting increased. No matter which way Leon turned, he felt Washington staring at him with a look of cold contempt.

As beads of sweat appeared on his brow, Leon developed a distinct feeling that George Washington was sending him a message from beyond the grave. With increasing uneasiness, Leon realized that Washington considered him to be a lowly, self-centered parasite feeding on the vitals of the government of the United States of America. It was a totally irrational feeling Leon knew, but as the event progressed, Leon could clearly see Washington staring at him with a gaze bordering on hatred. There was some awful truth emanating from the eyes of Washington. Leon Placke, the king of Washington's modern lobbyists, was being called on the carpet for his manipulation of the system of government by a man who had helped establish the nation.

Leon had important business with the Vice President to attend to at this event. He didn't need any interference from a man who had died in 1799. "The times and the functions of government have changed since you were alive, you dumb bastard! Go away and leave me alone," Leon snarled under his breath as he felt Washington's piercing gaze bore into the back of his neck just as the speaker touched on how Washington had personally intervened during the dark days of the Revolutionary War and prevented the Continental Army from making him America's dictator. With a growing sense of apprehensive awe, Leon realized George Washington would never fit into today's government because he actually turned down chances to grab power. Neither Leon nor anyone he knew in modern politics had ever done that. What quaint, old-fashioned ideas George Washington must have held as he made his many personal sacrifices to ensure the establishment of the United States of America!

Much to Leon's relief, it was finally Vice President Gore's turn to speak. Gore's brief oration focused on Washington's life-long interest in technology, correctly pointing out that Washington developed one of the most modern gristmills operating at the time, a profitable distillery and a cooperage producing shipping barrels. In a canny aside, Gore also managed to mention his own interest in technology issues. Leon thought the audience was impressed by the not-so-subtle reference to the commonality of Washington's and Gore's interest in technology. It was a good political move on the Vice President's part. The reporters covering the event would be sure to give Gore favorable coverage in the next morning's papers. After completing his remarks, the Vice President cut the ribbon and the restored George Washington's gristmill was once again opened to the public.

Actually it was a restoration of a recreation. Virtually all traces of the original mill George Washington built on Dogue Creek had disappeared by the 1850s. As plans were being developed for the bicentennial celebration of Washington's birth in 1932, interest was aroused in reconstructing the mill. The State of Virginia purchased the property on which the mill, distillery and cooperage had been located and a painstaking reconstruction of Washington's mill was erected, using many components from other old mills of the period. After operating many years as an historic exhibit, the mill was closed in September 1997 and turned over to the Mt. Vernon Ladies Association which had agreed to restore the mechanical components as part of an overall refurbishing project. After two years of work by Mt. Vernon's master craftsman, the mill was once again ready for public view.

As he and the other guests followed the Vice president into the musty building's ground floor, Leon was impressed by the fact that the mill looked as the original must have looked during its heyday in the 1790s. At the front of the group, Leon could overhear the guide carefully explaining to an attentive Vice President Gore how the 16 feet diameter breast wheel worked. Powered by water flowing through a millrace from the dam and millpond Washington constructed over a mile upstream, the wheel could produce a whopping 20 horsepower as it turned the wooden gears that drove the milling machinery. Leon wasn't much interested in listening to the details of how the master power gear, power gears and the hub gears interacted to transfer power to the millstones, but he did notice that Vice President Gore and others in the party seemed genuinely interested in how the 18th century machinery worked. Leon did think the conveyor system designed by Oliver Evans, the father of American industrial automation, was a good improvement. He found it amazing that little metal cups moving on leather belts had revolutionized the milling industry by increasing mill efficiency.

On the second floor, as he began to maneuver through the crowd to get closer to the Vice President, Leon heard the guide explain how the dust produced during the grinding process created an ever present danger of explosion and fire, making grain milling one of the most dangerous occupations of the time. As the group looked at the grinding stones, the guide told how Washington had, at considerable financial risk, installed two sets of grinding stones in the mill. One set made of granite was for grinding corn and a rough wheat for the local trade. The other set of expensive French Burr stones ground a fine, high-quality wheat flour that was sold at a premium price and was shipped to cities along the east coast.

By the time the group reached the sifting equipment on the third floor, Leon was next to the Vice President. He wondered how anyone could ever have considered the clanking, slow-moving wooden sifters to be state of the art. Leon maintained his place as the tour moved up the steep stairs to the storage areas located on the fourth floor. After viewing the termination of the gear shaft, pulley and conveyor systems, Leon knew they were finally through with their tour of George Washington's ancient technology and would soon be heading back outside to the tent for refreshments and serious modern world conversations.

As they exited by the ground floor door, the guide pointed out the old Sycamore tree standing next to the mill. It had been a young tree in Washington's time and George was said to have tied the reins of his horse to it during his daily visits to the mill. Suddenly, Leon felt the uncomfortable stare of Washington on him again and he heard a voice saying: "The name of my favorite horse was Magnolia. I rode her here more often than any other horse I owned. Tell the nice group of people my horse's name, if you please."

For a time Leon remained silent while Washington's stern face kept reappearing in front of him on the massive tree trunk. Finally, Leon gave in and blurted out, "The name of George Washington's favorite horse was Magnolia." As the others in the group turned to face him, Leon continued, "Washington rode that horse to the mill more often than any other horse he owned."

"Why Leon," Vice President Gore said, "I didn't know you were a student of George Washington. That's a interesting factual tidbit. Where did you come across it? "

Leon lied as he answered, "I heard it a couple years ago from someone who worked here before the mill was closed for renovation." The somewhat flustered VIP tour guide thanked Leon and said no one on the staff of Mt. Vernon knew the name of Washington's favorite horse. She would, however, be happy to research the archives to see if there was any mention of the horse's name in the plantation's records.

Leon heard Washington's voice speaking to him again. "Tell the lady to look in the margin of the stable records for the year 1799. The name of the horse is listed there." As the group looked at Leon in amazement, he said, "I can save you a lot of searching. You should find a notation with the name of the horse listed in it in the stable records for the year 1799."

The group crossed the small bridge over the channel carrying the spent water back to the creek. About 30 yards to the rear of the mill, they stopped to view the site where Washington's distillery had once stood. Although nothing remained but a few stones outlining the foundation, the distillery had once produced corn and rye whiskey, and it was thought, in later years, bourbon and brandy. The distillery opened by Washington, had continued to operate under various owners until sometime in the 1830s. It was a large operation. The tour guide informed the group that nearly 950 gallons of whiskey were inventoried at the time of Washington's death in December 1799. The distillery had been a real money-maker during the last years of Washington's life.

After the group returned to the tent to sample the refreshments, Leon got his ten minutes with the Vice President and went through the issues of interest to his clients. Two major oil companies were interested in learning Gore's views on a possible relaxation of the sanctions barring American firms from doing business with Iraq and Iran. A trio of manufacturing companies were interested in having the Vice President raise the matter of the slow pace of the privatization of the Egyptian economy with the President of Egypt during his next visit. The firms had tens of millions of dollars tied up in deals that were going nowhere because of the obstructionist tactics employed by Egyptian officials. Two high tech firms were worried about losing business in China if the U.S. government continued to impede the flow of technology exports to the country. A banking conglomerate wanted to find out if the Vice President would support legislation allowing them to move into domestic markets from which they were barred at the present time by anti-trust considerations. The changing of a few key words and lines of text in the existing law would allow them to reap enormous new profits.

Gore listened attentively as Leon covered the things his clients wanted from the government. As the photographer snapped a series the publicity shots, the Vice President made non-committal, somewhat affirmative promises to look into the matters. He had learned a long ago not to say no outright to a lobbyist's wish list. To do so would send Leon's clients shopping their agendas to other candidates and result in a immediate loss of important campaign contributions. The Vice President knew that most business contributors covered their bets by contributing to the candidates of both major parties. That ensured access to government decision makers no matter what party was in power. He didn't particularly like it, but it was the way the money machine worked. It was just another one of the hard, ugly, political facts of life in modern Washington.

The next morning, as he prepared to send the reports of his meeting with Vice President Gore to his to his clients, Leon was brutally reminded of how arduous the lobbying business had become. The synopsis of recent lobbying activity prepared by his staff showed he was in serious danger of being dethroned from his unofficial position as the king of the lobbyists. Many of Al Gore's former top advisors were making massive inroads in the local lobbying market. Peter Knight, who was orchestrating Gore's $55 million campaign fund raising strategy, had snagged contracts to represent telecommunications giant Bell Atlantic and Lockheed Martin, one of the nation's major defense contractors. Roy Neel, Gore's top advisor on telecommunications issues, had become the president of the U.S. Telephone Association at a salary of $500,000 per year. Tom Downey, a friend of Gore's since they had served in the House of Representatives together in the 1970s, had signed large lobbying contracts with Microsoft Corporation and Fuji Film Co. Jack Quinn, who had been the vice president's chief of staff and later a White House counsel, was now with a prominent Washington law firm. The firm had been hired by two software industry trade associations to represent them at a fee of $620,000 per year.

Leon could see that the hard-charging Washington insiders running Gore's campaign would sweep up many of his customers after the election if Gore won. More than anything else, clients wanted a lobbyist with access to the top levels of the White House. A Gore victory would give his present campaign advisors and managers enough of an edge in the presidential access market to garner themselves millions of dollars in new lobbying contracts after the new administration took office. Leon was sick at heart because the fickle fortunes of Washington politics were about to deal him a major blow. After many years at the top, he stood a good chance of being knocked out of the top slot of lobbying. In reality, the damage to Leon would be more psychological than financial. Even with the loss of some of his clients, Leon would still be earning an income many times the size of the average Washington wage-slave toiling at the daily drudgery of making the machinery of government work. Leon would continue to be invited to many more important social events than he could possibly attend. Although his ego would be severely bruised, Leon would have to learn to accept being shoved down into the second tier of Washington's power structure with a certain amount of good grace. The only other choice was to give up the struggle and leave town. That would be hard to do because Leon could never visualize himself as just another common working drudge . His proper place was here in Washington where the nation's affairs were decided.

As he brooded over the problems caused by the crude maneuvers of the clever newcomers to the lobbying game, the phone rang and a courteous voice said, "May I speak to Mr. Placke?"

"Yes," Leon answered, "this is Leon Placke speaking."

"Mr. Placke, this is Jane Mitchell. I am in charge of George Washington's personal papers at the Mt. Vernon library. I thought you would like to know we have confirmed the name of George Washington's horse by using the information you provided. Washington did have a favorite horse and it was named Magnolia. It took a little digging, but we found the stable records from 1799 that you mentioned. There is a note in the margin of one of them verifying the name of the horse. Since no one has looked at this particular record in nearly 100 years, would you mind telling me how you obtained the information?"

Leon was not going to admit he thought he heard George Washington speaking to him. People would think he was crazy, so Leon decided to tell a lie. "I can't remember exactly when or where I heard it. I think it was from someone who worked at Mt. Vernon several years ago. They may have seen it in an old book or in a now forgotten report on Washington. All those paintings of Washington displayed in the tent must have stimulated my memory. I know it sounds a little strange, but I don't have a better answer for you."

"Well, you were right and that is the important thing. I want to thank you very much for sharing the information with us. We are going to put up a sign next to the big tree explaining the story of the horse's name. It will be a nice addition to our storehouse of George Washington lore."

Across the room, on the wall filled with photographs of Leon greeting powerful politicians, Leon saw George Washington's scowling face slowly begin to appear. "Get the hell out of here," Leon shouted as he threw his precious Rolodex filled with the phone numbers of his important contacts at the spectral face emerging from the wall. The face disappeared as the Rolodex sailed through it and struck a photograph of Leon meeting with President Bush. The glass shattered as the photograph was knocked to the floor with a loud clatter.

"Excuse me, what did you say?" the voice on the other end of the phone line said.

"Nothing," Leon answered, somewhat chagrined. "I was speaking to someone else."

In the back of his mind Leon heard Washington's voice prompting him again, so he blurted out, "Did you know one of the mill employees named Tom Bell fell off the water wheel in the summer of 1791 and drowned in the tailrace? He was trying to repair one of the wheel braces when he slipped on the wet wood. Tom knocked himself unconscious as he fell into the water, his head striking the main shaft on the way down. He was dead by the time he was found by the other workers and pulled out of the water. There should be a notation in the 1791 miller's log mentioning Tom's death. Since the mill has been refurbished, maybe you could put a plaque next to the wheel commemorating the sad event. Tom was one of the best workers in the mill. He ought to be memorialized in some way."

"My heavens! How do you know all that?" Jane said.

"George Washington mentioned it to me," Leon stammered. "No, that's not what I meant to say! I mean I heard of the occurrence several years ago. Probably from the same source who told me the story about the horse. If you check the records, I'm sure you will find the incident mentioned," a nervous Leon answered.

"Well thank you very much for the new lead! You certainly have turned out to be an expert in gristmill lore. I will certainly do a search the flies and let you know what I find," Jane said as she ended the conversation.

Leon was looking at the mess on the floor when one of his staff stuck his head into the office. "What was the crash, I heard?" Bob said.

"Nothing important," Leon answered, "the Bush photograph fell off of the wall for some reason. I will take care of it myself, thanks."

Leon spent the rest of the day finishing the reports of his meeting with Vice President Gore and sending them to his clients. Although nothing else eventful happened, he was becoming worried about the annoying reoccurring visions of George Washington and his unnerving ability to hear Washington speaking to him. His mind was playing tricks on him. The smashing of a perfectly good photograph was a sign the problem was getting out of hand. Perhaps he should schedule an appointment with his psychiatrist and get to the root of the George Washington problem before it got worse. It was probably something very minor, triggered by the constant stress of being overworked by his client's incessant demands.

For the next two weeks everything was normal. Jane Mitchell from the Mt. Vernon library called back and confirmed the Tom Bell information

Leon had provided was correct in every detail. The unfortunate accident happened in July 1791. The staff was going to place a sign by the water wheel relating the details of the accident. Leon told her half-jokingly that George Washington would probably be happy with their decision because Tom was known to have been an exceptionally good employee and deserved to be remembered in the gristmill's history. Jane was so impressed by the depth of Leon's knowledge of the mill that she asked him to have lunch with her. Leon agreed in principle, but it could not be anytime soon. His schedule had no openings. He was too busy lobbying congressional committees with the legislative changes his irritable clients wanted him to get enacted into law.

A few days after Jane's call, Leon had the first of his many upsetting dreams. In the first one, he was on a surveying crew somewhere in western Virginia scratching his bug bites and holding a survey chain. A young George Washington was yelling at him to pay more attention to his work. The land survey they were doing for Lord Fairfax had to be done right the first time. Leon tried to dismiss the memory of the odd dream from his thoughts almost as soon as he awoke. He had no interest in the old land surveys of Virginia even if they had been done by George Washington. For days afterwards though, Leon could vividly recall how dangerous, hard and lonely the surveying work had been.

Several nights later, Leon was unnerved by a second dream. He found himself marching on a hot summer day in the middle of a column of British regulars moving through the dense forests of Pennsylvania. Sweat stung his eyes, his feet ached, the pack on his back felt like it weighed a ton and the musket he carried bit deeply into his shoulder. The sergeants treated him like the scum of the earth, screaming at him to close up the file and hold his place in the ranks. From conversations with the men marching to his left and right, Leon learned he was with one of the two regiments of regular British troops under the command of Major General Edward Braddock, a man known to be arrogant and more than a little bit unreasonable. On this campaign, Braddock's British regulars were accompanied by a good sized force of Virginia militia. Braddock had shown nothing but contempt for the Virginia soldiers; he considered them to be lazy, apathetic and nearly useless. The general and a captain of militia named George Washington argued constantly over the conduct of the campaign and Braddock's views of forest fighting.

Even though it had been slow going, Braddock and his 1,465 soldiers, 30 wagons, artillery and a number of pack horses were now only seven miles from French held Ft. Duquesne, the vital military installation which controlled the forks of the Ohio River. Even though on this Wednesday, July

9, 1755, there had been no sign of the French, precautions against ambush had been taken. Flanking parties were moving on both sides of the army, and the advance guard was well out in front. Behind the main body of troops came the wagons and pack horses, followed by a strong rear guard. The Monongahela River had been forded without incident and General Braddock soon expected to lay siege to the French fort.

Suddenly, from the front of the column, came the sound of musket fire as a mixed force of 900 French regulars, Canadians and native Americans collided with the advance guard. As the British advance guard was driven back to the main column, the regulars formed their normal tight formations and poured volleys of musket and cannon fire into the trees at an invisible enemy. Leon loaded and fired as rapidly as possible with the rest of the soldiers standing in the line of battle. While the French regulars and Canadians held their ground in front of the British, the Indians began to infiltrate the flanks. Soon the exposed British lines were being riddled from all sides. British soldiers were going down in heaps as enemy musket balls sometimes passed through two soldiers before lodging in a third. Leon heared the ugly sound of a musket ball tearing through flesh and bone as the trooper on his right was struck squarely in the chest and was knocked down backwards screaming in pain. Blood and brains spattered Leon as a shrieking apparition in full war paint emerged from the musket smoke and smashed the head of the soldier standing to Leon's left with a mighty swing of a war club. Before Leon had a chance to turn and fire, the fearsome enemy vanished back into the battle smoke.

The battle raged for nearly three hours and the British were on the verge of defeat. Although Leon and the other regulars continued to fire rapidly, they rarely hit one of the unseen enemy concealed in ravines and behind trees. General Braddock was shot down, critically wounded. On the flank, Leon could see Captain Washington, dressed in the blue uniform coat and red trousers of a militia officer, and his Virginia militia furiously exchanging lead with the enemy. During the course of the fighting, the rapidly moving Washington acquired four bullet holes in his coat and had two horses shot out from under him. Washington was attempting remove the wounded Braddock from the battlefield and organize the surviving troops for a retreat.

Leon could taste the dead soldier's brains which plastered his face and upper uniform. His nostrils were so choked with burnt gunpowder that he could hardly breathe. A musket ball whistled past his head as Captain Washington beckoned to the thin line of surviving regulars to join him. Leon had seen enough of Washington and the misery of battle. He threw down his smoking musket and ran as fast as he could for the safety of the ford on the

Monongahela River. He stopped and looked back once during his flight. Washington and the other surviving officers were working feverishly to save what remained of Braddock's army. It had been a terrible disaster for British arms. Braddock's force had been decimated, losing 977 of those engaged.

As Leon ran for his life, his foot caught in an exposed tree root and he was sent crashing headlong into the ground. Stunned by the fall, he awoke in a cold sweat to find himself on the floor next to his bed with his feet tangled in the sheets. The dream had been so real that he could still taste the dead soldier's brains. As he began to vomit, Leon scrambled to his feet and ran to the bathroom. He was so sickened by the battle experience that he had to take off two days from work in order to recover. When he felt better, he got a book from the library on General Braddock's ill-fated expedition. As he read about General Braddock's attempt to capture the site of modern Pittsburgh, Pennsylvania, Leon was shocked to learn that everything he dreamed actually happened. It was all very strange because Leon had never before in his life read anything about Braddock. What kind of tricks was his mind playing on him? Why was his strange dream so factually correct? It had to have something to do with George Washington, but what?

A week later, Leon was aggravated by another haunting dream. On the cold, snowy, Christmas night of 1776, Leon was nearly freezing to death as he pulled on an oar in one of the boats ferrying a ragged Continental army of 2,400 across the Delaware River. General George Washington planned to attack the Hessian force holding Trenton, New Jersey at first light on December 26. Few of the local inhabitants believed Washington and his often beaten, ragged troops could pull it off. Washington, now wearing the blue and gold uniform of the American army, looked terribly careworn to Leon as his small force embarked and moved off through the swirling snow in a desperate bid to strike a blow to keep the American Revolution from faltering. Thoroughly chilled to the bone, Leon stood by the stone house at McKonkey's ferry with a few other locals glumly awaiting word of the latest American disaster engineered by Washington. Later in the day, the news came. After a brief struggle, Trenton fell to the Americans at 9:30 in the morning. Washington won a startling victory, taking nearly 1,000 prisoners, capturing six cannon, 40 horses, over 1,000 muskets and 40 barrels of rum. The small group of fence-sitters with Leon at the ferry house looked at each other in disbelief. General Washington might not turn out to be a totally incompetent buffoon after all. Grudgingly, they had to admit George did know something about the business of being a general. Leon woke from the dream with a new appreciation of the trials and tribulations endured by George Washington, the military commander.

March 1999

Four days later, Leon was plagued by another bad dream. He was hungry, cold and wet on a miserable winter's day in 1777. Washington's battered Continental army was wintering at a terrible place in Pennsylvania called Valley Forge. Word has circulated throughout the dismal camp that General Washington has written to Congress saying: "This army must inevitably be reduced to one or the other of three things. Starve, dissolve or disperse, in order to obtain subsistence."

Soldiers became sick and died from the lack of proper food and adequate clothing. Leon was busy digging a burial trench in the frozen ground. No matter how fast he chopped at the unyielding earth, he could not stay ahead of the flow of dead soldiers being delivered by the collection parties. As he stood amid the rows of frozen dead, Leon saw General Washington, wrapped in his army greatcoat, approaching. There were tears in his eyes as the general swept his arm over the row of dead awaiting burial and he spoke to Leon, "These men paid the ultimate price to create the United States, Mr. Leon Placke! What price are you willing to pay to ensure the nation they created remains strong?" As the general's gaze drilled into the very core of Leon's being, Leon felt ashamed of himself and clutching his spade, slowly turned away. When Leon awoke warm and safe in his bed, he vowed not to put off a visit to his psychiatrist any longer. These dreams of Washington were taking too much of a toll on his mental well being.

The next morning at 10 a.m., Dr. Orasco Lopez listened intently as Leon recited his litany of troublesome dreams. The doctor was impressed by Leon's detailed knowledge of Washington's life and thought Leon ought to consider retiring and become a tour guide at one of the many historical sites commemorating Washington's achievements. Not being paid by his patients to make such glib suggestions, Dr. Lopez thought better of it, and refrained from making any comment. Something was nagging at his influential patient, but the doctor was not sure what it was. It was almost as if some kind of deep guilt complex was working itself out of Leon's psyche and manifesting itself in his dreams. Was Leon beginning to feel guilty because he had been the foremost lobbyist in Washington? Perhaps the hard years Leon had put in manipulating the political system in order to bring financial benefit to his clients were taking their toll.

Selling political influence was strenuous mental work, the doctor had no doubt of that. Nervous breakdowns were not an uncommon occurrence among the lobbyists inhabiting the nation's capital. Dr. Lopez knew all about dealing with the common mental breakdowns caused by the pressures of life, but he was not quite sure what to do about a lobbyist who was haunted by the spirit of George Washington. Leon Placke had come up with a totally new wrinkle in the mental problems affecting the capital's rich and powerful. His case would make an interesting item for the medical journal if Dr. Lopez could figure out the cause.

As Leon finished reciting his tale of woe, Dr. Lopez spoke, " I think you have been working too hard. Try to take a few days off and get some rest. It might also be a good idea to cut back on your schedule of social events and try to stay away from historical sites. I believe there was something you saw or did at the gristmill that triggered a reaction in your mind. It probably is related to stress in some way. You do have an unique problem and I'm not sure how to handle it. I have never seen a case quite like yours before. "

"Those dreams were so realistic, I actually felt I was participating in those history making events. The events were so real to me I was exhausted when I awoke. You don't think I'm going crazy, do you doctor?" Leon asked.

"No, having dreams about a national hero the likes of George Washington is not a sign of severe mental illness. Although younger people are usually the ones affected, I suppose there have been a few cases involving other people of your age. Consider it to be a kind of hero worship, a longing to be identified with a great and successful man. In your case, it's probably a sign you need to cut back on the dinner parties and get more sleep. You are not as young as you used to be, you know!"

"Thanks doctor. You make me feel better already. I was beginning to think I was going to have to spend most of my nights learning the lessons of early American history as taught by George Washington. I don't relish spending my nights wandering around in times past. It leaves me too tired to get any real work done for my clients in the morning."

"I'll give you a prescription for a sleeping aid. Take two pills each night before you turn in. You ought to try to also limit your intake of champagne and caviar. I know how you gulp the stuff down four or five nights a week at receptions when Congress is in session. It's not a healthy thing to be doing all the time. With Congress staying in session longer and longer every year, you are in danger of over stimulating yourself with all the rich food and drink. With the diet you eat, it's no wonder your mind has started playing tricks on you."

"When you are skinning your customers you should leave some skin on to grow again so that you can skin them again."
-Nikita Khruschev, 1961

A major American election would be held in the year 2000. With the coming political day of reckoning looming large in the minds of politicians, they were racing to fill their campaign coffers for the coming battle. The fund-raising circuit on Capitol Hill swung into high gear as a proliferation of fund raising events engulfed Washington. The uninhibited race for money was the result of a strategy implemented by the leaders in both parties. Their goal was to gain control of Congress no matter what the financial cost was. Once Congress was secure, there would always be many ways to recover the investment.

In order to find relief from his unsettling dreams, Leon followed Dr. Lopez's instructions to the letter as he moved through the money-driven social swirl. He limited his food intake at receptions to mostly vegetables, a dab of dip and mineral water. He delegated attendance and the delivery of the mandatory campaign contribution check to his subordinates on many occasions. Although his attendance was missed at these fund raisers, his generous check always erased any bad feelings remaining from his absence. Even with a reduced schedule, Leon was so busy lobbying and doling out campaign contributions on behalf of his clients that he was exhausted when he fell into bed late at night.

Leon and his senior and staff were breakfasted, lunched and dinnered out. In rapid succession, they attended a $1,000-a-person dinner for a New York congressman, a $500 breakfast for an Illinois congresswoman, a $2 million fund-raiser for the governor of Texas who was running for president, and a $500-a-plate barbecue for a representative from Georgia. In a little over three weeks, Leon and his staff attended 46 fund-raising events at which they presented checks on behalf of clients in the life insurance, railroad, pharmaceutical, trucking, banking, computer, steel and aircraft industries. Leon and his associates were transferring money from special interest groups to politicians as fast as their legs could carry them. Leon's office began to take on the appearance of a bank clearing house. It was becoming difficult to keep track of what check went where.

Ever alert to assaults on his lobbying turf, Leon was enraged to learn Deborah Steelman, a rival who competed with him for clients in the hospital and pharmaceutical industries, was given the unprecedented opportunity by the House leadership to address 223 Republican members of the House of Representatives in the Capitol basement. How the wily woman lobbyist managed to arrange it, Leon did not know. She was already earning over $2 million a year in fees from big pharmaceutical companies and was the top health care advisor to the Texas governor who was making a bid for the presidency.

The impact of Steelman's stunning coup had an immediate effect on Leon's bottom line. Within a few days, two of his clients curtly dispensed with the further need of Leon's services and signed on with Ms. Steelman's firm. It was obvious to industry observers that she had a higher degree of access to those who made the ultimate political decisions than did Leon. Because he tried to keep his overhead costs in line with his income projections, Leon was forced to cut costs. So he promptly blamed the humiliating debacle on his staff and fired two of them.

Leon had been outsmarted. He had been reminded once again that an intelligence failure in the unruly business of lobbying always meant a loss of clients. Being clever enough to reduce or block your competitor's access to those wielding power was just as important as maintaining your own foot in the door. Two of Leon's former staff members were now on the street scratching for work because they had ignored one of the cardinal rules of the business. They had failed to keep track of things and keep the boss informed of what the competition was doing.

As he mused over ways to counterattack and restore the luster to his blemished professional image, Leon felt besieged. From every nook and cranny of the capital, shark-like rivals emerged and tried to rip away chunks of his business. The struggle to represent the nation's powerful economic interest groups before the lawmakers of the land had grown more desperate. Former members of Congress, dollar hungry ex-staff aides from Capitol Hill and high officials leaving the Executive Branch were establishing new lobbying firms in the city at a record rate and going after Leon's established clients with a vengeance. Leon was engaged in a brutal struggle just to stay even. For every new client he gained, it seemed he lost one to a rival firm.

As he attended social fund-raisers and brooded over the savage state of the lobbying profession, Leon failed to realize he had not gotten his prescription refilled. It was probably as a result of the lack of medication that the dreams started again. Leon knew they had returned when the loud boom of a siege mortar shattered the silence of his bedroom. "Get down," the red-coated soldier crouching in the trench next to Leon said, "the Yankee bastards have fired another one." For a few seconds, Leon watched the shell with its sputtering fuse streaming sparks drop from the night sky. As he lay flattened against the floor of the squalid trench the concussion of the explosion lifted him a good six inches from the ground. As he slammed back down, Leon was showered by the clods of earth and stone the blast had thrown up.

Leon's red uniform was filthy and he stank something fierce. In the month of October in the year 1781, Leon found he had the misfortune to be trapped in the little port of Yorktown, Virginia with Lord Cornwallis and 6,000 British troops. The French navy had taken control of the entrance to Chesapeake Bay, cutting communications with other British forces. Outside the British lines, a force of 8,845 Americans and 8,000 French troops pushed their siege lines closer every day. If the British fleet did not arrive to drive away the French ships, Cornwallis and his hungry troops would be forced into surrender. The relentless boom of the big guns continued day and night as the siege wore on. Becoming hardened to the ordeal, Leon was no longer bothered by the rats scurrying constantly underfoot. Finally to Leon's relief, the siege ended. On a sunny October 19, 1781, the defeated British marched out between the files of French and American troops and laid down their arms.

As he moved forward in the line of surrendering British soldiers, many of them weeping openly, Leon saw a smiling General Washington astride his horse. The Virginia farmer-surveyor turned general had finally pulled it off. In mid-August, Washington had organized a daring large-scale movement of troops. In a bold move, they marched 450 miles south to Virginia, completely deceiving the British force holding New York. With the timely arrival of the French fleet in Chesapeake Bay, Cornwallis was trapped. The cream of the British Empire had been beaten by an unknown hick from the sticks. The world of kings and empires was turned upside down that day. As Leon placed his musket on the stack of surrendered weapons, the sharp sound of metal scraping against metal woke him up.

Looking about his bedroom, Leon felt out of place in the clean room because he had been sleeping outdoors in the dirt in the bottom of a British trench for weeks. He had to get up and take a shower to get rid of the stench. For days, the scene of the ranks of American, French and British troops lining the sunny surrender field stuck in his mind. Leon didn't go to the library to read about the British surrender at Yorktown because he knew he had seen the great event as it actually occurred. The British uniform button he found next to his bed in the morning convinced him of it. The antique appraiser who examined the artifact offered Leon $75 for it. On his next visit to Dr. Lopez, Leon was going to show the doctor the button. Maybe the good doctor could explain how it got into Leon's bedroom if Leon hadn't actually gone to Yorktown.

Dr. Orasco Lopez was not in the least bit amused by the uniform button and the appraiser's statement of authenticity that Leon presented. Instead of being impressed, the doctor was becoming extremely worried about Leon's mental stability. The man might be headed for a full-blown nervous breakdown for all he knew. "Leon," he said, "I don't have any idea how a British uniform button from the Revolutionary War got into your bedroom. Just because you had a bad dream about the British experience at Yorktown doesn't mean you were actually there. The button may have been rolling around in the room for years before you discovered it. It is just a sheer coincidence that you had the dream the night before you found the button. The two are in no way related. Do you understand what I am telling you?"

"Yes, I do," Leon replied. "But I can name the regiments and the order in which they marched to the surrender field for you, if you like. How did I come know those facts if I wasn't there? I am telling you doctor, I think George Washington is after me for a reason I do not understand! The button is another sign from him. I know he will be coming back again."

"Look Leon, you have to take your medication as I have prescribed or it won't do you any good. The reason you continue to have those annoying dreams is that you refuse to follow my advice. You are under a massive amount of work-related strain and the George Washington fixation you have developed is a symptom of a growing mental problem. If you won't take the pills the way you should, I recommend you enter my sanitarium for a month and get a complete rest. Don't drive yourself to the point of having a nervous breakdown."

"Do you think I am going to crack up?"

"If you don't slow down, you will. All the early symptoms are there. It's up to you to make the necessary adjustments in your lifestyle and take your medication. Don't let the prescription expire again. You have to take the pills everyday. "

"All right. I will take the pills faithfully and ease back on work a bit more. It will be a hard thing to do because all of my clients want things done, and done quickly. They want to make sure they are properly connected to the winners of the next election. You know how busy I am going to be until the election is over!"

"Leon, you have a simple choice to make. Either cut back on your high-pressure lobbying activities or crack up! There are no other alternatives. I can't tell you anything else to do. Look at it this way, if you go off the deep end, you will lose your entire business. If you take care of yourself now and follow my instructions, you will recover and can recoup the money you lost during the next election cycle. We have them every two years, you know. "

Leon thought the doctor could have been a little more diplomatic in expressing his opinions. For the size of the fee he charged for each visit, Dr. Lopez should have been less blunt. Although Leon didn't like the way he had been treated, he had to admit to himself the doctor was probably right. Leon jotted a note in his organizer to remind himself to take the pills faithfully and not let the prescription lapse again. As he walked down the street after leaving the doctor's office, Leon began to whistle the catchy little tune he heard the British band play at Yorktown. He could again see the ranks of troops standing in the sunlit field on a fine October day. Maybe his know-it-all shrink didn't know everything after all. Leon knew he was the only person living to have witnessed the British surrender at Yorktown. It made him feel a tad proud of himself.

April 1999

For the next seven weeks Leon was engaged in a massive political advocacy struggle on behalf of three of his clients as he lobbied congressional committees, the Departments of Commerce, State and Defense in an effort to blunt the government's attempt to tighten controls on sensitive technology being exported to China. Several of the communications manufacturing firms Leon represented stood to lose millions of dollars in sales if the controls were tightened. Leon worked the corridors of Congress and met with administration officials virtually around the clock. He organized a deluge of letters from CEO's, mid-level company managers and workers to members of Congress. The letters warned of massive layoffs in the industry if the China market was closed to American technology exports. The tactic worked because no elected representative wanted to be perceived by the voters as favoring a law that caused unemployment among Americans. The proposed controls were watered down enough in a joint congressional committee meeting so as not to interfere with the preponderance of technology items moving to the Peoples Republic of China. The loss of a major market for high technology products had been adverted. Most of the credit for the successful lobbying effort belonged to Leon Placke.

Leon and his staff were exhausted by their lobbying victory on behalf of American industry, having worked 16 and 18 hour days for over a month. It had been worth it in the end. The clients had been pleased with the result and the checks in payment for services rendered continued to flow into Leon's Washington lobbying firm. As he fell exhausted into bed the evening the campaign had been successfully concluded, Leon found himself back in Philadelphia during the summer of 1787.

George Washington had been elected the presiding officer of a group of 55 delegates from the various states who were taking on the weighty task of hammering out a new constitution for the United States of America. The group of delegates had been working since May 14, drafting text, making changes and arguing. Leon watched in fascination as the role of the office of the President of the United States was molded by the delegates to fit the personality of George Washington. As the summer wore on, the differences between the proponents of a strong central government and those favoring absolute rights for the states slowly worked out a compromise. On September 17, the delegates completed work on the new constitution and George Washington sent the document to Congress which ordered it sent to the state legislatures for ratification.

When Leon awoke he could remember the details of the session producing the U.S. Constitution as if it happened yesterday. On the floor next to his bed he found a parchment draft of the proposed Constitution with notes written by George Washington in the margins and on the back. His curiosity aroused, Leon took the historic papers to an appraiser. The document was found to be an original draft copy of the U.S. Constitution. It could easily bring Leon over $1 million if he decided to sell it at auction. Because Leon was very vague as to how he had come into possession of such a priceless historical artifact, the appraiser became suspicious and checked with the police to see if the theft of historical documents had been recently reported. He was startled when his suspicions proved unfounded, the police having no theft reports mentioning documents of the type Leon owned. How could a previously unknown draft copy of the Constitution of the United States of America suddenly surface after all these years, and in the hands of Leon Placke? Something was not right, but the appraiser had no idea of what it was.

A Fairfax County police detective didn't think so either. He remembered Leon's role in taking possession of the two boxes of historical artifacts which had ended up being sealed for the next 20 years and locked away in the National Archives. The detective also remembered a great deal of interest had been expressed in the matter by certain high-placed members of Congress and the intelligence agencies. That was why the case had been quickly and quietly removed from the jurisdiction of the local police. After weighing the evidence at hand, it was obvious to the suspicious policeman what had transpired. Leon Placke, the powerful lobbyist, had helped himself to some of the documents in the boxes during the time he was handling the matter for his powerful friends in Congress. After waiting a decent interval, the sly Mr. Placke was getting ready to put the rare documents he had purloined on the market and earn himself a nice sum of money with no one being the wiser.

The detective continued to think about the matter. Placke had been around the circles of Washington power a long time and was smart enough not to make mistakes. Powerful and greedy he was, stupid he was not. Perhaps he was in cahoots with someone or a group in Congress. It was quite possible that there was more than one individual involved in Mr. Placke's scheme to place rare historical documents on the market. The detective seethed inwardly because the local police had been treated shabbily by the federal authorities when they took over the case. Now was a good time to even the score, the detective thought, as he gleefully placed a call to the police liaison office at an intelligence agency. Let those know it all intelligence types deal with the misdeeds of Mr. Placke and his powerful friends in Congress. Had they not muddied the waters of the police investigation, the thief would now be in jail and those interesting Civil War artifacts and other papers would be on display at one of the local museums.

The detective's call set off the alarm bells in the Washington intelligence community. A hastily convened meeting was called to review the options. Was Placke working on his own? Was he fronting for an unknown number of members of Congress? How many others might be involved in the document marketing scheme with him? The clever plot had most likely been organized so the involved Congresspersons could deny everything if anything went wrong. The cover of complete deniability would make it very difficult to trace anything to anyone other than Leon Placke. The investigators might never find out who else was involved in the scheme if they nabbed Placke early on. Their allegations would bounce around for awhile in the newspapers and then be quickly forgotten by the general public and the Washington establishment. However, come the next budget cycle, the untouched, guilty Congresspersons would take their revenge on the upstart intelligence folks who had dared try to besmirch them. They would slash the agency budget authorizations to the bone. It was a moral dilemma of major proportions. How did one investigate a significant breech of public trust and, at the same time, not bite the hands that feed you?

The ladies and gentlemen sitting around the table knew it would have been better not to have become involved in the box hiding scheme in the first place. But they all knew they had no choice. Being totally responsive to the whims of Congress was one of those unwritten rules government agencies had to live by. Jumping to do the bidding of Congress was a requirement for getting next year's budget funded. It would probably be easier to assassinate the smart-ass Fairfax cop who brought the missing document problem to their attention than risk being burned politically during an attempt to resolve the matter in the proper way.

If the cop was dead, the problem might never surface again. They did a lot of ugly things in intelligence work, but killing a cop to avoid taking responsibility for a problem they helped create was going too far. Instead, they decided to use all the surreptitious means at their disposal to find out the extent of the involvement of members of Congress in Mr. Placke's document-marketing scheme. Once they knew the size of the group, they could take action. Information could be leaked to the press, provided to prosecutors or members of the opposition party. They would be doing the public a service by exposing the scam and cleaning out a few corrupt public officials in the process. If they got them all in one fell swoop, there would be no chance of a revengeful attack on the intelligence budget during the next funding cycle. It was a shame so many valuable resources had to be devoted to cleaning up a political mess, but there was no other option available.

Leon never noticed the small changes in his home. Had he been more attentive, he would have realized his house had been thoroughly searched by professionals. As it was, Leon had been too busy lobbying for tax breaks for business firms to notice many of his possessions had been slightly rearranged. Leon had led the massive lobbying effort which capitalized on the new era of government surpluses push through tax breaks for multinational corporations, utility companies, railroads, insurance firms, oil and gas operators, timber companies, the steel industry and small businesses. If the tax bill passed into law as Leon and his lobbying cohorts had left it, the Federal Treasury would be nicked for a $800 million loss in tax revenue during the next ten years.

Tax relief was a high priority among Leon's client firms. The stunning victory he had orchestrated in the committees of Congress that wrote tax laws would ensure that his clients would gratefully renew their contracts with him. In the largest never ending struggle in American politics, shifting the tax burden to someone else was a game played in deadly earnest. This time around, it was the business interests that got the win thanks to the tireless efforts of their high-powered lobbyists. With a projected national budget surplus of $3 billion coming over the next decade, it was an easy thing to push the lawmakers to do. As usual, no one in Congress seemed to worry about what would happen if the surplus didn't develop as planned.

During the swirling battle to rewrite the tax law, Leon's girlfriend mentioned that someone had been in her apartment. Nothing was missing, but someone had been there, that much she knew. Leon thought her a bit paranoid and dismissed the episode as the product of an over active imagination brought on by reading too many spy novels. To assuage her concerns, however, he had the locks on the condominium changed. Had he not been so focused on his lobbying activities, Leon would have noticed that he and his staff were being followed, their conversations monitored and one by one their dwellings carefully searched.

Thus far, it had been a lot of work with little useful result for the intelligence agents assigned to the case. They were now genuinely mystified by their lack of progress. They found nothing which would indicate how many historical documents Leon had in his possession and who in Congress might be working with him. The draft of the Constitution had been taken from Leon's safe deposit box, verified as authentic and returned. In all their searches, it was the only document they found. The agents knew they were dealing with extremely clever people who were masters in the art of deceit and manipulation, and having found no new evidence, the agents would have to sit back and await developments. They were not going to make a mistake by underestimating the craftiness of their opponents in the political sphere. This case could take a long time to solve. They were up against some of the best minds in American politics.

> **"Business? It's quite simple: it's other people's money."**
> **-Alexandre Dumas, 1824-98**

Smug with the knowledge of his tax bill victory, Leon attended a lavish reception hosted by one of his clients to celebrate the anticipated financial windfall. There he met and chatted briefly with a noted economist who thought tax reductions were a terrible idea at the present time because they would increase consumer spending, possibly triggering inflation in an already booming U.S. economy. That would force the Federal Reserve to increase interest rates, a move negating the benefit of the tax cut because it would increase the cost of money to consumers and business alike. The economist thought the best course was to let the projected budget surplus accumulate for awhile, perhaps using the revenue to pay down some of America's massive national debt. To accomplish that end, Congress would have to resist the ever present temptation to increase government spending. Increasing spending, the economist said, was as bad an option as the tax cut proposal.

Leon listened politely, but did not buy the economist's ideas. Leon was paid to look after his client's parochial interests. He did not give a damn about what might be best for the nation as a whole. Totally focused on making as much money for himself as he possibly could, Leon wasn't going to risk having his income cut by bringing unpopular economic positions to the attention of his clients. If corporate America wanted tax cuts, Leon would fight for tax cuts. Someone else could worry about the long-term consequences of the tax cuts to the national economy. It was none of Leon Placke's business.

After adroitly disentangling himself from the economist worrying about the economic health of the United States, Leon found himself with other guests discussing a topic more to his interest. Since January 1999, lawyers (over 4,000 of them) had contributed $3 million to Vice President Al Gore's election campaign. Texas Governor George W. Bush apparently was not as well liked by the legal community. He had taken in checks totaling $2.2 million from 3,000 lawyers. To everyone's surprise, Bill Bradley, who was battling Gore in the Democratic presidential primaries, had come out of nowhere with an extremely strong showing and collected more than $1.5 from 2,300 lawyers. Other than signifying lawyers were making unusually heavy political contributions during the primary season, it was also an indication that Bradley was going to give Gore a rough fight for the Democratic presidential nomination.

After dispensing with the presidential possibilities in the coming election, the conversation turned to a much more rewarding topic. Leon swelled with pride when he heard how well Washington's lobbying industry was thriving. According to a recently released report, lobbying expenditures were increasing roughly 13 percent a year, reaching $1.42 billion in 1998. As happy as he was to hear the good news about the healthy condition of the industry, the report wasn't all to Leon's liking. He learned there were now 20, 512 registered lobbyists competing with him in Washington for clients and their lobbying dollars. Overall though, the news about the fantastic growth of lobbying was uplifting. At least Leon was working in one of America's fastest growing industries, and one vital to the nation's welfare. Leon felt good as he left the reception. He had already forgotten the name of the wet-blanket economist with his pessimistic views.

"To know how to dissimulate is the knowledge of kings."
-Cardinal de Richelieu, 1641

As he waited for the valet to bring his Porsche from the parking garage, Leon listened with a little interest to the conversation of two of his acquaintances. They were discussing a poll conducted by respected Republican and Democratic pollsters that showed an alarming trend in public apathy towards politics. The poll found that slightly over 54 percent of Americans felt alienated from their government. These cynical American citizens believed the government was controlled by the political parties, lobbyists and the media. For them, it had ceased to be government of, by and for the people. It had become a government of, and for the moneyed special interests.

Leon chuckled to himself as he said his good nights, put the car into gear and sped out of the parking lot. Only 54 percent of America's mass of unwashed wage slaves had figured out they didn't count for anything except as a number on the Internal Revenue Service tax collection roles. "If those pathetic, dumb bastards want representation in Washington, they can hire me," Leon said to no one in particular as he shifted the Porsche into third gear. Leon did not sympathize with the poll findings. He had no use for run-of-the-mill tax paying morons and could care less for what any of them thought about anything.

Over a long period of years Leon had become a jaded Washingtonian, caring nothing for those who did not spend vast sums of money to influence the political decision making process. He controlled a lucrative piece of the Washington lobbying industry which was expanding, growing at robust annual rate of 13 percent and that was nothing to sneeze at. With the numbers looking so good, Leon might be able to add staff and launch a drive to expand his market share. In the competitive world of lobbying, it was a constant fight to increase hourly billings or risk fading into oblivion.

He was sure of one thing--Leon Placke didn't consider himself to be an average American. He had long been certain he was part of the nation's unofficial ruling elite. Republican or Democrat in the White House, it did not matter. Leon was there to see to it that those with the money to buy political influence got all they could. Lobbying had become an accepted part of the hallowed American political system and Leon saw no problem with it at all. Being able to contribute to the mundane everyday workings of American democracy had made him wealthy. The system was a little expensive and inefficient to operate he acknowledged, but that was a price the public ought to be happy to pay. The ungrateful louts in the hinterland should be praising lobbyists for the services they performed instead of constantly criticizing them.

It had been a long, tiring, but successful day so Leon was glad to hit the sheets. The pleasant dream in which he was handing out large checks to all the candidates for the Presidency and Congress was rudely interrupted by the intruding presence of George Washington. "Mr. President," Leon said with a degree of amazement as he looked at the man, "you look a great deal heavier than your famous portraits show."

"Like most people, controlling my weight was a constant battle for me as I grew older. Despite my best efforts to reduce my food intake, my weight increased from 175 pounds in 1760 to around 210 pounds by 1784. The artists of my era were kind enough not to over emphasize the additional flesh hanging on my bones in the portraits they painted of me in my later years."

"It was nice of them to do you the courtesy. Our modern photographers and painters would not be so kind. They like to show everything as it is. What can I do for you, Mr. President?" Leon asked.

"You don't have to refer to me as Mr. President. You can call me surveyor, farmer, businessman, captain, colonel or general if you like. I was all of those things before I became a politician. Filling a political role was a duty to be undertaken, not a career calling for me. Of all the work I did, I really enjoyed farming the most. It's too bad hardly anyone in your time remembers the contributions I tried to make to American agriculture. It was a tough row to hoe back then, nothing that worked well in England seemed to work in Virginia. I had to learn everything from scratch and work my way back up the ladder of knowledge."

"I see," said Leon somewhat discomfited by the great man's modesty regarding his political role. Leon thought George Washington would have a difficult time fitting into life in the modern capital, a city where politics counted for everything. Politics became a lucrative lifetime career for many of those who came to the city supposedly to serve the interests of the American people. Working the law, lobbying and politics was where the action was. As one of the successful new breed of political operatives, Leon was somewhat saddened to hear the first president of the United States was really nothing more than a common clod-kicker at heart. The man had absolutely no idea of how to spin-doctor an image of himself for public consumption.

Washington's mood changed abruptly as if he had been able to read Leon's mind. He shot Leon one of those now familiar stares of contempt as he said, "Leon Placke, you are among the lowest of the low. In your never ending quest for lobbying dollars you and your ilk have ruined the political system Jefferson, Madison and a host of others worked so hard to put into place. You sir, are a disgrace to the nation we created and an insult to our memory."

Leon, taken aback by the vicious, unprovoked attack on his character, stammered, "I only took advantage of the opportunities the political system you created offered to me. I provide a service to industries and individuals of influence who wish to exercise their right to petition the government."

"Now we are getting to the crux of the problem," Washington replied in an icy tone, "you and the rest of your career politicians, special interest groups and lobbying parasites have so debased the system we created, it has virtually ceased to function. Did you think we designed the American political system to serve the nation without any change or modification as the years passed? We did not! And we certainly did not invent it for you and your kind to run into the ground!"

Leon looked genuinely mystified as he said, "I don't really understand what you are talking about because we do everything according to the letter of the law."

"When we wrote the Constitution," Washington continued, "and established the three branches of government, the population of the United States was less than four million souls. We were a nation of farmers. The geographical center of population was 23 miles east of Baltimore, Maryland. We located the capital as near as possible to the center of the nation. At the time, the most central point in the country happened to be at what is now the District of Columbia, where the capital remains to this very day. The nation has grown in size. Why hasn't anyone moved the capital to the new center of the country?"

"I don't really know," Leon responded, "The question has never come up before. The capital stayed where it was, I guess, because you and the other founding fathers picked the site. No one wanted to tamper with what you put into place."

"I can see you are going to be about as easy to reason with as a New York City merchant who makes his money by supplying goods to His Majesty's army. The new capital was located in the District of Columbia because it was the center of the nation at the time. Where have you read anything in which we said we never wanted the capital to be moved? We assumed future generations would be capable of making the necessary adjustments in location as the country grew."

"The capital is just fine where it is," Leon angrily retorted. "It is even named in your honor! Why do you want it moved to the center of the country?"

"Leon, please try to understand we did our best to plan for building the nation and maintaining a democratic form of government! Neither I nor anyone else who was present at the founding of the nation thought our humble work would be used as an excuse for duty shirking by those coming after us. Naming a city after me does not excuse your generation from violating the spirit of the principles we put in place. As you certainly must be aware, democracy is a fragile thing. Having the capital located in the geographical center of the nation is a symbol of the equality of all the land. Therefore, it would have been wise to relocate the capital as the nation grew in size. The moves would have been in keeping with the standards of government we hoped later generations would follow."

"It would cost a fortune to move the seat of government to Kansas or wherever the center of the United States is now located. Congress would never approve the move. Besides, no one in politics in this day and age wants to live in the flat middle of the country. People like Bob Dole made lifetime careers out of avoiding having to go back to the boring hinterland. We modern Americans just do not see things the same way you did. We stopped being a nation of clod-kicking farmers a long time ago. Everyone I know is happy with the capital being right here in Washington, DC, just where you placed it!"

"When the capital was established, the country only reached as far to the west as the Allegheny mountains. Now it goes clear to Hawaii. I want you to bring this issue to the attention of the American people. Explain our reasoning, the intentions of the founding fathers. The people will understand why the capital should be moved."

"Why do you want me to bring up a matter I don't agree with in the least? There certainly must be others much better qualified for the task than I am! Why don't you go talk to Bob Dole? I hear he isn't doing much these days. I am a business lobbyist, not a capital mover. This is not in my line of work. Besides, as I said before, I think it is a really stupid idea!"

"Leon Placke, you are a scoundrel of the highest order! You would have made a fine minister for King George III. You earn your living from bending and twisting the American political system which I had a hand in creating, to give advantage to your selected special interests. It is now time you made a few personal sacrifices and gave something back to the nation! This is the time for you to cease being selfish, mean-spirited and milking the system for everything it is worth! You made plenty of money out of twisting laws to the benefit of your clients. Now it is time for you to do your duty and, for once in your sorry life, seek nothing in return but the grateful thanks of generations yet unborn. I know it is a difficult concept for a greedy person such as yourself to grasp. Hopefully, it is not too late for you to learn something about the meaning behind our system of governing. You may begin your lessons by talking to your lobbying cohorts about the advantages of moving the capital to the center of the land."

Leon felt a little ashamed as he said, "Well I guess, I could do that much for you if it will get you off of my back for awhile."

"Leon, I hoped you would see it my way because nothing worth having in life comes cheap. The political system in the United States has badly eroded, thanks in a large part to the activities of people like you. Having the lobbyist Leon Placke begin to espouse political reform in the United States would be no less an earth shaking event than the conversion of St. Paul. Being the unofficial king of the lobbyists, your words would carry a great deal of weight and attract the attention of the public. Besides moving the capital, there are a couple of other matters I also want you to bring to the attention of the American public."

"General Washington, you really ought to think about finding someone else for some of this work. I am willing to help you, but I can't do it all by myself. Since Bill Clinton will be looking for something to do when he leaves office, why don't you pay him a visit some night and explain your program to him? Being the current President, I'm sure he would be delighted to hear from you."

"I plan to ask him to take on the job of doing something about the national obsession with copulation. The preoccupation the population of the United States has with sex is a real problem, and Mr. Clinton appears to be well-qualified to address the matter. In my day sex was always around, but it wasn't a national fixation. Perhaps because we had to work from sunup to sundown six days week, we didn't have the time or energy to pay more attention to it. I'm going to ask President Clinton to help get America's focus off sex and put more energy into getting the national debt down to a manageable level. Maybe I should also ask him about increasing the nation's work week by several hours. Less sex and more work would help improve the country's economic health a great deal."

Leon was shocked and dismayed by what he had heard. No one in modern America would listen to such a crazy idea! George Washington had to be simplistic and naive beyond belief to even bring the subject up. Leon certainly wanted no part of the national less sex and more work plan Washington was proposing. It would not fly with the voters. It was preposterous! It would go nowhere politically! Happy to be let off the hook, Leon said, "General Washington, I agree with you completely! President Clinton is just the man to bring that important matter to the attention of the American people. Being an ex-president and a known expert on the subject of women, the voters will listen to him. I am sure of that."

"I thought so too," Washington replied. "I have tried several times to visit him in the Lincoln bedroom at the White House. But he is never there. The room is always occupied by campaign contributors who delight in being allowed to spend a night in what was once Abraham Lincoln's office. You would think President Clinton, the man charged with overseeing the welfare of the land, would want to spend a night or two there himself to gain a little inspiration. Abraham Lincoln had a mighty tough time of it when he was president. He had to make some very important decisions in that room, you know."

Here comes some more of that simple farmer's wisdom crap again, Leon thought as Washington went on. "Leon, the U.S. tax code is now complicated beyond all human understanding because of the slick changes you and your lobbyist friends constantly have Congress make to it. The tax law mess is one of the other matters of grave importance to the political health of the United States I want you to bring to the attention of the public."

"You mean you want me to do more besides trying to get people interested in the crazy idea of moving the capital out of the District of

Columbia? How much extra work do you think I am capable of? I have a business to run, you know! What else do you have in mind, Mr. farmer turned first President of the United States of America?" a much agitated Leon Placke sarcastically responded.

"Leon, please calm down and listen to what I have to say or I'll take you back to Valley Forge for another lesson in humility. When the 13 colonies opted for independence from His Britannic Majesty's government, it was not a sure thing. Barely 35 percent of the population supported the concept of independence, another third didn't care one way or another and one-third strongly supported the King. We who made the American Revolution opted to take the responsibility and risk the consequences. Had we lost the war, all the signers of the Declaration of Independence and others in leadership positions in the Continental government and army would have been shot or hanged. We chanced it, and by the grace of God, hard work, a little luck and help from France, we won. What we created is now being undone. The American public is rapidly losing faith in the miserable present state of American politics. I want you to set things right! You owe some small service to the nation that has provided you millions of dollars in lobbying income. I want you to change your degenerate ways and lead an American political renaissance."

Leon didn't like the sound of Washington's proposal at all, so he evasively replied, "It seems to me the checks and balances you established are still working well. I don't see why anything has to change. Congress legislates, the President administers and the courts make rulings. What more can you want?"

"The system of government we designed was for a nation of hard-working, self-sufficient farmers. It has become encrusted by hangers-on such as yourself and debased by the structural inefficiencies that have been allowed to develop over the years. The political process the founding fathers of the nation put in place needs to be streamlined and made relevant to the present needs of the country. It is absurd to think the single horse and plow you used on a ten acre field can efficiently plow a 100 acre field as well. Even a dumb clod-kicker such as myself knows you need a larger team of horses and a bigger plow, do you understand?"

"I don't know anything about plowing fields. I don't want anything to do with turning dirt with a horse and plow. I buy all my groceries at a supermarket. General Washington, you have lost me. Just what is it you are trying to say?"

"Have you ever killed, cleaned, plucked and cooked a chicken?"

"I never have killed a chicken in my life. I buy chicken in a nice package -

it comes all ready to cook, straight from a clean supermarket. Why on earth would I want to kill and pluck a chicken?"

"Leon, you have lost all appreciation for your humble national roots. One of the problems modern America faces is that its people have lost touch with the land and the mindset forged by a hard agricultural way of life. In losing all sense of how the land produces food and fiber, the people have also forgotten that our system of government was designed for a nation of farmers, or clod-kickers as you derisively call them. It was an era in which individual self-sacrifice and hard work was so common that the nation's founders simply took those traits for granted."

"The present sorry state of affairs could not have been foreseen when we established the rules of government. The individual self-denial and discipline we accepted as normal personality traits have become virtually extinct in modern American politics. Just look at yourself Leon! You are philosophically inclined to take every advantage of a government system we established in a time when no one would take unfair advantage of anyone, neighbors or government. As a consequence of the activities of people like you, the political system has been stressed to breaking! The functions of government have been debased to the point where the federal government's primary function is to dispense funds and tax breaks to the special interests having the right political connections. The purpose we had in establishing a new form of government has been rendered virtually meaningless in the present context of a Congress which wallows in a legislative sewer of providing handouts of one type or another to your clients."

Stung by the insult to his grab-all-you-can-get philosophy of legislative manipulation, Leon curtly asked, "Are you suggesting we go back to working on subsistence farms just so people can get the feel of the earth back into their fingers? You can't run an industrialized country like that! Why the national economy would collapse! It would be the ruin of the United States of America as a world power."

Washington sighed audibly as he continued after Leon's outburst, "You are missing the point entirely; let me try to explain it another way. When we established Congress, the constituent representation base for each member of the House of Representatives and the Senate was based on geography. Since there was little large-scale manufacturing and the majority of population worked in an agricultural economy, it was the fairest way to ensure equal political representation. We did it by state and congressional district. With nearly everyone engaged in farming, there was no need to consider other alternatives."

"It is a good system," Leon said. "Elections are held on the basis of the same geographical congressional districts and states to this day. Hardly anything has changed since you and the other framers of the Constitution set the precedent. Your fine work has stood the test of time. You can be very proud of it."

"Thank you for the compliment, but it was not supposed to be that way for all time. We perhaps incorrectly assumed those following us would change the basis of representation to suit the current needs of the nation. You have done us no honor by fossilizing and corrupting the system of representation we put into place. As you must be aware Leon, the United States ceased to be an agricultural nation many years ago. Its gross national product approaches eight trillion dollars per year. Agriculture accounts for a mere two percent of economic activity while industry contributes 23 percent and services 75 percent. Yet, the system of political representation remains virtually the same as it did when agriculture dominated the nation's economic activity."

Seeing the perplexed look on Leon's face, George Washington continued his explanation. "The seats in Congress continue to be apportioned on the same geographical basis as when everyone worked on a family farm. Who represents the interests of petroleum, motor vehicles, aerospace, telecommunications, chemicals, electronics, food processing, consumer goods, lumber, mining, insurance, banking, pharmaceuticals, advertising and the other economic activities of the nation in Congress?"

A look of comprehension slowly crept across Leon's face as he replied, "Why that has never been a problem, Mr. Washington. Every sector of the American economy is represented by a trade group of one sort or another. They hire talented lobbyists such as myself to present the views of the industry or labor group to Congress. The appropriate congressional committee considers these views in the preparation of legislation affecting the group's interests."

"Leon, you have grown extremely wealthy representing powerful special interests before Congress and government agencies. We never anticipated such a situation developing when we established the rules for our democratic form of government. Our political system was not designed to support the conniving deal-making activities of a massive number of moneyed special interest groups. You, the other lobbyists and a Congress thirsting for campaign contributions have perverted our creation and turned it into a playground for those currying special favor. An invisible empire of well-heeled special interests have taken control of the lawmaking process in Washington, DC!"

Seeing Leon shake his head in disagreement, Washington continued, "All right Leon, I see you disagree with me. Let me give you some examples of what I mean. In this year alone, Senate Majority Leader Trent Lott has received over $600,000 in contributions from real estate people and auto dealers. Senate Minority Leader Richard Gephardt has received almost the same amount of large contributions from brewers, unions and aerospace companies. Newt Gingrich, the former speaker of the House, did just as well, receiving a $800,00 contribution from a consumer conglomerate, $370,00 from textile interests and over $700,000 from brokers and investment firms. Congress, I'm afraid, has become an institution that is for sale to the highest bidder."

Leon cringed inwardly as Washington continued, "Don't try to tell me these contributions have no effect on the legislation Congress passes. Interest groups don't make contributions and pick up the tab for congressional junkets because they want to provide a public service. They want favors in return. Your damn special interests have also completely ingratiated themselves into an incestuous relationship with Congress by hiring former lawmakers and their aides as lobbyists!"

"The result is that no one ever leaves Washington after completing a stint in the so-called public service. The chance to manipulate the $1.8 trillion annual federal budget keeps people attracted to the city like honey draws flies. Whatever happened to the concept of service at a personal sacrifice? Then going back, after serving, to whatever you did beforehand for a living? In my day we knew what Alexander Pope meant when he said: 'But Satan is wiser than in days of yore, and tempts by making rich, not making poor.' You know exactly what I am talking about, don't you Leon? Lobbyists in the capital are spending over $700 million every six months. It's a growth industry serving no useful purpose, one which is obscenely growing at a faster rate than the information technology sector."

Leon knew Washington was right. He did much to help create the system the general was so eloquently denouncing. He knew quite well how his lobbying business functioned. "Well, I will have to admit things may have gotten slightly out of hand during the past few years. But you have to remember, the times have been good and no one seemed to care anything about what we did." he lamely responded.

Eyeing Leon malevolently, Washington spoke again. "The Congress no longer adequately represents the economic interests of the citizens of the United States of America. The system of representation the founding fathers instituted has been rendered obsolete by the growth and diversification of the economy. The Senate should remain organized on the basis of two senators from each state so as to maintain a broader geographical perspective in the national legislature."

"The House of Representatives has become a complete disaster and should be reorganized. The representatives to that body should be elected on the basis of an economic constituency instead of congressional district. Every sector of the American economy would be apportioned a number of representatives based on its contribution to the gross domestic product. Out of the 435 House seats, labor would be apportioned a number of representatives to elect. The other sectors of the economy such as agriculture, the information technology industry, medical, pharmaceuticals, steel , retail, real estate, vehicle manufacturing, aircraft, the legal profession, etc. would all be represented on the same proportional basis. Under the new system, lawyers could only represent the legal profession. A candidate for any of the other House seats would have to come from the economic sector he or she represented and agree to return to it when the term of office was completed. No more lifetime legislators would be allowed. Serving in Congress was supposed to be a duty and an honor, not a way to dispense favors to all your greedy friends. "

Leon was shocked! George Washington was proposing a system of congressional representation that would wipe out the largest part of the lobbying industry and severely limit influence peddling by people such as himself. "I have never heard of a more wild-eyed, radical proposal in my life," he said. "It will never be accepted by the American public! They don't like political changes. Your crazy idea destroys the very basis on which our successful political system has been built."

"Leon you are more selfish and shortsighted than I thought! A radical change was when the 13 British colonies in North America decided to dispense with the King of England and establish a new form of government. At the time, most of the world's population didn't think we could make it work because it was a radical idea far beyond the comprehension of most sensible men. Changing the current makeup of the House of Representatives is doing nothing more than bringing the basis of representation in Congress into line with national economic reality. As I told you before, we designed the system of representation when the nation was composed mostly of farmers, it was not a country with large and diverse economic sectors. People have always paid more attention to what is going on in their occupations than they do to happenings in the obsolete congressional district in which they reside."

"Under these circumstances, I believe the citizens would take a greater interest in national lawmaking and take the time to make a more informed

254

choice of the candidates running for office. The legislation in Congress would be improved because the body would once again represent the true economic interests of the nation's citizens, something it has not done effectively in close to a hundred years. As one who has contributed mightily to the current sorry state of affairs in the capital, I think you are ideally suited to bringing the matter of reforming the House of Representatives to the American people."

Leon was horrified by the concept George Washington was proposing. It would wipe out his lucrative influence peddling business and leave him unemployed. He decided to take a stand and argue his view of the matter. "You want me to talk people into moving the capital of the United States to the middle of nowhere and also change the composition of the House of Representatives? That is a very tall order. Have you ever considered the cost and how your program would work? Tell me how we can register voters by economic sector instead of by residence in a congressional district? Did you think of how we could solve that little problem Mr. President? It would require a massive, complex system of voter registration."

"You forget I have always had a deep appreciation for the application of technology. My gristmill and whiskey distillery were state of the art, always operating with the latest technological improvements available. Leon, go and apply a high tech solution to the problem! You ought to know modern computer systems can easily handle registering voters by occupation and economic interest. It is time to get the U. S. system of congressional representation updated. I want the legislative branch to function fairly as was our original intent. Leon, it's not an impossible job that I am asking you to do. The people are not stupid! They will understand the logic behind the concept. And while you are at it, stop using the names of the founding fathers in vain. We left you a system of government designed to be adaptable to change. Let me assure you and all the other modern political flunkies that the founders of this nation do not turn over in their graves every time a change is made. Stop using us as an excuse for avoiding doing the things you should!"

Leon wasn't sure what to do next so he remained silent as Washington continued, "Thanks to you and the other parasites, the cost of national lawmaking has gotten completely out of control during the past three decades. The people of the United States do not need to spend nearly $3 billion a year on Congress. With a new and realistic system of congressional representation in place, the 100 Senators and 435 members of the House of Representatives can go back to being citizen legislators again and stop trying to be proxy presidents. A reconstituted Congress will be able to spend less time in session, with no more than six months out of the year spent in the capital. The government could then reduce the number of congressional staff from the present 31,000 to a size more in keeping with the true needs of the legislative body, perhaps no more than 11,000."

"With Congress refocusing on its duties as intended by the Constitution, the White House ought to be able to cut its 1,000 member staff by at last 50 percent. Another 3,000 employees scattered throughout the federal agencies could be reassigned to productive work because there would be less congressional and White House correspondence for them to answer. With the economic interests of America once again fairly represented in Congress as the founders of the nation intended, the need for lobbyists would diminish greatly. Can you measure up to the task, Leon? I want you to lead an American political revolution! A real revolution, not one of those phony ones promoted by the self-serving political hacks interested in keeping their fingers in the federal cash box! Do you understand?"

"If the number of lobbyists goes down, I will be out of a job," Leon retorted. "How do you think I am going to make a living? I would have to close up my firm and find some other way to earn money. Why should I reform myself out of a very good job?"

"You are an attorney, a supposedly respected member of the bar. You could go back to practicing real law, trying cases in court, writing wills, etc. Leon, you could run for elected office or retire-- you have plenty of money. Whatever course you choose, you would be forever remembered for performing a great service to the nation. The country will be better off without the class of legislator-lawyer-lobbyists who have taken over the affairs of government in the years since the end of World War II. You played a big part in creating the problem. Now do your duty and help resolve it! Otherwise, one of these fine days, the entire system will come crashing down on top of you! Remember the mess in France in 1789? Russia in 1917? It will happen here if you don't get the system cleaned up. The militia movement, the growing distrust of the federal government and low voter turnout are symptoms of a citizenry's mistrust of a political system that has become dysfunctional. Leon! You must educate the people to see the need to reform the system before it's too late!"

With a deep sense of unease, Leon finally relented and reluctantly agreed to start the ball rolling on the political reforms President George Washington wanted instituted, although he was completely unsure of how to go about it. Leon could not tell people the proposals for reforming the government came from George Washington. If he mentioned Washington as the author of the concept, Leon knew he would be sent on a one way trip to a mental ward. No one would believe the long-dead Washington had prodded the city's most successful lobbyist into turning his back on the system under which he had amassed great wealth and power.

The fact that the reforms would destroy Leon's power base and his lucrative income would make Leon's sanity automatically suspect in Washington's law-making circles. No sane lobbyist or legislator in the capital of the United States of America would ever consider doing anything that would adversely impact on one's ability to gain and control political power. Having power or access to those wielding power translated into the ability to earn big money. Everyone in Washington knew and accepted that fact as the foundation on which the lobbying industry was built. It was something never to be tampered with by anyone, Republican, Democrat, lobbyist or bureaucrat. It was how the system worked.

"We have the power to do any damn fool thing we want to do, and we seem to do it about every ten minutes."
-Senator J. William Fulbright, 1952

True to his word, Leon began his campaign by raising George Washington's reform proposals during the many lunches he attended with incumbent members of Congress. Their views on the seditious plan were quickly made clear to Leon. Every member of member of Congress he spoke to was completely appalled by the political heresy Leon espoused. The lawmakers couldn't believe what they were hearing. Over lunches whose cost would be billed to a client, Leon Placke, the unofficial king of the lobbyists, was seriously suggesting lawmakers ought to demolish the political system that enriched them. By the fifth luncheon, Leon knew the legislators were not interested in supporting any of his proposals. They frankly saw no need to change a system that treated them so well. When Leon broached the matter of simmering citizen discontent, he was bluntly told that the average American didn't care one iota about how the political system functioned. One of Leon's luncheon guests, who was well-versed in the nuances of the language of diplomacy, strongly suggested to Leon that he ought to remove his head from his rectal orifice and stop all the talk about wrecking the system that supported Washington's law making establishment in style.

Leon took the message to heart. He now understood the congressional incumbents had absolutely no interest in backing any serious reform proposal. He was going to have to find support in other quarters for the changes to the political system that George Washington had charged him with implementing. Leon sat gloomily at his desk, completely deflated by his

257

humiliating failure with Congress and thought about his next move. As he mulled over the few remaining options, his mind wandered back to a glorious long-ago October day at Yorktown, Virginia. Leon could see the lines of red-coated British troops marching to the field of surrender as clearly as if it had happened this morning. The memory of George Washington and his selfless sacrifices moved Leon deeply. It was proving to be completely incompatible with the culture of a modern capital city in which the exercise of political power and the money it attracted, counted for everything. Leon was anxious to go out and try again. His wretched experience with his friends on Capitol Hill had taught him that doing George Washington's bidding was going to be far more difficult than he had expected.

May 1999

The influence peddling industry in the nation's capital had a very good year in 1998, with the top ten law and lobbying firms earning in excess of $110 million. 1999 was proving to be a better year, income was surging 18 percent ahead of last year's levels. To celebrate the good fortune smiling on the lawyers and lobbyists prowling the capital, the Washington Society of Solicitors rented the large and ornate grand entrance room on the first floor of the Department of Commerce building for the social occasion they held in the merry month of May. The building, which had been completed in 1932 and opened by President Hoover, had just the touch of elegance the society's members felt they deserved in a year when the money was rolling in.

Expectations were high. Corporations, labor unions and wealthy individuals contributed over $220 million in unregulated soft money contributions to the national political parties during the 1997-98 campaign. A good sized portion of those funds eventually filtered down to the society's members as payment for services in one form or another. With the 2000 election looming, over $55 million had already flowed into the coffers of the national parties. Attack ads were flashing across television screens, mass mailings of inflammatory political diatribe were going out, and the Washington Society of Solicitors was gleefully celebrating the anticipated flood of money yet to come.

With powerful behind-the-scenes shakers and movers attending, the society's party would be given a nice write up in the society pages of the newspapers in a city known for its elegant power dinners and large receptions. The Commerce building had been constructed before the age of air conditioning. The grand entrance room with its ornate solid brass doors, high ceilings and elaborate decor was a relic from an era of genteel refinement and good taste. It was the perfect place for the solicitors to socialize because they were comfortable being in surroundings radiating a sense of wealth and power.

Lavish buffet tables, groaning under loads of tastefully arranged culinary delights, stood against the walls at opposite ends of the room. If any of the 650 guests didn't care to sample the lobster, oysters or clams, they could try the halibut or roast beef. For those cursed with counting calories, an exquisite selection of fresh and cooked vegetables offered a degree of solace. Delicate pastries, fresh strawberries, raspberries, figs, almond-cream filled tortes and a large selection of fruits completed the feast. Strategically located along the two other walls were four bars busily dispensing fruit juices, soft drinks, fine wines and liquor. Carefully balancing plates of food, lawyers employed by the government mixed with those from the city's major law firms as they traded legal anecdotes and hints regarding the course of proposed enforcement actions. As they talked, they eagerly researched the possible lucrative employment opportunities dangled before them by the private sector firms. Staff members from the powerful committees of Congress bantered about pending legislation with lobbyists eager to shape the laws to fit their clients' interests. If they could not maximize advantage, they aimed to minimize the damage to their client's welfare. In the rough and tumble world of Washington lobbying, they got paid either way.

Leon was munching on strawberries and washing them down with a good quality champagne as he circulated among the happy group. It didn't take long for him to realize he had to face the negative repercussions generated by his ill-conceived series of lunches with members of Congress. Word of his ludicrous political reform proposals had circulated rapidly through Washington's close-knit legal and lobbying communities. Leon was bombarded by inquiries from hostile society members demanding to know why he had broached such an obscene topic with Congress. As one who epitomized everything the system represented, Leon's sudden obsession with proposals to demolish the way the legislative process operated made him appear to the society's members as an outright traitor to his class. "Leon, you bastard! Just because you got yours, doesn't give you the right to stop me from getting mine," a young lawyer who worked deep in the bowels of one of the big lobbying firms hissed through a lobster-filled mouth as Leon passed.

"Leon we are all very disappointed in you! I can't believe the man who made the concept of the titanium career triangle work so well for himself would so foolishly abandon the concept. You were, until very recently, the idol of all the young lawyers in this city. Why would you tell the lawmakers in Congress you thought our system has to be changed? Have you taken complete leave of your senses?" an old acquaintance fired back at him after Leon had extended his greetings.

Other red-faced lobbyists shouted a series of questions at Leon in rapid succession.

"Our friends in Congress are totally shocked and dismayed by your asinine reform proposals. What has gotten into you, Leon? Are you trying to destroy the lobbying industry and all that we stand for? If the public gets wind of those half-witted ideas of yours and takes a liking to them, we will all be in bankruptcy court in no time flat, you included! You of all people should know better than to bring that reform crap to the attention of Capitol Hill! Why are you trying to ruin such a good thing?"

A tall, well-dressed lawyer, widely known for the free legal work he performed for liberal causes, pushed his way through the crowd to Leon's side. "How could you impugn our great democratic system of electing members of Congress by having the impudence to suggest it needs to be changed? When Leon looked him without answering, the outraged lawyer continued, "You insulted the intelligence of our lawmakers with your disgusting prattle! The American people don't want or need reforms. They should consider themselves lucky because they have the best government money can buy!" Seeing that Leon, who was calmly eating another strawberry, was not going to reply, the lawyer finished by saying, "You are a disgrace to the lobbying profession. Why don't you check yourself into a mental hospital and see if anything can be done to help restore the function of your addled brain!"

Having had enough of the verbal dressing down, an angry Leon replied, "Where do you think I got the ideas for reforming the system of congressional representation from?"

"Most likely from some idiot who doesn't have any idea of how a great democracy such as ours has to work! Perhaps from a simple fool with absolutely no political sense! The real question to answer is why you, of all people, would waste your valuable time by bringing the matter to the attention of Congress," responded the lawyer.

"You are partially correct," Leon said. "The ideas came from a simple, straight forward farmer by the name of George Washington. He doesn't like the way things are going in the country and has been jumping all over me for months to go out and get something done about it. I'm trying to do what he asked me to do for him. If you don't like the sound of the reforms, why don't you take the matter up with Mr. Washington?"

"Now I know for sure you have gone completely mad," said the incensed lawyer. "Washington has been dead for nearly 200 years. You could not possibly have gotten those ridiculous proposals from him. Being the astute politician he was, he would never consider such crazy notions if he were alive in this day and age. You need to get serious medical help for your delusions before you ruin yourself and take the lobbying business down with you." With that said, the lawyer turned and stalked away. Leon, watching him go, took another sip of champagne.

Leon had enough of the unbridled hostility, so he drifted to the fringes of the group, no longer interested in trying renew old friendships. He knew it would be a waste of time. He was only going to catch more hell for trying to promote George Washington's concepts. As he stood by himself, ostracized by the lobbying community, a lawyer representing real estate interests in Kansas came over and told him that not everyone held the high degree of contempt for him that was being displayed by the opponents of reform. The lawyers representing the real estate industry were split. While those with interests in Washington saw moving the seat of government as an unmitigated national disaster, those with interests in Kansas saw it as an opportunity of unparalleled proportions. She wanted Leon to know that his proposal to move the federal government to the center of the country had her complete support. It would be good for the nation and better for her real estate clients. It was real win-win situation. She urged Leon to keep up the good work. Leon felt slightly better as he watched the shapely woman walk over to the nearest bar.

As Leon continued his solo journey around the fringes of the crowded room, his thoughts drifted back to the 1969-72 period when Maurice Stans was the Secretary of Commerce under President Richard Nixon. Mr. Stans had maintained an immense, unregulated shush fund of unreported campaign contributions in a safe located in his office on the fifth floor. The secret fund came to light when the Watergate scandal swept Nixon out of office. Watergate was so long ago that Leon could not remember if Stans went to jail or not for his role in the affair. It seemed a minor event when he compared it to the cost and scope of the political scandals in Washington in recent times.

Independent counsel Ken Starr's ongoing investigation of President Clinton was nearing $60 million in costs, while the President was in hock to his lawyers to the tune of $5 million for the time they spent defending him. Lawrence Walsh ran an eight year investigation into the Iran-contra affair costing over $47 million. The bill for an investigation of HUD during the Reagan administration came to $28 million. Investigations into the conduct of Clinton political appointees: Mike Espy, Henry Cisneros, Bruce Babbitt and Alexis Harman had rung up another $25 million in costs so far. Leon began to think George Washington had a valid point. Things were really getting out of hand in the modern capital. He couldn't argue with Washington's desire to make the changes needed to save the system from destroying itself.

As he admired the craftsmanship of one of the building's fabulous brass doors, Leon recalled that the late Secretary of Commerce, Ronald H. Brown, who died in a plane crash while leading a trade mission in 1996, had also been under investigation. The probe was terminated at a cost of a mere $3 million at the time of his death. When Brown became commerce secretary, he brought in many of the staff from the Democratic National Committee and placed them in key management positions in the department. They made sure the firms making financial contributions to the Democratic party got the best seats on the trade missions led by the secretary. When the current secretary, William M. Daley took over, he promised Congress he would restore the department's tarnished public image. He said he would review the procedures alleged to favor the participation of Democratic contributors on overseas trade missions.

Daley also stated he would eliminate 100 of the 256 political positions in the department. Leon thought the 100 of the party faithful Daley had been forced to let go had been quietly picked up by other agencies. Commerce also had a reputation in both Republican and Democratic administrations as a place where political operatives could park themselves while seeking to develop ties to the business community. Both parties used the place as type of employment office to help party workers find good jobs in industry. Only a few days ago, Leon had seen nothing wrong with the program because it helped the political parties function. The costs were part of the price the taxpayers paid for politics. Now, after his meeting with George Washington, he saw it in a new light. It was a rip-off, a waste of tax dollars and ought to be ended.

John Huang had become the most famous political fund raiser in recent history by pushing the art of collecting money for presidential campaigns to new and exciting limits. Huang had the high and distinct honor of meeting President Clinton 15 times during the many visits he made to the White House between 1993 and 1996. His trendy involvement with the Lippo Group (an Indonesian banking and real estate conglomerate), a large number of foreign contributors and China inspired those who worked to raise campaign funds from the masses of the electorate. After a lengthy investigation, the criticism of John's unorthodox methods ended as he pleaded guilty to a single felony count. It was part of a plea agreement giving him no jail time. Huang had cut a lot of corners while raising money. His standing among fund raisers increased to celebrity status when they realized he had gotten away with a lot and had only been given a slap on the wrist after being caught.

For approximately 18 months, the trend-setting Mr. Huang occupied the position of Deputy Assistant Secretary of Commerce for international economic policy. His former office, entered through room 3868A on the eighth corridor of the third floor of the Commerce building, became a kind of shrine to aspiring fund raisers, regardless of party affiliation. Commerce Department officials, embarrassed over the volume of classified commercial intelligence data Mr. Huang had available to him during his stint in economic policy making, would have preferred the sorry episode be forgotten. The name of the bureau in which Mr. Huang worked had its name changed from "International Economic Policy" to "Market Access and Compliance" as part of the program to erase the unhappy memory left by Mr. Huang's tenure.

Bending the rules during the tedious struggle to raise campaign contributions was what all fund raisers had to do on occasion. Not one of them believed the laughable fiction that contributors gave freely and without expecting anything in return. In the real world of the Washington political commodity market, politicians sold access to their power to alter the tax code, make laws and apportion $1.8 trillion in yearly federal expenditures to donors willing to provide the large sums of money necessary to finance political campaigns. Through his fund raising endeavors, John Huang had often gotten to see the president. Who cared if a little of the money he collected was a bit tainted? His access to the most important person in the government was a very marketable commodity. People paid well for it.

With trade between the United States and Indonesia running at eight billion dollars per year, traders could profit handsomely from advance knowledge of U.S. government actions influencing the import-export markets. Those fund raisers, hoping to follow in the footsteps of Mr. Huang, did not doubt for a second that he used his access to secret commercial data for personal gain during his stint in the Commerce Department. By dropping the right bit of bid pricing information, the status of a product market, advance notice of a change in trade policy or a coming trade sanction to those with a competitive need, Huang must have been handsomely compensated. Why else would he have given up a banking job paying $200,000 per year to grub in the thankless boiler room of campaign fund raising? They knew John Huang was a lot smarter than that. He probably stashed the funds acquired during his stint in Washington in banks around the world. John Huang was taking a minor hit by pleading guilty to a felony, but it was worth the financial gain. John Huang was a legend in the eyes of the fund raisers because he had cleverly taken advantage of the opportunities Washington offered. It would never get any better than that for any of them.

Around 11 p.m., a group of 35 members of the Washington Society of Solicitors, many of them well-lubricated by drink, quietly left the festivities through a rear door opening on the stairs. Led by a reluctant security guard with a ring of door keys, the group climbed to the third floor, heading for John Huang's former office on the eighth corridor. His government-issued desk, chair, credenza, bookcases and file cabinets were still there, no doubt being used by an incumbent functionary of far less vision. The visitors sat in the chair once occupied by the famous Mr. Huang and reverently touched the desk and other office paraphernalia as they whispered about the exploits of the great man. He had seen through the charade of Washington's silly fund raising games and had taken the system for all that it was worth. While there would never be a plaque placed on the office door as a reminder of Huang's exploits, the cleverness of what he accomplished while occupying the office would remain an inspiration to the solicitors. To duplicate what John had done was the worthy goal of many of them. As they discussed the finer points of political fund raising, they agreed wholeheartedly among themselves to purchase the office furnishings when the government offered them for sale as surplus property. There would be nothing finer than to own a piece of furniture from the office of the man they deeply admired, a man who had beaten the system. A memento from this celebrated office would occupy a place of honor in their homes or offices for years to come.

Finding that very few of the guests were willing to speak to him, Leon tagged along with the group moving through the doorway since he had nothing better to do. They passed the entrance to the second floor hallway on which Leon had borrowed an office a few months ago as he neatly put an end to the potential political embarrassment created by Bob Vargo's discovery of the Confederate papers. So much had happened recently that Leon had forgotten all about the man who found two containers of Civil War documents. As the assemblage of solicitors moved down the third floor corridor to John Huang's former office, Leon wondered if Bob had wisely spent the hush money he had received. Leon assumed the documents he had taken from Vargo were still sitting in the national archives, out of sight and out of mind. As he listened to the fund raisers talk glowingly about John Huang, Leon began to think he had misjudged the man. John Huang represented the new generation of political operative, one who milked the system for everything he or she could get from it. According to the ecstatic young men and women gathering in the office, John Huang had done a much better job of it than Leon could ever have imagined.

As the group of solicitors chatted about Huang's phenomenal exploits, Leon saw again what George Washington had been trying to drum into his head. National politics had gotten completely out of control. With each election cycle, the costs of campaigning got higher, the campaigns more vicious, the voter turnout lower. The 2000 election was not going to be any different. It was rapidly on the way to becoming a mammoth spending spree. Twenty-five years after Congress passed a law to restrain the flow of money into presidential campaigns, the candidates were blasting open the flood gates to an unprecedented amount of unregulated spending. When the 1974 act was written, the lawmakers thought they had devised a way to shift the dialing for dollars back to discussing issues. The financial preparations for the 2000 presidential campaign were bitter proof that the lawmakers had failed miserably. By the end of the first quarter of 1999, Al Gore had already raised over eight million dollars, George W. Bush nearly that much. The total raised by the ten competing presidential hopefuls was a whopping $30.7 million.

"Government does not solve problems; it subsidizes them."
-Ronald Reagan, 1972

To underwrite the enormous costs of modern campaigning, funds had to be raised in ever increasing amounts. In 1999, new records were being set. The AFL-CIO allocated $46 million to help Democrats retake the House of Representatives, while corporations poured funds into efforts to thwart them. The fund raising community was pleased when one Washington political action committee dinner raised a record setting $550,000 from the attending mix of technology company executives, bankers, accountants, lawmakers, lobbyists and consultants. To take advantage of the offerings of the computer age, candidates operated web sites to recruit volunteers, organize events, spread messages and raise money.

A legion of professional pollsters, media consultants and policy planners worked on the fringe of the American election system, turning it into a lucrative, expensive public relations spectacle. Snappy television commercials marketed politicians running for office to the voters in much the same way as dog food was hustled by advertising companies. The system was truly out of kilter and Leon felt a tinge of shame for the role he played over the years in making it so. Changing the basis of representation for one of the houses of Congress would do a great deal to simplify the convoluted system and restore a semblance of normality to how America elected its legislators. George Washington's reforms were fairly simple. Why had neither of the major political parties not proposed similar changes long before now? Leon already knew the answer. His proposal to change how Congress worked had been flatly rebuffed by his lawmaker friends because they liked things the way they were. Both parties had a vested interest in keeping the present system in place.

Capitol Hill was a grand bazaar where the champions of special interests regularly tacked a bewildering mass of riders containing costly perks and financial breaks for constituent special interest groups onto bills funding military operations and disaster relief. The political gamesmanship pitted Republicans against Democrats on occasion. At other times, the regions of the country against each other; and every now and then, the Congress against the White House. Creative new ways of looking out for special interests were

266

constantly devised by the 435 members of the House of Representatives and the 100 members of the Senate as they hid gifts for their political friends deep in federal budget. The lawmakers and the 31,000 employees who served them were proud to have created the world's most expensive legislative body as they churned out the laws that regulated the affairs of the nation.

Leon had been a part of the system that took care of the needs of the special interest groups. His intimate knowledge of the ins and outs of lawmaking in Washington provided him with a substantial income and a high degree of respect in lawmaking and lobbying circles. Now that he was challenging the system which he had helped build, he found himself becoming increasingly isolated from the Washington establishment. It was a clear case of do as I say, not as I do. The Washington establishment, which had absolutely no compunction about demanding sacrifices from the rest of the nation, was not about to make a sacrifice itself. It had become an indispensable institution, too vital to the national interest to consider change. Unwilling to accept the fact that a massive bureaucracy dedicated to producing an endless flow of bewildering legislation was the antithesis of what the nation's founders had worked to create, the current lawmakers of the United States saw Leon Placke as a dangerous renegade, a traitor and a fool. Despite the constant political wrangling, Republicans and Democrats did agree unanimously among themselves that Leon Placke's crazy ideas were not for them.

June 1999

Dr. Orasco Lopez was becoming exasperated with Leon's rambling tales of his effort to reform the government. He knew for a fact that Leon could not have been in touch with George Washington and bluntly told him so. Whatever guilt complex was driving Leon's fertile mind to create imagined meetings with Washington would have to be dug out when they met in future sessions. In the meantime, he increased the strength of Leon's stress-reducing prescription and instructed him to get more rest. Dr. Lopez was perplexed; he could not figure out what was driving Leon to self-destruction. Even though Leon realized the political changes he was advocating meant the end of his successful lobbying practice, he seemed bent on pursuing the idiotic scheme despite the high personal cost.

It was all very odd. This reform fixation of Leon's was a case for the medical journals. Hopefully, he could help Leon get over this absurd reform craze before Leon did more damage to his career. Why would an individual with a strong vested interest in the present state of political arrangements suddenly decide they were bringing ruin to the nation and start advocating radical reforms as a solution? If the changes Leon was pushing were ever implemented, the Washington region would lose close to 100,000 jobs as the political establishment imploded. No sane person in Washington wanted that. The impact on real estate values would be horrific, the all powerful Congress would be a mere shadow of its present robust self, the White House staff would shrink drastically and the influence peddling industry would be virtually wiped out. As a medical practitioner with ties to the lawmaking elite, Dr. Lopez didn't relish the idea of losing clients, so he had more than a professional interest in getting Leon cured. Leon had become a menace to the lobbying profession. If he continued with his deranged notions, he could ruin them both.

As Congress stayed in session longer each year churning out a deluge of new laws, the business of the lobbying industry increased. Washington, DC had more lawyers per capita than any other city on earth. While he had once been immensely proud of the fact, Leon now considered it a symptom of a parasitic sickness in need of a drastic cure.

As Leon strolled past the White House walking west on Pennsylvania Avenue, eventually passing the blocks of lobbying and law firm offices, he was shunned by the legal and lobbying community. When they saw him coming, many of his former professional peers crossed the street rather than make contact with the man who had become the abhorrent leper of the lobbying world.

Leon seemed not to care. George Washington had been good enough to show him where he had gone wrong and Leon was determined to do Mr. Washington's bidding by helping get things back on the right track. As he turned up 21st Street, passing more offices dedicated to lobbying, passersby noticed that Leon Placke was marching in step to the beat of an unseen drum and whistling a catchy tune. As they passed in the opposite direction, one of a pair of pedestrians responded to his walking partner's question, "I heard that tune played at a Fourth of July celebration many years ago. It's a old tune dating back to the Revolutionary War. I wonder where that fellow heard it because it hasn't been played for years." Then turning and looking back at Leon he added, "The old gentleman is marching like he was in the ranks of someone's army. What do you suppose has gotten into him?"

The drum beating the cadence grew louder in Leon's mind as he marched. As clouds of choking black powder smoke drifted by, Leon could see a line of tough British regulars up ahead exchanging volleys with the advancing American line. Leon furiously rammed home another musket ball, cocked his musket and awaited the command to fire. When the officer on horseback next to Leon gave the order, a sheet of flame erupted from the battle line, staggering the British. Pushing forward, Leon reloaded and fired again. Screaming like a fiend from hell, Leon went forward on the double-quick. As he ran, Leon turned to glance at the horseman riding by his side and was startled to see George Washington. The look of contempt the general had often given him was gone. George Washington was actually smiling at him. "Drive them Leon. Do whatever it takes," Washington said as British musket balls whistled by. The Americans fired once more, ripping holes in the red-coated line which began to disintegrate under the well-directed fire.

Still shouting at the top of his lungs as lines of troops collided, Leon savagely knocked aside the thrust of a British rifleman and drove his bayonet deep into the man's body just below the white cross belts on his chest. Invigorated by the feel of cold steel driving into human flesh, Leon yanked the bayonet out of the sagging, lifeless body and delivered a smashing blow to the head of another British soldier with the butt of his musket. That did it. The impact of the attack broke the British line. They were fleeing the field in disorder. As Leon stood amid the carnage, he turned and asked General Washington, "We drove them from the field general. What do we do next?"

George Washington didn't answer because he wasn't there. Leon was standing on the sidewalk in front of the building that housed his office, people staring at him in disbelief. It didn't matter. Leon knew what had to be done. He was going to change the way the government operated in the city named after the general and first president of the United States. He would never forget the broad grin on the face of George Washington as they charged across the field. Leon even felt a tinge of regret because he had dodged the draft in his younger days. Serving as a citizen-soldier might be one of the costs of maintaining a viable democracy. The tradition had been established by George Washington's ragged little army. Leon was sorry he didn't see it that way years ago.

Leon went up to his office and began to reflect on the gloomy mess in Washington he had helped to create. It was all there, outlined in the reports he read. The federal government was a good tenant. It spent $924 million on rent in the Washington metropolitan area every year to house many of the 340,900 federal employees in the region. Leon knew that savvy building owners had learned a long ago that it did not hurt to contribute lavishly to the political campaigns. It could prove to be the winning edge in a tight bid competition. Uncle Sam had grown into an unwitting supporter of the paper industry as Americans spent seven billion hours a year filling out government forms. The Internal Revenue Service, which oversaw the complicated tax code written by Congress, accounted for nearly 80 percent of the time as taxpayers struggled with confusing tax forms.

The White House controlled the filling of more than 3,000 government jobs, ensuring that a loyal cadre of political supporters would carry out the President's wishes. Most of those 3,000 political appointees being paid an average of over $100,000 a year, would be out of work after the 2000 election. The new president would bring a new group of supporters into town to share the Washington experience with him. The problem was that many of the those in outgoing administration had discovered they had grown to like the place, they didn't want to leave town. Some would have the clout to pull enough stings to convert their present job from a political appointment to civil service. The others would seek staff positions in Congress, or would swell the ever growing ranks of the lawyers and lobbyists working the city.

While the Clinton administration was taking credit for cutting more than 350,000 jobs from the government rolls through defense downsizing and the reinventing government effort that transferred functions to local governments, it was rapidly creating new positions for the politically favored at the top levels of the bureaucracy. It had created as many new job titles as the preceding seven administrations had done over a 33 year period. This created a new problem because the managers often fought with each other over the allocation of scarce employees. No one wanted to be a political manager and not have a big staff to boss around.

The number of presidential appointees and senior executives expanded from 451 in 1960 to over 3,000 today. In some agencies, 30 to 40 suffocating bureaucratic layers separated the front line employees from the agency head. The creation of layer upon layer of political managers had become so acute that a nonpartisan management group had recommended reducing the number by a third or more. Because no one in the White House was sympathetic to a less top heavy government work force, the recommendation was politically naïve. No politician with a grasp of the costs of political campaigns in this day and age could support such a proposal. The costs of winning office kept going up, leaving the winning candidate deeply indebted to the many who wanted to come to Washington and be part of a president's administration.

The cost of the expensive political pay backs also showed up in other areas. Trips by the president to Africa, China and Chile cost the Treasury Department an impressive $72 million. A good number of the 2,200 people traveling with the president, including those on the advance teams, went as a reward for past political services. They were owed for the past aid and comfort given the president, so it was difficult to turn down their requests to go on a trip. It was much easier to roll with the flow, to send five people to do the work one could have easily handled.

Not everything in Washington was exactly the way the politicians said it was. Leon heard from reliable sources that nearly 17 million people worked directly or indirectly for the federal government. Somewhat shocked by the high numbers, Leon found he could not argue with the actuality of the math when one considered the $200 billion spent annually by the federal government on contracts created 5.6 million jobs. The $55 billion the federal government dispensed in grants to various entities created another 2.4 million jobs. And federal regulatory mandates required the addition of another 4.7 million positions to the employment rolls of state, county, and city governments.

It was another case of the selective use of statistical data, an incumbent administration not quite telling the public the whole story. President Clinton often made assertions that he was reducing the role of the federal government and bringing the era of big government to a close. The President overstated the case a bit. As an old Washington hand, Leon considered it nothing more than a mild truth in advertising problem. While it was true the number of people working directly for the federal government was down, the total number of individuals who earned their livelihood from it probably had increased slightly. No one was complaining. The voters appeared happy with the fact that federal tax dollars were creating jobs for private contractors instead of government employees. Leon saw it as a shrewd political move. It was a cleverly presented political illusion designed to create a new reality in the public's perception. It was the politically smart thing to do, Leon had to admit, because it pandered to the preconceived notions held dear by liberals and conservatives alike.

Sometimes American political leaders took the liberty of hoodwinking the public as they went about the business of leading the nation. As he was reflecting on the impact of the government employee numbers game, Leon realized he had discovered the best laid political stratagem of the last quarter of the twentieth century. As Leon thought about President Clinton's clever public relations ploy, his thoughts were rudely interrupted by a distant drum roll. As Leon saw the British regulars coming in a line of battle with bayonets fixed, he snapped back to reality. No, the Clinton administration's program to reinvent the government had not resulted in any real gain for the American people. It was a political slight-of-hand, the very kind of thing George Washington had been incensed about. This latest mini-fraud on the public trust was another example of the problems caused by a system gone bad. Once again inspired to change things, Leon went back to planning how he was going to get the general public interested in George Washington's reform proposals.

The Fairfax County police detective was relentless in his pursuit of finding out how Leon Placke had come into possession of a draft copy of the U.S. Constitution. He was so focused on digging out the facts that some of his fellow officers believed he had been cursed with an uncompromising conscience and an unquenchable thirst for the truth that would one day get him into big trouble. They thought the day had finally come on a Friday afternoon in May when Senator Harry Byrd of West Virginia, who was driving west in a rented Cadillac on Route 50 near the Fair Oaks shopping mall, rear-ended a Ford van. It was not much of an accident, the damage to the vehicles was less than $3,000. As was standard police practice in such instances, the senator was ticketed for following too closely.

The minor fender bender soon turned into an event of constitutional significance because the police commander tore up the ticket. A little-known article of the U.S. Constitution gives members of Congress immunity from arrest when Congress is in session except for cases involving treason, felony and breech of the peace. It was never clear whether the police commander or the senator first raised the issue of immunity. The senator was known to carry a copy of the U.S. Constitution in his pocket, quoting from it when it suited his purposes. The police commander knew that the powerful senator could, with a single phone call, adversely affect the amount of the federal financial aid and grants received by the Fairfax County Police Department. Because the police commander did not want to risk giving offense to the man holding the purse strings, he tore up the ticket. He and the senator chatted amicably at the police station while the senator waited for an aide to bring another car.

When he heard of the matter, the detective reacted forcefully, arguing the ticket should be reinstated because the provision was written to protect members of Congress from harassment as they traveled across country by horse and buggy. It had nothing to do with a misdemeanor automobile traffic ticket issued in the communications rich year of 1999. As the matter came to the attention of the press, learned constitutional law authorities agreed with the detective's conclusion, but for other reasons. In their infinite legal wisdom, they ruled the traffic violation should have been construed as a breach of the peace and the ticket should have been allowed to stand. After four decades in the Senate, the senator, who considered the U.S. Constitution the same as holy writ, saw a firestorm of negative publicity coming his way. He brought the matter to a quick conclusion by asking for a reinstatement of the ticket and paid the fine. His civil liability in the accident was never at issue. His insurance would pay for the repair of the damaged vehicles. Once the ticket was paid, the press lost interest and moved on to other matters.

The detective's constant inquiries into the Placke matter aggravated those who would have preferred to let well enough alone. He firmly believed Placke had purloined the priceless draft copy of the Constitution before the containers of documents had been sealed and stored in the National Archives. His views finally came to the attention of a congressman who had not been privy to the original plan to keep the unsettling Civil War papers out of circulation. The congressman deeply resented being left out of the loop by the other members, so he launched his own investigation. Much to the chagrin of his fellow lawmakers who advised him not to meddle, he had the collection of Confederate Secretary of State Judah P. Benjamin's papers opened to the public. The sleazy attempt to hide the papers immediately became an major embarrassment for those who had taken part in it. The reporters wanted to know why a prominent Washington lobbyist concealed old revolvers and documents from the public. Why had certain members of Congress urged him to do so? What was so important about boxes of old papers that they had to be classified? Government employees had been bribed with free vacations at taxpayer expense to keep them silent. The individual who found the documents had been bought off.

The scandal caught the attention of the nation and those involved tried desperately to shift their share of blame onto Leon Placke. No one in Congress could recall ever having asked Leon to undertake such a dastardly deed on their behalf. It was agreed by all on Capitol Hill that crazy old Leon had acted alone, for what reason they did not know. Leon had usurped his position of trust by attempting to deceive the public. Americans had every right to see the historical documents Placke had tried to hide from public view. With the cat now out of the bag, everyone hurried to congratulate the congressman for his fine work in bringing Placke's transgressions into the open. The affair highlighted the urgent need to revise government document classification procedures and a committee was established to duly study the matter. Controls were going to be put into place to ensure such a thing could not happen again. The public's right to know was going to be protected.

The detective was startled to find nothing in the boxes to indicate a copy of the Constitution had ever been part of the collection. It would have been completely out of place among the Benjamin papers, none of which appeared to be older than the time of the Civil War. A draft of the U.S. Constitution would have already been of historical significance in 1865. If it was in his possession, why would Benjamin stick it in a box of government records to be hidden out of harm's way? It made no sense since unlike the other papers, the draft would not help Benjamin in his effort to survive a treason trial.

A check of archives showed no mention of a draft copy of the Constitution having been in Richmond at the time of the Civil War. Therefore the detective downheartedly concluded, Mr. Benjamin did not have the document in his possession and could not have packed it into his now famous boxes. Placke must have obtained the document from another source since it had absolutely no relation to other Civil War era memorabilia. Placke had more than once in recent days hinted at George Washington being the source of the priceless paper. The draft appeared to be one of Washington's working copies, saved by someone at the convention that wrote the U.S. Constitution. Although never before seen, it was not a stolen document. Perhaps it was a inventive forgery, the detective thought. But why would Placke be preaching about reforming Congress while he used a forged document as a prop? It did not make any sense. Maybe Leon Placke had really gone off the deep end. The puzzled detective knew only one thing for certain. Although the document had George Washington's handwriting all over it, Washington never gave it to Placke.

As historians and reporters dug into the stacks of Confederate records, it wasn't long before the congressman who played a role in bringing the papers to light found himself in a predicament. Two of his largest campaign contributors, upon seeing their cherished family names sullied by revelations contained in Benjamin's papers, angrily withdrew their financial support. With the most powerful financial supporters in his district miffed, the congressman knew he was going down to sure defeat in the coming 2000 election. His role in exposing old Civil War truths had brought him nothing more than unhappy contributors and an empty campaign fund.

Because he wanted to stay in Washington, the congressman began trying to line up employment with legal and lobbying firms. Unfortunately, he received no job offers from those who had recently congratulated him for looking out for the public's interest. In private conversations, he was told he had acted like a imbecile, bringing disgrace upon them by disrupting critical campaign fund raising operations. Looking out for the public's right to information was one thing, being stupid enough to aggravate large campaign donors was another. The Washington establishment had no use for a man foolish enough to lose his major sources of funding before the campaign season had even begun. With doors slamming in his face all over town, the congressman saw his dreams of power and glory fade. He had violated the unwritten rule of never letting the truth interfere with the real or imagined needs of those who funded the big political game.

The grim truths emerging from the Benjamin papers cut deeply across the fabric of American society. Two senators and three members of the House of Representatives from the old Confederate States were scandalized when the names of their much-heralded ancestors appeared on the list of Confederate army deserters. All across the South, hallowed family myths were demolished as it was revealed that a large number of the men who later claimed to have fought with the Confederacy to the bitter end had, in actuality, deserted the Rebel military forces much earlier in the war. The true nature of the wartime conduct of many a revered ancestor came as a devastating shock to the moneyed elite. Many a fine old family portrait was removed from its place of honor in the living room and hustled to the attic by horrified descendants not particularly appreciative of the assault on sacred family values. Since the belittling information came from documents once safely out of circulation in the government achieves, many of the candidates running for reelection felt the sting of the growing unhappiness as their insulted campaign contributors switched their financial support to other candidates. The ugly cloud of historical accuracy unleashed by the long-dead Confederate Secretary of State swept across the nation, destroying many a family legend and shortening many of the lists of political contributors.

In the North, the reaction was equally as unpleasant. In the years since the end of the Civil War, the population had conveniently forgotten that many people had disagreed strongly with all or some of Abraham Lincoln's war policies and voted against him. As newspapers and journals published articles, the reexamination of old historical facts was deeply resented by those who saw their forebears' names smeared across the headlines. The uncomfortable evidence of abetting the enemy in wartime by selling weapons, medicines and other necessaries was extremely offensive to the many fine families whose ancestors had profited handsomely from the activity. The evidence that many Northern political operatives had taken Confederate gold while working to defeat Abraham Lincoln in the election of 1864, offended many an old-line family. They reacted with unabashed horror when confronted with confirmation of what their ancestors had done . Like their Southern brothers and sisters, the rich Northerners relieved their feelings of shame and guilt by focusing their blame for the unpleasant publicity on the modern politicians. Outraged by the humiliation of it all, they promptly switched their financial allegiance to those candidates for office untainted by the Benjamin papers affair.

All across the nation, financial contributors, both private and corporate, recoiled from the ugly barrage of truths flowing from Mr. Benjamin's long-lost papers. Local historical society meetings were no longer boring and poorly attended events. They were now jammed to capacity as a new generation found an interest in the scandalizing reality of a bygone era. Even some of those who were personally burned by the revelations in the documents had to admit Benjamin's papers had rekindled an immense interest in genealogy and the events of the Civil War. It was as if a cynical Judah P. Benjamin had reached out from his grave and dragged everyone back in time to face the real ugliness of wartime America. The savagery of the Confederacy's clandestine warfare made a fascinating topic of discussion. Debates raged over the role played in those activities by Confederate President Davis. Why had his U.S. citizenship been restored? Was it the result of a political whitewash of the facts by a naïve later generation not having the slightest clue as to the mean methods Davis had used? As the debate raged, the Davis burial site in Richmond's Hollywood Cemetery became swamped by tourists. An admission ticketing system had to be established to control the flow of visitors to the grave of the only president of the Confederate States of America.

Richmond's city council was dismayed. It had just concluded a divisive debate over the status of a portrait of General Robert E. Lee that had been installed on the city's new walkway along the James River. After much deliberation, the council agreed to have it removed because the city's large African-American community viewed Lee as a traitor and a defender of the institution of slavery. It was finally agreed by the city fathers that modern Richmond didn't need to be reminded of its role as the capital of the nation that went to war to preserve slavery. The matter had barely been laid to rest when other African-American groups, composed mostly of young professionals, began to demand Lee's picture be restored to the river walk. For better or worse they argued, General Lee was part of the city's history. Had he not pressured the Confederate government and Virginia to raise units of Negro troops during the war? The Benjamin papers affair was bringing swarms of tourists to the city. Visitors were walking the streets searching for the sites on which Confederate office buildings and the homes of Confederate officials had once stood. Lee was a big tourist drawing card. Put the old general's picture back on the walkway wall, they demanded. Stuck between the competing demands of the two groups, the unhappy council agreed to revisit the issue again.

At the Ohio State University's medical school, someone remembered the dusty photograph of Dr. Cyrus Bellnapp hanging on a wall in a little used rear hallway. It was moved out of limbo into a place of prominence when it was realized the doctor was the same Cyrus Bellnapp who was involved with the Benjamin papers. Everyone had read that Bellnapp was one of the two soldiers who had hidden the infamous Benjamin papers at Centreville in 1865. The great fighter of medical infection had never revealed to anyone during his lifetime that he had been one of the Negro soldiers put into uniform by the state of Virginia during the closing months of the war. The man who had learned his doctoring skills in a military hospital in wartime Richmond and had gone on to a respected medical career had also been a Rebel soldier honorably paroled with Lee's army at the time of surrender .

There was no debate in Richmond when a large portrait of Dr. Bellnapp was unveiled on the James River walkway before a crowd of nearly 5,000 on Sgt. Cyrus Bellnapp Day. The slave, surgeon's assistant, loyal Confederate soldier and doctor of medicine became Richmond's favorite personality overnight. His face began appearing on ashtrays, coffee mugs, posters, and tote bags. To have been caught in the worst of all possible worlds - a Negro soldier fighting for the Confederacy- fired the imagination of the city. A extensive research effort was undertaken to learn more about the ill-fated blacks who had tossed in their lot with the army of the dying Confederacy. They had to be the unluckiest of all the unfortunates caught up in the cauldron of the Civil War. People clamored to learn more about the last-ditch Southern effort to field gray-clad Negro troops.

A hundred miles to the north in Washington, DC, Leon Placke found himself almost as famous as Sgt. Cyrus Bellnapp, but for different reasons. His role in stashing the documents in the National Achieves had brought him a high degree of notoriety. As no one else would admit to having been involved with Leon's deplorable act of hiding historical documents, he had to take the heat generated by the fiasco by himself. As he made the rounds of the TV talk shows with his attention-getting draft copy of U.S. Constitution, he talked freely of how national lawmakers actually conducted their business. Leon talked about the high degree of influence wielded by large campaign contributors, the deals for special interests cut behind closed doors in Congress and the ownership of the government. Leon said, "We have the best government large sums of money can buy. Your average American can be proud of the fact it is not sold cheaply."

Although his constant references to George Washington made him mentally suspect, to the horror of many on Capitol Hill, people began to seriously take an interest in Leon's plan to change the composition of Congress. Leon Placke might be a little crazy, but much of what he was advocating made sense. The system of representation was certainly out of date and had become subject to abuse because it failed to keep pace with the economic changes occurring since the 1790s. Leon's reform ideas began to be discussed openly and often by the voters. Some even took a liking to the idea of moving the capital to the center of the country. If that was where the founding fathers had wanted it to be, the capital should have been moved as the nation grew. "Better late than never" was the watchword of a recently founded group that dedicated itself to the concept of moving the seat of government. The Washington established was horrified by the heresies Placke was foisting off on the gullible common people.

Senators and representatives were not enamored with the growing volume of mail expressing interest in the revolutionary ideas espoused by the reformed lobbyist named Leon Placke. It was all very annoying, this talk of reorganizing the House of Representatives along lines reflecting the economic components of the American economy. While it made sense in theory, no one with a vested interest in Washington wanted anything to do with the idea. Something was going to have to be done to silence Leon before the situation got completely out of hand. Leon's clients began to abandon him because of his involvement in hiding the Civil War papers, but Leon didn't seem to care one iota about the lost revenue. He was more interested in talking about his plan to reform the government than in taking care of his lobbying business. It was a sure sign to many in the city that Leon Placke had finally gone completely insane.

July 1999

The Secretary of Commerce was sitting in his spacious 5th floor office overlooking 15th Street and the Ellipse nursing a splitting headache. He had just concluded a testy meeting with representatives of the Government of South Africa who had expressed their unhappiness with the small amount of U.S. investment flowing into the country. They wanted the Secretary to do more to encourage American firms to invest. The visitors had also stated their displeasure with the negative tone of a recent television special highlighting the growing problem of lawlessness sweeping South Africa. Under instructions from the White House to do what he could to help, the Secretary agreed to bring a trade and investment mission to the country. Given the seedy state of the South African economy and a legal system that often left foreign investors in the lurch, he realized it would be a difficult mission to pull together. The trade mission would also serve a useful purpose. It would provide a forum in which to press upon South African officials the need to continue economic reforms and remove the impediments to foreign investment.

The Secretary's already tough day was not going to get any better. In the afternoon, he had another contentious meeting scheduled with visitors from the People's Republic of China. The Secretary realized America must squarely face the challenge posed by China. Could the Chinese leadership manage economic development, control political discontent and avoid military conflict as a new century dawned? As a rapidly developing one-party state, China posed a growing dilemma for the United States. Its appalling human rights violations cast a pall on the bilateral relationship between the two countries. In 1989 at Tiananmen Square, 5,000 pro-democracy demonstrators were killed and another 10,000 injured. China's poor human rights record, its actions in Tibet, abortion policies and the lack of religious freedom did not sit well with many Americans and their representatives in Congress.

As heirs to a long tradition of strong central control, the Chinese leadership didn't understand the American concerns. After all, the Chinese were among the oldest civilized people on earth, first unified as an empire around 200 BC. By 110 AD, they were bartering Chinese ginger and silk for the Roman Empire's gold, silver and wine. For 2,000 years, successor dynasties rose and fell. Through long and bitter experience, the people had become a nation of hardened survivors. When the central government was strong, the nation mostly prospered. When it was weak, the country declined, suffering from the ravages of invasion and internal banditry.

Social problems not withstanding, China was on the move. By using a peculiar blend of Communist orthodoxy and free market economics, the government doubled the country's gross national product during the decade of the 1990s. China was the most successful developing economy in the world, consistently producing growth rates in excess of eight percent. However, with a population of 1.2 billion scrunched in an area only slightly larger than the United States, the country also faced monumental growing pains. As the Chinese government continued efforts to remake the communist economic system into a more market-oriented one, it had to deal with over 300,000 money-losing state-owned enterprises which had to be made productive or closed. One positive sign of change was that private businesses now accounted for over 25 percent of the country's economic activity. With over 20 million workers a year looking for work in the cities, the government was betting that the private sector could generate a massive amount of new jobs and provide employment opportunities.

There was a real fear among a number of U.S. analysts that as the old system was dismantled, the weak Chinese social safety net might not be able to handle the millions of laid-off rural workers, thereby increasing domestic dissatisfaction. The Secretary did not care to venture a guess as to how long the Chinese government's huge security apparatus could coexist unmodified with a developing market economy. The more the economic program succeeded, the more the internal pressure for political reform would increase. Lurching uncertainly into the future, China was bringing with it a host of problems for everyone.

Reversing the attempt to isolate China after it had gone Communist in 1949, President Richard Nixon reestablished contact with the nation in 1972. Since then, economic ties had flourished as U.S. firms invested approximately $11 billion in the country. Each year, America imported products valued at $55 billion from China while exporting goods worth only $14 billion to it. The large and chronic trade deficit was also becoming a thorny problem in the U.S.-China relationship.

The Secretary felt trapped in a mass of Pacific Ocean problems that never seemed to go away. In 1898, William McKinley, our 25th president and a veteran of the fierce fighting in the Shenandoah Valley during the Civil War, annexed Hawaii. Also in that fateful year, the U.S. quickly won the Spanish-American War, acquired control of the Philippine Islands and became a Pacific Ocean power. As an ugly harbinger of what the coming century would bring, 50,000 American troops had to be committed to suppressing a guerrilla war in the newly acquired Philippines because many Filipinos were opposed to trading rule by Spain for rule by the United States. During the struggle that lasted until 1902, U.S. forces suffered approximately 6,000 casualties. American involvement in Pacific affairs came at a high price in the twentieth century. As he pondered the complex China issue, the Secretary fervently hoped that American soldiers would not be fighting in the Pacific region again in 2002.

The Secretary thought William McKinley must be about the only person of his era whose name had not been mentioned in the Civil War papers that had been the talk of Washington for the past several weeks. Leon Placke, who was right in the middle of the Civil War papers mess, was also now running around town saying President Washington had helped him develop his government reform proposals. Feeling the need for a bit of help with China problems, the Secretary wondered if crazy Leon, who claimed to have the ability to communicate with dead U.S. Presidents, could speak with President McKinley. It was with high expectations that the United States plunged grandly into the Pacific a hundred years ago. Whether the 21st century turned out to be as bloody as the 20th would be determined in a large part by how U.S.-China relations developed. Having presided over the initial involvement of the United States in the Pacific, McKinley might have some good insights on how to handle China. The Secretary sighed, put aside the silly idea of calling Leon, and went back to work thinking about what he was going to say at the China meeting.

The Secretary did not want to ask the White House for advice because President Clinton was too busy feeling people's pain on a host of domestic issues to be of much help on international matters. As if China was not a big enough of a problem, he also had to deal with a Middle East interest group coming to see him that evening. The Arab-Americans wanted more emphasis placed on aid to the Palestinian private sector. It was a touchy subject because a test program costing the U.S. government $1.5 million during the past two years had already flopped badly. The funds had been frittered away on seminars and dinner speeches and had not developed any of the intended new business ventures in the Palestinian controlled areas. Being significant contributors to the party, these visitors could not be brushed off lightly. Something would have to be done for them.

Since his visitors were not going to be gladdened by the report on the failed project, it was not going to be an enjoyable evening. It would probably result in the threat of political pressure being applied to the White House if more good money was not thrown after bad. His first priority was to keep the powerful domestic political constituency happy even if it cost a few tax dollars. Sometimes the Secretary thought the Middle East region was cursed. Maybe it was really the location where the end of the world would take place. Many people claimed it to be so. The problems in the region seemed over time to defy the best efforts of sensible people to bring about a resolution. After having poured over $70 billion in U.S. aid to Israel over a period of a half century, the peace process still seemed nowhere near fruition. It was a damnable dance that led to nowhere, a frustrating one step forward and one step backward pace that always seemed to leave the situation worse off.

Things were a little better on the eastern edge of the unstable region. With the U.S. importing over 50 percent of the oil it consumed, the American economy was becoming increasingly intertwined with those of the Middle East oil producing nations. A major blow-up in the region could shatter the American economy if the petroleum supply lines were cut for any length of time. The war to liberate Kuwait from Iraqi clutches may have been the first of America's oil wars. Because no one could predict what misfortune Iran or Iraq might set loose in the future, the Persian Gulf remained a hotbed of U.S. military involvement. In an interdependent global economy, the vital oil supply lines to Europe, Asia and North America had to be held open and it was the U.S. troops who were doing most of the holding.

"Greed is all right, by the way....I think greed is healthy. You can be greedy and still feel good about yourself."
-Ivan F. Boesky, 1986

It was so quiet in the Secretary's office that Commerce Department chief of staff, H. Muncaster Swindell, thought his boss had dozed off behind his big desk. Not wishing to interrupt the deep thoughts of the Secretary of Commerce, Muncaster gazed idly out of the window at the tourists filling the Ellipse seating stands on the other side of 15th Street as he waited for the Secretary's final instructions for the afternoon's meeting arrangements. Something unusual was going on over there. The tourists were leaving the seats and gathering around a man who appeared to be making a speech. Picking up the binoculars on the window ledge, Muncaster focused on a sight that made his blood boil. He saw the contemptible fool Leon Placke haranguing a crowd of tourists waiting to visit the White House. Muncaster told the preoccupied Secretary he would be back in 20 minutes as he headed for the door. He wanted to find out for himself what the deranged Leon Placke was up to this time.

Muncaster was not really interested in international trade or foreign officials, but since the only political job he was offered in Washington was chief of staff in the Commerce Department, he took it. He thought he deserved it and more because he had worked extremely hard for the Clinton-Gore ticket in 1996, sometimes putting in 18 hours a day as he supervised bumper sticker distribution, arranged speech venues and 30 second photo opportunities designed to make the evening television news. Muncaster did not relish being stuck in meetings with the Chinese Communists. Let someone else worry about the boring, weighty issues of economic development, war and peace. Muncaster's sole objective was to put his law degree to maximum use by establishing a money-making lobbying practice in the capital sometime in the near future. The time he was spending in the position of chief of staff could translate into millions of dollars in influence industry income for him if he avoided getting bogged down in the unprofitable details of running his office.

In his exulted position of political trust, Muncaster ruthlessly controlled the flow of correspondence in and out of the Department of Commerce with the able assistance of a carefully selected staff of 50 former campaign workers. It was a tough job, but he loved evaluating the incoming letters and ranking them by political priority. Correspondence from individuals and corporations making the largest political contributions ranked first on his scale of one to ten. The numerical rankings then descended down through those individuals and entities making increasingly smaller contributions, ending finally in the dead-end slots numbered eight through ten. These last two categories, Muncaster contemptuously reserved for those who had contributed nothing financially, but had the audacity to ask for government help of some type or another.

The Department's formidable resources were employed to serve the needs of those individuals and companies assigned places in Muncaster's top three categories. He adored the constant exposure and interaction as he coordinated the administration's position and cut deals with powerful people on Capitol Hill and in the White House. He saw to it that the government did everything humanly possible to make life easier for his top-ranked constituents, making sure in the process they remembered the helping hand of H. Muncaster Swindell.

It stood to reason that those entities unfortunate enough to be assigned the lower priorities on Muncaster's grand scale got less attention and service because Muncaster shoved their requests down into the bowels of the bureaucracy. Since the working-level employees were already busily slaving to meet the endless number of high priority demands generated by Muncaster's top-ranked requests, very little was actually done for those outside the Washington power loop. The second-rate citizens ignorant of how

Washington operated, usually received a short letter from a low-level bureaucrat thanking them for their interest and advising them in a nice way that they were out of luck. While he strove mightily to meet all the needs of the big contributors, Muncaster was equally adamant in seeing to it that the lesser people got a response of one type or another. Being politically savvy, he knew it would make the politically insignificant people feel good about themselves and the elected officials in Washington, DC who looked out for the welfare of the nation.

Muncaster carefully gathered all useful information in a separate set of files. When he left government, many of the untutored people who had written the department would receive a letter advising them of the benefits of retaining H. Muncaster Swindell as their eyes and ears in Washington. Being appallingly ignorant of how things worked, these dolts obviously needed to hire a newly-minted lobbyist to get things done from them. At work, Muncaster had access to a gold mine of potential clients and devoted himself to making as many valuable contacts as he could. Muncaster realized life was never going to get any better than it was at the present time because the government was paying him over $100,000 per year while he devoted most of his effort to building a base for his future lobbying career. It was Muncaster's reward for having actively participated in the election. He was part of the reasonable overhead costs the American people had to bear as the price paid for making the great American democratic process work.

Muncaster pragmatically viewed Washington as the financial sump pit of the nation. Much like an efficient sewer system, federal tax revenues flowed into the capital where the eminent lawmakers labored over the arduous process of dividing up the money among the numerous competing interest groups. With so many competing special interests, decision making often became a stressful undertaking requiring a great deal of tact, patience and negotiating ability. Muncaster shrewdly realized real political power came with the process of handling nearly $2 trillion a year. A lot of favors could be done for friends who would then be beholden to you. It was a matter of building yourself a sound supporting web of contacts, the sort of thing Leon Placke often spoke so eloquently about before he became deranged.

Although it was never mentioned publicly by those elected to serve the people, laboring in Washington also meant having the ability to exercise raw political power. Because you had won an election through a process of rigorous political combat, you now had the right to pull the strings controlling American society. It was the closest one could come in this day and age to ruling, as did the kings of old, over the affairs of the ordinary mortals who grubbed to make a living. Power was an addictive tonic because it was exhilarating to control the fortunes of others. You helped create or destroy wealth, make war and arbitrate justice. Unfortunately, the founding fathers, fearing the human weaknesses of individuals of Muncaster's ilk and the sovereign power of kings, had made ruling America a difficult endeavor. It took some time for Muncaster to figure out that many of the obstacles placed in the way of the exercise of undiluted power by the men of George Washington's era could be circumvented through clever effort.

Muncaster could see the various political groups beginning to coalesce in the run-up to the 2000 elections. In their attempts to rally support, Vice President Gore and Senator Bradley had already made campaign promises to spend every penny of the available federal budget surplus for the next 10 years. The projected $1 trillion surplus was going to go into programs generating greater political power for the party. The wily Republicans, on the other hand, were courting other centers of power as they promised a $792 billion tax cut over a ten year period that also got rid of most of the projected budget surplus. While taxes were chopped at the federal level, it was cynically assumed that Republican party officials at the state and local level would be ready to grab the revenue windfall by hiking local taxes.

The American voters were going to be given a clear choice in the election held in the year 2000. They could keep political power concentrated in Washington by electing Democrats or they could dissipate some of it to the local level by electing Republicans. Either way, the total financial cost to the taxpayers came out about the same. Muncaster was amazed how close the total spending projections for each party's program matched the other. The real political battle was going to be over which centers of influence were going to get the money.

As he watched events unfold, Muncaster worried about the state of the Democrat's political crusade. The leading opponent, George W. Bush had already raised $52 million in contributions while Vice President Al Gore seemed to be getting steadily derailed in the contest for dollars by an unexpected strong showing by former Senator Bill Bradley. Bradley had come out of nowhere and was giving the Vice President a real battle for the party's presidential nomination.

Despite his loathing of Republican policies, Muncaster was enthralled by the vast fund raising machine Bush had cobbled together. It was doing so well that Bush was rumored to be taking the unheard of step of not accepting any federal election funds for his campaign effort. In many ways, Muncaster admired the Republican money gathering juggernaut because being able to do deals in a money-flush political environment was where the real action was. He sincerely hoped the Democrats got themselves organized before

Bush got too financially strong to beat. If Bush won the coming election, Muncaster would soon be on the streets of Washington looking for a job along with a couple of thousand other out of work Democratic political operatives. Being tossed out of his cushy job after the election would not help him get his lobbying career off the ground. Having to start work in an environment that diminished his marketability was a thought he didn't like to dwell on.

> **"Corporation. An ingenious device for obtaining individual profit without individual responsibility."**
> **-Ambrose Bierce, 1842-1914**

Not everything worked out for Muncaster as he labored to fulfill the wishes of political contributors. Sometime things went wrong and big problems emerged. In those cases, it was better to duck for cover and turn the mess over to the spin-doctors to clean up. He had worked a little too hard on getting export licenses approved for Hughes Electronics Corporation and Loral Space and Communications, Ltd. As a result, Muncaster, the Commerce Department and the White House were caught off guard when the firms were accused of damaging U. S. national security by providing Chinese engineers with the technical rocketry data that could have assisted China's ballistic missile development program. In a rare show of bipartisanship, a devastating report by a congressional committee clobbered the administration for thoughtlessly loosening high-tech export restrictions to benefit the two American firms. The embarrassed Secretary made Muncaster personally write responses to the hundreds of letters the Department of Commerce received from angry citizens accusing it of selling out national security.

As he wrote for hours on end, Muncaster became quite incensed at the stupid, knee-jerk reaction of the American masses. He deeply resented wasting his valuable time answering the mail from a bunch of nobodies who were worried about being blasted to bits by a Chinese missile utilizing the best technology America had to sell. It had been only a slight error in judgment on his part. How was he supposed to know the firms could not be trusted once they got into bed with the Chinese rocket people? How on earth was H. Muncaster Swindell supposed to anticipate that corporate greed would win out over national security concerns? American firms were not supposed to bite the helping hand of the administration and embarrass the political leadership. Muncaster was deeply offended by the conduct of the companies. These corporate types had absolutely no sense of honor or fair play. In retrospect, Muncaster decided he should not have recommended the approval of the licenses.

As the uproar continued, the U.S. satellite industry and the Department of Commerce were staggered when Congress decided to transfer the control of licenses from Commerce to the State Department. Satellite exports were placed under the same stringent licensing requirements as foreign weapon sales. In this shift of jurisdiction, Congress did not provide the State Department with additional funding to do the extra work. Nor did it move any workers from the Commerce Department where they no longer had anything to do. So many U.S. makers of satellite components found themselves in an untenable position of having to respond to bids in 60 days while it took over 90 days to obtain license rulings from the backlogged Office of Defense Controls at the State Department. No one in the capital cared anything about the plight of the small component part manufacturers because the large majority fell in the bottom range of Muncaster's grand scale. They had made no political contributions, so they had no voice to make themselves heard. Like a band of ignorant peasants caught between the contending armies of kings, the small firms were cut down on the commercial battlefield of the global economy because they happened to be in the wrong place at the wrong time.

Still smarting over the embarrassing accusations that it had allowed Hughes to skirt American export regulations for years while it landed deals in China, the Clinton administration struck back at the ungrateful firm. Senior government officials flatly rejected a $600 million sale of communications satellites to China. Hughes, which had made a science out of exploiting loopholes in the export regulations, was being disciplined by a damaging blow to the corporate bottom line. In the aftermath of the lesson in corporate responsibility, Hughes stockholders became incensed, a few corporate heads rolled and the Chinese, not having the slightest clue as to what the Americans were trying to prove, shrugged their shoulders and began negotiations with French and German satellite providers. Although he had labored hard in the halls of government on behalf of Hughes, Muncaster survived the firestorm. He crossed off a couple of names from his list of prospective future corporate clients and got back to the work of looking out for the public interests of other big campaign contributors. The bewildered drudges sitting around in the licensing bureau with nothing to do soon found themselves being sucked into Muncaster's world of providing friendly service to those smart enough to know how to successfully play the political game.

The flap over missile technology and satellites was quickly forgotten as the bitter partisan debate over how to conduct the national census engulfed

Washington. The Constitution of the United States required a census to be taken every ten 10 years, the next one in the year 2000. The party in power got a monumental gift once a decade as the Commerce Department's Bureau of the Census geared up to fulfill the constitutional mandate. There were hundreds of millions of dollars to spend on renting office space, equipment, printing forms and hiring the legions of temporary census takers. It was a politicians' dream, a cornucopia of contracts and jobs to give out. Muncaster saw to it that contributors in good standing got first crack at offering leases, local service contracts and providing supplies.

A number of the of the temporary jobs at the census management level paid $20 to $30 an hour. Muncaster finagled things so loyal party members got to the forefront of the hiring line. Applications from the less fortunate were purposely misplaced, interviews were conducted on short notice and in difficult to reach locations. The normally vocal Republicans remained strangely silent. They were honoring the tacit bipartisan agreement reached long ago, one in which the party out of power agreed to keep its hands off of the census plum. It was delight to be enjoyed solely by the party in power when census time rolled around. The Republicans would respectfully wait because they knew their turn would come in the future.

The census was no longer the simple, straight forward enumeration of the nation's population and economic underpinnings envisioned by the nation's founders. For the 2000 census, the Census Bureau would mail about 94 million questionnaires to American households and deliver an additional 22 million by hand in its effort to count everyone in the United States. There was a problem because disillusioned Americans, filled with revulsion, distrust or fear of the government, were failing to return the forms in increasing numbers, causing the count to became skewed. Only 65 percent of households returned the forms in 1990, down from 70 percent in 1980.

Beside giving a snapshot of the nation's population trends and economic health, a number of politically important matters were also at stake. Because the apportionment of congressional seats and federal funds was based on census population data, an undercount would leave many programs and state populations shortchanged. To make up for the projected undercount, the Democrats proposed using statistical samples to cover the difference. While not quite in line with the intent of the Constitution, sampling would solve the undercount problem to the advantage of the Democrats. Naturally, the Republicans were dead set against a solution that favored the opposition party. As the bruising political battle over sampling moved to the Supreme Court, the only thing certain about the rules for the 2000 census was that they would be extremely complex and tangled, perhaps to the point of being unworkable in the field.

Such considerations were not the concern of the warring politicians; they did not have to make the program work. Muncaster and his cronies could have cared less. The census workers would be left to figure out things for themselves as the best they could. They were willing to hire all the people needed to get the vital job done, even create two sets of data if it was required to meet the court's ruling. The fact that the integrity of a census system, which had been in place since 1790, was in danger of being destroyed didn't bother them in the least.

In his elegant office, Frank Duester, Ph.D., literally drooled over the prospects of many new contracts coming his way. Washington's unparalleled master of statistical manipulation saw the coming breakdown of the soundness of census data as a signed, blank check. He would take the resulting mishmash of confusing data and make an analysis support whatever position his clients were willing to pay for. Frank saw wonderful things happening for him in the wake of the coming census debacle. Like a vulture on a battlefield covered with fresh dead, Frank was preparing for a feast. He urged both the Republicans and Democrats to fight to the last on the issue. The more statistical chaos their infighting generated, the better for the business of Frank Duester, Ph.D. He could see that the political battles surrounding the year 2000 census were going to generate a massive amount of new business for him. In the new millennium, Frank was going to have to beef up the capacity of his sophisticated computer systems and add to his staff in order to meet his client's needs.

Even though he had once been an admirer of the smooth operating style of Leon Placke, Muncaster had grown to despise the man in recent weeks. The bizarre conversion of Leon from Washington insider to political reformer unsettled Muncaster to no end. Leon's diabolical plan to revamp representation in the House of Representatives along national economic lines instead of by geographical district was an abomination to Muncaster. If the despicable plan was ever implemented, it would snuff out Muncaster's chosen path to power and riches. One of the consequences of Leon's horrid proposal would be the demise of the lobbying industry. Influence peddling in Washington would be reduced to a mere shadow of the current robust industry now bringing in hundreds of millions of dollars a year in revenue.

Muncaster didn't agree with Leon's recent ludicrous pronouncements that massive amounts of money in politics was bad, lobbying was dirty and special interests were slimy. To Muncaster's way of thinking, lobbyists were vital because they acted as the voices of the people in telling Congress what they wanted to be done. Big money in politics was not an evil. It was a sign of the high level of sophistication finally reached by the American political process. Money opened doors. Those willing to spend cash rightfully deserved a larger voice in the management of national affairs than those dullards who didn't. Paying for political access was not corrupting, it was simply a fine manifestation of basic human nature at work. Spending money to influence politics was a form of free speech and ought to be clearly protected by the First Amendment. Muncaster wanted no part of campaign finance reform. He wanted America to spend even larger sums of money on politics. Politicians had made America the richest nation on earth. They deserved a fair share of the national financial bounty. The taxpayers ought to be happy to be paying for it.

As he strode across the grass on the Ellipse towards Leon and the tourists he was addressing, Muncaster remembered an incident from long ago. Magnusan T. Butler had come to Washington to work for President Lyndon Johnson in 1964. As the Vietnam war expanded, sucking in a growing number of American troops, Magnusan got to spend a considerable amount of time in the White House situation room helping the President pick bombing targets. He enjoyed it immensely as the aircraft rose from aircraft carriers in the China Sea and bases in Thailand to do his bidding. In 1966, President Johnson called a halt in the bombing campaign, one of the many called during the war. After the North Vietnamese failed to respond to the peace gesture, Johnson turned on the bombing again. Magnusan and some other interns decided to launch a raid on the Ho Chi Minh trail, using planes from the base at Ubon in Thailand. As the F4-C Phantom jets screamed in on the target, the North Vietnamese gunners blasted them from the sky. The trail's defenders had not been idle. They had used the lull afforded by the bombing halt to bring in new radar-controlled antiaircraft guns. When President Johnson left office, Magnusan found a job with one of Washington's major law firms and did quite well for himself for a number of years.

While entertaining clients over expensive lunches, Magnusan liked to relate his experiences helping President Johnson pick bombing targets. It impressed his guests immensely because it showed Magnusan had access to the top of the power pyramid. He knew how to get to the right people in Washington. One evening at a reception, as he was relating his experiences, he had the bad luck to run into one of the few surviving pilots who had flown on the mission over the Ho Chi Minh trail. The pilot told Magnusan in grisly detail how the planes went down, victims of the new antiaircraft guns. He described how one pilot, sprayed by burning hydraulic fluid from ruptured lines, had screamed in agony over the radio as his plane hurtled to earth. The crew member riding in the second seat had managed to eject from the doomed fighter plane and landed safely, but was killed by the North Vietnamese before the rescue helicopters could reach him.

The grim wartime tale shattered Magnusan. From then on, he was constantly haunted by the image of a burning pilot dressed in a U.S. Air Force flying suit. Often frequented by the phantom from the past, Magnusan lost interest in his work. The work hours which could be charged to clients dropped so low that he was not earning enough for the firm to cover his salary. He was let go. Magnusan went back to Texas and eventually became a preacher. He was famous for his fiery sermons and church programs that bolstered the dirt poor community in which he had chosen to live.

Muncaster figured something similar to what had ruined Magnusan had affected Leon Placke. While he had no idea of what was haunting the once capable lobbyist, Muncaster had no intention of letting Leon stir up the masses by preaching a political line that would destroy the power and the good life enjoyed by Washington's lobbying community. If Leon had changed his mind about lobbying, he should leave Washington, as Magnusan had done, and do his good works in some other location. Leon wasn't wanted or needed here any longer. His usefulness to the Washington power structure had ended.

As he neared the group of tourists, Muncaster heard Leon say, "So you see how the seats in Congress were originally allocated at a time when our largest economic sector was farming. With farming being the major economic activity in the country at the time, the founding fathers had no reason to consider the distribution of congressional seats by any means other than on a geographical basis. If we were truly interested in following the intent of the founders, we would allot the distribution of congressional seats on the basis of economic activity. As farming declined in relative importance, congressional representation should have been redistributed to the manufacturing, retail and services sectors based on their contribution to the gross domestic product. By failing to keep congressional representation in line with what the founding fathers intended, we brought about a cluttering of the political landscape with lobbyists."

"Most of the campaign contributions a member of Congress receives comes from the economic interests he or she supports in committee, not from the voters in the obsolete geographical district represented. If we realign the seats in the House of Representatives to reflect the sectors of our mighty economy, we will virtually eliminate the need for lobbyists, reduce the time Congress is in session and the number of convoluted laws passed each year.

We abandoned the concepts of the founding fathers when we failed to make changes as the economy developed. I am asking you to help me make things right again! Will you do it?"

"I never heard my congressman say anything sensible like that," a man said as he moved forward to shake Leon's hand. "Why do you suppose our lawmakers never brought this matter up?" " Tell us more," a woman said as she pushed closer to the speaker who had captured her full attention. "Damn it all," muttered Muncaster, "The old fool is really getting these people stirred up with his stupid political reform talk."

As Leon answered the questions posed by the attentive crowd , a number of members of the Washington Society of Solicitors came by. They were mostly tax lawyers who had attended a morning seminar on helping clients deal with the psychological stresses generated by preparing income tax forms. Surveys had shown that a tax lawyer who clearly understood the taxpayer's distressed state of mind, could increase net income by 15 percent. The seminar was the hottest thing going in Washington, being completely sold out for its two week run. Since Muncaster was a well-known society member, the group came over to ask him what Leon was doing. They too had heard of the treasonous pronouncements Mr. Placke was spreading. His constant harping on his lunatic congressional reform proposals was rapidly costing him what little respect remained for him in the lobbying community. Muncaster told them it was very sad to see a once great lobbyist disintegrate before their very eyes. The suave, sophisticated mover and shaker they all had admired and respected for many years was no more. In his place was a wild-eyed imbecile who had totally lost touch with everything of real importance. Muncaster was sure Leon was having a nervous breakdown. The solicitors could see for themselves how much he desperately needed help. Why else would Leon choose to make a fool out of himself by stooping so low as to waste his time by addressing a group of innocuous tourists?

The Society of Washington Solicitors was indebted to Leon for laying the foundations of the city's powerful influence industry. In consideration of Leon's past service to the society, Muncaster suggested they remove Leon from the group of gullible tourists he was shamelessly haranguing, and get him to Dr. Lopez for treatment. More than any other doctor, Dr. Lopez understood the stresses of lobbying because he was the world's leading authority on lobbyist burn-out syndrome. Perhaps the doctor could pack Leon off to his sanitarium for a few weeks of therapy and rest.

At the very least, Leon needed to be sedated and gotten off the streets before his wacky ideas got more public attention. Look how the crazy old fool had already infected this group of innocent tourists with the political garbage he was passing off as reform. Neither the Washington Society of Solicitors, Congress, or the booming lobbying profession could tolerate having this mad man on the loose any longer. They had to act decisively before Leon's antics endangered their incomes. With Muncaster's mention of potential income damage, the group's thinking quickly crystallized. They were more than willing to help Muncaster get Leon to the medical attention he direly needed.

The society members circled around the large captivated flock of tourists standing before Leon and approached him from behind. Their assistance was coming not a moment too soon because Leon had already made converts of many of the gullible sightseers. They were telling Leon they knew he had more common sense than any of their elected representatives. Would he be willing to come to their home towns and share his message of hope with their friends and neighbors? They would gather attentive audiences to hear his astounding message of reform. Leon had put his finger on what had gone wrong in Washington. The tourists were eager to help him in any way they could to get his message out to the American public.

The apprehensive solicitors quickly surrounded Leon. J. Dawson Howell, a massive man who fixed things on Capitol Hill for the largest corporations, put a friendly arm around Leon's shoulder saying, "Leon, you look really tired! I'll bet a little rest will do you a world of good. You have said enough to these nice people for the time being. Why don't you come with us now and let us help you?" " Leon, we have come to help you in your time of need," said another lawyer. "Dear old friend, please accept the helping hand we are offering you. We want to help you get back to being your normal self as soon as possible," a third society member chimed in.

J. Dawson had almost extracted Leon from the clutches of the crowd of wide-eyed tourists when one of them snapped, "I don't think you have a right to take Mr. Placke anyplace." That said, he grabbed Leon's arm, halting his movement away from the admiring audience. J. Dawson glared at the upstart from the back country saying, "Sir, please take your hands off of Mr. Placke! It is now time for him to come with us. We are going to see to it that this poor man gets the proper medical attention he so richly deserves."

"And just who in the hell do you think you are to be doing that?" the tourist shot back, not letting go of his hold on Leon's arm.

Angered by the lack of proper respect shown by the nonentity, J. Dawson retorted, "I am a respected member of the Washington Society of Solicitors! Now, please remove your hands from Placke. He is very ill. He must be placed in the care of a competent medical professional."

"Did you hear that?" the man shouted to the crowd of edgy tourists. "This no-good, low-down, creature is one of those crooked lobbyists Mr. Placke told us about!" Turning back to face J. Dawson, he spat out, "You take your filthy hands off Mr. Placke! He sure as hell isn't going anyplace with the likes of you!"

An impeccably dressed tax lawyer tried to calm things. "Look sir," he said, "Mr. Placke's welfare is really not any concern of yours. Why don't you just run along and take the nice White House tour the National Park Service has waiting for you? We will take care of things here, I assure you."

The tourist was unconvinced as he replied, "Kiss my ass, legal beagle! Mr. Placke doesn't look sick to me! And he doesn't need any help from you! I'm not letting you take Mr. Placke away because I've seen in the movies what you Washington slime balls do to whistle blowers. He is going to stay right here with us so we can keep him safe. We will also see to it he gets home later."

"You are ignorant of the facts of the matter, sir! Besides lacking in basic manners, you are completely misjudging this situation. We are Mr. Placke's true friends, no harm will come to him in our care. We all want him to get well."

"Boy, you must think I'm stupid as a gate post! Mr. Placke has just finished telling us about the sweet racket you folks have got going for yourselves. I'm busting my ass to make a living in Kentucky while you stinking lobbyists are skimming off the cream from everything in Washington! What you really want to do is shut him up! You don't want him talking to working people like us because you are afraid we will catch on to the game you are playing!"

"I assure you that is not the case at all! Mr. Placke is on the verge of a nervous breakdown. He desperately needs rest and medical care. With the proper help, I'm sure he will recover completely. He will be free to talk to you again after he has recovered."

"What does he need to recover from? That he is no longer willing to keep quiet about the sleazy shit you pull off in Washington with our tax money? That America gets sold down the river to the highest bidder by the politicians of both political parties? That lobbyists are secretly running the country behind the backs of us common people? Mr. Placke doesn't need any medical treatment from people like you! He can tell right from wrong by himself! Now, you let go of his arm Mr. big shot before I get mad and whip your ass!"

The situation was spiraling rapidly out of control. Sensing the other tourists were ready to support the loudmouth yokel, J. Dawson knew the time had come to act. It was now or never. He gave a mighty yank in an attempt to pull Leon free from the agitated tourist's grip. To his consternation, he found he had badly misjudged things because the stocky man from the sticks had anticipated his move. Leon arms got stretched as the man dug in his heels and maintained his hold. With roars of rage, the other tourists swarmed forward to help him. No one was sure who struck the first blow, but J. Dawson let go of Leon as he crumpled to his knees, holding his profusely bleeding nose between his hands. As three other solicitors stepped into the fray and tried to move Leon towards a waiting cab, the fight was on.

Those who produced food and material for a living battled with those who bent the rules to get favors for special interests in Washington. A forklift operator sparred with a tax lawyer. A grocery clerk slugged it out toe-to-toe with a lobbyist. A landscaper hammered a trade law practitioner. It was class warfare modern American style. Those who wore $1000 suits and lunched at the best eating establishments found themselves beset by a howling mob of outlet mall shoppers who ate their lunch from boxes.

Muncaster was amazed by the ferocity displayed by the motley assemblage of nondescript tourists as Leon suddenly became animated and led them in the attack. The old jerk acted like he was opening the first battle of the second American Revolution. Their plan in shambles, the stunned solicitors had no choice but to fight off the shrieking horde of tourists and hope they could quickly reach the safety of police protection.

It had been a very slow news day for the reporters covering the White House. As the rolling brawl spilled from the Ellipse onto E street in the rear of the White House, the bored TV crews came running to film it. By the time the combatants were nearing 15th Street, the police were arriving in full force. Trapped in the swirling maelstrom, Muncaster vented his rage against the taxpaying scum that dared threaten his chosen life style. He knocked one of the crazed tourists into a concrete planter box with an uppercut, turned to his right and sent another sprawling with a very low blow. Leon, who had just smashed a much younger lobbyist's head against the White House fence, saw Muncaster in action and came charging over. Muncaster easily parried Leon's wild right swing, but completely misjudged the older man's ability to use his left. The blow caught him squarely on the jaw. The last thing Muncaster remembered before slipping into unconsciousness was the eerie, strange glow in Leon's eyes. The old guy must really be high on something. As Muncaster went down to the pavement, the TV cameras filmed the action for the evening news broadcasts.

The city of Washington had never seen anything like it. Some of its best and brightest lobbyists were brawling in the streets with sightseers. Flushed with their victory over the forces of malfeasance, the excited tourists spilled their guts before the TV cameras, telling how the solicitors had tried to kidnap Placke after he had spoken to them about the dire need to reform the lawmaking establishment. They had stopped the cunning band of lobbyists from silencing the prophet of reform. They had saved Leon from an unknown, awful fate at the hands of the evil lobbyists. Like the common people who had flocked to George Washington's standard during the American Revolution, they had dealt an oppressive establishment a righteous blow. Nursing skinned knuckles and bruised faces, they vowed to carry on Leon's fight to implement reform when they got home.

Although they were stunned by the crude tactics used by the usually smooth-operating lobbyists, the police were not overly impressed with the tourists' version of events either. Brawling in the back of the White House was not good for the capital's image, no matter how just the cause. After a considerable amount of discussion, the police charged Leon, who should have known better as the former dean of the lobbying corps, with inciting the riot. When he could not make bail, Leon was tossed into jail. The tourists who had fought by his side were released with a stern warning not to take the law into their own hands again, no matter how much they disliked lobbyists. Their sentences were suspended on the condition they leave the city as soon as they completed their sightseeing. The police also made it clear their safety could not be guaranteed in a city swarming with lawyers and lobbyists, any one of whom might be out to revenge the insult to professional honor.

To the dismay of the lobbying community which hoped Leon would be out of circulation for at least 30 days, Leon was not in jail long. When the story of the altercation between the lobbyists and tourists hit the evening news, over 3,000 offers to post Leon's bail flooded into the police department from all over the country. Leon also found himself in demand as a speaker. Invitations were pouring in by the time he was released from jail.

Leon's speedy trial pushed political events off of the front pages for a few days. As onlookers watched, a mob of unruly tourists marched around the outside of the court building chanting, "Down with rule by lobbyists. Set America free!" Inside the courtroom, the stern judge found Leon guilty and slapped him with an example-setting fine of $77,000. The judge made it clear to Leon that the judicial system was not going to tolerate a publicity-seeking turncoat lobbyist leading riots in the streets behind the White House. The next time Leon was arrested, he could expect to go straight to jail for a long time.

The large fine did not halt Leon's reform effort. The money was quickly raised from the large number of his uncouth supporters milling in the streets. Deeply offended by the show of support for Leon, the Washington Society of Solicitors retaliated for the embarrassment inflicted on the organization by striking Leon's name from its list of esteemed members. Placke's professional conduct was also an issue. A petition calling for his ouster from the bar was quickly rushed through. Washington's attorneys agreed that Leon Placke was unfit to engage in the practice of law. Leon was promptly given the papers advising him that his money-making days were over.

Leon had been tried, convicted and disbarred in a matter of days. Needing a little time to sort things out in his mind, he drove across the Potomac River, then south, down the George Washington Parkway past Mt. Vernon. Turning right on the Mt. Vernon Memorial Highway, he soon reached the parking lot of George Washington's gristmill. As he sat on a picnic table in the darkness watching the slowly moving water in Dogue Creek, it wasn't hard for Leon to imagine himself back in the time when the silent mill was a viable commercial facility. Everything was simple and easier in George Washington's time, all problems were easily solvable in an age when wooden gears and water power were considered high tech.

How hard was it for a person to be successful in an age when ocean going ships were so small, they could come up this backwater of a creek to load flour, whiskey and tobacco? Leon was looking at the modern highway that ran between the head of the creek and the mill, trying to figure out where Washington's loading pier had been located. The site was probably buried under the bridge abutments, he thought. It could also have been be on the far side of the highway or maybe on this side. It wouldn't have been very large because small boats had been used to move the cargo to the anchored ships. Leon was watching a small fish as it jumped for insects when he heard a voice saying, "So you think we had it so easy, do you Leon?" As he turned on the seat to see who was speaking to him, Leon could see George Washington calmly tying his horse to the big sycamore tree next to the mill's door.

Still thinking about the complexities of modern life which overwhelmed him, Leon answered the question as Washington strode over and sat down on the other side of the table. "I think you did because it was a much simpler time in which to live. Everything you attempted to do worked out well for you. Your life was nothing but a string of unbroken successes. You went on to lasting fame and glory because life was a lot easier to live in the 1700s."

Washington was looking at the tree. "When I built the mill," he said, "the sycamore was hardly six inches across at the widest part of its trunk. Now it's over six feet in diameter, don't you think? A couple of hundred years will do wonders for a tree in a good location." "It certainly dwarfs everything thing else around here," Leon said in agreement.

Turning back to face Leon, Washington said, "Everything always looks easy to people after someone else has already done it for the first time. Don't you dare to believe all those fables about me never failing at anything. Let me tell you how hard it really was. Let's start with my looks. My face was pitted with small pox scars and I had another big scar on my jaw caused by the removal of an ulcerated tooth. Those feature flaws certainly didn't help me much with wooing the ladies of my time. Although my work kept me outdoors much of the time, I had an uncanny ability to catch colds, no matter how hard I tried to avoid them. Malarial fevers and agues struck me often, settling in my bones, always giving me twinges of pain. I also caught dysentery more often than the other soldiers I served with. I never seemed to get adjusted to being in the field with the army."

Leon couldn't believe what he was hearing. The great American icon, George Washington, suffered from all the ills of normal men. "I had no idea you had so many physical ailments, I thought you never had a sick day in your life! In your portraits, you always look so healthy. Weren't you tall also, about 6 feet, 2 inches in height?"

Washington continued, "You are correct as to the matter of my height. Everyone has forgotten about my ills because they don't fit with the image people like to hold of me. Do you want to know what my first big disappointment in life was? When I was young, I had my heart set on going to sea with the British Navy, like my elder half-brother. My mother would not hear of it because of the danger. She refused to let me go. The pain of seeing my future as a seafaring man disappear hurt me for months afterwards.

"What was I going to do? Being the younger son of a second marriage, I was due only a modest inheritance. So, I became a surveyor, and a rather good one, by the age of 16. Although dangerous and lonely work, surveying was a lucrative and respectful profession for a young gentleman of little property. It also opened my eyes to the potential this great land held. I saw it firsthand because I tromped the wilderness myself, often with only one or two others for company."

"It was because of my brother's unfortunate early death that I eventually inherited Mt. Vernon and became a farmer. I made a go of it, experimenting with fertilizers and crop rotation and battling the soil exhaustion which came from tobacco growing. When I was away from Mt. Vernon, production always dropped because too many of my overseers were inefficient. Upon my return to the farm, I found crops drooping in fields torn with gullies and the animals becoming smaller from the poor breeding practices. I got a paltry three pounds of wool per fleece while farmers in England were getting 11 pounds. My wheat crop was destroyed by rust more than once. Excessive rain and drought took their tolls. It was a hard life, full of the setbacks dealt by nature and unreliable men."

"Do you have any idea of what it was like to sell tobacco through a merchant-factor in England? The tough businessman who shipped me the manufactured goods I needed after he had sold my tobacco? The lack of manufacturing in Virginia put planters such as myself forever in the factor's debt. He paid the lowest possible price for my tobacco and shipped me inferior goods at high prices in return. If a piece of machinery was missing a part, I had to wait a whole year for the next shipment to come from England. In the meantime the machine sat idle, producing nothing of value for man or beast."

"I never thought of life in colonial times as being beset by so many problems. I always pictured it as an easy life, living off of the fat of the land so to speak," Leon replied. "If you were so interested in farming, what were you doing soldiering so much of the time? It seems to me you were doing quite well as a farmer."

"I was not without military ambition during my younger years. While serving with the Virginia militia, I got blamed for provoking the French forces in the border country. It stemmed from an incident caused by the shooting of a Frenchman who later claimed to be on a diplomatic mission. I didn't know he was under diplomatic immunity when we shot him. It turned out to be a tempest in a teapot, no lasting damage done. France and England were going to go to war no matter what I did, so it made little difference in the end."

"In 1755, when General Edward Braddock moved against French-held Ft. Duquesne at the forks of the Ohio River, he took me and nine companies of Virginia militia with him. The expedition ended in a terrible disaster. Our army was virtually wiped out and Braddock died from his wounds on the retreat. I did learn from the experience. I found out I could lead men while under enemy fire. The next campaign was with General Forbes. We slowly pushed across Pennsylvania and finally captured Ft. Duquesne in November 1758, securing the vast Ohio territory for England."

"I hoped to obtain a commission in the regular British army as a reward for my services with the militia. But it was not to be. I was rejected by the King's army because the regular English officers held a very low opinion of us colonials. They viewed us as inferiors. As I abandoned my ambition for a regular army career, I resigned from the militia and concentrated my efforts on farming. In my mind, I also began to see myself less as an Englishman and more of an American. Being rejected by the British army and the infernal dealings with the factors in London put me firmly on the road leading to my eventual participation in the American Revolution."

"I never knew you wanted to join the British army," Leon said. "It sure was lucky for the future United States that you didn't become a British officer. Where would we be today if you had been fighting on the side of the British?"

"Enough of this talking about me," Washington replied. "You seem to have had a rather rough time of it yourself lately. The message you are trying to bring to the public is unpopular in many quarters of the capital. The entrenched foes of reform will do everything they can to silence you. Are you sure you want to continue with our crusade? The personal cost could be very high."

"I have already reaped a massive amount of trouble as a reward for helping you," Leon said. "The solicitors have expelled me from the society. And I have lost access to most of my valuable contacts in Washington. I am no longer a member of the legal profession, having been stricken from the rolls of the bar association. My former friends now see me as a threat to the income of all lobbyists. Many in Congress would like to see me committed to an asylum or run out of town. What other choice do I have?"

"Let's not get overly righteous Leon! You have been in the capital for many years, working hard to help create the present muddle. The bloating of the staffs working at the White House and Congress, a bureaucracy top-heavy with ineffectual layers of managers and the explosive expansion of the lobbying industry are due directly to the efforts of cynical, self-centered, selfish individuals such as yourself. Since you helped create the predicament, should you not share the responsibility for cleaning it up?

George Washington looked directly into Leon's eyes as he continued, "Pandering to the whims of special interests and pushing the costs of political campaigns to exorbitant levels are not what we had in mind when the government was created. We established three distinct branches to efficiently do the necessary work of governing. One of our major goals was to bind the disparate states into a common whole that would support and foster economic growth. Your generation has debased our endeavors by promoting factionalism, making government a trivial source of handouts and by encouraging citizens to try to shift their legitimate share of the tax burden to others."

"We were not a group of stupid people, Leon! We were well acquainted with the problems faced by the Greek and Roman Republics and European kings. We tried to mitigate as much as possible the impact the inherent flaws in human nature have on the process of governing. To our credit, it worked fairly well, until your disgusting class of nation-wreckers began to come along in the 1960s. As a result of the trends you helped start, the city of

Washington is rife with scandal. President Clinton has barely survived an impeachment caused by his sexual misconduct. Special prosecutors have spent over $60 million in taxpayer funds investigating the shenanigans of the President and his political friends."

"In the 1980s, the nation was rocked by the Iran-Contra scandal as members of the White House staff traded missiles for hostages in Iran and secretly funded a war in Latin America. The savings and loan scandal, ultimately cost the poor taxpayers $500 billion as they paid for the mistakes made by a Congress shirking its responsibilities and doing the bidding of the banking lobby. The degrading emphasis placed on dirty tricks in political campaigning led directly to the Watergate scandal and cost President Nixon his presidency. It is not a national record to be proud of by any stretch of the imagination."

"Leon, with each passing year, the situation grows worse. As the cost of getting elected to public office increases, every new president creates more jobs for his loyal campaign workers and contributors. With a bloated staff of political hacks cluttering the halls of the White House, the President is effectively cut off from the people in government who should be getting information to him. Congress has done virtually the same thing as it has expanded its number of employees. It never goes out session, being too busy dispensing endless favors to interest groups and lobbyists. Things are really going downhill Leon! Are you proud of what you helped create?"

"That's not really fair of you, General Washington! You make it sound as if I spent my working lifetime corrupting the system. I only worked in the capital. I was never in a position of responsibility for setting the tone of how things got done. The big people at the top did that, both the Republicans and Democrats."

Washington smiled as he said, "Well, I can honestly say you did not cause the capital to stay rooted in the District of Columbia for 200 years. There was a great deal of talk about moving it to a new location before the British burned it in 1814. After the war ended, donations poured in from all over the country to help pay for rebuilding. The idea of moving the capital then faded away. People seemed determined to keep it located in the District of Columbia to show the King of England that merely burning public buildings doesn't bring a republic down."

"However Leon, you did everything you could to promote the excesses of the lobbying and the influence peddling business. Leon, you never did anything to halt or even to slow the insidious process for nearly 30 years. You didn't earn your unofficial title as being the king of the lobbyists for doing anything to curb the insatiable appetite of the special interest groups.

As you enriched yourself immensely by lobbying, you completely lost sight of how the government should operate."

"Do you remember anything about the critical time when an American president spoke to the nation and said: 'The attack yesterday on the Hawaiian Islands has caused severe damage to American naval and military forces. I regret to tell you that very many American lives have been lost... Yesterday the Japanese government also launched an attack against Malaya. Last night Japanese forces attacked Hong Kong. Last night Japanese forces attacked Guam. Last night Japanese forces attacked the Philippine Islands. Last night the Japanese attacked Wake island. And this morning the Japanese attacked Midway Island.'"

"That was long before my time. It sounds like something President Roosevelt might have said in the days after the Japanese attacked Pearl Harbor," Leon replied.

"I quoted from President Franklin D. Roosevelt's speech to the Congress asking for a declaration of war against Japan on December 8, 1941. Presidents do make mistakes, Leon. Roosevelt in his capacity as Commander-in- Chief oversaw a big one. His commanders failed to notice the large Japanese fleet composed of six carriers, two battleships, three cruisers and several destroyers as it sailed across the Pacific Ocean to attack the Hawaiian Islands. Unfortunately, that was also the last time the Congress of the United States fulfilled its constitutional responsibility by declaring a state of war. These days, Congress continually commits troops to combat situations by passing watery resolutions and shifting the responsibility to the President. What would your friends in Congress do if an incident like the attack on Pearl Harbor happened today?"

Leon remained silent as Washington continued to lecture him. "Don't you think elected officials ought to take the responsibility for telling the American people about the dangerous problems caused by the break-up of the Soviet Union and the potential new problems coming with the rise of China? What about the growing threat of attack on the United States by missiles carrying chemical, biological or nuclear weapons from the growing number of rogue states? Is the trade deficit, which has been running at $25 billion a month for years, a good or bad thing for the economy of the country? What about the new economic curse plaguing the world? The unregulated flows of global capital that roil the waters of the emerging global economy and create havoc in developing economies? The population of the world has just surpassed six billion. What is the impact of the expanding world population going to be on the United States? Only a complete nincompoop would say world population trends are an unimportant issue having no effect on the future of the United States."

"Leon, the situation in our capital has to be changed! You are the person who is going to have to stir things up, get the public interested in setting things right again! Tom Jefferson had a gift for putting difficult concepts into written words which people could understand. He was always so much better at it than I was. He put our thoughts on the necessity for government bodies to adapt and change into eloquent prose: 'I am not an advocate for frequent changes in laws and constitutions. But laws and institutions must go hand in hand with the progress of the human mind. As that becomes more developed, more enlightened, as new discoveries are made, new truths discovered and manners and opinions change, with change of circumstances, institutions must advance also to keep pace with the times.' No one could have said it any better than that. Leon, go help the moribund institutions of the U.S. government adjust to the times in which you live! Let the words Tom Jefferson penned guide you in your endeavor!"

Leon didn't respond immediately. He was in the process of absorbing the ramifications of the positions George Washington had presented. After some thought, Leon reluctantly admitted to himself that Washington was right. Leon could not deny that he had used his privileged status to do all he could to expand the tentacles of the influence industry over the years. He had also callously disregarded the greater national good as he relentlessly pushed the agendas of special interests, earning himself a tidy profit for his work. He was about to tell George Washington he agreed with his main points when he was interrupted by the voice of a park ranger. "Excuse me sir," the ranger said, "the park is closed. Sleeping on the park picnic tables overnight is not allowed. I am going to have to ask you to leave."

"I wasn't sleeping," Leon groggily replied. "I was having a serious discussion with George Washington about the state of current national affairs." As he stiffly stood up, Leon realized he shouldn't have said that. There was no George Washington sitting on the opposite seat of the picnic table, nor was Washington's horse tied to the big sycamore tree. Leon felt a bit foolish as the ranger escorted him to his car, the only one remaining in the gravel parking lot.

As Leon unlocked the door of his car, the night wind was rustling the leaves of the enormous tree, making a very relaxing sound. Leon was pleased he had come to the gristmill. The chat with George Washington had cleared the cobwebs of indecision from his mind. As he entered his car, the ranger kept a respectful distance, one hand on his holstered sidearm. Leon didn't care if the ranger thought him slightly crazy. Leon Placke was re-inspired. He was not going to let George Washington down. He was going to make amends to the citizenry for the way he selfishly expanded the capital's lobbying business and in the process mangled the Founding Fathers' concept of government by the people. Leon Placke was going to come clean with the people of the United States. He would pay the price George Washington demanded of him and get started on the task of cleaning up the mess in the capital he had helped to create.

August 1999

Leon went to Mt. Vernon and, with a bit of forceful persuasion, got himself admitted to George Washington's private study. Built in 1774-75, the study occupied one end of the house, separated from the rest of the dwelling by a hall and a staircase to the master bedroom above. In their conversation a few nights ago, Washington told Leon he had also used it as a dressing room, keeping his clothes and chamber pot there as well. George would come down the stairwell before 7 a.m., light the fire and begin writing correspondence. Leon looked at the shelves where Washington's 900-volume library had been stored, and leafed through the surviving maps and charts. Some of the survey maps from Washington's younger years had the trees and water painted in color. Leon put his hand on the terrestrial globe Washington purchased from England in 1790. It showed the United States as an independent nation.

Snickering, modern lawmakers considered George Washington naïve, dull, boring and a bit aloof, a real stick-in-the- mud from the old school. They had to pay homage to the man who founded the country on occasion, but that didn't prevent them from considering George Washington to be completely lacking in the traits needed to succeed in modern political life. From his personal encounters with the man, Leon knew Washington to be dignified, steady and truthful. Those traits were looking pretty good to Leon about now since he knew they had mostly disappeared from the White House and Congress.

A rock star heard of the commotion Leon's reform proposals were stirring up during a stop his concert tour made in Washington. He was so impressed by the sincerity exhibited by the reformed lobbyist who was denouncing the excesses of the lobbying establishment that he offered Leon the use of his bus when his tour was completed.

It was a generous offer, made by the star over the strident objections of his accountant, who was dead set against it. The accountant firmly believed the donation of bus services was not tax deductible and ought not to be made. Putting an expensive bus and driver at the disposal of a political nut case made no financial sense. In an attempt to salvage something from the expensive blunder the rock star was making, the accountant asked the IRS for a special ruling on the deductibility of the donation. Perhaps the IRS would allow a percentage of the bus costs to be deducted because it was actually a donation in kind to a worthy political purpose. If that didn't work, the accountant would try to write off the costs as a business advertising expense. Since the bus still had the star's name on it, carrying Placke through the countryside might hopefully be construed as a new way for the star to advertise. Every time the bus stopped and Placke gave a speech, people would see the rock star's name. The accountant also thought about having Placke sell the rock star's tapes and CDs at each stop. If he could convince Placke to do it, the bus expenses would be deductible for sure

The rock star was true to his word. Two weeks later, with the plush bus and its driver at his disposal, Leon was ready to go on the road. He was going to speak on the dire need to reform the nation's lawmaking establishment and of the evils of uncontrolled campaign costs and lobbying to anyone who would take the time to listen. Leon's help in scheduling stops was coming from the citizens who had fought alongside him on the mean political streets of Washington on the glorious day they thwarted the plan of the Washington Society of Solicitors to kidnap Leon. These tourists had been the first to join Leon in his righteous battle to curb the insidious political power of the lobbyists.

A long time ago, accompanied by an unknown colonial officer named George Washington, General Braddock's ill-fated army had marched out of Ft. Cumberland as it began its failed attempt to capture the forks of the Ohio. In honor of Washington's baptism of fire, Leon decided to begin his speaking tour in Cumberland, Maryland.

Leon warmed his audience to his topic by pointing out that while the IRS dutifully collects $1.8 trillion in taxes per year, it can't reconcile its own books with Treasury Department records. If the IRS spent less time dealing with the complicated tax law changes the lobbyists continually got inserted in the tax code, it just might be able to spend a little more time on more important matters. Next, Leon said what was going on in Congress was getting far beyond the point of shame. At the very time Republican lawmakers were solemnly proposing a 1.4 percent across the board spending cut to keep budget expenditures within guidelines, dissolute members of both parties were busy burying billions of dollars worth of projects for pet special interests deep in the budget's fine print.

The struggle between the White House and Congress over the details of conducting the 2000 census was rapidly pushing up the cost to the taxpayers from $4 billion to $7 billion. While politicians with no interest in controlling the cost to the taxpayers feuded, the public got stuck with paying the bill for their petty partisan games.

Leon bluntly told the small crowd gathered in the school gym, "America has the best government money can buy. What you have to remember is that nothing your representatives in Washington give to Cumberland is free. You pay for it every April 15! You are being skinned financially by the power-seeking staffs of the White House and Congress and the greedy, deal-doing lobbyists who stalk the streets of the nation's capital."

Leon exhorted the crowd to demand a reduction in the size of the congressional staff, a 50 percent staff cut, including interns, at the White House, controls on soft money contributions to political campaigns and the redistribution of the seats in the House of Representatives on the basis of national economic sectors. The out-of-date geographical system now in place was being shamelessly abused. It must be brought in line with economic reality so that the lobbying industry, which had run amuck during the previous 25 years, could be phased out of existence. Leon ended his talk by pointing out the founders of the nation had never intended for the system of congressional representation to remain frozen forever on the basis of assumptions made in the days when nearly everyone was a farmer. The attendees were overwhelmed, never having heard such a disconcerting speech before. It would take time for the disquieting issues Leon had raised to sink in.

Leon went on to Ligonier and Washington, Pennsylvania, Wheeling, West Virginia, Newark and Greenville, Ohio. At each stop, the crowds grew larger as word of Leon's electrifying message spread. Leon Placke, the reformed lobbyist, had seen the light and was now preaching political redemption. He had turned his back on everything which had made him rich and was now working to save Congress from itself. As Leon's bus headed for Ft. Wayne, Indiana, the influence industry in the capital began to worry because the old fool was going to try to close down the lobbying industry he had helped create. To make matters worse, people were listening to his message. Leon was endangering the very basis of how things got done in Washington. As those with a vested interest in the present system of congressional representation and the lobbying industry gathered to consider their options, Leon moved on to Paducah, Kentucky, a barbecue and another speech.

H. Muncaster Swindell was mortified. He was the laughing stock of the government. Everyone in the Commerce Department had seen the video tape of Muncaster being flattened by Leon Placke during the street brawl between the solicitors and the sightseers. To add insult to injury, the Secretary had read him the riot act for his involvement in the tawdry attempt to silence Placke. Coming on the heels of the scandal involving the reserving of seats on prestigious international trade missions for special political contributors, charges of intended census data manipulation, and the untidiness of the scheme to hide the unflattering Civil War documents, the bungled attempt to silence Leon Placke was not particularly pleasing to high administration officials.

Muncaster's sore jaw still ached. His cozy political job was in jeopardy and his vision of future wealth and power as a Washington insider was being endangered by a madman traveling the back roads of the nation in a borrowed bus. Muncaster was going to make killing Leon Placke the highest of his priorities. He would get himself up to speed on the Civil War document issue, use that to get close to Leon and then figure out a way to get Placke out of circulation for good. Muncaster would do whatever it took to take Leon Placke out of action. His future in Washington was at stake. Placke was not going to ruin his chances for becoming one of Washington's best deal-doers.

> **"Such is the brutalization of commercial ethics in this country that no one can feel anything anymore delicate than the velvet touch of a soft buck."**
>
> **-Raymond Chandler, 1949**

If Leon's brainless reform scheme could be snuffed out before the tax-paying masses of mindless little people took a liking to it, Muncaster saw many opportunities waiting for him after he left the Commerce Department. His knowledge of export control laws and what Congress would permit someone with influence to get away with, was a very marketable skill in these days of austere defense budgets.

The once free-spending Pentagon was living with a procurement budget only half the size of what it had been at the height of the Cold War. Beginning in 1995, the U.S. defense industry launched a full-scale export drive when President Clinton approved the changes in arms export policy giving economic concerns equal weight with national security considerations. Industry and government became partners, pushing high-tech U.S. arms to all nations with the funds to pay for the latest in lethal weaponry. As a result of the sales drive, the United States now led the world in arms exports, holding a hefty 44 percent share of the $35 billion spent annually on arms worldwide.

In the late 1990s, U.S. arms exports were holding at a steady $14 to $16 billion per year. In the meantime, overall Pentagon procurement fell from a high of $100 billion annually during the Regan-era build up to less than half that amount by 1999. Defense spending supporters justified the high level of international sales as an major asset because the sales helped cover many of the costs of new technology development. Critics of military spending argued that the foreign sales were just another thin excuse for continuing the out-of-control global arms race. They said the United States was not under-armed because it was spending more than twice as much on defense as all of its potential enemies combined. And spreading the latest weaponry around the globe was doing nothing to help the U.S. defend itself from potential aggressors. It was only upping the level of the military technology used in local wars.

Muncaster wasn't interested in the philosophical debates surrounding the pros and cons of foreign arms sales. The pursuit of foreign sales by American companies translated into work requiring the services of a good lobbyist. The merger of Daimler Chrysler Aerospace, AG and Aerospatiale Matra, SA recently created the world's third-largest defense company with annual sales of $28 billion. The new entity was going to compete head-on with Boeing which had sales of $56 billion a year, and Lockheed Martin which was doing business valued at $23 billion a year. Somewhere in all those billions lay the opportunities for Muncaster to help his future clients split legal hairs as they waded through the long process of getting sales approved by the U.S. government.

To develop his future client base, Muncaster had to focus a great deal of attention on building up a solid list of contacts. Since the disagreeable Secretary had chastised him for helping the solicitors in their hour of need, Muncaster felt absolutely no misgivings about developing his client files on government time. He had labored too hard in the last political campaign to have to put up with being treated like a common civil servant.

Maybe it had something to do with the air in Washington, Muncaster thought. Once safely in place, ungrateful senior political appointees always seemed to quickly forget who it was who did the hard grunt work necessary for them to gain the much coveted position of political power. Muncaster firmly believed the election victor had a moral obligation to share the spoils of victory with those who had sacrificed their time and talent to make the election win possible. Under those rules, Muncaster felt he deserved all he could profitably wring from the time he spent at the Commerce Department. He saw no problem in aggressively using the resources available to him to ensure he was properly rewarded when his days a lower level political appointee came to an end. Personal gain from a political appointment was not a bad thing. Why else would Muncaster have worked in politics? He had no time at all for those who talked about the old fashioned ideals of service to the nation. That kind of talk belonged to a doddering previous generation and had no place in modern Washington.

September 1999

"Finality is not the language of politics."
-Benjamin Disraeli, 1859

Muncaster was incensed. Leon Placke had stood on the steps of Abraham Lincoln's home in Springfield, Illinois and told the listeners jamming the street in front of the house that Washington's lobbyists had a vested interest in keeping the tax code, which he said was stack of documents over seven feet tall, as complicated as possible. Why? Because there was money to be made in dealing with the legal complexities of a convoluted tax code. Leon had further stated that Congress sold itself time and again to the selfish special interests that poured the big dollars into congressional campaigns. After the election, the interest groups lined up to reap the rewards dispensed by a compliant Congress through special earmarked appropriations in the annual federal budget. Because Congress no longer represented the economic realities of national life, rapacious lobbyists had moved in to fill the void. Leon raged about the need to redistribute the seats in the House of Representatives along rational economic lines and thereby remove the curse of big-dollar lobbying from the national legislative process. He amply colored his remarks with examples of the underhanded deals he pulled off during his days as a master lobbyist.

Leon also said the founding fathers of the nation had been against establishing family political dynasties. As such, Leon viewed President Bill Clinton's plan to purchase a $1.35 million dollar house in New York as nothing more than an attempt by the Clinton family to retain a grasp on political power after the President left office. The President's wife, Hillary Clinton, was going to use the house as a legal residence so she could run for a seat in the U.S. Senate. Trading one seat of power for another was not in keeping with the founding fathers' concept of public service. Bill and Hillary Clinton should follow the example set by George Washington, Leon was quoted as saying. They should leave the capital and go back to Arkansas, get jobs and work to pay off the $5 million in legal debts they owed. Being President of the United States did not entitle anyone to try to maintain a hold on political power by cleverly switching it to another family member. That kind of power grabbing was what had ruined the economies of many countries in the past. It should not be permitted to happen here.

Giving up the perks of political power was tough on the ego, but that was

313

the way things were supposed to be in the United States. Bill Clinton was a U.S. President, not a Roman emperor. He had no right to arrange a special backdoor access to the federal treasury through his wife, Leon was reported to have said. Muncaster thought Leon Placke was a sorry piece of ungrateful trash. Not only was he unfairly attacking the First Family's right to keep their fingers in the federal money trough awhile longer, he was destroying the public image of Washington's indispensable lobbying profession. Muncaster had no idea what was driving the terribly demented man. He decided time was running out. If he didn't act soon, Leon would wreck every thing Muncaster loved about Washington, DC.

Muncaster's attempt to use Leon's role in the Civil War document affair as a way to legally silence him had come to naught. While Muncaster found plenty evidence of illegal actions which could be used against Leon, there were overriding mitigating circumstances that prevented him from taking these matters to the police. Leon had acted on the wishes of a number of powerful lawmakers. If Muncaster had Leon charged with a crime, he was also going to implicate some of the very people in Congress he hoped to cozy up to in the future. The tantalizing Civil War papers issue could not be used as a method to remove Leon from circulation because it would also ruin Muncaster's future access to Congress.

The nasty truths oozing out of the papers ordered hidden by Confederate Secretary of State Benjamin had already taken a large toll of corporate and private political campaign contributors. Despite the substantial damage done to the political money-raising establishment, the matter had to remain dormant because Muncaster did not want to in anyway jeopardize his future relations with Congress. If he got Placke sent to jail, a number of potential future patrons on the Capitol Hill would be going along with him. Playing a part in jailing members of Congress was not what Muncaster wanted the inhabitants of Capitol Hill to remember him for.

Muncaster read that Dwayne O. Andreas was in town. He was the retired grain company executive who pioneered the art of corporate campaign financing while building one of the country's biggest food processing empires. Dwayne Andreas had courted politicians across the political spectrum, from Hubert Humphrey to Richard Nixon, from Bob Dole to Mikhail Gorbachev. He set an example for business executives seeking to build support across political party lines and national boundaries. At the time of Watergate, President Nixon had $100,000 in unmarked bills from Dwayne Andreas in the White House safe.

Unfortunately, Andreas's legacy was tarnished a bit more by a criminal price-fixing case that cost his firm $100 million in fines in 1995. It was a matter of little importance in Washington political circles because Mr. Andreas would always be fondly remembered for other reasons. His strategy of lavishing contributions on both Republicans and Democrats became the model for other corporate executives seeking to influence the national political agenda. Unlike Leon Placke, Dwayne Andreas had not gone soft in the head as he aged. Muncaster wished he could get himself on the gentleman's schedule for a few minutes. There were so many things he would like to learn from the undisputed master of the art of corporate political giving.

From his vantage point in the Commerce Department, Muncaster sadly watched the opportunities fly by. A corporate bidding team including Lockheed Martin Corporation, won a 15-year, $10 billion dollar contract to maintain aircraft engines for the U.S. Air Force. That contract came on the heels of a NASA operations contract worth $6 billion that Lockheed had won a few months earlier. General Dynamics made an unsolicited $2 billion offer to acquire Newport News Shipbuilding, Inc. Because of antitrust considerations in the defense sector, someone was going to pick up a good piece of work pushing the deal through Congress and the Department of Defense bureaucracy. Had Muncaster gotten wind of the deal before hand, he could have made a quick $3.50 a share on Newport News stock as it jumped in value in response to the surprise General Dynamics bid. What good was having a lot of friends in Washington if they weren't going to tell you what was going on?

Americans were spending more than $6 billion a year on vitamins, minerals, herbal remedies and dietary supplements. Consumption had increased an astounding 62 percent since 1984. Muncaster decided to check into who was representing these eager manufacturers in Washington. Maybe he could line up a couple of future clients who were in the rapidly expanding supplement business.

Muncaster was informed of a new trend sweeping across corporate America by a friendly stockbroker who shared a table at lunch with him. Firms were spinning off parts of their businesses and investors were heartily cheering the change. Muncaster read how the Hewlett-Packard Company became the latest company to divide itself into two publicly traded entities. It joined such corporate titans as AT&T, ITT, PepsiCo and DuPont in revamping their corporate structures by chopping them into smaller pieces. The spin-offs were very popular with investors because they were a tax-free way to give existing stockholders a dividend in the form of a additional stock. It was a trend in corporate affairs Muncaster was completely missing. He didn't have a clue as to who was handling matters for the splitting firms on

Capitol Hill. As a result of his oversight, a big bundle of money was destined to go into the pocket of some other lobbyist.

Muncaster was not pleased to learn that the U.S. was cracking down on Chinese attempts to acquire nuclear data. The unexpected furor erupted because designs for U.S. Trident missile warheads had somehow found their way into Chinese hands. The pilfered data could have saved China as much as four years in designing their own weapons. A major U.S. government counterespionage investigation was underway, involving nuclear experts at the national laboratories at Los Alamos and Sandia in New Mexico and Lawrence Livermore in California.

Muncaster knew from experience that serious national security lapses were a very bad thing for incumbent politicians because they got the common citizenry uptight and stirred up a host of grave problems. Someone could get fired if the security breech was bad enough. Muncaster hoped none of the blame could be pinned on sloppy work done by the Commerce Department's export licensing section. Although he didn't like to admit it, he had been spending far too much time at work on developing his future business prospects. Maybe he should have paid a little more attention to the export security papers that kept coming across his desk. At any rate, Muncaster didn't need another scandal of any type to sort through. Figuring out how to permanently take care of Leon Placke was more than enough work for one person.

Muncaster was elated to learn the $110 billion boost in defense spending proposed by the Clinton administration was surviving the congressional budget battles with very little in the way of changes. Congress, in its infinite wisdom, might even add a few billion to the amount of the administration's request as it finalized the budget. Muncaster didn't care if $2.5 billion of the increase was earmarked to pay for the deployment of 7,000 troops in Bosnia. The items of interest to him were the billions of dollars going to buy spare parts for trucks, tanks, ships and aircraft. Some of the companies bidding on those government contracts probably could be convinced they needed the services of a good lobbyist familiar with how the government worked.

"Mediocrity in politics is not to be despised. Greatness is not needed."

-Hans Enzenberger, 1990

In a disrespectful slap at the administration, the Congressional Budget Office warned that the President's well-publicized approach to funding the Social Security System would not prevent the system from running out of money in about ten years. Almost at the same time as it warned of the failing Social Security system, the budget office released new budget projections forecasting federal surpluses of nearly $800 billion over the next ten years. That report delighted many on Capitol Hill because dividing up the surplus was going to be a very enjoyable experience. Lobbyists, special interest groups and members of Congress got ready to lay claim to a slice of the surplus for their pet projects.

Muncaster was stunned to learn that the competitive tensions generated by the global economy were beginning to ruin relations between the closest of allies. In a blow to America's well-scrubbed image, the German government forced the United States to recall three CIA agents who were caught while recruiting German citizens to engage in economic espionage work. When it came to competing for business in the cutthroat international marketplace, no country had any friends. To win the global trade battles, companies competing for worldwide contracts needed every fragment of useful commercial intelligence they could get. Maybe the American agents needed to be better trained in the future to avoid getting exposed. If it happened in a less-friendly place than Germany, they could easily end up dead instead of expelled.

Vice President Gore was running into problems with his bid for the presidential nomination on the Democratic ticket. His overwhelming lead had completely disappeared. He and Senator Bradley were now running almost neck and neck. To help negate his image as a Washington insider, Gore was moving his campaign headquarters to Nashville, Tennessee. Muncaster's extensive investigation into the Civil War papers incident had uncovered the story of the Confederate soldier who had survived the crushing defeat at Nashville and ended up moving to Virginia after the war. Muncaster hoped Nashville would treat Al Gore better in the year 2000 than it had General Hood's Confederate army in late 1864. Although he never mentioned it to others, Muncaster had begun to believe Leon Placke had put a hex of some sort on Gore's campaign. Everything started to fall apart about the time Leon turned his back on his lucrative lobbying business, launched his anti-lobbyist crusade and started to call for campaign finance reform and the remaking of Congress.

Muncaster barely read a report stating President Clinton had pledged to forgive the $5.7 billion debt owed to the United States by 36 of the world's most desperately poor countries. Countries that bad off were of no interest to Muncaster because they probably couldn't afford to hire a lobbyist in Washington, even on a part-time basis.

Muncaster got a chuckle out of a story in one of the papers regarding G.

Gordon Liddy, the mastermind of the Watergate burglary. The tough former Republican political operative, with nine felony convictions on his record, now stood accused by one of his neighbors of moving property survey stakes. Maybe crazy Leon could bring the ghost of George Washington to the property and have him run a honest survey for the pair of feuding property owners. Liddy was said to be as tough as nails, but not even Liddy was likely to be tough enough to take on George Washington and his 20th century mouthpiece, Leon Placke. Muncaster gave serious consideration to giving Liddy a call. He might in the spirit of bipartisan cooperation, be interested in taking a contract to put an end to Placke's life. Liddy should not be too hard to find. Since being released from federal prison, he had become a syndicated radio talk show host in the northern Virginia suburbs of Washington. It would be a true service to the nation if Liddy killed Placke. It would be a far more noble deed to do than breaking into the campaign offices of the opposition party in order to satisfy the whims of a paranoid president.

Muncaster was disappointed to find out how much the police lacked a sense of real justice. No matter how hard he tried, they would not give him the list of the names and home addresses of the people who had been arrested with Leon Placke. With it, Muncaster had hoped to be able to plot Leon's route across the country, then take a few days off and intercept the lunatic in one of the small towns he was frequenting. Without access to list, Muncaster had no idea where Placke would make his next appearance. The unpretentious tourists who had been mentally seduced by the cunning traitor to the lobbying industry seemed to have all come from nondescript places no one of Muncaster's stature would have normally ever have cared to visit.

As Muncaster brooded, word came that Placke had crossed the Mississippi River and riled up a good-sized crowd at Cape Girardeau on the Missouri side. Placke began his rabble rousing by mentioning President Clinton had signed legislation that would double the pay of future presidents and raise the salaries of members of Congress effective January 2001. The next president would receive a salary of $400,000 a year. Members of Congress got a 3.4 percent raise, bringing the annual pay for most members to $141,300.

Leon said the cost of operating 61 Federal regulatory agencies had reached an all-time high of $18 billion a year. While the cost of regulation was going up, the new Speaker of the House, J. Dennis Hastert, was pouring $350,000 every three months into the political action committees he controlled. Much of the money came from industries the government regulated. Leon continued with his usual harangue on the bloated staffs of the White House and Congress, the need to change the basis of congressional seating, campaign finance reform and how Democrats and Republicans alike played hell with the audience's tax money at budget appropriation time.

Leon stated that voter turnout in the United States was falling below 50 percent during elections because the people had lost control of the government to the lobbyists and special interest groups. He noted that although Americans were voting less, they were going to prison in ever increasing numbers. The number of adults imprisoned had more than doubled in the last 12 years, reaching its highest level ever. American jails and prisons held 1.8 million people, second only in the world to Russia in the number of individuals incarcerated. He also took a jab at Washington's double standard by saying that while President Clinton sat in the White House managing the affairs of the country, his own staff was not paying its taxes on time. Nearly 14 percent of the White House staff had not gotten tax payments to Uncle Sam on time in 1999.

Leon could no longer be considered an inconsequential joke by the Washington establishment because a massive volume of letters and calls supporting his proposals were beginning to pour into the White House and Congress. Leon's speeches, a strange mishmash of fact and personal recollections, were having a devastating impact on the minds of the unsophisticated voters Leon addressed. Disagree as they might on many issues, the White House and Congress were united as one in their growing fear of the nauseating ideas Leon Placke was spreading across the land.

Feisty Senator John McCain borrowed part of Leon's reform package and launched his bid for the Republican nomination by calling for reform of the political financing system. As McCain entered the race, former Vice President Dan Quayle had to call it quits due to a lack of campaign contributions. While Republican party strategists worried about the party's uncanny ability to compound its negative image in the eyes of the voters, Vice President Gore's campaign mailed another 500,000 letters to prospective contributors. It was politics as usual Muncaster thought, people working hard to make political inroads during the primary season.

Muncaster read an interesting story about an indicted lobbyist accused of stealing campaign contributions and taking payoffs. Despite an indictment by a federal grand jury, the female lobbyist was still raking in hundreds of thousands of dollars in lobbying fees. In the realpolitik world of Washington lobbying, her access to the powers in Congress was not affected by the indictment, so the majority of her clients decided to stick with her. Muncaster was deeply affected by the show of good common sense displayed by the lobbyist's clients.

Not so good was the news that a federal appeals court had reinstated criminal charges against a Democratic party fund raiser charged with conspiring to funnel illegal campaign contributions to the 1996 Clinton-Gore reelection campaign. Muncaster didn't understand what all the fuss was about, only a paltry $100,000 was involved. It was hardly enough for a sensible court to bother with. The appeals court ought to be devoting its time to more serious matters.

Muncaster was annoyed to learn some people never figured out how to do things properly in Washington. He thought that the Secretary of Energy's embarrassing order to remove the brother of a department director from the consulting payroll was a downright silly example of such shortsightedness. It was a waste of a good opportunity. Muncaster could have set up a contract and subcontracts which would have made things look legal. The brother could have been given a contract netting him $70 an hour for the service he provided. If only people had the sense to ask a few questions, many sticky embarrassments could be easily avoided.

Muncaster was pleased to learn the lawyer who had defended Monica S. Lewinsky's mother had made his mark in the legal world. He had joined one of the larger Washington law firms as a partner. It was a position paying him about $375,000 a year.

The former Speaker of the House, Newt Gingrich, appeared to be getting himself slowly back together after leading the party to defeat and wrecking his career. Although he had agreed to pay a $300,000 penalty for his misleading statements to the ethics committee, the IRS had recently cleared his foundation of charges that it had violated its tax-exempt status. Muncaster felt a degree of sympathy for the fallen Republican leader because his savage political attacks had often backfired. At times, Gingrich had been a very great help to the Democrats.

The tobacco industry had been most generous in its lobbying expenditures. It spent $58 million to keep unfavorable legislation from becoming law in Congress. As he finished reading the report, Muncaster had the feeling that Leon Placke would soon be misinterpreting much of the same material in his talks to the unsophisticated plebeians in America's outer provinces. Leon had absolutely no business stirring these people up. Let them watch their TV shows, shop at their malls and pay their taxes on time as all dutiful citizens should.

The Occupational Safety and Health Administration was readying a new set of rules for the modern workplace. The rules would require employers to ensure that workers were less likely to succumb to an array of injuries to the back, neck, wrist and arms. The objective was worthy, to reduce injuries that come from constant overexertion, awkward postures, or equipment not suited to the size or strength of the worker. As with many standards created in the pristine vacuum of Washington rule-making, this set of rules had a number of built-in flaws that would make compliance difficult. Because the regulations would have far-reaching effects in the nation's industries and offices, employers' groups were fighting in Congress to halt enforcement of the rules.

Muncaster knew the safety rules were complicated and confusing. He didn't want them made any easier to understand because a high degree of confusion would generate a substantial amount of new business for Washington's lobbyists. The unworkable tax code was generating thousands of opportunities yearly. If the safety regulations could be made as obtuse, additional thousands of lobbying opportunities would develop. Muncaster decided to have a few of his analysts work on an economic analysis of the rules' potential economic impact. If the dollar amount was large enough, he might give up the idea of working in the defense sector and shift his focus to the opportunities emerging in the field of occupational safety.

He had to be brutally tough in getting the analysis started because some of his staff balked at an undertaking which was clearly in the jurisdiction of another department. Muncaster was extremely annoyed because they dared question his faultless judgment. These unimaginative, bureaucratic lower-life forms simply didn't understand that what was good for H. Muncaster Swindell was also automatically good for America. They were paid to work on the projects he assigned, not sit there and think about the reasons why he assigned them. Muncaster's hard work during the previous election campaign had earned him the right to supervise these ninnies as he saw fit. It took several acrimonious meetings for Muncaster to get his analysts straightened out on what exactly he wanted from the analysis of the economic impact of the new safety rules.

As his group of reluctant dimwits dutifully cranked up their computers, Muncaster found another item that attracted his interest. He read that American foundations were giving away approximately $82 billion a year to finance worthy charitable activities. According to the IRS, individual Americans took tax deductions for charitable contributions for another $102 billion a year. Tax-free philanthropy had a tremendous impact in the United States when one considered the sheer volume of money flowing in the system. Where was all the money going and what was it doing? As soon as the safety regulations project was completed, his analysts would be tasked to find the answer.

Muncaster was also enthralled by the fact that Richard Mellon Scaife, the Pittsburgh billionaire and patron of conservative causes, had pumped $340 million into the conservative foundations he controlled over the last 40 years. As he absent-mindedly watched the untrustworthy tourists moving on the sidewalk below his window, Muncaster wondered if there was a rich liberal donor out there someplace, someone who wanted to pump a few hundred million dollars into liberal causes. If there was, Muncaster knew he was just the right man for the job. He would love to be in charge of handing out someone else's money to groveling petitioners. It would be a position worthy of his many multifaceted talents. With a job like that, doors would open to him all over the capital. Those who dispensed money in Washington were treated with the utmost respect by all the myriad components of the Washington establishment. Money had a truly unique way of transcending the gulf created by partisan party politics.

October 1999

Leon Placke was in Lawrence, Kansas, a town rewarded for its pro-Union stance during the Civil War by being virtually obliterated by Quantrell's Confederate guerrillas. Leon was telling his listeners not to be believe the often repeated campaign promise that politicians would cut taxes. Americans, Leon argued, were not so much against taxation without representation as they were against all taxation of any kind. The American fascination with shifting the tax burden to someone else had, in Leon's opinion, created an overly complicated tax code that generated a financial windfall for lobbyists, tax accountants and lawyers. Clever politicians had used the deep-seated hatred of taxes to manipulate the voting masses on more than one occasion. It was a never ending charade which brought with it no change in the overall tax burden Americans carried. While Americans were paying less in federal taxes than they did 20 years ago, they were not paying less of their income to the combination of federal, state and local tax collectors. As politicians cut federal taxes with fanfare, state and local taxes were quietly allowed to increase as these jurisdictions picked up the slack left by the cut backs in federal programs.

Leon announced it was time to put an end to the hype the pandering politicians were using as a smoke screen to confuse voters. Did the audience know that the so-called rich were actually paying a sizable share of federal taxes? The top 1.5 percent of taxpayers paid an astounding 37 percent of all the federal taxes collected last year. Leon said the real problem the voters needed to face was the tangled tax system which had become a tremendous overhead expense to the U.S. economy. The economic drag caused by the confusing tax system was never mentioned as a serious problem by the Washington establishment because they were quite happy with things as they were. The massive IRS bureaucracy, lawyers, accountants and politicians all had a stake in leaving the existing system alone.

Leon said the forgotten savings and loan debacle of a few years ago had cost the American taxpayers $500 billion to clean up. Why had Congress removed most government controls from the savings and loan industry while at the same time keeping the government responsible for making good the losses suffered by insured depositors? The $500 billion loss was directly attributable to the ludicrous changes a short-sighted Congress made in the laws to please the lobbyists. Another massive change in the banking regulations was ready to be enacted into law by Congress. The supporters of the legislation said the new regulations would enable banks, securities firms and insurance companies to more easily merge with one another. The new laws would allow the banking and financial industry to catch up with trends already underway in the financial community, making the system more efficient and better able to offer services at a lower price. The more efficient the industry is, the better off everybody was going to be.

Leon told his listeners that he had heard it all before. The backers of the savings and loan legislation said exactly the same thing as that disastrous bill wound itself through the committees of Congress. Did the people know that this latest industry-dream-come true law came with a hidden cost for the consumer? Not only did it shred old-fashioned notions about privacy, it also took away an individual's control over the personal information routinely cited as the most sensitive. It was going to be open season on the poor consumer's financial information files as the firms traded data among themselves. Stockbrokers were going to be able to do internal reviews of your checking account information and bank clerks were going to push discounted insurance coverage based on reviews of your insurance records. The sales pitches were going to come from all sides as the prohibitions against sharing information disappeared. Leon suggested to his listeners that the time might be right to raise the matter of consumer privacy with government officials.

Treasury Secretary Lawrence H. Summers was not amused by the volume of letters descending upon the United States Treasury Department. In a much publicized response to the outcry of consumers, he appealed to Congress to include better protection for personal financial data in the pending banking reorganization bill. Secretary Summers dryly warned that the administration would be pressing the financial industry to give people more control over how companies used their financial data. Privately, Summers wondered why Leon Placke was out in midlands stirring up the people. Leon had changed in some way. He never seemed to care about the interests of consumers before. What had gotten into the man?

As one of the nation's leading economists, Summers knew a overhaul of banking regulations was long overdue. So much was at stake that it had to become the law of the land even if a few consumer interests got mangled in the process. Summers also knew that the national economy operated in a constant state of turmoil. In the $7.6 trillion U.S. economy, nothing stayed the same for very long. As new technologies emerged, whole industries developed virtually overnight as new businesses started up. The grinding competition caused casualties as obsolete firms went out of business. Hopefully, as workers lost jobs in declining industry sectors, they would find employment in the ones that were growing. There was one big problem. The theory didn't always hold true in the real world of work because of the skills needed. While there were close to 25,000 jobs open in the computer field in the Washington metropolitan area, those individuals on the unemployment rolls did not have the skills required to fill them. It was a depressing situation. Jobs were going begging while at the same time people remained unemployed. Economics was not called the dismal science for nothing.

Secretary Summers could understand Leon's new-found concern regarding the privacy of consumer financial data. It was a legitimate issue. What intrigued Summers the most, however, was Leon's plan to redistribute the seats in the U.S. House of Representatives on the basis of economic sectors instead of by geographical congressional district. His keen mind could see the logic behind the proposal because it made eminent economic sense. As one of the nation's brightest economists, Summers could not argue with the reasoning behind Leon's proposal to bring congressional representation in line with the economic changes which had occurred in the nation during the past 200 years.

What Summers could not understand was why Leon Placke, who was one of the most astute lobbyists in Washington, had raised an issue that collided head-on with the entrenched interests in Congress and Washington's powerful lobbying community. The forces of Capitol Hill and Lobbyist's Row would pulverize Leon in any fight over the redistribution of congressional seats. It seemed as if Leon was on some sort of a suicide mission. All economic logic aside, Summers didn't see the matter as one whose political time had come. What was driving Leon to push an issue that would take ten years or longer to work itself through the political process? Leon had absolutely nothing to gain from promoting the idea. He was in danger of losing the accumulated benefits of a lifetime's work as a lobbyist in Washington by championing a proposal that was an abomination to sitting members of Congress and all the city's lobbyists.

Leon's proposal made no sense in the current political climate. But then Lawrence H. Summers had not achieved professional success by avoiding the investigation of unpopular economic ideas. His curiosity was aroused. He wanted to test Leon's proposal. How had the lobbyist come by such a fascinating economic idea? The Secretary of the Treasury made a note in his reminder pad to call Leon for lunch sometime after Leon, the father of the new theory of congressional reorganization, got tired of riding around the countryside and returned to the capital.

Secretary Summers turned his attention to other matters. His inspector general had just issued a report stating federal officials did a lousy job policing money laundering schemes at the nation's banks. The report was going to be a real hot political potato, an embarrassment for the Treasury Department and the nation's banking community. The U.S. had become the largest repository of ill-gotten financial gains in world. In the lucrative world of private banking, banks were moving money around the world at the behest of wealthy clients interested in avoiding taxes and government scrutiny. Money obtained by ill-gotten means was being laundered through a complex web of transactions that made its origins and ultimate owner hard to trace. Hundreds of millions of dollars in dirty money was floating around the U.S. banking system. The laws for controlling such activity were inadequate and the few laws that did exist were rarely enforced.

The report was an indictment of a banking community that did not feel particularly constrained by the regulations. It was ironic that at the same time the laws governing the compartmentalization of banking and the financial services industry were being loosened, the banking establishment was being exposed for engaging in money laundering activities.

Summers knew what was coming next. New laws with the teeth needed to control money laundering would be passed by Congress and Treasury's enforcement agencies would be strengthened. It was a real mess to clean up. But then no one ever went wrong by underestimating the extent to which human greed would push things to the limit in monetary affairs. The bankers had brought it upon themselves.

There was better news in the next report the Treasury Secretary read. The jobless rate was down to 4.1 percent for October, the lowest in 30 years. There were 129.3 million Americans working at jobs. The booming economy was adding nearly 160,000 new jobs a month. Summers was extremely proud of the fact that the U.S. economic expansion, which began in the spring of 1991, was still proceeding at a healthy pace and appeared to be on track to become the longest in American history. President Clinton might have a miserable set of personal ethics, but history would have to record that he made excellent choices in filling the government's top financial and economic positions. Clinton deserved a lot of credit for letting his low-key team of economic specialists alone while they managed the booming economy which had become the envy of the world. When it came to the state of the national economy, not even the Republicans voiced complaints.

Although he was cheered by the favorable employment statistics, Summers could not get Leon's radical proposal to overhaul Congress out of his mind. After finishing reading the reports, he turned on his computer and began working up analyses that would prove or disprove if Leon's fascinating plan had economic merit. If it did, Summers would be ready with his statistical data when Leon's congressional reform proposal evolved into a hot political issue. Summers would really enjoy going before a congressional committee and telling the pompous group of sanctimonious legislators on Capitol Hill that their organizational structure was obsolete.

As his computer began to spit out reams of supporting data, Summers could see no good reason why Congress should not be reorganized. Everything else in the American economy was in a perpetual state of upheaval, it was the price the nation had to pay for economic progress. Maybe it was high time for a change at Congress. The institution ought not be exempt from paying its share of the bill for national prosperity. Having a Congress that accurately reflected America's economic structure would be good for the country because it would take a great deal of the stress out of politics. Leon Placke's idea was not as crazy as it seemed at first glance. Modernizing Congress was something that had simply been overlooked for 200 years.

As Secretary Summers brooded over his charts and graphs, the heady brew of national politics continued to churn outside the Treasury building. Elizabeth Dole dropped out of the race for the Republican presidential nomination, citing difficulties in raising campaign funds as the reason. As she became the fifth Republican to pull out of the race for the White House, one disgusted political consultant said, "We're turning the nominating process of both parties into nothing more than a contest based on the lifestyles of the rich and famous." "Many good candidates never get to the point where the voters get to say one way or another how they feel about them. The primary races have turned into nothing more than a game at which only the richest endowed of candidates can play," said another appalled observer of the campaign financing business.

Congress passed a $269 billion defense bill containing many benefits for special business interests hidden at strategic places in the voluminous pages of small print. Then, in order to stay under the overall budgetary caps on spending, the straight-faced Republicans in Congress continued to push for the 1.4 percent across the board spending cut that was being vigorously opposed by the White House. Dividing up the tax dollars was proving to be a very difficult undertaking for both Congress and the White House. Reaching an agreement on how to spend the tax wealth was proving to be much harder than expected. It was hoped by all in Washington that America's taxpayers appreciated the fantastic amount of effort put forth by the Executive and Legislative branches as they squabbled and very slowly crafted the national budget.

In order to win favorable treatment from the U.S. Government on a host of issues, Russian business groups were spending millions on the services of

Washington's lawyers and influence peddlers. As the Russian economy staggered on the verge of chaos, little was being said by Washington's decision-makers about the mismanagement and corruption that was knocking the bottom out of Russia's attempts to get its economy working.

Despite the interest stirred up in the topic of reforming campaign financing by Leon Placke as he traveled across country, the Senate voted down a campaign finance reform bill. The move guaranteed politicians of both parties access to millions of dollars in soft money contributions during the coming campaign. In their collective wisdom, the lawmakers ruled that the gigantic financial contributions special interest groups made to incumbent members of Congress and other selected candidates had absolutely no corrupting influence on American politics. Instead of being a national problem, the congressional majority viewed unlimited campaign contributions as a lubricant to stimulate the free flow of ideas in the public domain.

Washington insiders smiled at the little white lie being promulgated by Congress because they knew exactly how the system worked. Political contributions bought access to officials, a guarantee of a respectful hearing from those involved in deciding how things got done in the country. Busy elected officials in Washington didn't have a lot of time to waste; they had to set priorities. No time could be spared for those failing to make a contribution.

While it was very true that political contributors never got everything they wanted, they managed to get more than anyone else. If you were interested in affecting the political decisions made in Washington, you had better be willing to pay your dues. No payment, no play. It was as simple as that. There was absolutely no room for cheapskates in a capital where the games were played for extremely high stakes.

Texas Governor George W. Bush was running the most lavish spending primary campaign ever undertaken by a presidential front-runner. He spent nearly $13 million during the previous three months, leaving him with $37 million from his national fund raising effort still in the bank. Despite Mr. Bush's overwhelming lead in the race to the Republican nomination, Senator John McCain, who argued for campaign finance reform, was suddenly emerging as a credible challenger.

An unhappy Republican party reported to its leadership that America's businesses were neatly hedging their political bets this year. They were not being nearly as loyal to the Republican party as they had been in previous years. America's business interests were splitting their giving evenly between the Republicans and Democrats running for seats in the House of

Representatives. The party saw it as a worrisome trend. What was happening to the country?

"Politics is a place of humble hopes and strangely modest requirements, where all are good who are not criminal and all are wise who are not ridiculously otherwise."
-Frank Moore Colby, 1926

As the Republican-controlled Congress struggled to complete work on the federal budget, it relied to an unprecedented degree on creative accounting practices to boost spending beyond what the rules allowed. The legal but sleazy and unethical process, gave the trend-setting lawmakers an extra $46 billion to spend on defense, farms, education and other programs. When lawmakers had the many needs of special interests to take care of, it was often difficult to stay within the boundaries of acceptable accounting practices. The lawmakers had to allow themselves a degree of flexibility in order to meet their many political obligations.

As Congress was creatively spending money, Richard Holbrooke, the new U.S. Ambassador to the United Nations, announced it would be a good idea if the United States paid the $1.7 billion in back dues it owed to the organization. A reluctant Congress was prepared to pay only about $112 million on the balance owed, just enough to keep the U.S. from being expelled from the organization's general assembly. The Congress currently in session in Washington didn't want to be reminded of the high hopes the United States had for the United Nations when it fostered the establishment of the organization in the dark aftermath of World War II.

The AFL-CIO endorsed Vice President Gore's bid for the presidency, despite the fact polls showed former Senator Bill Bradley rapidly gaining ground on him. In New York, Hillary Rodham Clinton, the nation's first lady, used the opportunity of her 52nd birthday to collect $1million for her Senate campaign at a combination fund raiser and birthday bash. Not to be outdone in the race for campaign funds, Representative Tom DeLay, the House Whip, used a network of lobbyists to gather more than $15 million in contributions for needy Republican congressional candidates.

A large number of Washington's jaded lobbyists were hedging their bets by not forgetting the Democrats had a good chance to regain control of Congress in the 2000 elections. To the delight of the Democrats in Congress, there was an avalanche of soft money cascading into their congressional campaign committee's coffers. If the disgruntled voters decided to put a Republican in the White House and Democrats back in control of Congress, it would be fine with the Democrats on Capitol Hill. They would be happy to exchange roles with Republicans if that was what the voters wanted.

President Clinton vetoed the $792 million Republican tax cut bill, killing all chances for tax reduction for the remainder of the year. Having already made plans to spend the money, Congress was not overly dissatisfied with the presidential rejection. President Clinton would have to take the political heat for not cutting taxes, while members of Congress could honestly say they tried to give a few dollars back to the taxpayers. Although they would never admit it to the public, Congress was more than happy to have been let off the hook by the President. As the tax money flowed in, members of Congress saw to it that it went to where it would do them the most good during next year's election. With limited funds to dispense and unlimited demands from constituents to meet, it took the focused concentration of the best legal minds in Washington to hammer out spending bills that would pass bipartisan muster.

The Senate rejected the Comprehensive Test Ban Treaty, dealing a devastating blow to a pact that was at the center of global efforts to curb the spread of nuclear weapons. As part of the on-going power struggle between Capitol Hill and the White House, the Senate took the opportunity to embarrass President Clinton with the crude blow to the nation's foreign policy agenda. In other parts of the world, the Senate's rejection of the treaty was seen as a clear sign that the United States was no longer interested in limiting the spread of nuclear weapons. Many foreigners thought the Americans had a new super weapon ready to bring off the drawing boards and into the testing phase. It was so very much like the Americans to continually tell other nations that they should not build nuclear bombs while America readied a new one in secret. Countries such as Iran, Iraq, India, Pakistan and North Korea, who were deep into their own weapons development programs, anxiously waited to see what the cynical Americans did next.

In the heart of the old Confederacy, the state of Mississippi found itself awash in federal largess as Senate Majority Leader Trent Lott did his best to take good care of folks back home. Lott, who portrayed himself to the voters of Mississippi as a fiscal conservative who wanted to reign in big government spending, obviously felt the brunt of any government spending cutbacks should be dutifully shouldered by the citizens of the other 49 states of the Union. The state of Mississippi was going to get every federal dollar, program and grant he could shove her way.

All things considered, it had been business pretty much as usual in Washington during a busy October. The politicians made the usual large number of lofty public promises and then negated them in the deals they cut behind closed doors. Nearly anyone of any importance was in a good mood because it was going to be a very good year for the White House and Congress. The latest IRS reports projected a continual rise in tax revenues for the foreseeable future.

November 1999

The annoying has-been Leon Placke was somewhere in the middle of the wheat growing region of the United States speaking to startled audiences about the dire need to change the basis of congressional representation. The crowds responded enthusiastically when Leon argued for removing a few thousand employees from Congress, a law-making establishment that generated countless drafts of bills and engaged in a never-ending string of fund raising events. Leon didn't want the people to be fired. He wanted the government to put more of its human resources to work on matters like the $19 billion in improper payments nine of the federal agencies paid out during the last fiscal year. As astounding as the $19 billion loss to the government was, it was only the tip of the iceberg. No one in Washington knew for sure exactly how much money the federal government incorrectly handed out each year. Prudent fiscal management was just not a high priority in a city where the emphasis was on political deal making and appointed agency heads were focused on lining up their next job and helping candidates win elections.

An independent counsel decided not to seek indictments against Interior Secretary Bruce Babbitt or anyone else involved in the Interior Department's rejection of a permit to allow an Indian gambling casino to open in Wisconsin. After an 18-month investigation, the independent counsel was unable to turn up any evidence to support allegations of illegal political interference in the decision-making process. Secretary Babbitt, who was one of five Clinton cabinet officials investigated by independent counsels, denied any wrongdoing on his part. The controversy stemmed from an attempt by three Chippewa tribes to open an off-reservation casino on the site of a money-losing dog racing track. Other tribes opposed the project because it would compete with their own lucrative gaming facilities, contributed more than $350,000 to the Democrats during the 1996 campaign. Despite the sizable political contribution from the tribes opposed to the new casino, Babbitt steadfastly denied that the White House or the Democratic National Committee had improperly influenced the Interior Department's decision to reject the license application. The weighty financial contributions of the opponents to the license had absolutely no impact on the bureaucratic mechanics the Interior Department used to weigh the merits of a gambling license application. Washington insiders chortled over the independent counsel's finding that money bought no influence in Washington.

A committee of the U.S. House of Representatives voted unanimously to grant John Huang, the super campaign fund raiser and former Commerce Department official, immunity if he would testify publicly about his role in the 1996 campaign finance scandals. Huang was considered a key witness because investigators believed he could map the illicit fund raising connections running from foreign countries to the White House.

Not everyone in Washington was overly happy that Mr. Huang had finally agreed to testify. There were a number of individuals on Capitol Hill who fervently hoped that Mr. Huang understood that he did not have to mention any foreign sources of campaign contributions that may have ended up going to members of Congress. In these days of giant, interlocking companies competing in a global economy, it was often difficult for a U.S. Senator or Representative to determine the ultimate source of all financial contributions received during the frenzy of a political campaign. With the United States being the world's largest trading nation, learning the source of every last nickel and dime contributed to a congressional campaign by multinational companies and Washington's lobbying corps was an almost impossible task. Mr. Huang had to be cautioned as to the extent of the testimony he was prepared to give.

Because Huang had no real expertise on the intricate internal workings of Congress, he might inadvertently stray into matters of no interest to the grand legislative body of the United States. It was a well known fact in Washington that Congress was only interested in learning the facts about foreign financial contributions that may have been made to the President's election campaign. It was definitely not interested in hearing about any foreign contributions that may have filtered into the races for seats in Congress. The smug lawmakers on Capitol Hill knew that while foreign contributions might easily contaminate presidential decision-making, they could never taint the deliberations of the upright individuals in Congress.

Bill Bradley, the former NBA player and U.S. Senator, collected $1.5 million for his presidential campaign war chest at a fund raiser held at New York City's Madison Square Garden. A crowd of 7,500 came to meet Bradley and other basketball stars in what was viewed by Washington insiders as a very colorless political event. Many of the guests paid only $50 to attend.

What kind of nondescript voter was Bradley trying to appeal to? A mere fifty bucks was considered chump change in the high-rolling, fund raising affairs carried out in the nation's capital. The people Bradley courted counted for absolutely nothing in the select ranking of national special interest groups. They were merely part of America's vast, invisible middle class. They were only expected to work hard and pay their taxes on time. The management of the nation could be left in the capable hands of better qualified groups.

However, because the polls showed Bradley steadily drawing closer to Vice President Gore in the race for the Democratic presidential nomination, Bradley was a man who needed close watching. If he somehow managed to pull off a political upset, Washington's insiders would have to nimbly and quickly jump onto his bandwagon. Having access to the new administration occupying the White House was a vital ingredient for successful lobbying. Access had to be quickly established during the first weeks the new President was in office. To fail to do so meant immediate financial loss because clients had no use for a lobbyist who had couldn't keep his or her foot in the door to the President's home. A degree of access had to be achieved, no matter what the financial cost.

All over Washington, crafty lobbyists prepared their contingency plans. If Bill Bradley won the nomination, he would suddenly find himself besieged by a couple thousand of new, best friends that he never knew he had. If he went on to win the general election, the lobbyists would begin calling the White House shortly after inauguration day to remind the new President of their steadfast past support for his candidacy. If he lost the election, Bradley would never hear from Washington's influence industry again because the lobbying community had no use for someone out of power. Bill Bradley would be nothing more than an expense item on lobbying accounting reports, an expensive but necessary covering bet that didn't pan out.

President Clinton and Congress were inching closer to a final agreement on spending the nation's tax dollars for the fiscal year. As in so many past years, wrangling between the White House and Congress had caused the nation's budget to be late in preparation. Unlike the common taxpayers who were forced to file their tax returns by a set deadline or face severe penalties, nothing of consequence happened to the elected leaders of the land if the federal budget was not ready on time. These super-wise chieftains had carefully exempted themselves from the rules they made for everyone else to live by. As the White House and Congress battled over who got to spend what, the masses of taxpayers went to work every day to pay the costs of a budget process that had degenerated into a highly inefficient arrangement.

With more than a half-dozen backed-up spending bills awaiting final congressional action, lobbyists for a variety of corporate interests took advantage of the last minute confusion to sneak in provisions that would never have been given a second look by the harried lawmakers if the proceedings had been better organized, more leisurely and open. The hectic pace of the lobbying activity was testimony to the enormous stakes the unfolding legislation held for big business. The changing of a few words in a pending piece of legislation could mean extra profits, exemption from taxes or a large reduction in overhead costs.

As the lobbyists struggled frantically to get their favorite budget items included, no one in Washington seemed to notice that the long budgetary war between the White House and Congress was seriously eroding the credibility of the government in the minds of many citizens. These clear-thinking common folk saw the partisan struggle over the nation's cash box as nothing more than a cynical political show put on for their benefit by the two parties as they struggled over the right to divide up tax receipts. Very few people believed an honest effort was being made to reach an agreement on the country's real needs. The Washington budget charade was nothing more than a tawdry example of the excesses of two-party government at its worst.

In a stunning ruling that sent reverberations throughout the high-tech world, a federal judge slammed Microsoft for wielding monopoly power over its rivals. Although the issue was complicated, the government might eventually decide to force the software giant to break itself up. When an angry Microsoft vowed to fight the charges in court, Washington's lawyers and lobbyists let out a lusty cheer. The stakes were enormous, the company rich. Working for the plaintiff or the defense didn't matter. If the court battles continued for years, the fees would just keep rolling in. Washington's litigating community suddenly had a lot to be thankful for during the coming holiday season.

The Defense Department announced it had spent $100 million to study the causes of Gulf War Syndrome since 1994. A new study that looked at the possible effects of nerve gas protection said the use of the drug pyridostigmine bromide could not be ruled out as a cause of the lingering illness in some veterans. About $17 million was being spent on studying the effects of the drug which had been used by 250,000 soldiers during the war. Were there conditions present in the Gulf that made the drug toxic? Were there unusual interactions between it and other chemicals commonly in use such as insect repellents and insecticides? No one was sure. Finding out what caused Gulf War Syndrome was part of the price the U.S. was paying to keep the vital oil supply lines from the Middle East open. It was one of the hidden costs of being involved in the interdependent global economy. Like it or not, America was stuck in an oil supply situation over which it had little control.

H. Muncaster Swindell was frustrated. The revival of the John Huang affair in Congress meant Commerce employees had to spend thousands of hours going through the documents in the departmental files, searching for the ones meeting the requirements of a congressional committee subpoena.

Muncaster found it difficult to get his surly staff motivated to do the work. It was almost as though they resented the fact he had not bothered to take the time to properly mark and record the location of the files the last time they had been reviewed. So what if he had been a little careless? It really didn't matter to Muncaster because he didn't gave a damn what his staff thought of him. The grubby, low-lifers who worked for him lacked the brains to grasp the implications of the larger, more important political picture. Their sole purpose in the grand scheme of things was to labor for their daily bread and the promise of a pension. They worked in dreary jobs that involved making sure Muncaster got what he could get for himself out of the time he spent in government.

Muncaster saw his attempt to establish lobbying links with Lockheed Martin, the nation's largest defense contractor fall flat. A series of catastrophic failures involving the Lockheed Titan IV rockets used in satellite launches plus the loss of a $4.5 billion contract to supply the U.S. government with top-secret spy satellites had seriously damaged the firm's profitability. The cascade of misfortune and management mistakes drove down the price of the company's stock, wiping out $14 billion in shareholder equity and infuriating major stockholders. The company's president and executive vice president had been forced to resign. The firm was retrenching; it was not hiring any new lobbyists.

In a move designed to expand his fields of expertise, Muncaster tried to get himself assigned as member of the U.S. delegation to the new round of global negotiations aimed at lowering trade barriers. Because he had not acted quickly enough, Muncaster found himself out-maneuvered by individuals with better access to the higher-levels of the White House. In a devastating setback to his career expansion plans, Muncaster learned he was not going to be one of those spending time in Geneva, Switzerland at taxpayers' expense. The rejection left him thoroughly dejected. He had hoped to be able to hang around the fringes of the talks for a couple of months while he advantageously used his free time to see the other sights of Europe.

Muncaster sat glumly on the sidelines watching morosely as the U.S. and China, after 13 years of talks, reached an agreement to bring China formally into the community of world trading nations. As a result of the trade deal, American firms were going to have better access to China's potential market of 1.3 billion consumers. And for better or worse, China was going to continue to reshape its economy along market driven lines. Hopefully, over the long-term the pact would provide solid benefits to both nations as China's growing economy led to a expansion in trade with the United States. The potential economic benefits to the populations of the United States and China didn't matter in the slightest to Muncaster because he knew it could take as long as 20 years for the agreement to produce major results. As such, he was more interested in the lobbying potential the new U.S.-China trade relationship provided. Since American firms were investing $1.5 billion a year in China, and China was shipping goods valued at $71 billion to the U.S. annually, there had to be a piece of the action for him somewhere in all those billions of trade-related dollars.

In the fiercely competitive world of Washington lobbying, Muncaster found the market for China lobbyists saturated. Former White House officials, Senators, Congresspersons and the large established lobbying firms had already grabbed the best work. The only job Muncaster found open was far beneath his talent level. Charting the trends of the measly $14 billion a year in goods that the U.S. shipped to China was not going to get Muncaster where he wanted to go. While U.S. exports were going to continue to rise as China's antiquated industrial plant modernized, Muncaster saw no big dollar lobbying fees coming out of forecasting export trends. Unable to find a lobbying position that would pay him what he thought he was worth, Muncaster decided to forget about China and the rest of the Pacific region. He would have to look elsewhere. There was no use in wasting his time on a region that did not appreciate his true value.

One of the best kept secrets in Washington was that politics really paid well. The vast majority of Americans didn't realize the act of electing a new president and members of Congress had grown into an elaborate, big spending enterprise. As the election battles raged across the land, a top-level campaign manager could easily earn $160,000 per year plus all kinds of present and future perks. Those with a good knowledge of the advertising game could tap into the vast sums being spent by the political campaigns on TV and print media to establish and keep the candidate's image in front of the of the voters.

Vice President Gore had raised a hefty $29 million in contributions through September 30, 1999 and his campaign had already furiously spent $14 million of that sum on preliminary primary strategies and long-term public image building efforts. Once the nomination was secured in August 2000, the Vice President would automatically collect an additional $63 million in federal election funds to help finance his presidential campaign. His top aides were quietly working with President Clinton's cabinet officials, urging them to schedule as many official events as possible during the winter and spring. That way, as Gore traveled the country handing out federal grants, giving speeches and posing at photo opportunities, the travel costs could legally be charged to the Vice President's office as an official government expense. The money Gore's campaign saved by using this clever little gimmick would provide a nice cushion of surplus cash to be advantageously used in the final struggle with the Republicans in the autumn election. In Washington's insider political circles, this unpublicized and widely used tactic was known as effectively using the power of being an incumbent office holder. Republicans and Democrats alike admired Gore's strategy to milk the Vice President's office for everything it was worth. It was the politically correct thing to do in the era of big, expensive political campaigns.

Muncaster thoroughly admired the creative way business got done in Washington. The ingenious creativity displayed by American politicians as they financed political campaigns and did favors for special interest groups made Washington the most fascinating and intellectually stimulating city in the world. The day-to-day affairs of America's beloved democratic process had a heady, exhilarating effect on minds trained in legal matters. It was the ultimate place to test one's power to achieve professional and political ends; there was no other place like it on earth. Having obtained his present government position on the basis of having devoted a large amount of time to the previous presidential campaign, Muncaster began to seriously consider trying to obtain a position on Al Gore's campaign staff. If Gore won the election, Muncaster would be able to claim at least two more years on the federal payroll in Washington as his reward for services performed. If he obtained a position at an agency with a higher profile than the stodgy Commerce Department, Muncaster could greatly expand his base of future lobbying contacts and acquire loads of marketable knowledge in the process.

In a sudden switch in campaign tactics, the incumbent Vice President of the United States moved his campaign offices out of Washington. Because the polls showed a strong link in the minds of the voters between Vice President Gore and President Clinton, Gore's political strategists thought it wise to put some physical distance between the Vice President and the scandal-ridden Clinton administration he had loyally served for nearly two terms in office. Vice President Gore ditched his blue suits, note cards and the title of Vice President when he opened his presidential campaign headquarters in Nashville, Tennessee. As part of his new image, the now folksy Al Gore sported a knit shirt and cowboy boots as he told onlookers: "Home is not only a place, it's an idea. Home is where we start from; home is where we learn our values."

The foreign diplomats assigned to Washington were deeply perplexed by the Vice President's attempt to create an illusion of being nothing more than an average American from Tennessee. After much discussion among themselves, they decided that only in America would the government's second highest executive launch a campaign for the nation's highest office by disassociating himself from his current role in the government. The United States might be the birthplace of modern democracy, but the strange, expensive rituals American politicians followed to get themselves elected to office were simply not understood by many members of Washington's diplomatic corps. Trying to explain the outlandish activities occurring during an American election to the government back home was a most difficult task. It made being a diplomat assigned to Washington during an election year the most miserable of occupations. If one honestly and diligently reported what was taking place in American election campaigns, there was a real risk of being recalled to one's home country and being sent to an insane asylum.

Perplexing to unsophisticated onlookers as it might be, there was an advantage to running a presidential campaign out of a former medical building in the Tennessee capital. It was much cheaper than Washington; Gore's campaign was saving $47,000 a month in rent alone. Tony Coelho, a former member of Congress and regarded as one of the nation's best political tacticians, was overseeing the management of Gore's election drive. Since leaving Congress in 1989, as a result of a scandal involving a $100,000 junk bond investment, Coelho had proved he was more than capable of competing in the private sector. After a mere decade in the investment business, his net worth was estimated to exceed $55 million. Having succeeded financially in the rough and tumble business world, Coelho was out to reestablish a political legacy for himself as he feverishly worked to get Al Gore elected to the White House. Serving at no salary, Coelho was cutting costs, firing staff and remaking an organization which had become notoriously pompous and ineffective.

As Gore closed the gap with Republican George W. Bush in the national polls, he also found himself locked in a dead heat with Bill Bradley in the first Democratic primary state of New Hampshire. It was a crystal-clear sign to many quick-judging political observers that Gore's campaign remained in a state of disarray. Others were not so sure. They believed Coelho would have Gore's campaign machinery finely- tuned by the time hard electioneering began. Only a complete fool would underestimate Coelho's ability to marshal his forces and hit with bone-jarring fury when the real battle for elective office got underway. Some cynics went so far as to say that the rumors of faltering and disorganization were nothing more than a smoke screen purposely spread by the ruthlessly efficient Coelho in an effort to lull the opposition into believing Gore's campaign was on the rocks.

The fidgety Coelho was extremely busy, beginning his workday at 5 a.m.

Muncaster called Nashville repeatedly for several days in attempts to reach the master political tactician. When he finally did get through, Muncaster was jolted to learn his chances for joining Team Gore were nonexistent. What was left unsaid by the diplomatic Coelho as he firmly rejected Muncaster's offer to work for the campaign was the fact that Muncaster was considered to be seriously damaged political goods. Muncaster's brawl with the tourists behind the White House showed a total lack of judgment and an objectionable tendency to attract unfavorable publicity. Hiring an individual who had engaged in fisticuffs with a group voters was not an act considered to be politically prudent. The very act of hiring such a jerk would bring a flurry of unflattering news stories and immediately detract attention from efforts to build the candidate's image. Being politically astute, Muncaster understood what the gracious evasions coming over the phone line from Nashville really meant. With the clarity of perfect 20/20 hindsight, he now realized that his little altercation with Leon Placke and the group of tourists had done irreparable damage to his reputation.

In the political environs of Washington, voters were like fine china, they had to be handled very gently at all times. Instead of showing the expected deference to voters willing to cast ballots in the November 2000 election, Muncaster had committed the ultimate political no-no by physically beating them up. As a direct result of the ugly fight Muncaster provoked, wacky old Leon Placke was touring the country and raising many deeply embarrassing questions about how Washington's political elite carried out the nation's business. Placke's outrageous aspersions could cause problems for Republicans and Democrats alike if the voters began to take a serious interest in the procedural matters they usually blissfully ignored. Placke was shredding the cherished myths surrounding the management of representative politics that both parties had worked to keep in place for many years.

Placke's call for changes to current system of electing representatives was most unwelcome to establishment Republicans and Democrats. Placke, for reasons which defied the comprehension of Washington's shakers and movers, was trying to destroy the basis on which many a good life in Washington was built. His call for the reorganization of the House of Representatives was completely unacceptable to the city's lobbyists and politicians because they saw it as a threat to their way of life. Leon Placke had turned into the worst kind of a subversive. He was out to wreck the best run political system in the world, one that he had been an integral part of for many years. The right of free speech clearly did not apply to the ravings of a deranged man bent on destroying the most financially profitable aspects of politics. Under these trying circumstances, no one in Washington's

341

leadership circles would seriously oppose the silencing of Leon Placke. No questions would be raised as to legalities of how it was done. Permanently closing the mouth of Placke had become a matter of pest control, no different than exterminating a disease carrying rat.

> **"To choose one's victim, to prepare one's plan minutely, to slake an implacable vengeance, and then to bed…there is nothing sweeter in the world."**
>
> **-Joseph Stalin, 193?**

Seeing himself shut out of the most lucrative presidential campaign in American history, Muncaster's hatred of Leon Placke soared. Muncaster vowed to get even with the sorry bastard who had betrayed the lobbying profession and wrecked Muncaster's career prospects. Had Leon been sensible and gone to the needed medical treatment, there would not have been a fight and Muncaster would now have been welcome to join Gore's election team. Leon Placke had absolutely no right to crush the high aspirations of H. Muncaster Swindell. Despite a veneer of political sophistication, Leon had turned out to be nothing other than a good-for-nothing cretin who had turned savagely against the lobbying profession that had made him rich. He must not be allowed to get away with such a display of ingratitude to the men and women who lubricated the process of government. As a furious Muncaster clearly saw it, Placke had seriously derailed his plans for the lobbying career he planned to begin after he completed his stint at the Commerce Department.

Now violently agitated, Muncaster decided to get his revenge by liquidating Placke in a way that defied police detection. It would be a masterfully planned crime, one worthy of his powerful intellectual abilities. With Placke and his reform nonsense out of the way, Muncaster's sagging fortunes would quickly reverse themselves as Washington's thankful lobbyists expressed their gratitude for his selfless act in a hundred quiet little helpful ways. Invitations to dinners attended by powerful people with the right connections, along with a generous batch of client referrals and lobbying subcontracts would go a long way towards making Muncaster whole again. Muncaster had worked hard for the political system. If he acted in its behalf, he knew he would reap his fair share of the rewards. As with other powerful groups, Washington insiders always took good care of their own.

As Al Gore reinvented himself into a common man in Nashville, George W. Bush was distancing himself from the unpopular congressional wing of the Republican party. He soundly criticized the Republicans in Congress for trying to balance the budget on the backs of the poor. He followed that stinging jab to his party's right wing with another verbal blast as he announced his party had been too enamored in believing that the free market could solve all social problems while ignoring the role of government. The managers of the Democratic party's candidates cringed in political pain. They knew the wily Texas governor and Republican contender for the presidential nomination had launched a major drive to reach out to independents and suburbanites who were turned off by the extremes of both parties. Bush was offering something attractive to swing voters with his talk of reshaping compassionate conservatism. Telephones rang as polls were immediately taken to determine the impact of Bush's strategy. Counter-positions had to be quickly developed. The Democrats had to come up with a new plan that would save more money and help more of the poor. The battle for the hearts and minds of the independent voters had begun.

Despite the flurry of activity, it was too early to tell what the impact of Bush's efforts to attract the independent voter might be. Despite the months of political skirmishing and millions of dollars spent on pre-primary political advertising, more than 64 percent of eligible voters described themselves as still undecided. It was clear to those who made a living marketing politicians to the public that the citizenry was genuinely bored by the early onset of the political silly season. The message coming back with the poll results was that the selection of candidates could easily wait until closer to the election in November 2000. For the present, Americans were more interested in enjoying the rewards of a booming economy. In recently released government statistics, the economic growth rate for the third quarter of the year had been revised upward to 5.5.percent. Inflation was low. Families were purchasing new cars, houses, furnishings and taking long vacations. The times were good. The economic expansion, which was nearing its ninth anniversary, was showing no sign of slowing down. Although reviled and condemned in many quarters for his personal misconduct, President Clinton was presiding over record-setting good economic times.

Leon Placke was swinging through the revitalizing towns of the old rust belt, waxing eloquent on his now familiar refrain of reorganizing the House of Representatives, controlling unlimited political contributions, reducing the power of special interest groups and limiting the role of lobbyists. Leon told his audiences he knew that they were more interested in the political agendas of candidates who promised things that would benefit them personally. Government funding for abortions, education aid, tax cuts, benefits to the working poor, universal medical insurance and private school vouchers were the things the voters wanted to hear about. The number and type of these programs to be dispensed by the federal government to the American public was dependent upon which party won the Presidency and control of Congress.

"Now let me tell you something that no politician in this country will tell you," Leon said to his audience. "Why don't the candidates running for office address such matters as why we want to fight wars in which the military suffers no casualties while at the same time we ignore the fact that the United States has the highest homicide rate in the industrialized world? Why are we are outraged if American soldiers are killed in the line of duty in foreign lands, but don't bat an eye lash if our neighbors kill themselves in ever-growing numbers on Saturday night? Do you know that the amount of illegal narcotics flowing into the U.S. has a value equal to eight percent of all the world's international trade? It is an expensive and socially destructive way to indulge our baser appetites because addicts rob and kill to get money to support their drug habits. Yet, you don't hear much about the uncontrollable drug problem from politicians because they have been busy playing it safe, gaining a victory over cigarette manufacturers and tobacco growers."

"What about the growing lack of personal responsibility in America? One in three of us commits some kind of theft at work such as stealing money or supplies or faking illness. Shoplifting from retail establishments is at an all time high, a real national disgrace. Stealing has become an accepted way of life. Visitors to one of our beautiful national parks are pilfering petrified wood at the rate of 12 tons per year, not caring if there is anything for future visitors to see. Profanity-spewing, abusive fans are constantly ruining attendance at sporting events for other patrons. Folks, we cannot steal and cheat ourselves into greater prosperity while at the same time allowing the basic unit of all human societies, the family, to fall apart!"

"We want unlimited government provided benefits, but at the same time we work diligently to shift the burden for paying the necessary taxes to others. Over a period of 50 years, we spent hundreds of trillions of dollars to bring about the fall of the Soviet Union. Since then, Russia has remained mired in economic chaos despite attempts at reform and billions of dollars in international aid. Why is there no criticism of the current U.S. economic policy towards Russia heard from the candidates? Are we going to sit back placidly watching our television sets until some former Red Army corporal seizes power, restores Communism and restarts the Cold War? It's time we stop worrying so much about getting more benefits out of our government and start worrying a little bit more about the mess we are leaving behind for the next generation to clean up. It is up to you, the voters, to start asking candidates to answer the hard questions on which our national survival depends."

From his many years of experience in Washington, Leon knew that above all else, Americans like to feel good about themselves. Across the nation, from Maine to California, there was an undefined smug feeling of being somehow superior to all other mortals on earth. To take full advantage of this little-noticed American character trait, the nation's politicians never missed a chance to puff up the voters' egos by spreading platitudes as they trolled for votes. In a political environment based on the mutual deception of voters and politicians, it was little wonder that Leon's scathing speech caught his listeners' attention. Since Leon was a former representative of the parasite class inhabiting Washington, he probably knew what he was talking about. Maybe everyday people should care a little more about what was happening in Russia and China. Even if Communism was dead for the present, it could make a comeback if international economic chaos wasn't controlled. As the upset people absorbed the gist of Leon's nasty little speech, it also flashed like a meteor across the national media screens. If Leon Placke kept at it, there would be no politics as usual during the current campaign season.

December 1999

"Woe unto you, lawyers! for ye have taken away the key of knowledge: ye entered not in yourselves, and them that were entering in ye hindered."

-Bible, New Testament, Luke 11:52

All good things have to come to an end. Leon had to return the bus to the rock star who was readying his troop of performers and technicians for a another concert tour. As he rode back to Washington, Leon felt that he had accomplished a great deal. Among other things, the public was beginning to see the need for revamping Congress and curbing the excesses of the lobbying industry. While it would take some time to educate the people to the dire need for implementing reform, Leon was confident he could see the task through to completion. Leon had made an admirable start on keeping his promise to George Washington and he felt genuinely good about himself. Much better than he had felt in years. Without the use of the bus, he would have to spend the next few weeks getting his neglected business affairs in order, and limit his speaking engagements to occasional talks with sightseers waiting to tour the White House.

Once back in the capital, it didn't take Leon long to realize how unwelcome he really was. His attacks on Washington insiders and their way of doing things had earned him a dose of the bipartisan enmity usually reserved for foreign enemies during wartime. Politician or lobbyist, it made no difference. No one in Washington wanted to have any more to do with Leon Placke. In Congress, Republicans and Democrats continued to differ on many issues of national importance. Behind the closed doors of the committee rooms, however, they could easily agree on the fact that Leon Placke had to go, the sooner the better for America's body politic. Placke was a real and present danger to the basic fabric of the existing two party system and Washington's lucrative influence peddling industry.

On an early winter's day, Leon walked up 17th Street toward K and M Streets. The chill he felt inside was not so much from the cold westerly wind as it was from the hatred and rejection displayed by his former friends and business acquaintances. They refused to speak to him. Not one would accept his phone calls or respond to his emails. On Capitol Hill, it was more of the same treatment. Although Leon could get into the office buildings, he was bluntly turned away for the individual offices where he had in the past often been the most welcome of guests.

Leon found himself about as beloved in Washington as the British troops who captured the city in the hot and humid summer of 1814. As they taught the haughty Americans a lesson in military humility as they burned all the public buildings, the British arsonists set off an inferno seen from 50 miles away. Leon could understand why he was viewed in much the same way as the invading British had been. His intellectual torching of the operations of the White House and Congress was leaving burn marks on the political establishment far worse than smoking ruins left behind by the British. Buildings could always be rebuilt after the invaders departed; a population's naive belief in political myths could not be as easily reestablished once it was destroyed.

Lonely and dejected, Leon sat at the far-end of the bar in one his old haunts and drank a silent toast to the British soldiers, sailors and marines who captured Washington after a hard 50 mile march from their landing site on the Patuxent River. Leon and the British had one thing in common. There was no monument to the exploits of the British invasion force in the American capital, and Leon knew there would never be one to his effort to force reform upon the entrenched interests in Congress and the lobbying industry.

As Leon brooded over his double Martini with four olives in chilly Washington, across the country in sunny California, Yogesh K. Gandhi was sentenced to a year in prison for mail fraud, tax evasion and making political contributions while using funds provided by a foreigner. Gandhi was a key figure in an illegal $325,000 contribution to the Democratic Party in 1996. He was also ordered by the sentencing judge to pay more than $327,000 in back taxes to the Internal Revenue Service.

A final accounting of government spending confirmed Congress exceeded the Fiscal Year 2000 spending ceiling by $37 billion and had relied heavily on the Social Security surplus to cover the additional outlays. The report, which was purposely ignored in most of Washington's power circles, also warned that if Congress continued to spend at the same rate, the surplus would turn into a deficit within a couple of years. Although the Republican-controlled Congress and the Clinton administration fell well short of their stated goal of adhering to the spending limitations agreed to with much public fanfare in their 1997 balanced-budget deal, no one at the White House or in Congress appeared inclined to give the overspending so much as a second thought. The leadership of both parties knew the voters paid little attention to boring matters such as the federal budget. Who really cared if gimmicks, such as declaring the 2000 census to be an emergency, were used to circumvent spending constraints?

Republican presidential front-runner George W. Bush unveiled an ambitious $1.1 trillion tax-cut package for the coming decade that would be solely financed by future budget surpluses. Democratic presidential candidate Bill Bradley called for the United States to reduce its unilateral overseas intervention and instead work with the United Nations and other international organizations to build security in a world lacking the Cold War's predictability. If elected, Bradley said he would work to restore the mindset of the Cold War, when men and women of goodwill joined together to do what was in America's best interest. He wanted to restore the vanished foreign policy consensus which once held that all domestic political divisions stopped at the water's edge. In other words, the foreign affairs of the nation ought to be conducted in a way which benefited the nation. In dictatorships, monarchies and democracies worldwide, Bradley's bold policy statement raised no objections. Sometimes restating the obvious sounded good on the campaign trail.

The vast differences in the laws governing the conduct of those who wanted to be the nation's next president and those controlling the activities of the average citizen were clearly evident. According to federal law, the completing candidates in New Hampshire's first-in- the- nation presidential primary were supposed to abide by a $600,000 campaign spending limit. By the clever use of well-placed regulatory loopholes, shrewd presidential contenders could easily wink at the law and stretch the limit into a $6 million spending spree. Surprisingly, no one thought it odd that this fiscal ruse was occurring at the same time the candidates were deluging the voters with information attesting to their unyielding dedication to honesty and integrity. It was another example of Washington sanctioned campaign programming at its best, complex, easily circumvented and difficult to understand. By using a complicated but legal slight of hand, the candidates could pump millions into the vital campaign and still remain in technical compliance with the regulations. In one often used practice, candidates could utilize an exemption which enabled them to claim half of their expenditures in New Hampshire as fund raising costs, costs that did not count against the campaign spending limits.

The World Trade Organization (WTO) opened a meeting in Seattle, Washington. The 3,000 WTO delegates were going to formally begin talks leading to a new round of trade liberalization negotiations. As representatives of the world's leading trading nation, the United States delegation was prepared to press for an end to subsidized farm exports and argue for opening the global banking and telecommunications markets wider to American firms. Instead of attending staid opening ceremonies, the shocked delegates found themselves trapped in their hotels by an angry army of anti-trade protesters. In what was politely termed by apologists as the largest act of civil disobedience in modern U.S. history, the rioters disrupted the meeting, burned vehicles and looted downtown stores. Although the chief U.S. trade negotiator, Charlene Barshefsky, tried to put the best face on the situation by saying the failed discussions had been a success, it was obvious the street chaos ruined the talks. The message that came with the clouds of tear gas and looted Seattle storefronts was that the terms of the free trade debate in the United States had changed. Labor unions, some farmers, feminists, environmentalists, defenders of butterflies, right-wing nationalists and left-wing anarchists all demanded to have a say in future trade talks.

The rioters who battled police and trashed downtown Seattle had no memory of the fretful days following the end of World War II. In those desperate times, the global trading system had been reestablished as a war-ruined group of nations made an effort to spur global economic efficiency and hopefully avoid future destructive wars. For 50 years, the dogged handiwork of the early trade visionaries had worked relatively well as trade expanded and the standards of living around the globe steadily improved. The outpouring of opposition to the Seattle talks severely shook the free-trade wing of the Democratic party to its core. The spectacular collapse of the Seattle conference amid a firestorm of riot and protest sent the unprepared global traders reeling and running for cover.

As the architects of the battle for Seattle gleefully savored their victory over free trade, not a single politician in the vapid White House or Congress had the courage to inform the nation of what had been destroyed. As the forces of isolationism and reactionary nationalism stalked the land unchallenged, politicians ignored the bitter lesson learned from the Smoot-Hawley tariff of 1930 which raised U.S. tariffs to the highest point in history and caused a sharp drop in foreign trade. In the waning days of 1999, no one wanted to remind the nation of the cost of America's role in the fiasco that made the Great Depression worse. As the rioters pushed the country on the first steps of a retreat that would end behind a new tariff wall, the most important issue facing politicians was winning the 2000 election. They could easily afford to let a future generation worry about paying the price for their current head-in-the sand attitude.

The Census Bureau, which Congress funded on an emergency basis to conduct the census taken once every ten years, released a preliminary report showing the fastest growing states were in the South and West. As a result,

15 states would win or lose seats in the House of Representatives based on population shifts. Every state would get at least one seat in the 435 member House, and the remaining 385 seats would be divided by using a complicated formula based on population and growth, the intent being to create congressional districts of equal size. It was good news for the Republicans who dominated at least half of the state governments and tended to do best in the growing regions. In terms of being able to control the outcome within the states, the Republicans were in the best position of a half century.

"Politics will eventually be replaced by imagery. The politician will be only too happy to abdicate in favor of his image, because the image will be much more powerful than he could ever be."
-Marshall McLuhan, June 1971

The big business of selecting America's new president continued to pump vast sums money through the nation's economy. Democrat Bill Bradley and Republican John McCain translated their growing political momentum in New Hampshire into their best fund raising performances of the year. In Bradley's case, he outpaced the incumbent Vice President in fund raising for two quarters in a row, raising more than $8 million since September. Bradley's year-end tally put him at nearly $28 million overall, bringing him essentially even with Gore for the entire year of 1999.

McCain's fund raising surge in the last few months was even more rapid, taking him from the $3 million raised in the third quarter to over $6 million raised between October and December. But McCain's total of nearly $16 million for the year still left him far behind Bush, who had harvested a cool $65 million while conducting the best financed campaign in history. Bush had done so well in raising contributions that he could afford to continue to turn down the federal matching funds that were his for the asking.

In the Democratic race, both candidates were expected to have about $20 million (including federal matching funds) to spend during the January to March 2000 primary season in which the nomination would be decided. As the political strategists planned campaigns, field workers were dispatched to critical states, consultants hired, and TV and print media advertising prepared. In taking the art of vote trolling one step further, Bradley added a sociologist to his Iowa headquarters staff. The sociologist, who was busy crunching numbers 16 hours a day, was targeting precincts where the sociological indicators showed Bradley had the best chance of making inroads against Vice President Gore.

The dramatic increase in the amount of money flowing to the candidates was a new phenomenon, a real windfall for the capital's political operators. Fueled by a strong economy, well-heeled contributors in unexpectedly large numbers were opening their checkbooks to both parties. The torrent of contributions was shattering all previous assumptions about what it was possible for a presidential campaign to raise. The amount of money collected during the 1999 pre-election year easily topped the $26 million President Clinton raised in 1995 when he was an incumbent famous for his fund raising abilities. Along with the nation's economy, America's electioneering business was having its best year ever.

Shunted to the sidelines of the generously funded political wars, a crestfallen Muncaster watched the flood of money pass him by. He had been reduced to the unenviable position of joining the ranks of Washington's lowest of the low, of being part of an administration leaving office after the next election. As he sat in his spacious office on the fifth floor of the Commerce building partly listening to his visitors talk about an international trade problem, Muncaster's thoughts turned to a more important matter, the removal of Leon Placke from the Washington scene. In a few more days he would be ready to make his move, his preparations were nearly complete. With Placke out of the way, Muncaster's fortunes were sure to improve. He would once again be a man worthy of respect and admiration as he attended the trendy social functions sponsored by the Washington Society of Solicitors. He would no longer be a fading political nonentity clinging by his fingernails to the outermost ring of Washington's circles of power. H. Muncaster Swindell would soon be back on the road to becoming a successful power broker in the capital of the United States of America.

The clamorous voices of his business guests rudely brought Muncaster back to the unpleasant reality of the meeting. Ordinarily, Muncaster would not have debased himself by dealing with a group of politically insignificant individuals who, as a computer check revealed, had not made a single political contribution to anyone during the past five years. These unenlightened citizens, so unwise in the workings and ways of politics, would have been quickly shunted down to a lowly office director along with instructions to be handled in a proper but perfunctory manner.

The problem was that these were not ordinary times with the general election less than a year away. Muncaster's visitors, a trio of self-made irrigation equipment manufacturers, happened to be constituents of a Congressman facing a tough uphill battle for reelection. Since their business was well-known in the congressional district, the Congressman wanted the government to expeditiously resolve a sticky international business problem for them. A resolution of the problem would send a strong signal to voters back home that the Congressman cared enough about them to cut through the layers of an indifferent, entrenched Washington bureaucracy and solve a problem for a deserving local firm. If handled correctly, the matter would be advantageously reported on the business pages of the local newspapers. On a slow news day, it might even get a 45 second spot on the 6 p.m. local news.

Because the other top departmental officials begged off, Muncaster found himself stuck with hosting the meeting. Due to the fact he had an impressive title, Muncaster was forced to sit and listen to the gripes of people who built watering equipment for trees and bushes for a living. It was a tedious way to spend the afternoon, a complete waste of his talents. His trio of guests were excitedly droning on about how they had started their irrigation equipment manufacturing firm, worked for years on improving irrigation technology and had been granted several patents.

As he listened to the seemingly never ending tirade of trivia, Muncaster glanced out of the window. Across the Ellipse, he could see a group of tourists gathering around an individual. As his blood pressure rose, Muncaster knew instinctively who the individual was. Leon Placke, the contemptible traitor to the influence industry had come back to town to spread more obnoxious drivel on the need for changing the representational basis of half of Congress and in the process, snuff out most of Washington's moneymaking lobbying industry. Lamentable as it was, Placke had become a tourist destination in his own right. It was unfortunate that the tourists, who had little comprehension of the intricate workings of government, gathered every two days to listen spellbound to the subversive ranting of Leon Placke. The situation was turning dangerous. Vendors were hawking coffee mugs and clothing inscribed with Placke's dire messages on the need to reform the Washington establishment. If Placke got his way with the voters, Washington's lobbyists would rapidly become an endangered species. Muncaster once again vowed to himself to halt the activities of the un-American lunatic who had lost all appreciation for the bounties bestowed by the nation's political system. Everything in Washington worked so well, why didn't Placke have the good sense to leave things alone?

As Muncaster watched the crowd around Placke grow larger, his guests finally stopped speaking. Attuned to sensing the awkward silences generated by the politically uninitiated citizenry, Muncaster immediately broke the silence by saying, "Thank you for the very informative presentation on the establishment and growth of your firm. You can certainly be proud of what you have accomplished in the field of irrigation. The products you have developed and brought to market certainly have helped reduce the consumption of water in our nation's agricultural endeavors. It is contributions of firms such as yours that makes the American economy function so extremely well. You have the wholehearted thanks of the entire Clinton Administration for the fine work you have done in water conservation. Now, would you be so kind as to give me a few more of the details regarding the current problem you have encountered trying to market your products internationally?"

Too polite to mention they had already covered the topic once, the firm's president responded, "Certainly Mr. Swindell, please interrupt at any time you have a question. As you probably are aware, the Middle East and North Africa are areas suffering from an acute water shortage. At the encouragement of our local Department of Commerce District Office, we began promoting our irrigation equipment overseas. We make a fair number sales in Europe, some in Asia. Our sales to Mexico have really begun to climb during the past year. We have developed steady customers in Egypt, Tunisia and Morocco. After a slow beginning, our sales to Saudi Arabia, Kuwait and the other Persian Gulf countries have been steadily improving."

"We have also made several sales to Israel and shipped a $440,000 order to Syria. The Syrian order is the one that has turned into a big nightmare for us. The Syrian purchaser has informed us that the government has seized our shipment because it violates the Arab boycott of Israel. So, we have three containers on the docks at the port of Latakia and our Syrian purchaser is in danger of being arrested for attempting to bring prohibited material into the country. And our company stands to lose a substantial amount of money if the material is confiscated."

"If the products were made in the United States, why did the Syrian authorities seize them?" Muncaster asked. He was developing a feeling that this was not going to be an easy problem to resolve. It would be a terrible imposition to him if he had to devote several weeks of his time to getting the matter straightened out. Because a Congressman was involved, Muncaster couldn't weasel out of the mess by suggesting to his visitors, as he often did, that they retain the services of a good Washington lawyer.

"According to the Office of Antiboycott Compliance, which incidentally is part of your Commerce Department, a number of the Arab countries boycott the products of American firms if the product is considered to be helpful to the development of the Israeli economy. Once it becomes blacklisted, the offending company cannot ship its products to the participating Arab countries. The Syrian Government says our firm is on their list of boycotted firms, therefore our products cannot be imported into Syria."

Muncaster felt a bit foolish. Perhaps he should have spent less time dreaming about getting even with Leon Placke and spent more of it doing research on this problem. Never at a loss for words because of his superb legal training, Muncaster quickly recovered his confidence and replied, "Didn't you ship the material by using an irrevocable letter of credit to protect yourself from financial loss? If you had, you would have been paid by the bank even if the goods were confiscated by the Syrian government at some point in the transaction."

"We have been active in international trade for a few years sir," coolly answered the president of the irrigation firm. "We were smart enough to use the proper letter of credit. Under Syrian banking regulations, however, there is a 60 day waiting period for all bank payments that begins after the goods are landed at the customs warehouse. The long waiting time is due to government's strict rationing of foreign exchange. Because our shipment was found to violate the Syrian boycott law, the banking regulations were overridden by our supposedly criminal act. The Syrian bank does not have to meet the obligations of the letter of credit. We don't have to be paid and our shipment doesn't have to be returned because we have committed what passes for a crime under Syrian import law. That is why we asked our Congressman to see if he could get our government to help us. We believe we have done nothing wrong. Our firm is a victim of the convoluted Syrian system of laws and regulations"

Muncaster was now totally focused on the issue. The tricky and twisted Syrian regulations that snared unsuspecting foreign firms like a spider web catches flies, were a brilliant piece of legal composition. It rivaled anything Washington's finest lawyers could produce. Muncaster had a sudden warm feeling of kinship with the lawyers working in the countries of the Old World. On occasion, they displayed brilliant flashes of legal perceptiveness. Of course, Muncaster was not going to tell these dull irrigation equipment builders what was really on his mind. Putting on his best I feel your pain, you can depend on your government to help you expression, he said, "Gentlemen, you may rest assured that I will personally take the responsibility for investigating the travesty committed against your company. You may tell the Congressman that the U.S. Department of Commerce will do all that is necessary to get your merchandise back or else see that you get paid for it."

"Why thank you very much for your offer of assistance, Mr. Swindell. Our Congressman said we could count on your fine agency for help. There is just one more thing I should mention. Our Syrian customer has been slapped around some by the Syrian police because he purchased prohibited goods. Do you suppose the U.S. Government could also put in a good word for him? He is trying to improve tomato production for a group of farmers living in the eastern desert. He had no intention of doing anything illegal. His project is part of a larger effort to improve Syria's irrigation techniques and has been approved by the UN's agricultural aid program."

"I'll be happy to look into it for you," said Muncaster as he showed his visitors to the door. It had turned into a productive meeting after all. Muncaster was going to be able to score big points with the Congressman for helping his constituents. He was going to be able to talk with the staff at UN headquarters in New York City, maybe spend a few days there while he researched the matter. And he had learned a few new legal tricks in the process. To come out on top, all he had to do was arrange to get the confiscated goods returned to the U.S. or have the bank pay the letter of credit. That should not be too difficult an undertaking for the powerful chief of staff of the Commerce Department. He ought to be able to foist most of the really heavy lifting off on the American Embassy staff in Damascus. If things didn't work out, he could always shift the blame onto them. Everyone already knew America's diplomats were sadly lacking in ability when the time came for them to assist American companies. It was the type of situation Muncaster loved. He could take all the credit for himself if the matter was satisfactorily resolved, blame another party if it was not, and have someone else do most of the work.

January 2000

"Those who have been once intoxicated with power, and have derived any kind of emolument from it, even though but for one year, never can willingly abandon it. They may be distressed in the midst of all their power; but they will never look to anything but power for their relief."

-Edmund Burke 1791

The resolution of irrigation firm's problem would have to wait for a few days because Muncaster was busy finalizing his plan to eliminate Leon Placke. The first item in the extensive set of files Muncaster opened was a copy of a map drawn by a Union army officer of the Confederate fortifications around Centreville. It delineated the system of Rebel field works, forts and trench lines alike. According to the briefing memorandum accompanying the document, a Union army engineer mapped the Rebel defense line after the Confederate army withdrew from northern Virginia in the spring of 1862. There were no Confederate records in the file. They were believed to have been destroyed in the fires set by General Lee's army when Richmond was abandoned. Muncaster next looked at copies of the paroled prisoner passes for Sergeant Cyrus Bellnapp and Lieutenant Colonel Matthew Chambon issued at Appomattox Courthouse, Virginia in April 1865. Because the two soldiers were not attached to Lee's Army of Northern Virginia, the paroling officers had not recorded their names on the unit rosters. Instead, they filled out duplicates of the passes and included them in the records shipped to Washington. The copies had remained undisturbed for over 100 years until Muncaster sent his minions searching for them.

The third item was a map of the Civil War military defenses of Washington. In an irregular circle around the city, which was much smaller in the 1860s, Muncaster saw Ft. Sumner, Ft. Reno, Ft. Stevens, Ft. Totten, Ft. DuPont, Ft. Foote, Ft. Willard, Ft. Lyon, Ft. Ward, Ft. Cocoran and others. There were approximately 70 forts in the District of Columbia, Virginia and Maryland. When he compared the old map to a modern one of Washington and its suburbs, Muncaster was amazed to see many of the fortification sites still existed. They had become parks tucked away in the subdivisions, only their names gave an indication of their once deadly purpose. It was very interesting stuff, Muncaster thought. It would make good background material for the conversations he was going to have with Leon Placke.

Muncaster read summaries of the material the Confederate Secretaries of State and War sent to be buried at Centreville in the closing days of the Civil War. In Muncaster's judgment, Leon Placke did provide a notable service to Washington's politicians when he had the documents classified and stored at the National Archives. It must have been the last lucid thing Placke did before he went off the deep end, before he set out on his crazy mission to remake the House of Representatives and destroy the lobbying profession. Muncaster agreed with the decision to hide the documents. There would have been absolutely no harm done if the Confederate papers had remained hidden for another 20 years. No one had a pressing need to read through a big list of Confederate army deserters or Benjamin's personal list of prominent Northerners who took exception to Lincoln's Emancipation Proclamation. Opening the documents to public scrutiny had only aggravated many influential political donors; there had been no benefit to Washington's politicians at all.

As he read, Muncaster began to understand why so many upright, solid political contributors had been disgraced when the documents became public. The startling contents of the Confederate papers proved to be an acute embarrassment to many modern corporations and the prominent descendants of Civil War military and political personalities. It was no wonder the unwise airing of the papers crimped the generosity of many loyal political contributors. Who in this day and age needed to be reminded their ancestors smuggled war materials, were Confederate deserters, or worked to defeat Abraham Lincoln in a long ago election? The Confederate documents had become the source material of new books, each one destroying an old corporate or family legend. Muncaster thought the general public ought to have more respect for the memories held dear by those who financed the political system. The past should have been left at rest; it didn't need to be dredged up to impede the hectic pace of modern political fund raising.

There wasn't much information on the illegal Strawderman whiskey distilling business in the files. A few birth and death notices, old census records and a small jug. The worn jug, which looked like it would hold about a quart, fascinated Muncaster as he turned it over in his hands. The faded but still legible inscription on the jug's face read: "Strawderman's Finest." It dated from the 1860s and was used by William Strawderman when he sold whiskey to Union and Confederate troops and the saloons of Washington. It was a piece of history, a tangible link with the region's hard-drinking past. The jug had been found in an antique store located in the old section of the City of Alexandria, not far from the streets of fine old restored homes now inhabited by many of Washington's prominent lobbyists.

Reading on, Muncaster learned that some of William's whiskey-making skills had been successfully passed down through the generations. Moonshining continued to be a traditional way of life in Virginia; the profits were high and the risk of going to jail was low. The state's illegal whiskey makers were producing over 600,000 gallons of untaxed whiskey annually, costing the state and federal governments millions in lost tax revenue. There was nothing indicating that any of the modern moonshiners claimed to be working with George Washington's recipes. All traces of George Washington's contribution to art of making fine whiskey had unfortunately been lost during the passage of time.

"Few men have virtue to withstand the highest bidder"
-George Washington, 1779

As Muncaster meditated on the cultural consequences of the loss of George Washington's whiskey formulas and the potential monetary rewards of rediscovering them, his phone rang. It was Michael Greene, the department's head of human resources. Greene was a living legend at the Commerce Department because, over a period of years, he turned himself into an indispensable asset to each new incoming Secretary of Commerce. While hewing to the letter of the voluminous government personnel regulations, Greene could almost magically create as many new political jobs as the new Secretary desired. So good was Greene's work, that none of his creative job position descriptions had ever been overturned on appeal. He was a master wordsmith, a loyal career professional who delivered without question whatever his political masters wanted. Because he was such an outstanding civil servant, Greene received the highest evaluations and the maximum amount of performance bonuses permitted by law.

The fact that Greene's program ballooned the department's personnel cost by several million dollars a year was ignored by his superiors. To keep matters legal and within budgetary guidelines, Greene accessed a slush fund hidden deep in the human resources budget. By not filling a number of jobs in the lower ranks, Greene always maintained the fund at a level needed to fill positions of importance.

Not having been warned about the realities of Greene's power, a somewhat naive but dedicated budget officer learned the hard way not to question Michael Greene's budgeting methods. After she began investigating the unusually large number of dollars parked in one of the miscellaneous categories of the human resources budget, she suddenly found herself transferred to inventorying wire nuts in government electrical shops. After three months of continual counting, it finally dawned on the budget officer that regulations were not written to be uniformly enforced, especially when the desires of those at the higher levels were affected. As a result of the unfortunate incident, Mr. Greene's remarkable budget arrangements were never challenged by anyone again.

Muncaster respected Greene because Greene knew his place in the bureaucracy and understood how things worked. "Mr. Swindell, I have come across a small problem that I believe you should be made aware of," said Greene. "What is it?" Muncaster responded, "I certainly hope it is nothing too serious."

"I am sure it is just a misunderstanding," said Greene. "Two of the employees detailed to your office on a temporary basis have filed grievances because they have been researching records in the National Archives for the past month. They claim the Civil War era material they are collecting is for the personal use of someone in the Secretary's office. They believe it is irrelevant to the mission of the Commerce Department and a waste of their time. Being relatively new employees with little understanding of the broad scope of our departmental mandate, I'm sure they misunderstood the reason why you have them researching these seemingly strange subjects."

"I am delighted you brought the matter to my attention because there is a very good reason why they are doing the research," Muncaster responded. "The White House has asked the Secretary to be the main speaker at a meeting of eastern U.S. land developers. The speech is on the need to preserve Civil War historical sites while building shopping centers, strip malls and housing subdivisions. It will be a newsworthy event, so my entire office is working on the speech. Getting all the gritty background details together has been a lot of tedious work." Muncaster wasn't worried his ruse would ever be discovered. It was no big deal because speeches got written all the time for events that were later canceled. The cancellation of this speaking engagement would soon be forgotten. No one would ever check to see if it had ever really been on the speaking schedule in the first place.

"That's good to know," Greene answered. "I assumed there was a good reason for the large expenditure of labor. I know you are very busy, but would you mind talking to the immediate supervisor of those employees? It would be best to get their grievance petitions withdrawn as soon as possible. We don't want some nosy newspaper picking up the story and blowing it out of proportion. Maintaining a clean departmental public image is a vital concern for us, especially after the messy aftermath of the John Huang affair."

"I have always believed we have a responsibility to look out for the welfare of our hard-working employees. I'll make time in my schedule and get this unfortunate misunderstanding taken care of right away. I will have everything back to normal before the close of business today. I really appreciate you being on top of things and for alerting me to the situation. Misunderstandings of this type need to be nipped in the bud before they get out of hand. Mike, dedicated employees such as yourself are the backbone of this department. Keep up the good work!" Muncaster said as he hung up.

The Office of Controlled Correspondence was the heart of Muncaster's bureaucratic empire. The unit, staffed by people loyal only to the political party in power, evaluated the importance of all incoming correspondence, assigned a priority status and had the responsibility for ensuring an answer went out in a timely manner. As part of the process, the sender's record of political contributions was checked against a continually updated master computer file. The computer terminal, kept under lock and key, was more closely guarded than the top secret commercial intelligence reports that came into the Commerce Department from all over the world.

The draft response for sensitive Priority A correspondence had to be returned to the Office of Controlled Correspondence within three working days. Once the outgoing letter was prepared in final form, the Secretary or Deputy Secretary of Commerce signed it. The office sent Priority B correspondence to Under Secretaries and Assistant Secretaries to answer within seven working days. Priority C letters went to Deputy Assistant Secretaries to be answered within ten days. Priority D material went to Office Directors with a 14 day response deadline. Priority E did not have to be answered. It was forwarded to lower-level offices for information purposes only.

The system over which Muncaster presided provided political oversight, flexibility, meticulous record keeping and absolute control over the Department's employees. It was a large operation because at any given time, 500 pieces of correspondence were in various stages of processing. Like most systems, the correspondence control regime did not always work perfectly. Because drafting answers to letters was boring work, many of the higher officials reassigned the task to those of lower rank. It was not uncommon for the luckless individuals at the bottom of the bureaucracy to be slaving over five Priority A projects, seven priority B jobs and three Priority C letters at the same time. As long as the deadlines were met, Muncaster didn't care how long the employees stayed at their desks at night. What was good for his political party was automatically good for the nation. The civil servants were provided by the taxpayers to be worked hard by those who had been smart enough to win the last election.

Barbara Adolfo, the head of Muncaster's controlled correspondence unit, was a tireless campaign worker who was rewarded with the high honor and grave responsibility of assigning the final correspondence priorities. Because she was blindly loyal to the party's agenda and unquestioningly followed instructions, Muncaster trusted her judgment implicitly. "Let me explain the situation to you," Barbara said to the two disgruntled employees seated in front of her desk. "Mr. Swindell is deeply offended by your awful accusations of misconduct. That having been said, he feels a degree of responsibility for letting the misunderstanding get out of hand. He knows he should have informed you of the important reason why you were assigned to research the archives. Since he is very busy, I'm sure you understand how he could have easily overlooked such a minor matter. Because you felt badly used on our last project, Mr. Swindell wants to make your next assignment a good one."

"Once you sign these forms withdrawing your grievances, I'll give you travel orders for a four week stay in Bahrain. While there, you will research the potential for trade missions, trade shows and the economic sectors having developmental potential. We want you to bring back a 35 page report of your findings. You can do research in the morning and write the report while sitting on the lovely beach in the afternoon. I'll give you a laptop computer to take along. Be careful with it. Please don't allow any sand to get into it. Since it is difficult work and a long flight, we are also authorizing a three day rest stop for you in Paris on the way back."

As the eager employees signed the release forms, Barbara pushed the travel orders across the table. The State of Bahrain, situated in the Persian Gulf off the coast of Saudi Arabia and not far from Iraq and Iran, was vital to the strategic military interests of the United States. The fleet of U.S. warships constantly patrolling the Gulf had access to the port and supply base located on the island state. Bahrain was also a very lovely place to visit during the winter months.

The American Embassy was surprised to learn two researchers were coming for a month long stay. Their visit had some vague connection with the economic projections Washington agencies were preparing on the Gulf's oil producing countries. The visitors would have an easy job because most of the data they were seeking was already in the embassy files. Why they didn't ask for the material to be mailed or faxed to them was something no one in the embassy could figure out. Knowing better than to ask questions, the embassy staff also gathered together all the information they could locate on the island's tourist attractions. It would give the visitors something to do with all their free time.

"Power is the great aphrodisiac"

-Henry Kissinger, 1971

Taking decisive action was the hallmark of being a true executive. As a hardened goal-oriented leader, Muncaster was proud of how quickly he had disposed of the annoying personnel matter. As the two happy Commerce employees departed for the airport, Muncaster got back to what was important, completing his plan for the eradication of Leon Placke. As an expert in reviewing reports prepared by others, Muncaster readily noticed something was missing from the extensive files spread before him. There was no mention of how Leon Placke acquired the draft copy of the U.S. Constitution. The rare document, on temporary loan from Placke, was on display at the National Archives building. Placke never fully explained how he acquired the valuable record that had George Washington's handwritten notes scrawled all over it. He continued to stick by his preposterous story which no one in the capital believed. Placke repeatedly said that the document had been given to him by George Washington. Leon Placke's unbelievable explanation was just another indication to Muncaster that Placke had completely lost his mind. Placke had turned against the lobbying profession and was claiming George Washington's ghost had made him do it. Placke was nuts and that was all there was to the matter.

Much to the chagrin of Washington insiders, many tourists saw the document in a different light. To these gullible bumpkins, the draft copy of the Constitution was positive proof that Placke's effort to reform the Washington establishment was guided by the spirit of one of the nation's founding fathers. As they crowded around the well-guarded display case, the tourists could read the notes in George Washington's handwriting in the margins and between the paragraphs of the draft copy: "The capital of the country should be located in the middle of the land, equally distant from points north to south and east to west. Once established, it can be moved periodically as the nation expands to the west, as I expect it will."

Another of the notes read: "We are a nation of farmers at this time. The convention is apportioning the seats in the houses of Congress on the basis of geography. Should we allow representation to based on field of endeavor at a later time? As the nation's manufacturing industries grow and become more diverse, would it not be better to have the members of one of the houses elected on the basis of the craft or occupation of the inhabitants?"

"In the future, the nation's bakers, gunsmiths, blacksmiths and farmers will have more in common politically with those engaged in the same profession than they will have with the other people living in their localities.

Transportation and the mails are sure to improve in the future. Will those coming after us remember to adjust the basis upon which the seats in Congress are allocated?"

As a steady stream of visitors filed by the encased document, the capital's establishment remained stymied in its attempt to discredit Placke's story. The document was checked by a dozen experts and found to be authentic. Because the rare piece of paper had not been reported stolen, there was no way Placke could be charged with theft. Muncaster thought it was most unfortunate Placke was the document's lucky discoverer because the long lost piece of old parchment was giving Placke's crazy reform ideas an aura of unshakable credibility. Finding the rare document probably had also contributed to Placke's mental collapse. As his mental processes disintegrated, Placke began to actually believe George Washington was talking to him, the old paper serving to reinforce the delusion.

Muncaster began to wade through another stack of government reports. He paid no attention to the November 1999 trade figures. Increases in the imports of cars and consumer goods pushed the United States trade deficit to a record $26.5 billion, a 3.5 percent rise from October. Muncaster wasted no time reading the arguments over whether the growing deficit was good or bad, or if anything should be done about it.

Instead, he fixed his attention on a report showing the lobbying industry had earned $697 million for the first six months of 1999. Washington's lobbyists were earning a cool $116 million a month to lobby Congress and federal agencies. Muncaster nearly drooled as he read the good news. The health care industry led the pack in lobbying expenditures, spending $95.5 million. The communications and technology sector spent $94.6 million; the finance and insurance industry, $89.8 million; energy and natural resources, $71 million; transportation, $57.7 million; business and retail services, $51.4 million; manufacturing, $36.7 million; agriculture, $34.8 million; and a mixture of single issue groups, $26.7 million. The city's dynamic influence industry would be in danger of being swept away if Placke's silly ideas took hold among the voters. The power of the lobbying dollar would be diluted, a way of life would end. Placke had to be stopped before he did more serious damage to the lobbying profession.

The Labor Department retreated from a policy interpretation that had explicitly stated employers were responsible for federal health and safety violations occurring in their employees' homes. The overzealous government regulators suddenly realized they had overstepped the bounds of reason.

In a historic first, Hillary Clinton, the First Lady of the United States, moved out of the White House and took up residence in a $1.7 million home located in Chappaqua, New York. Ms. Clinton was establishing the legal residency required for her race to win a U.S. Senate seat from New York. Jaded Washington insiders applauded the Clinton family's ingenuity. They saw it as a cleverly disguised effort to maintain a grasp on at least a few of the levers of federal power. Everyone in Washington knew how senators made deals involving federal budget dollars behind the scenes. It was the power to affect the budget that made suffering through the terrible ordeal of a campaign so worthwhile.

> **"Power, like a desolating pestilence,**
> **Pollutes whate'er it touches."**
>
> **-Percy Bysshe Shelly, 1792- 1822**

The U.S. Treasury Department sent $16.9 million in checks to presidential candidates authorized to receive federal matching-funds. The Democratic National Committee sadly reported it was behind in its fund raising efforts. It collected only $40 million in 1999, significantly behind the $58 million raised by the Republicans. The race between Al Gore and Bill Bradley turned nasty as their dedicated campaign workers took to engaging in fisticuffs, picketing and disrupting each other's events.

President Clinton nominated Alan Greenspan for a fourth four-year term as head of the Federal Reserve, the nation's central bank. Greenspan was widely credited with pursuing a set of interest rate policies that helped keep inflation low while encouraging strong economic growth. The U.S. Government announced the final revenue collection figures for 1999, it had collected $1.7 trillion. As part of President Clinton's final opportunity to shape the nation's spending and tax policies, the White House announced a plan to motivate Americans to put aside money for retirement and establish new tax breaks for the 44 million people lacking health insurance.

A nonprofit investigative group published a book alleging big donors swayed the policies of both the Democrats and Republicans. The book stated that all the leading presidential candidates running this year were beholden to some degree to the special interests which funded their political careers. As knowing Washington lobbyists snickered, the offended candidates roundly denounced the book's unwarranted attack on the integrity of the nation's leading politicians. The candidates made it clear that elected officials never did crass favors for donors, they made their decisions based solely on what was best for the country. The massive amount of political contributions they were receiving were merely an aid in doing what they already were pledged to do.

As they solemnly listened to the political braying, the lobbyists knew what was being left unsaid. What was good for the country often happened to be good for campaign donors. Non-contributors were irrelevant because they were not part of the political process. If their interests got mangled a little in the complex process of governing the country, it was too bad. Everyone with any sense at all knew what the unwritten rules were: "If you want a voice in political decision making, donate to a campaign. Pay your dues to the club of democracy or get run over by those who did."

The small sign next to the tourist seating stands on the Ellipse said Leon Placke would speak at 2 p. m. Officials had tried to get Placke barred from the property because he was a public nuisance, upsetting the visitors waiting to tour the White House. The attempt to ban Placke from the property had not worked. The infuriated tourists demanded he be permitted to speak on the site. Mobs of visitors also jammed the Archives building to view the draft copy of the Constitution on the three days per week when Placke spoke on the Ellipse. It seemed to harried officials that every visitor to the capital city planned an itinerary which included listening to Leon Placke speak and viewing the draft of the U.S. Constitution. Placke was a vexation, creating traffic jams and arousing a degree of hostility in the usually placid tourists. Even now in the dead of winter, a group gathered to listen to the most hated man in Washington speak.

Placke began by saying Congress no longer functioned as the nation's founders intended. The people knew instinctively something was going wrong. Fifty percent of the U.S. population disapproved of how Congress performed, although they were not sure of the reason. Placke went on to say it was because Congress no longer represented the interests of the people as a whole, having been captured by well-financed special interests and lobbyists. Congress had to be updated to reflect the current economic makeup of the nation. The awesome behind-the-scenes power of the lobbyists had to be broken. The U.S. House of Representatives should be elected on the basis of modern economic sectors, not by obsolete geographical congressional districts. The current system of districting had lost its political vitality sometime after the nation industrialized. There was nothing in the Constitution which precluded making such a change. George Washington had even made a few notes on the topic when the Constitution was being written. Leon encouraged his listeners to go to the Archives and read them.

"We can also slash the White House staff by 50 percent," Placke continued. "The President doesn't need 400 people working frantically to get his profile on TV each and every night. While the White House staff chases media exposure for the President, no one monitors the endless creation of new of jobs to be filled by loyal campaign workers. In some parts of the government, 30 to 40 bureaucratic layers now separate the front line employee from the agency head. It's impossible for the bottom to hear the top when messages go through dozens of interpretations on their journey down the line."

"The president has to spend less time seeking media exposure and do what he is supposed to do, manage his managers. Did you know that of the 340,000 federal employees working in the Washington metropolitan area, 75,000 don't have enough work to occupy them for a full day because of the poorly managed flow of work? If the President and his senior Cabinet officials did what you paid them to do, these under utilized employees would be working on productive tasks. Do you care if this problem is resolved? Why should you care? Because it is your tax money which is being wasted, not the funds of the political parties. The situation has gone to ridiculous extremes. In one federal agency employees sit around with nothing to do while a block away another agency is hiring employees. Make any sense? Of course it doesn't, but it is a fact of life in Washington! You need to tell the President and Congress to stop spending so much of their time smiling into the TV cameras and start managing the operations of the government." Placke ended his speech to a loud round of applause from the assemblage of tourists.

A short time later, calls from irate citizens started pouring into congressional offices and the White House. As the phones began to ring, the staffs mobilized because they knew Leon Placke had once again roused the rabble. Placke's unsophisticated fans were an annoying distraction because they diverted vital resources from the real issue facing the politicians, maintaining the best possible access to the $1.8 trillion federal budget. The Republicans had no time to worry about Placke's trivial concerns regarding the management of government resources. They were too busy trying to save the nation from itself. Republicans knew in their hearts that the Democrats were only one small step removed from Communism. The leftist liberals of the Democratic party wanted to turn the United States into a socialist state, a country in which the federal government dominated every facet of life. The Democrats wanted to tax and spend as they went about ruthlessly snuffing out the spirit of free enterprise in the United States of America.

The Democrats mistrusted Republicans because they were nothing more than latent fascists disguised as free market advocates. Republicans cared nothing for common people. Their interests were focused solely on looking out for the welfare of big business. When the Republicans were in power, America's business fat cats got richer while everyone else suffered and the environment was degraded. The Democrats did not have time to worry about little management matters. They were preoccupied with the daunting task of trying to pass meaningful social legislation while at the same time curbing the insatiable appetite of "Corporate America." The voters should be thanking them, not wasting time listening to the ridiculous drivel spouted by Leon Placke. To have to spend time responding to the telephone calls of quasi-literate sightseers three times a week was almost more than one could endure. Placke was nothing but an agitator of the uninformed. He ought to be sent to an asylum before he disrupted the critical functioning of the entire political system.

As Placke's listeners dispersed at the conclusion of his speech, a group of about 20 walked down Pennsylvania Avenue toward the Treasury Department talking about how the political parties and lobbyists had let the country down. Still incensed by the points raised in Placke's speech, the angry people pooled their change as they halted at pay phone outside the Treasury building. They wanted to vent their outrage at the sorry state of affairs by calling the White House and members of Congress.

As the noisy mob milled around the public phone outside of her window, Jennifer Wentworth paid no attention to them as she sat at her desk in an office on the first floor of the Treasury building reading a book. She had done a lot reading during the past eight years because she was rarely given any work to do. Despite having nothing to occupy her time, she came to work punctually each day to avoid giving her superiors the slightest excuse for taking disciplinary action.

After graduating from a prestigious law school, Jennifer Wentworth moved to Washington during the last year of the administration of President Reagan and stayed on during President Bush's term of office. Jennifer had a fine job at Treasury keeping track of the soaring national debt. Working with the big numbers gave her a feeling of fulfillment because every month the debt totals she tallied appeared on newscasts and in the papers. Having developed a good degree of political understanding while computing the soaring national debt, Jennifer realized President Bush was not going to be reelected because the voters did not understand why the ever increasing national debt under Republican Presidents was supposed to be a good thing. In the past, Republicans had always stood for balanced budgets. The confused voters deeply resented the Republican switch to the free spending ways of the Democrats. What were they supposed to expect next? A spendthrift Democratic administration that tried to balance the budget? The blurring of the political roles of the parties was very disconcerting to the electorate. As a consequence of the confusion, the fickle voters were going to toss President Bush out of office.

Taking the advice of a friend who knew about such things, Jennifer went to see Michael Greene at the Commerce Department to inquire about the subtleties of converting from a political to a career position. The affable Mr. Green was always willing to be of service to government employees with needs. Over a two hour, $85 lunch paid for by Jennifer, Greene outlined how the little known transfer procedure worked. The conversion, which always became highly popular near the end of an administration's term of office, was called "burrowing-in." Once the transfer papers were approved by Treasury higher-ups, Jennifer was quietly moved into a job in the career service. She was no longer part of the Bush administration. She had become just another drab, non-political government employee.

As the disheartened political appointees of the Bush administration began to drift out of town after the election defeat, Michael Greene presented the advance team of the incoming Clinton administration a copy of his extensive list of individuals who had burrowed-in. Greene knew the routine well, having approached every incoming administration regardless of party, in the same manner for the past 15 years. Greene suggested that the untrustworthy leftover miscreants, who were little better than spies for the defeated party, be isolated from other employees. Not wishing to have Republican infiltrators contaminating the politically innocent general workforce, President Clinton's people heartily thanked Greene for his initiative and valuable personnel management insights. Most of the betrayed job converters got bored with doing nothing after a few months. By the end of the first year of the Clinton administration, the majority had resigned and left the government payroll. For his skill in overseeing human resources operations, Michael Greene was presented a cash performance award at a ceremony held at the White House.

Jennifer Wentworth was stubborn. She had stayed at Treasury reading law reviews and doing occasional clerical assignments for the entire eight years of President Clinton's two terms of office. Being an enterprising individual, she also made herself useful by preparing tax returns, drafting powers of attorney and writing wills for anyone who asked. Because she freely dispensed legal services to employees, Jennifer was not hassled by her supervisors.

Jennifer's familiar world of national debt data crumbled as the Clinton administration had the audacity to balance the federal budget. The national debt was no longer rising; it stopped being a front page news item. Greatly disappointed by the turn of events, Jennifer focused her sights squarely on the future. If the Republicans won the autumn election, she would become somebody important again. Perhaps she would be assigned to the prestigious position of monitoring the soaring budget surplus which now dominated the financial news. Of course, if Republican policies got the national debt climbing again, she would be happy go back to monitoring those numbers.

As she sat idly turning the pages of her book, Jennifer was visible to the angry people on the street. The tourists lined up to use the pay phone soon noticed Jennifer wasn't doing any work. "That must be one of these under-employed bureaucrats Leon mentioned," said one. "She has nothing to do but read a book?" commented another as the line moved forward in front of Jennifer's window. As the phone calls protesting the wasteful work assignments of government workers were made, the group watched Jennifer, their anger rising. "She's never going to get busy, I'll bet she sits there all day long doing nothing," said one frustrated individual as the last of the phone calls were completed. Angrily, he pried up one of the decorative stones neatly fitted around the base of a crab apple tree planted next to the sidewalk. "This ought to get her moving," he shouted as he heaved the stone through the office window. Jennifer jumped up as the window shattered, glass flying everywhere. The stone landed on her desk, bounced and hit the wall, knocking a large hole into it before falling to the to the floor.

As a stunned Jennifer Wentworth watched in horror, the fist-waving mob on the street shouted, "Get to work you lazy bureaucrat! Stop wasting our tax money! Why are you sitting there doing nothing?" The breaking glass set off an alarm, alerting the security guards who came running, weapons at the ready. The tourists were arrested for vandalism, but they did not remain silent. As they sat at the police station trying to arrange bail, the nightly national TV news featured a story on their window breaking escapade. It was also splashed across the front pages of the next morning's newspapers.

Treasury officials reacted vigorously to the crisis by ordering drapes for all first floor office windows. After a survey of visibility from the street was completed, employees on the first floor were instructed not to open the drapes more than 18 inches. As the other federal agencies followed Treasury's lead, a deluge of drapery orders overwhelmed the local installation companies. As punishment for her thoughtless act, Jennifer was banished to windowless interior office. If she had not previously made arrangements to prepare the tax returns of 87 of her coworkers and supervisors, her punishment would have been much more severe.

"To rely upon conviction, devotion, and other excellent spiritual qualities—that is not to be taken seriously in politics."
-Vladimir I. Lenin, 1922

Along with the world's highest density of lawyers and lobbyists, Washington is also generously endowed with a large number of think tanks, institutes and policy shops that formulate policy options and publish papers on every issue having the financial backing of an interest group. Because the matter of redundant government employees suddenly gained notoriety, the policy community responded by producing a blizzard of papers covering all sides of the issue. A left-leaning think tank duly reported Leon's numbers to be highly inflated. It found no more than 24,368 federal employees in the Washington metropolitan area idle on any given day of the work week. A right-leaning institute countered, claiming Placke's figures were too low. According to the institute's scientific survey, 103,243 federal employees in the Washington metropolitan area often performed less than four hours of real work on at least two days a week.

The Office of Personnel Management, the agency in charge of all federal employees, issued a rebuttal paper stating it was unable to define what was meant by "real work." As an alternative, it suggested a study be done on the number of employees who came to work on time each day. An ad hoc bipartisan coalition of former political appointees announced the issue was bogus. If the lunch meeting schedules of the higher-ups were kept up to date, travel arrangements were properly made and speeches and press releases prepared on time, the lower-level employees were functioning as well as could be expected. Nothing else was deemed to be relevant to the proper conduct of the nation's business. The people of the nation ought not let themselves be mislead by false issues that could hamper the proper functioning of the democratic process.

Never missing an opportunity to voice an opinion, Congress rushed into print a 95 page report accusing the Executive Branch of failing to properly manage and motivate government personnel. Too many top-level federal executives spent little of their time managing the organizations they were in charge of, rampant waste was everywhere. Government programs were in disarray and it was all the fault of the corrupt President and his crooked, deal-doing subordinates.

Insulted and humiliated by the tasteless, manner-breaching attack, the White House retaliated with a scathing 110 page report blaming all government waste and inefficiency on Congress. Personal corruption was not the issue. The most honest of managers could not function in the morass of conflicting laws and regulations that a Congress, bought off by lobbyists and special interests, churned out faster than a normal person could read. It must be delightful to sit on Capitol Hill enacting laws while being free of the responsibility of carrying them out. The White House then threw down the gantlet. The geniuses occupying Congress were cordially invited to come down to the other end of Pennsylvania Avenue and try their hand at being managers in the regulatory swamp Congress had created. If they could do any better than the President and his cabinet, the country would be proud of them.

Stunned by the vicious breech of political etiquette, Congress wasn't sure what to do next. To its great relief, the Supreme Court stepped into the raging war of words, solemnly pointing out that any blurring of the separate functions of the Executive Branch and Congress would be immediately declared unconstitutional. For the first time in 50 years, the entire Congress was delighted with a Supreme Court ruling. Maybe the crotchety court had a useful function in the American scheme of things after all.

Federal Reserve Chairman Alan Greenspan strongly urged Congress to use the burgeoning federal budget surplus to pay down the national debt rather than using the money to finance new spending programs and tax cuts. From Greenspan's point of view, that would be the best means of employing the surplus because it would ensure the future financial health of the nation by freeing private capital for investment while reducing the government's debt servicing costs. To the tax cutters and spenders in Congress, Greenspan's message did not sit well. They would have to find ways to work around his unpalatable suggestion because none of the special interest groups making large political contributions cared anything at all about debt reduction.

The U. S. Chamber of Commerce, in an effort to improve its standing with Congress, announced it was raising $8 million to support pro-business candidates engaged in close election races. Senator Orrin G. Hatch of Utah, who had hoped to become the Republican's fallback choice for the presidential nomination if George W. Bush stumbled, closed down his failing campaign and threw his support behind the Texas governor. Although he couldn't win the presidential nomination, Hatch had no intention of leaving politics. After withdrawing from the presidential race, Hatch announced plans to seek a fifth term as senator.

At the arms control talks in Geneva, Russia suggested reducing the number of nuclear warheads held by each side to 1,500. The U.S. countered with an offer to keep 2,000 to 2,500 warheads in service. U.S. arms negotiators believed the smaller number proposed by the Russians would not be sufficient for a credible nuclear deterrent. In Kosovo, the U.S. Army began a probe into the behavior of American soldiers mired in the thankless peace keeping mission. It seemed that a few of the frustrated troopers trying to keep peace in the caldron of feuding local factions had grown tired of taking abuse. They had taken to knocking a number of uncooperative civilians around.

In the longest (89 minutes) State of the Union address of his presidency, President Clinton proposed an agenda including a variety of tax cuts and spending programs. The President was launching an activist spending agenda during the final year of his second term in office. As the President enumerated the spending proposals he planned to send to Congress, everyone conveniently forgot the gist of his 1996 State of the Union address, the one in which he said that the era of big government was over. The sound economic advice that Greenspan had recently given Congress was not accorded much of a priority by the President. Wiping out the $5.7 trillion federal debt would take until at least 2015, maybe longer, depending on other presidential and congressional spending priorities.

February 2000

"Those in possession of absolute power can not only prophesy and make their prophecies come true, but they can also lie and make their lies come true."

-Eric Hoffer, 1955

A longtime Democratic fund raiser for Vice President Gore went on trial for disguising contributions to the Clinton-Gore campaign and other politicians during 1993-96. During those years, she allegedly steered thousands of dollars in illegal donations through straw donors. Two Buddhist nuns, who were prospective witnesses in the case, fled the United States. After learning the nuns had moved to Taiwan, the irritated trial judge issued bench warrants for their arrest.

Texas governor George W. Bush filed reports revealing he raised $69 million in campaign contributions during 1999 while his campaign expenses for the year amounted to $37 million. Bush raised and spent more money than any other presidential candidate ever did during a primary campaign year. The news cheered Washington insiders because much of the money went to local political service companies. As the firms prepared themselves for another banner sales year, Senator John McCain unexpectedly trounced George W. Bush in the New Hampshire primary. In the Democratic race, incumbent Vice president Al Gore maintained a slim lead over former basketball star and U.S. Senator, Bill Bradley.

Muncaster had a difficult time reaching Leon Placke. The once mighty lobbying firm of Placke and Associates, Inc. was practically out of business. Its glory days of lobbying Congress and federal agencies were over. The firm had been reduced to nothing more than an answering service, a sure sign that Placke's role as Washington's most renown influence peddler was at an end. The calls to Placke's number now consisted of nothing more than thank you messages from tourists who had heard him speak on the Ellipse.

Nevertheless Muncaster was annoyed by Placke's lack of adherence to the rules of Washington protocol. Although he was now a powerless political nonentity, Placke should have retained the decency to promptly return the phone calls of high administration officials the likes of H. Muncaster Swindell. After his third call in the same number of days brought no response, Muncaster changed his tactics. On his fourth call, Muncaster left a message stating he had uncovered new information relating to the Civil War materials Placke had tried to hide in the National Archives. Would Placke care to see the information? Muncaster no longer had any interest in blocking Placke's political program, crazy as it was. Muncaster only wanted to renew their damaged friendship. Could they let bygones be bygones?

Muncaster's gambit worked. Placke returned his call, and agreed to meet. Muncaster would have to do the driving because Placke's car had been repossessed. "The sorry bastard has really hit rock bottom. I'm truly doing everyone in Washington a favor by putting an end to his miserable reform prattle," Muncaster joyously muttered to himself as he poured the moonshine whiskey he had purchased during a recent trip to southwestern Virginia into the antique jug. Muncaster had been careful to leave room in the jug for the pulverized pile of sleeping pills he now slowly added. As the crushed pills slid from the piece of folded stationary he gently tapped on jug's rim, Muncaster reread the brightly colored warning label on the pill container. In bold letters was a warning that the prescription medicine should not be taken when alcohol was consumed. Mixing the two would result in severe drowsiness leading to possible fatal consequences. After firmly corking the jug, Muncaster filled a silver flask with more of the moonshine whiskey. The stuff was strong, it had a real kick to it. Three good swigs would knock a normal man out. After loading the jug, flask and an exquisite selection of expensive finger foods into the trunk of his car, Muncaster piled his collection of maps and reports onto the back seat. He was ready to go.

After winding slowly through Washington's endless late morning traffic, Muncaster saw Leon waiting for him on the corner of 18th and K streets. "Good morning Leon, how are you this fine day?" Muncaster uttered in his best polite, politically correct voice as he reached over and opened the car's right front door.

"Oh, I've had better days," Leon responded as he climbed into the front seat next to Muncaster. "But things could be a lot worse, so I don't waste time complaining. Giving speeches to the tourists keeps me good and busy."

"You are well on the way to becoming Washington's man of the hour," Muncaster dryly said. "Your reform ideas are being noticed by the presidential aspirants. John McCain has co-opted a lot of your reform agenda and has begun using it in his speeches. His heated attack on Washington's iron triangle of big money, lobbyists and legislation had the masses, excuse me, I mean the people on their feet cheering. Leon, you sly dog, have you gone and started writing campaign speeches for McCain?"

"No I haven't. A couple of his campaign aides listened to me speak on the Ellipse. They saw how well my ideas were being received by the tourists and decided to add one of my reform themes to John's speeches. The incestuous political situation in Washington is starting to be noticed by the voters, reform is catching on. It may turn out to be a major issue in this year's election. The average American voter is starting to see how both the Democrats and Republicans milk the system for all that it is worth."

Muncaster was not about to let the verbal jab pass, so he acidly replied, "Now hold on for just a minute Mr. ex-lobbyist who knows all! There's nothing wrong with lobbyists being involved with candidates. Special interests are merely another way the people can express their will in an organized fashion. Loaning corporate jets, contributing to campaigns and establishing positions on important political issues are all part of making our wonderful democracy work."

"You miss the point completely," Leon answered. " Our system of pouring money into political campaigns has gotten out of control. A run for office has to begin two years prior to an election. The extra time and money spent adds nothing but cost to political campaigns. Politics has become a well-paid business in the United States. Those who want favors know they have to spend money to gain access to power. Once the candidate is elected, it's time to provide favors in return for the financial support previously given."

"What you are criticizing is nothing more than a healthy democratic process at work," retorted Muncaster. "There's nothing wrong with it at all. If people want to spend a little money to gain political influence, so be it. People ought to be free to invest in politics, it is good for the country and better for those who work in the political establishment. Managing a campaign is an important job, more important than managing a store, I might add. Please stop knocking those who make money in politics! It isn't like you never made the big bucks by playing the political favors game yourself! You didn't earn your title of being the king of the lobbyists for doing nothing in the political deal-making arena!"

Leon let the remark pass as he responded, "Big money is corrupting the system. It has gotten totally out of control during the last ten years. The Republic is going to be destroyed if the problem isn't fixed soon. Our system of government was not founded on the basis of big money controlling everything. It is not supposed to be a government of, and for the politicians and special interests. By the end of next month, George W. Bush will have raised $74 million in campaign contributions. Al Gore about half that amount. Do you really believe the so-called Pioneers, each of whom has collected over $100,000 for Bush, are not going to have any influence if he wins the election? Bush's financiers are up in arms because he lost the New

Hampshire primary to John McCain. If the money doesn't matter, why are they so bent out of shape?"

"I'll tell you why," Muncaster said. "McCain has started using some of your reform bullshit to stir up the masses. Poor George W. Bush now has had to spend close to $40 million of his campaign war chest to fight McCain in the early primaries because of an irrelevant issue you dug up. Of all people, you ought to know better! Why do you insist on agitating the voting masses with things that are only the business of those of us who work in Washington? Why should anyone care how much it costs to operate the White House and Congress? No one noticed the high overhead costs until you started shooting your stupid mouth off!"

"President James Buchanan once said: 'When the birthday of George Washington shall be forgotten, liberty will have perished from the earth.' I want to help revitalize the country by spreading Washington's basic beliefs and values across the nation. We have strayed far from the path Washington laid out for the country! We have put the government up for sale to the highest bidder! Washington was soldier, surveyor and farmer before he became a politician. Now, we are governed by those who spend their lifetimes getting themselves elected to public office so they can spend our tax dollars."

As Muncaster switched lanes, Leon continued, "Things have really gotten bad. The power that comes with politics is like an infectious disease, many people can't let it go of power once they have exercised it. For the first time in the history of the United States, the wife of an incumbent president has moved out of the White House to run for the U.S. Senate. I think it is just another way for the Clintons to keep their fingers in the five hundred dollar drawer of the federal treasury. Hillary Clinton loves political power more than the President does. Neither of them want to let it go completely because they are both hooked on exercising political power."

"I don't see how Hillary Clinton's run for the U.S. Senate has anything to do with the values of George Washington," Muncaster said sarcastically as he looked over his shoulder and changed lanes again. "Lots of people stay in the capital to work after a stint in politics, there is great opportunity here for those of us with political smarts. Of course, if your nutty idea about reapportioning the seats in the House of Representatives catches on, lobbying will be as dead an industry as the manufacture of buggy whips. Don't think it hasn't been noticed by people that you only got interested in halting the evils of lobbying after you made yourself a nice big bundle of money in the business. Now that you have gotten yours, no one else is supposed to be able to make a buck doing political deals? Your whole program has the strong smell of hypocrisy about it! You have no right to be giving the shaft to everyone else in the business!"

Leon dropped his head and looked down at his scruffy shoes. "I know it looks bad, like I am the worst sort of swindler. However, George Washington pointed out the errors of my ways to me. As a consequence of his intervention, I am a changed man. A man charged with bringing reform to the system! To bring it back into conformity with the goals of Washington and the other founders of the nation!"

Muncaster interrupted, "I can't help but notice George Washington has been dead quite a number of years! So, how does he talk to you? I suppose you also expect me to believe he handed you a draft copy of the Constitution of the United States? You know, the one you have been showing all over town! What you need to do is stop telling tall tales and get yourself to a good shrink. You have a serious mental problem, not to mention one giant sized ego. Deluding yourself into believing George Washington would stoop so low as to pick you as his agent of reform is sure sign of a mind losing touch with reality, of one desperately in need of the best medical help all of your money can buy."

Muncaster didn't really care what Leon was going to say next. He could see Leon was crazy as a loon. It wouldn't have been a problem if Leon had only wandered around the streets not bothering anyone, but Leon had taken to spreading outrageously seditious ideas throughout the electorate. Leon had also refused to seek treatment for his illness and rebuffed the assistance of his friends. He was a danger to the Washington establishment and that was the reason why Muncaster was taking him for his last ride.

Leon looked up from his shoes and glanced at Muncaster. "You already know how I met George Washington, having heard the story at least ten times from my former friends. Since you think I'm lying, I'm not going to bore you by going over it with you again. Instead, let's talk about the real issue--money and its influence on modern politics. How many of the 196,000 people who have contributed to the Bush campaign expect something back from him if he wins the election? How many of his 149 full time staff are going to be waiting in line for a political job? How many of his big contributors want to come to Washington for a couple of years at government expense? What is the going price for an ambassadorship these days, a contribution of $150,000 or more?

"Washington fund raising dinners have become an end in themselves. Last Wednesday night, the Democratic Congressional Campaign Committee took in $7.3 million. On Thursday night, the Republicans pulled in $7.2 million at their event. Most of the money came from lobbyists covering their bases with both parties, to keep a foot in the door no matter who wins. To raise that kind of dough, you have to sell a lot of tables with ten lobbyists or company representatives to a table. They all have their list of things they want from Congress: tax breaks, less strict regulations, a competitive advantage, a license to rip-off the public. They will all be there to collect after the election, you can bet on that."

"That's how our glorious democracy works," Muncaster responded. "And it works one hell of a lot better now than it will when that stupid idea of yours--of having the economic interests of the nation neatly represented in the Congress--catches on. Why do you want to change something when it works so well? The dolts outside of the capital don't care one damn about the art of politics. Why not leave them to spend their time at the movies or watching TV at home? Why does the high cost of elections cause you so much grief? Politics puts money into our local economy and creates jobs for the political industry. All the money campaigns spend goes for advertising, polling, catering, payrolls, postage, and chartered jets. A fund raising dinner by a candidate is a major boost for business in any city. You ought to view election costs as hidden tax paid by the special interests so they can be heard by the politicians. You know how the system works? The companies you hold part ownership in are doing quite well this election year, are they not?"

After doing a quick mental calculation Leon answered, "It has been a very good year, profits are up 130 percent. My share has kept me in shelter and food despite the collapse of my lobbying business."

"Leon, why don't you forget about your so-called reform schemes and go back to making money out of the political system like everyone else in Washington? You were doing quite well for yourself before you went off on that stupid reform kick of yours!"

In a barely audible voice Leon answered Muncaster's question. "I can't. Our political system is in falling apart right before my eyes. The costs of lobbying, elections and excessive layers of political bureaucracy are pushing the system to the breaking point. The crisis has slowly been building for years, my job is to bring about change before everything collapses into chaos. The people are losing faith in our system. Nearly 50 percent of the eligible voters don't brother to cast a ballot because they have turned cynical about politics. Who can blame them when they see John Huang is testifying as a government witness against his old friend Maria Hsia, confirming that illegal funds were raised for Clinton and Gore. On the other side, the New York Republican state party is trying to keep John McCain off of the ballot in the state. Talk about democracy in action!"

As an annoyed Muncaster stared straight ahead at the highway, Leon continued: "President Clinton has submitted a $1.84 trillion dollar budget to Congress. It's 2.5 percent higher than last year's. Why is it going up if the era of big government is over? Clinton proposes to increase aid to farmers, help the Internet, bolster national defense, expand health care coverage and build 17 new federal prisons. It's all very nice, useful to the nation, few will argue about that. But what about the deal the President and Congress made to spend the Social Security surplus to pay down the national debt? Why don't the Social Security funds stay in the Social Security account so they can be used to pay future retirees?"

"It's just a deceptive accounting gimmick foisted over on the American people so they will be mislead into believing the government is doing more things for them. In the real world, where the rest of America has to live, such dishonesty would bring the practitioner a stiff jail sentence. Who exempted President Clinton and Congress from reality? Have you seen anything in the Constitution covering it? It's just part of the game the Washington establishment plays with the welfare of the country! Do you want to talk about all the goodies for special interests buried deep in the budget where no one can find them? How much do they cost each year? Who gave the President and Congress the right to squander $10 or $11 billion dollars a year to benefit those who bankroll campaigns? The system is sick, I tell you! Why do you think George Washington is so worried about the nation's future?"

Keeping his eyes on the road, Muncaster frostily responded. "George Washington doesn't think anything anymore Leon, he's dead! Why can't you get that fact through that thick head of yours once and for all! By the way, who appointed you to criticize the actions of the President and Congress? Who cares if a few billion dollars get used to help the political friends of the two major parties? Money is the lubricant that makes American democracy work. It is an important part of getting things done efficiently; it sets clear priorities everyone understands. You pay to play in the game." Although he did his best not to show it, the loathing and contempt Muncaster felt for the idiot seated next to him was beginning to show. He had to keep himself under tight control or Placke would begin to suspect he was not being taken on a purely social outing.

After they had driven a few miles in stony silence, Muncaster said, "Look Leon, I don't want to keep arguing politics with you. I know your views have changed, you have become anti-Washington establishment, anti-Congress and anti-White House. I don't understand it, but I'll accept it, okay? Let's drop the subject of present day politics and stick to the matter of the Civil War papers. I thought you'd be interested in my new material because of the big stink the contents of Benjamin's boxes caused some of the leading personalities of the country. Talk about shattering images in the North and South, those papers did it! They really made a lot of powerful people and corporations mad as hell. The list of Confederate deserters destroyed thousands of embellished family histories. Next best was the information on the Northerners who secretly worked to toss Abe Lincoln out of office in the election of 1864. That didn't set well with a lot of big donors in the North."

"Old Judah Benjamin's papers rubbed the ugly realities of war into the faces of a modern generation of dilettantes. You and Mr. Benjamin have really stirred up things around here. Since you hate life in the capital so much, why don't you go someplace else and teach a course in revisionist Civil War history? Although no school around here would touch you with a ten foot pole, almost any college outside the beltway probably would be glad to have you because your name is recognized nationally."

As he spoke Muncaster turned off of Interstate Highway 66 onto a two lane road. A few miles further on, he turned onto a narrower road not much wider than a driveway. Two miles later, it came to a dead-end in front of the remains of a six- story tall stone structure that had burned sometime in the recent past. "What happened to the building?" Leon asked as he stared at the roofless, windowless ruin.

Muncaster replied as he opened the car door and stepped out. "What you see is the remains of what was Chapman's mill. It was damaged during the Civil War and rebuilt some time thereafter. The mill continued to operate until the 1950s. Then it went out of business and the building was sealed up. Although it was not open to the public, it was a famous site. The damage you see now was recent, caused by vandals when they set fire to it a couple of years ago." As they walked to the ruin, he continued, "I thought you'd like to see it because the two soldiers Benjamin sent from Richmond to stash the infamous boxes of documents camped here one night."

"You have to be kidding. How did you know that?" Leon said as he looked into the building at the debris left by the fire.

"I found all kinds of interesting information when searching the old records. There was a lieutenant colonel and a sergeant. The colonel's name was Matthew Chambon. The sergeant was Cyrus Bellnapp. They must have been a couple of tough customers because neither ever talked about their trip to anyone afterwards. It was probably because Benjamin or Breckinridge swore them to secrecy. It's hard to imagine in this day and age, but in those days a man's word was his bond. Having taken an oath, they took their secret to the grave with them. Back then it was not at all like it is today with everyone blabbing everything to the papers and the TV reporters day and night."

The pair walked around the mill ruins, passed the railroad track and stood on the bank of the swiftly flowing stream called Broad Run. It was easy to see why the mill was built at this location. The ample supply of water powering the grinding wheels made it productive all year long. Later, when the railroad threaded its way through the gap in the mountains the tracks ran close by the mill, providing for the easy rail movement of raw and finished products. As they stood watching the rushing water Muncaster said, " Do you know what the most amazing fact I learned about your Confederate soldiers was?"

"I don't have the slightest idea," Leon responded. He was engrossed in watching the rushing water swirl around a large rock. He wondered how much of the rock had been worn away by the swift water in the years since Chambon and Bellnapp had camped here. How fast did water erode stone? It couldn't have been very much, perhaps no more than an inch. The stones and the stream were a constant in time. They were about the same in 1865 as they were today. Leon was looking at virtually the same landscape as the soldiers had. It gave him a sense of comfort, of having something in common with men he could never meet. The splashing water made a restful, soothing sound, one that slowly lulled away the cares of the world. It was an ideal place to spend a night. He could easily understand why the soldiers stopped here.

Leon began to realize Muncaster was talking to him, when he heard him say, "Bellnapp was a black man."

He answered, "What do you mean by black?"

"He was an African -American, you know, a Negro as they were called in those days."

"You must be kidding. Why on earth would a black man be in the Confederate army?"

"It is true. I know because I checked a couple of sources. There were a number of Negro men in Confederate uniform near the end of the war. The total number is unknown because the records were lost when Richmond fell. When the Confederates began enlisting Negroes in the army, Bellnapp happened to be one of those who signed up. Its anyone's guess as to why he would join an army already beaten and fighting a war to keep slavery alive. One thing is for sure, we will never find out his reasons because we can't ask him. Some day someone will decide the subject is worth the time it takes to write a book. It would make fascinating reading."

As he turned away from staring into the rushing water all Leon said was, "He must have had very good reasons to do what he did." Leon would have liked to know what possessed the man to enlist and then go on a desperate mission for a dying government. What did he have to gain? What could have motivated him to do such a thing?

It turned into one of those infrequent February days when the temperature climbs into the low 60s, giving a hint of the spring yet to come. After they walked back to the car basking in the unseasonable warmth and sunshine, Muncaster retrieved the papers from the back seat of the car and spread them on the hood. "These should interest you," said Muncaster as he handed Leon two documents. " These are copies of the paroles for Bellnapp and Chambon. Richmond fell during the time they were on the road. After they hid the boxes of documents, they somehow got themselves surrendered along with Lee's army at Appomattox. They were probably trying to catch up with the army or the fleeing Confederate government when the fighting ended."

Leon looked at the paroled prisoner passes. They certainly weren't fancy, having been printed in great haste by the Union army printers who set up a temporary print shop in the village of Appomattox after the surrender. "Where did you find these?" he asked.

Muncaster was flattered to be asked the question. "A person in my position has available the services of a large number of skilled personnel. I put a few of them to work researching the National Archives in Washington, the records of the Museum of the Confederacy in Richmond and a number of lesser document collections. I was able to collect quite a bit of information about your soldiers and their boxes of papers. Since the documents those interesting characters hid a long time ago created a stir in the high social circles of this modern age, I thought they warranted an investment in research time."

"The soldiers tried to give the location of the hidden papers to former Confederate officials after the war ended. That turned out to be an impossible task because the Rebel leaders were fleeing for their lives, many left the country to avoid being charged with treason. As time went by, there were no trials. No one was going to visit the hangman. Not being of any use to anyone, the papers were forgotten as the former Confederate leaders went about picking up the pieces of their lives. Here is a copy of a note Chambon sent to John C. Breckinridge," Muncaster said as he handed Leon a copy of a letter. "It was discovered in a collection of Breckinridge's papers. It took some doing to find it. Until now, no one had any idea of what it related to. Breckinridge knew it was important because he kept it."

" Here is an engineer's drawing of Rebel defenses at Centreville and a map showing the fortifications around Washington," Muncaster said as he handed more papers to Leon. "We know that in their later years both Chambon and Bellnapp came back to this area at least once. These are the records and press clippings from the ceremonies marking the 50th anniversary of the first battle of Bull Run in the early 1900s. Both are listed among the attendees," Muncaster said as he pushed the stack of files across the hood.

"By time of the anniversary ceremonies, Bellnapp had become a respected research physician at the Ohio State University. He had done a lot of work on the cause of infections and their prevention. His experiences in the military hospitals of Richmond during the war got him interested in the problem. You have to give the man credit, he was among the first to notice the relationship between sanitation practices and the spread of infection in wounds. It's hard to believe people didn't know enough back then to boil their medical instruments." As he finished speaking, Muncaster added the Bellnapp file to the stack Leon was examining.

It was pleasant standing beside the car under a warming sun, the sound of the rushing water softly audible in the distance. Leon spent a leisurely hour reading through the materials Muncaster had brought with him. When he finished, Muncaster suggested they take the time to visit some of the sites mentioned in the files before returning to Washington. His curiosity aroused, Lean readily agreed. Although they had been dead for years, Leon was beginning to feel as though he knew Bellnapp and Chambon on a personal basis. As a result of their travel to Centreville, he had gotten into a great deal of trouble. He might as well take the time to see the sites connected with their visit. It had already destroyed his previous career.

Muncaster expertly retraced the route to Interstate 66 and headed east. Ten miles later, he exited the interstate at Sudley Road, turning north. In a few minutes he made a right turn into the parking lot of the Manassas Battlefield Park. "The serious fighting occurred here," he said as they emerged from the vehicle. "In July 1861, the Union army tried to capture Manassas Junction. The Confederates were defending a line running along this side of Bull Run, a stream with steep sides, very difficult for cannon and army wagons to cross. Part of the Union army crossed upstream some distance from here and drove down in this direction, crumbling the flank of the Confederate line as they came. In the afternoon, the Confederates were able to halt the attack on this ground. They managed to bring up reinforcements and counterattacked, forcing the exhausted Union troops into a retreat that turned into a complete route as the green troops panicked and fled to the rear."

As he spoke, Muncaster gestured, pointing out the features of the terrain that had played a role in the battle. As he listened, Leon found it hard to believe that this rolling, pleasant countryside was once savagely fought over by contending armies. The reminders were here though, and they were difficult to ignore. The silent cannon occupied the same positions from which they had once belched death. The house in which an unfortunate old woman had been killed by an artillery shell was clearly visible. A monument to the fallen made of a reddish stones sat on a hilltop. The crudely constructed memorial had been erected by soldiers before the war ended. Looming large on the brow of the ridge in front of him was an enormous statue of General Thomas J. Jackson. Here, he earned the name of "Stonewall" for his exploits during the battle.

Muncaster continued, "After being defeated, the Union Army fled back to Washington without stopping. Fearing an attack by the Confederates, a shocked federal government frantically went to work fortifying the city. Washington became so well defended that the Confederates never attacked the place, although they occupied most of the territory between here and there." As Muncaster related the sequence of events, they walked around examining the battlefield and then returned to the car.

Exiting the parking lot, Muncaster made a right turn, traveling north on Sudley Road. At the intersection of Route 29, he turned right, pointing out to Leon the historic Stone House which stood at the intersection. After proceeding east, Muncaster stopped to show Leon the old stone bridge crossing Bull Run. A few miles further east, he turned left onto Stone Road, stopping at what looked to Leon like a park with a long, tree-covered mound running through it. Leon thought the earthen sculpture was in a odd place, winding as it did through the middle of a housing development.

As the car halted, Muncaster said, "The Confederate army was never strong enough to attack Washington. So in October 1861, it pulled back to the high ground around Centreville and established a fortified defense line that it occupied for the winter. The earthen wall before you is one of the few remaining sections of a line of fortifications that was once over six miles long. Although the years have worn it down and trees have established themselves, these old defenses are still over six feet high. Some of these works must have been 10-12 feet high in their day. Can you imagine the amount of labor expended in building them? It was a tremendous military engineering effort, constructed by hand, with pick and shovel. Early in the war, it was one of the most strongly fortified positions on the continent. The Centreville line was so strong that the Union army decided not to attack it. When they finally launched another offensive they went in another direction, avoiding this line entirely."

Muncaster continued speaking as he drove back to Route 29. " Having spent the autumn and winter of 1861-62 here, the Confederate troops were intimately familiar with the area. By 1865, however, this region no longer had any major military significance because the fighting had shifted down to Richmond and Petersburg. Being close to Washington, it did offer Benjamin what he needed, a safe place to stash his papers. You have to give the man a lot of credit. Had he been put on trail for treason, he would have been able to put up one hell of a good defense with all the stuff he packed in those two boxes. Also, as he called in his chips, tons of money and political support would have come to him from his friends in the North."

"One of the soldiers--the one named Chambon-- was in the artillery during the early part of the war. Having spent a number of months here, he would have known where all the ammunition storehouses and other storage sites were located. That is why he was picked to make the trip."

As he spoke, Muncaster made a left turn on Pickwick Road and pulled the car to the curb in front of a historical marker located between two houses. "If you look at the diagram of the fortification line, you will see that it ran west-to-east just to the north of the village of Centreville. At a large fort located on a prominent hilltop, the line changed direction and ran north-to-south along the west bank of Little Rocky Run. The big linchpin fort that hinged the lines is located at the end of this path. Let's walk down to it."

As he sauntered behind Muncaster, Leon noticed the narrow path followed the floor of an old trench. The vine and brush covered walls on either side of him gave no indication they had been erected by desperate men during wartime. Because they had made such a good job of it, there had been no fighting here. The soldiers who had labored on these forgotten fortifications had gone on to fight and perhaps die in other places that were now famous locations in the history books. The fort itself, when they finally reached it, was massive. Even though covered by trees and scrub, Leon could see how it commanded the approaches to Centreville. Whoever laid out the fort and its supporting trench line had a good eye for picking the defensive features of the terrain.

After returning to the car, they drove a few blocks to Wharton Lane, where another of the old forts stood. After showing Leon its position on the map of fortifications, Muncaster drove into a church parking lot situated just off the intersection of Wharton Lane and Mt. Gilead Road. He told Leon they would have to park here and walk to the next site which was nearby. Muncaster took a covered package out of the trunk and locked the car. He was sure no one would notice his vehicle in the church lot because visitors were coming and going all the time. As they walked through the church cemetery, Muncaster mentioned that a unknown number of Civil War soldiers had been buried here. Many of the graves had lost their markers in the years after the war, so now no one knew how many or exactly where on the grounds they were buried. They had walked only a few hundred yards on Mt. Gilead Road when Muncaster halted at an iron gate in front of what appeared to be a very old house situated in the middle of large park-like green space filled with stately trees.

"This is a notable place," Muncaster said as he asked Leon to lift the latch and push open the heavy iron gate. He knew the part-time caretaker, a rather eccentric professor at George Mason University was not on the premises. The professor was teaching classes and would not be back until evening. The professor had a good deal. In exchange for living rent free, he resided in the house and made minor repairs now and then. Initially, the arrangement was supposed to last for only a few months until the county government and the local historical society raised the money to turn the old house into a museum. Even in these boom times, the large sums of money needed for the renovation of historical properties were hard to come by. The restoration project had been put on hold due to the slowness of the fund raising effort and the professor was now nearing the end of his second year as a historical house sitter.

As they walked up the curved driveway toward the house, Muncaster said, "It was a very disgruntled Confederate army that entrenched around Centreville during the October of 1861. The war had not ended quickly as the majority of soldiers had expected. The city of Washington remained firmly in Union hands and foreign governments were expressing little interest in recognizing the Confederacy as an independent nation. As the glum army settled in, General Joseph E. Johnston opted to use this dwelling as his personal quarters. It was only a short walk to the Grigsby House that the army was using as headquarters. The Grigsby House, was located just west of here on the other side of those town houses, at what is now approximately Route 28 and the entrance ramp to I66."

Leon looked in the direction Muncaster was pointing. He could see the entrance ramp to the interstate on the other side of the townhouses, the traffic moving swiftly. It was a relatively close location, the distance could easily be walked in less than five minutes. "Given the army's stay at Centreville was going to be a long one," Muncaster continued, "living in separate quarters would afford General Johnston some relief from the constant pressure and unrelenting commotion of the headquarters building."

Leon had expected to see a large mansion house situated on the spacious grounds, a fitting place for a general to reside. The small dwelling before him was a total disappointment; it looked more like a large shed. If this was the best Centreville had to offer a general, it must have been a real down-in-the-heels dump of a village at the time of the Civil War. As he peered into the windows, the rooms looked nondescript, small and cramped. Living there afforded one shelter from the elements and not much else. Other than being very old, the house didn't have anything going for it at all. It and its few dilapidated outbuildings were sad relics left from the long ago days when great armies tromped across the region. Over a century ago, Centreville was a place of national military significance. Now, it was just a name of part of the sprawling high-tech suburbs that occupied the Virginia side of the nation's capital.

Although the house was a disappointment to Leon, the grounds were something else, a true delight. The large, ivy-covered deciduous trees and evergreen Magnolias gave the place a feel of genteel elegance, the look of a proper country estate. The small house sat unobtrusively on three acres of beautifully landscaped grounds. At the rear of the property, Leon could see the headstones peeking through the periwinkle that elegantly carpeted the family cemetery plot. Muncaster said the graves dated back to the period of the Revolutionary War. To right of the old burial ground was a line of Civil War earthworks, the same type they had been looking at for the better part of the day. In his wisdom, General Johnston had ordered a line of defensive trenches and artillery positions built across the backyard of his temporary home. At least the army engineers had the decency to run the trench line around the small graveyard. The owners of the house must have been dismayed to find their property so torn up when they returned after the army moved out in March 1862.

Muncaster was in a good mood as they walked around the grounds admiring the large trees and shrubs, many of which had to be over a 100 years old. His plan was working to perfection. Leon, the dirty turncoat, remained relaxed and unsuspecting. More importantly, they had not been seen as they entered the secluded property. The site was also well-screened from the view of anyone casually passing on the road. "I brought a little something to eat and drink," Muncaster said. "Why don't we sit here among the trees and enjoy the wonderful afternoon sunshine and have lunch." As Leon settled himself against the base of a large oak tree, Muncaster opened the blanket he was carrying and sat himself and the basket on it, facing Leon. As he watched Muncaster unpack the contents, Leon said, "All the walking in the open air has given me quite an appetite. I certainly appreciate you being thoughtful enough to provide lunch."

As Muncaster unpacked the two bottles of mineral water, plastic cups, an assortment of fine cheeses, French bread, tins of caviar, exotic imported spreads and crackers, he watched Leon hungrily eye the feast he was neatly arranging. "I'll bet this no good useless piece of shit hasn't eaten this well in months," Muncaster said to himself under his breath as he placed the jug and flask next to the array of foods. The treacherous swine who had turned against the lobbying profession was about to get his due.

"This is something you might be interested in," Muncaster said as he handed Leon the jug, being careful to leave no finger prints. "This is one of the few surviving jugs we can actually trace back to William Strawderman. If you recall, he was the moonshine whiskey maker who sold to the Union and Confederate forces alike. We believe he also supplied a few of the saloons and at least one of the whorehouses in Washington with whiskey during the war. The old coot lived on a farm located next to the Warrenton Turnpike which is now Route 29. His only fame was due to his claim of making his whiskey exactly the same way George Washington did. The site of his farm is not far from Little Rocky Run. The house is now owned by a developer and has been boarded up for years, but we can stop to see it on the way back if you like."

"This thing is heavy," Leon responded as he took the jug. What's in it?"

"I developed an interest in the people and events surrounding the Civil War as I did my research on the papers. I dug up quite a pile of information and the jug in the process. In keeping with the spirit of the times, I filled it and my flask with top-grade moonshine from southwest Virginia. I thought it would be interesting to try the same stuff the soldiers drank when they were here. Why don't you give it a try," Muncaster said as he unscrewed the flask cap and took a sip. "Wow, this is strong stuff! It's got a real kick to it!" he squeaked as he hurriedly reached for one of the bottles of mineral water.

Although his throat was burning, Muncaster was overjoyed as Leon uncorked the jug and took a stiff swig. "Wash it down with that," he said pointing to the second bottle of mineral water. "Now, let's dig into some of this food. It's not good to drink on an empty stomach." As he spoke, Muncaster handed Leon a large paper plate loaded down with cheeses, bread, and a host of other tasty treats.

As the sat in the balmy sunshine eating and drinking, Muncaster mentioned the historical significance of the house and property. General Johnston quarreled often and long with Confederate President Jefferson Davis while Johnston resided at Centreville. The feud between the general and president, which grew white hot during Johnston's stay in the house, had dire consequences for the Confederacy in 1864 when Davis relieved him as the commander of the army defending Atlanta, Georgia. Johnston's replacement blundered badly and lost the city to the Union army in a defeat that sealed the eventual doom of the Rebel cause. The psychological drama played out between a senior general and a president on these grounds was worthy of a better sign, Muncaster said. Since no battles had been fought in the fortifications, it was the old village of Centreville's only real historical significance.

"Practical politics consists in ignoring facts."
-Henry B. Adams, 1907

Leon agreed with Muncaster's statement and then abruptly changed the subject. "Muncaster," he said, "I really believe the costs of operating the government have gotten completely out of control. The tax payers are being taken to the cleaners by both parties. Why should it cost nearly $3 billion a year to operate Congress? "

Muncaster gave Leon a pained look before replying. "It is money well-spent. It's for the benefit of the American democratic process. It's payment for making the laws of the land. It's an overhead cost of running the best government in the world. The American citizens should be happy to pay."

"That's a bunch of crap, Muncaster and you know it! The founding fathers never intended for Congress to have 31,000 employees and stay in session the year around."

"The country has changed a great deal since your friend George Washington was around to get things started. The legislative role has had to expand to keep up with the needs of the country."

Leon continued to press his point. "Congress could function quite nicely if its staff was only half the present size. The high cost of getting elected to Congress has caused its members to create a mass of jobs for the people who want to spend some time in Washington. The White House is doing the same thing. It costs $300 million a year to operate the President's office and pay for the 1,000 people stumbling over themselves in the hallways. What do most of those people do? I'll tell you! Nothing of any value to the nation. They write memos to each other and to other government agencies! The blizzard of useless paperwork they create keeps 10,000 government workers tied up doing nothing but answering the stuff."

Leon continued to eat and sip whiskey as he talked. That being a good sign, Muncaster kept the conversation going. "Well, I will have to admit things may have gotten slightly out of hand during the past 20 years. I move a lot of papers back and forth between Congress and the White House all day long. So I can see the situation has gotten somewhat out of control. There are certain days when my office can't keep up with the flow. Email has only made things worse. Now we have to watch the computers and the incoming mail at the same time. The paperwork reduction act doesn't apply to government operations, so the only solution is to hire more staff to handle the increased number of letters and messages."

"That's the problem, Muncaster! More staff just leads to a larger volume of paper. They make the problem continually worse, not better! If we reorganized the House of Representatives along economic lines instead of by obsolete geographical districts, Congress could stay out of session six months of the year. There is, you know, no good reason for a legislature to be in session the year around. Congress is not supposed to assume the powers of the President, no matter how much our lawmakers would like to expand their power base. If the right changes were made to our political system, the staffs of Congress and White House would shrink by over 50 percent and the lobbying industry would be reduced in size by 80 percent. We could do so much so easily to restore the people's faith in their system of government. Why, if we succeeded, people might even take a serious interest in voting again!"

"Leon, the people of this great country don't care a damn about making things efficient in Washington. That's the kind work people do in the private sector to compete more effectively and try to stay in business. Efficiency is an economic concept, not a political one. It has absolutely no application to how our government works! We do things to make people feel good about themselves, and no one questions the costs of doing it. "

"Leon, the Washington establishment is not going to put itself out of business just so some yokel in Indiana can have a government that runs itself on the cheap. Our system of political patronage, power through lobbying, and the expansion of staffs provides income for a lot of people. The money spent on elections shows up on the bottom line of the companies providing writers, media exposure and advertising. It puts dollars into the pockets of people like you. Why not just leave things alone? Things are working fine for everyone who counts for anything."

Leon was becoming angry. "How can you say things are just fine! The Congress has been bought by big-money special interests! The same goes for the White House! The never ending need for money has totally corrupted the political system. It's time you took a hard look at how things really are in Washington. Let me give you a few examples. Maria Hsia, a longtime associate of Vice President Gore, has just been convicted of channeling more than $100,000 in illegal contributions to Democratic candidates in 1996. She could be sentenced to as much as 25 years in prison."

Leon continued to continue to tick-off his list of political wrong doing. "An independent counsel is finishing an investigation of Labor Secretary Alexis M. Herman who is charged with seeking hundreds of thousands of dollars in illegal campaign contributions. This is the seventh independent counsel investigation of a Clinton administration official. So far, these investigations have cost the poor taxpayers over $95 million, Don't tell me nothing is wrong in Washington!"

"Don't get all bent out of shape over such minor matters, Leon! The lawyers are happy to have the work. The bulk of the money filters to our friends in the capital, so why should we care if there have been relatively few indictments by the independent counsels during the past six years. A lawyer billing for hours is also a consumer who purchases goods and services. You shouldn't get too uptight over the few bucks being spent to lubricate the political process because it all goes for a worthy cause."

"Muncaster, it's not a little bit of money! We are talking about big money buying tremendous amounts of political influence. The fund raising in the Senate race in New York is an example. Rudolph Giuliani has already raised $19 million so far this year. Hillary Rodham Clinton, the absentee first lady who wants to become a U.S. Senator, has pulled in $12 million. She has also cleverly nicked the White House operating accounts for close to $185,000 to pay for her travel to New York. It's another fine example of how we do things in the nation's capital, spending tax dollars to promote one's own interests."

Muncaster smiled as Leon continued. "I suppose you expect me to believe the big contributors don't expect to get anything back from their friends in Congress? Might they not want something useful like the application of a little political pressure to prevent a tightening of the rules controlling the hours a truck driver can be on the road without a break? Increasing the sleep time of drivers will cost the industry money, so you know they will be dead set against it. Never mind that we know for sure that truck driver fatigue is responsible for 800 fatalities annually. What about the little noticed effort to loosen the standards governing factory-made housing? Who cares if the units blow down in a 50 mile an hour wind. No one lives in those things but trailer trash and they don't contribute to political campaigns! Do you see any movement to loosen the building codes for houses costing $400,000 and up, the ones the lobbyists live in? Of course not! They wouldn't stand for it because occupant safety is a serious concern at those economic levels. I've been a lobbyist for over 30 years. Damn it, Muncaster, I know what political contributions can buy!"

Leon rambled on as Muncaster did his best to pretend he was interested in what Leon had to say. "We need a good dose of reform because the political establishment in this country has lost touch with reality. The White House lamely says it has to spend $3 million to restore thousands of missing email messages that should have been produced for congressional investigations. You and I know it was only another deliberate blatant attempt to avoid responsibility."

"The Republicans are no better. The champions of big business recently sent out a fund raising letter to small givers denouncing Clinton's plan to spend the Social Security surplus on left-wing, social engineering schemes. The letter turned out to be a major embarrassment for the Republican party because a couple of the schemes mentioned -- sewer repair in Salt Lake City, Utah and research funds for reindeer herds in Alaska- - were specifically placed in the budget by senior Republican lawmakers. The humiliating fiasco brought about by the ill-conceived Republican letter points out clearly what everyone in the country instinctively feels-- that there are no real standards for anything in Washington."

"Everything is for sale to the highest bidder. Republicans routinely denounce Democrats for doing the same things they do and vice versa! Are we supposed to believe that left-wing social engineering schemes are no longer left-wing social engineering schemes when the powers of the Republican party support them? While all this ridiculous playacting and posturing is going on in the House of Representatives and the Senate, who looks out for the welfare of the nation? It is certainly is not the occupants of the White House and Congress. Everyone in town is too busy taking care of political friends, chasing campaign contributions and conniving to see that the needs of special interests are included in the federal budget to have any time to worry about the United States of America."

"It is a damn sorry state of affairs, if you ask me. I think it is time to shake up the rotten establishment and get the government back on the path George Washington outlined for us. Congress needs to be knocked back into its rightful role as a legislative body. The president needs to be moved away from his never ending series of photo opportunities and sent back to work in the Oval Office. He really only needs to appear on TV once a week at the most. We all know what he looks like."

As he listened to Leon, who was conformably leaning against a large tree trunk, rave on, Muncaster was becoming worried. They had been sitting here eating, drinking and talking for nearly an hour. The drugged moonshine was having no effect on Leon. He remained wide awake and completely talkative. What had gone wrong? Maybe something in the strong shine had negated the active ingredients of the sleeping drug. Muncaster now wished he had stuck to store bought whiskey because its effects were well known. What if nothing happened to Leon? Or worse, suppose he got sick later and ended up in a hospital. Muncaster was sure to be charged with attempted murder after they pumped out the old fool's stomach and found the drug concoction. Muncaster was having the same sinking feeling he felt on late Friday afternoons when the Secretary threw a big pile of rush projects on his desk and wrecked his plans for the weekend.

Leon had been eating and drinking the best foods and liquid refreshments Washington had to offer for many years. Perhaps over time, his system had built up a massive tolerance to whatever he put into his stomach. It was not uncommon for a lobbyist to converse, eat, drink and go without sleep for a couple of days if he or she was in hot pursuit of legislation that helped a client. Once the adrenaline got flowing, they stayed keyed-up until the deal got done. Lobbyists were very goal-oriented people in that respect.

Muncaster was trapped in the yard of an old house with a madman who didn't have decency enough to die when he was poisoned. How long could they sit here before another visitor came along and discovered them? The one thing all Civil War buffs had in common was they liked to talk. The last thing Muncaster wanted was for someone to try to begin a conversation while he was in the company of Leon Placke. That would surely increase the chances of the cops placing him at the scene of Leon's death. Once the police made an identification, they would be all over him like ants on a gob of honey. He would be out of wiggle room, it would be very difficult to avoid being implicated.

As he sat watching Leon, Muncaster thought about the Russian monk, Rasputin, who developed a degree of political power from his association with the Russian royal family in the early days of World War I. Rasputin must have been a lot like Leon. After Rasputin had been poisoned by those wishing to remove his embarrassing presence from the governing circles of Russia, he refused to die and finally had to be shot to death on a public street. As Muncaster remembered, it had been a very messy affair.

Muncaster cursed himself for failing to prepare for all possible contingencies. He had no back-up plan to use if the drug did not do its work. By not being fully prepared to shift to an alternate plan, Muncaster realized that he lacked a lot of what was needed to be a successful murderer or a political shaker and mover in Washington. He would have to work on sharpening his skills if he was going to make it in the dog-eat-dog world of lobbying.

Leon was never going to shut up and Muncaster was growing more desperate by the minute. Not sure of what to do next, he stood up. Perhaps if he looked around, he could find a large rock and bash the old fart in the head with it. He would still be in the clear if he got off the property unseen before the house-sitting professor returned. "Excuse me," he said to Leon. "I'm

395

going to walk over to the fortification over there and stretch my legs. Want to come along?"

"Maybe I should," Leon responded. "It wouldn't hurt to walk off the effects of the delightful food and drink you so thoughtfully provided."

As Leon began to push himself up, his legs suddenly gave out and he slid back down against the tree trunk. "On second thought, I feel tired, so I think I'll just sit here for a few minus and rest. You go right ahead without me," he sleepily muttered.

"No problem," Muncaster said. "I'll just walk around the yard and come back for you in a few minutes." He was overjoyed. Although it had taken over a nerve-wracking hour, the sleeping prescription mixed in the booze was finally taking effect. With a little more luck, the pain-in-the-ass Leon Placke would not be bothering anyone in Washington ever again.

Leon felt good. He didn't have a care in the world on this balmy day. As he began to comfortably doze, the refrain of a old song began to wander across his relaxing mind. "While soft falls the dew on the face of the dead, the picket is off duty forever. All quiet along the Potomac tonight." Leon tried his best to remember what a picket was. Picket fences didn't have a face, so that couldn't be it. Then it came to him. Although he couldn't remember exactly at what period in the nation's history it was, at some time in the old days, army sentries were sometimes called pickets. Leon tried to figure out why a picket died on the bank of the Potomac River, gave up thinking about it, and slid into a deep, untroubled sleep.

Muncaster walked to the fortification, being careful to keep out of sight of the road. The large mound-like structure of grass covered earth had been an artillery position containing six guns. The dips in the wall from which cannon had once protruded were still visible. The quiet suburban road must have been of major military significance at one time because the bastion had been built to control it. The connecting trench line running to the right crossed the road and ran between two houses on the other side of the street. It had once gone all the way to the large fort they had visited earlier. To the left, the trench line ran in a westerly direction across the rear of the property and abruptly halted. From that point onward it had been obliterated by the new home construction on the other side of the property line. Having satisfied himself that General Johnston's military engineers knew what they were doing a hundred plus years ago, Muncaster slowly walked back to check on Leon's condition. He found Leon slumped against the tree, either fast asleep or unconscious. When Muncaster gave him a nudge it was apparent that the unresponsive Leon was slipping away. Muncaster gleefully concluded the trouble making days of Leon Placke were coming to a well-deserved end.

Muncaster carefully cleaned up the leftovers, taking everything with him except the whiskey jug, one of water bottles and the food containers with only Leon's fingerprints on them. He made his way back to the large iron gate, closing it with a hand wrapped in a napkin so as not to leave any of his prints. There were no cars on the road as Muncaster walked slowly back to the church parking lot pausing now and then and pretending to admire the shrubs and trees along the way.

Crossing the intersecting street, he entered the graveyard, and not wanting to look out of place, stopped by a large magnolia tree to read an inscription on a headstone. It was the final resting place of two Confederate soldiers executed by a firing squad in early 1862. The two Louisiana toughs had gotten themselves drunk, precipitated a wild brawl in camp and then tried to stick a knife into the lieutenant who tried to break up the fight. For their transgression, they had been tried by courts-martial, convicted and shot. As he read, Muncaster began to feel a degree of affinity with the commander who ordered the long-ago executions. The two soldiers had gone before the firing squad as a demonstration to the unruly rank and file that army discipline could not be breached without penalty. For many of the same reasons the army commander had acted to eliminate a bad influence on his troops, Muncaster had executed Leon Placke. His undisciplined behavior had become a threat to the orderly functioning of the Washington establishment.

The only difference between the two executions was that Muncaster had been forced to act in private. The general in charge of the Confederate executions was James Longstreet. Muncaster made a mental note to look up his biography because the incident would provide an interesting topic of conversation. Muncaster was also stuck by the fact that the more things changed, the more they stayed the same. He and the general had done what had to be done to keep order. Muncaster felt good, as a future Washington lobbyist with a great deal of potential should.

After threading his way through the cemetery, Muncaster climbed into his car and exited the church parking lot. He was sure he hadn't been noticed because no one paid the slightest attention to the constant stream of Civil War buffs who were forever wandering around the place. Leaving the backwater of the old village of Centreville behind, Muncaster made a left turn on Route 29. Shortly after crossing the bridge over Little Rocky Run, he passed the neglected, boarded-up Strawderman house on the left side of the road. "Here's to you William," Muncaster said laughingly as he threw the old structure a salute with a wave of his arm. "In your time and in mine, too much strong drink can have bad consequences for those who imbibe too much."

As he drove back to Washington becoming more upbeat with each passing minute, Muncaster ruminated over the knowledge he had gained from the headstone in the graveyard. So those who stood to benefit from what he had done would remember his notable service to the lobbying community, Muncaster mentally composed an inscription for Leon's tombstone. He decided it should read: "Here lies a traitor to the lobbying profession. Executed by H. Muncaster Swindell on behalf of the Washington Establishment." Of course it couldn't really be stated that way, but Muncaster enjoyed thinking about it.

The lobbying community, however, now owed him a great deal for taking the initiative and silencing Leon Placke before he did more damage. It was mentally invigorating to think about the ways he could collect the rewards due him. In his mind's eye, he could see a roomful of thankful lobbyists rising to give him a standing ovation. For his disposal of Leon Placke, H. Muncaster Swindell would be warmly welcomed to take his place among the city's lobbying elite. In a few years, he would surpass the record established by the memorable Mr. Placke as he became the ultimate Washington insider. Muncaster would be the man to call if a politically sensitive deal had to get done. With his unparalleled access to the White House, Congress and government agencies, Muncaster would be the most celebrated lobbyist the capital of the United States had ever seen. Muncaster was elated. His plan had come together perfectly. Muncaster was right where he wanted to be, involved enough in the matter to gain a degree of career boosting publicity, but legally beyond suspicion as a suspect in the death of the double-crosser who betrayed Washington's most hallowed institution.

May 2000

"Not necessity, not desire—no, the love of power is the demon of men. Let them have everything—health, food, a place to live, entertainment—they are and remain unhappy and low-spirited: for the demon waits and waits and will be satisfied."

-Friedrich Nietzsche, 1881

Having learned in politics that the best defense is a good offense, Muncaster called the police after the discovery of Leon's corpse was mentioned on the evening news the day after Leon died. According to Muncaster's version of events, he and Leon had traveled to Chapman's mill and then made stops at a few locations along the old Confederate fortification line. In the afternoon, Leon asked to be dropped off near the church saying he wanted to walk around the area before meeting unspecified friends for dinner at a nearby eatery. His friends would see to it he got home. After dinner, they would take him to the Vienna Metro station. From there, Leon planned to ride the subway back to Washington.

Leon had a paper bag with him. Although Muncaster had not seen its contents, it must have contained the jug of whiskey and the other items found near the body. Sometime after bidding Muncaster goodbye, Leon must have walked to the house, sat himself down at the base of the tree and killed himself. Muncaster showed the police the maps and documents he had taken on the excursion. The fingerprints matched. Further police investigation turned up witnesses who remembered seeing Muncaster and Leon at two of the sites. They appeared to the onlookers to be two visitors with an interest in the Civil War, nothing unusual was noticed. Muncaster's story checked out, appearing to be truthful in all respects.

The house-sitting professor was another matter. He became so distraught upon being informed that a dead man had been found in his yard that, for a time, the police thought he was faking and trying to hide something. It didn't seem logical to the suspicious police officers that the person who occupied this particular dwelling would become completely unglued over the discovery of a set of modern human remains. Any person who had such qualms regarding proximity to the dead would not have dared to live in old Centreville. During the Civil War, dead and the dying soldiers had filled the village after two battles. Many of the superstitious local residents believed the restless spirits of the departed soldiery still haunted the place, the police knew that. From time to time, officers responded to calls reporting the sighting of blue or gray phantoms near what were once the main roads of the village. However, after careful checking, the professor's alibi held. He was at George Mason University at the time Leon Placke died. Reliable witnesses vouched for his presence on campus, he could not have been involved in any way.

After evaluating the evidence, the police determined Leon committed suicide. He probably selected the historical house as the location of his final act because his career had begun to unravel after his attempt to conceal the Civil War papers from the public. Until their recent discovery, the Confederate government documents and artifacts that had embarrassed many prominent individuals and institutions had been buried at Centreville. It was easy to understand why the troubled, nearly bankrupt, out-of-work former lobbyist had gravitated to General Johnston's temporary home. It was secluded, seldom visited at this time of the year and easily accessible. Placke's strange contention that he had developed a relationship with George Washington made the selection of this location even more obvious. As much as he might have desired to do so, Placke could never have killed himself at George Washington's Mt. Vernon home or gristmill. Those were busy places, constantly patrolled by security guards. All the evidence pointed to the one conclusion, no foul play was involved. With all the investigators in agreement, the bizarre case of Leon Placke's death was closed.

There was no sorrow in Washington over the passing of Leon Placke. Having been the last person of consequence to see Placke alive made Muncaster an instant Washington luminary. Washington society buzzed with speculation regarding the extent of his involvement. How had he so ingeniously silenced the scourge of the Washington establishment? He was bombarded with invitations to Capitol Hill social events and to lunches with the city's high-powered lobbyists. Even the usually cantankerous Secretary of Commerce began treating him with a new sense of respect. The possibility that Muncaster may have had a hand in Placke's demise, made Muncaster a person worth knowing. No one in the national seat of political intrigue was naive enough to believe Muncaster had taken Placke for an innocent ride through the Virginia countryside merely to view an old mill and fortifications. H. Muncaster Swindell found himself the capital's man of the hour. He had crossed the line between talking about policy and taking action, and got away with murder.

After months of preparation, protesters brought a large chuck of Washington to a close as they attempted to disrupt the Washington meetings of the World Bank and the International Monetary Fund. Although the protest was not the tear gas drenched street battle over global capitalism as had previously occurred in Seattle, the strains imposed by the rapidly changing global economy were apparent. The vast cross-border flows of goods, money, people and information made rich and poor nations, workers and multinational firms, more than a bit nervous. The workers blamed the capitalists for their troubles while the environmentalists condemned the global firms for fostering environmental devastation. At the same time, in the less-developed nations, people struggled to gain access to clean water, motor vehicles and television sets despite the impediments imposed on their economic development by flawed political systems.

In the national political arena, the two major parties ended their internal bloodletting. In February, multimillionaire candidate Steve Forbes dropped out of the Republican presidential race after a poor showing in the Delaware primary. A few days later, conservative activist Gary Bauer shut down his presidential campaign, saying his message had caught on with the other candidates. In March, Senator John McCain called it quits after warning the Republican party to heed his call for reform or risk slipping into political obsolescence. Former Senator Bill Bradley, who at one point in the primary campaign appeared to a formidable challenger for the Democratic nomination, also gave up his quest for the White House. As the dust from the expensive, bruising primary contests began to settle, the winners-- Vice President Al Gore and Texas Governor George W. Bush--began to hurl barbs at each other in earnest. Behind the scenes, they renewed the scramble to line up contributions for their election campaigns.

The peace deal, brokered by the United States and other nations in Sierra Leone, disintegrated as the rebels captured and took hostage hundreds of the UN peacekeepers assigned to keep peace between the warring factions. In Boston, Vice President Gore made a speech in which he sketched out a foreign policy based on a broad engagement with vital partners, and a willingness to move swiftly to counter threats posed by rogue states. He said it was time to abandon the cold war mentality propagated by his Republican opponent, Texas Governor George W. Bush. Polls reported the voter fatigue with President Clinton was rapidly changing to nostalgia because the Clinton years had been, in general, good ones for the nation. Six months before the election of his successor, there was a growing realization among voters that, no matter how they felt about Clinton's personal life, as a political talent President Clinton was in a class far above his contemporaries.

President Clinton had also been a blessing to the legal profession. The new independent counsel, Robert W. Ray, asked the Justice Department for

$3.5 million to cover the expenses incurred in the continuing investigation of President Clinton's relationship with Monica Lewinsky.

George W. Bush, speaking before a major Republican fundraising dinner attended by 1500 guests, vowed to end the arms race of anger and return civility and integrity to the bitterly divided partisan politics of Washington. The black-tie gala netted him $21 million in contributions. Hillary Rodham Clinton's U.S. Senate campaign office in New York returned a $22,000 contribution from a Miami businesswoman who played a role in obtaining a 1996 donation to the Democratic Party from an international drug trafficker.

Democrats in the U.S. House of Representatives filed a civil suit against the Majority Whip, Republican Tom DeLay. The suit alleged DeLay pressured contributors into donating to the Republican Party and then placed those funds into the hands of nonprofit political groups that did not disclose their donors or how the money was spent. The quick-witted DeLay had apparently established a shadow political organization that evaded the already weak campaign finance laws by funneling donations into secretive organizations. Afraid that the DeLay controlled groups were about to flood certain congressional races with money, the Democrats launched their preemptive legal action.

A large Washington law firm reported it had been paid $440,000 to help protect an investor group's interests in a Siberian oil field during a Washington-based lobbying battle with a competing group. The payment was for work to ensure the State Department and the Export Import Bank would not renege on the U.S. government backing for the project loan guarantees.

"Politics is just like show business, you have a hell of an opening, coast for a while and then have a hell of a close."
-Ronald Reagan, 1966

The Washington establishment was in its glory. Presidential and congressional candidates were going to spend a whopping $3 billion on political campaigns in the year 2000, a hefty 50 percent increase over the amount spent during the 1996 election. In the city's political consulting businesses, the exalted strategists and specialized technicians who made and remade candidates, decided which issues were important to voters, raised money and produced television ads, were gearing up for a record season. It was a good time to be in the business end of politics. A good media strategist could earn $1 million a year by creating and placing winning attack ads on television. In the hyper-political environment of the 2000 elections, $600 million was going to be spent getting televised messages out to the voters.

The frenzied buying of air time was already underway. Media schedulers were blocking out prime time slots, often also netting themselves a fat commission for the time commitment. In other offices, political fund raisers were establishing a foothold on the Internet. With nearly 60 million American households online, running a fund raising campaign online was a new way into the pockets of potential contributors.

A rash of fund raising dinners swept the country. A Saturday night Beverly Hills benefit for the Democratic National Committee netted $2.8 million, mostly from Hollywood's movie-making set. At a fund raiser in Louisiana, President Clinton raised more than $400,000 for the same committee at a luncheon speech attended by a mere 40 donors. In a downtown New York city hotel, the President's presence brought over $2 million into the Democrat's coffers. A few days later, Vice President Gore raised $3.5 million for the Democrat's war chest from a group of Florida trial lawyers.

In the American pay-to-play political system, campaign contributions guaranteed access to politicians. The times were obliging to Republicans and Democrats alike as political donors wrote bigger checks and more often. Contributions of $100,000 were becoming so commonplace they were hardly worth noting. Once a rarity in politics, contributions ranging in size from $200,000 to $350,000 were now flowing in a steady stream into the treasuries of both parties from wealthy individuals, corporations, labor unions and anyone else with a desire to influence policy-making or legislation. In Congress, a group of electronics firms were pressing legislators to normalize trade relations with China and credit industry lobbyists were pushing to tighten consumer bankruptcy laws. Congress continued to struggle with finalizing the $1.8 trillion federal budget, trying to ensure there was a little something in it for everyone.

President Clinton was readying a financial privacy protection law that would give consumers sweeping new powers to control how corporations shared customer information. While the proposed legislation was praised by consumer groups, industry executives thought it was far too stringent. The corporate lobbying cadre was put on notice. The law protecting consumer privacy had to be watered down before passage. In Colorado, the regional director of the Environmental Protection Agency's Denver office was suspended for illegally helping to raise money for congressional candidates in his region.

Wealthy Texas businessman Sam Wyly, who spent $2.5 million on ads praising George W. Bush and his record on the environment, received an award for his environmental work. Dallas businessman, Fred Meyer was named by Bush to take charge of the Republican National Committee's general election fund raising effort.

The White House sent to Congress a thick package of email correspondence dealing with former intern Monica Lewinsky which it said had been lost due to computer glitches. Because of consumer resistance to genetically altered potatoes, the McDonalds Corporation instructed its growers not to plant them despite proven improved crop growth and less need for chemicals. Two no-show Buddhist nuns were indicted for failing to appear as government witnesses at a trial in which a Democratic party fund raiser was convicted of arranging illegal contributions.

The State Department charged Lockheed Martin Corporation with violating the Arms Export Control act. The firm had provided rocket motor assistance to the Chinese. Although Lockheed Martin faced as much as $15 million in fines, leniency was expected. The firm's political action committee had, after all, donated more than $1 million to Republicans and Democrats during the last election. The CIA fired one intelligence officer and reprimanded six others for making the errors that led to the mistaken bombing of the Chinese Embassy in Belgrade during NATO's air attacks against Yugoslavia.

A study by the Centers for Disease Control and Prevention concluded that cheap beer led to higher rates of gonorrhea. Alcohol was found to be directly linked to risky sexual behavior among young people. The cheaper the beer, the more young people could afford to drink and the easier it was for them to get into trouble. In a stunning decision, the Clinton White House formally designated AIDS as a threat to U.S. national security because it could topple foreign governments, touch off ethnic wars and undo free-market democracies. Budget requests to combat AIDS overseas were immediately doubled to $254 million and a new White House interagency working group was established.

A research group found fault with many of the performance reports recently issued by the largest federal agencies. These reports, which were required by law, were supposed to disclose to taxpayers what they were getting for their money. The research group also hinted that Congress was doing a poor job of holding agencies accountable to the taxpayers because it was spending too much of its time playing partisan politics and not overseeing the vast operations of the U.S. Government. The research group's findings were not well-received well on Capitol Hill. Congress acted unusually swiftly, the research group's contract with Congress was terminated.

In the first big antitrust case of the new century, the U.S. Department of

Justice won a court decision against Microsoft Corporation proposing that the company be split in two. Microsoft had come to dominate the personal computer operating systems software market in a relatively sort period of time and was ruthlessly exterminating all vestiges of competition. The firm vowed to fight the ruling, saying the problem was not with Microsoft, but with the American system of justice. The case was being closely watched by the Washington establishment because of the large legal costs involved. The lawyers, however, did not have the lucrative Microsoft playing field to themselves. Microsoft had poured $4.6 million into its lobbying effort during 1999. Monopolistic or not, Microsoft had become one of the darlings of the Washington establishment.

In a change of heart, Ralph Reed, a prominent lobbyist, shocked Microsoft and Washington when he issued a statement of regret for taking on the job of drumming up nationwide grass-roots support for the firm just as the software giant was embarking on its legal battle with the Justice Department. Reed had been hired to curry favor with anyone having access to the leading politicians of both parties. Issuing a statement of regret for doing what one was hired to do was a very unusual practice for a lobbyist. Leon Placke had gone crazy, was Ralph Reed the next lobbyist to go? Some in the business thought the professionalism of lobbyists was falling to a new low.

In current election spending, Microsoft had given Democrats over $8 million and the Republicans another $8.6 million. When Bill Gates, Microsoft's chairman, swept through Capitol Hill a few days after a federal judge had branded the company a lawbreaking monopoly, Gates found he still had many friends in the lawmaking establishment. He was treated with the deference and respect due a national business superstar. In Congress, many on both sides of the aisle let it be loudly known that the government was being too tough on the firm which had done so much to develop America's vast information industry. Mr. Gates was also greeted warmly by the President at the White House. Gates sat next to the President and was the featured speaker at the White House conference on the new economy. Gates didn't seem too worried. Even if Microsoft was broken up, analysts predicted the value of the stock in the two reorganized firms would continue to rise. As a major stockholder, Bill Gates was not going to lose, no matter what the legal outcome.

In Arkansas, President Clinton was battling to keep his license to practice law. A group had begun an effort to have him disbarred on the grounds that his evasive testimony in the Paula Jones sexual harassment case violated the code of conduct for lawyers. The politically hot potato of disbarring a sitting president from the practice of law was to be taken up by the Arkansas

Committee on Professional Conduct. It was another major embarrassment for the President. He had already been found in contempt for making false statements by the U.S. District Court judge who presided over the original case. In a bold display of new legal strategy, President Clinton argued in his defense that many categories of responses which are misleading, evasive, nonresponsive or frustrating are nevertheless not legally false. This also included literally truthful answers that imply facts that are not true. Every lawyer and lobbyist in Washington was closely following the proceedings. It was going to be a true battle of the best legal minds money could buy.

Muncaster found there was a downside to his new-found fame. The many rounds of socializing had added over five pounds to his weight in a few short weeks. Being too gracious to turn down a free meal and drinks, Muncaster decided he was going to have to make room for exercise time in his busy schedule. It was either that, or start buying larger clothes.

With the unanimous blessing of Congress, the Secretary of Commerce announced a new $22 million trade enforcement program to monitor the Chinese Government and ensure it lived up to its trade commitments. With a rapid response team of trade specialists, the enforcement program was to be the largest ever directed at another country. Muncaster's growing prominence served him well. When the management positions for the enforcement team were created, Muncaster was selected for one of the top jobs although he knew nothing about China and very little about international trade matters. What counted most was his numerous new patrons in high places. Muncaster was well regarded on Capitol Hill and throughout the lobbying community. Muncaster was delighted with the way things were going, a substantial pay raise and unlimited access to Washington's top decision makers were enough to brighten anyone's day. With a larger staff at his disposal, Muncaster could comfortably concentrate his efforts on developing lobbying contacts while fobbing the work onto the backs of the civil servants.

Arrogance fit Muncaster's personality perfectly, like an expensive glove on the hand of a pretender to a medieval throne. As he lunched with the best legal minds in the city, Muncaster adroitly dodged all questions as to how Leon Placke had met his end. He and his hosts did have many a good laugh over whether or not Leon's demise should be considered murder. It was a serious ethical question worthy of much deep thought. All agreed that other legal considerations didn't apply in this case. To investigate the matter and make an arrest would be an monumental and tragic waste of police and prosecutor's time. It was a matter of ignoring the legal technicalities in order not to interfere with something that was right and just in its own right. This was one of those times, as any good lawyer understood, when it was in the best interest of justice to do nothing.

The conversation then turned, as it always did at Washington power lunches, to the state of national politics. John McCain had put the bitterness of the primary battles behind him and endorsed George W. Bush as the Republican candidate for president. While they agreed on the need to reform education, health care, the military and Social Security, McCain remained adamant about the need for campaign finance reform. Muncaster and his luncheon partners thought it was likely McCain had been incurably infected with Leon's crazy ideas. McCain's many years as a prisoner of war in Vietnam probably had rendered his mind susceptible to such oddball ideas. Why else would he hang on to a concept of no interest to anyone else in Washington?

McCain's spirited primary campaign had forced Bush to spend tons of money to beat him, putting a serious dent in Bush's campaign war chest. McCain also publicly stated he would not accept an offer to run as Bush's vice president. Although out of the race, polls showed the feisty McCain still appealing to 23 percent of the voters. If Bush was going to whip Al Gore in the November election, he had to get McCain involved in his campaign. Muncaster's luncheon partners thought Bush ought to offer McCain a cabinet post, Secretary of Defense would be most appropriate, and use his potential participation in the new administration as a drawing card to attract the independent-minded swing voters so crucial to winning the election. If Bush was going to win, the Republicans were going to have to learn to live with at least some of McCain's unpleasant campaign reform proposals. That thought wasn't all that appealing to those seated at the table. After all, Vice President Al Gore was a fine man and quite capable of leading the nation. Would the interests of Washington's lobbying elite be better served by a Gore presidency?

While Mucaster and his cohorts lunched on culinary delights and imbibed the finest spirits at one of Washington's most exclusive restaurants, military engineers were struggling with the complex problem of building an antimissile defense system. President Clinton was scheduled to decide during the autumn whether to make an all out push to build the missile shield by 2005, a date by which intelligence agencies warned certain rogue states would have ballistic missiles capable of reaching the United States. The estimated costs of the National Missile Defense system ranged between $12 and $60 billion, an almost prohibitive cost . Although the costs were deemed high, the alternative was much worse. None of the nation's leaders wanted to be placed in the position of having to explain at some future date how a missile fired from a rogue state managed to hit a major American city. As serious as it was, the threat of urban incineration by missile attack was not a matter the politicians cared to push to the forefront in their discussions with voters because they instinctively knew Americans did not like to hear discomforting news from candidates for high office. A mere 50 years after the Japanese Imperial Navy won a smashing victory at Pearl Harbor, the people of the United States had fully slipped back into the habit of underestimating the abilities of potential adversaries.

An email virus known as the "love bug" raged through the world's computers causing $8 billion in damage as it destroyed computer files and disabled systems. The FBI and police agencies throughout the world were searching for the perpetrator. In Richmond, Virginia, the NAACP and the Sons of Confederate Veterans were exchanging heated words over a Confederate history month proclamation issued by the governor. In the graveyards of Virginia, the Union and Confederate soldiers paid no heed to the controversy. Their long-ago sacrifices had evolved into the foundation of the state's $12 billion-a-year tourism industry.

The amount of energy used by one American was equivalent to that used by three Germans, six Mexicans and 14 Chinese. In the Persian Gulf, the oil fueling a large part of the world's economy continued to flow unimpeded out of wells from Oman to Kuwait as American military aircraft flew constant patrols over Iraq. In the United States, the people blissfully ignored anything having to do with the U.S. military campaign that successfully drove the Iraqi invaders out of Kuwait. It was almost as if America's first oil war fought only a few years previously, had never happened.

In Washington, a contract employee hired by the U.S. Department of Education to manage its telephone and computer needs pleaded guilty to carrying out a scheme which bilked the government out of more than $1 million. The employee had avoided suspicion because he steered telephones, computers and other equipment to the Education Department employees who were overseeing his work.

The overlap between corporate money and public policy was an open secret in Washington. While energy deregulation did not interest the average American, it was of extraordinary interest to the $300 billion a year power industry. Over lunch with new friends, Muncaster learned the details of how some of the nation's largest electric utilities had funneled millions of dollars through two secret front groups -- one with Republican ties, the other linked to the Democrats-- in a lobbying effort to stop Congress from deregulating the electric utility industry. The goal of the $17 million undertaking was to prevent the undesirable legislation from moving forward in Congress.

Muncaster was electrified as he listened to how the organizers had launched a massive radio ad campaign and barraged selected members of Congress with volumes of telegrams and letters in their successful effort to bottle up the legislation. Thinking of everything, they shrewdly made their effort look like a spontaneous outpouring of genuine interest from the voters back home. Muncaster was fascinated by the cleverness demonstrated by this first rate piece of lobbying work. It was far superior to anything the late Leon Placke could have done, even in his glory days as the undisputed king of the lobbyists. As he conversed with his table partners, Muncaster was nearly overcome by a burst of patriotic fervor. He definitely wanted to put his law degree to work helping to make the big decisions affecting the American public.

The missing White House email files continued to roil the political waters. Investigators discovered that four White House computer specialists had been warned of extremely dire consequences if they talked to outsiders about the computer glitch that kept the thousands of email messages requested by subpoenas from being located. Investigators also found no attempt had been made to fix the underlying computer programming errors even though the cause was known. It suspiciously appeared as though senior White House officials did not want the glitch fixed because it allowed them to avoid turning over an accumulation of missing email messages subpoenaed during a criminal investigation of the administration.

Loyalty to one's political benefactor had always been highly regarded in Washington, regardless of the party involved. For her valuable service to the Clinton administration, the woman who silenced the computer specialists was rewarded with promotion to the position of chief of information at the Department of Labor. Although many Americans were horrified by the revelation that the White House deliberately hindered a criminal investigation, Muncaster thought it to have been a gutsy move. The woman had what it took to make it in the capital city. Although she would most likely be out of a job after the November election, Muncaster wanted to meet her. He knew she had a great future in the lobbying profession.

China was worried. Its top arms negotiator warned the United States that its proposed system to shoot down missiles could neutralize China's own defenses, forcing China to deploy more warheads. China, as a developing country, did not want to spend its precious resources to counter the proposed U.S. system. The Chinese government, however, could not simply rely on U.S. assurances that the American missile shield would be designed to protect the United States from attack by smaller rogue states such as North Korea, Iraq and Iran.

Foreign intelligence agencies, noting Washington's slavish preoccupation with media coverage, had not been idle. The FBI told a House of Representatives hearing that foreign spies, working undercover as news correspondents, had gained unescorted access to the State Department. Stung by yet another reported security lapse, Secretary of State Madeleine Albright called for an internal investigation saying, "we obviously don't want spies posing as journalists." President Clinton, who daily received the highest-level intelligence briefings, agreed the issue should be looked into and blandly said it was the first time he had heard of the allegation. After all, these lethal international security matters had nothing at all to do with real political issues. Mixing it up with the voters and telling them what they wanted to hear was where the real action was.

Muncaster was being run ragged. His busy social schedule often precluded him from putting in more than five hours per day at his office. In order to rectify the lack of attention to his official duties, Muncaster manipulated the human resources system he knew so well and obtained pay raises for two of his most trusted subordinates. Having thus guaranteed their cooperation, Muncaster charged them with the weighty task of covering for him and managing the flow of work during his long absences.

A notice from the White House reminding federal agencies to inform employees of their obligations to the taxpaying public during the reduction of waste, fraud and abuse week arrived on Muncaster's desk about the same time as the approved pay raise documents came from the human resources department. As he finished a draft memorandum to departmental employees encouraging them to avoid wastage of paper, pens and other office materials, Muncaster saw not the slightest tinge of hypocrisy in his actions. After all, Washington was a city in which the Golden Rule had been slightly changed to: "do as I say and not as I do." It was the most important rule newcomers to government service had to quickly learn.

After being in Washington for a few months, only a complete blockhead would fail to realize that those at the top of the political pyramid were exempt from the rules that stringently governed the conduct of those occupying the lower levels. What was lauded as a shrewd action if undertaken by an upper level intellectual was, at the same time, an immediate firing offense if attempted by some mindless slob situated on the lower rungs of the bureaucratic structure. Over the years, Muncaster had always been surprised by the large number of people who had difficulty grasping this simple concept. He also noticed that those who wanted to make it big in the capital absorbed the implications quickly. It was the most vital of the ingredients necessary to a successful career.

Muncaster gave the draft message on curbing waste to the auto pen operator to affix the signature of the Secretary as he departed for another important luncheon meeting. His hosts of the day were considered to be at the forefront of developing new lobbying techniques. They believed members of Congress were too busy making speeches and raising campaign contributions to have time to study national issues and properly legislate the laws of the land. To help ease the hectic pace of legislators' everyday life, the lobbyists had taken upon themselves the mundane task of drafting the legislation to be introduced in Congress. At the urging of a coalition of pesticide manufacturers, agricultural organizations and food processors, the brazen lobbyists prepared a draft law weakening the regulation of dangerous pesticides. After a lengthy search, the lobbyists found a sympathetic House member from California who introduced the legislation as his own creation. Within a few weeks, a majority of the members of the House of Representatives and 38 U.S. Senators had signed onto the legislation as cosponsors, virtually ensuring its passage.

The lobbyists, who had been well compensated for their work, outlined to Muncaster the legislative areas in which they saw lucrative possibilities for applying their specialized brand of technical legislative assistance. Anticipating a bright future for their firm, these new generation lobbyists were boldly taking advantage of the trend toward specialization in Congress. Muncaster had to admit that his hosts were on target. Locked into a life of raising campaign funds and denouncing vile opponents, the good members of Congress could ill afford the time to investigate and prepare legislation. The growing void would have to be filled by professional lobbyists. As loyal, patriotic Americans, it was the least they could do. Muncaster was proud to have made the acquaintance of a fine band of distinguished professionals who were making a valuable contribution to the nation's welfare.

"Finishing second in the Olympics gets you silver. Finishing second in politics gets you oblivion,"

-Richard M. Nixon, 1988

Muncaster and his friends next discussed the growing interest of Americans in politics. All types of special interest groups were rushing to finance components of the 2000 election. By taking advantage of legal loopholes, large sums of money from undisclosed sources was pouring into campaigns. Secret money was running television ads, sending mailings and paying for telephone calls to voters that mentioned candidates by name and promoted specific agendas. About $160 million in uncontrolled so called soft

411

money had been raised thus far in the campaign, divided about equally between the Republicans and Democrats. It didn't matter the slightest to Muncaster that the voters had little or no idea of who was paying to influence them. It was an essential part of the refined political media blitz aimed at enticing a vote out of a voter by any means possible.

After departing from his gracious friends who also mentioned their gratitude for any assistance he may have provided to the departure of Leon Placke, Muncaster headed back to the office after the leisurely three hour lunch. He had to catch up on his reading. Keeping oneself informed of the issues of the day was a requirement of his job. And as one never knew when something might come along that would be of personal benefit, Muncaster willingly devoted a great deal of time to the task. He began with a report stating the amount of U.S. currency in circulation had risen from $3 billion in 1910 to $517 billion in 2000. It meant nothing to Muncaster, so he tossed it into the trash can. Next was an intelligence appraisal of the new oil field in the northern Caspian Sea off the coast of Kazakhstan. It was going to be a large one, containing between 8 and 50 billion barrels of oil. Although the new field would make the Clinton administration's proposal to build a $2.4 billion, 1,000 mile pipeline to Turkish ports viable, Muncaster wasn't interested in the project because the old guard lobbying firms had all the oil firms as clients. The report went into the trash.

The next item was a staff paper outlining the auto makers' worries over potential changes in the corporate average fuel economy standards set by Congress. The combination of higher gasoline prices and lobbying by environmentalists had provoked Congress into considering tightening the standards. A change would cost manufacturers a bundle if they were forced to improve the fuel efficiency of new models. Costly as it might be to the bottom line and stockholders dividends, the car problem was of no concern to Muncaster. The ranks of the auto industry's lobbyists were chock-full, no opportunity there for him.

A runaway blaze started by the National Park Service devastated a sizable part of Los Alamos, New Mexico along with 42,000 acres of public and private land. Damage estimates were hovering near $1 billion. Interior Secretary Bruce Babbitt was confident the government would provide financial aid to the stricken residents. Although the destruction of a good sized part of a town by a fire set by a government agency was a sad affair, the information was of no use to Muncaster. He tossed the report. In the next document he read, the Treasury Department proudly announced the government was running a surplus of $124 billion thus far in the fiscal year. As he discarded the Treasury news release, Muncaster wondered if the amount of the mentioned surplus was before or after the expenses of the Los Alamos fire fiasco had been paid.

Muncaster carefully read the campaign news digest prepared by a watchdog group. George W. Bush had sent letters seeking advice on choosing a running mate to 450 leading Republicans. What was Bush going to do if 300 of the party stalwarts responded by saying they were the best choice available for the Vice Presidency? Vice President Gore's top advisors met in Nashville to figure out ways to improve Gore's dull TV persona, review test-market ad results and sign a new three-month $10 million advertising contract. Senate Republicans were pressuring high tech companies to ante-up money for advertisements supporting vulnerable Republican incumbents. The ad hoc groups fronting the fund raising effort could accept donations of any size from any source and did not have to disclose their donors. Used ferociously by both parties, these front groups had become a fixture of modern campaigning as the cost of America's political wars skyrocketed. The concept appealed to Muncaster. He saw himself organizing at least a couple of front organizations once he became an established lobbyist. They offered a brilliant new way to gain access to those at the seat of power.

The notice that saccharin, an artificial sweetener, was being dropped from the government's list of cancer causing chemicals went into the trash. It was soon followed by a lengthy, scholarly paper outlining the differences between Governor Bush's and Vice President Gore's proposals to save Social Security and Medicare, the government's two most expensive entitlement programs. In an otherwise dull election year, both parties had already embarked on a campaign of sowing the fear of coming Social Security and Medicare insolvency among the voters. The resulting panic among the politically unsophisticated masses was supposed to pay dividends at the polls. Depending on whose gruesome political ads you believed, only the Republicans or the Democrats were blessed with the ability to save these programs from future bankruptcy and provide for elderly Americans.

The House of Representatives overwhelmingly rejected a legislative initiative to streamline the federal budget process. It was a major setback for the small band of House reformers who had been advocating changes to the year-end stalemates that often crippled the operation of the government.

Microsoft's lobbying largess was paying off. Its well-financed behind the scenes campaign to generate public support was winning allies in the fight to block the government's plan to split the firm into two parts. Microsoft was gaining supporters in Congress in direct proportion to the amount of money it spent.

Diagnosed with cancer and beset by a failing marriage, New York city mayor Rudy Giuliani withdrew from the race for the U.S. Senate.

Representative Rick Lazio replaced him in the expensive battle with Hillary Rodham Clinton. Too bad Giuliani had pulled out. His marital infidelities would have given the Democrats a wonderful chance to lambaste a Republican with the morality issue for a change.

"The louder he talked of his honor, the faster we counted our spoons."

-Ralph Waldo Emerson, 1870

Muncaster would use the gist of most of these interesting tidbits to stimulate conversation during his luncheon meetings. It would demonstrate to his guests that he was extremely well versed in the important issues of the day. Retrieving a copy of President Clinton's financial disclosure statement from near the bottom of the stack of reading materials, Muncaster began a careful study of the complicated form. The President's annual disclosure listing all gifts worth more than $250 riveted his attention as he read through the columns of figures. Discreetly sandwiched among the gifts of golf clubs, suits, cuff links, china, sofas, crystal and a leather jacket was a $2.25 million gift from the trust fund created to pay his legal bills.

On another page, the disclosure statement revealed the President had substantial liabilities, owing a combined $10 million to three law firms for services rendered during the Monica Lewinsky scandal and impeachment trial. Muncaster thought the $10 million legal liability was probably overstated because no sensible law firm was going to actually bill the President at the top rate. At some point during the payment settlement, the President was going to apply pressure and negotiate a deep discount for himself. His power to deal was for real and his astute lawyers knew it. Having a former President out and about spreading the word that he had been screwed to the wall financially by a bunch of greedy shysters was not a recommendation the firms were seeking.

Still, the President was going to leave office with a sizable legal debt hanging over his head. Perhaps like servants of old, the President would have to indenture himself to the law firms and work off the debt. It would not take him very long to do it in Washington because having an ex-president on staff would attract many big dollar clients to the firms. He was after all, a man with in-depth executive experience and legal expertise.

With the Arkansas Supreme Court's disciplinary committee recommending that President Clinton be disbarred for serious misconduct, the President might have to work as a consultant and not as a lawyer. The committee found the misleading answers he gave during the Paula Jones sexual harassment case fell far short of the required standards for all lawyers. Because he was a former state attorney general and Yale Law School graduate, the President was supposed to know better. In his rebuttal, the President argued that while his answers were evasive and misleading they were not legally false. It was a position Washington's legal and lobbying communities understood and supported wholeheartedly. Even if President Clinton joined Richard M. Nixon as the only president to lose his law license due to unethical behavior, he would not want from a lack gainful employment. Those who lived the good life splitting legal hairs in Washington would stand by their man.

While they might be unappreciated elsewhere, the President's formidable legal skills were greatly admired by a Washington establishment willing to back up its admiration with money. The Democratic National Committee's national tribute to President Clinton set a new record as it pulled in $26 million from the 12,000 who dined on southern style barbecue dishes in Washington's downtown sports arena. The best and most expensive tables were filled by the city's lobbyists eagerly discussing the interesting nuances of the President's legal defense. The new interpretations of what legally constituted truth were riveting the attention of the appreciative city.

The federal government was responsible for overseeing many of the nation's safety programs. In another example of the Washington philosophy of do as I say and not as I do that Muncaster loved so dearly, the General Accounting Office found 903 federal buildings collectively needing $4 billion worth of repairs or renovations. While it was busily sticking its nose into the business of everyone else, the government was allowing its own office buildings to fall into serious disrepair.

The remaining were useless pieces such as the U.S. Patent and Trademark Office document reporting the agency granted 94,096 patents last year, more than ever before in the history of the United States. Muncaster trashed it and a number of others dealing with international economic matters and returned his attention to the fascinating presidential financial disclosure statement. He had barely resumed leafing through its pages when a quaint voice interrupted his thoughts. "Sir, if I may say so, the patents granted by United States Government are worthy of a bit more of your attention. They are the life's blood of this nation's material progress and the foundation of its economic well being. If I may also be so bold as to mention, the establishment of patent protection was one of the proudest achievements of my presidency."

Muncaster wasn't in the mood for jokes, no matter how good the mimicry of old style English was. As he spun in his executive chair to face the uninvited intruder, he spat out, "Buzz off you goddamn ass hole, can't you see I busy!" Expecting to see someone as he swiveled around, Muncaster was stunned to find no one else in the room. On the wall, in the direction the voice had come from, he was startled to see that the large photograph of President Clinton had somehow changed into one of George Washington. As Muncaster watched with unbelieving eyes, the image of Washington slowly faded and the familiar current President's smiling countenance emerged again in its rightful place in the frame. As the picture changed before his eyes, Muncaster realized he had been working too hard and decided to call it a day. The heavy concentration on reading must have had seriously overtaxed his tired brain.

In the subbasement of the Commerce building far below Muncaster's grand office, was a little-visited storage room known informally to the housekeeping staff as the room of the "righteous ins and the putrid outs." In a temperature controlled environment, the large room housed the property belonging to the executive office of the Secretary of Commerce. The desk used by Herbert Hoover when he served as Commerce Secretary was there along with the safe used to stash secret campaign funds during the Nixon years, a jumble of once-used expensive furniture, gifts from admirers and foreign visitors and two massive steel racks jammed with expensively framed portraits.

For as long as anyone could remember, every Secretary of Commerce had a costly official portrait painted at taxpayer's expense. It was one of the perks of the cabinet position usually reserved for the richest business contributor of either party. Since Secretaries usually stayed in office for an average of 18 months, a large number of portraits had accumulated over the years. Ages ago, a building manager, whose name was forgotten, brought in the two large racks of shelving and arranged the Democrats in one rack and the Republicans on the other. To make things easier for the staff who had to be ready to change the portraits on demand, he made the two nicely engraved wood signs which were inconspicuously lodged on the inside of the racks where they could not be seen by the infrequent visitor.

For the past 20 years, it had been customary after each election for the housekeeping staff to assemble in the storage room a few days after the election to partake of a small buffet meal and drink a champagne toast in honor of the change in administrations. If the current party in power had gone down to electoral defeat, the highlight of the event was the solemn switching of the signs from one rack to another by the staff member with the most years on the job. The social gathering made the housekeepers' life much easier. By checking the easily remembered signs they were assured of always selecting from the current politically correct rack of portraits. The sign system was an iron-clad guarantee against the humiliation of lugging a painting of a Democrat into the executive offices when the Republicans were in power and vice versa.

Along with removing the furniture and ordering new carpeting and drapes, it was the housekeepers' duty to remove the portraiture of the defeated party lining the hallways of the executive offices and assist the politically victorious in selecting the replacements to grace the walls for as long as the voters would allow. It was a nerve-wracking task that consumed weeks because the newcomers often fought among themselves over the selection of their favorite former secretary, the arrangement of the portraits and background color schemes. A portrait might have to be changed six or seven times before agreement was reached. While these weighty choices were being made, a steady stream of framed possibilities moved flawlessly up and, if rejected, back down the building's freight elevator. Because so many portraits were available, it was possible to change them all every few months during a political party's full tenure and not exhaust the supply.

Muncaster cared nothing about the ridiculous selection process or the deplorable waste of housekeepers' time it caused. All he cared about was visitors being impressed by the gallery of former secretaries lining hallways linking the executive suites. As he locked his office door and entered the brightly lit hallway, he was immediately struck by the change. All the pictorial representations of the mighty were gone, replaced by a hodgepodge of paintings of George Washington. Washington as a child, Washington as a surveyor, Washington as a Virginia militia soldier, Washington as a farmer, Washington at his gristmill, Washington as a Continental Army General, Washington at the Constitutional Convention and Washington as President. As he walked down the hallway to the guard post at the exit, Muncaster was irritated by the tasteless, tacky display. In the middle of all the Washington art work was a poorly done painting of two Confederate soldiers, one white, the other black. It didn't fit at all with the Washington theme. Why was it displayed here? Inscribed on the frame's unstylish name plate was the simple notation, "They did their duty." Muncaster was uncomfortable with the glowering, unfriendly look of the Washington canvases in the exhibit, they seemed to hold him in contempt. It was the one thing all the pictures had in common.

The guard sitting at the executive office entrance was bored. There wasn't much traffic going by her post this time of the day and she had two hours remaining on this shift to work. The security station was installed at the entrance, not so much as protection against terrorists as it was to keep unwanted people from randomly traipsing in and out of the executive suites.

417

The incident that brought about the guard placement was enshrined in departmental lore and eagerly passed from one administration to another. Every new Secretary ordered new furniture and rearranged the office, placing everything in a position opposite to the placement used by his or her predecessor. As the furniture moved, so did the main entrance to the Secretary's cavernous suite. With three doors to choose from, the one not blocked by furniture always became the entrance after the extensive remodeling project was completed.

After one of the frequent changes of furnishings, an employee was rushing to the Secretary's office with an updated briefing memorandum for a pending meeting with a foreign dignitary. Reading the paper as he walked, he entered what had formerly been the entrance and promptly tripped over a coffee table and fell against an end table, smashing it and also breaking a lamp as he hit the floor. The mess was quickly cleaned up in the minutes remaining before the meeting and the dazed man was dispatched to a hospital for treatment of the contusions on his head and a large gash on his leg. It was decided at that time to establish a guard post to keep unsolicited people out. One of the many new administrative aides on the payroll would be called to the guard post to accept the papers and deliver them to the off-limit inner sanctum. The aides were all qualified to open the door and place papers on the secretary's desk. There would be no further risk of embarrassing accidents caused by uncoordinated employees.

The guard looked up as Muncaster approached with a troubled look on his face. "May I help you Mr. Swindell?" she politely said.

"Do you know why the paintings in the hallway have been changed? Who authorized the switch?" Muncaster queried.

"What changes, sir? I don't know of any," the puzzled security guard responded.

"All the paintings in the main executive hallway have been changed. Do you know why it was done?" Muncaster asked.

"Mr. Swindell, I've been here the better part of the day! There have been no changes made since I've been here. Those paintings are the exact same ones that were hanging there yesterday, I'm sure of it."

"Damn it! I just came down the hall. The pictures have been changed! Someone had to do it! Maybe if you made an effort to stay awake on the job, you might notice a little of what goes on around here!"

Insulted by Muncaster's remark, the guard's annoyance turned to cold fury. "Don't insult me! I see everything that goes on around here! I know damn well how to do my job! You want to examine the pictures? Let's go down the hall and check them right now!" With that said, the guard stood up and with one hand on the holstered weapon on her hip, ordered Muncaster to follow her back down the hall.

"Now tell me, what do you see?" the angry guard sneered as she turned to face Muncaster. Muncaster was dumbfounded as he stared at the rows of portraits. The grand array of former commerce secretaries had returned, George Washington and the Confederates were gone. "I don't know what to say," he stammered. "When I came through here a few minutes ago these were all paintings of George Washington, with the exception of one which was of two Confederate soldiers. Now they have all changed back to normal again."

The guard looked at him in disbelief. "Why would we put up a display of George Washington paintings in the executive hallway of the Commerce Department?" she coldly asked. "Look, lawyer boy! Whatever it is you're smoking, shooting-up or drinking has started to affect your mind. You better get off of whatever the stuff is right away, before you lose your cushy job and land in jail to boot." When Muncaster said nothing she continued, "I have taken all the crap I'm going to take from you today. Just march yourself out of here and get your self treated. The next time you hallucinate on my watch, it gets reported. Do you understand me?" As the suspicious guard watched, Muncaster turned and quickly walked down the long hallway and out the exit. The guard was fighting to hold her impulses in check. In the back of her mind, she heard a strangely accented voice telling her it would be all right if she went ahead and shot Muncaster in the back. Stuck here in the hallway of the high and mighty, guarding these power-mad weirdoes must be getting to her. She was going to ask for transfer to a more normal guard post the first thing in the morning.

June 2000

"The fundamental concept in social science is Power, in the same sense in which Energy is the fundamental concept in physics."

-Bertrand Russell, 1938

It took Muncaster several days to recover from the verbal beating he received from the surly guard. The insolent bitch had some nerve to accuse him of being a drunk or doing drugs. For a time, he thought about pulling a few strings and getting her fired, but changed his mind and let the matter drop. He didn't want to risk an investigation because the guard was sure to use his outburst over the changed portraits in the hallway as a defense for her actions. It would raise questions about his mental state and place him in a very bad light. Instead of addressing the disrespectful behavior of the guard, the focus of the investigation would shift to his conduct and those damn George Washington portraits he saw. What about the voice he heard in his office? He couldn't explain that either. If he pressed charges, the guard would make him look like a fool and enjoy doing it. His many enemies would grab the opportunity to make him a departmental laughing stock and the guard would become a hero of sorts. It was a no-win situation. He had been given the shaft and there was nothing he could do about.

An important senator's office called and strongly hinted Muncaster ought stop playing games and accept the luncheon invitation offered by Dr.Ken Morgan. Morgan was researching a project of some sort and had been trying in vain for weeks to get on Muncaster's engagement calendar. Muncaster, thinking Morgan would be a complete waste of his time, had been making one excuse after another in the hope Morgan would give up. In the tried and true ways of Washington hard ball, Morgan somehow conned the senator into applying pressure and Muncaster buckled, he had no choice. He could not afford to anger the senator.

To compensate for his trouble, Muncaster vowed to stick Dr. Morgan with a large lunch tab. He knew no one on Capitol Hill would fault him for it even if Morgan had the guts to complain. To make doubly sure he could eat his fill, he purposely skipped breakfast on the day of the meeting. After the usual introductions, as a stunned Dr. Morgan looked on, Muncaster ordered the $49.95 imported sea food entree and two glasses of white wine at $14.95 each to wash it down. If Muncaster was going to have to answer this dimwit's questions, he was going to do it in the proper style. By the time coffee and desert arrived, the pleasure of Muncaster's company was going to cost the eminent Dr. Morgan at least $100. Perhaps the next time he would not be so insistent on having a meeting.

As he stuffed his face, Muncaster was not impressed to learn Dr. Morgan was from a college in the Pittsburgh area and was writing a research paper on unusual sightings of George Washington. The article would undoubtedly be published in some scholarly journal, read by very few people and quickly forgotten. Muncaster wanted to find out how this scrounge of a professor had gotten enough clout to get a senator to intercede for him. Because Morgan wanted to maintain access to the powerful on Capitol Hill, he had to treat Dr. Morgan with a certain amount of respect. There had to be more to Morgan than met the eye. Maybe he did campaign consulting or polling work on a part time basis for the senator.

Dr. Ken Morgan recovered graciously from the shock of Muncaster's ostentatious ordering spree. He swallowed another bite of his moderately priced fish sandwich and began the serious part of the conversation, the reason for the meeting. "I had hoped to be able to meet with Leon Placke, but unfortunately he passed away before I had a chance to contact him. As I understand it, you were one of the last people to see Mr. Placke alive."

"Yes that's true," Muncaster replied. "We spent part of a pleasant day visiting the Civil War sites related to Leon's unfortunate involvement with a batch of Confederate government papers. You may have read about them in the newspapers, they turned out to be quite an impressive find." When Dr. Morgan nodded in the affirmative, Muncaster continued, "During the time we were together, poor, dear, Leon never once gave any indication that he planned to take his own life. He seemed so relaxed at the time. I was really shocked when I learned the sad news. I still spend many a sleepless night thinking about it! If only I had been more perceptive, Leon would still be among us!" Muncaster stopped talking, pretended to wipe away a tear and finally took a big sip from one of the wine glasses. "It still pains me to talk about it," he said in a choked voice.

Putting down his glass of iced tea, Dr. Morgan sympathetically answered, "You can't keep blaming yourself for something you had no control over. Leon was a good actor. He would have had no difficulty hiding his true intentions from you. If he didn't want you to know about his planned suicide, there is no way you could have guessed at what he planned to do. Leon Placke was a true master of deception. He was able to fool the best and brightest all the time."

"I guess you are right," Muncaster said. "Leon was the best lobbyist this town ever saw. For many years, he expanded the influence of the lobbying profession as he cut all types of trend-setting political deals for his many clients. He was also the consummate role player. Leon always appeared sincere when he made his pitch. Everyone in town knows he was better at projecting sincerity than most of the other lobbyists. If you had the cash to play the big stakes lobbying game, Leon could really make you believe he felt your pain as he lobbied for your agenda!"

Looking directly at his host, Muncaster continued, "It makes me feel much better to hear from an impartial observer such as yourself that I didn't overlook something on the dreadful day Leon died. Perhaps it's time for me to stop worrying about why I was unable to help Leon when he needed it the most. I should face reality and accept the fact that Leon had me and his other friends completely fooled. We never suspected, never had even the slightest indication that our dear friend Leon was planning to do himself in."

Dr. Morgan was completely taken in by Muncaster's first-rate performance. "What's done is done," he said. "And," he continued, "it ought to be obvious to anyone with half a functioning brain that there was nothing you could do about it. Now if you don't mind, I'd like to change the subject. The question I am seeking to answer is why the late Mr. Placke decided to turn his back on the system that made him powerful, successful and rich? His conversion, and I use the term loosely you understand, seems to have taken place at the same time he began believing he was communicating with George Washington. It is the Washington aspect of the Placke affair that intrigues me. You may find this hard to believe, but Leon was not the first person to claim he saw Washington. Reported sightings of George Washington have occurred throughout U.S. history. I have found evidence of Washington making appearances during times of grave national crisis."

Muncaster was annoyed and tried hard not to show it. "You mean to tell me there have been other mentally unbalanced people running around claiming to be having conversations with George Washington? I suppose it is possible because people are always having nervous breakdowns and as a result, could easily imagine all kinds of strange things. Washington is certainly famous, so a certain percentage of the loonies probably think they see him. Mentally ill people probably have been seeing and talking to imaginary images of George Washington for many years."

Dr. Morgan smiled as he answered, "I can tell you find the possibility of George Washington making appearances to living men hard to believe. Most rational people do, including myself. Although I don't claim to understand it, I have found evidence of George Washington appearing to people at critical times in U.S. history. Now, before you say I'm crazy, let me say a few words about what I have discovered during my research. It may help you to see the Washington sightings from a new angle and aid us in figuring out why Mr. Placke insisted he was following George Washington's guidance. I admit, I would have written Leon off as just another slightly deranged person had it not been for the draft copy of the U.S. Constitution Leon claimed Washington had given to him. It was the appearance of this previously undiscovered priceless document that attracted my attention. The document had to come from some heretofore undisclosed cache of Washington papers. But from where? There have been no discoveries of important Washington memorabilia in years. The strange saga of Leon Placke is worth investigating because Leon had ownership of a political document with Washington's handwritten notes on it. If Washington didn't give the paper to him, where did Leon get it? The other papers surviving from the Constitutional Convention have been in museums, libraries or private collections for years. Whose long-forgotten coat pocket did this one come out of, if it wasn't George Washington's? Where has the document been for all these years?"

"I see your point," Muncaster intruppted. "It was the draft of the Constitution more than anything else that solidified Leon's credibility with the common people. There are many in this nation who firmly believe George Washington gave the paper to Leon as a visible symbol of his reform movement. It was a volatile mix! George Washington coming back from the dead to enlist our best lobbyist in leading an attack on the excesses of the ruling establishment. When it could not be proved the document came from another source, Leon's strange reform ideas began to spread like wildfire among the politically unsophisticated. People are still standing in line for hours to view the piece of paper George Washington allegedly gave Leon Placke! It continues to make quite an impact on the tourists. Dr. Morgan, please excuse my interruption and continue with your discussion of your findings." Having finished the first glass of wine, Muncaster started sipping the second.

"The reward of one duty is the power to fulfill another."
-George Eliot, 1874

Dr. Morgan thought he now had Muncaster's undivided attention so he continued, "More than any of his contemporaries, George Washington was responsible for the establishment of the United States of America. Modern Americans have absolutely no idea of how close the British came to snuffing out the rebellion in their North American colonies. After the lofty words declaring American independence were written, it was George Washington who masterfully managed to keep the woefully inadequate Continental army in the fight over the long haul. He had to contend with British irregulars and their Native American allies on the frontier while at the same time waging a conventional war against the tough British regulars. It was Washington who held the American army together, he prevented it from mutinying on more than one occasion. Through those tough and terrible times, Washington set an example by refusing to consider all offers to make him America's king or dictator. And he never lost hope as the seemingly endless war dragged on year after year. Finally, with French assistance, Washington was able to force the surrender of the British force at Yorktown. That victory convinced the King of England of the futility of continuing the expensive struggle."

"As the victorious colonies bumbled along the path to nationhood, it was retired General Washington who made an indelible mark as he presided over the convention that hammered out the Constitution of the United States. As they worked, the delegates molded the duties of the nation's president to fit the personality of George Washington. While serving two terms as the first President of the United States, Washington's conduct in office completed the list of the awesome contributions he made to getting America established on a firm footing. When Washington stepped down and voluntarily gave up the power of high office, the stunned leaders of the world took notice. Something new, different and trend-setting was taking place in the strange new nation called the United States of America."

"George Washington returned to his farm and gristmill and, in the last years of his life, built a distillery to produce whiskey. When he died in 1799, Washington was well on the way, and quite deservedly I believe, to becoming one of America's great heroes. After his death, however, Washington's home at Mt. Vernon, slowly sank into disrepair. By the late 1850s, John Augustine Washington, Jr., the first President's great-grandnephew, was firmly caught in the cycle of land ruination George Washington had labored so hard to change. The farm, that was George Washington's pride and joy, had become a money loser. As a result of years of neglect, the roof of the mansion sagged, the walls were unpainted and the pillared portico was propped up with raw wooden beams. On the eve of the Civil War, Washington's home was in as bad as shape as the federal Union that he helped establish."

"As the Union splintered into two pieces, John Augustine Washington turned his back on George Washington's legacy and sided with the Confederacy. John's military career was a short one. He was killed fighting for the Southern cause in September 1861. Although both the Union and Confederate authorities claimed allegiance to George Washington's principles and often invoked his name in support of their respective war efforts, I believe the evidence shows George Washington was and always remained a pro-Union man. Although he made appearances to Union troops on two critical occasions during the Civil War, he never appeared to the Confederates."

As Muncaster began to believe he was having lunch with a man as crazy as Leon Placke had been, Dr. Morgan stoically continued his story. "In early July 1863, the Confederate army commanded by Robert E. Lee was in southern Pennsylvania fighting a critical battle at the small town of Gettysburg. During the first day's fighting, Lee's forces routed the Union troops, capturing thousands and sending the remainder retreating through the town in disarray. Lee was now just a hair's breath away from winning the victory that could secure independence for the Confederacy. If he smashed the Union army on this field, he could move on to capture Baltimore or Washington and thereby knock the bottom out of the Union war effort."

"As the bitter struggle on the first day drew to a close, Lee's grand plan began to unravel for a reason over which he had no control. As the bits and pieces of shattered Union army units fell back, George Washington, in full military uniform and mounted upon a white horse, appeared among the retreating troops. Following Washington's instructions, the shattered units coalesced into a strong new defensive line along the fish-hook shaped high ground south of town. It was against this strong defensive position that Lee unsuccessfully hurled his army during the following two days. In the end, Lee was repulsed with appalling losses and forced to withdraw to Virginia."

"A number of years after the war ended, Joshua L. Chamberlain, a reliable observer who rose from pre-war college professor to Union army general, interviewed the Union veterans and included references to their sightings of George Washington on the battlefield in his memoirs. Whether they were real or imagined, Chamberlain credited Washington's appearances, coming as they did at a critical point in the battle, with giving the beleaguered Union troops the morale boost they needed to rally and hold. Chamberlain was no casual observer, he fought in the battle from the second day onward and was awarded the Congressional Medal of Honor for his actions. As he arrived on the battlefield, Chamberlain overheard the rank and file troops talking excitedly about seeing General Washington on the previous day. I am sure that Washington's appearances at Gettysburg were the first time he came to the aid of the nation after his death. Although I have carefully searched the records, there is no mention of anyone sighting George Washington prior to the Civil War."

Muncaster was so stunned he ordered another glass of wine. This guy was even crazier than Leon Placke. Why was he wasting his time trying to convince Muncaster that George Washington would come back from the dead to help the United States? Leon had tried to convince people of the same stupid thing when he began prattling about reforming the capital's political establishment. Was this fixation with George Washington the result of a new virus disease that affected a certain type of people? Muncaster took a big swallow of wine and decided listening to Dr. Morgan's implausible story was the price he was obligated to pay for a free lunch. He wondered if the senator had any idea of how seriously deranged the man was. The senator had no right to force Muncaster into meeting with this demented individual.

Dr. Morgan began speaking again. "About a year later in August 1864, I found the second substantiated instance of George Washington coming to the aid of his beloved nation. During that hot, long ago summer, Abraham Lincoln's war policies were failing. Despite three years of fighting, a horrendous number of casualties, crushing new taxes and a rising mountain of war debt, the Union had been unable to defeat the Confederacy. The North was war weary, its people in despair. The Democrats, hoping to bring the hated Lincoln administration down, were promising to end the war by making peace with the Confederacy after they won the election. Unless something changed drastically and quickly, Lincoln was going to be soundly defeated in the election scheduled for November 1864."

"During the last days of August 1864, General Sherman led a large part of his army in an wide arc to the west and south of Atlanta. Having grown tired of endlessly blasting away at Atlanta's stout defenses, Sherman was cutting loose, gambling that he could force the fall of the city by severing the last railroad supply line controlled by the Confederates. Confederate General William Hardee and his army corps were in Sherman's path, defending a vital stretch of the Macon railroad. Hardee got wind of Sherman's maneuver and sent an urgent telegraph message to Atlanta reporting Sherman's location and appealing for reinforcements. About the time the message left Hardee's headquarters, George Washington appeared among the advance elements of Sherman's army. Washington urged the soldiers, who were still miles away from the railroad, to speed-up the advance. At the time, every soldier in Sherman's army was able to recognize General Washington when he saw him. Washington's face was as familiar to them as their own because the likeness of George Washington hung in every schoolhouse and in most of the homes in the nation. Inspired by the national hero's presence in their ranks, the dusty Union columns shook out their battle flags, shifted into attack formation and lunged forward."

"Washington, waving his hat and urging them on, rode in the forefront with the inspired troops as they raced across the final miles to the railroad.

Although his troops offered a spirited defense, Hardee's command was overwhelmed by the on-rushing horde of animated blue-clad troopers that enveloped the position and drove the Confederates from the railroad line. Now cut off from supplies, Atlanta fell to Sherman in early September. When the news of Atlanta's capture reached the North, the people reacted with unbridled joy and the mood of the voters changed. Atlanta's fall was a clear indication the Confederacy was tottering on the verge of ruin. The much maligned, but vindicated Abraham Lincoln was reelected President. It had been a severe test of America's political system, with the President of the nation opting to run for reelection in the middle of a civil war. With Lincoln back in office for a second term, the war would be fought to a finish and the Union saved. The nettlesome issues of slavery and secession would die with the Confederacy."

Not wishing to waste his breath arguing with an obviously deranged man, Muncaster sat silently sipping his wine as Dr. Morgan continued, "There were no sightings of George Washington in the years following the Civil War. Washington never made an appearance during the Indian Wars, the Spanish-American War, the Philippine Insurrection or World War I. Based on the evidence, I have to conclude that Washington only appears at times of grave national crisis, when the very survival of the nation is at stake."

"The third sighting of Washington will prove my point. After a 78 year interlude, the United States was again in mortal danger as George Washington came to the assistance of his country. In June 1942, the military forces of the Japanese Empire were rampaging across the Pacific, they had been winning victories virtually non-stop for six months. Seeking to stretch Japan's perimeter of control eastward and destroy what remained of the U.S. Navy, the Japanese decided to capture Midway Island situated about 1,100 miles northwest of Pearl Harbor. In the largest operation mounted thus far in the war, the Japanese Navy assembled a fleet of 145 warships and 600 carrier-based planes to do the job. To counter the massive Japanese force, the U.S. Navy scraped together everything available, including two carrier groups, and positioned them near Midway to blunt the Japanese invasion. If the outclassed Americans were going to win a battle in which ships fought out of sight of each other, they had to surprise the Japanese fleet with a strike by the U.S. carrier based planes."

"The American patrol planes went up on flight after flight, finding nothing. On the afternoon of June 3, 1942, a patrol plane flying at the outer limit of its range was turning back when the astounded pilot spotted George Washington riding his horse across the cloud bank next to the aircraft. Although he risked crashing into the sea if he flew on, the pilot turned the aircraft in the direction Washington pointed his saber. After about 15 minutes of flying with Washington riding alongside the aircraft, Washington pointed his saber down through a small hole in the dense cloud cover and the aircraft crew saw the mighty Japanese armada spread out on the sea below them. The patrol aircraft radioed the position of the Japanese fleet as it limped back to base, its engines running on fuel vapors."

"On June 4, the battle began when the Japanese hit Midway with a punishing air attack. After the Japanese aircraft had returned to their carriers to refuel and rearm, the Americans planes struck, catching the Japanese carriers with their flight decks full of bombs and refueling planes. In the ensuing melee, four Japanese carriers were destroyed. By the time the battle ended on June 7, the Japanese had lost 322 aircraft along with four carriers sunk and two heavy cruisers and three destroyers heavily damaged. The Americans paid a heavy price for victory, losing the carrier Yorktown, a destroyer and 147 aircraft. As a result of the bloody engagement, Midway remained in American hands and the severely battered Japanese fleet was forced to switch to defensive operations. The string of Japanese victories in the Pacific had come to an end. The United States had taken the first big step toward victory in World War II."

"To the best of my knowledge, George Washington never appeared to anyone again during World War II. For the next 47 years, there were no sightings. None, until Leon Placke began claiming George Washington had convinced him to abandon his lucrative lobbying practice and take on the thankless task of reforming the political establishment. Mr. Swindell, do you want to know what I think is going on?"

Although he really could care less what this blabbering idiot had on his warped mind, Muncaster responded in the politest free-luncheon-guest tone he could muster, "I certainly do, Dr. Morgan. Your story has been quite thought provoking so far. I was never aware of the Washington sighting incidents you mentioned. It almost sounds as if George Washington continually looks out for our nation's welfare."

"That's it exactly," a delighted Dr. Morgan responded. "Washington has only made appearances when the country is in deadly danger. I believe George Washington was working through Leon Placke because the country is in a very serious crisis."

"I played by the rules of politics as I found them."
                                                    -Richard M. Nixon, 1990

"I don't see how you can draw such a conclusion from the facts you have been outlining for the last hour," Muncaster retorted. "The United States is at peace, the cold war has been won. We are the world's only remaining superpower. Times are good. The economy has been setting growth records and the federal budget deficit has stopped growing. Where is the crisis of such a magnitude as to require George Washington's intervention? What war are we in danger of losing? The United States is facing no deadly danger that would require Washington's assistance! I am using your exact words to emphasize my point! If, as you say, Washington shows up to help the nation in times of crisis, he certainly would not have wasted his time on Leon Placke. The country is not in any danger of any sort right now!"

"Mr. Swindell, I beg to differ with you on that point! While no foreign power is our military equal, the political infrastructure of our nation is rapidly rotting out. With political campaign costs at astronomical levels, Congress readily auctions itself to well-heeled, special interest groups. Congress hardly goes out of session anymore because its grossly oversized staff spends too much time catering to the legislative needs of big campaign contributors. At the White House things are even worse. The bloated pack of White House hangers-on are forever thinking up new ways to curry favor with the President's political friends so they can squeeze them for money during the next election. The Executive Branch of the United States Government has become the largest cash cow in the world, a trophy worth having at nearly any price. The candidate elected to be President has control of a cash box for four years that has $1.8 billion a year pouring into it."

"The expensive, brainwashing, propaganda blitzes that pass for political campaigning are a disgrace to the process established by the founding fathers! Our system is languishing, Mr. Swindell! One of the symptoms of the seriousness of the illness is the huge numbers of lobbyists infesting the capital city. They are the maggots feasting on the rotten flesh of the decaying American political system."

"Our political system has been so abused it is reaching its breaking point. Half of the eligible voters are so disgusted with the way big-money has corrupted politics, they will not waste the time on election day to cast a ballot. A democracy with such problems is on the way to ruin. Things need to be fixed soon or America's great democratic experiment won't survive much longer. We are in crisis because our political system has stagnated, it has not kept pace with America's growing economy. George Washington is rightfully worried about the state of the nation. That's why he got after Leon Placke to start getting reforms moving. We have to change the basis of representation in the House of Representatives so America's economic sectors will again be represented fairly in Congress as the nation's founders intended. Once we abandon the obsolete concept of representation based on geographical district, a big part of our problem is solved. The obscene lobbying industry will shrink back to an appropriate size!"

"We also have to reinvigorate the cherished concept of the citizen politican, someone who makes a real sacrifice by serving in Congress or the Executive Branch. When the Constitution was written, it was never envisioned that participation in politics would be a lifetime calling for the chosen few. Our citizens are supposed to donate a few years of their time to governing the Republic. If we went back to that concept, it would help get the sky-high costs of political campaigning under control."

"Beware of the politically obsessed. They are often bright and interesting, but they have something missing in their natures; there is a hole, an empty place, and they use politics to fill it up. It leaves them somehow misshapen."

-Peggy Noonan, 1990

Muncaster ordered another glass of wine. He would continue to listen to this strange litany as long as Dr. Morgan was willing to pay. As the wine was served, Dr. Morgan was saying, "The framers of the Constitution had experience with the foibles of human nature. They did their level-best to negate the temptations posed by unbridled power and greedy self-interest. George Washington himself set a high standard when he refused to serve more than two terms as President and freely gave up political power to go back to his life as a farmer. I'll tell you plainly Mr. Swindell, we need to have dedicated people like George Washington in government again! Not the crass political animals we have now! Those who spend 20, 30 and more years in the capital working to build up power bases so they can broker favors and lobby after leaving government. In many cases, they switch sides if the money is right and work against the causes they championed while in government service."

"Politics in this country has become an expensive undertaking, controlled by people who make a lifetime career out of selling access to the federal budget. Special interests have bought the U.S. political system, the White House, the U.S. Senate and the House of Representatives. The crisis we face is as plain as your reflection in a mirror, Mr. Swindell! How can you not see it! There is no mystery as to why George Washington made his appearances to Leon Placke! George Washington looks out for our country, lends a helping hand in times of national crisis. The crisis we face right now is

431

caused by a political system which has turned itself into a big spending business, one that has lost touch with the concepts on which our nation was founded."

Muncaster had just about reached the limit of his endurance. The simpleton seated across the table had swallowed Leon Placke's tall tale hook, line and sinker. Dr. Ken Morgan actually believed all the nonsense about George Washington and the need to reform America's free-spending political system. The stuff about Washington appearing during the Civil War and World War II was interesting, but linking it to modern politics and political campaigns was carrying matters too far. Things were just fine with the political system as far as Muncaster was concerned. The real problem was these wide-eyed reform fanatics, they never knew when to stop.

Muncaster knew there was no use wasting time trying to reason with the man. Instead, he opted to use his diplomatic skills and extract himself from Morgan's clutches. Feigning a degree of interest in the crackpot theory was always the best policy to follow in cases like these. "Dr. Morgan," Muncaster said in a voice betraying no hint of the actual exasperation he felt, "I would like to congratulate you on a fine piece of research work. Your careful investigation of the George Washington appearances have yielded truly astounding results. You make a strong case for taking seriously the bedrock principles of government laid down by George Washington and his contemporaries."

As Dr. Morgan looked at him Muncaster continued, "I wish there was more I could do to contribute to your worthwhile project, but unfortunately Leon never shared the details of his meetings with George Washington with me. On our last outing, Leon never once mentioned Washington by name. We did, however, have many mutual friends. I will be happy to make inquiries and ask if Leon spoke to any of them about his personal meetings with Washington. Once Leon's previous acquaintances learn from me how fascinating and interesting your project is, I'm sure those with any knowledge of the subject will be anxious to help you."

After a few more minutes of mouthing bold-faced lies and bland pleasantries, Muncaster excused himself, leaving Dr. Morgan stuck with his worthless promises and the hefty luncheon bill. Muncaster had no intention of helping Morgan in any way. While he was certainly going to tell his friends about his encounter with the laughable eccentric who was searching for people who had seen George Washington's ghost, Muncaster would do nothing that might bring the slightest bit of publicity to the reform related story Morgan was chasing. The sooner people forgot about Leon's insane reform schemes, the better it would be for the nation.

432

"Man is by nature a political animal."

-Aristotle, 343 B. C.

"Politics are now nothing more than a means of rising in the world. With this sole view do men engage in politics, and their whole conduct proceeds upon it."

-Samuel Johnson, 1775

Returning to his office, Muncaster spent the remainder of the afternoon catching up on political events. The first item on the large stack of papers in his in-box contained the most uplifting news he had heard in weeks. During his first days in office in January 1993, President Clinton signed a tough new executive order tightening the restrictions covering those who would leave his administration for a lobbying career. Now that his term in office was winding down, the President was having second thoughts. The policy requiring senior administration officials to wait five years after leaving government before they lobbied any federal agency for which they had any responsibility was under review and would be relaxed during the waning days of the Clinton administration. President Clinton's bold words stating his lobbying ban would help "uphold the highest possible ethical standards and guarantee that members of this administration will be looking out for the American people and not themselves" were quietly being retired. President Clinton was not a foolish man. He had the infinite good sense to remove the roadblock he had placed in the way of his own future employment. Muncaster was elated to learn that the safeguards against abuses in the revolving door between government and the lobbying profession were going to be relaxed. The President was doing the right thing for the Washington establishment.

The pre-election campaign promises were flying thick and fast. Governor George W. Bush outlined a $2.3 billion educational plan emphasizing math and science. Vice President Gore countered by offering a retirement savings proposal costing $35 billion a year. Both candidates and oil industry executives hurled charges at each other regarding the responsibility for the Midwest's surging gasoline prices. An elated White House announced the government's ten year budget surplus projection had grown to $4 trillion. Taking note of the plethora of funds available, the Republicans in Congress indicated they might be able to cut some spending deals with the President. He should send his people over to talk. Governor Bush visited Philadelphia and proposed slashing the federal workforce by two percent. He said the cut would help bring discipline to government operations. Of course, staffing at the White House and Congress would automatically be exempted from the cut.

As Muncaster flipped through the pages of the reports, he saw that lawyers and law firms had contributed $50 million to lubricate the political process thus far in the election year. Computer firms lagged far behind, contributing a paltry $13 million. The winner in New Jersey's Democratic senate primary race reported spending $34 million of his own money to saturate the state with political messages. How was he ever going to get that much money back? That was the question Muncaster would have liked to ask him.

The federal government was becoming slower in collecting the debts owed to it. The amount of outstanding non-tax debt climbed to a record $59 billion, according to a report. The Democrats in the U.S. Senate were demonstrating a new gusto in fund raising. They had raised $40 million from business interests, stunning the Republicans who had collected $42 million from the same business groups. It was a clear indication of a massive change in the political contributions landscape. The Senate Republicans were losing their proud hold on big business contributions.

Muncaster smiled while reading the next article. While Vice President Gore was promising to spend billions of federal dollars to better the lot of average Americans, a family renting a house from him in Carthage, Tennessee struggled with overflowing toilets and backed-up sinks. After a Nashville television station aired the story and chided the Vice President for being a slumlord, Al Gore ordered his property manager to get busy and fix the plumbing problems.

Because it cut out an expensive layer of costly litigation, Washington's lawyers were not enamored with the federal judge's ruling allowing the government to bypass the U.S. Court of Appeals and take the Microsoft antitrust case directly to the Supreme Court.

Muncaster heartily agreed with the bipartisan political decision to bury the World Health Organization report that cast aspirations on U.S. health care spending. Although the United States spent more money than any other nation on healthcare, it ranked in a lowly 15th place on an overall index measuring the efficiency of healthcare delivery. The American healthcare system lagged far behind those of Japan, most Western European countries, Canada and Australia. As he filed away his copy of the report, Muncaster could see why it was a good idea not to thrust these cheerless facts upon the American public during an election campaign. It would only divert attention from the really important issues the politicians wanted to bring to the attention of the voters.

"The political arena leaves one no alternative, one must either be a dunce or a rogue."

-Emma Goldman, 1910

"A passion for politics stems usually from an insatiable need, either for power, or for friendship and adulation, or a combination of both."

-Fawn M. Brodie, 1974

Muncaster tilted back his chair and placed his feet on the top of his desk. The summary of social events at the upcoming political conventions so arduously prepared by the Washington Society of Solicitors was going to be very enjoyable reading. The Society had prepared the agenda for its many members planning to spend a day or two at one or both of the conventions. The conventions were a highlight, they were where the political action was during the late summer of a presidential election year. The Republicans would meet in Philadelphia beginning July 31, the Democrats would convene their festivities in Los Angeles two weeks later.

The political conventions were the Super Bowl of sucking up to the moneyed interests and then shaking them down. Big contributors were pampered and then hit up for more money. The political parties could extract money from captive audiences because all the die-hard political supporters were in one place. Some of the more ambitious fetes at both conventions were sponsored by the trade associations who were underwriting the costs. Lobbyists and special interest groups would be entitled to quality time with lawmakers at the receptions which often cost six figures. The fact that large companies were hosting lavish social events for the officials who regulated them did not seem to be a problem at convention time.

At both conventions, donor perks varied with the size of the contribution check. A $5,000 contributor was entitled to one free hotel room while a $50,000 contributor got two free rooms. A $100,000 contributor received three free rooms at the best hotel and dinner with an important politician interested in learning the contributor's views and legislative needs.

At the Philadelphia convention, Senate Republicans would host a plush golf tournament for donors of $5,000 or more. There would also be a sports luncheon featuring NASCAR drivers and a dinner buffet with big-screen television sets and a choir. If you were interested in hobnobbing while mixing informally, a huge Texas style barbecue was yours for the asking.

In Los Angeles, people contributing $5,000 or more to the Democratic Congressional Campaign Committee would be driven to a gala opening celebration at the best restaurant in Beverly Hills. Two days later, AT&T would treat the Democratic Senatorial Campaign Committee's top donors to dinner at the same restaurant. Another political action committee was holding a bash at the Playboy Mansion. It was going to be a fabulous event, making invitations difficult to obtain for those who were not well-connected.

The Republican National Committee expected to raise $3 million from the Philadelphia affair. The Democrats expected a like amount from the party's partygoers in Los Angeles. The extra business for caterers and florists was a big boost to the economies of the two cities, a well-deserved reward for assisting the electioneering process. At some point during the festivities in Philadelphia and Los Angeles, the political parties would take the time to formalize the selection of the candidates running for President in the autumn election.

Although some supposedly rational people in Washington found it impossible to defend the current campaign finance system, everyone wanted to get invited to as many of the parties and celebrations as they could. In the best tradition of a true democracy, there was going to be a little something for everyone at the conventions. If a person could not afford to attend the grand events, there were plenty of others to pick from. Governors, state parties and political action committees were hosting their own dinners, golf tournaments and hospitality suites. Any reasonable donation would get you in the door and entitle you to share your views on how to make America a better place with a like- minded group. Muncaster was going to take a few days off and go to Los Angeles. As he drew circles around the events he wanted to attend, Muncaster thought of the capital's golden rule. It was simple and straightforward-- those with the gold made the rules. Anyone with an ounce of sense understood it. Once an individual grasped that concept, it was quite easy to prosper in Washington, DC.

Muncaster didn't care that 25 years after Congress approved federal funding for national political campaigns in an effort to limit political spending, the cost of this year's nominating extravaganzas had soared past $100 million. The role of official money was reduced to little more than a down payment on the playground for contributors and lobbyists. Each of the major parties received $13.5 million from the U.S. Treasury to stage the summer's conventions. Because of the federal money, the parties could not take cash subsidies from corporations, although they were accepting plane and train tickets, the use of automobiles, computers, and Web services.

Host committees in Philadelphia and Los Angeles were also collecting unlimited tax-deductible gifts from major companies in order to create unforgettable conventions for the attendees. Under the host committee system, corporations could give any amount they desired in cash and services. As he read through the impressive listing of $1 million corporate donors, Muncaster realized Corporate America was pulling out all the stops to impress a diverse and influential group of political shakers and movers. It was a tried and true system working at its very best. People gave money because they wanted access. They wanted their phone calls promptly answered by someone at the top level of government, not by some impotent nobody buried deep in the bureaucracy.

Muncaster saw nothing wrong with this system because all successful getting things done depended upon relationships. Not taking the time to carefully cultivate powerful relationships was a mistake to be avoided in the capital. Without relationships, you were nothing but a common individual. Being common meant you definitely were not part of the Washington establishment. You were merely a powerless cog in the mighty economic engine of the United States. Neither Muncaster nor anyone else in politics believed corporations were making these massive donations because they supported a pristine political process, or that they gave so generously out of purely civic pride. This was no grade school civic exercise. Access to the politically powerful and big tax deductions was what corporate convention support was all about.

The material marking the 50th anniversary of the beginning of the Korean War was of little interest to Muncaster. He didn't like to waste his time reading about the sacrifices the little people often made for the good of the nation. Muncaster was not impressed with the statistics; the 628,333 dead suffered by the United Nations forces, or that a woefully unprepared U.S. military had expended 36,516 American lives while toughing out the war. The fact that the bloody sacrifices made in Korea laid the groundwork for much of the economic prosperity of modern Asia wasn't worth more than a casual glance from Muncaster.

As aging veterans gathered at the capital's Korean War memorial to sadly honor the lost friends who had done so much to shape the modern world, Muncaster got bored with the subject of the Korean War and tossed the file into the wastebasket. He had better things to do than ponder the implications of a truce now nearly 50 years old. The 37,000 U.S. troops stationed on the Korean peninsula could stay there until hell froze over for all he cared.

July 2000

"We mean by politics the peoples business—the most important business there is."

-Adlai Stevenson, 1955

"Politics is the reflex of the business and industrial world."

-Emma Goldman, 1910

"Politics is war without bloodshed while war is politics with bloodshed."

-Mao Zedong, 1938

Important things were happening in Washington. The U.S. House of Representatives voted to give members of Congress a $3,800 cost-of- living pay raise in 2001. The robust economy and surging federal budget surplus entitled the lawmakers to a raise in their $141,300 base annual salaries. There was virtually no debate on the issue which passed in a matter of minutes, a majority of Democrats and Republicans supporting the measure.

As of July1, House Democrats had $37.4 million in campaign funds in the bank, $15 million more than House Republicans. Democratic strategists believed they were on the way to picking up the six seats needed to depose the vile Republican majority. The size of the financial war chest was due to Democratic leadership's ruthlessness in demanding that members raise vast sums by appearing at events and working the telephones. Although the Democrats held the lead in collecting money for House races, the Republican National Committee had $53 million in its accounts, a hefty $20 million more than the rival Democratic National Committee.

Labor Unions dramatically stepped up their political giving, showering the Democratic Party with record amounts of soft money donations taken from Union treasuries. With the major political campaigns of the year yet to be waged, labor unions had already anted-up $15 million. Leading House Republicans argued for the abolition of all limits on campaign contributions as they voted down Senator John McCain's campaign reform proposals. The Washington establishment was delighted with the forthright attack on campaign contribution limits. Funding political activities was a personal right, another type of expression guaranteed under the Constitution. Of course, the higher the amount of political spending, the better it would be for the capital's professional campaign strategists, media advisors, policy designers, mass mailers and lobbyists.

The U.S. economy was growing at a vigorous 5.2 percent annual rate, surprising analysts who had predicted a significant slowdown because of moderating consumer spending. Instead of slowing, the growth rate was being maintained by exceptionally strong increases in business spending for new plants, equipment and inventories that offset the pullback by shoppers. Both the White House and Congress rushed out press releases trying to take credit for the pleasant national economic performance. Neither the White House nor Congress hurried to take the credit when the Middle East peace talks held at Camp David, Maryland failed. If and when Israel and the Palestinians agreed to a peace settlement, the U.S. taxpayers were going fund it. Estimates indicated that it was going to cost approximately $15 billion in U.S. aid spread over a several year period to make it work.

In true bipartisan fashion, Washington's political leadership ignored federal budget projections indicating much of the expected surplus was going to be consumed by current programs, leaving relatively little for other initiatives. It was not polite in an election year to draw attention to the fact that the trillions of dollars in anticipated budget surpluses were already spoken for. In reality, there was very little money available to finance the new programs and tax cuts proposed by Al Gore and George W. Bush. Sometime after the election was over, the new President and Congress might get around to advising the people of the true state of the budget situation.

A Commerce Department official admitted in an affidavit that subpoenaed records concerning contributions to the Democratic Party by participants invited to join departmental trade missions were wrongfully withheld despite legitimate demands they be produced. The presiding U.S. district court judge concluded that Commerce officials systemically concealed documents explaining how seats on overseas trade missions were used to reward Democratic Party contributors. At about the same time, another federal judge chastised the White House for failing to produce subpoenaed email correspondence, saying the explanations for the long delay were preposterous. The judge ordered a special round of hearings to determine the best way to restore and search the missing email files.

In an unprecedented rebuke to a sitting president, an Arkansas Supreme Court Committee filed suit to strip President Clinton of his license to practice law. Saying President Clinton lacked the overall fitness to be a lawyer, the committee accused Clinton of engaging in serious misconduct in the Monica Lewinsky affair, including giving false testimony that damaged the reputation of the legal profession. In Little Rock, Arkansas, Seth Ward died. Mr. Ward was a retired businessman who had gained national attention for his involvement with the Clintons in what became known as the Whitewater scandals.

Although the citizenship program looked extremely suspicious, it was not implemented to further inappropriate political ends said the Justice Department. An investigation found the program to accelerate the citizenship application process was not designed to pad the voter roles before the 1996 investigations, but the investigators admitted some White House officials may have taken advantage of it to boost Democratic election prospects. A summer season of high anxiety began on Capitol Hill as people working for retiring members of Congress began looking for new jobs. Washington's lobbying firms expected to be flooded with resumes from their good friends leaving Capitol Hill.

Muncaster's nightmares began a few nights after he celebrated the 4th of July as guest at a rooftop party held at one of Washington's finer hotels. He was delighted to receive the invitation because it was a sign he was becoming an important person, one able to socialize in the higher circles. It also meant he would not have to mix with the masses crowding the Mall to watch the fireworks display. From the rooftop vantage point, the spectacular pyrotechnics could be viewed while enjoying the fine food, libations and company of those who were politically aware. A number of absorbing discussions regarding the legislative needs of clients took place during the festivities and a number of impressive political bargains were struck. As the social evening concluded, Muncaster was duly impressed with how things had gone. Those who managed America from behind the scenes knew how to celebrate the nation's birthday in style. He was looking forward to becoming more closely associated with those who, for the right price, made big things happen in the capital for special people.

Muncaster 's sound sleep was disrupted by an annoying, repeated tapping at the foot of his bed. As he became aware of a unwanted presence in the room, Muncaster shot upright and grabbed his automatic pistol from the night stand, clicked off the safety and aimed at the intruder. "Make one move and you're a dead man," Muncaster said. "I can't miss at this range. Just stand there while I call the police." Muncaster also noticed the room was oddly chilly. It also smelled of stale human sweat and hard-ridden horses.

"The pistol won't do you any good at all," the intruder responded unconcernedly in a strangely accented voice. Muncaster had heard the voice before. It was the same voice he heard in his office on the day when the George Washington portrait appeared on the wall. "Since I am already deceased," continued the intruder, "the police will be of no help to you in this matter. Mr. Swindell, I have come to discuss a grave situation with you, so let us waste no more time on irrelevant conversation. Surely you did not believe I would permit you to murder my associate in a matter of great national importance, Mr. Leon Placke, and avoid punishment? No sir, I could never permit myself do that! I am here to remind you of your duty. To ask you to confess your guilt for Mr. Placke's murder, and accept the responsibility for your despicable act."

What the hell was going on in his bedroom? As Muncaster's eyes grew accustomed to the darkness, he made out the figure of George Washington, clad in a mud spattered military uniform, standing at the foot of his bed with his hands folded unthreateningly in front of him. Although he was taken aback by the strange sight and smell, Muncaster's keen legal reflexes did not fail him. Quickly recovering his wits, Muncaster defensively replied, "General you are mistaken. Placke was no great shakes as your messenger. He was a disruptive idiot. I did your memory and the country a great service by putting an end to his incendiary nonsense."

General Washington neither moved nor changed his expression as he calmly said, "The United States of America is in crisis. The process of government is being debauched by those professing to serve the public interest while seeking personal gain and power at public expense. If you will recall sir, Mr. Placke was acting as my town crier, seeking to alert the American people to sorry state of affairs existing in the federal capital."

Muncaster decided not to interrupt as the general continued, "I'll tell you plainly Mr. Swindell, having this disgusting city, this cesspool of greed and special interest deals named after me is an insult to my name and the memory of all the men who fought the war for independence. We did not throw off the English yoke to establish a nation so self-indulgent and degenerate as this."

This ghost of Washington or whatever it was, was talking crazy, just like Leon Placke. Muncaster was not going to let the vile attack on the political establishment pass and he fired back a rebuttal, "General, excuse me for saying this, but don't you see how good things are in the United States? The economy is at an all-time high and unemployment is down as far as it can go. I would say sir, and the record supports it, that there is nothing wrong with the way the business of governing is conducted in Washington, DC. We have, I believe, achieved a perfect working democracy. Our disinterested citizens are blessed with the best system of government in the world. Once the preserve of mere part-timers, politics has grown into a professional endeavor. The parties will spend $2 per each vote cast on media messages during the coming election. Think of the number of rewarding jobs such an undertaking creates. Instead of criticizing us, you ought to be proud of what we have built on the strong foundation you established. Times change, what worked in your day will not work in our complex, interdependent information age society. Why don't you go back to your grave and leave us alone to manage things as we see fit?"

"I'm not here to debate the merits of sorely needed political reform with you, sir! Since I participated in the founding of the nation, I should have thought you would at least give me credit for knowing what the founders intended," Washington retorted. "My only purpose in coming here tonight is to ask you to confess to the murder of a good man, the one named Leon Placke. You poisoned him and then sullied his honor by making it look as though he took his own life. A murder has been committed, Mr. Swindell. You must now pay the price for your foul deed. Go tell the constables what you did and accept the consequences."

Muncaster sat in bed holding the pistol, making no response. Legal definitions aside, killing Placke was no crime, it was a public service. George Washington waited a moment before continuing, "If you do not of your own accord confess to the crime, I will see to it that you are vigorously encouraged to do so. Of that you may be assured! Doing what is right is difficult, Mr. Swindell. For once in your life set aside your deceptive ways, go against your instincts, do the honorable thing!"

Washington again waited for a response from Muncaster. When none came, he said, "Sir, I see we can come to no agreement on this matter this night. Very well then! Perhaps it is time you were taught a lesson! One that will open your eyes to the loathsome level to which you have sunk. Mr. Swindell, what I now say, I say to you in all sincerity. There always have been good men who fight valiantly for bad causes, and in so doing, raise the cost of victory to hideously high levels. This bitter truth you will learn first-hand! It is a truth that all those who govern or advise those who govern must learn and understand."

Not waiting for Muncaster to comment, the apparition standing at the foot of the bed turned smartly and faded from sight. Although Muncaster was shaken by the brazen invasion of his privacy, he was unmoved by Washington's appeal to his better nature. Despite the threats made by his strange visitor, Muncaster had no intention of going to the cops. Why should he? He had been forced to act in the best interest of the Washington lobbyists only because Placke had selfishly refused countless offers of medical assistance. Placke was a betrayer, a lowlife bent on changing the very rules that had allowed him to become rich. Trying to deny others the lucrative benefits of a lobbying career was the ultimate hypocritical move by a man who had made a reputation in the capital as the king of the lobbyists. The back-stabbing asshole deserved everything he got. As he lay down to resume his interrupted rest, Muncaster tried to make sense out of George Washington's babbling. He didn't understand any of the vague crap about good men and bad causes. In the busy world of politics, the only bad cause Muncaster knew of, was the one without any funding.

The malodorous smells in Muncaster's bedroom lingered for days despite his best efforts to air out the room. The sensory reminder of George Washington's visit lingered so strongly that he finally brought in a fumigator. As he worked, the fumigator couldn't imagine why anyone would leave old, stale, sweaty riding cloths lying around for so long that the smell seeped into every nook and cranny of the bedroom. He wondered what Muncaster finally did with the clothing that made the room smell so badly.

A few nights later, Muncaster received another massive shock. He awoke to find himself in a place where the heat was oppressive and the stench bad enough to gag a maggot. He was outside a whitewashed hospital building, surrounded by at least a hundred wounded soldiers. They were a sorry lot, suffering from all types of wounds and some looking as if they had lain untreated in the summer heat for days. Inside the open door of the building, Muncaster could see two surgeons, one a white man, the other a black man, and a few assistants frantically working on patients. As a flabbergasted Muncaster observed the gory scene, the black surgeon saw him and beckoned to him with a wave of his bloody bone saw to come in and help. Horrified by the macabre scene, Muncaster ignored the doctor's entreaties and stood rooted to the ground. There was no way anyone was going to get him to go into that primitive operating room.

After finishing with the wounded soldier on his table, the surgeon put down his saw, wiped his bloody hands on his apron and started for the door clearly intending to bring Muncaster into the operating room. As the surgeon approached he said, "Please sir, could you assist us for a few hours? We are so desperately short of help." As the blood-spattered surgeon came to within a few feet of him, Muncaster suddenly realized where he was. The surgeon's southern drawl and the gray uniforms of the wounded made it plain as day. Muncaster was at one of Richmond's Civil War military hospitals. The surgeon standing before him was none other than Cyrus Bellnapp, one of the soldiers who had hidden the Confederate government papers at Centreville.

Muncaster wanted nothing to do with Bellnapp or his blood-soaked misery. Finding his finely honed legal skills of no use in this wretched situation, Muncaster lost his composure and shrieked, "Damn it, keep away from me!" as he turned and ran for his life. Looking back over his shoulder as he fled down the dirt road, Muncaster saw the blood spattered surgeon, a fly-covered pile of amputated limbs and the mass of wounded waiting for treatment. Muncaster ran as fast as he could to get out of there, passing ambulances and supply wagons going in the opposite direction. He was growing tired and gasping for breath when he ran right into his bedroom wall. The jarring impact stunned him, broke his nose and sent him reeling backward in pain.

As he later sat in the hospital emergency room holding ice packs on his swollen nose and bruised forehead, Muncaster could not get the repulsive scene at Cyrus Bellnapp's hospital out of his mind. As his shattered nose throbbed, Muncaster came to realize that Bellnapp was one of those good men involved in a bad cause that George Washington had warned him about.

His swollen nose had not completely receded to its normal size when, a few nights later, Muncaster was tormented by a second nightmare. He found himself straining with the other members of a gun crew to manhandle a newly arrived cannon into position. Moving the iron monster was tough, hard work. Using rope, block, tackle and muscle power, the gunners slowly inched the piece forward and up the incline to the firing port. As they heaved and pushed, Muncaster realized he had been to this place before. He had been here with Leon Placke, on the last day of day Leon's life! To his dismay, Muncaster found himself struggling to help position an artillery piece in the Confederate fortifications at Centreville, Virginia during the first year of the Civil War.

The loud crack of a rope parting under excessive strain was a warning that all was not well. Now out of control, the loose cannon hurled backward down the incline. To get out of its path, Muncaster dove to the side, crashing into one of the access trench's wooden interior walls. As the free swinging big gun sailed by his head, Muncaster could read the manufacturer's markings stamped on the cannon. He saw the words "Tredegar, Richmond, VA" in capital letters flash closely by his face. With a terrific jolt, the cannon slammed into the ground 15 feet behind him, sending clods of dirt flying in all directions. As soldiers came running to reclaim the wayward gun, Muncaster congratulated himself on his narrow escape. He had barely avoided being crushed by the iron monster.

As Muncaster tried to regain his feet in the dirty trench, the fortification disappeared and he found himself painfully draped over the tipped-over chest of drawers in his bedroom. He must have dove directly into it from his bed, knocking it over. The same doctor who had treated him on his last visit was on duty in the emergency room. While diagnosing Mncaster's three bruised and cracked ribs, the doctor told him he ought to start taking it a bit easier. This was Muncaster's second visit to the hospital in as many weeks. As

Muncaster lay on the emergency room bed waiting for the sedative to ease his pain to take effect, he tried to remember the name of the other good man involved with a bad cause. It was Chambon or something like that. He was the ex-artillerist who accompanied Bellnap to Centreville. He had gotten himself blown up at Centreville when the Confederates evacuated the place early in the war's second year and had met Bellnapp while recovering in the hospital. As he fitfully drifted off to sleep, Muncaster remembered telling Leon Placke about him. The contents of Muncaster's extensive data files, gathered for his own use at much expense to the government, were coming back to haunt him. Sneaky George Washington must have gone through those files without Muncaster's knowledge. The vengeful, miserable bastard was now using the information to generate the appalling nightmares that tormented Muncaster.

His sudden proneness to accident conferred a degree of celebrity status upon him. As he slowly hobbled down the halls of the Commerce Department with his sore ribs and mashed nose, Muncaster's deplorable condition attracted sympathy from few and smirks of delight from many. As word of Muncaster's misfortune spread, it brightened the day for a large number of the building's inhabitants. To the numerous people Muncaster routinely treated like dirt, it appeared as if justice was finally being done. They were delighted that Muncaster, who was known to be one of the capital's sleaziest manipulators, was falling on hard times in a big way. Commerce workers were pleased to see Muncaster receiving at least a partial measure of what was due him. With undisguised glee, they waited to see what would happen next to the arrogant scoundrel they had grown to despise.

The many fans of Muncaster's misfortune didn't have a long wait. Jolted from a restless sleep a week later, Muncaster found himself thrust into a wartime hell of equal opportunity at the Tredegar Iron Works on Richmond's James River waterfront. Producing nearly half of all Confederate artillery pieces, the five acre Tredegar complex was a bedlam of never-ending activity. Iron smelters lit up the night sky as 800 laborers, both black and white, free and slave, toiled around the clock in the smoke and heat to manufacture cannon for the Rebel government. Muncaster was in the gun foundry, working with a sweating crew filling a cannon mold with molten iron. Large ladles of flaming iron had to be maneuvered from the furnace to the gun cast set in the floor. As the ladles were trundled over in rapid succession, they had to be tilted and emptied into the narrow opening at the casting's top. Speed was essential because, if the prior load cooled before the next batch was dumped, the cannon casting would be ruined.

The heat was intense as the pouring progressed. Already grimy and on the verge of heat prostration, Muncaster was worrying about burning his hair and eyebrows when something went wrong with one of the large ladles moving the superheated molten iron. A hissing stream of the stuff spewed onto the floor, racing toward him. To avoid being fried alive, Muncaster threw down his tools as he dove out of the fiery stream's path. To his amazement, Muncaster didn't crash into anything because he found himself able to float in the air. As he watched, the other members of the crew grabbed shovels and frenziedly threw up dikes of sand around the bubbling, molten mass to contain it.

No longer wishing to be involved with those who worked with scorching iron, Muncaster steered himself toward an open window. As he glided outside, he saw the Tredegar complex buildings, the Confederate States Armory, the broad James River and the coal and iron ore barges tied along the bank of the canal waiting to be unloaded. Floating was so much nicer than working in the dirt and heat. A full moon was up. The scene below looked like something one saw in one of those old oil paintings in an art museum. The glow of the fire-belching furnaces was actually pleasant to watch from a distance. Looking in the other direction, Muncaster saw the Confederate capitol building, and the Confederate White House perched on the hills. Bellnapp's hospital was also around here someplace. Muncaster wanted to make sure he steered himself clear of that wretched site.

Being able to float above the fray while others struggled with fiery chaos should have been a warning to Muncaster that something was about to go wrong. Muncaster's pleasant free floating experience came to an abrupt end when he crash landed at the foot of the stairs in his home. Pain shoot through his body as the bones in his twisted leg snapped and his face smacked into the wall. After some agonizing moments, he recovered enough of his senses to be able to drag himself across the floor to the kitchen. Dazedly fumbling with the phone, Muncaster managed to call for an ambulance. It was his third and most serious accident within the same number of weeks. In what was becoming a neighborhood ritual, Muncaster was transported to the hospital. There, the doctors placed his fractured leg in a cast. His nose, smashed for a second time, was gently worked into a shape somewhat similar to the original.

Two of Muncaster's previously cracked ribs had been broken. Muncaster grimaced as the doctors pushed them back into place. As he lay immobilized, Muncaster groggily came to the conclusion that he had lost the battle he was waging with the most determined of foes. The uncompromising George Washington had beaten him to a pulp. Washington had demonstrated to Muncaster who was in charge. Bad things were going to continue to happen until Muncaster accidentally killed himself or gave in to Washington's demand and admitted to Placke's murder. Stiff, sore and barely able to move, Muncaster had come to the end of the road. With no little degree of difficulty, he picked up the bedside phone and asked the hospital operator to connect him with the homicide division. Confessing to Placke's murder was infinitely better than risking another of the ghastly nighttime confrontations with the past orchestrated by George Washington. As he hung up the phone, Muncaster began to weep. Not from any degree of remorse for what he had done, but because he had been beaten by a putrid, stick-in-the mud with old fashioned ideas.

"All voting is a sort of gaming, like checkers or backgammon, with a slight moral tinge to it, a playing with right and wrong.
-Henry David Thoreau, 1849

"Son, in politics you've got to learn that overnight chicken shit can turn to chicken salad."
-Lyndon B. Johnson, 1958

"The human being is in the most literal sense a political animal, not merely a gregarious animal, but an animal which can individuate itself only in the midst of society."
-Karl Marx, 1857

The Washington establishment was launching the 2000 election melodrama onto the national stage. It was the grandest of political plays, one with millions of spectators, and the Washington establishment loved it. The ad writers, pollsters, television spot creators, policy constructors, speech writers, mass mailers, fund raisers, lobbyists and politicians were ready to play their roles in the miracle of democracy spectacle that would pump hundreds of millions of dollars into the business side of politics.

To win election, a candidate had to artfully burnish his or her image while outmaneuvering and denigrating the opponent. The voter had to be pandered to and amused at the same time. The voter was fickle, well-intentioned, but unsophisticated and easily duped.

The friends and supporters of a candidate's position were quick studies in learning what was needed to save the country. All opponents and their supporters were selfish, desiring to ruin the country in order to achieve their greedy ends. They were intellectually arrogant at best, chronic liars at worst, and prone to all sort of evil machinations. A candidate's contributors gave large sums of money to campaigns solely out of a sense of civic duty or to ensure they could lawfully petition their government at a later date. The opponent's contributors were crassly buying access to government, expecting to be rewarded handsomely in one form or the other after the election.

While everyone in the business worked ceaselessly to promote these stereotypes as the money rolled in, they knew it was really a matter of the pot calling the kettle black. That's what made the political business so interesting, being able to do what one condemned the opposition for doing. In the political industry, the concept had always worked well. Nothing would ever have to change until the dull-witted voters caught on to the game. And no one presently actively engaged in politics expected that day to come anytime soon.

The two political conventions were over. The television audience watching the convention coverage was the smallest in decades, but delegate entertainment was the most lavish ever. The cruises on corporate yachts in Philadelphia, lunches with the elite of Beverly Hills, evening receptions and the hospitality suites provided by special interest groups and lobbyists had receded to pleasant memories in the minds of the attendees. The nation's lawmakers relished the memory of being the guests of honor at the splendid events paid for by the corporations they regulated.

The fact that all of the extravagance was part of a sorry American political trend didn't matter to the partying attendees. As conventions evolved into more spectacle than political selection process, the social events increasingly took over as the venue where the real business of politics got done. It was where the parties raised money, candidates schmoozed with potential donors and corporations and unions gained goodwill from politicians. For those having business with the government, it ensured access to those with the power to change or waive the rules. Giving people good food on china plates was a quid pro quo sort of a thing. Those paying the bills for the lavish affairs wanted the legislators to fondly remember them later when their help was needed.

Some who wrote the big checks to the Democratic Party were not smiling because they had been given the impression that $500,000 was the going rate for a skybox at the Los Angeles convention center. So much money had been raised and the availability schedules so poorly coordinated that many donors were forced to share boxes or limit their use to alternate days. It was another sign of the Democratic Party's tortured relationship with money, grasping for as much as it could get while pausing for occasional bouts of self-flagellation. Although the Democrats declared themselves to be the party of the people, those who gave the most got the best of everything at the convention. A 500-seat restaurant was reserved for big donors, with guards stationed at the doors to carefully scrutinize passes. Inside the posh eatery, fund raisers, large donors, those serving in Congress and lobbyists mingled and discussed the important issues of the day.

On the campaign trail, Democrats regularly assailed pharmaceutical companies, cigarette makers and the gun lobby. At the convention, the same ostracized groups the Democrats loved to bash in public paid for a large number of the sun-up to sun-down smorgasbord of events held to honor Democratic delegates and lawmakers. The National Rifle Association and two large tobacco companies underwrote a party at the Santa Monica pier for conservative Blue Dog Democrats. Two other large drug makers helped sponsor the $40,000 "Mardi Gras Goes Hollywood" bash at Paramount Studios. As the Democrats castigated the Republican nominees of the "Grand Oil Party," they thoroughly enjoyed the hospitality provided by Texaco, Chevron Corporation, and Occidental Petroleum. With a new found respect for family values taking precedent, the sold out Democratic fund raiser scheduled for the Playboy Mansion was abruptly moved to Universal Studios. Vice President Gore had objected strongly to the venue, claiming it would embarrass the party.

The Republicans left Philadelphia vowing to launch a $100 million dollar campaign to get wavering voters to go to the polls in November. Over the radio and television airwaves, by phone, through the mail and by knocking on doors, the party was going to pay to boost the turnout among those who seemed most likely to come down on the side of Republican candidates. The coming election was expected to continue the trend of low voter participation, with less than half of those eligible expected to cast a ballot. This shocking piece of political intelligence made getting a percentage of the unmotivated to vote critical to the outcome of the election. If the party could get a fraction of America's couch potatoes up long enough to vote, they would have the election in the bag.

With the conventions over, the struggle for votes in the coming election intensified. With the nation in the midst of the longest period of economic prosperity in its history, Vice President Gore officially took charge of the party apparatus. He claimed credit for converting big budget deficits into the largest surplus ever, lowering inflation and creating 22 million new jobs. He promised tax cuts to help people save for college, pay for health insurance and child care. He also said he would end the marriage penalty tax. The Vice President, however, would not go along with a huge tax cut for the wealthy at the expense of everyone else. It would wreck the good economy and in the process make rich Republicans even richer.

The Republicans countered by accusing the Democrats of promoting class warfare and partisan division. Texas Governor George W. Bush promised to spend $1 billion on education while claiming he did not want to increase the federal government's role in education. The Republicans thought the voters were in the mood for a dose of prosperity mixed with compassionate conservatism. The Democrats, realizing they could not ride the economy alone to victory, abandoned their resistance to religious programs and began to talk openly about faith. The nation's economic house was fixed, they said. It was time to start worrying about getting the state of America's moral house in order.

In the aftermath of the well-scripted conventions, polls showed the candidates in a statistical tie for the lead. The candidates heatedly campaigned, Gore attacking and slashing along the banks of the Mississippi River while Bush fought ferociously in the west. As the candidates waged war on one another, the government released a report showing the American prison population now topped 1.3 million. An additional five million Americans were out of prison on probation and parole. There being no political mileage in the news, neither party rushed forward to claim credit for the policies behind the mind-boggling statistics. Another government report revealed that the foreign trips taken by President Clinton and other administration officials since 1997 had cost the taxpayers $292 million. It cost $51,100 an hour to transport the President by air. The Republicans thought briefly about making an issue out of the high travel costs, but then decided the security, communications, decoy aircraft and large number of advance people were a justifiable part of the overhead costs of running the nation. If they won the election, they weren't planning to skimp on overseas travel. Republican office holders, like their Democratic counterparts, liked to travel in a manner befitting the ruling class of a great nation.

Thousands of miles of pipeline crisscross the United States. Many of the lines had been in continuous use for 20, 30, 40 years and longer. Without warning, a 30-inch natural gas pipeline buried six feet underground in New Mexico ruptured. The resulting explosion carved a crater in the landscape 86 feet long, 50 feet wide and 20 feet deep and killed the 11 people camping nearby. The federal official in charge of pipeline inspections admitted that not much pipeline inspecting was being done these days. The agency didn't have the funds to hire inspectors for the maze of aging lines winding across the United States. While official Washington was shaken by the size of the disaster, no one saw a link between the ever rising costs of political overhead and the unavailability of funds to pay for pipeline inspections.

An unpublished government study listed the United States as the world's biggest arms exporter with shipments more than five times greater than second place Britain. The U.S. had active arms deals with developing countries valued at over $25 billion, a respectable 35 percent share of a very competitive market. The study also said national defense did not come cheap. America's hefty outlay of $276 billion for military weaponry accounted for 33 percent of the world's spending on weapons.

Democrats reacted with cold fury to the news that the troublesome independent counsel had impaneled a new grand jury to consider evidence on whether President Clinton should be indicted after he leaves office on charges arising from the Monica Lewinsky affair. The leak undoubtedly was made by Republicans in an effort to detract from Vice President Gore's brilliantly orchestrated campaign. Senator John Breaux of Louisiana called the timing of the news release, "the most political act that I think I have seen in my lifetime." Breaux's statement immediately attracted wide attention, coming as it did, from one of the most astute political deal-doers ever to sit in the Senate.

Robert W. Ray, the current independent counsel, issued a terse statement saying his office didn't release the information. Enraged White officials knew he was lying. Ray, a no-good dirt bag with big ambitions, was probably in league with one of the right-wing conspiracies trying to bring President Clinton down. As the scorching accusations flew back and forth across Washington's political no-man's land like poorly-aimed artillery shells, a federal judge sitting on the panel of judges overseeing the independent counsel's investigation, abruptly brought the political bombardment to a halt. The judge, a Democrat appointed by President Carter, admitted he had inadvertently let word of the new grand jury slip to a reporter. The judge's forthright admission raised another prickly legal question. Was the judge's mistaken disclosure of the grand jury's target a violation of grand jury secrecy laws? Because the bungling judge was a Democrat, the angry Democrats weren't quite sure what to do next. It would have been much simpler if the source of the leak had been a Republican. Wrong-doing could then have been righteously railed at and a great deal of favorable media coverage could have been created for the party.

Totaling more than $52 million, the cost f the Clinton probe was setting new records. The investigators, attorneys, consultants, and computer analysts contracted to the independent counsel were working overtime. When Attorney General Janet Reno announced she was refusing to name a special counsel to investigate the 1996 campaign fund raising tactics of Vice President Al Gore, many in Washington were disappointed. Another well-funded independent counsel investigation would have been the source of many good paying jobs and a host of new contracts.

A White House lawyer asked the presiding federal judge to end the probe of missing email files. With a straight face, the attorney said all the email files sought by the judge had been handed over. The White House had done its best to meet the court's demands and had not tried to deceive the judge in any way. The federal judge didn't believe the lawyer was telling the truth. Instead of ending the seven-month inquiry, the untrusting judge called a former White House counsel to testify as to what he knew about the thousands of supposedly lost Clinton administration email messages. The judge thought it peculiar that an administration claiming to have invented the Internet and priding itself on being on the cutting edge of information age technology couldn't locate the email files demanded by the court.

Only days before its scheduled release, the Republican National Committee canceled the airing of a harsh television ad that attacked Vice President Gore's creditability by using misleading excerpts from a six-year old interview. Enraged by the violation of her freedom of speech rights and insulted by the slap at her clever creativity, the ad's designer resigned in a huff and took a job with a firm creating TV spots for the Democrats. With millions of dollars in unregulated soft money donations financing political ad campaigns, there were plenty of good ad writer jobs available in Washington. As a political professional, she had options. She did not have to accept the humiliation of having her creativity questioned.

After accepting the Democratic presidential nomination, Vice President Gore unleashed a series of blistering attacks on health maintenance organizations and drug makers, savaging the former for denying healthcare to patients and the latter for keeping prescription drug prices high. Gore's populist onslaught created a somewhat awkward situation for his running mate, Senator Joseph Lieberman. Over the years, big pharmaceutical companies and health insurers had been among the most generous donors to Senator Lieberman. The Democratic ticket he so joyously joined in Los Angeles was now savagely biting the hands that loyally funded him for years. There was nothing he could do but try to maintain a dignified silence. What was preached in Washington was often not practiced after the election was over. Things were sure to get back to normal after the political harangues quieted down.

In a clear violation of the understanding that Labor Day was the traditional kickoff for the fall campaign, Democrats launched a surprise blitz of attack ads on six vulnerable Republican House candidates. As the rolling barrage of brutal messages came howling over the television airwaves into the six congressional districts and catching the Republicans napping, the battle for control of the next Congress began in earnest. As stunned Republicans scrambled frantically through a furious hail of visual and verbal shrapnel to unlimber their political guns and return fire, it was clear that the first victory in the televised skirmishing had gone to the Democrats. Flushed with an unprecedented amount of cash, the tough Democratic warriors in Congress were hell-bent on wresting control of that establishment from the Republicans. If the American people wanted to change the party controlling the White House, they ought to also be persuaded to do the same with Congress.

As the dust kicked-up by the quick-stepping legions of political shock troops swirled through Washington's streets, the shocking news of Muncaster Swindell's hospital bed confession rocked Washington's lobbying establishment to its core. It was simply unimaginable to the lobbyists and media warriors that an aspiring lobbyist would sink so low as to take the life of one of the city's best and brightest political fixers. Such a deed was a violation of the lobbying code of ethics and would result in Muncaster's immediate expulsion from the prestigious Washington Society of Solicitors. Worse yet, there was bound to be a rekindling of public interest in Leon Placke's crazy reform proposals as the murder case went to trial. Big and expensive political campaigns were underway. Washington insiders didn't want Placke's weird ideas dredged up again because they would draw the spotlight away from the ongoing campaigns. Muncaster's sense of timing was really pathetic. On that point, the city's political operatives, lawyers and lobbyists were in agreement. If he had been a true gentleman, Muncaster would have had the decency to wait until the election was over before he confessed to Placke's murder.

The battered person lying in the hospital bed was in sad shape. His badly bruised nose looked as though it had been flattened by a hammer. As the two police detectives listened, Muncaster related the details of how he had killed Leon Placke. As Muncaster rambled, the detectives couldn't help wondering if he might not still be under the influence of the strong sedatives given to ease the pain of his many injuries. With Washington, DC having one of the nation's highest homicide rates, the overworked detectives were pleasantly surprised to learn the crime had been committed in Fairfax County, not in their jurisdiction. Trying hard to hide their sense of relief, they told Muncaster his statement would be forwarded to the county authorities, who would contact him shortly. With Muncaster incapacitated by his injuries, there was no real rush. Muncaster wasn't going to go anywhere very soon.

Two days later, the Fairfax County homicide detectives appeared at the hospital and Muncaster repeated his confession for a second time. The police officers found themselves discussing a murder with a well-connected government official who had in the past weeks taken to diving down stairways and crashing headfirst into floors and walls. This same unstable individual was also insisting on confessing to a murder because a ghost was demanding that he do so.

Despite the initial skepticism of the police, the details of Muncaster's confession checked out after investigation. Leon Placke had been killed by H. Muncaster Swindell, who then cleverly covered his tracks by making it appear as though Placke had committed suicide. The murder had been well-planned, the police had been completely fooled, never even suspecting the crime occurred. As such, Muncaster was never under the slightest hint of suspicion. So why did he decide to confess after he had gotten away with the crime? The detectives never gave any credibility to Muncaster's irrational insistence on blaming George Washington for forcing him to admit his guilt.

The real explanation for the ingenious method of murder, the subsequent change of heart and confession was lodged somewhere the dark recesses of Muncaster's warped mind. From all outward appearances, it was clear Muncaster was insane. Had he been insane when he committed the murder or had his deep sense of guilt pushed him over the edge later? Although they had a true confession, the homicide detectives wanted to have a psychiatrist evaluate Muncaster's mental condition. The prosecutor would need to know precisely when Muncaster had lost his sanity. It was going to be a be difficult matter to determine because Muncaster was in the business of politics. He could easily have been insane for a number of years and no one in the industry would have noticed. While the police were trying to find someone willing to take on the laborious task, the Washington Society of Solicitors sprang into action.

"Without money honor is merely a disease."

-Jean Racine, 1669

A delegation from the society approached Dr. Orasco Lopez, the well-regarded psychiatrist who tended to the needs of the lobbying community, and offered him a proposition. Because Muncaster was a current society member and Placke a former member, the society was concerned about the potential for negative publicity the murder trial would bring with it. Would Dr. Lopez be interested in evaluating Muncaster Swindell? The society wanted a trustworthy professional handling the project, not a neophyte picked randomly off of a roster of police service providers. Although he was honored by the offer, Dr. Lopez always adhered to the highest standards of ethical conduct in his patient dealings. There was a slight problem with the proposal his distinguished visitors had placed before him and he was felt obligated to point it out. If he accepted the $40,000 payment offered by the society, he was ethically bound to name the society as his client on the evaluation he would submit to the court. He would also have to pay tax on the income earned. On the other hand, if $40,000 in $20 and $50 bills magically appeared on his desk, Dr. Lopez would volunteer his services out of a strong sense of civic duty and he would not have to report the income to the IRS.

As an unpaid volunteer, his objective psychiatric evaluation of Muncaster Swindell would be untainted by any link to the society. The society would be able to distance itself from the unsavory killing of a former member who was known to have been agitating to change certain Washington political practices. The confessed murderer, Muncaster Swindell, was a current member of the society in good standing. It was an open secret in town that Placke's reforms would have hit society members hard in their pocketbooks if they had been adopted. As ideology and self-interest went hand-in-hand, the members couldn't pretend to sorry to be rid of Placke. It was a very delicate situation. The evaluator could not leave any clues behind if the reputation of the society was to be protected. The delegation immediately saw the wisdom of Dr. Lopez's astute observations, and in the finest tradition of Washington deal-making, heartily agreed to the good doctor's terms.

Dr. Lopez had been a student of Soviet psychiatric methods and had adapted a few of the Soviet procedures to his practice in the nation's capital. When the occasion demanded, Dr. Lopez always delivered the analytical result desired by those wielding power. The society's delegation was reassured by the doctor's adherence to this principle of conduct. There was now no doubt that Muncaster Swindell would be found to be insane. It was likely, based upon Dr. Lopez's thorough evaluation, that Muncaster would be discretely committed to an institution for the criminally insane. The burdensome expense and publicity of a public trial would be avoided completely. The messy business of Leon Placke's unwanted reforms and Muncaster Swindell's rash indiscretion would be quietly put to bed once and for all. The indelicate matters of a bloated White House staff, a dysfunctional Congress, the scandalous impact of special interest money and a government overrun by lobbyists would not be raised to distract the voters during the ongoing moneymaking political campaign season.

Centreville had not seen such embarrassment since overconfident, picnic basket laden Washington hot-shots had parked along the ridge to watch the Union army whip the Rebels at the battle of first battle of Manassas in 1861. The most powerful and influential lobbyist in Washington had been killed at a Centreville historical site and the local police had been duped to the point of missing the crime completely. They had been hood-winked by a quick-witted killer from the upper rungs of the national political bureaucracy. If the murderer hadn't taken to falling down stairs and breaking his bones, the inept police would have been none the wiser. Even when the killer first confessed, the police had been skeptical. The chagrined police waited for a torrent of abuse to begin. The charges of incompetence, demands for an investigation and reorganization of the force always followed in the wake of an incident of this type.

Strangely, nothing happened. There were no calls to the County Board of Supervisors from irate members of Congress, lawyers, lobbyists or the professional police haters. The mystified police were even more pleasantly surprised when Dr. Lopez volunteered to evaluate Muncaster's mental condition at no charge to the county. Having such a respected professional involved in the matter would help remove some of the humiliation remaining from the miscued call on the cause of Placke's death. The esteemed Dr. Lopez made numerous calls and visits, covering all the bases at the police department and the prosecutor's office before he began. Everyone anxiously awaited the expert analysis his all-inclusive and impartial evaluation would produce.

Dr. Lopez would have loved to been able take Muncaster to another location and test the Soviet electrical shock methods on him that he had read about. After a few days of treatment, he'd be willing to bet he'd have the bed-ridden bastard willing to sign any statement placed before him. People stupid enough to cause problems for those who paid the bills for national endeavors ought to be quickly disposed of. Dr. Lopez considered bringing the transformer and wires he had purchased from a Moscow institution's surplus property sale to the hospital, but wasn't sure he could make it work because the screams of his patient would be hard to explain to the staff. Unable to experiment, Dr. Lopez decided to use the tried-and-true interview option. With clipboard in hand as he entered the room, he announced, "Hi, Muncaster, I'm Dr. Orasco Lopez. Your friends in Washington have sent me to help you. Although you may not remember it, we have met at a number of society social events in the past."

"I appreciate your concern," Muncaster responded, looking up from his bed. "But I'm afraid you're too late. I've already admitted to the police I disposed of Leon Placke."

"True enough. It's unfortunate, however, you did not take the time to speak with a good criminal attorney before you made your confession. With all your experience, you should know very well how the law works! I would've thought you would have had the good sense to do it! But the lost opportunity is now merely water over the dam and we have to go on the best we can."

"Your friends want me to explore the mitigating circumstances we can use in your defense. Our plan is to go for a minimum sentence, one supported by an insanity plea that will overwhelm the court, the press and the general public! My task is to convince the judge and jury to go easy on you by pointing out you weren't responsible for your actions. That you were really the victim, not the perpetrator! I think its quite doable, if you will help. Please begin by telling me how you planned and implemented the removal of the pest also known as Leon Placke. How did it actually happen? I'll sort out the items we can use in your defense and ignore the remainder. With your permission, I'll take notes because I'll be testifying on your behalf later."

Muncaster felt better than he had in days. His powerful friends in Washington's political and lobbying communities had not abandoned him. With their help, the price he had to pay because he had been forced by George Washington's henchmen into admitting he knocked off Leon Placke would be a small one. The lawyers of Washington were, after all, leading experts in the art of getting their clients the lightest of all possible sentences. With the assistance of the brilliant Dr. Lopez, Muncaster's defense would be crafted to appeal to the biases of both liberals and conservatives. As such, it would be hard to break. Dr. Orasco Lopez didn't work for cheap. His friends must have put up a large sum of money to get the noted doctor to take the case.

"It's all that goddamn George Washington's fault," Muncaster said as he began to tell his version of events.

"What did you say? Say it again, please," responded a surprised Dr. Lopez as he wrote. This assignment might turn out to be a lot easier than he thought. Muncaster Swindell probably was loony. If so, so much the better. The less time he had to spend on this case, the higher his profit margin would be.

Muncaster repeated himself and continued, "George Washington has come back from the grave to make life miserable for our modern political establishment. He went after Leon Placke with a vengeance. He harassed poor Leon unmercifully, until he couldn't take it anymore. To get Washington off of his back, Leon finally agreed to give up his lobbying practice and take up the stupid cause of promoting Washington's bullshit political reform agenda. You know the garbage Leon talked about: cutting back the bloated White House and Congressional staffs, change the way the House of Representatives is apportioned, eliminate lobbyists and the influence of the soft money contributed by special interest groups. The dumbest of all George Washington's moronic schemes was the idea of moving the capital to the center of the country. Just because Washington placed the capital in the center of the nation in days when everyone plowed with horses, doesn't mean we have to move it to keep up with his obsolete concepts."

"This is very interesting Muncaster! If I understand you correctly, you are saying one of the nation's long dead founders thinks our political system has been corrupted and ought to be changed? You actually believe this ghost is pressuring the living to institute reforms, to get the nation back on the track of following the founding fathers' tenets?"

"Yes, I think he sees it that way! The problem is George Washington doesn't understand there is nothing wrong with things they way they are! The political decision-making system in this country works fine. Why would we change it? The political parties are happy, the political industry does well financially and those willing to invest money in the political process get all the help from government they can afford to buy. George Washington's thinking is outmoded, totally out of step with our modern political system. The old shit is stuck in a time-warp! He thinks duty, personal sacrifice, honor and integrity are important political ingredients! Who believes that debilitated crap nowadays? It belongs to a time when the country was full of subsistence farmers."

As Dr. Lopez scribbled a few notes and drew a lot of doodles on his pad, Muncaster continued, "George Washington loves this country, no doubt about that. In the past, he appeared during times of crisis to help save the nation. He came twice during the Civil War and at least once during World War II. He loves the country so much that he keeps trying push his misguided, obsolete ideas down our throats. He doesn't know when to quit! He doesn't understand his help isn't needed in our information age. I don't understand why he keeps at it! Maybe sleeping outside on the hard ground for so many years affected his mind, made him mean. Look at me doctor, I am a product of his handiwork! George Washington has nearly gotten me killed!"

"George Washington did this to you? Dr. Lopez said as he waved his arm over Muncaster's extensive injuries. "My lord, what happened? Did the brute from antiquity come into your home and attack you?"

"No, he didn't do it himself," Muncaster replied. "He's too smart for that! He sent two goddamn Confederate soldiers to do the job for him. You know, the same two who buried the boxes of documents at Centerville near the end of the Civil War. The very same papers that got Leon Placke into so much hot water when he tried to help his friends in Congress by hiding the documents from the public."

This was preposterous, better than funniest TV sitcom! As he tried not to laugh, Dr. Lopez looked up from his notes saying, "Muncaster, I'm afraid I don't understand the time frame of events. It seems to me our historical epochs are getting slightly mixed up. Please explain to me how George Washington could send two Confederate soldiers to brutally beat you to within an inch of your life? After all, Washington was a general in the Revolutionary War and it occurred long before the Civil War. Why didn't he send some of his Revolutionary War troops or just knock you around himself? From all I've heard, he was a fairly rough individual, one quite capable of taking care of himself. This is an important matter! We can't be mixing up historical periods because the court will have difficulty following the sequence of events."

"How would I know?" Muncaster answered. I can't read the mind of living person, much less the one of a dead man. No, wait a minute! I remember Washington saying something about teaching me a bitter lesson. It had something to do with good men fighting well for bad causes and raising the ultimate price of winning, or some such nonsense! That's why the two Confederates were involved. They had a bad cause, but fought well and to the bitter end for it. We are supposed to respect them for doing their duty as they saw it, I guess."

Dr. Lopez asked another question. "You seem to gotten to know George Washington quite well. Did he talk to you a great deal? Did he appear in person or did you only hear his voice?"

"Oh, George Washington never gives up once he starts something! He's tough as an old nail and isn't the least bit shy. I met him a number of times. I remember one time he came directly from a military campaign. He smelled to high heaven of stale sweat and horses. It nearly gagged me. He must not have had a bath for weeks."

"What about the Confederate soldiers who assaulted you at Washington's behest? Did they appear in person or just speak to you?"

"No, you don't understand! They didn't beat me up! They used a much more subtle method than a direct physical assault. I'd go to bed the same way I normally do, only to wake later and suddenly find myself in some strange place. One night, I found myself at a Confederate military hospital in Richmond. There I was, standing smack in the middle of a group of wounded soldiers outside of an operating hut. It was awful! I can still see the flies buzzing over the wounds, bloody bandages, the appalling stench. The black

Rebel soldier was inside the building, working as a surgeon in a primitive operating room. He was short of help and kept trying to get me to assist him in cutting off arms and legs. When he came after me, I ran down the dirt road leading back to town to get away from him. I also ran right back into reality and fell down the stairs in my own home."

"He never struck you? This black man who served in the Confederate Army? What was he doing at the hospital in the first place?"

"He was a slave. He started working at the hospital, Chimborazo, it was called, on Richmond's east side, in the war's early days. He trained himself in surgery and worked there for most of the war. He joined the army during the war's last days and went to Centreville to hide the now infamous Confederate papers. After the war, he became a noted medical research doctor at the Ohio State University. For as long as he lived, he never told anyone about the papers he helped hide."

Dr. Lopez paused in his writing and looked hard at the pathetic wreck of a man lying before him. Muncaster suffered from a peculiar mixture of delusions, of that there was no doubt. His nightmarish apparitions had a certain lively texture to them, enough to make them almost believable. His mental fabrication of the past colliding with the present was a combination good enough to be the subject of an article in a medical journal. Dr. Lopez decided he would write a piece on the "Muncaster Syndrome." The livid fantasies, the blending of history and psychosis would be entertaining reading if nothing else. "Tell me more," he said. "I understand your problem. I feel your pain. I want to help you."

Encouraged by the doctor's seemingly real interest, Muncaster continued, "The other Confederate was a lieutenant colonel of artillery, stationed at Centreville during the first year of the war. He was seriously injured in an explosion when the Confederates evacuated northern Virginia in early 1862. After long stay in the hospital, he recovered well enough to be assigned to the Ordnance Bureau. Being unfit for field service, he was an inspector or government technical representative until the time the higher-ups picked him to carry the papers to northern Virginia. I think he spent a lot of time at the Tredegar Iron Works overseeing cannon production. I saw the scoundrel there when I got dumped into the gun foundry building one night. I found myself working with a crew pouring molten iron into cannon molds. It was a hellish place, hot, full of fire, smoke and grime. As we were casting a cannon, one of the ladles moving the liquid iron sprang a leak. To avoid being burned, I jumped out of the way and found my self able to float in the air. I floated myself right out of an open window and got the hell out of there."

"Was this colonel the cause of your injuries? Did he chase after you like the surgeon did? What specifically did he do to you?" the doctor asked.

"He didn't do anything! After the molten iron leaked, I floated away from the building. The next thing I remember, I fell down the stairs in my house again. I broke several ribs and my leg when I hit the floor and the wall at the bottom of the stairs. The only other thing I know about the colonel is that he lived for a long time after the war and never revealed his role in stashing the documents to anyone. I guess he and the other guy took their oaths of secrecy seriously."

"How did you get to the hospital? Did George Washington or the Confederate soldiers help you?"

"Not in the least bit! I think I knocked myself out when I crashed into the floor or wall at the bottom of the stairs, which one it was, I'm not sure. When I woke up in a great deal of pain, I managed to crawl to the phone in my kitchen, pull it down from the countertop and call 911. The ambulance paramedics patched me up and took me to the hospital."

"Dr. Lopez, why on earth would you think either Washington or his Confederate cronies would do anything to help me? The three of them are nothing but vindictive savages, completely uncivilized and unfit for life in modern society! They're weird as all get out! They lived by some damn code of honor and let it rule their lives! I think they tried to kill me because I don't believe in that old fashioned honor crap. George Washington really had it in for me! The mean old son-of-a-bitch told me so himself! He was going to keep making ghostly things happen to me until I agreed to tell the police the truth, how I killed Leon Placke."

"There is one more thing you should know, doctor! George Washington has absolutely no respect for a person's rights. He's nothing but a hooligan who doesn't mind using excessive force when it suits his ends! Oh, I wish I could sue him for the misery he has inflicted on me! No one will believe me when I tell them George Washington is a damn hypocrite! He helped write the Constitution that guarantees me my rights as a citizen. My rights! The very same rights he trampled when he ran rough-shod over me! It was George Washington who turned me into the physical wreck you see in this bed! Why, I would have gotten away with liquidating Leon Placke as clean as a whistle if George Washington had stayed the hell out of my affairs! He will cause lots of other problems for people, you know! The folks who run the country nowadays have to watch out for his tricks! They don't need George Washington sticking his very old nose into national affairs. Who needs his worn-out concepts in this day and age?"

Dr. Lopez continued taking a few notes as Muncaster rambled on. "The political establishment owes me big time, Republicans and Democrats alike.

What do suppose would have happened during the campaign now underway if Placke had been allowed to live and continue to agitate the masses? Neither Mr. Bush nor Mr. Gore wants to be bombarded by hundreds of questions regarding our current operating procedures and what is to be done about the mess. No candidate for Congress wants to answer embarrassing questions about special interest money, lobbying deals, or allocating the seats in House of Representatives on the basis of economic sectors! With Placke gone, we don't have to worry about any of it! The reform issues are dead! We're back to politics as usual. I saved the asses of everyone in the political business by doing a number on Placke. If the asinine ideas Placke got from George Washington ever took hold with the stupid voters, nearly half the people in the capital would end up being unemployed. We don't want that, do we doctor? Do you see why I had to act, to nip Placke's half-witted reform plans in the bud?"

"Your tremendous contribution to the welfare of our organization has not been forgotten, Muncaster. Everyone with a stake in keeping things as they are, is indebted to you! Committing murder, however, is against the law. The ability of your friends to assist you is somewhat constrained by that legal technicality. While they deeply appreciate what you have done, we must proceed cautiously because we do not want to draw anymore attention to the late Mr. Placke's deformed views. Under no circumstances, do we want to risk stirring up the ignorant, unappreciative populace again. We want to keep Placke's unseemly proposals completely out of sight during the remainder of the campaign season."

As Muncaster nodded his agreement, Dr. Lopez continued. "I'm sure your brilliant legal friends will be able to plea bargain on your behalf, get you off with minimal jail time. In our hearts, we know removing the threat to our society ought to be rewarded, not punished. But you must realize our hands are tied to a certain extent because we do not invite public scrutiny of our work. We must observe the niceties of the law, you know, so the common people will maintain respect for it. Keeping the average American uninterested in how we broker political deals has to be a high priority in this matter. I guarantee our attorneys will do their best for you. They are well aware of the clear and present danger Placke's disruptive schemes posed to the pocketbooks of our capital's sacred institutions."

Dr. Lopez looked directly into Muncaster's eyes as he continued outlining his plan of action. "The court will not be a problem, the society has already fixed things there. It is you I worry about! How will you handle your phantoms, Muncaster? How do you intend to control George Washington and his destructive Confederate helpers? As you previously stated, they were the ones who coerced you into confessing in the first place. How will you react if they come after you again? Can you resist them if they appear during the court proceedings? How do we know you will not make a fool out of yourself and wreck our well-crafted plan to save you?"

Muncaster lay quietly thinking for a moment. After a long pause he answered Dr. Lopez's question. "Let's use George Washington's dedication to his code of honor against him! I think I can give him the shaft by holding him to his word! He told me I had to confess the murder to the police. The old pain-in-the-ass never said anything about my having to do time for the crime. I have done what he demanded and legally fulfilled my part of the bargain. He is now obligated to leave me alone since his honor has been satisfied. When this sorry little episode blows over, I intend to get my career back on track. With nearly everyone in the capital in my debt, I ought to have enough collectable chits to last me two lifetimes as a lobbyist. As I see it, I'm off the hook after the trial. After I go free, George Washington can take his code of honor and stick it right up his ass!"

"I see," said Dr. Lopez as he slowly put down his pen. Quick-witted as he was, Muncaster failed to understand that no one in the political arena wanted to keep a confessed murderer employed in the capital. It was bad for the public image, a constant reminder of past things gone wrong. Having the man who killed Leon Placke going to the White House or Congress to do deals was not exactly what the ruling establishment had in mind. Although he had performed a valuable service by ridding the capital of Placke's presence, in the process of doing so, Muncaster had converted himself into tainted goods requiring disposition. It was Dr. Lopez's job to see to it that Muncaster went quietly and quickly into oblivion. His usefulness to the society was at an end.

August 2000

"If there were no bad people there would be no good lawyers."
-Charles Dickens, 1841

Muncaster was well enough to be transferred to the Fairfax County Adult Detention Center, located about 20 miles west of the capital city, where he would remain incarcerated until trial. As Muncaster settled into his jail cell, Dr. Lopez submitted his report to the judicial authorities. The prominent doctor found Muncaster to be certifiably insane. His patient suffered from severe and permanent emotional turbulence. He was beset by violent intrusive thoughts and delusions of a vast magnitude. H. Muncaster Swindell was vicious and suffered from uncontrollable rages. He displayed all the symptoms of a classic psychopath, being totally self-centered and ruthless in achieving his goals. Muncaster had admitted to killing a man and showed absolutely no sense of remorse for his crime.

He was so mentally unbalanced that he was unable to distinguish the past from the present. He often held conversations with phantoms he believed had the power to physically attack and injure him. Muncaster was unable to control his actions, having suffered permanent physical injury on at least two occasions, by diving down flights of stairs. He was, in the doctor's judgment, a serious danger to himself and society. He was so deranged that he was incapable of standing trial. Due the number and complexity of his mental disorders, it would require many years of treatment to restore Muncaster's mental facilities to a point where he could distinguish right from wrong. Dr. Lopez recommended convening a special judicial hearing to consider committing the dangerous and mentally incompetent H. Muncaster Swindell to a facility for the criminally insane.

Rarely did such a prominent professional as Dr. Lopez donate so much of his precious time to the cause of justice. The county authorities were most appreciative of the thorough evaluation and analysis the distinguished doctor provided. The Washington Society of Solicitors was also delighted with the doctor's recommendation. To maximize its return on its hefty investment in the project, the governing board of the society ordered two trusted, up-and-coming members to volunteer their services to the county to help expedite the commitment proceedings.

According to the polls, Al Gore and George W. Bush were locked in a dead-even race for the White House. Gore consolidated the gains he made at his nominating convention and erased the summer-long gap between him and his opponent. President Clinton presided over a Middle East peace conference. Although he tried his best to get the Israelis and Palestinians to hammer out a final peace accord, the conference failed. Until the protagonists agreed on a settlement, the U.S. taxpayer would continue to finance the slow-moving peace process by providing financial aid to both sides. The House of Representatives failed to override President Clinton's veto of legislation repealing the estate tax. With the veto upheld, Republican leaders conceded that their two-year -long drive to enact tax relief had collapsed. The Democrats rejoiced because they had prevented the rich from getting richer.

Despite a booming economy, nearly 30 million Americans, of whom 12 million were children, did not have enough to eat on a regular basis. Although food insecurity was declining as a national problem, some thought it remained annoyingly high given the most prosperous economy in history. While there was a shortage of money to provide food for the poor, there was no shortage of cash to fund national politics. The unregulated soft money donations to the two major political parties hit a record $256 million as corporations, labor unions and wealthy individuals preferred politics to feeding the hungry. The reason was simple enough. The hungry had no access to the nation's rulers, so it was smarter to invest the $250 million in political endeavors. Taking advantage of the congressional recess, President Clinton appointed three large political contributors to ambassadorships. The three had raised over $900,000 for the party in power and therefore deserved to represent the United States in Slovakia, Norway and Barbados.

September 2000

The booming American economy was consuming energy at a prodigious rate. Responding to global fears about a looming energy crisis, the Organization of Petroleum Exporting Countries agreed to raise production by 800,000 barrels a day in the hope of curtailing the surge in crude oil prices and lessening the possibility of a heating oil shortage in North America during the coming winter.

Congress reconvened after its summer recess and began to quietly insert favorite pork-barrel projects into appropriations bills. The lawmakers on both sides of the aisle considered satisfying the needs of political contributors and powerful constituents as the top priority for the closing session of the current Congress. The addition of pet projects to appropriations bills was a hallowed bipartisan tradition conducted in a legislative house of mirrors. While loudly denouncing the practice of distributing political pork in public, the legislators cut their deals in private. It was a nerve-wracking scramble to gain the votes necessary to help those who had helped you. The dealing was uncomplicated; if you support my project, I will vote for yours.

The White House released a photograph of a smiling Representative Rick Lazio shaking hands with Yasser Arafat. Lazio, who was in a hotly contested race for a Senate seat from New York with Hillary Clinton, was not amused as he scampered to explain himself to the enraged voters. As he was being roundly denounced for being a terrorist lover, Lazio seemed to have forgotten he had criticized the first lady for hugging Arafat's wife during a recent visit she had made to the Middle East.

In South Brunswick, New Jersey, the parents of eight and nine year old boys fought after a disagreement about whether a coach could stand behind the goal line got out of control. Although a dozen parents and coaches engaged in the fist fight, no one was seriously injured and police made no arrests.

Senator Joseph Lieberman went raiding deep into Texas, carrying the political offensive into George W. Bush's backyard. Slashing at the Republican candidate's record as state governor, Lieberman's foray netted $1.7 million in political contributions.

A government study found the entertainment industry to be aggressively marketing violent movies, music and games to children even though the material carried ratings or labels warning it was appropriate only for mature audiences. Recent poll results showed that many parents believed their children were being bombarded incessantly by violent advertising images from the entertainment industry. In a bold shift of tactics, President Clinton and Vice President Gore threatened the entertainment industry with harsh regulation if the makers of explicit and violent movies, recordings and games do not stop aiming advertisements at children.

In striking at Hollywood, the Democrats were attacking one of their most reliable sources of financial support and opening themselves to criticism that they lack credibility on the issue. Executives of the film, television and recording industries had already donated more than $13 million to the Gore for president campaign. In light of the startling attack on free enterprise and freedom of expression, it was not immediately known if the current level of Hollywood financial support would continue. The feelings of those in the entertainment industry were deeply hurt. They didn't like being accused of warping the minds of innocent children

A government report warned of vital national interests becoming increasingly vulnerable to computer attack by hackers and cyber-terrorists. Overall, the federal agencies inspected were given a dismal D- grade for poor computer security. A fourth of the 24 agencies checked received failing grades. The agencies responded to the report by making pleas for more money to deal with the problem. Despite the fact that nearly $2 billion had been requested to fund cyber-security in President Clinton's fiscal 2001 budget, government-wide efforts to improve computer security were hampered by a patchwork of funding and oversight structures in both the executive and legislative branches. Although no one in a Washington leadership position was quite sure what to do about the problem, it was not considered a big crisis because the polls showed the voters had no interest in it.

The date for Mr. H. Muncaster Swindell's commitment hearing was set. The court administrative officer decided to hold the session in the unused courtroom in the old courthouse building. All the rooms in the modern facility next door were already booked, and since the group was small and the hearing scheduled to be a short one, the old courtroom would do. Besides, the sanity hearing involved an individual claiming to have spoken to George Washington. Why not spice up the drama a bit by holding the hearing in a building nearly as old as Washington himself? A copy of the great man's will was put on display from time to time at the old courthouse. Maybe the subject of the hearing would like spend a little time reading it while his lawyers did their work. Using the old courtroom was also a clever way to get even, to let people know the administrator didn't like being pushed around. There had been an unprecedented amount of pressure from important people placed on the administrator to get the hearing scheduled at the earliest possible date. The bunch of eager, overbearing smart-asses could now sit in the old, cramped room as a reward for the headaches they caused the overworked administrator.

Many veterans have a tendency to hold on to items because they are a source of memories of days gone by. A shirt that saw one through a hard campaign hangs in a closet. A canteen that once held wine shared with a departed friend is packed in a box in an attic. Boots, duffel bags, helmets caps and cartridge belts sit in dusty basement corners. General George Washington was no exception to the rule, the man almost never threw anything away. As a result of his frugal habit, a traveling display of Washington's military memorabilia was about to open in the old courtroom for a ten day run. The traveling display cases filled with worn boots, a coat or two, buttons, sashes, belts, a saber, a pair of pistols, saddlebags, camp chest, field desk and other assorted odds and ends were arriving daily and lined the walls of the room. The display was scheduled to open for public viewing three days after Muncaster's hearing.

As the star witness, Dr. Lopez looked forward to performing in the old courtroom. He knew his spellbinding oration would ring throughout the historic chamber. The photographs of him testifying would make excellent additions to his office wall of fame display. As he walked toward the entrance, he stopped to admire a large bed of coleus plants planted under one of the large trees on the lawn. The brightly colored plants in this bed had been allowed to flower. In the well-tended beds surrounding his Washington office building, the buds of the coleus flowers had always been pinched off. On this warm day, the flowering beds on the courthouse lawn were alive with bees. Was it regional preference or the liability issue that dictated how coleus plants were maintained? What was the county's liability if someone was stung by an errant bee? Governing a great nation was a difficult task. A mere 20 miles from the capital, the local people were already forgetting the implications of the rule of law.

Dr. Lopez liked to keep up with events in the capital's expansive system of law and rule making. His pleasing personality and open mind made him a favorite of Washington's highly stressed legislative, legal and lobbying communities. The luncheon intermission in today's sanity hearing was going to be an enjoyable event because there were a number of issues the doctor wanted to discuss with the other society members attending the hearing. The independent counsel had ended the Whitewater investigation by stating the evidence was insufficient to show any criminal wrongdoing by President Clinton or First Lady and senatorial candidate, Hillary Rodam Clinton. Were the Clintons innocent or had they been legally able to cover their tracks in the matter? Washington's lawyers would be discussing these nuances among themselves for weeks to come. The President remained under investigation for making false statements in the Monica Lewinsky affair. Was the independent counsel planning to prosecute him after he left office? Because much of the $52 million cost of the Clinton probe had gone to his clients, Dr. Lopez had been able to increase his fees in accordance with rule of supply and demand.

The United States promised to strictly monitor the new trade pact with China. A newly created interagency body could curb imports and initiate complaints to the World Trade Organization if China broke the rules. Dr. Lopez was interested in learning which lobbying firms were involved in this exciting new international project. Iraq launched another aggressive effort to weaken the crippling sanctions imposed on it after the Persian Gulf War. With oil prices at an all time high, trade with its neighbors improving and the world becoming disinterested with the UN embargo, Saddam Hussein was again on the move. Were any of the big lobbying firms planning to pick up the dormant Iraqi account? Dr. Lopez had to give Saddam credit. Despite U.S. efforts to be rid of him, he had outlasted President Bush and was on the verge of surviving President Clinton's term of office.

Despite the robust economy, troubled loans by banks to U.S. businesses had more than doubled to over $100 billion. With banking regulators becoming worried, it might be time to lobby Congress for relief. Dr. Lopez wouldn't mind learning which lobbying firms were going to make the push. Congress and the White House were locked in a battle over key spending bills. The deadlock meant Congress would be unable to wrap up work on the budget by the time it adjourned on October 6. What were the chances of Congress coming back for a special session? Dr. Lopez had to know. He might have to change his vacation plans to accommodate his hard-working Capitol Hill clients.

With $208 million in soft money contributions safely in the bank, the political parties were desperately chasing hard money contributions. The hard money contributions, legally defined as personal contributions to individual candidates and limited to an overall annual cap of $25,000, were needed to leverage the soft money bank accounts. To keep within the law, the parties had to spend at a ratio of 35 percent hard money to 65 percent soft money. Dr. Lopez loved a good race. He wanted to know which party was ahead in the money chasing game?

The sheriff's deputies had already unlocked the doors of the old courtroom. As Dr. Lopez approached on the winding brick pathway, he noticed many of the participants were already there. The hearing judge was inside talking to the attorney representing the prosecutor's office and the defense lawyers volunteered by the society. Chatting amicably outside, were two homicide investigators, a lawyer from the commonwealth's attorney's office, a representative from detention services, a social services investigator, three members of the society of solicitors and a person from the convention and visitors bureau. A growing number of visitors were flocking to the site of Leon Placke's murder, spending money in local restaurants and spending nights in local hotels and motels. The conventions and visitors bureau wanted to ensure it got firsthand facts to include in its new brochure and the new signs going up at the historical site. The focus of the program was changing to a peculiar blending of Civil War events and Leon Placke's last days.

Being able to tap two distinct sources of tourist revenue at one site was a blessing. The place had become so busy the house-sitting professor had moved out and the neighbors were complaining about the lack of adequate parking space. The grass under the tree where Leon Placke died had been worn away, forcing the erection of a chained enclosure around the base of the tree to keep the teary-eyed visitors at a respectful distance. Leon Placke and his bizarre menagerie of George Washington inspired political reforms were marketable commodities. The bureau's goal was to keep the visitors coming, to keep money pumping into the local economy. The martyred Leon Placke was on the way to becoming a legend. He was outdrawing the Civil War enthusiasts by a ratio of 5 to 1. The forlorn old house now had regular visiting hours, an admission charge and a full-time staff.

The members of Washington Society of Solicitors and Dr. Lopez were horrified by the news. Wasn't it just like the ungrateful multitude to focus on a lunatic and his fringe ideas while ignoring the expensive political campaigns being waged for their votes? The last thing the lobbying community wanted was for Leon Placke's place of death to become a shrine. Just how deep was the dead man's hold on the minds of the little people anyhow? To find out, a pollster would be dispatched to the site three times a week to collect data. The troublesome Placke virus infecting the body politic was proving extremely resistant. It was not going to die out if ignored, so it had to be eradicated. Once a complete profile of the typical Placke admirer was developed, a full-blown ad campaign lampooning Placke's ideas would be created and aimed at the target audience. It would be an expensive undertaking, utilizing the print media and TV, but it had to be done. Cost was no object. As soon as the national election was over, bipartisan funding for the project to discredit the memory of Leon Placke would be readily made available.

As Muncaster understood the plan from his friends in the society, his redemption came in two phases. During the first phase, Muncaster would be declared insane and committed to an institution without having to go through the ordeal of standing trail for murder. In phase two, after decent interval of perhaps 12 months or whenever public interest in the matter had sufficiently died down, Muncaster would be reevaluated and found to have been remarkably cured. At that point, his support groups would be unleashed to take up Muncaster's case and launch a well-financed crusade for his release. Having been found insane at the time of the murder, the newly cured Muncaster could not be tried for a crime committed when he was not in possession of his mental faculties. To keep this bright, caring, reinvented man institutionalized would be a travesty, an insult to the innate American sense of fair play and reasonable justice. His friends would orchestrate the pressure groups, see to it that Muncaster's release became a national cause. Once set free, he would then be able to take his rightful place among the lobbyists beholden to him after he had made the rounds of the talk shows.

"I would be loath to speak ill of any person who I do not know deserves it, but I am afraid he is an attorney."
-Samuel Johnson, 1770

In the finest tradition of legal deception, Muncaster's friends neglected to advise him of the deal's fine print. While phase one was contractually guaranteed, carved into stone so to speak, phase two was an option to be exercised solely at their discretion. With Muncaster's usefulness to the Washington establishment over, no one anticipated a time coming when he might be of service again. The phase two option would not be exercised. If Dr. Lopez did his job well today, it would be years before any shrink at the institution even thought about opening Muncaster's case file.

With judge finally firmly planted behind the bench, the hearing got underway at 9:15 a.m. Handcuffed because of his violent nature, Muncaster sat unconcernedly at the front table next to his two able defense attorneys. In the first order of business, the judge called the two homicide investigators to testify. They outlined the premeditated nature of the crime, Muncaster's methodology, diagrammed the crime scene, retraced the victim's and Muncaster's movements and reiterated the details of Muncaster's confession.

Turning to the defense lawyers, the judge said, "Have you anything to add? Are there any points in the testimony presented you wish to refute? Do you wish to cross examine the witnesses?"

Taking his eyes off of the attractive court reporter busily typing in the corner of the room, Muncaster's lead defense attorney slowly responded, "No, your honor. The testimony just concluded is a fair and nearly impartial representation of how the unfortunate incident unfolded. We do not dispute the facts presented and would like to take this opportunity to commend the detectives for their fine investigative work." The judge looked up, a bit startled at the remark. Never before in all his years on the bench had he ever heard a defense attorney compliment the police for doing anything right.

"Very well then," said the bewildered judge. "The facts of the case will be recorded in the record as being undisputed. Since all parties present agree that the subject of this hearing, Mr. H. Muncaster Swindell, did commit the crime of murder, let us move on to the subject of the state of his sanity." Almost reverently, the judge called the noted Dr. Orasco Lopez to the witness stand. After swearing to tell the whole truth, and nothing but the truth, Dr. Lopez presented the results of his in-depth evaluation of Muncaster's metal state. The great psychological showman was in his element, citing test results, personal observation and reams of clinical data. He alternated between being seated at the witness stand and standing before a series of exquisitely detailed, large flip charts he positioned on an easel as he made his presentation. Dr. Lopez concluded his lengthy statement by giving his expert opinion. He found the subject of the hearing to be certifiably insane. The man was not, at the time of the murder, or at the present time, responsible for his brutal actions. Muncaster had to be institutionalized so his neuroses -driven, uncontrollable violent behavior would not endanger anyone else. Dr. Lopez believed it would take many years of treatment to restore Muncaster's mental condition to a state where he was able to be held responsible for his acts.

As the great practitioner strode back to his seat after being dismissed by the judge, the room fell into awed silence. Never before had they heard such a lucid explanation of the diseases affecting a tortured human mind. As he looked at the society members present, Dr. Lopez could tell by their respectful expressions that he had earned his pay this day.

After some moments of reflection, the judge called on the prosecutor. "Your Honor," the prosecutor said as she stood to address the court, "We in the prosecutor's office are a very civilized people. It is not our intent to prosecute an insane individual for doing evil deeds over which he had no control. The previous testimony clearly shows the defendant was not responsible for his conduct at the time he committed the crime of murder. The cause of justice would not be served by going to trial. We wave the right to bring the defendant to trial for premeditated murder on the condition that he be directly remanded to an institution for the criminally insane and housed there until such time as his mental state improves."

As the prosecutor sat down, the judge turned to the defense attorneys. "Your Honor," said the second of Muncaster's attorneys, "We believe our client's best interest would be served by following the course of action recommended by the esteemed prosecutor. In his testimony, Dr. Lopez has demonstrated the causes of, and proven the determination of Mr. Swindell's insanity beyond a reasonable shadow of a doubt. Our client is seriously mentally ill, in need of a caring society's help, not its punishment! Over time with proper treatment, Mr. Swindell might again become a useful and productive member of society. Until then, we agree that he should be confined to an institution for his own good and that of the population at large. Our client's interests and the interests of Fairfax County and the Commonwealth of Virginia are one and the same in this matter."

Before the judge could make a response, Muncaster leaped to his feet, shouting, "You should give me a medal for what I did, not lock me up! I exterminated a piece of filthy vermin! I took it upon myself to rid Washington's political environment of a hazardous, contaminating substance bent on destroying our awesome political process! He was a piece of trash, a traitor and a renegade! Leon Placke deserved to die!" As the deputies rushed to restrain him, it was obvious to everyone in the courtroom that Muncaster was mentally gone, completely unrepentant and unable to fend for his interests. It was exactly the impression Muncaster wanted to leave with those present at the hearing because it would make his cure look even more miraculous later.

Thunderstorms blow in from the west in Fairfax County, Virginia. They form over the eastern edge of the Blue Ridge and Bull Run mountains, gain strength over the hot plains around Manassas and often strike with sudden fury during the sweltering summer months. As the deputies forced Muncaster back into his chair, one of the periodic summer storms announced its presence with high winds, darkness, claps of thunder, sheets of driving rain and bolts of lightening. Being nothing unusual for the time of year, no one in the courtroom was particularly concerned about the abrupt change in weather. The rain would pour for a short time and the fast-moving storm would move on, crossing Washington, DC and eastern Maryland and dissipate somewhere out over the Atlantic Ocean.

As thunder rattled the windows and rain fell in torrents, Muncaster uttered a fearsome shriek. The more liberal of the courtroom's inhabitants looked at the deputies pressing Muncaster back into his chair, automatically assuming an act of police brutality was in progress. Not so in this case. Muncaster was staring out the window, the deputies barely restraining him. Out in the rain amid the bright lighting flashes, Muncaster saw what no one else in the courtroom could see, the figure of a vengeful horseman. George Washington was out there, coat collar turned up against the blowing rain, the water pouring off his worn campaign hat. As Muncaster screamed, "Oh, please help me! He has come to kill me! I know it!" Washington slowly raised his arm and pointed his gloved hand directly at Muncaster. At that same instant, a bolt of lighting blasted through the window, leaping across the room in a fiery arc. It hit the floor in front of the startled judge, bounced and slammed directly into Muncaster. The defense attorneys, deputies and Muncaster were sent flying as the table at which they were seated exploded into fragments. Witnesses later recalled how Muncaster's handcuffs glowed like a light bulb as his body went airborne.

As terror-struck Dr. Lopez watched, the bolt next slammed into the wall and ricocheted down into the display case containing Washington's saber. The secure, shatterproof case with a lifetime guarantee against breakage shattered into thousands of pieces as the bolt struck. The last thing Dr. Lopez saw in this life was George Washington's saber sailing gracefully through the air as it glided toward him. Dr. Lopez died almost instantly. Run through by the saber as if an 18th century swordsman had expertly guided the blade that skewered his vitals.

The thunderclap accompanying the lighting bolt was deafening, leaving the ears of those in the courtroom still living cruelly ringing. The courtroom was a shambles. The bolt had blown a two foot deep crater in the floor and scorched a three foot wide patch of wall. Plaster and brick dust hung in the air, pieces of table, display case and chunks of the floor and wall were scattered everywhere. Surprisingly, no one else was seriously hurt. The deputies, although tossed violently about, were uninjured. The defense attorneys picked themselves up off the floor thankfully realizing they only suffered strange, but relatively minor burns to their tongues.

H. Muncaster Swindell was dead, electrocuted by the direct strike of the lighting bolt. Dr. Lopez was also dead. He lay slumped in his chair, his mouth hanging open, his blood streaming to the floor. The hilt of the old saber protruded from his front, a portion of the blade that had gone through him stuck out of his back between the rungs of the chair.

As abruptly as it came, the thunderstorm departed. As the deafened, bewildered survivors staggered out of the courtroom wreckage into daylight, the clouds were moving east and the sun was beginning to shine. It had been an odd weather phenomenon. The radar tracking record showed the storm breaking up almost immediately after passing the courthouse. No one could recall a storm of such immense magnitude dissipating so rapidly before.

There were a number of other questions puzzling the accident investigators carefully picking through the wreckage. How could a bolt of lighting have struck the courtroom when the entire courthouse building was wired with sophisticated devices to protect against lighting strike? The murderous bolt had entered the room horizontally, through a window. Its path violated the standard pattern followed by lighting bolts as they moved from cloud to ground. None of the experts could offer an explanation for the killer bolt's unusual travel path. It simply defied all logic.

The coroner had a queasy feeling about something strange and unusual being involved in the case. Although Muncaster had been killed by the lightning strike, the coroner had never seen a corpse with such a look of abject terror frozen on its face. What had Muncaster seen in the moments before he died? This might be a matter better answered by the religious community because Muncaster looked as though he had seen some sort of a terrible supernatural apparition. What it was, the coroner didn't know.

Tests failed to duplicate the catastrophic failure of the case housing George Washington's saber. The investigators could not determine why the case exploded when struck. The manufacturer's consulting engineers studied the matter, ran tests, but could not ascertain a cause. Even more puzzling for the coroner and investigators was the flight path of the saber. No one could explain how the blade came to be launched into the air in such a way as to cross the courtroom and impale Dr. Lopez. The weapon itself offered another mystery. It had not been used for 200 years. For the last five years, it had been safely locked in the display case. When it was checked, the blade edge was as smooth and sharp as if someone had sharpened it yesterday, using the same care and implements as an expert owner would have used in the 18th century.

The only happy member of the ill-fated courthouse gathering was the representative from the convention and visitors bureau. The series of events transpiring in the courtroom and the tantalizing list of unanswered questions were prime material for the new brochure and a series of explanatory signs. The eerie courtroom happenings would greatly embellish the legend of Leon Placke. The old courtroom was on the way to becoming another visitor stop on the Placke tour. People were already coming to visit the site even though the place was a total wreck.

In the old days, the dirt track that passed for a road ran from George Washington's Mt. Vernon home to his gristmill. It meandered in a north-westerly direction across his fields, crossing Dogue Creek at a shallow, upstream ford. A group of archeologists excavating the distillery site on the gristmill property were amused to see a horseman watering his horse at the old creek crossing. The rider watched them work while his horse drank, then waved, turned and rode away. "That fellow must have spent a small fortune outfitting himself to look like George Washington," one of the diggers said as she stood to stretch. "He looked so much like Washington, I could have sworn it was really him." Breaking into a smile, one of the other archeologists responded, "You know you have been working on this project too long when you begin to see old George riding about the place. However, I will have to admit that was the best Washington look-alike I have ever seen. Why do you suppose he is wasting his time retracing the route of the old road? With most of it now covered with houses, it's a complete waste of his time. Dressed as he is, he would be better off traveling along the modern highway where more people could see him."

There was a sudden rash of other George Washington sightings. He was seen near Trenton, New Jersey, in the old part of New York city and Boston. He appeared at Williamsburg and Yorktown in Virginia. He was spotted in an old graveyard in eastern Pennsylvania standing with head bowed before the grave of a long-dead and forgotten miller. Ignoring the jibes of his neighbors for supporting a lost cause and the threat of British reprisal, the miller had done his duty. He had defiantly stood by his millstones, keeping them grinding during the darkest days of the Revolution. He was one of the few to send flour to Washington's starving army while the dandies of Philadelphia entertained the occupying British.

There were sightings of Washington in the old frontier settlements of the Shenandoah Valley. He was spotted prowling the forks of the Ohio river near the site of the old French fort. A startled park ranger saw him at the Gettysburg battlefield. A naval aviator was grounded temporarily for reporting Washington near Midway Island far out in the Pacific Ocean.

The presidential candidates were increasing attacks on each other as the election neared. George W. Bush declared the U.S. education system to be in a recession and promised to spend a $1 billion a year to fix it if elected. Vice President Gore countered by blasting drug manufacturers for making too much money and offered a government prescription drug plan with savings for nearly everyone. Both candidates claimed to know how to save the Medicare, Social Security and flood insurance programs. While each accused the other of being in the pocket of special interests, neither mentioned cutting the bloated White House staff or questioning the massive number of people on the payroll of Congress. Also not a discussible issue was how the deal-making Congress divided up the trillions in tax revenues wrung out of the American people. There was complete agreement among the presidential candidates on one matter, the soaring costs of campaigning. Regardless of who won the election, the price of an ambassadorship was going to jump significantly after this expensive political war was over.

As the candidates debated on TV and spouted promises of freebies for everyone, the American public focused intently on what they were going to get for nothing from their government. Forgotten were the old rules: a dollar saved is a dollar earned; there is no free lunch; and everything has an ultimate price. That you worked hard until you died in an effort to make things better for the next generation was a rule of life that no longer applied in the United States of America. Since the political attack ads made the average voter feel slighted and cheated by life, neither candidate dared mention that compared with wage earners in most European countries, the paycheck deductions for Americans were relatively modest. The average single wage earner in the United States had deductions of 25.8 percent. In Denmark the rate was 43.4 percent; Germany, 42.4 percent; Belgium, 41.8 percent; the Netherlands, 34.4 percent and Norway, 29.6 percent.

The White House announced that 404 people had stayed over night in the executive mansion since Hillary Rodham Clinton had launched her campaign for the U.S. Senate. The grateful guests were also donors, contributing over $600,00 to her campaign effort. Republicans salivated at the prospect of regaining control of the White House. With a little better organization and planning, they could run 810 people through the facility during a comparable period of time It could be a real money maker for the party.

The Clinton administration had been good for the capital's lawyers. All told, the five independent counsels investigating Clinton administration officials spent more than $100 million. Despite all the investigating, former housing secretary Henry G. Cisneros had been the only official convicted of anything. Still to come, however, was the decision on whether to prosecute Bill Clinton after he left office on charges stemming from the Lewinsky affair. Regardless of party affiliation, the city's lawyers were genuinely sorry to see the Clinton presidency come to an end. It had been good to them, and what was good for the capital's lawyers was automatically good for the nation.

"It could be probably be shown by facts and figures that there is no distinctly native American criminal class except Congress."
-Mark Twain, 1897

The freewheeling money culture dominating Capitol Hill was in evidence as lawmakers of both parties aggressively solicited contributions from corporate lobbyists. Special access to those who wielded the power to make or change laws was available to those smart enough and willing to pay the price. A few members of Congress and 30 lobbyists flew off to Los Vegas for a golf tournament and a round of partying. It was understood by everyone involved that there would be plenty of time to discuss the important legislative needs of clients during the trip.

After dallying until the last minute, Congress was forced to consider 11 long-stalled domestic spending bills now stuffed with special projects, many of them added in a last-minute flurry of back room bargaining. In a chaotic round of closed-door negotiations, representatives of the White House, Senate and House of Representatives got down to the serious business of finally agreeing on how to spend a lot of federal budget dollars. Special water and science projects, tax advantages for a few, special exemption from regulations, beneficial changes in laws for certain interest groups, agricultural trade with Cuba, land preservation, crop loss insurance, environmental provisions, prescription drug imports and the new standards for measuring drunk driving were on the negotiating table. As the lawmakers struggled to complete the people's business, they also tried to steer a number of parochial projects to states and districts in which members faced tight election races. There being little bipartisan agreement and not enough money to fund everything on the wish list, the bargaining was intense as Congress and the White House attempted to fulfill their unofficial mandate to take care of those who had contributed financially to the political process.

The American people could be proud of how Congress slaved night and day to make the country's democratic process work as corporations, trade associations and special interest groups scrambled to get their legislative desires included in the spending bills. Members listened politely as a horde of well-tailored, IOU collecting, business lobbyists pleaded for the special provisions they wanted inserted in the last minute legislation. AT&T was fighting for relief from a Federal Communications Commission ruling limiting its ownership of cable stations. General Electric sought a delay in a federal order to clean up toxic sediments in the Hudson River. The credit industry was attempting to overturn rules protecting the privacy of Social Security cardholders. The thoroughbred racing industry wanted to use the Internet for off-track betting. Cummins Engine and its allies battled to delay the implementation of new EPA rules on diesel fuel and engines. The National Association of Broadcasters wanted to restrict the licensing of lower-power FM stations that were mainly operated by schools, universities and minority groups. The accounting industry strove to weaken SEC rules aimed at preventing conflicts of interest in big stock and business deals.

President Clinton's Middle East peace initiative collapsed as Palestinians rioted and Israeli forces struck retaliatory blows. In Yemen's Aden harbor, 17 sailors aboard the USS Cole were killed in a suicide attack that blew a massive hole in the side of the ship. World oil supplies were dangerously tight. There was virtually no excess production capacity available anywhere on the globe. Demand continued to increase as the Asian economies began to recover from recession. Stung by higher fuel prices for their large and expensive vehicles, Americans began to grumble to their political representatives about the unfairness of the situation.

President Clinton and Congress came to an agreement on a number of spending programs costing $80 billion. The President signed the hodgepodge bill that relaxed trade sanctions against Cuba, expanded importation of low-cost drugs, provided emergency assistance to farmers and enabled low-income families to own a car and remain eligible for food stamps. "I decided that on balance that this bill advances the interests of the American people," said President Clinton as he solemnly signed the spending measure with a flourish at a White House ceremony. He also signed the $310 billion defense appropriations bill that Congress sent over.

A federal judge and the White House continued to duel over missing email messages subpoenaed by the court. The judge considered the White House stalling tactics so outrageous that he began deliberating contempt-of-court proceedings. Despite the judge's irritation, it was clear to court observers that the stalling strategy worked. The missing messages were not going to be processed or produced until after the voters had chosen a new president.

Congress remained in session, meeting at night and on Saturdays, as the White House and Republican congressional leaders slowly chipped away at their differences. While the constant political wrangling delayed the passage of the remaining budget items, the operation of the federal government was funded for a few days at time. Disputes raged over education funding, Medicare financing, tax cuts for businesses, immigration law changes, subsidized school construction bonds, telephone tax repeal, assisted suicide and union wage scales. If the impasse continued, it was likely the struggle between the White House and Congress would go right up to the November election. Behind the scenes, however, bipartisan deals were worked out to accommodate a number of the needs of the major political contributors to both parties.

The Republican congressional leaders were confident that the party would benefit in the coming election if they took a confrontational stand with the President on the remaining spending and tax issues. The President vetoed a spending bill that would have allowed a congressional pay raise after House Republican leaders torpedoed an agreement on education spending. The veto of the $33 billion appropriations bill left the budget talks between the White House and Congress in shambles. With $113 billion in spending yet to be agreed upon, President Clinton decided to tough it out. Since he was going to be out of a job in a matter of days, he didn't really care if the balky Congress would be forced to meet in an unusual post-election session to finish its neglected business.

November 2000

With the new fiscal year already a month old, President Clinton and Congress continued to abdicate their constitutional responsibilities as they locked horns in partisan budget warfare. Many of the annual spending bills essential to the operation of government were left dangling in limbo as Congress and the White House hurled insults at one another. For months, many in Congress assumed the Republican leaders would quickly cut a deal with President Clinton so the members would have time to return home and campaign. As budget negotiations dragged on weeks beyond their deadline, tensions rose on Capitol Hill as President Clinton insisted on signing the continuing resolutions necessary to keep the government functioning one day at a time.

The furious election-eve bickering almost triggered a trade war with Europe. A number of American tax breaks for businesses had been ruled illegal under World Trade Organization rules and had to be changed or rescinded by November 1. The bill to replace $4 billion in tax breaks for big exporters with a revised tax regime that would meet the requirements of the world trading rules died on the floor of Congress when embattled House leaders refused to bring it up for a vote. Because the necessary changes had not been made to the U.S. laws, the European Union was legally free to retaliate by slapping 100 percent tariff rates on $4 billion worth of U.S. products, effectively shutting them out of the European marketplace. The fact that American workers might be laid off as a result of the inability of Congress to do its job didn't seem to worry anyone on Capitol Hill. One congressional spokesman said, "Hopefully the Europeans understand that our government doesn't move quickly just before a major election. If they don't, I'm not concerned because it doesn't affect my reelection chances."

Congressional leaders abandoned efforts to complete a final budget and tax deal with President Clinton before the election and agreed to return for a lame-duck session on November 14. The lawmakers and the president knew the final accord on the unresolved budget items would be heavily shaped by election results. Both parties were betting they would be better off politically by digging in their heels. Republicans believed they could rally the conservatives by standing up to Clinton, while Democrats used the standoff to emphasize the Republicans were incapable of managing Congress. Neither party dared inform the voters that a lame-duck session was a dangerous thing. The many members who were retiring or were defeated would be an open conduit to lobbyists trying to get special provisions added to bills. When the extra session of Congress was announced, the capital's lobbying industry joyously began working overtime. When Congress came back to town, they would be ready and waiting.

The price of selecting America's political leaders continued to rocket skyward. Over $3 billion had been spent to influence an election in which barely 51 percent of eligible voters cast a ballot. Despite the unprecedented campaign spending, America was rewarded with an election that ended in a virtual tie. As dumfounded voters watched in dismay, there was no winner and the election remained in doubt. Vice President Gore held a slight lead over Governor Bush in the popular vote. In the electoral college, Gore led Bush 260 to 246. With 270 electoral votes needed to win, the 32 undecided votes would decide the election.

The battle of the ballot came down to Florida where Bush retained a tenuous lead in the popular vote. The candidate winning Florida and its 25 electoral votes would win the election. For the first time in a century, the power of the electoral college was apparent. Bush could win the electoral vote and win the Presidency even though he lagged in the popular vote. Gore, who had won the national popular vote could still lose the election. Both parties began hurling charges and counter charges of voter fraud as the Democrats demanded recounts in Florida. The state became the center of a legal battleground as the parties fought in the courts for the state's winning margin of votes. As the big political guns belched forth a steady stream of complaints and insults, the political parties and the nation became even more polarized.

In Congress, the Republicans retained a slight edge in the House of Representatives while the Senate was split 50-50. It was a clear sign the voters had given neither party a mandate to govern on its own. In a campaign in which over $100 million was raised outside of the state, the First Lady of the United States, Hillary Rodham Clinton was elected U.S. Senator from New York. In January 2001, she would take her seat in an institution that had recently tried her husband during his impeachment. The Washington establishment, which had never seen an election this close in many years, eagerly readied itself for the new round of deal-making that would begin when the lame-duck session of Congress began. Big business was going to try to tweak legislation to its benefit while big labor readied a massive counter-agenda.

Although they would have to wait for a final decision on a new President, the innumerable financial backers of both candidates were eagerly and anxiously lining up to collect their rewards. Large contributors signaled their interest in appointment as ambassadors to prestigious countries or high government positions while loyal campaign workers ferociously competed with each other for one of the thousands of political jobs the new administration would be handing out. It was also time to publish or perish. With less than three months remaining for regulators in the Clinton administration to issue the rules they wanted to see on the books before leaving office, new federal regulations began pouring off Washington's printing presses in rapid succession.

December 2000

After 36 days of halted and resumed partial vote recounts in selected counties in Florida, endless court battles and conflicting lower court rulings, the Supreme Court of the United States handed down a ruling that ended Vice President Gore's hopes for overturning his narrow loss (537 votes) in the state. With Florida's 25 electoral votes firmly beyond his reach, the Vice President graciously conceded defeat to Mr. Bush as the nation heaved a collective sigh of relief. The expensive election from hell was finally over.

Although Texas Governor George W. Bush secured the electoral college majority (271) required to become the 43rd president, he lost the popular vote to Vice President Gore by 539,897 votes. The final tally gave Gore 50,996,064 popular votes to Bush's 50,456,167. Green Party candidate Ralph Nader collected 2,864,810 votes; Reform Party nominee Patrick Buchanan took 448,750 and Harry Browne got 386,024. Nationwide, voter turnout amounted to 105,380,929 ballots cast, or 51.2 percent of those eligible to vote. Despite all the campaign money spent, the 2000 election ranked among those elections with the lowest percent of voter turnout. The results were another clear indication the downward trend in American voter participation was continuing unabated. As late as the 1960 election, 62.8 percent of eligible voters still thought enough of the election process to take the time to go to the polls and vote.

The lame-duck Congress and the White House were nearing agreement on a $109 billion spending bill for education, health and labor programs. The two sides were also ready to compromise on spending an additional $37 billion on Medicare and Medicaid programs. With completion of the federal budget already months behind schedule, Congress continued to vote stopgap funds on a daily basis to keep the government running.

Hong Kong's homicide rate of 1.23 per 100,000 people was among the lowest of any major city in the world. Despite rather large recent declines, New York's murder rate remained 15 times higher. Neither Congress nor the White House thought the interesting statistic was worth bringing to the attention of the American public.

Although the new fiscal year began on October 1, Congress and the White House didn't reach agreement on four of the 13 annual spending bills until December 15. With time running out, the bickering, lame-duck Congress finally agreed to a final budget deal with President Clinton totaling $109 billion, up $14 billion over last year's levels. As negotiations between the

White House and Congress dragged on, the colossal final package became a magnet for hundreds of millions of dollars worth of members' pet projects. "I think this shows that if you wait to do the major spending bills at the last minute, you end up spending so much more," a senator on the budget committee wryly observed. "It's a fair trade-off though," he continued, "The advantage of waiting is that it is so much easier to help your friends and deliver on promises made. After all, that's what brings in the contributions and gets me reelected. Overall, I'm more than satisfied with the results we have achieved."

The House approved the measure, 292 to 60, and the Senate adopted it by voice vote. With the last of the spending deals finally done, Congress had authorized federal spending totaling $1.8 trillion for the fiscal year. The votes closed the books on a Congress that began with Clinton's impeachment trial, then deadlocked for 18 months over everything from campaign finance reform to Medicare prescription drug benefits and finally ended weeks after the results of the November election left the next Congress even more politically divided. Clinton hailed the budget agreement as an unprecedented increase in spending for his national priorities. The members of Congress congratulated themselves for the fine job they had done in taking care of America's needs. With the last order of business completed, the lame-duck session of the contentious 106th Congress closed up shop and the members headed for the airports.

The 107th Congress would begin deliberating the nation's business in January 2001, its members happy with the $3,800 pay raise that had been included in the final spending package passed by the previous Congress. The annual salaries of members of the new Congress would total $145,100. Along with a lavish package of benefits, the higher salaries would make the strain of serving the people of the United States a bit more tolerable. The Washington establishment was contented. Leon Placke was gone for good and things were going to be the same as before. No one had any interest in addressing the problems of dysfunctional government appropriation and management procedures, the gross lack of national budget accountability, an outmoded system of congressional representation, the astronomically high costs of elections or the persuasive influence of lobbyists and special interest groups.

Despite his reputation for being extremely partisan, House Majority Whip Tom Delay began to quietly forge alliances with conservative Democrats. A coalition between Delay and conservative Democrats could prove critical if President-elect Bush intended to move on issues such as tax cuts and defense spending. House Minority Leader, Richard Gephardt, was alarmed by

DeLay's foray onto his turf. He moved to blunt the contacts, saying Delay was only seeking to establish ties with the Democrats in order to promote a conservative agenda.

Federal Reserve officials were surprised by the speed of the deterioration in the outlook for the U.S. economy. They acknowledged they might soon have to cut interest rates to help boost growth. An alarmed President-elect Bush stepped up his warnings about the state of the economy. Bush's complaints irked the White House which considered them to be nothing more than an attempt to promote his tax cut plan at the expense of market confidence. Not sure of what was going on, investors began pulling out of stocks and the market slid downward.

New York Senator-elect Hillary Rodham Clinton accepted an $8 million advance for a book about her eight scandal-fraught and politically interesting years as first lady. As an author, she was going to be very busy during the weeks before Congress opened. A professional ghostwriter had to be selected and a writing outline developed. The book announcement did not mention if any of the book's potential earnings would go to pay some of the outstanding Clinton family legal bills. In the publishing world, the sizable advance was not considered unusually large because the book was going to be written by the most famous woman in the world. As such, it was sure to be a best seller when it reached the bookstores in early 2003.

The first census results indicated the U. S. population had reached 281,421,906. President-elect Bush announced a plan to pay for most of his $30 million inauguration costs with large private donations. Watchdog groups said this was another opportunity for wealthy interests to contribute money in order to gain access and influence. Washington insiders, on the other hand, thought it was a grand idea and began lining up to underwrite the cost in $100,000 increments.

What did it all mean? With George Washington reported across the river from the capital in old Alexandria, Virginia, a gnawing sense of unease began to develop in many quarters of the national political establishment. With a restless spirit roaming the land, a few of the weaker souls began to believe George Washington was searching for a replacement for Leon Placke and that he would not rest until he found him or her. To counter the problem, a quiet search was begun for a way to make the unwanted spirit of the nation's founder go away. His old-fashioned ideals had absolutely no part to play in modern national politics. They were irrelevant and out-of-date and ought to stay consigned to their place in the history books. The White House astrologer was duly consulted and agreed to develop a plan for a special spirit suppression project if it was properly funded from bipartisan sources.

How long was George Washington's search going to continue? Who might the general and first president be looking for to help him by taking up the just cause of getting the nation back on the right track ?

Senator John McCain was sitting the Senate dining room eating lunch by himself. Since he had begun pushing the matter of campaign finance reform as a legislative issue his popularity with his colleagues in Congress had fallen. McCain was pleasantly surprised when Senator Russell Feingold, the equally despised cosponsor of the proposed reform legislation, sat down in the chair on the opposite side of the table. "Good afternoon Russ," McCain greeted his fellow reformer as he looked up from the papers he was reading. "I've been reading about the murder of Leon Placke and the bizarre death of his killer, Muncaster Swindell. It's a very strange situation, especially with people seeing George Washington all over the country. I feel sorry about Leon's murder, because I used some of his ideas in my primary campaign."

Feingold spoke. "I've seen him too, you know. I've seen George Washington. He was siting outside my window on his horse. Sitting there, looking at me, like he was waiting for me to do something."

McCain didn't look one bit surprised as he responded, "That's good, I'm glad to hear it. I wasn't going to tell anyone, but he appeared to me too. On his horse, just like you said. He gave me a look, the likes of which I'll never forget."

"We can't let the spirit of George Washington down! We have to reintroduce our campaign finance bill again when Congress reconvenes," Feingold said.

"It will be a tough fight because everyone is against it," McCain responded. "But let's do it! We'll be bound for hell or glory, one way or the other."

"We probably will catch a lot of hell and find very little glory in what we are doing," Feingold quietly said as the two men stood up to leave the dining room.

March 2001

The campaign finance reform legislation was met with undisguised derision and contempt in Congress when the two maverick senators introduced their bill during the opening session. The bill had no support. The bill's opponents were certain it would never be become law. It would dangle on the fringes of the legislative process for awhile and then die a natural death because the concept of reform was an anathema to Congress, the capital's special interest groups and the lobbying profession.

As the months went by, things began to slowly change. One by one, pale, bedraggled senators came in to the Senate chamber and announced they were reconsidering their position on the issue and throwing their support behind the McCain-Feingold bill. The unofficial reason for their change of mind was they wanted to have nothing more to do with the haunting spectral visits or the fearful nightly trips through America's bloody and violent past. As much as they disliked reforming the way political campaigns were financed, they were being forced by circumstances beyond their control to do the right thing. In a stunning reversal of fortune and to the surprise of everyone in the capital, the McCain-Feingold bill was approved by the Senate.

As support for the measure began to mount, a bleary-eyed President announced at a early morning staff meeting that he was changing his position on the matter. He would be willing to sign the campaign finance reform legislation when it came to the White House for signature. When one of the startled meeting participants asked him what had brought about such a sudden change of heart, the President angrily retorted, "Go down to Mt. Vernon. Sit yourself down next to Washington's tomb and spend the night! Then come back here in the morning and tell me if you don't see the matter in a different light!" Everyone in the room could see that something had gotten to the President, really gotten under his skin. Since he was in such a rotten mood, they decided not to ask any more questions.

The opponents of campaign finance reform rallied their forces and prepared to smother the legislation when it reached the House of Representatives. House leaders confidently predicted they would gut the measure of all substance during debate on the floor of the House or failing that, would bury the despised legislation so deeply in a joint conference committee that it would never again see the light of day. Senators McCain and Feingold made no comment. They knew this was only the first shot in what was going to a long battle to implement political reform. They also knew they could count on the help of a strong ally. The members of the House of Representatives were about to be taught a jarring lesson by the spirit of a man from America's past.

"Where there are no rights, there are no duties."
-Henri Benjamin Constant de Rebecque, 1797

* * *